FOX DEN

BOOKS

Oregon

The Trilogy of Tinna
Copyright © 2017 by Miranda Mayer

Fox Den Books may be ordered through booksellers or by contacting

Fox Den Books
PO Box 39
Brightwood, OR 97011

Fox Den Books rev. date 5/1/2017

10th Anniversary Trilogy Edition

By Miranda Mayer
Copyright © 2007-2017 Miranda Mayer
www.mirandamayer.com

BOOK 1

TINNA'S PROMISE

MIRANDA MAYER

CHAPTER 1

Taneth was an oddball and a troublemaker; there was no doubt about that. He'd carved himself quite the reputation among his fellow students with his loud mouth and explosive declarations. He certainly wasn't going to disappoint them when he'd gotten them all so well conditioned to his outbursts. It was so expected of him, that the few times he had nothing to say, the group would fall into an uncomfortable span of silence, wondering when he would eventually and predictably chime in. This particular day, he did not fail his fellow students, and interrupted the professor as he usually did.

"Nonsense," Taneth called out. "Our essence is as fragile as the flesh it inhabits! We lend ourselves all these special exceptions to the basic rules of life because we hold ourselves so above other creatures. Souls…spirits. That's all a crock. We are slaves to the physical body and are subject to its whim, and to the whims of chaos! Do we really think ourselves so separated and above everything else that we would be immune to such a vulgar concept as death?"

It was no mystery to anyone who knew Taneth even for a short time, that he was a staunch atheist. He never failed to make his opinions known in any forum where faith or myth was open to discussion, sometimes even when it wasn't.

"We imagine our minds are just resting temporarily within the flesh. We make up all sorts of stories to explain why that would be. But in truth, we are held prisoner by it until the sad day of death and our precious soul will rot away as surely as the flesh will." He paused, and took a long, deep breath before going on. "We have seen case after case where a man is injured in the head, and he loses his ability to reason, conceptualize, or create, loses his conscience, his ability to recognize and show emotions—all the things that make up the so-

3

called superiority we imagine we possess—gone. Why? Because something in his brain was injured; because the body and the mind are irrefutably linked, and the mind cannot exist without the body. It is not because their spirits have abandoned them, it is because our souls, and our spirits are naught but functions the same as breathing and walking are, and are subject to the same afflictions of the body. It can be killed even while the body lives!"

Taneth was a tall, lean fellow, with mousy brown hair and a neatly clipped beard. He was twenty-two years old. He had a very angular, long face, and a scholarly look to his features. He wore the mandated chasuble robes that all students of Hildercross wore; a simple red-wine-colored wool gown with simple cotton lining. His longish hair was tied back in a thong. He had a serious furrow in his brow, wrinkling the tattooed mark that identified him as a man of Knowledge. The subtle black tattoo followed his hairline from the widow's peak to the outer corner of his left eye, festooned with strange glyphs and figures. He straightened the front of his chasuble and continued with his outburst.

"So answer me this: How immortal is our soul if a freak accident, a well-placed injury, can in one fell swoop, destroy all the qualities that make the spirit and the mind exceptional above all other beasts? I am astounded that you, Professor Nelnath, are certified to instruct in this fine institution with such a despicable arsenal of lies and untruths! It is the poisoning of young minds with fairy tales!"

"Sit down, Wetal Taneth," the Professor yelled. Taneth, as usual, did not comply, and continued to stand, shifting back and forth on his feet as if confused by his own impulses. The professor gestured for him to sit again, doing so with such violence that his generous sleeve snapped and flopped about in an undignified manner. Taneth sat, appearing stupefied by his own inability to control his actions.

"What you fail to understand, time and again, is that learning is about exploring opinion, and basing your own judgments on a series of ideas. Not a single idea, but opening your mind and basing your self-created idea upon the knowledge of many. I am not preaching nonsense as you so injudiciously implied." The professor leaned on the large table in the center of his dais with his hands flat on the stone, leaning his body toward the students. "I am encouraging the art of contemplation and debate by presenting as many theories I can possibly teach someone as thick-headed as you! Now for the last time—keep your bloody mouth shut for the next few—although precious—moments so that the other students may actually glean something from this class for a change without one of your untimely interruptions." The professor stood silently, glaring at the unmoving young fellow until he deemed that the silent battle for control between them had finally ended.

The professor then pushed himself upright again, keeping his glare fast on Taneth in order to capture the tiniest indication of impending insubordination, and continued his lecture from the point where it had been cut off. He was a man in his late years, wizened and worn by decades of teaching an impossible number of exceptionally bright young people. This Hildercross Academy was one of many Oromoii High Throne-sponsored institutions dedicated to finding the youngest, brightest children of the land, and training them to be the single source of education and medicine for the people they served. These students before him had been under his tutelage and that of many other professors since they were six years old. Not all of them made it to graduation, granted, but the ones who did were valued members of society. He had trouble imagining that Taneth could turn out to be anything more than a troublesome burden to anyone with the misfortune of having him in his or her service.

Taneth sat still, although his eyes blazed. To him, there was no reason, logic, or explanation why the others accepted such stifling conditions and saw his behavior as inappropriate. It burned him that they all just sat there, and listened, and absorbed, or even reflected away like light to mirrors, all these so-called facts without the slightest indication of stimulation, or question. Did they have no brains? Did they have no understanding? So little is our time on this plain, thought he, that we should spend it all questing to pry the true knowledge from ignorance. Instead, they sit, and absorb dogma and speculation, and accept it as being learned and educated, and function pretentiously throughout their lives as educated and knowledgeable people.

That's the big lie! Taneth's eyes darkened. He felt some days that it was Him versus the World. His friends would say: "Taneth, you mean to tell me that you think you're right and the whole world is wrong?" His nod would produce words such as "How arrogant" from their ignorant little mouths. He frowned as he thought of the hypocrisy of the institution. It was said to be a place where great minds were found. But instead, it was where their notion of "Great Minds" were molded and shaped to their specifications and standards, which to Taneth, left a great deal to be desired.

"Hypocrites," he whispered to himself. The girl beside him, by the name of Cezine, a particularly devoted zealot of the all-knowing professor, turned and glared at him, eyes narrowed into two evil slits. She was a pale little fair-haired creature with bright blue eyes and pretty pink lips. Her cheeks were freckled with soft-colored spots. She could have been pretty, Taneth thought, if she weren't such a vacuous mouth-breather. It reminded Taneth of his days as a child, where a group of nameless youths from his village called him names and shot him harsh, reprimanding glares for being different. She was no longer a child, however, so the action, as puerile as it was, was strangely appropriate to his opinion of her and the institution he felt at that moment. He felt an urge to give her some sort of highly inappropriate gesture that would be of great insult to her. His urge could not be stifled. He needed some amusement, and at the moment, the professor was trusting enough to turn his back to the class to pull down a large schematic of the spread of various belief systems through the known world.

So, Taneth, in all his oddity, jabbed his hand into the air in front of her face, with only the index finger and pinky pointing up. Her mouth formed a shocked little "O" and she raised her hand, and smacked him across the face. Without the slightest hesitation, as if the law of equal and opposite reactions had been put into effect, as soon as her hand had left contact with his face, his rose, and he smacked her with equal force across her face. She screamed and jumped to her feet, touching her tender skin, and pointed an accusing finger at Taneth, who sat with his arms crossed and a look of utter bliss upon his features. It was a look that implied that Taneth had fulfilled a secret, greatly desired fantasy at that very moment.

"He hit me!" she screamed.

The professor, as if defeated, took a moment before he'd even turn and look at the face he knew very well would be Taneth's. He paused to sag his shoulders and sigh. He did turn however, and said nothing, leaning onto the lectern and crossing his arms, washing his hands of this entirely.

"You seem to forget that your hand was first lifted against me. It was an instinctive act of defense," Taneth said smugly, propping his feet on the back of the seat in front of him.

"How dare you!" she whined, her eyes filled with tears. "How dare you! You coward! How low can one sink to find pleasure in hitting a woman?"

"I beg to differ on that statement, Cezine. You are no woman. You are a cow, a bovine, a heifer, trudging along, chewing her cud and following the herd," he retorted.

For some reason, he simply didn't care anymore. He didn't care about her feelings, or the wrath of the professor. He didn't care about the consequences of his behavior this day, nor the days to follow. He simply went with his feelings. He followed his anger, and his disappointment, and let all the things that had infuriated him before find an outlet at last. He decided that whatever was to come, he could certainly withstand it far better than to endure another day of being force-fed so-called facts created by an unending chain of extremely lazy, stupid people, who wasted entire lifetimes fabricating these "truths" while they sat on their chamber pots scratching their fat behinds.

CHAPTER 2

"As of this day, Taneth, you are expelled from Hildercross and restricted from enrollment at any and all schools related to Hildercross in Oromoii. That means tat, including this fine place, you are forbidden to enter Redhall, Cliffside, Eldercross, Methcrene, Morston, Schellville, Arestain, Montsummet, Delse, Nuvram, Inthrop, Highfeld, and Inithran in this empire alone. Let us not omit the other countries, shall we?" The headmaster turned a page in his tome, wearing a self-satisfied grin upon his face as his finger found the next list he was to read. Taneth's father, Methix, who had been summoned for Taneth's dismissal, shook his head in disgust, listening with shame as the headmaster continued on with the list of schools Taneth was forever banned from. "In Weuunilan, if you should ever see fit to culture yourself by crossing its border, these schools will not accept you: Britecreek, Harwood, Nevprair, and Tavino. So, even if you chose to go to Weuunilan for an education, you'd be deprived sorely, for those four schools are the only schools. Pity," he said with a happy smile.

Taneth simply crossed his legs and let his eyes wander to the ceiling. Oromoii was the largest empire on the continent, and in part had the largest collection of High Throne-sponsored schools. The High Throne, however, had such schools in other empires as well. It was well known that they were amongst the best in quality and prestige. Of course, that was according to the herd of blank eyed, mooing collectives they churned out of their doors on a yearly basis. To Taneth, such praise and acclaim was relative—seeing where it was coming from. He stifled a smirk as the headmaster stared at him as if expecting some response from Taneth.

His father sat hunched in a chair against the far wall, glaring flaming daggers at his son.

"Let's see…The Isle of Gales, oh, oh dear. Only one school of this level there, and what's this?" the headmaster continued, and pointed at the name. "It's one of ours. How sad," His look of pity was so exaggerated it looked as if someone had squashed his features and they'd stuck that way. Taneth ignored him as he went from page to page, orally dictating every school that would not accept Taneth, including schools across the great waters and among the isles. The headmaster closed the book and sighed, taking in another breath of air to continue his tirade.

"That leaves, oh, perhaps seven or eight schools unaffiliated with the High Throne that will offer something close to our level of education—about a hundred more if you'll settle for something more your level. Our quality is not matched however, and of course, the prestige of being among the distinguished alumni of Hildercross will be lost to you. You will have to school with the dunces and the people not advantaged enough to afford a true education. But that's how things go, I suppose," He lifted the tome and carried it back to a shelf. "You could do that, or you could consider just dropping out of the educational process altogether, and taking up basket-weaving or something, farming, peasantry, whatever suits your mad little fancy. You're free now, isn't that what you wished? Being expelled with only three months to graduation, well, we all know that's not a good thing. You go back to school somewhere; you have to start all over again!"

He fiddled and fidgeted with the items on the shelf, trying hard to act as if this were not a lark for him. Taneth's gaze fell onto the glowering headmaster, and he sat up in his chair, thrumming his fingers on the armrests.

"What have you to say, boy?" Taneth's father asked in a bear-like growl.

"Nothing. I'm neither sorry nor regretful. I simply have no desire to explain myself in any way, for I need not. I think the school should explain itself."

"That's it," Methix said through clamped teeth. He stood. "You are not only expelled from this school, you're expelled from my life! Until you come to understand what you have done, and have apologized and explained your faults sufficiently to hope for forgiveness, you are not to speak to me, your family, your mother, or enter your home again."

"My home? What home? You carted me off the moment I was capable of cognitive thought. It's no loss to me. You cannot punish me, Father"—he directed his casual gaze at the headmaster—"nor can you. Nobody can. You can glare and mock, and what infuriates you both is you know all too well that I am beyond your control. Let's face it: I never was under your control. All the leniency, and the warnings ..." he paused, and sighed, "never mind. I'm not going to waste another moment explaining anything to you. I don't have to, or need to. I don't answer to either of you." He used the armrests to lift himself from the chair, gave both men a final glance before clicking the door latch behind him.

The corridor connecting the school to the dormitories seemed longer than it really was. The walk to his rooms seemed to last forever—as if he couldn't be free of this place soon enough. He found his room, and gathered his sparse belongings, stuffing them unceremoniously into a large shoulder pack. He slung the strap diagonally across his chest, and put on a floppy hat. He made no scene as he left. Doors of the dormitory opened as word got 'round, and faces peered at him as he walked through. He maintained a dignified façade as he passed the throngs of students cheering and clapping in joy at his departure. They jeered and threw balled-up parchments at him as he passed. He simply kept his gaze high, and his mind focused upon the task ahead: to make it outside the edifice without losing control of his anger.

The teachers waited, clustered in the main hall by the door, making a great show of dividing themselves into two groups flanking the sides of the open door, forcing him to pass through them in humiliation to escape. They laughed, jeered, and roused chants with the students, gesturing him to pass through them to the outside.

"Taneth, Taneth, leaves at last! Taneth, Taneth, outward cast! Leave us, leave us, Taneth, now. Choose to stay, we'll throw you out!" they chanted, fists jabbing into the air on every other syllable. He was amazed they had the capability to maintain such a complicated task with such meager resources in their heads. He walked toward the crowd, and through the chasm between the groups, maintaining every shred of his dignity he could muster. He looked cheerful, and happy to be leaving this place. His gaze did not avoid a single set of eyes that sought to challenge him. He straightened the rim of his hat, and walked through, his step energetic and his spine rigid. As long as he could maintain it, he held his head high and kept his face smiling.

When he was sure he was out of their sight, he slumped his shoulders and slowed his gait. He ignored and went around the little town at the foot of the hill upon which Hildercross sat. It wasn't long before he was stooped against the foot of a tree among some unknown wilderness beyond the civilized world, face in his hands.

He was terrified. His whole life had been dedicated to learning, sheltered and nurtured in the school environment from the moment he had developed speech. His knowledge was vast, but he knew it meant nothing when he sat alone on an unused road with no future or prospects. No gold, no valuable items—only a bag of clothing, some trinkets and a few books, and his pale, smooth hands.

"I can tell every species of tree around me, but I cannot decide what to do" He sighed. He was miserable—yet he was liberated. He sat against that tree for another hour, attempting to organize his actions for the next few days. But it occurred to him that what he was doing was useless, for in all truth, he had no idea what to expect. He knew absolutely nothing of the real world. Books could not truly teach life skills. He stood after some time, and trudged along at his own pace, examining things such as leaves, and twigs, small animals and trees—creating a catalog of the species and the genus of each thing he saw. It kept his mind occupied, and suppressed his fear of what was to come.

Taneth had slept in a ball in the comfortable furrow of a Noab tree's roots. The roots that snaked from the trunk in thick, vertical ribbons created many labyrinthine nooks and crannies wherein a person could be somewhat protected from the elements. The dense canopy had shielded him from the morning rain, and he woke covered in dots of dew. He shook off the humus that clung to his vestments, and did his allotted time of yawning and stretching before gathering his things and moving along his way.

He was famished. He hadn't eaten since the morning of his dismissal, yesterday, and his stomach was giving him a hollow sensation, a sunken feeling that made air bubbles rattle and groan through his intestines. He had an enormous headache, either from hunger or from sleeping in a strange place and waking wide-eyed every time a creature grunted, squeaked, or tooted during the night. He looked, felt, and was, miserable. His hair was filled with burrs, his hem of his chasuble was soaked and darkened from the humid floor of the forest, and his underarms emitted an odor that sent all forms of fauna into a flight of terror. His gait was a trudge, his feet were sore, his calves threatened to bind up into a cramp if he turned his foot one millimeter the wrong way, his nose ran, and his eyes had crusted things on them which he preferred not to describe. All in all, he was a disgusting mess. And this was only one day free of the school!

Taneth came to this realization as he walked. He paused and assessed his inferior condition, and suddenly got angry at himself. If I am like this only one day upon my freedom, the future outlook spells doom! he thought. How can this be? I shall not allow this to happen! He picked up his pace, and tramped through the undergrowth, leaving the path and heading toward the thicker parts of the wood, certain he would find water there.

His instincts were right. He found a narrow river that moved languidly through the forest floor, snaking around tree roots as if they had been there before it had. It was too slow to be dangerous and too quick to be stagnant and green. There were rocks shoved up to the sides of the riverbed, put there at some point in the past, perhaps during spring when the snows melted, when the river became swollen and fast-moving. The rocks were smooth and rounded, and strewn along the bends, there were also larger ones in the middle, creating resting spots for swimmers, human or animal. It made a lovely picture. The water made little noise; a waterborne creature somewhere along its length created the occasional ripple or splash.

Taneth smiled. Another new thing for him. How sheltered he had been indeed. He studied the patterns of the gentle curls and vortexes of liquid on the surface, the occasional bubble, or twig riding the gentle current. He reached down and touched the surface, testing the temperature. He shucked his clothes without a second thought and dove in. Taneth soaked in the sensation of the cool water flowing over his skin as he swam beneath the still surface, looking at the clear water above and around him, stones smooth below him, and the surface sparkling above. He pumped his way to the surface and emerged with a gasp for air, but taking only a moment to breathe, he re-submerged like a large fish, his feet flapping the surface as if the flukes of a whale.

It was miraculous to him, how this water felt and tasted. It was so different from the stale water of the fountain pools of Hildercross, which were recycled and sometimes green—and one could not avoid touching slimy fish they kept there to keep the water clean. Here, it was naturally clean. It tasted sweet, it was clear as glass, and only the slight distortions created by his own movement seemed to mar the span of his vision. He took another breath and dove in again, scaring up a school of silver fish that flashed and flickered as spots of light hit them from above. For that second, Taneth understood the meaning of happiness. He emerged from the water refreshed and amused by the way his body seemed heavier.

He was clean now, and he drank his fill of the water. Taneth cleaned his clothing on one of the smooth stones, battering out the stains with a handful of pebbles from the riverbed. He bathed in the sun while his clothes dried. He slept a bit. The warmth of the sun, and the comfort of the long, swaying reeds in which he rested was enough to overcome his will to remain awake. The night of interrupted sleep owed his body a great debt. And the morning repaid it tenfold. He rose even more refreshed. And starving. He foraged about for some edible foods, and thanks to his learned ways, he found various forms of leaf and berry. He caught a fish with his bare hands, and wrapped it in the fragrant leaves of a leaf-pine, and cooked it over a small fire.

When he had eaten, and put out the fire, he sat for a long time in the afternoon weaving together a reed mat for his comfort and, pleased he could put this skill he had deemed useless to work, heard himself chuckling at the thought that he was doing what the headmaster had so rudely suggested: basket-weaving. He then dressed and was along his way. This time, he ignored the paths, and forged straight through the forest, following the river. He crossed the river upstream where it was running shallow and vivaciously. He hopped over the exposed stones, and found his footing on the opposite shore.

He'd walked miles, he wagered, and yet the forest persisted—as did the river. He glanced at the sky, and the sunlight that managed to penetrate the leafy canopy of boughs above, and kept walking, hungry yet again. He flopped down in the humus to rest, and pulled off his shoes, wincing at the odor. He scrubbed his feet clean in the water, pleased to have this undulating, refreshing companion on his journey. He unrolled his fresh new mat and lay down on it, took out his thick tunic, balled it up, and lay his head on it. There, his fatigue, his resolve, his loss, and his gains, all culminated in a heavy sleep, and an active dream. He woke the next morning drowsy and headachy. He gathered his wits and his belongings, and continued on. He began to think he'd never find another human being again.

He traveled a total of three and a half days, surviving on his own wits and determination. As the river curved, he followed, and to his delight, it led him to a tiny little community. He knew their kind as soon as he saw the gates of the village. The runes in the wood of the twin pylons marking the village entrance were stylized horses. Horses of all sizes and shapes, in all poses. He knew this design, and he knew these people worshipped the horse as the Supreme Being. They believed that the horse created man to serve them. He also knew that these were honest, good, hard-working people.

Their beliefs were the most prevalent in this region; they were the People of the Horse God, Arak. He stumbled through the gates, and observed their small portion of the world. Five buildings, no more. The main hall was an enormous construct that blended so well into the forest it was nearly invisible. It was partially underground;

the roof was a soft steeple upon which the forest life grew as if it were the earth itself—trees and bushes alike. The only sign of it being created by man was the flat, richly painted face of the building, with a huge wooden door, with two inset doors nested within each other. One to open and air the hall out, the second to allow access to larger things, and the third for people.

The second was an edifice of almost equal enormity, and equal invisibility. The only difference was a wooden horse carved onto the face of the hall. This was the stable and holy place. The other buildings were smaller, yet just as old—each with its own small forest acting as a roof. All were more than halfway underground. So old were some that the trees created suspended root systems that hung down from the roofs and found the earth below. If they were to destroy the house, the tree would stand independently with a roof-shaped arch under its trunk, the roots creating two tangled walls on each side. All the buildings were built to circle a large center, where in the middle stood an ancient oak, trimmed and pruned to perfection, causing the canopy to grow into one of the finest domes of leaves Taneth had ever seen. He knew this was the Founder's Tree, the oak that was planted over the body of their village founder—the tree alleged to possess the spirit of the person buried beneath it. It was a burial practice of their culture. The people of the Horse God created forests of oaks instead of gloomy graveyards. They believed the growing sapling would soak up the essence of the body under its roots, and eventually absorb the spirit of the deceased entangled in its roots—he thought it a wonderful way to prolong the life and the memory of a loved one. The ground was paved in ruddy granite slabs around the Founder's Tree; the rest was clean-swept dirt.

On this hot day, not a soul was to be seen. The doors were closed to keep in the coolness of the earth inside the cozy buildings. He heard horse snorts and children giggling. He walked to the oak and sat down, mumbling a quiet greeting to the tree, his feet aching, his emotions wasted. He sat for a long moment, just listening to the chickens scratch and the people stir inside their great hall. No sooner did he think of leaving, when somebody exited the main hall, and strode across the forum, startled by the sight of the disheveled young man leaning against their sacred oak.

"Who are you?" the man asked. Taneth simply looked up at him, and sighed. The man studied Taneth's markings and turned on his heel, flinging the door of the main hall open, and shouted, "There's a Wiseman here from the forest!"

The people of the village poured from the main hall, and surrounded Taneth to stare at him in astonishment. "I'm not a Wiseman," Taneth confessed. "I was expelled from the academy shortly before I was able to complete my schooling."

The man who had seen him first stooped before him and stared deeply into his eyes. "How many months is a horse's gestation period?"

"Eleven."

"How many nails go into a horse shoe?"

"Seven."

"In the tales of creation, why was the horse cast from the realms of the human gods?"

"Because he won a contest of strength against the High God, Lasul."

"How did he regain not only access to the realm of gods, but win the throne of the High God?"

"He imprisoned Lasul upon this firmament, and covered him with burning rock. Lasul now stands as the highest mountain, Fureen," Taneth blurted out, tired of this game of trivia.

"You know everything you need to know to be called a Wiseman around here. Come inside." The man stretched out his hand, Taneth grasped it, and the leader pulled Taneth to his feet. "I am Rigerd, I am leader here."

Taneth took in the sight of this impressive man. He was very tall, his shoulders were wide and strong, and he had a narrow waist and thick thighs; he had the look of a man who worked very hard. He had a red beard, plaited into a hundred tiny braids, and then those braids braided into three large ones. His matching ferruginous hair was short, so much so it looked like the fuzz on a fresh summer peach. He had two thick loops of silver through his ears, and the mark of a leader etched on his cheek, a simple arrangement of dots making a curved line under his right eye.

"I am Taneth."

"You look hungry and exhausted. Come inside the hall, and join us for our midday repast and rest," He guided Taneth with his great big hand, patting the boy's back in a friendly fashion as he led him into the hall. The community surrounded him as they walked back to the hall. There, they crowded into the narrow entranceway. Some began to file through a hallway, and others through the second corridor. Soon, it was just Taneth and the leader Rigerd waiting to go in.

The leader gestured for Taneth to follow, and he led him into the third entranceway to the main hall. The room was deserted. People had already eaten here, and had headed back into their personal spaces to sleep. There was food still, sitting on the communal table that stretched the length of the room. He gestured for Taneth to sit, and he did. He waited until Rigerd gave him silent permission to help himself before he began eating voraciously. His hand found the tall pile of crispy bacon, which melted in his mouth.

Rigerd sat down, and propped his elbows on the table. "Why were you expelled from that school?" he asked, nudging his chin in a general eastward direction. "Uh, Hindercross, Hildercrest, whatever it's called."

The school was a well-known source for Wisemen for many surrounding communities. This academy served a wide area adjacent to the hill it sat upon. "Hildercross, yes. I was indeed expelled. I didn't behave according to their standards," Taneth said around a mouthful of food, artfully displaying the half-chewed contents as he did.

"Yet you knew that you had only a short time to go until you completed your schooling ..."

"Yes," He swallowed, and gave Rigerd a single, exaggerated nod.

"And it did not motivate you to keep to yourself until you were certain you were free to do so?"

"No. Frankly, Rigerd, I didn't want to be known for graduating from a place that has such ridiculous standards. I did adhere to them before, barely, clinging to the edge with the tips of my fingers, but as time went on, I grew more and more discontented with their ways." He grabbed three more strips of the bacon, and then reached for the grain stew, slapping some out of the ladle into one of the empty wooden bowls stacked beside the concoction. He grasped a thick wooden spoon and took a large heaping spoonful from the bowl of porridge, relishing the mix of soft grain meal, forest nuts, and bits of beefy meat.

"Why? What ways?"

"I do not appreciate a school that encourages no individuality. Not unlike your herd of horses, the people where I was schooled were led this way and that, told to be such a way, and accepted it as readily as the mares accept the authority of the lead stallion. I showed my individuality subtly at first, and they quelled it. Then I tried a bit more obviously, hoping to make them respect and realize it ... only to be squashed again. Lastly, I had become known for my outbursts

17

and disagreements, which I confess I formulated simply for the act of being heard, but I did it thinking it would have some effect. It was getting me nowhere, only achieving a growing resentment from the student body and faculty." He paused, taking a bite of a strip of bacon, and then a spoonful of the delicious gruel. He reached for the remains of a loaf of bread, tearing off a bit to eat with his porridge.

"And then I just lost all control—or desire for control, perhaps" he said with a half smile. "I looked at the face of one of the students beside me, and realized that nothing I could do would matter enough to make anyone respect my individuality. That it was simply never going to be respected or allowed—even outside the school when I serve. It was a future I could not bear to choose. So, I did something rash enough to cause and assist my dismissal. It had to be something bad enough to have my father come to the school. Normally, my father would pay the school some measure of gold to keep me, and the school has always known that having me as a student, troublesome as I was, was a sound investment. So they never would have expelled me unless I did something to truly upset both my father and the school. Otherwise, I'd have been reprimanded as before, and left in the school to rot, and then forced to take a post somewhere where I would be stifled and miserable." Taneth shrugged and took a chicken leg from a platter of baked fowl. He bit into the drumstick, chewing ungracefully, his eyes cast to the side as he remembered the past few days.

"So how many years were you shy of completion?"

"Just three months, actually," Taneth responded. Rigerd cringed.

"So, technically, you're almost graduated. What were you missing?"

"Nothing. Just a few lectures I've heard before, the ceremonies, of course, and a few more sessions on ancient theology" He tossed the bone into a dish, and wiped his mouth with his sleeve, returning to scrape the thin layer of gruel still left in his bowl. He then crammed another thick slice of bacon into his mouth, sighing in the breath that indicated he was nearing fullness, but seemed unlikely to slow down just yet.

"By ceremonies, you mean the Ceremonies of Induction?"

"Yes," Taneth answered, reaching for a tomato to bite into.

"I have a proposition for you then, Wiseman. You stay here for a while, and help us contend with a problem concerning a form of annoying rodent, and you will receive all you need for your journey from us, including a very fine horse."

18

"Rodents?"

"And as a topper, we have a Holyman who can perform our own rites of induction upon you, and you can leave this place a true Wiseman—at least to my people, leaving you free to find a place to serve among my kind anywhere."

"Why would you do this?"

"Because we need your help. This is the first time we've ever been plagued with these rodents, and we haven't a clue what to do. We have a theory that they arrived with some Gypsies who passed through recently. There are so many already, rodents, I mean. Perhaps you can help. I hope you can." Taneth gazed at Rigerd for a long moment. He took another bite of his tomato, the juice and seeds running down his chin. He wiped it off with his sleeve, and furrowed his brow.

"Is there a shortage of smart people here as to require you to solicit the help from a complete stranger?" he asked bluntly.

Yes." Rigerd's reply was as equally curt.

Taneth shrugged. "Then why not? I've no pressing engagements elsewhere." He laughed easily. Rigerd smiled. "You have a place here as long as you like." He stood. Taneth stood as well, sufficiently gorged. Rigerd led him back to the entranceway, into the foyer, where he entered the left corridor. Taneth followed, amazed how large the interior of this edifice was, and how dark and cool it was. They walked through a long and shadowy passageway, lit only superficially by small lamps. There were arched doorways into personal apartments here. He led Taneth to the last door on the end. He opened it. It was a large apartment, made for a full family, Taneth assumed. There was already furniture inside, and three narrow windows let light in from the outside. There were wooden shutters that could slide right into the frames and lock in, should the weather or other factors deem it necessary. There was a single enormous bed in a partially walled-in cubby area. It seemed out of place, as if too fine to be of this place.

"It belonged to our own Wiseman," Rigerd explained, noting Taneth's expression. "These quarters are those of our past Wiseman, who died last winter in a blizzard; he'd lost himself in the forests. We found him dead some distance off from camp, frozen solid. He was very old, and stubborn. Didn't like to be told not to do things. Poor fellow." The leader shook his head regrettably, and sighed.

"Everything here was his. It is now yours until you decide to leave or stay."

"Are you trying to lure in your own Wiseman?"

"Perhaps. But we won't impose any expectations upon you. We welcome the intelligence and knowledge you bring. And we will enjoy it as long as you decide to make this place home. As long as you are here, you will be treated as one of our clan."

"It is timely I came, then."

"I was going to petition your academy this coming week. It seems Arak has perhaps had a hand in this. You should keep that in mind while you decide. It's not good to second-guess the will of the Horse God. Now, if you don't mind, I need to go back out into that intolerable heat. We've a mare that is dropping foal, and I must see to it that there is enough bedding for her. Make yourself at home, Taneth. The summons cord will bring you someone to attend to your needs. Here, the Wiseman is like the Holyman, and ranks among the Council of Five Elders. Here he is worthy of our servitude. Take advantage of it" He closed the door and left the bedraggled young man to himself.

Taneth's eyes wandered to the cord. He shook his head, and walked to the heavy chest of drawers under the windows, pulling out the top drawer. There was a neat stack of underclothes, clean and folded. The next drawer revealed the telltale chasubles of a Wiseman, all the same bland green color, all generic in size, and all clean and tempting. There were woolen ones for winter and linen ones for summer. There were little horse-shapes carved from cedar peppered inside the drawers to deter fabric-eating creatures. He scanned the room. His small kitchen area was complete with combined fireplace, stove, and oven. It was a layered hearth, with one fire to provide heat for the grilled iron, the spit, and the pothook, as well as a stone cubby wherein one would place a roll of freshly risen dough to bake. It appeared as if the man before him had never cooked or baked. The irons were simply blackened without sign of use, and the oven still immaculate, void of darkened flour markings or such.

There were some pots and pans hanging from hooks above this hearth. Families cooked in their homes, and brought their dishes out to be shared with the community. Everyone ate together. Children played together, families shared food, materials, and resources, unlike the market based community he knew at Hildercross.

He sighed, kicking off his worn shoes, and digging his toes into the sheep's-wool carpeting that covered the floor. The carpet had been patched together from diamonds of sheep's wool of varying shades, made into a large quilted pad to the dimensions of the room, and laid down onto the cold slate floor. It was thick and soft and the padding within made walking a pleasure. How he wished for a bath. His eyes wandered back up to the cord, and again he shook his head. It seemed almost rude to make such a request. He sat on the edge of the bed and stared at his feet.

There was a gentle knock on the door. A young girl's face appeared in the crack as it swung partially open. "Our leader told me to attend to you, sir."

"I didn't pull the—"

"Our leader anticipated you, sir. What may I do for you?"

He looked up, and clutched his hands together. "Do you think a bath would be possible?" he asked, somewhat sheepishly. She smiled and nodded, vanishing from the doorway. A few minutes later, two men entered, carrying a large copper tub with little brass horses galloping around the sides of it, and women began to enter one after the other, filling the tub with buckets of warmed water. One gave him some soap, obviously made right in this little village. It had been poured into a mold in the shape of, unsurprisingly, a horse. Taneth smiled. They stopped coming as suddenly as they had started, and they left him to enjoy his bath. He cleaned himself up, soaked out his days' worth of grime, trimmed his goatee back down to something more manageable and neat, scraping off the stubble that marred its manicured lines, tied his hair back and borrowed some of the old Wiseman's clothing. He remained barefoot, relieved to be rid of his shoes—he had always been someone who preferred to go without anything on his feet, and with the soft carpet beneath his feet to the clean slate of the rest of the lodge, he knew this was the perfect place to enjoy this secret little habit of his.

He left his room when he was finished and sauntered along the corridor and entered the main hall again. There he found a group of children playing with a small puppy by the cool empty hearth. He sat with them, played with the puppy, and found himself held captive by the children once they discovered he had story-telling capabilities.

When the hottest hours of the afternoon were past, the children grasped his hands, and pulled him outside into the waxing evening. The twin moons were just beginning to appear in the sky. The breeze had come to bless them. The children involved him in a game of hide and seek, and were soon again gathered 'round him as he wound the tale of the moons. Their eyes were all tied fast to his hands and face as he gestured and recounted the tale with dramatic flair.

He added his own embellishments to the stories, changing some of the main characters into horses, and into the enemies of horses, the ground dragon, and the prairie lion. The children were fascinated with each word, clutching their little hands to their mouths in horror as he described the battles and the faces of the villains.

Rigerd's people were pretty much all outside the lodges, tending to the horses, lingering nearby to hear his tales, lighting the circle of lamps that hung from the tree limbs and ran the perimeter of the forum. The lamps were assisted in their task of shedding light by dancing fireflies glowing a soft luminous green in blinking flares. Smells of food cooked on wood fires rose up into the air, and pads, blankets, and quilts were placed out for the children to sit on while Taneth wove tales for them. This evening was a defining moment for the young man. It would be the second and most profound occasion when Taneth knew happiness. Pure unabashed happiness. He suddenly loved these people, their complexity and their simplicity, their absolute trust in him to be as they, good and kind, and the way they included him at once into their fold. They had no idea who he was, yet they took him in and respected him as he had never been respected in his life.

"And so the moons appeared in the sky—the ever-watching round eyes of Ashakul, who promised never to allow the night-sky cloak to be stolen from him again. But as the days passed, Ashakul's eyes closed, for he cannot stay awake for so long. And every day, his lids get heavier, and heavier … and when he has slept enough, he will rise to watch wide-eyed for the thief Uthano, again and again," he concluded.

The children applauded and rose from their riveted silence like a sudden explosion, from sitting to running in the blink of an eye, coursing around his legs in a river of juveniles, using him as a shield from the fists of others. They stampeded into the trees, filled with stored energy from sitting still for such a long time. He seemed lost for a moment. There were no longer children to attend to, and the others seemed so preoccupied.

Rigerd called him from the front of the Horse Hall. "Taneth, come see this!" he shouted. The people stopped their many tasks, exchanged glances and, clapping hands, ran into the main hall shouting praises. Taneth crossed the forum, pausing for the occasional citizen to pass by. He reached Rigerd, and the man opened the large door of the hall, heaving it open with all his might. Inside, the smell of fresh straw and hay was overwhelming.

There was almost no smell of horse, so to speak. These people revered the horse. One was never to live a moment in an environment unworthy of a creature of divine creation. The Horse Hall was clean to the point of obsession. The side walls were lined with large, airy stalls, and the center was a slate-paved aisle interspersed with soft-colored pebbles in undulating mosaic designs. Dominating the center of the floor was a large stone table.

Rigerd led him to a huge stall that consumed the back end of the structure. Inside, a single mare stood, head low, eyes dampened and ears drooping, her gaunt, drained, angled face highlighted by the many lamps lighting up the stable. Fifteen horses could have fit in this stall with room to stretch. The walls were tiled in mosaic nearly all the way to the incline of the root-laden roof. The floor of the stall was knee-deep in straw as fresh as the morning.

The mare sighed so wearily, even Taneth felt her burden. She made a bit of a groaning sound and dug the straw around with her left front hoof. She then moved a bit, and lowered herself carefully onto her front knees, letting her back end follow more slowly and carefully. Strangely, all her care came to no avail, for her own weight made her fall with a bit of a tired thud on the golden bed of straw.

She sighed again and laid her head down. The townspeople began to arrive, each carrying a small package in their hands. They lay the packages on the table, and gathered in front of the stall, sinking down cross-legged before the half wall, waiting patiently with the mare. The Holyman arrived at this point. He was bedecked in a mask of a horse, and a covering that emulated the fur and mane of a horse. Pieces of reed and leaf stuck out from his form, and the tall mask swayed unsteadily on his head. He managed to keep his footing, no matter how precariously out of balance the ridiculously tall mask made him, and made his way through the aisle the people left for him. Rigerd moved Taneth back a few steps, and made room for the Holyman.

The wide stall doors were pushed back so all could see the mare within and he began to chant. Taneth had read about their rituals, but it was so much better for him to understand the people he had studied, being here firsthand to observe them. He watched the Holyman's dance, but his gaze never remained long upon him, nor the people. He concentrated on the bay mare lying on the hay, her soft muzzle opening wide for a tired breath to pass. Taneth so wanted to be closer. He was afraid to upset their ceremonies, but this was the first true birth he would ever see. He glanced at Rigerd, who seemed to be watching Taneth's reactions.

"She looks so tired …"

"Bearing a child of such size is not an easy task," Rigerd replied. Taneth nodded   thoughtfully.

"Might I be able to get a bit closer? I cannot see anything," Taneth asked. Rigerd shrugged.

"Come," he said, giving Taneth a wave to follow him. They stepped into the straw, ignoring the dancing Holyman. Rigerd led Taneth to within a few meters of the mare. Taneth sat down in the straw and waited. He watched her flanks quiver, and her swollen belly convulse. At that point, everything else seemed to disappear. The Holyman, the people, the walls around them—all Taneth could see and hear was the mare's struggle and her heavy, ragged breaths. It seemed like forever before the white membrane began to show.

"She broke water some time ago. I feared it would be a breach birth, but look: There are the little hooves," Rigerd intruded upon Taneth's quiet, focused world with his statement. He leaned forward and pointed to the membrane. All Taneth could see was the alien protrusion. The mare heaved again, and the protrusion grew. This time, Taneth saw the shape of little hooves within the silvery covering. His throat tightened up. His eyes remained fast to the mare, in fear of missing a thing. The mare heaved again, and the lump of the foal's nose appeared. It was hard work for the mare. She would push, and there would be great progress, and then the contraction would relax, and the foal would slip back in. It seemed as if she wouldn't be able to sustain these efforts for much longer. But suddenly, with one heave, the whole assemblage of limbs and amniotic fluids slid out of the mare into an ungainly heap behind her. He only then noticed that the Holyman made no noise; the people went still as well.

Taneth watched in amazement as the mare lifted her head, and laid her muzzle on this thing. The membrane was slightly torn, and the form lay still within. The mare began to lick away the constricting birth sack. Taneth now saw for the first time the tiny black body and the awkward, stick-like legs of this baby. It had its eyes closed and its head pressed against the fronts of its tiny legs. Taneth thought it was dead. Some licking and prodding from the mother proved him wrong, however.

The little horse jerked ungracefully, and splayed its legs all at once. It struggled and wavered as if tipsy. Taneth's eyes glossed over. Tears slid down his cheeks unnoticed as he watched this small miracle shake its head and prop its tiny knees up. Such coordination for so new a thing. It was amazing that an animal such as the horse could be so aware within moments of its birth, and yet human babies remained objects of high maintenance for years beyond the day of their birth.

Perhaps this animal was worthy of its revered status in this place.

Taneth did not know how much time had passed when the foal began its first attempts to stand. The mother had long since found her own footing and ejected the afterbirth, which was gathered hastily by a town's person and taken to be buried under the roots of an ancestor's tree. The mother cleaned and prodded her gangly child. It struggled and splayed its legs in all directions, searching for a manner in which to stand.

And it did. Wobbling unsteadily. The mother's doting muzzle did not help his effort as she investigated every corner of this new thing beside her. The little colt grew confident on its sticks beneath his small body, and attempted to step forward, nearly falling. A few more tries, and he was happily nuzzling his little muzzle into the mother's teats in search of his first meal. Taneth sat in the stall watching the pair for a long, long time. He could not control his reaction to this amazing thing, the second defining moment in his life. His eyes were red and his nose runny. It was the most beautiful act of nature he had ever witnessed.

He turned to share this with Rigerd, and found him gone. Everyone was gone. The stall doors stood half closed. They'd left him to sit with their worshipped mare alone to learn from her. And to look upon Taphenus, the newborn stallion. He knew that this was his name. They were all named so, new stallions; it was an ancient word for "honored one" Taneth made his way slowly back to the community house, ignorant of the knowing glances that were traded back and forth from the people lingering about inside. There was a silent consensus among them that they had just gained a new Wiseman.

CHAPTER 3

Tinna smiled to herself, stooping over the soft, downy nest of the khari goose she'd felled with her arrow. She had found to her delight that it was a nesting goose, and made it her business to find the object itself, looking forward to fresh goose eggs, as well as a soft material to apply to something useful. She had found exactly what she had hoped for. The eggs were still warm from their mother's downy underbelly. She gathered them up, placing them gently into her shoulder pouch. She then carefully peeled away the mat of soft goose down upon which the eggs had been laid, rolled it up, and ferreted it away into another pouch that contained most of her things.

Khari geese were small for their species, not much larger than a mallard duck. They had long, graceful, deep-blue necks, and black-and-tan bodies. The long pinfeather wings had the same deep blue as the neck. Tinna plucked them out with care, placing the iridescent beauties aside, but threw all the others in front of her feet. She plucked the goose with a practiced hand, finishing her task quickly and efficiently. She gutted and spitted the goose, leaning it on a tree while she crouched above a circle of stones, using a flint and an old, dulled dagger to attain a small flame. She added tinder, and then the wood she had collected, steepling it over the growing flame. She jabbed her forked branches into the earth beside the fire, and reached for her goose. To her utter fury, she discovered the goose was gone. She stood, looking around with a tight frown on her face. She swung her head around, her blue-feather-tipped braids flaring out in a dance of color.

"Hello?!" she shouted, hearing nothing, smelling nothing. She reached for her crossbow, pointing it into the thick growth around her small clearing. Not a sound could be heard except for the wind. She glowered, glancing at what she had left: seven eggs only slightly bigger than chicken eggs. She stooped over them, and gathered them up, reaching for her single cast-iron fire pot, complete with legs to stand above a blaze. She ungracefully jammed the item into the fire, causing an explosion of sparks, and began cracking the eggs into the pot one after the other, and breaking them up with a well-used wooden spoon.

She added some salt from her stores, and a few other dried herbs she kept on hand. She looked around like a wary bird, stirring her eggs absentmindedly as she scanned the trees for the thief. When she decided her scrambled goose eggs were sufficiently done, she simply lifted the pot off the fire by its handle, and plopped it in front of her. Using the same spoon she'd cooked them with, she ate, brows furrowed, eyes focusing on the area where the goose had been.

This wasn't the first time someone or something had stolen her food. She was being followed by someone who appeared to enjoy stealing her food—and did so with such stealth, Tinna wondered if he were invisible. He left no trail on the ground and made no sound … it was making Tinna crazy. It was forcing her to seek out a place where there were more people, where she hoped this invisible thief could not dare to come.

She had had to bypass the school on the hill and the subsequent noisy town at its foot. Despite her knowledge that northerners were more tolerant a people than her own, she did not have any desire to be mired for any length of time amongst an entire city's worth of them. Even if they were better about not saying anything about her obvious differences, they had yet to master hiding their indiscreet stares and whispers. She appreciated the efforts the northerners made to appear unperturbed by having a Thran amongst them, but she tried habitually not to subject herself to too much of these efforts.

She frowned to herself as she trudged along after eating, looking occasionally behind her with animal-like quickness, hoping to catch a glimpse of her stalker. She smelled horses occasionally, when the wind came from the northwest. This meant a community of horse-folk. She'd encountered some of those people near the prairie lands in the first leg of her long journey, and found them to be infinitely delightful and good people. She would stop there for a while. Perhaps her stalker would grow tired of waiting for her to strike out again, and would leave her once and for all.

She found the path worn into the old earth by generations of horse riders packing it down with their hooves. She reached the village by just after sunrise, and smiled at the smell of fresh bread baking, emanating from one of the many lodges open to the forum-like center that held smiling, welcoming faces.

Taneth's two months among the people of Thamatoch made him forget about any desire he'd ever had of being anywhere else. The people had been so welcoming to him; he was immediately made to feel a member of the clan. The horse he'd seen born was named as his own companion; he'd been given his own apartments in the Summer Lodge; he sat with the council of elders at the community hearth; soon he didn't care whether or not he had some great mission to prove his father and the school wrong—all those things seemed long ago and quite vague and unimportant now. He and Rigerd had become as thick as thieves—finding a very strong bond of friendship despite their having very little in common except a strong mutual respect for one another. Taneth had taken only three days after his arrival to formally accept the proposal to remain as their Wiseman. He was initiated a month before, and now he served his people. He educated the children, tended to the ill and wounded, and did all the thinking and inventing to benefit the clan. He had complete autonomy in his work, was trusted explicitly by all he served, and enjoyed a position of some reverence, which was a plus.

The mouse problem he had solved with his knowledge of natural plant poisons. And he had found his intelligence to be useful for many other things, such as providing a plan for running water to the stable and the other lodges, using clay pipes. He was working with Khaim the potter on the pipes, figuring out how to make them link together in a manner that would prevent leaking. Rigerd was coordinating the herders, who were leading the horses back to their summer pasture for the day. It was a crisp morning, the sun was rising with a particular strength this day, and the dew was just beginning to burn away. The community was taking advantage of the cool hours of the morning to do all the things that needed to be done out of doors before it became too hot, including the baking, which produced a tremendous amount of heat in and of itself.

* * * *

Tinna walked right into the scene. She saw an immense, towering, and muscled character standing with his arms crossed—the clan's chieftain by his markings—overlooking a lady potter and a young, quite handsome Wiseman who had yet to attain the full set of tattoo markings of his position, but wore the garb of his station. They were working on some clay tubes and the chieftain seemed intrigued by the process. Tinna appreciated the northern ways ... one could always tell a person's place in their society by their clothing and markings. The Holyman and the herders were just leaving the center of the village with a cluster of horses, probably taking them out to pasture for the day. Children ran about, women wove baskets, sewed garments, and worked standing looms while chattering like hens. The aroma of yeasty bread permeated the scene.

It took a moment for someone to notice the unkempt girl enter the forum. Rigerd looked up first, and then Taneth. He stood up straight, and glanced at the leader.

"A Thran," Taneth said. "I've heard of them. This is my first time ever seeing one." He couldn't take his eyes from her. She was so beautiful, his breath caught in his throat at the sight of her. She was not very tall; in fact, she was petite. She had beautiful raven-black curls of hair; so long it brushed the nape of her back.

Her eyes were such a deep luminous black; they could have been made of hematite. Her legs were strong and muscular, covered in smooth, flawless, olive-colored skin. She had exotic almond-shaped eyes that were slanted just a bit, like a cat. She had full, pouting lips that made Taneth bite his own at the sight of them.

She wore the clothing typical of a Thran, a short, thin, gathered linen skirt sewn to the bottom of a wide hip-belt. The belt itself was set low on her flat tummy, clinging to hips, revealing the soft, elegant curve of skin just above the crease between the thigh and her body. She wore a linen top of the same thickness as her skirt, clinging to a pair of perfect, rounded little breasts that were almost visible through the fabric. Taneth had to avert his eyes to keep control of his mind.

"Mmm. They can be trouble," Rigerd grumbled. "Their ways are strange. They can also be a bit militant and confrontational, from what I hear. If she is a Thran, I hope she doesn't want to stay." He sighed. He then went into a subdued but welcome mode, as was required of him as a leader. He walked up to the woman, and lowered his gaze in a curt bow, placing his fist on his right shoulder.

"I am Rigerd, leader of the Clan Thamatoch. Welcome to our village named for our clan."

"Aitinna of Ymnoth," she replied. Her voice was low and velvety. Taneth liked the quality of it very much. It seemed to strike his core ... like the strumming of a harp string. He'd reacted to women before, but never this strongly—it made his neck flush, and his throat itch. He kept clearing his throat nervously, attempting quite badly to watch her discreetly while Rigerd spoke to her.

"I seek shelter. I am willing to work for my keep."

Her eyes kept glancing over at Taneth, too, every time he harrumphed, which only made him more nervous and embarrassed. It was nigh impossible to study her properly through the haze of sheer attraction he felt. He turned to the knowledge he had of her people to distract him from his boyish response. He'd read books about her kind: They were people of the south; they tended to have common features, and were less varied in appearance as northerners were; they mostly had black hair and brown eyes; their skin was usually made for their sunnier, temperate climate ... and the deep, exotic, olive-tone that Taneth finally understood. It was hard to imagine such a skin color without ever seeing it. It was so much richer than he'd imagined. Glowing even. This girl was much that he expected in a Thran based on the descriptions of her culture, but there were some inconsistencies that confused him. There were her unusually high cheekbones, the seductive tilt of her eyes and her diminutive height. She did have the black hair comprised of hundreds of tight ringlets—that was consistent with what he knew. She had most of them tied back in a thick tail, leaving only a select few to coil down the sides of her face and onto her shoulders—and she also had a few attractive little braids decorated with the bright, royal-blue feathers of the summer goose, which were also a norm for her kind. Something to do with age, he remembered.

The clothing, he recollected, was made of the linen her people were known for, and the soft suede they also exported. She was visibly recognizable as a Thran on the most part. However, the fact that she was up north, alone, went against everything he knew about her culture. Her people were insular and even bitter against non-matriarchal societies. They kept themselves within their mountainous borders, and the only ones who ventured out were unwanted by those they left behind. What was it that had made her abandon her comfortable status of female superiority, to be frowned on by northern, woman-oppressing savages?

His eyes took in her whole being, looking for the answer. She carried a large pack on her back with a campfire pot dangling from it, a shoulder bag, a crossbow—a purely Thran weapon—on her hip, with a small quiver on the same belt filled to capacity with small arrow bolts. She had soil imbedded on her knees, the front of her soft suede calf boots, and on the palms of her hands. She was pretty dirty, to say the least. She looked gaunt as well, as if she wasn't getting enough to eat. There was something about her that he couldn't quite place—something unusual. If I knew more about her people, I'll wager I could figure it out just by what I see of her this moment, he thought, angered by the limitations his lack of knowledge caused him. Taneth liked to know everything. Understand everything. Not knowing left him unprepared. And uncomfortable.

"You are welcome here. As long as you respect our ways," Rigerd said with a stern glance. She did not show any offense at his words.

"I respect the ways of all people," she replied. She glanced at Khaim and Taneth, wondering in passing what they could possibly be doing with those pipes.

"Taneth, show her to the visitor's quarters, would you?" Rigerd asked. Tinna turned to look at this Wiseman named Taneth, noticing the stricken look on his face when his leader made the request of him. His neck and ears were red, and he coughed and fidgeted. He nodded finally, jumping into action, and held his hand out toward the second long-house, nearly tripping over a stray toy as he led her along.

Young people who'd recently married and were building their first home together were the ones who mainly inhabited this particular lodge. The third long-house was the home of the elderly, who preferred their own quiet part of the village, free of squealing children and other such disturbances. The guest hearth was in the second lodge, known as the Spring Lodge. It was the lodge that was blessed for fertility, and where all new children were born. The Summer Lodge was where the larger families, and the leaders lived. The meeting lodge was the Autumn Lodge; nobody lived in it. All ceremonies and gatherings were held there, and it acted as a formal temple to the horse god aside from the more informal ones in Horse Hall.

Taneth led her to the Spring Lodge. Sitting outside were the youngest of the married women, some no more than sixteen. They chatted, and learned things from one another, doing their projects in the morning sun under the dappled shadow of the great oak. They looked up at Taneth, some blushing and smiling at him. He received warm greetings from them. The warmth faded immediately when they saw Tinna, evolving into a collective gaze of mistrust.

"This is Aitinna. She will be staying with us for a while," he introduced her. A young woman smiled shyly, admiring the woman with a look of envy. She was Rhoa, who lived in the Spring Lodge with her sister, who was married but one year. Rhoa had been forced to live with the newlyweds because her father had died, and her sister did not want her alone yet at such a tender age of seventeen.

32

She was a pretty little thing, albeit a bit strange in her taste in clothes and such. She was often treated badly by the other girls because of her different tastes and odd behavior. She was an introvert, and enjoyed her time alone. She hated to be forced to sit in the group with her sister to do crafts she despised. When she saw the Thran, her heart leapt. She'd often created little fantasy scenarios in her head of her becoming a Thran, wearing those daring clothes, and the feathers, and having utter freedom to do as she wished, learning to defend herself, and be the dominant sex. She jumped to her feet.

Tinna studied her in a quick glance—thick and wavy auburn hair loose and wild with little braids randomly peppering her scalp. Her eyes were wide and curious, a quality Aitinna appreciated. They were also a deep, lovely golden brown. She was small, like Tinna, about the same height, but certainly less muscular, and uncoordinated and clumsy in her movements.

"Welcome, Aitinna," Rhoa said. "Will you be staying at the guest quarters?"

"Yes, she will," Taneth said, his face still a deep red. Tinna noticed he harrumphed between every other word when he was flustered.

"I will show her in, Taneth. Thank you." She smiled and led Tinna away from Taneth. As they stepped through the doorway into the darkened hall, he heard the girl, Rhoa ask:

"You are Thran? I've always wanted to meet a Thran ..." Her voice faded as they disappeared into the darkness of the hall, the door swinging shut behind them. The other women looked at Taneth questioningly.

"Rigerd agreed to let her stay?" one of the older girls asked in disbelief, brow arched quizzically. Taneth noted how her hands never stopped working the loom as she looked up at him.

"He did. He asked her to respect our ways. I think she will. She seems like she knows this land, and she's been up north long enough to learn a few lessons about cultural sensitivity," he reassured them. They trusted him for his word. He'd given them no reason to think otherwise. They nodded, returning to their activities.

Taneth found Rigerd, who'd gone to help some of the remaining men clean the stalls out while they were vacant. Taneth checked on his new friend Taphenus, whom he had named Fox, because he had shown slyness in his very strong personality. He always tried to escape the stall—he was fiercely independent for a young foal. He wasn't glued to his dam like most babies. He was too fascinated with people, and all the interesting things they carried with them that were delightful to nibble on, including hands and fingers. It was acceptable before he'd grown his milk teeth, but of course now, it could hurt.

He and his mother were being prepared to be led to the paddock. Rigerd smiled at Taneth when he entered the darkened stable.

"Pretty little thing," he noted. Taneth nodded, reaching for Fox's soft little muzzle. Immediately, he grabbed onto Taneth's fingers. Taneth ignored him, letting him nibble away to his delight.

"Keep an eye on her, though," Rigerd said. "I find it difficult to trust her kind"

"I've read a great deal about her culture. I'm familiar with her ways. I shall watch her. But as I told the girls at the Spring Lodge, it seems she's been up north for some time, and she seems quite familiar with our culture. I don't think she'll be much trouble"

"She's really quite pretty," Rigerd repeated, arching a brow and looking through the huge opening of the stable at the Spring Lodge.

"She is," Taneth agreed, his ears growing pink again. Being around normal people again afforded him the opportunity to learn social skills. The students he's grown up with were not at all social beings—they were dedicated scholars. His experience was limited to the city at the foot of the school, and he hardly went there anyway. At Thamatoch, however, he'd become an object of adoration from the moment he'd arrived. Young girls living in the Summer Lodge often stood outside his door every morning to greet him, and would fight over who would respond to his summons for assistance with certain projects or needs, and stand about giggling under the shady oak, eyes all locked on him.

Rigerd often made hints that he should feel free to court someone, and consider mating with a girl. But Taneth didn't feel quite ready yet to father children or live with someone day in and day out. He was so curious about his world, and he had so many ideas and things he wanted to do, that he didn't want to be limited by being responsible for the needs of another person. Not yet. But it seemed that Rigerd was hinting again. Rigerd thought perhaps an educated man, a man of the world such as Taneth, would find the village women not worldly enough for his tastes. He thought that perhaps an exotic creature from a matriarchal society, with a perpetual bone to pick with all men, would be an adequate challenge for a man of his intelligence.

"What sort of things would suit her … to earn her keep, of course?"

"Well, she's Thran. She has the ability to make that amazing leather...Maybe we can hunt for some fresh meat, and give her the hides to work," Taneth suggested, thinking about the wide panel of that very soft suede hugging her narrow hips and clinging to her flat tummy. The fine quality linen skirt that brushed her golden, perfectly hewn thighs. Rigerd cleared his throat, scratching his head.

"Anyway, I'm going to help the fellows finish up the stalls. I think you should go back to Khaim and work on those pipes." Taneth joined Khaim as Rigerd suggested, giving her a few more suggestions for the pipes before preparing for his afternoon session with the children.

CHAPTER 4

Four days later, Tinna entered the main lodge quite warily. The hottest hours of the day had come, and everyone had all but vanished. She didn't mind the heat, and would have stayed outdoors, but as usual, the place was a ghost town during this time. She had finished washing her dirty clothes and all such things the day before, running out of activities to fill this void of time. She ventured out of her little room this day, hoping to find some occupation, one person who was still awake … something, anything. The young women out front had gone to their own respective little apartments, and were napping through the midday. She padded through the courtyard under the sweltering oak tree. She entered the main lodge, poking her head in first. The lodge was quiet, except far in the back, Wiseman Taneth was sitting at the table with a young boy, leaning in to hear the boy's whispers. His little eyes were puffy and his cheeks reddened from tears He was a sad-looking little creature, with the appearance of a retired fighter, all sinew and bones, with eyes that betrayed a terrible experience that made him look old.

Tinna knew that look, and instantly understood the slumped, frightened posture. Her heart went out to him straight away. The wary child looked up at Tinna the moment he sensed her, and Taneth followed the child's gaze. "Aitinna," he said, gesturing for her to sit at the huge table with them.

"Tinna," she muttered, her voice breaking. "Call me Tinna," she replied, clearing the frog from her throat. She smiled wanly, sinking down on the bench across the table from him. "'Ai' is a formal appellation, much like Miss," she explained.

Taneth nodded, glad to have this little tidbit of knowledge to add to his growing mental-encyclopedia on Tinna. She hadn't been around this man too much, but whenever she was in his company, she found herself increasingly uncomfortable—mostly because of the discomfort he seemed to display whenever she was around.

"Is it like Miss? Are there different forms of this word, as there is a Mr. or Mrs.?" he asked, rattling out the words at incredible speed. She smiled inwardly. He found comfort in learning new things. It gave him a chance to communicate in a way he was fully comfortable with. Tinna cocked her head and arched her brows.

"Yes. The names of women of high stature and rank are prefixed with Na-ai. Young girls, ones in training and apprenticing, are given the title of Iri before their given name. I was once Iritinna. I shall one day be Na-aitinna."

"And the male counterparts to these appellations?" Taneth asked, his face devoid of expectation, only filled with a wonderful curiosity. Tinna's ears and cheeks grew hot, and she dropped her gaze, for she knew with northerners this was a sore subject. She shook her head. "The men are not permitted such embellishments as they are thought to be unworthy of them." There was an uncomfortable silence, and Taneth inhaled and then exhaled. His voice however, broke the quiet moment.

"Hanru and I were just having a little chat before you arrived. Are you hungry?" Tinna glanced up at him, not expecting him to just leave the subject without making some pointed comment about her culture. He looked quite unaffected by the statement she'd made, and was distracted again by the boy.

"No. The girl, uh, Rhoa, shared her meal with me. I was just looking for something to do." Taneth found that he liked her accent very much. She'd been among them for four days now. She did not participate in all their activities, and acted quite shy and withdrawn when everyone was gathered. She remained on the most part to herself, sometimes engaging Taneth in a halting conversation about her people, but infrequently, and it was mostly a conversation that was erratic at best, and that usually tapered into uncomfortable silences. It was typically because he was only really comfortable when he was trying to learn about her people—which was a safely impersonal subject—and if she wasn't willing to talk about her culture, he really didn't know how to initiate chat about anything else. So he would start harrumphing again, and eventually move away in order to prevent further embarrassment. She did spend some time showing the women of the Spring Lodge some of her methods of tanning with some hides they'd gotten from the storage room in the Summer Lodge. Rhoa was her greatest admirer, and the two spent most of their time together, whether Aitinna willed it so or not, it seemed. But Rhoa was quite determined to be her friend. So far,

Tinna had yet to be devoid of something to do … this was a first for her to be bored and restless.

Taneth had never actually seen her have to seek out company or a project before now. This moment was a surprise to Taneth. A pleasant one at that. The unexpectedness of her arrival caught him slightly off guard, but because there was already a task at hand, there was no need to flounder for words or activities to span the silence. He had Hanru, and an objective in mind—that alone made the discomfort wash away.

"Well. Your timing is excellent. Hanru was asking if I would help him with a little task. Perhaps you can assist." She looked more closely at Hanru. She saw a great deal more to add to the story she was building about him. The child had a difficult life. The old scars on his arms, the burn marks on his neck and the sunken eyes, spoke a great deal about his existence. He did seem to like the Wiseman a great deal, and she had noticed him occasionally since she arrived, trailing about behind the man like a little shadow. She gave him a little smile, and he returned it, but a very shy one, his face moving slowly behind Taneth's arm. "Do you not sleep?" she asked Taneth, a brow arching, looking directly into Taneth's eyes.

This directness of her gaze threw Taneth off stride quite often. Her eyes were very intense, and he often couldn't look in them. They incited a number of reactions he feared she'd see—it was easier to appear distracted by something over her shoulder, or act as if he had some grit under his nail that required his immediate attention while he talked.

"I've had trouble assimilating that part of their routine just yet." He laughed uneasily. "This is usually an intensive study hour for me, and sometimes I use the time to write books."

"How long have you served these people as knowledge-keeper again?"

"Two months," he replied.

he had thought it longer for some reason, but she now remembered him telling her that a day ago. Perhaps it was because he had integrated so well with the clan, it made him seem less like an outsider than anyone else would in so little time.

"Shall we go?" he asked.

Tinna could only consent. She was bored and uncomfortable. She noted in this small interchange with Taneth, that despite his agitation around her, he had very much figured out who he was somewhere along the line, and even with his fidgety hands and itchy throat, he could be relied upon to be exactly who he presented himself to be. His questions were always questions to slake an ever-thirsty curiosity, and he seemed to accept just about everything she had to say at face value Everyone else interacted with her in some different mode, somewhat wary and distanced, except for Rhoa, who was harder to get rid of than an infestation of lice, and equally as annoying. She smiled to herself, and looked at the man and the boy. She had to give him credit for that. She never felt like a stranger with the Wiseman. His reactions were obvious and sometimes disconcerting, but she could rest assured it wasn't because he was uncomfortable that she was a Thran. It was because he was attracted to her, and vastly inexperienced with women; and that, she could handle. Taneth nodded to Hanru, and they all rose.

They crossed the forum and left the village, heading into the trees via a narrow but very worn path. The little boy held a small wooden box. Inside was a small puppy that had been killed tragically—a large bird of prey had attempted to make off with the boy's little dog, from what Tinna understood, and couldn't keep hold of the whelp, dropping him from high. Poor Hanru was inconsolable.

Taneth explained to Tinna what the situation was as they picked through the dense forest. On their way out to this mysterious destination, Taneth uprooted an oak sapling, and they continued on. Tinna found herself liking this fellow even more as they marched along. He was very smart, but unlike most of the products of the academies, he was very human. He was especially good with the sad little boy. He spent most of his time sympathizing with the child, whose lower lip trembled and nose dribbled as he cried over his lost puppy.

Tinna empathized with his loss. She had once had a canine companion on her travels, but he'd perished from old age only this past winter. The cold of the northern winters proved too much for her southern dog to bear. She lamented this to herself as she followed the tall man and the small boy through the trees.

The sun was at the zenith when they reached their destination, which was a small glade surrounded by towering oaks. There was a little brook washing over a bed of smooth stones running right through the center of the glade. It was a place often used. There was a tattered trail to the water's edge, and a number of signs of children having taken possession of this special place. There were small wooden animals lying about here and there, a doll propped up against a tree, and a wooden splashing bucket by the brook.

"Now ... where do you want to put Nibbler?" Taneth asked. The boy pointed a sad finger at a small grassy plot on the far side of

40

the clearing near the place where the brook emerged from the darkness of the forest.

"Is that a good place?" Taneth asked. The boy nodded.

"They're all 'fraid of that place," he said. "Nobody will go there." It was a tad intimidating through the eyes of a child, Tinna thought. The brook emerged from a cavernous leafy mouth, and the entire end of the clearing on that side seemed ominous and dark because of the dense growth edging the glade.

"We'll have to tear up those little trees trying to occupy that space," Taneth said. The boy nodded, crossing the shallow brook with his bare feet. Taneth and Tinna followed. They turned right toward the plot by the dense foliage. It was an ideal place, Taneth thought. The sun shone brightly, uninhibited by the canopies of the looming trees nearby. There were a large variety of plants attempting to take up this precious spot. The three began to pull them up, one after the other.

Once there was sufficient space cleared, Taneth went back to get the tall sapling, carrying it back across the brook to where the boy and Tinna stood. The boy took the small spade he had tied to his belt. He put the box in Tinna's hands and stooped, beginning to dig through the rich, loamy soil—fresh smelling from their vigorous weeding. Taneth took over for a while, letting the boy keep the tree with wilting leaves from toppling over. Taneth dug a sizable hole. Tinna suddenly realized what the tree had to do with the whole thing. She'd never actually seen a northern burial before, but she had heard of the ritual. Her feeling of uselessness suddenly vanished, as she unexpectedly did.

"Where did the lady go?" Hanru asked.

Taneth looked up, his face smudged with dirt. "I don't know. She'll be back; she's got Nibbler," He climbed out of the hole, brushing his gown off. "In the meantime, go get that bucket and fill it up with some leaf litter from under the trees there." The boy obeyed, returning with the desired goods, having braved the darkness of the dense growth to gather it.

Taneth sprinkled the hole with the dark, rich-smelling humus. He then told the boy to get the bucket and fill it with water. He wondered where Tinna had gone, but just as he was about to lose his patience she returned, carrying a rainbow of colorful wildflowers. She handed the boy the box with Nibbler inside it, and sat down on a large granite rock. Her hands danced over the bundle of flowers. Taneth knew what she was doing and hid a soft smile.

41

"Everything's ready," he declared when the boy gave him the bucket of water.

"It's time. Tinna? We're about to begin." The boy looked up at the woman, who looked tall from his perspective.

She carried her freshly made garlands of forest blossoms to the site of the newly dug hole, quite fascinated. She sat down with crossed legs at the edge of the hole as the boy had, holding the box with Nibbler inside. Taneth stood beside the hole, reaching for his hip bag where he kept his collection of herbs. Tinna was instantly intrigued by his collection, having a sizable one of her own. She was becoming increasingly interested in this character that was so different from his other Wiseman brethren. They were never so easy-going and real. They were healers and educators, usually cocky and arrogant from a lifetime of being marinated in a cesspool of self-importance. Hardly ever did they care to the level that they would dig a hole to plant an oak for a dead puppy. He sprinkled some lavender into the hole, chanting out some words of blessing.

"Of the earth to the earth, out of death there is rebirth ..." These were sacred words. He was committing a crime against protocol, using the ceremony for a human death to bury naught but a small dog. He was also treading on the Holyman's territory, which was only permitted in certain circumstances. But it didn't matter. It was for a dog. And a lost boy. Tinna also knew that in this community it would not be frowned upon. She saw a goodness in the people, and especially in the leader, Rigerd. They would approve of this attempt to assuage a boy's grief. Taneth opened the box the boy held, lifting the tiny carcass out of it, feeling a sudden pang of sadness for this helpless innocent thing taken so young.

"May this shell feed this tree. May the roots release the essence. May the tree absorb the soul. May the tree become the life. May it live long, with dignity. May it watch over us all, and serve as counsel to all who seek its wisdom," he rambled, sprinkling a mélange of herbs, blessing the bed in which both the tree and the puppy would rest. He lay the puppy down, and buried him a bit, sprinkling more herbs on the thin layer of soil covering him. "Bless this life, young as it was. Of the earth to the earth; out of death there is rebirth," he said, remembering the words he'd read in his books. He then lifted the tree, and laid it gently over the puppy.

"Let us all pack the soil in around the roots."

The three set to work shoving the dirt back into the hole, and pressing it hard into the shallow roots of the juvenile tree. Taneth poured the water all around the roots occasionally; continuing to pack the dirt in layer by layer, making sure the tree was properly hydrated. When they were done, they were muddy and tired.

Tinna reached for her garlands. "In my land, the dead are honored with gifts of flowers and ribbons before they are cremated on a pyre. I have made some garlands for your friend. May I lay them at the foot of his tree?" The boy nodded, smiling wanly. Tinna, resting on her knees, leaned forward and looped the garlands around the trunk, fastening them shut. "Is this a fitting tribute, do you think?" she asked Hanru. He nodded.

"You must give Nibbler water every day for the next three days," Taneth instructed the boy. "Speak to him. It will encourage his essence to leave the shell and take over the tree. The tree will gain strength if you pay him sufficient attention to make him want to possess this new body. But once he does take over, it doesn't mean you can neglect him. He will do well if you pay him tributes, and keep him apprised of what's going on in the community. Keep vines from growing up his trunk, and weeds from growing around the roots. Talk to him of the things he loved."

"He liked this." Hanru withdrew a thick log of felted sheep's wool from his tunic. It had the appearance of being ravaged by a playful young canine.

"He still does, I'm sure. It is customary to give gifts to the tree. You tie them to the branches, loosely so that it won't inhibit the growth of the tree. They will be carried up to the sky as the tree grows," Taneth explained. Taneth pulled a thick flax cord from his hip bag, and tied it tightly around the felted toy, then tied it to a high branch of the eight-foot sapling.

"It is in his hands now. Whether he decides to leave his shell and take residence in this young tree ... You can help him make the transition. You promise to do that?" Hanru nodded. "Good. We will leave you to wake his essence from his sleep. You should talk to him. Tell him how much you miss him" The boy nodded, still kneeling next to the tree.

Taneth gestured to Tinna, and she stood, following him out of the glade. "I can't imagine I was of great help, but I'm glad you asked me along," she said. Taneth smiled through his dirty face. "You were a great help," he replied gently, his eyes lingering fleetingly on her own dark irises.

"That was good of you to do what you did for the boy— stepping on the Holyman's toes, perhaps, but it was nice nonetheless."

"I am permitted to perform that ritual too, under their laws. That is why I know the ceremony; the Holyman showed it to me. But yes, I did overstep my bounds." He smiled shyly, eyes on the path ahead. Tinna walked beside him reflectively.

"It's a beautiful way to go," she said. "I think I like it more than fire," she admitted.

Taneth stopped, nodding. "Come, let me show you something." He began to walk faster, taking another path that branched from this one. Tinna followed, curious and pleased at the same time. He was getting easier around her; at least it felt that way. He had an expectant smile as he led her through the maze of paths in the forest around the village. He stopped abruptly, and lifted his head. "We're almost there, but listen," he whispered. She listened. And she heard the faint sound of glass tinkling together, and what sounded like metal, as well. Taneth led her up a rise, and over, stopping at the crest. Tinna's eyes widened. This was a sacred place indeed.

Before them was the village cemetery. By that definition, it meant it was an oak forest. Oaks of all ages, planted haphazardly, wherever a good circle of sun had offered a sapling opportunity to grow. And there were hundreds. Thick and narrow trunks alike, the ground clean of leaf litter, paths winding around the root bases like lace—it was unbelievable. Acorns were piled in neat cone-shaped heaps here and there in some bizarre act of reverence for the dead that lay entangled in the roots of these trees. Above, the branches of these ancestral trees were festooned with items, put there by loving hands. Wind chimes of copper covered in a green patina, colored-glass tied onto mobiles that sang and shimmered in the wind, toys, dolls, tools, horseshoes, whatever would have meant something to someone at some time was tied up there.

"I remember when I first came to the village, and saw the Founder's Tree, I remembered reading about this custom. I thought it lovely then—poetic, however idealistic. Then Rigerd brought me out here just before my official induction as Wiseman, so I could understand his people better. Understand their relationship to the world. Standing here, it struck me very hard. It brought tears to my eyes. I have always been most adverse to any spirituality, Aitinna, I thought it weak and frivolous, a desperate attempt to stanch the fear of death. But Arak help me ... I stood here with Rigerd, and I could feel them. Every one of them. It's strange, and it doesn't mean I've gone and become some mindless zealot, but I think I understood it better at that moment—that the love of those who survived them keeps them alive. It's like this forest breathes, and if you stand still, and listen, you can hear them whisper." He closed his eyes, and smiled softly. Tinna stared at him for a moment. It was a side of him that surprised her. She turned her gaze onto this wonderful place of death. It was alive. Peaceful, vibrant, and comforting. The leaves hissed in the breeze and yes, it did sound like voices.

The cacophony of noise made by the tokens in the branches gave it all the more mystery. But it was the care that the people of Thamatoch took in cleaning the forest floor that made the whole place appear almost unnatural and otherworldly. It was beautiful beyond words, and so was this man who stood there, with his eyes closed, listening to the dead speak. All discomfort blew away in the breeze right then, for both Taneth and his quiet, dark-haired companion.

Taneth's eyes snapped open and he turned his head to look down at her intent gaze. "Amazing, isn't it?" She nodded, noticing the attractive little wrinkles that appeared under his jaw when he turned his head like that.

"As I said, much more dignified and beautiful than fire." She sighed. He nodded.

"Let's leave them to themselves. They're probably sick of the living by now." He hopped down the rise, and returned to the path. "The pup's tree isn't with the others, because I'm not sure if the villagers would appreciate that, but nonetheless, there's a sense of closure for the boy, and it's done in a way that's comforting and familiar to Hanru," he surmised, falling back into a comfortable stride again as the path leveled out.

Tinna nodded, smiling wanly. "It will give him great comfort to know that the puppy isn't really gone forever."

"Yes. Poor boy. He was very much attached to the pup. He doesn't have many friends. He's a bit of a loner. He has a troubled life. And with all those things against him, he is also brighter than the other children. That puppy not only brought him joy, but also brought him the attention of those who envied him having the little dog. He lost a great deal when Nibbler died. And seeing it happen was very traumatic for him as well."

"Poor thing. Where did he get the dog?"

"Some Gypsies came through a few months past. Their mongrels had a litter of pups. The Soothsayer gave it to him when she saw the ostracized boy, making a great event of it."

"I see. So there are no dogs readily available here?"

"No, nobody breeds them in this village because they don't need them for herding." He shrugged. "I shall go to the academy tomorrow. There's a settlement at the foot of the old fortification where I am certain I can find a young dog for Hanru," she decided.

"I don't want him to neglect the tree. A new pup would distract him," Taneth warned her. "These people believe that if the tree dies, the soul underneath has refused to leave this world … it's very distressing to them." She smiled.

"I shall help him," she declared.

Suddenly, Taneth stopped, and held his fingers up to his lips. She furrowed her brows in puzzlement. "Hear that?" he whispered.

She shook her head, wondering if he was trying to hear the chimes and glass of the cemetery again. She heard only the trees waving their branches in time with the gusts of wind, but nothing else. "What?" she whispered in return.

Taneth didn't answer, he only stood very still, and tuning his hearing onto something she obviously wasn't hearing. She tried to listen, but caught nothing. He was looking up now, at the trees. All she saw were limbs moving in the wind. Taneth then suddenly moved again, back toward the village. She followed at his heels, wondering why he seemed so preoccupied. When they entered the village square, he turned to her.

"You bring a Nimrath with you," he snapped. She furrowed her brow again, confused. She had no idea what a Nimrath was. She said exactly that.

"Oh come now—" he chided her, dubious of her claim. He saw the utter confusion in her eyes, and suddenly believed her. "You travel alone, yes?" She nodded, crossing to a new bench under the oak to sit. He followed, standing over her. "Did you ever glimpse anyone nearby when you thought yourself alone?"

"No." Then she paused, thinking it was silly to pursue the thought that entered her mind, but she felt comfortable with Taneth now, and just went with it. "But I have … felt … someone. And then there were these stupid things, like my food vanishing without a trace of anyone ever being there." She laughed uncomfortably, fearing he would mock her.

He did not. Instead he nodded knowingly. "No tracks?"

"That's the strangest thing; I could have easily marked it up as a clever little forest animal stealing my food, but there were no tracks."

"That's because they don't travel on the ground, they travel in the trees." Tinna's mouth opened in disbelief.

"What exactly is this thing?"

"Well, to be perfectly honest, nobody really knows what they are. They are shaped like us, only smaller. They have skin that can mimic its surroundings, and blend right into the trees. They have rarely been seen because they blend so well. And they seldom actually walk on the forest floor," he said, summarizing his knowledge of these mysterious entities. "They are thieves. They steal everything, and have been known to abduct people, mostly children, and pets, too. There were some around Hildercross during my teenage years that created some serious problems with the locals, and we had to be grilled over and over again on what to keep an eye out for in order to avoid running into one. I've been increasingly sensitive to those lessons since I've come out here, but Rigerd says there's little sign of them. I heard something up there, Aitinna. I certainly heard something. And the movement of the limbs was like something heavy was affecting them."

"How bizarre." Tinna blanched a little, swallowing hard.

"They don't venture too close to settlements because they don't like to be seen. Somewhere along the line they learned to avoid human settlements in general.

Every once in a while, however, they come in droves and strike at communities … it's almost like a small-scale war. They inflict significant damage and then vanish for years. I've a theory it's a retribution attack, for something we've done to them, but who knows for what, when we don't even know the face of our attackers?"

"Why was it following me?" she asked. "And from where? How long did it plan to follow me, or do you think it wanted to abduct me?" she rambled, standing up again. "Will it go away? Why is it here if it fears settlements? Do you think it's going to be one of those war-strikes?"

"Slow down, Tinna," he grunted. "But I'm afraid for Hanru. I think we should go back and get him."

"Yes. I'll go for him. But perhaps you should tell Rigerd that there's one of those… Nim… Nim… Nimthings roaming about at the fringes of the village," she suggested.

"Good idea." Just as he said that, Hanru came into the forum, looking sad, but certainly lightened a bit. Tinna ran over to the boy, and picked him up, relieved to see that he was all right. She looked flustered. Taneth gestured to her to follow him into the main lodge.

The residents of the Summer Lodge were just rising from their long siesta when Taneth and the others entered. Hanru's mother Rhana yanked him out of Tinna's arms and thrust him onto the ground. "Where have you been? What were you doing with that

47

southern whore?" she hissed, squeezing his arm very tightly. Hanru squirmed out of her grasp, and shoved his mother away, running to Taneth. Rigerd appeared.

"Where have you been?" he snapped.

"We had a little ceremony of transition for Nibbler," Taneth retorted in a low, shameful voice. Rigerd couldn't answer to that, and Rhana frowned darkly. Rigerd simply crossed his arms, and Rhana left.

"We have a bit of a problem," Taneth said. "It seems a Nimrath has followed our guest here." Rigerd furrowed his brow, and he leapt instantly into action, barking out orders.

CHAPTER 5

Tinna was busying herself gathering up the mess she'd made showing a young girl how to make the soft suede her people were known for. Most of the villagers were at rest. Taneth wasn't; he and Hanru had gone to see the tree and give it water. They returned during the hottest hour, spotting Tinna, who was just finishing her task, and getting onto her feet. They walked toward her. Hanru, hungry for the attention both she and Taneth gave him, ran to her. Tinna picked him up, bouncing him a little bit as he sat on her strong arm. He was sad. Poor thing.

There were bruises on his arm from where his mother had squeezed him. The boy always had a new mark at the beginning of each day. It was growing close to intolerable for both Tinna and Taneth to see this happening to the boy. Taneth wasn't sure what to do about it, and Tinna knew it wasn't her place to step in, however tempted she was to pummel that woman's face into her skull.

"How's Nibbles?" Tinna asked, tickling him under his chin.

"He's wonderful," Taneth exclaimed with an overly excited tone. Tinna pursed her lips, and brushed some of the boy's flyaway hairs from his forehead.

"Do you miss him?"

Hanru nodded. "He was my friend," he muttered, his tone rising in pitch with each word. He was soon sniffling and weeping again.

"I know," Tinna cooed. "But you'll have a new little dog soon," she said. "And he'll be just as wonderful a friend as Nibbles was."

"Really?" Hanru asked. Taneth frowned.

"Really. So you had better start thinking up a good name for your new friend. And make sure you take good care of Nibbles—because I am going to go and get you a new puppy very soon."

"You promise?"

"I promise!" she declared. "You make a promise; you give your word—you break that promise, you owe all who heard!" Tinna sang.

49

The boy giggled over his tears. Hanru hugged his arms around Tinna's neck; his eyes clamped tightly shut. Taneth gave Tinna a disapproving shake of the head. He left Tinna and Hanru together to go take a short nap before everyone awoke expecting stories from him.

That night, Taneth found Tinna after the evening meal. She was just helping a girl with her tanning mixture, and was washing her hands in the small fountain Khaim and Taneth had installed in the entranceway of the main lodge to experiment with their "running water" pipes.

"Tinna, you shouldn't promise that boy things. His life is comprised of broken promises and shattered hopes. It's cruel."

"I have no intention of breaking my promise to Hanru, Taneth," Tinna grunted, trying to scrub the tallow from between her fingers. Taneth watched her silently for a moment, finding himself lost in the movement of her graceful fingers. He was growing to care for this woman a great deal.

"Was there anything else you wanted to reprimand me for?" she asked sarcastically.

"No." He laughed uneasily. He realized he did a lot of that, telling her what to do and what not to do. He felt bad, reaching up and massaging the back of his neck. He thought he'd like to spend more positive time with her, but wasn't sure how. "I'm going to do some work on some of the books I have here … mainly copying a few so that everyone can have access to the information without harming the original. Perhaps you could assist me."

"How could I be of any help?"

"You know how to write?"

"Yes. And I write in your language very well," she added, with a bit of a proud smile.

"Excellent. You can help me copy some texts." She thought about it for a moment, and then nodded.

"I'll get some things, and meet you at the main table," she offered.

Taneth nodded and watched her leave the lodge, jogging across the lighted forum to the Spring Lodge on her magnificently muscled legs. She returned when he'd set out the books he wanted copied, and some blank books he'd ordered and just received from the town near Hildercross. She arrived carrying a small pillow to pad her side of the bench, and had changed into some different clothes, a pair of leggings, and a loose, floppy tunic. Gone were the small skirts and short tops since she'd arrived. He thought perhaps the people of Thamatoch made her feel a bit uncomfortable for it.

She settled down at the bench, and looked over the supplies he'd laid out.

"What do I start with?" she asked, her eyes bright.

Taneth was suddenly overwhelmed by her presence, by her eagerness to take part in his project, by the flash of her eyes and the casual smile on her face. He cleared his throat and grinned clumsily. "Uh … any of these books … you can start any of these. Here's a blank one. It has many more pages than the text you're copying. I'm hoping to fit more than one book in the blank ones; they're expensive. Rigerd wasn't too pleased with the cost," he rambled.

Tinna watched him fidget and squirm, very well familiar with such things. She was an experienced woman. Thran culture encouraged their women to be forward and confident in all of their endeavors, including sexuality. She knew

Taneth was attracted to her—and she to him. Normally, she would not hesitate to engage with a man she was attracted to, but something held her back with Taneth. He deserved more than the usual romp, and she found that perhaps it was because she respected him—and understood that he would come with strings attached, which she wasn't too sure about. She liked him, she liked Thamatoch, and she liked Hanru. But it was too soon to think long-term in any case—and thoughts of any intimate interactions with Taneth would automatically require long-term planning. For now, she contented herself with things as they were. She reached out and picked up the huge tome filled with blank pages. She opened it up to the first page and then grabbed one of the smaller books, flipping it open to read the title and copy it onto the page she decided would be the contents. Taneth watched her over his own work. They hardly spoke, but somehow communicated volumes.

Finally, Taneth broke the silence. "You've been with us for some time, and I know I've pestered you a good deal about your people, but if you'd indulge me a bit more, there are some other things I'd like to know—I feel there are great gaps of knowledge that need to be filled, and I cannot stand gaps," he joked.

Tinna looked up from her writing, which he noted was a bit uneven and messy. It made no difference to him, she had not been rapped on the knuckles for bad penmanship as he had, and he thought her all the more fortunate for it. He liked the way the lines flowed like water.

"Well … if you've spent your life completely ignorant of the existence of my world, then you're probably better off," she grunted. He made as if he had ignored that statement and went on. "Why did you leave your home? Your people are generally insular, are they not? It's rare to see a Thran outside the borders unless ordered to be there, or they are fugitive. Are you a fugitive?" he asked with a playful smile. She shook her head.

"I did not get along well down there. I am not pure Thran. They made sure I was reminded of that."

"Really." He put his quill down and stared at her. "You're not half northern … what is your shared heritage?"

"One of my parents was a Gypsy," she mumbled, focusing too hard on writing a particular word.

Taneth thought perhaps she expected him to judge her, and that was why she looked away. He didn't understand the attitude toward the nomadic people, especially her people, who were known to persecute them. He shook his head and sighed. It made a lot of sense now, those details that didn't seem consistent with what he understood about her people before. He felt relieved to have this understanding now.

"I can see the traits now that you mention it. It's very becoming, that combination." Tinna's eyes remained locked on her work. "Are you a warrior then?"

"I was. I was Kanindra," she decided to just tell him. She didn't know why, but she thought it was best he know now.

"I recall that word from school … but I don't remember its meaning."

"I was an assassin grade warrior." His hand froze, and he stared at her.

"It's the least respected of all the Guild's grades, but I think they decided since I was already inferior to them with my mixed blood, I should have been all too grateful for their choice to allow me to serve at any level," she said; hoping the impact of what she just said would be lost somehow in the words. But she saw no impact at all. She saw him take it in and keep writing with a thoughtful smile on his face.

"That's amazing," he finally said. "Thran are the best-trained warriors in the world. And you are of the Kanindra. I imagine you're a force to be reckoned with." His smile was crooked, his face betraying a bit of pride in her. She found herself speechless by his reaction. They did not speak for a long moment, and then she sighed.

"I don't do that anymore. It offers nothing positive to the world."

"I'm sure you have plenty of positive things to offer the world, Aitinna." Taneth looked directly at her, the admiration plain in his eyes.

"I think sometimes my Gypsy blood makes me drift about, but mainly, I think it's because I'm looking for someplace or something where I can feel like I can contribute without killing," she admitted. He stared at her, and she at him, both hands still on the books, quills resting above each page.

"You have a place here—doing exactly what you are doing now, or doing whatever you enjoy doing. You have a place here with us," he said. She glanced down and looked through her work. She hid her expression, not even sure herself what it was. She liked him. She liked him very much. Tinna was walking toward the edge of the trees carrying a pack when Taneth came running at her. "Where do you think you're going?" he snapped, grabbing her arm and jerking her back.

She tore her arm from his grip, and rubbed the place where his fingers had dug into her skin, glaring at him. "To the village ... for the puppy," she answered, brows arched and face confused. Part of her liked that he was so concerned about her, and that her going away for a day or two made him so agitated. She suppressed a smile, and gazed at his handsome face.

"Are you mad?" Taneth was frantic. "There's a Nimrath out there."

"Who's done nothing but steal food from me. I survived well enough," she muttered, frankly growing bored with the panic this invisible foe had created in the village. She had obviously been traveling some time with the thing, and it had never harmed her. Besides, she was a Thran after all, and quite capable of taking care of herself.

"We don't know what they do to people...people just disappear. You cannot just venture out there on your own like that; the puppy can wait." "For what? The Nimrath to get tired of waiting?" She laughed, shaking her head, turning her shoulder as if to go. Taneth's hand stopped her, turning her back again. "It's still out there. Galrai's loom is gone, complete with weeks' worth of weaving."

Tinna wondered what a tree-dwelling invisible what's-it would have to do with a woman's loom ... really. She suspected it was Galrai's aunt who took it, the woman took everything, she even took one of Tinna's hides she'd been working on, but she didn't want to be so rude as to say such a thing. "I traveled this forest for nine weeks before I found this village. That thing was with me most of the way, and did not do anything more than nick the occasional food item, and cause me periods of brief paranoia every so often. That's it. I want to get Hanru a new puppy. I promised him!" she replied stubbornly.

Taneth had been teaching his morning reading session to the villagers, first the adults, and then the children. Rhoa had interrupted his adult class to alert him that Tinna was planning to leave the village. Rhoa had seen Tinna leaving her apartment and noting her packs and travel garb, asked her where she was going.

She was instantly alarmed by Tinna's response—the whole village had been told to remain indoors or very close to their lodges. Rigerd had assembled a hunting party to flush out and somehow get rid of the Nimrath before a child vanished. She was so frightened for Tinna she had rushed to the Wiseman immediately. Taneth had leapt up from his lesson, and run out, Rhoa at his heels. She stood behind them as Taneth berated a very stubborn but admirable Tinna. She seemed quite resolved to go. He knew deep down she'd be fine, but he didn't want her to go. Not yet.

"She doesn't have to go alone. I'll go with her. She's armed anyway, and I can be there to watch her back, so to speak," Rhoa volunteered. Taneth stopped in mid-reprimand and clapped his mouth shut, quite unprepared for the offer. He threw his hands up and stalked away. Rhoa grinned at Tinna, who gave her the very first approving smile Rhoa had ever gotten from her newly acquired mentor. "I'll go get some good boots on, and some supplies. Please wait for me."

Tinna nodded, watching the young girl run off to the Spring Lodge. That was one thing Rhoa was good at: She could run. Most of the people of Thamatoch ran with the horses and were very practiced and fast. The clumsy girl was transformed when she ran into a smooth, liquid entity. She was quick in her errand, and was soon at Tinna's side.

Tinna gave her another smile, rather pleased with Rhoa for a change. As a mean, she found the girl's constant presence mostly bothersome, but for once, she was glad the girl had spoken up. She would have gone, regardless, that was a given; but somehow what Taneth thought mattered to Tinna. She knew that despite his knowledge that she was able to take care of herself, he could not keep from being concerned. She didn't really need Rhoa along, but if it made him feel better, and gave her the freedom to go, she would make do with things as they were. She frowned inwardly as they found the cool shelter of the dense forest, climbing over the roots, and jumping down into the ruts. She found herself growing very much attached to this little community. In her short time with them, she caught herself making long-range plans. This set off a little alarm in her head that tolled incessantly—move on, move on ... it sang. But she felt so drawn to the comfort and acceptance of the village. She really liked Taneth—he was the first young man ever to make her think twice about her lifestyle.

Well, she mused; I suppose I can worry about all that when I get back from getting a little pup for Hanru Her throat tightened up when she thought of Hanru; she pressed her lips together and clenched her jaw bones. She loved that boy. She found great commonality in his situation and his relationship with his mother. He didn't have a father, either. He'd been invisible until Taneth arrived. That she knew from her heart. She saw it in the way the boy clung to the Wiseman. From the morning of the burial she had formed a fondness for Hanru, and in part, a deep respect for Taneth for acknowledging the boy's existence.

Rhoa slipped and fell on the hard, slick soil that was so black it made a dark streak on Rhoa's calf. Tinna asked her if she was all right, and Rhoa only laughed and blushed, hiding her embarrassed face from Tinna. "Why do you travel through the forests, Aitinna?" Rhoa asked a little while later. Tinna gripped the straps of her pack, and climbed a rather knotty tangle of above-ground roots, leaning over to use her hand to steady herself. She jumped down the other side, and waited for Rhoa to appear before replying.

"I like to travel. It's in my blood."

"Really?"

"I have Gypsy blood in my veins," Tinna confided.

Rhoa seemed very surprised by this admission. "Really?"

"Yes. I do."

"Really?"

"Goodness, Rhoa, don't you know another word?"

The girl blushed again, moving ahead of her on a deer path. "You don't have the mannerisms of Gypsies," Rhoa pointed out a few minutes later, after waiting for Tinna to check her bearings. Tinna set the direction, moving off the deer path, and up a rather rocky rise.

"I was fathered by a Gypsy man. I wasn't raised by them," she retorted, digging her foot into a nook and heaving her body upward.

Rhoa followed, a bit winded by the effort, hugging one of the trees that clung tenuously to the sharp incline so she could pause for a breath. Tinna stopped, looking down from her boulder, waiting for Rhoa to catch up.

"Who raised you then?"

"My mother." Tinna was growing increasingly uncomfortable with the girl's questions.

"Did your father help?" Rhoa asked in between gasps for air.

"My father was a Gypsy. My mother not. She became pregnant with me. You certainly know what sort of reaction any family would have with such a shameful act."

"Yes … I suppose I do," Rhoa said, her voice breaking. She climbed up to Tinna's boulder.

"My mother traveled with the Gypsies for some months while she carried me. But she did not wish to leave her life behind for a nomadic existence, nor could she return home in disgrace—with a half-blood child. She decided to start anew, try to raise me somewhere where I would be more accepted, perhaps. She left my father. She took me with her. She set up residence in Khamamar. She raised me there." Tinna was surprised at the ease with which the words flowed out.

"Well, I think it's stupid that she had to hide your existence from her immediate family. Those things don't matter here. It's a shame they still do in your land."

I know, Tinna thought. She didn't reply.

"Why did you leave your mother?" Tinna shrugged, her mind going to Hanru for a second. "Because I was not accepted, even by my mother. Khamamar was perhaps better than other places, but it was still a difficult life for me. So I left when I was old enough. And I think I left mostly because traveling is in my blood."

The conversation had cycled back to where it had begun, and Rhoa saw that Tinna had made it do so for a reason. She did not ask any more questions for now. She simply followed the surefooted Tinna over the rise of the high hill, and down into the forest that seemed never to end. In the distance, like an island in an ocean of trees, towered the spires of Hildercross.

Taneth was plagued with worry for the rest of the day. Rigerd noticed how distracted he was, and sat down with him at the dinner table. "You worried about the girls?" he asked.

"I should have gone with them."

"You had a responsibility to fulfill here," Rigerd grunted.

"The Nimrath—"

"Tinna was right. She's managed on her own for months, and she'll see to Rhoa being safe. You've learned about her kind; they're very self-sufficient, women of her kind. Not to be trifled with. I've met a Thran or two in my time. They look deceivingly small and gentle, but they are nothing of the sort, mark my words." Rigerd laughed. "They'll be fine."

Taneth nodded, feeling guilty that he hadn't worked harder to keep them from going. He looked at Rigerd and emitted a heavy sigh, picking at his food. "I suppose they will be all right. But I will feel directly responsible if something happens to them."

Rigerd patted his back gruffly. Taneth's appreciation for Rigerd's friendship was great, especially at a time like this. Hanru climbed into the spot Rigerd left when he withdrew to counsel someone else. He leaned on Taneth's arm. Taneth lifted it and put it 'round the boy's shoulders, tucking his little head against him.

"What's wrong, Hanru?" he asked.

"Ilma said the Nimrath will get me and take me into the forest never to be seen again."

"Ilma is a spoiled, rotten little bully."

"I want to go to the tree … give it water, but Rigerd won't let me."

"I'll go with you." He could use a distraction. He took the boy's hand and left the table, the two walking past Hanru's mother, who ignored him. She was sitting inside their apartment, door wide open, leaning over the table top, snoring.

CHAPTER 6

Tinna's first impression of the man on the large horse was that he was undoubtedly of noble blood. He had that look they all had—that unidentifiable yet unmistakable common set of features they all shared from breeding exclusively within the same circles for thousands of years. Long horse-like teeth and nose, bored, half-closed eyes, jaunty golden hair. So typical of northern high-bloods. He looked down at them at first with a small but visible curl to his lip, but it softened when he saw Tinna. He got that look men got; desire mixed with something else she could never identify.

"Welcome to Mount Klatna," he said, as if it were his home and he was inviting them in. Above them, the academy that Taneth had left months before loomed against the sky.

Tinna ignored his gaze, and moved 'round the equine obstruction. Rhoa followed, gawking at the man as she walked past him, stumbling unceremoniously over one of the cobbles. She ran to catch up with Tinna, who'd managed to stride quite far ahead among the growing crowd of people—the poor girl was terrified, but keeping her fear internalized. This was a trade town, and a student town ... there was a strong presence of the scholars of the academy above, as well as a loud merchant contingent festooning the streets with kiosks, carts, and even their own bodies draped in merchandise. This was too large a place, too bustling and loud for Rhoa; she was close to panic every second Tinna was out of eyeshot.

"Who was that?" she gasped, trying very hard to maintain Tinna's fast pace.

"Probably the landlord," Tinna grunted. "There's a good place." She pointed up the street to a faded, water-warped sign indicating that it was an inn. "We can stay overnight and leave tomorrow, after I've found a puppy for Hanru."

Rhoa could not conceal her excited smile, looking forward to seeing Hanru's little round face beaming as the new puppy she would acquire for him licked his chin. She could almost touch the image it was so vivid. She followed Tinna into the old post-and-beam building. It smelled strongly of a mix of ale, boiled cabbage, mildew, pipe smoke, and age. It was no luxurious place, that was for certain. They were met by a portly woman with a cheerful smile. She led them into the large room that served as both a dining hall for the guests and a tavern.

"You girls look tired. It just so happens that the most accommodating and comfortable room has just been vacated. It's all clean, and there are two beds, and there is a water pump inside so you can freshen up. We take our evening meals after sundown for about two hours. You can always purchase a snack if you miss the meal ..." The woman rattled on, waddling down a corridor that was clearly built for someone far leaner than the hostess. She managed nonetheless, paying little heed to the close quarters as she prattled away.

They emerged into a very small courtyard surrounded by the guestrooms. There were two doors for each of the three sides, leading into narrow little quarters. The doorway from which they emerged shared the back wall with another guest apartment. The lady moved immediately to that door. "It gets the most warmth because it shares a wall with the tavern," she explained, lifting the latch. "And because it shares the same wall, it's the only one that has its own pump from the well. I put the best of our furnishings in here too, so we can have something with a little more luxury for our better customers ..."

Tinna wished she'd just shut up and move out of the way so they could get inside and close her out.

She did finally move, and when she vanished into the corridor again, she was still talking. Rhoa had never left the forest before, and she was in a strange state of shock by all the sights and sounds that Tinna seemed to take completely for granted. Tinna hadn't realized this was Rhoa's first visit to any non-Araki settlement, until she caught sight of the look of amazement on her face as she'd gazed around the bustling town. She was now completely exhausted by the long, three-day hike through the forest. She threw her bag down, and flopped onto the first bed she saw, ignoring the fine, but somewhat threadbare chairs and furnishings. Tinna glanced at Rhoa, and smiled. The girl had scarce laid her head on the pillow and she was out.

Tinna resolved to set aside some time to take Rhoa around. But while she was still awake and active, she decided to go and scout out some possibilities. Perhaps find a breeder, and also, find a means to pay for their room. She changed her clothes after freshening up with the incredibly cold water from the water pump. She ventured out into the city in search of puppies.

Rhoa grunted and rubbed her nose with her hand, pushing away the thing disturbing her from her sleep. She felt warm, wet kisses all over her face. She jerked from her slumber and propped herself up on her elbow. The source of her annoyance wagged his short little tail, and rushed at her again.

"My goodness, Tinna, that was fast!"

"You've been out for six hours. It was time enough for me to visit a number of breeders. Meet the new puppy," Tinna said.

Rhoa sat up, and picked the thing up. It was very small, and very young—too little to be taken away from his mother. His ears were still thick and rubbery, and he was only as tall as Rhoa's ankle. "It's too young, probably not fully weaned—"

"He eats solids. I've fed him already, and he responded by duly depositing a healthy coil of poop on the floor, albeit a small one."

"But he shouldn't be taken from his mother so soon," Rhoa whined, hugging the squirmy little puppy to her shoulder.

"He had no mother. I visited a number of breeders, as I said before. Most of the pups were too old, inbred, or costly to bother with. I was sent by a particularly snobby breeder to a shelter where the strays are collected. This little fellow was found in the forest only this morning, next to his emaciated, dead siblings, mother nowhere to be found. He was in a basket with a number of strays, feral and gentle; I thought he'd have a better chance at life if I took him. The rest of the dogs were older and stronger, so I didn't feel particularly piteous toward them. He was just a speck amongst them, cowering in his basket in corner of the pen, surrounded by barking dogs. I chose him. I think he and Hanru will suit each other very well."

"He is positively adorable," Rhoa admitted. "What are you doing?"

"The proprietress suggested we take advantage of the laundering service to have our clothes cleaned for tomorrow. So I'm taking my clothes off. You should too, and don't forget to put your other articles of clothing in the pile. We can rest here and eat in our rooms she said, until our clothing is cleaned, and then we can explore the town tonight."

Rhoa's face blanched. "Must we? It's awfully…awful out there. There are too many people." Tinna was surprised by Rhoa's fear; she'd expected the girl to be raring to see the sights. Instead, she was intimidated by it all. She clutched the puppy in her hands.

"I understand your fear, I really do. I have my own set of aversions that make visiting any city a task for me, but I have a companion this time, so I thought I'd take advantage of it; make it more comfortable for us both. But we needn't go out at all, Rhoa. I was only suggesting it."

"I'm all right where I am. Besides, we can't leave little puppy by himself," she reasoned. It was obvious poor Rhoa was terrified. Tinna smiled.

"We'll have a nice dinner here in our room, and light a good, blazing fire. We can rest, play with the little dog, and be off at the crack of dawn before the market opens. The sooner we're home, the better," she said, before realizing what she'd said. Home. Rhoa took it in stride, nodding enthusiastically at this much better plan. Tinna reached into the sack of items she'd collected on her shopping spree.

She spilled the items out on her bed, and sat down. She sorted through them, picking up a thin, rectangular box made of fine wood. She wondered if it was appropriate to give Taneth a gift, but she hadn't been able to resist it when she saw it. Her hands caressed the well-made box. She slid her nail under the little latch, lifting it off the hook. She opened the lid and smiled. Appropriate or not, it really did suit him so well, that she would be forgiven regardless. It was a fine stylus. It was made from leather-wood, thin and gracefully tapered to a sharp little point. The nib was made of gold. It rested in a silken bed. Next to it was a very small vial made of shiny silver. The opening was just the right size for the stylus to fit, and it was tightly corked up, keeping contained the finest Karrian ink, the merchant had claimed. Alongside of that was a neat row of nine replacement nibs, all shining and new. She closed up the box, and put it down, sorting through her other purchases.

She had bought a box of six new arrow bolts made from a new alloy the name of which escaped her. She had bought a length of soft linen to make into some new summer tunics when she had some time to sew them. She paused as she looked at the fabric, smiling wanly to herself. She knew this meant something, no matter how trite it seemed. It meant she planned to stay in Thamatoch for some time. She hadn't thought of that when she was purchasing the fabric, only after, while she inventoried it among her possessions.

She put her acquisitions into her now empty packs, and picked up her bundle of soiled clothing. She dumped them unceremoniously onto the chair, and pulled her leggings off. She decided for now she wouldn't tell Rhoa how she got the gold to make her purchases. She wasn't sure how the news would be taken.

"I think I'm going to warm up some water for a good wash."

"I wish I'd brought something to do." Rhoa sighed. "It isn't often I get time entirely to myself. My sister and her husband take up a good deal of my time."

"Why don't you come out with me before I commit to a bath and to the laundry? We can purchase a project for you to do. We can go out and be back within an hour. We can even take the pup," Tinna said, enhancing her previous suggestion.

"Then we can come back, have our clothes cleaned, have dinner and relax." Rhoa seemed as if she were about to decline right off, but hesitated, pursing her lips.

"I suppose, if it's only for a little while. But you must promise not to walk so quickly. I could barely keep up on our way into the city, and I'm so afraid of getting lost out there." Tinna nodded reassuringly, pulling on the clothes she had just taken off. The two girls set off, Rhoa holding the new dog in the crook of her arm.

Rhoa was afraid, obviously. The town was a large and bustling place, next to the complete peace and harmony of Thamatoch. She clung to Tinna's side as they browsed the market district, clutching the puppy to her chest as if he too felt as terrified and lost as she did. After only a short while, Rhoa realized she was annoyed by the complete lack of natural things in this city. They'd cleared everything that had once grown here to build their homes and businesses, and left no room for trees to grow among the buildings. It made everything seem unnaturally open and exposed. Trees were comfort to Rhoa. She tried to concentrate on not being afraid. Tinna seemed glad to be out and about. She didn't really buy anything, but she did stop to admire a number of things, all of which Rhoa found both surprising and telling about her strange but admirable companion.

Tinna liked pretty fabrics. Not just finely designed ones, but also the most expensive and reserved for only those select few who were rich enough to afford them: the finest silks that changed tones when turned in a different light, some embroidered, others adorned with patterns of tiny seed-sized glass beads, and she had a taste for velvets, always stopping to run her hand along the soft material, a whimsical smile crossing her lips as the merchant tried to sell it to her.

Tinna also liked weapons. She had a habit of slowing, and often stopping to poke around at the tables where certain weapons were being sold. The greatest draw for Tinna was a shining blade, but she seemed to retreat from the glinting metal before she could actually touch it. It was as if it were habit for her to reach out and test a sword or dagger's weight in her hand, to feel the cool metal encased in her warm fingers. She would pause, and reach out tentatively to the weapons that called to her: all the very polished, sharp, and artful in design. Her hand would snap back in self-reprimand, and she'd glance at Rhoa to see if she'd been watching, before pretending to admire some other less interesting item, such as a longbow or a fighting spear. Rhoa recognized guilt in Tinna's eyes, and found that intriguing. As Tinna slowed to admire a collection of miniature dolls on display among pieces of furniture scaled to their size, Rhoa was truly surprised.

"Look," Tinna told Rhoa, stooping low over the table. "Look at that tiny little chair. Even the legs are turned." She pointed it out, a strange smile on her face.

"They are quite detailed, aren't they? Seems too fragile for a child."

"These things here, these are not meant for children. Are they?" she asked the man who sat behind the stall, carefully carving a tiny face into a head no bigger than a hazelnut.

The man's eyes widened and he shook his head. "I cannot prevent all of my merchandise from falling into the hands of a child, unfortunately, but I try. I certainly don't like to imagine any one of my things being handled by anyone incapable of understanding the amount of work I put into them."

Tinna nodded in full understanding.

Rhoa thought it was bizarre, and even a bit silly. "They're dolls … toys." She laughed.

Tinna and the merchant looked at her as if she'd spoken words against Arak himself.

"There are some who understand these things to be more than just toys. They are sculpture … art," he bragged.

Rhoa shook her head incredulously, and Tinna reached down to pick up a very small doll appropriately dressed as a Wiseman. She showed it to Rhoa, who giggled. Tinna smiled. "These small things…they are their own world. And you can make perfect worlds with these little dolls and their accoutrements." She smiled in a faraway fashion, studying the little Taneth, turning the wooden doll in her hand. "People find escape in so many ways. This is just one of many. Perhaps it is much like child's play, but there's nothing wrong with being child-like sometimes. Who was it who decided that with responsibility one must sacrifice innocence? That's a crock." She put the miniature Wiseman back to sit on his little chair by his little desk covered in little parchments. "They're treasures," Tinna complimented the miniature-maker. He nodded his thanks, returning to his work with a smile curled onto his lips.

"You like those things then? Little dolls?"

"I like the furniture mostly," Tinna admitted. "There was this girl I once knew who had a whole doll house. It was furnished with all the furniture one would expect from such a house, had all the occupants, including the slaves, and a couple of Thran guardians even! Oh, I envied her. She hardly touched it … I imagined that the artisan who made it for her spent hours bent over each little item making it perfect, and she didn't care about it at all. I'd still trade my left arm for that house and its accessories, even today."

"It's hard to imagine you playing with toys." Rhoa giggled.

"We all have our toys. It's nothing to laugh about." Rhoa shook her head in denial.

"I don't have any such thing!"

Tinna laughed and paused at a table where a very old woman sold beaded necklaces, anklets, earrings, and all sorts of ornaments for the body, and had a gigantic selection of ready-made items to choose from.

"You of all of those at Thamatoch are guilty of playing with toys; remember, I share a lodge with you." Tinna shook her finger at Rhoa, whose brow arched in puzzlement. "The collection of carved horses you have? An astounding assortment for one owner, even by the standards of your fellow Araki."

Rhoa blushed. "Those aren't toys … they're not meant to be played with."

Tinna's brow rose and she gave Rhoa a sidelong glance, smirking dubiously before picking up a particularly pretty necklace of blue-glass beads. Rhoa nuzzled the puppy with a defiant look on her face. Tinna put the necklace on her neck, and asked Rhoa what she thought; and receiving naught but a shrug, she rifled through other items, asking the old woman a number of banal questions. It was only after, as they made their way back from buying Rhoa a drop spindle and a small sack of raw fleece did Rhoa realize Tinna was still wearing the necklace and hadn't paid for it.

"Tinna, you made off with that necklace by accident!" Rhoa gasped. Tinna looked at her in surprise, and shook her head with a smile. "Goodness no. It was no accident." Tinna trotted up the stairs to the inn, and went inside. Rhoa followed, a bit flabbergasted by Tinna's ways. Little did she know that the spindle and wool were byproducts of a very similar act on Tinna's part. She would remain ignorant of that fact all that night while Tinna taught Rhoa how to spin her own yarn.

* * * *

The explosion was so enormous, it lifted Rhoa off the ground, over Tinna, who she saw in mid-flight rolling heels over head. Rhoa's grasp of the little dog never wavered. She curled herself into a tight ball around the puppy, anticipating the inevitable crash to the ground. She fell on her shoulder, knocking the wind out of her lungs. Tinna fell within but a few centimeters from her. Rhoa was wheezing for air, her lungs feeling as if they had collapsed. She then found the tiniest bit of air seeping through her strangled wheeze, and tried to pull as much in with it as possible. Her lungs suddenly filled—so suddenly it actually hurt more than the stabbing pain in her shoulder. The puppy whimpered. Rhoa's eyes opened again, and she saw only Tinna's still silhouette lying on her side, against a balloon of fire consuming Klatna and the great school above it, Hildercross.

Rhoa sat up, wincing in pain. "By the Gods ..." she muttered between gasps. She crawled to Tinna, and rolled her onto her back. The woman groaned and sat up, looking with sheer disbelief at the fireball that was once the town they'd stayed in. "What was that?"

"I don't know, but I'm glad we left so early," Rhoa moaned, making a bit of a squeal when she tried to move her arm.

Tinna's head spun around and she frowned. "You dislocated your shoulder." She stood up, stumbling a bit. She had several deep scratches on her cheek and forehead, but seemed not to notice, focused as she was on Rhoa's shoulder.

"Put the puppy down," she commanded. She made Rhoa lie down on the ground, planted her foot on her shoulder, and picked up Rhoa's limp arm. She glanced at the girl, whose face reflected the insufferable pain she felt, and smiled wanly. "This is going to hurt."

CHAPTER 7

It was him, the man who'd greeted them at the gates of the doomed town. He was sitting on a large rock next to an exhausted horse, staring blankly at the ground. He didn't even react to their arrival. Tinna moved to stand in front of him, noticing a deep sorrow in the sag of his shoulders. He finally looked up, eyes drained.

"You got out," he said. "That's good."

"What happened?" Rhoa asked.

"Search me. My whole grant is gone. The town, the people...everything," he whispered, digging his fingers deep into the hair on the sides of his head, and burying the ball of his hand into his eye sockets. "I just went over to Insdale to collect my winnings from Sir Rodol. Why I decided to do it today, instead of tomorrow or yesterday, who knows."

"What would do th—a thing like this?" Rhoa suddenly burst into tears. Her arm hurt so much, perhaps less sharply than it did when it was dislocated, but it hurt nonetheless. She was anguished, and frightened, and suffering. But the confusion was the worst of all. Tinna had decided to head immediately back to the village, and not look back. They were not even two miles away from the demolished town when they found this defeated character.

"Where are you going?" he asked. Tinna jutted her chin to the west.

"Where?"

"My village," Rhoa volunteered before Tinna could shut her up.

He stood, looking at Tinna sheepishly. "You wouldn't mind if I go with you, would you?"

"Yes, I'd mind. Whatever did that"—Tinna pointed toward the smoking hole that had once been a city. Even the academy on top of the hill was naught but a ruin—"might be looking for you, and Gods forbid I put Rhoa, or the pup, or myself for that matter, in such peril."

She gestured to Rhoa to go, and they did, circling 'round the hopeless landlord and his horse.

"I want to get home NOW!" Rhoa shouted. Tinna frowned, crouching in that savage sort of way she did, looking around. "I swear to you I saw it, and honestly, I saw it on the way here, too. I'm afraid...It's stalking you, and I came with you, how stupid was I?"

"I'm trying to sleep ... could you please not shout so much?" the nobleman grunted from under his cloak. He'd gone with them despite Tinna's objections, following them with some difficulty, trying to lead his reluctant horse along as well. Both of the girls seemed resigned to his company, and largely ignored his mutterings.

"Both of you shut your mouths!" Tinna barked. The flames of the campfire made her face look frightful.

"The puppy needs to eat. Rhoa, soften up some of that dried meat in the soup for him," she commanded, looking around, listening to every creak of a branch and hiss of the wind. She wished she could hear whatever it was Taneth heard that day. She was terrified too, but if Rhoa were to pick up the scent of Tinna's fear, she would panic. She was already too close to the edge to begin with. She calmed down a bit, concentrating on the task of feeding the puppy. Tinna hunched by the fire, crossbow in hand, eyes fruitlessly scanning the blackness pressing in against the weak yellow light of their fire while the tiny dog lapped small bits of softened meat from the tips of her fingers.

Draphen hardly ever lost control. Everything he did was calculated and deliberate. It was his nature. The nature of his kind. It was survival. Survival against the ground dwellers. His people could be described as single-minded. They had to be, he supposed. They had a limited environment that was constantly under threat by the ever-destructive and fearful ground-dwellers. Everything his people had become, had evolved to make them most efficient in this environment. So they never strayed from their common views and thoughts, and barely ever disagreed. Draphen, however, was yanked out of this pattern of behavior by a rather intriguing intruder.

She had made him think things he'd never thought before. Caused him to consider different modes of behavior, and do things on impulse rather than planned. He had decided he liked this woman very much, and chose to follow her—leaving his clan and striking out on his own. Of course, he had to steal from the girl in order to complete this journey with her, for he had nobody to hunt with, as he would have if he had stayed with his clan. He could conceal himself well, and the girl was not exactly as attuned to the signs of his kind as the ground-dwellers were. He tried not to steal too much from her. He would not eat for a few days, and then eat a great deal in one sitting, pilfering rather large amounts of her supplies at once.

He made her nervous. He could smell her fear when he made himself "known" to her. But he did not really panic her. He knew she was not someone to be trifled with. He'd seen her hunt with her arrow-thrower, and she was very good and extremely dexterous. He found her face most pleasing. He'd seen many ground-dwellers in his time, but none with features like hers. They were much like his people, save for her deep, olive-toned skin. His people had the same dark features like hers, and yet hers still showed a deeply exotic dissimilarity to anyone within his realm of experience. It made him wonder about the world outside his own, which was never done among his kind. There was no other world but the canopy villages, and the treeways of heavy boughs. There were no discussions of interesting things, or any debates among his own kind like he had heard her and her other girl companion have. Aitinna had broadened his world by leaps and bounds by just passing through a glade where Draphen happened to be enjoying the sun. He wasn't like most others of his kind. He did not kill ground-dwellers. He attributed his departure from his comfortable life to his difference, and he never looked back once.

He was distressed when he saw Aitinna with the tall, robed man from the village. But she left him—to journey with her new companion. But now she was returning, and with another man besides. He was quite beside himself. She was his. He invested all this time in her, that man however, had not, and with such danger around all of them, Tinna would need an ally who understood what was happening, not some stupid horse-rider. He did understand that Tinna was unaware of him for the most part. He had no idea how to go about making himself known to her, especially with the other girl and that idiot trailing behind them. So how? The dragons would be returning soon. He could smell them. He had to get Tinna out of there as soon as possible.

Tinna smelled something familiar: heat. She felt hard bony fingers wrapping around her arms, and her body being dragged along; she had no control of her own movements. She heard Rhoa groaning. It had come so quickly. It was raining, and that didn't help. Rhoa thought it was the Nimrath but was harshly surprised to see bird-dragons emerging from the sheets of rain. They spit their venomous spines before the girls could react. Above, their larger and more intelligent cousins roared and soared. Tinna suddenly had a

69

sharp fear for the village … But her thoughts soon clouded from the spines that had pierced her temple and her cheek, numbing her face first. She drooled ungracefully as they dragged her wherever it was they wanted to take her. She rolled her eyes to take in as much of the scene as possible. It was indeed the landlord they wanted…She fumed in her paralysis, for she knew it was he who had led these beasts to them.

Suddenly, Tinna became aware of a scuffle, and a horrid hissing. She tried her very hardest to see what was going on, but was put in a worse position when the two bird-dragons dropped her unceremoniously to find out what the scuffle was about. Her head lolled to the right, where she saw Rhoa with her face pointed away from her, the puppy squirming inside her bag where she had put him to keep him dry. The stupid nobleman's foot was right by her head. When she got her muscles back, she would waste no time killing him, Tinna resolved acidly. The scuffle was growing increasingly frantic. She wished she could move, even just a little. She saw something strange, and then realized what it was.

It was a foot. A foot that reflected the background almost perfectly. She felt a hand from this being take hold of her arm, trying to lift her, all the while doing whatever it could to keep the bird-dragons at bay. She could see the bird-dragons now, moving into her line of vision. She saw their large clawed feet, much like those of the larger dragon's talons, but scaled down. They were biped, but not as intelligent as their larger, airborne cousins. They were easily manipulated, and were very often used as instruments of war, the first line of soldiers and henchmen. She wondered what the nobleman had done to merit the rage of someone powerful enough to solicit the assistance of bird-dragons, let alone that of the noble dragons themselves.

The camouflaged feet were very dexterous in their movements, but the insistence of their owner to get Tinna up was its downfall. She heard the sound of spitting, and her vision was filled with the confusing sight of the background falling before her in the shape of a man. The paralysis spread, and she watched in amazement as the camouflage melted away to reveal skin. Was this the Nimrath? she wondered. The bird-dragons poked at him, equally surprised to see this display.

He apparently lost his ability to blend in with the surroundings when paralyzed by these beasts. The bird-dragons then lost interest in the Nimrath's skin, and the claws grasped Tinna's arms again, and continued dragging her along. Rhoa's head dangled, collecting twigs and leaves in her fine auburn-colored hair, which was also wet from the rain. Finally the dragging stopped, and they were dropped to the earth, which was burnt, and smelled strongly of creosote, the rain, and the ashes.

Tinna heard air ballooning through a leathery membrane. It was the sound of incredible power, keeping aloft a considerable bulk. The reason why the ground around Tinna was charred finally dawned on her: She realized they'd reached the clearing the dragons had made for themselves.

"Crate them. I've no idea who these others are, but if they were with him, they should be of some interest to Lothos," someone muttered. The bird-dragons writhed in compliance to this commanding voice, and the people were again on the move. They were dumped into a large wooden crate in a single tangle of limbs. The cover was closed over them, and in the din of bird-dragon hisses, and huge wings flapping, the crate was lifted up into the air as if it were made of feather down.

"Oh Gods …" Rhoa moaned. "Tinna, can you feel the puppy? Can you move and check on the puppy?"

"I can move my arms a bit. It's so dark, it's hard to tell who's who."

"That's me," a male voice grunted.

"Oh, sorry. Ah … Here you are, Rhoa. The puppy is fine. He's biting my hand." Rhoa heard a relieved smile in Tinna's exclamation. "I can move a bit here … hold on, I'll get off whoever legs I'm sitting on."

"Oh, my goodness, that's better." The man moaned in relief. There was a good deal of shifting about in the crate, but one body remained still. "Who's that?" Rhoa asked, touching him.

"I think it's the Nimrath, Rhoa," Tinna said, pulling her own leg up and shimmying her body to rest against the crate's wall. "I saw it blending into the leaves, and then change into normal after those lizards knocked him out."

"There's a Nimrath in here with us?" the nobleman asked. "I've never seen a Nimrath before …"

"Without the camouflage he looks quite ordinary from what I saw."

"Tinna … what's happening here?" Rhoa abruptly seemed to take into account what was going on around them.

"Gods, woman … did your really just ask that? You must be as vacuous as a half-wit." The man spat snidely. Tinna frowned in the darkness.

"She's a forest-dweller, you idiot. She's never seen bird-dragons, let alone real dragons. It was her first visit to any settlement outside her own when we went to your ill-fated town. I suggest you soften your tone when you address her; you're already on very thin ice with me, as it is. You exposed us to this peril, and I am holding you completely responsible for it. It's fortunate that these monsters got to us before we reached her home, because if you'd brought them there, I would have killed you right at that moment," she snarled.

Rhoa was cooing at the puppy. She'd obviously gotten her arms back under control, and was using them to check on the little dog she took care of so diligently. She'd even dislocated her shoulder protecting him, something Tinna would never forget; she was extremely impressed with Rhoa's actions. The Nimrath stirred. Everyone recoiled a bit from his moving limbs. They all fell quiet, listening with baited breath to the movements of this unfamiliar entity among them.

The breathing quickened from his corner of the box. Draphen's eyes, equipped with dense receptors to pick up even the tiniest shred of light, made out the subtle shapes of the people occupying the box with him. He lifted his fingers and touched the crate's wall, pleased to feel the familiar grain of wood under his specially evolved fingers. He lay his hand flat on the surface, letting the infinitely small tendrils take a grip on the many imperfections on the surface. His muscles were weak, for sure. Those things had spat some needle things at him and paralyzed him. He'd never seen the small dragons before … they were quick and had keen senses. He would remember that next time he encountered them. He took control of his limbs enough to climb up the side of the crate, and find a comfortable place in a corner above them all, keeping an eye on them, but out of their way as well.

"Where'd he go?"

"I think he climbed up there."

"Climbed?"

"Yes. Like a lizard," Tinna affirmed.

"Do you think he understands us?"

"I have no idea. I know less about Nimraths than you do, Rhoa. You forget I'd never heard of them until I came to Thamatoch. I wish Taneth were here."

"I wish I were home."

"They don't talk. They're not human," the nobleman muttered.

"He looked human to me," Tinna retorted. "If you don't have anything useful to offer, I suggest you shut your mouth. I really don't think it's very smart to continually remind me of your presence in this small space … it might cause me to do something you might just regret," she warned him in the darkness. The crate creaked around them.

"You know, I'm getting right tired of having you tell me what to do. Do you have any idea who I am?"

"Whoever you think you are, you forget that anyone and everything you were titled to assert power over has been burnt to a crisp, so who you are is clearly irrelevant as of this point. You're nobody now. You're an idiot locked in a wooden crate with a Thran, who is growing increasingly impatient with you," Rhoa said. Tinna was quite proud of the statement, and rewarded it with a laugh.

"How can you laugh in this situation?" He barked. "You're mad!"

"All the more reason for you to shut up." Tinna sighed, feeling quite a bit better. "Rhoa, do you have anything left for food in your pack? I'm hungry."

The joints of the wooden crate groaned as the dragons tightened its grip. It was a precursor to what turned out to be a deafening roar. They heard the sheer power of it bubbling through the body of the dragon before exiting its huge maw in an earsplitting cry that shook the heavens.

"We must be arriving," the noble guessed, voice betraying his apprehension. Rhoa made a noise of exasperation at the very sound of the man's voice, persisting in his desire to talk. Tinna imagined she'd rolled her eyes as well. She heard Rhoa rifling blindly through her bag, and then something else.

"Listen," Tinna muttered. Another roar, obviously far distant, replied to their transporter's call. "We're not arriving anywhere."

"What does that mean?"

"That we've got a long way to go still. They're carrying us by relay. I wonder how many times we'll change hands before we get to wherever we're to go?" Tinna wondered.

"Would he know? It is him they wanted after all, and his land they reduced to cinders," Rhoa growled.

Tinna waited for the man to reply, but he did not. "You owe us at least an explanation."

"I have no idea who attacked my land," he snapped. "There are a number of people I could imagine capable of such a thing, but none of them powerful enough to have the support of the dragons. I'm as without a clue as you are." He crossed his arms in the dark, and pulled his knees up to his chin. He heard the women whispering to one another, and then smelled the rich odor of dried, smoked venison. His mouth watered as he heard the women eating the jerky. The Nimrath stirred as well. Rhoa, in an act of uncharacteristic boldness, reached for some of the jerky, and held it up. "Have some," she said to the Nimrath. "If you understand me, it's for you. You must be hungry, too."

A tentative hand slid through the blackness, finding the hardened, leathery piece of meat with his sensitive fingers. She felt it being pulled gently from her hand, and with a self-satisfied smile, she returned to her own snacking, taking a special kind of pleasure in hearing the mastication of the mysterious Nimrath as he gobbled up the piece of jerky, relishing the spices and the smoky taste. He was genuinely grateful, and he realized in a strange epiphany, that this was the first time he ever knew of that a ground-dweller had ever been known to offer something to one of his kind. It made the jerky taste all the more delicious.

CHAPTER 8

"Oh gods, what a fool I was to let them go!" Taneth shouted, arms waving. Rigerd looked quite distressed. The wildlife of the forest had given them their first signs of it, showing uncharacteristic agitation and anxiety, that gave the people of Thamatoch an idea that something was amiss to the east—that was then followed by the smoke from great fires that darkened the late summer sky. The horses were spooked as well, and that was enough to put everyone in Thamatoch on edge.

Runners had been dispatched, and scouts sent eastward to assess the situation. The residents were as skittish as the horses. Rigerd had ordered a "cover down" and Taneth's current tantrum was occurring in the middle of the execution of this command. The people ran out to the forests, and returned with uprooted young trees. Others helped to saw barrels in half, and to find other means to pot the large root systems of the trees. They surrounded the huge oak, which largely covered the forum to begin with. They peppered the potted trees around the bare spots. Taneth understood the purpose immediately, as well aware as Rigerd and the people of the village that dragons were nearby and were being atypically destructive.

"Taneth, as much as I worry about the ladies, I cannot distract myself for their sake when the entire village is at stake," Rigerd grumbled.

Taneth frowned darkly. "They were out there, Rigerd. Who knows what's happened to them?"

"Exactly, and you can either stand there and speculate, or you can help your people," Rigerd barked, stalking off.

Taneth took pause at what Rigerd had just said. He'd never had a people. He smiled tightly to himself, and followed the huge man. The open forum was looking more like a nursery for burial trees now. People were dragging water to feed the shocked plants, in hopes that they wouldn't react too adversely to being uprooted and moved to constraining pots. Taneth helped drag one into a spot where the paved area could be seen from above. People covered up the chimneys with diffusers on top of the lodge. The horses were brought back from pasture, and stabled.

Soon, the community retired to their lodges, eyes cast to the ceiling. For some reason that was neither planned nor even agreed upon, the villagers cooked in their own apartments and ate there that night, too afraid to concern themselves with Taneth's needs. Taneth was enjoying the rare occasion of not only eating a meal on his own, a meal of his own choice, and cooking it too, since the act of feeding Taneth was a highly competed for activity amongst the villagers. Normally, he rarely had the chance to decide what he wanted to eat; that was usually decided for him by whoever won the battle for the right to cook for him at that particular meal.

He changed from his robes into his old breeches and a loose tunic, and padded bout barefoot, unconsciously enjoying the sensation of walking on the soft, warm floor padding to the cool hard surface of the hearth's apron. He'd selected a young pheasant for himself from the hunting party's spoils. He was entitled to whatever he liked, being the village Wiseman, but given the rare occasion when he could cook for himself, he would always chose humbly; a bit of deer, a small chicken…This day, everyone seemed to be grabbing their own pieces of venison from the storage room and paid him little heed. It wasn't hard for him to pick up on their unspoken desire to be alone with close family in what was growing into a crisis. So Taneth decided to go all out, since he had no family or other such comforts, and took his own pheasant and a small basketful of other ingredients for a special meal.

He found himself quite pleased and enjoying the luxury of orchestrating his own meal, and made almost a ceremony of it. He washed his pheasant and put it aside—the task seemed to set his worries aside for a while. He had always enjoyed cooking, even at the academy. He often thought that if he hadn't been so bright as to be sent to the academy, that he would have become a great cook. Perhaps the head cook for the high throne. The memory made him smile a bit over his task, rubbing an emulsion of herbs and black-nut oil all over the pheasant.

He then began slicing up fresh pine onions, and some dark, richly red, yellow-leaf tubers. He chopped off the bitter leaves for which it was named with a sharp knife, and began cutting the tuber up into tiny blocks. He tossed the onions and his tiny blocks of tuber into a pot, hanging it over the fire. He tossed in a pat of rendered lard. He let his mind focus only on his dinner. He chopped up some stale bread, some pine nuts and walnuts, throwing it all into the pot that was now sizzling, and sending up a delicious aroma of onions and the mild, but unmistakable smell of yellow-leaf tuber. He stirred the contents, allowing the flavors to marry before taking the pot off the fire. He began to stuff the pheasant with the steaming mixture. He trussed the bird up with twine, and hung it a good height above the fire by the pothook.

Nama, a round and delightful matron who lived with the residents of the Summer Lodge, had seen him puttering about the community pantry earlier and smiled at him and said, "I'm making some bread. Would you like me to make you a loaf?"

He shook his head. "I'm determined to make everything on my own tonight," he declared proudly.

Nama understood his subdued glee at this concept, and instead offered him the raw dough. He had followed her back to her apartments, where she handed him a linen-lined basket that held an unimpressive, mottled, off-white lump of dough at the bottom. He put it on a special proofing shelf on the hearth unit, and left it there during most of the afternoon, and was delighted to discover it had tripled its size when he returned, smelling richly of the yeast and the tart berries that the yeast had been rendered from. He dumped it out of the basket and slid it into the baking oven. Tonight he would eat like a king! he decided. There was a little knock at the door, and it opened without his bidding. Taneth was about to shout a reprimand at the rude intruder but caught himself when he saw Hanru's little face appear in the doorway.

"Hello there, Han. To what do I owe the hon—" It was then he noticed the boy's swollen eye and cheekbone. Taneth pulled him in the door, and closed it behind them, his lips tightened, and his jaw rippled. He had to calm down the instant he saw Hanru's face. He paced his breathing and swallowed hard, biting down on his tongue and squeezing his eyes shut while he waged a battle with his rage. When he managed to wrest the anger from his system enough to be coherent, he picked the boy up, and put him on the edge of the bed. "You wait right here, Hanru … don't move. In fact, you are in charge of seeing to supper. I'll be right back."

He stormed out of his apartment and banged loudly on Rigerd's door. There was a grunt of annoyance in response, and the door jerked open to reveal a very mussed up, and very naked Rigerd. Taneth had no time to apologize. He was furious, and Rigerd saw it at once.

"What is it, Taneth?"

"Hanru just came to my apartment. He's been beaten again. The whole side of his face will be purple tomorrow. I'm tired of the inaction, Rigerd. We cannot allow this to go on under this roof. I am the village Wiseman, Rigerd, and until now, I've respected your reticence, but right now, I'm exercising my right to address this situation, and I am coming to you to demand we do something about this at once or so help me, I'll go to her and wring her bloody neck myself!"

Rigerd's brow tightened into a patch of wrinkles and he set his lips into an angry line. He'd never seen Taneth this angry before. He was a bit impressed; until this point, he hadn't been sure the young man had it in him. He did, obviously, and Rigerd could do nothing else but respect Taneth's resolve, and decided not to interfere anymore. It was indeed Taneth's right to decide on this—he was responsible for the health of the people of Thamatoch, and this fell under his jurisdiction. And now he stood before Rigerd and was commanding him to act. Rigerd decided to do as his Wiseman ordered.

"I'll be right out." He closed the door. Taneth heard Rigerd's wife's protests, a quick, gruff explanation from the towering leader, and words of concern and anger. Rigerd stomped out of his apartments, pulling a jerkin over his disheveled hair. He jerked his head at Taneth to follow him to the apartment belonging to Hanru's mother. The door was partly open. Rigerd pushed it open. The woman was sitting on her bed, staring at the floor. There was vomit in the corner that reeked of spirits, and broken, clay bottles scattered around.

She looked up at Rigerd and Taneth with a sneer. "Get out of here."

"We are a people, Rhana. We have rules," Rigerd growled in his deep voice.

"You have broken them for the last time."

"Pcha!" She laughed, sitting up a bit. "What are you going to do? Put me in stocks? Have me whipped by the Founder's Tree?" She chuckled at her own cleverness, shaking her head at such pathetic attempts at intimidation.

"You know what happens to people who harm children of the clan, Rhana."

She didn't even look at him. "Probably a punishment no worse than being burdened with the bastard of a man who didn't have the balls to raise his own creation. He made me carry it, and feed it day after day and left me to enjoy his life wherever he went, while here I suffered because of his seed, knowing no joy except the peace that this gives me." She thrust a clay bottle toward them before taking a swig. Her face was full of bitterness and hatred.

"Well, you may now go and find the joy he cheated you of. Collect your things and be gone from here before morning," Rigerd said. It was as if she didn't hear it for a moment, but registered the command after some strange delay. She looked up and her brow wrinkled.

"What?"

"You will never show your face in our village again. Your place in our clan has been forfeited, and you are no more under the protection of the Horse God. He would never protect anyone who seeks to harm her own child. Hanru remains with us. You will leave our territory and never return. If you do not, you will be driven from here by the people in the most humiliating manner possible. You have two hours." Rigerd then pulled the door shut with such a slam it shook the lodge, making some of the packed soil sift down from the root-entwined ceiling. He looked at Taneth with a look of resigned sadness.

"I will take Hanru, Rigerd. I've a special fondness for the boy."

"And he does you," Rigerd replied, patting Taneth's shoulder. "I've been avoiding doing this for a year, Taneth. I should have sent her away before, but the boy … who can take on another child? Fortunately, you came. He loves you. You're the only person who has ever really taken notice of him. I'm ashamed of that now. We did nothing, and I am truly ashamed." The sound of pottery shattering against a wall startled them. Rhana roared in fury inside.

"I'd have someone watch her. That sort of anger can't be very good. If she's capable of doing what she does to Hanru, she's probably capable of about anything."

"Good notion. You are a wise man, Wiseman." Rigerd sighed. He walked to an apartment across the way to ask Lotno to keep an eye on the woman and see to her departure.

Taneth returned to his apartment. Hanru was sitting on the floor, looking at the bird dangling above the fire. The fat was falling onto the embers, causing rich-smelling flares and hisses. Taneth tried to smile at Hanru. "It's getting nice and brown. Good," he said, sinking down into a cross-legged position next to the boy.

Hanru was hurt. Taneth sighed, and reached for his little basket of herbs and remedies, pulling it over to his knee. He carefully sorted through the balms and elixirs, picking out what he needed. He then with a soft touch treated the bruising on the boy's face, trying to bite back his fury as he did. When he was done, he kicked the basket back to its place, and looked at Hanru. The boy, needing some comfort, leaned onto Taneth's side. Taneth put his arm 'round his back and squeezed him twice, feeling the sting of tears in his eyes for the boy's suffering. He cleared his throat, fearful of how to present his next words to the traumatized boy.

"Han. How would you feel about coming to live with me?" he asked. Hanru sat up, his eyes filling with tears. He threw his little arms 'round Taneth's neck, sobbing and whimpering. He heard the boy say

"I want to very much, Teacher," between sniffles.

Taneth pulled him onto his lap, the boy still latched onto him like a little monkey. He could feel the warm tears wetting up his shoulder and neck. "Your mother is going away. Rigerd said she has to go. Does that make you sad, Hanru?"

The boy shook his head. "I want her to go away. I want her to go away. I want you to be my daddy, and I want to forget her. I want her to stop hurting me," the boy cried, his words partially muffled in Taneth's tunic.

Taneth rubbed the boy's back, shaking his head at the pitiable situation this boy has had to endure all his life, being made to feel like a burden, unwanted and hated. Taneth decided to dispel that myth first off. "Well, I would be very happy to be your daddy, Hanru. Nobody will ever hurt you again. And you will never see her again. You will be my son, Hanru. You can start all afresh, starting with a delicious dinner. How does that sound?" Taneth lifted his hand and wiped away the tears he'd wept for the boy. Hanru clung to him for another moment, and then leaned back, nodding his head and rubbing his puffy, swollen eyes with the ball of his hand.

"Good. We'll find you some clean clothes, and have a nice supper, all right?" Hanru nodded again. Taneth left to ask if Rigerd's wife had some old clothes from her boys. She gave him quite the armful, pleased to get rid of the things.

When he returned, the aroma of the cooked pheasant filled the apartment, and the fragrance of hot bread permeated everything. It was very well baked, even a bit too much. The crust would be very hard and crunchy. But that didn't bother Taneth. He liked bread with a hard, delicious crust, and a soft, bubbled inside. He put it on the counter to cool, and hung the bird upside down to brown the top for a bit.

He checked Hanru's bruises to see how the balms worked, and put on some compresses with mint and thatch-pine needles to keep the swelling down. He dressed the boy in some of Rigerd's sons' old clothes. The boy obviously thought himself unworthy of such finely made clothing from the way he sort of drew into himself, and away from the garments hanging from his own little frame. They sat down at the small table against the wall, and ate. Hanru ate sparingly. He looked exhausted. While he had a warm bath, Taneth and Rigerd worked to set up a suspended bed over Taneth's, so the boy would have a place to sleep. It was a simple task of hooking some chains into the iron rings already in place in the thick wooden rafters above. They then pulled one of the many bed platforms from the storage area, which happened to be next door to Rhana's apartment, hung it on the chains by the corresponding rings at each corner and unrolled the feather and down mattress onto the platform.

Rigerd's kind wife, Eletha, provided him with linens, and shoes for the boy, as well as a large trunk of other items, including some of their long-gone sons' toys. She seemed to love the idea of spoiling the boy, and was very much pleased that their newly acquired Wiseman had such a big, compassionate heart. She was touched by his kindness to the boy even before, and now she was overwhelmed by his adoption of the child. He was teaching a lesson to all of them, and she would make sure everyone learned it. It was a late night. Luckily the bed was set up quickly and the freshly bathed and tired child was tucked in to sleep for the night. Taneth sorted through the many things in the trunk that Eletha provided, and could not contain his gratefulness for Rigerd. For his people. For the clan. He let himself weep openly over the trunk of toys and clothes, wiping his eyes with a look of personal embarrassment, but he was worried. Worried for Tinna.

In the short time he had spent with her, he had found himself very attracted to her. He found her little actions in regards to Hanru very touching, let alone going on a long journey to replace his lost puppy. He knew he could love her, and he already cared such a deal for her for what she was doing. He should not have let her go alone with only a young girl to help her. She could be in great peril for all he knew Taneth stubbornly refused to consider even the slightest possibility of her and Rhoa being among the dead of Hildercross … He couldn't permit himself to believe anyone could hurt Tinna.

He chastised himself for his stupidity, allowing them to go to the town, wondering what he could do. He realized there was really nothing he could do. Not now. He was responsible for a fragile young soul who needed every free moment of his time to help him heal his body and spirit.

He picked up a little wooden horse, elegantly carved from a fine-grained hardwood, sanded smooth and waxed to bring out the intricate grain. He put it on the bed next to the boy, who was sleeping peacefully. Probably for the first time in his life, Taneth thought. He pushed some of the boy's ill-trimmed hair from his little forehead, and tugged the blanket up to Hanru's chin. He was glad the boy was safe with him now. He only wished Tinna were, too.

CHAPTER 9

Tinna was never really one to be in peril, at least by the standards of normal people. She had always been strong, self-sufficient, self-confident and fearless. She seemed to have everything under control and the situation well assessed, at least as far as Rhoa was concerned, who could only keep her own panic at bay if she thought that. She needed to believe that Tinna would get her out of this. She voiced her concern to Tinna when they changed to their third dragon-carrier.

"I made a promise to bring Hanru a puppy, and I damn right will," she said in a determined mutter. Rhoa heard her mussing about in her packs, and the familiar click of arrows being loaded into her crossbow. The nobleman had actually fallen asleep and was snoring loudly, and the Nimrath still clung to the corner above them.

"What are you doing that for?"

"We're going to land soon. I want to be prepared."

"It's fortunate those things didn't take your weapon when they captured us."

"Bird-dragons are not known for their intelligence. Thankfully," she added.

Rhoa nodded in the dark, as if anyone could really see her do it. She felt Tinna's elbow graze her shoulder as she strapped her bag on tightly, indicating that Rhoa should do the same. The pup was asleep in his own little pouch that hung from Rhoa's neck on top of her own bag, which she also wore strapped over one shoulder and diagonally across her torso. She made sure the strap was still as strong as it had been, and that the flap was tightly closed.

Tinna closed her eyes and began to meditate, crossbow resting on her knee. She was blocking out everything that wasn't relevant to the next few minutes, her senses focused on the sounds outside the crate, and setting aside the person she'd become for the person she once was. Rhoa was about to get a firsthand look at exactly what being a "Thran" really meant.

* * * *

Aitinna was well prepared for the effect of bright light pouring into the crate after her eyes had been adjusted to the darkness for so long. She simply listened. She let her arrows fly where her ears told her, and at the same time, she leapt toward the light, crashing out of the crate and falling with a roll. She heard more hisses, and her hand loaded and shot so quickly, it seemed nearly impossible. She opened her eyes and bit down on her tongue, keeping her eyes open despite the searing pain burning into the back of her skull. She made out some figures against the light, and shot at them, keeping them at bay long enough to get onto her feet. Once she had gained her footing, she was off. She leapt off her feet, and twisted her body in mid-flight, directing her feet at the head of one assailant while twisting around to shoot an arrow at another. This was her last bolt, and after it flew, she threw the crossbow before she even reached the ground again. Draphen had escaped almost exactly when the woman exploded out of the crate like some feral, rabid animal.

Her exit allowed him to get out unnoticed, and provided him long enough to turn himself into the surroundings. He watched his beloved with awe. She was like a cat, he surmised. Like the large cats that roamed the rocky slopes near his clan's home. She seemed to suspend herself in the air she leapt so high. She was amazing. Almost terrifying. Her limbs could not have been better coordinated and disciplined. Even encumbered by her own packs, she was graceful.

She'd pulled a knife from the side of one of her assailants and crouched, swiping the thing off its feet with her leg before kicking it in the head and burying the knife in its gut. She took on the next attacker without the slightest hesitation, flowing from one killing to the next. Draphen suddenly realized that there was an icy fear in his stomach as he watched her. He swallowed hard, and cowered into a corner of the stone walls. He heard a squeal of terror and was distracted by the Rhoa girl being dragged out of the crate by one of those lizard things. Draphen felt a surge of anger at the lizard. That girl had been kind to him. Shared her food with him. He went after that lizard with no reserve. He was nearly blown over by a gust of wind in doing so.

"Contain that rabble!" a powerful voice shouted over the chaotic scene.

Tinna had killed almost all the bird-dragons that had been sent to retrieve them. Rhoa's assailant was being attacked by air shaped like a man, and the nobleman cowered in the crate. Aitinna was lifted off the ground, a great claw wrapped around her body. She struggled to no avail, and screamed out her frustration. The great dragon then reached for Rhoa, tilting his great head in puzzlement as he watched a bird-dragon struggling with what appeared to be nothing.

"NIMRATH," Tinna's captor bellowed out of his huge mouth. They didn't speak well, for certain. They were not made to speak. They had no lips that could form sounds. They relied only on their tongues and their throaty growls to articulate human words. When they spoke, it was so inconceivably loud and bass, that it rattled the bones of all around. The bird-dragon stopped struggling the moment the superior dragon spoke. Draphen had withdrawn his attack, slinking into shadow of a wooden walkway overhanging the wall above.

"Never mind that," the first, less impressive voice muttered. "Where's the idiot?"

"THERE," the dragon breathed, his breath like a hot, bread oven. The huge muzzle pointed into the crate. An extremely muscular man came 'round the dragon into Tinna's line of sight. He walked up to the crate and pulled the nobleman out by his collar. He threw him several meters, landing in front of the dragon.

"Get up," the towering man hissed. The nobleman got to his feet, rubbing his head where he'd hit the hard stone, scraping off a good measure of the top layer of skin on his temple. "You were given your chance to decide. You chose. Now you have nothing and are nothing. You will be imprisoned with the rest of the infidels that chose the high throne. Your friends will die, for we have no use for them."

"They're not my friends," the nobleman spat out. "You can let them go."

"Please … do you think me an idiot?" The huge man laughed.

"Really. That bitch even threatened to kill me I don't know how many times. As annoying as the woman is, I cannot in all good conscience allow her or the others to be part of this. I just can't." The nobleman attempted to be noble—odd as the concept was.

The muscular man who commanded the dragons glanced at the woman in the dragon's claws. "That little thing threatened you?" He laughed again.

"I believe she's just proved her skill," the nobleman said, gesturing at the dead bird-dragons littering the strange stone bailey where they had arrived in the crate.

"SHE IS WELL CAPABLE OF ANYTHING," the dragon hissed with a touch of admiration for the little thing struggling in his claw. There was then a deep rumbling belly laugh rising up through the dragon's enormous neck. He obviously found the deaths of nearly eleven perfectly good bird-dragons very amusing.

"Then why were they found in your company?"

"I followed them—I had no more home to return to, and I feared showing my face in any other haunts. I thought perhaps their village would shelter me. They're just common horse-worshippers. As much as I despise them, I cannot justify their being punished for something I did."

The muscular man stood still, pondering this for a bit. He glanced at the Thran, and then the other woman who he assumed was the real horse-worshipper. They seemed innocuous enough for who they were. He was personally impressed with the Thran, and wondered why one of her kind had become a horse-worshipper. But he had not time to humor his musings. He had an empire to help take over. He didn't wish to waste any more time with common folk when he had this nobleman to add to his growing collection of unseated nobility.

"Do what you wish with them, great one. If you find the Nimrath, get him out of here as well."

"AS YOU WISH," The great dragon stirred, beginning to lumber about in the small space, making as if he were about to find his way free of the bailey and the surrounding skirting walls.

Draphen ran from his hiding place and clutched his entire body onto the scaly tail of the dragon, using his tree-gripping hands and feet to glom himself onto the scaled surface and hold on for dear life. As if this were a signal for him to go, the huge dragon unfurled his tremendous wingspan, and put both Tinna and Rhoa into his mouth, careful to close only his teeth around them. They rolled on his strange, cat-like tongue, which was slightly damp and very raspy. Tinna stood up and planted her hands on the ridged, wet ceiling of his mouth to steady herself while she gazed out from between his carefully parted teeth. Rhoa was simply sat in a tight ball, knees drawn up, with a look of utter disbelief on her pretty face. The dragon climbed up one of the walls. It turned out to be a high parapet of an outer bailey of this immense fortification.

They had been deposited in the high bailey by the third dragon that had transported them. This was another dragon. One of great rank. His elegantly curved horns and spines showed his great age, as well. He scaled the wall with little effort, taking his bulk even higher by climbing   via a looming guard tower. Once he attained the elevation he desired, he launched himself off, falling a good distance before stretching out his immense wingspan, and leveling out into a stomach-lurching glide. He flapped his immense wings, and they rose a bit. He did that again and again until he'd glided above the tallest tower, and caught some thermals, and circled even higher. He seemed to be delighting in frightening his passengers.

"Let me out of here!" Rhoa shouted.

The dragon tilted his head to one side, as if acknowledging her, rolling her onto her side in the process. She bellowed out her displeasure, and staggered unsteadily to her feet, moving to Tinna's side. The woman gazed out of the sizable gap in the teeth, and Rhoa looked down from there at the earth far below. The dragon opened his mouth a bit more. Rhoa looked at Tinna with complete confusion. "Does he expect us to jump?"

"Girl, sometimes your ignorance astounds me."

Tinna crouched, and ducked under the top row of teeth, clutching one of his beautiful fangs to steady herself. She reached his canine, clutched it in her arms, and used it to swivel around. She stepped over the bottom teeth onto the ridge of his lip. She clutched the rim of scales that bordered his upper lip, and sidled gingerly down the head, wind buffeting her as she passed his enormous eye. The vertical iris followed her. She found the large spiny protrusions of the dragon's cheeks, and used them to scale up to the place behind his head, where the thick bony crown rose up, creating a shield against the violent wind. She crawled up to the tender skin under the crown, and settled in, waiting for Rhoa to gather up the courage to follow.

The girl never stopped screaming from the start to when she crawled in the space behind the dragon's crest. She cursed Tinna and called her every dirty name she could think of and some she just made up on the spot. Her hands were trembling so terribly, she couldn't hold on to anything, and so she pushed herself up against the crest and stayed there, cursing under her breath. Tinna reached into her bag, and pulled out a sweater she'd had so long she had a sentimental attachment to it. It was wool, and moth-eaten, but it was still warm. She gave it to Rhoa, and helped her put it on. Rhoa stopped cursing after that, and only then did she think to check on the puppy.

The dragon dove after an hour or so, falling through clouds tinted orange by the setting sun. Draphen had managed to find a comfortable place sitting between four large spines bristling from the tip of the dragon's tail. He held the top of each horn in front of him with a death grip, never once thinking in his entire life that he'd be riding on a dragon's tail high above the forest. He was terrified and exhilarated. And he found he liked the way dragon scales looked on his own skin. He did not wish anyone to see him in his natural form; he was sure his nakedness would embarrass the women, and he feared they would find him horrifying and ugly. When the dragon dove, he glommed his hands and feet to the animal, feeling his body lift off the tail because of the sudden drop, wondering how the girls could stay on this thing, if he barely could.

They emerged from the layers of clouds above a huge plain, something Rhoa had never seen. Despite the fact that horses were creatures from this environment, her people had long found the forests a far better and safer place to live, and once they brought their horses there, they never looked back. Soon enough, the People of the Horse God forgot they had originated in such a habitat. The dragon dove low, scaring a herd of plains sheep. Tinna was standing up behind his head, gripping the edge of his crown, wind in her face, howling with delight from the exhilaration. Rhoa remained tucked under the safe overhang, having a hard enough time looking at the grass below going by in a blur.

The dragon began to slow, and when they thought he was so slow that he would fall, he rose up a bit, flared out his wings, and lofted down on the ballooned air captured in the stretched membranes. He landed so softly they hardly knew he'd touched ground. Rhoa wasted no time in sliding off the dragon to the ground. She fell to her knees when she reached the cherished firmament and let the trembling ebb away. Tinna, on the other hand took her time, climbed down his long arm, and took a moment to touch his great face that filled her entire field of vision.

"THE CITY WILL GIVE YOU WHAT YOU NEED TO GET HOME. GET THOSE THINGS AND GET OUT OF THERE AS SOON AS YOU CAN; IT IS A DANGEROUS PLACE. I WOULD TAKE YOU FARTHER, BUT I REALLY CANNOT. I HAVE A WAR TO WAGE," the dragon instructed. "YOU ARE A WORTHY WOMAN. YOU HAVE EARNED YOUR FREEDOM BY YOUR STRENGTH ALONE. HAD I MORE TIME, I WOULD HAVE LIKED TO KNOW YOU BETTER. I THINK WE MIGHT HAVE BEEN EXCELLENT FRIENDS." Tinna was so overwhelmed with honor by his words, she felt the burn of tears in her eyes, which she blinked back.

"THE NIMRATH IS WITH YOU AGAIN. BRING HIM BACK TO HIS TREES. THIS IS NOT HIS PLACE IN THE WORLD."

"I will. I thank you, honorable dragon."

"I THINK YOU DESERVE TO KNOW MY NAME. I AM LEDRORAN. WHAT ARE YOU CALLED?"

"Aitinna. Aitinna of Ymnoth," she said, giving him a polite bow.

The dragon came very close and touched her forehead with his huge muzzle.

"I AM PLEASED TO KNOW YOU."

"I am honored to have made your acquaintance," she replied.

The dragon then backed up a few steps, and walked away, waiting until he was a good distance from the three of them before he lifted his enormous bulk off the ground, beating his great wings, flattening the grass under them with the sheer force of the air he moved. He finally got high enough to catch the warm drafts rising from some freshly ploughed fields nearby, and circled up into the clouds, vanishing among the powdery pink wisps.

"By Ulai that was AMAZING!" Aitinna screamed, leaping about like an exuberant child. Rhoa glared at her in disbelief.

"I would give my arm to have that dragon come back and take me with him!" Tinna cried out emphatically. Rhoa was completely in awe of the Aitinna she was coming to know in this new world. It was a far more aggressive, impulsive, and fearless Tinna. The woman had a death wish. "Where are we?"

"I haven't a bloody clue, nor do I care! Look at this! We're so far from where we began this morning … days and weeks worth of ground travel … almost nothing for a dragon! Gods, that was AMAZING!" Tinna jutted her arms straight out from her sides and turned a full circle, stopping to face a huge, sprawling city that occupied an entire valley below them. Her arms dropped at the sight of it.

Rhoa hadn't noticed it either, but upon seeing it, her face turned white, and her jaw dropped. "We're not going there, are we?" The place made the town at the school look like a one-horse village.

"Of course we are. We're out of food, low on money, I need a new weapon, and we need to find out where in the name of Ulai we are," Aitinna said, grinning again. She began to march down the hill toward the city with a long, impatient stride. Rhoa got to her feet, holding the tiny dog to her so he wouldn't be shaken up too much from her jogging.

Aitinna's confident stride was soon interrupted; she slammed full on into something very hard and fell backward onto her bum. She looked disoriented for a moment. Rhoa realized it was the

Nimrath she'd run into when she made out just the faintest outline of a man within the view, the camouflage momentarily disturbed by the impact of the Thran hitting it.

"You cannot leave me here." It was a desperate voice. The open space made him feel tiny and nervous. This was the first time he'd made even the smallest noise. The girls were surprised by this. They didn't know if he could speak, let alone speak their language. "You have to take me from this place. Please." His voice was trembling, his accent was very strong, but his command was good.

"You've been following us since the beginning, this is not time to stop," Tinna muttered, getting to her feet, and dusting the grass from her rump. "I can't believe you speak our tongue and have said not a bloody word since you decided to show yourself, so to speak."

"We're not stupid. We learn languages just like you do," he muttered self-protectively.

"It's important to know how the enemy communicates."

"Whatever." Rhoa sighed intolerantly. It was just too much for her to take in all at once, so her way of dealing with it was to act as if the absurd were normal.

"Let's go then," Tinna commanded, moving around the invisible obstruction. Both Rhoa and the Nimrath balked.

"I can't go into that city," Draphen yelled.

"Why not?"

"Too much movement. I can't blend into that kind of movement."

"Then don't blend," Rhoa said logically.

"I can't not."

"Why not?"

"I've no clothes. And I look different from you."

"Everyone looks different in big cities; nobody will even notice. Come along. We'll find you something to wear in the city, maybe even before we get there."

Aitinna continued down the hill, accelerating as she did, skipping like a girl. Rhoa and Draphen followed, the only evidence of his being present beside the young girl was the grass being flattened under his stride.

"Here you are." Tinna threw a large wad of men's clothing at nothing. The clothes stopped abruptly in mid-air.

"Where are these from?" Rhoa asked, touching the rather fine, threaded wool. It was of unusually high quality.

90

"From him." Tinna's thumb pointed back over her shoulder. They looked, noticing a pair of naked legs protruding from some prickly blackberry bushes.

"Did you kill—?"

"NO!" Tinna snapped. "Why do you assume I would just kill someone arbitrarily?

I did what I did back at the fortification because I had no other recourse!" she shouted defensively. "I just gave him a bit of a bonk on the head. Put the bloody clothes on, Nimrath, I'm starving, and the puppy is probably hungry as well. We've got to keep him healthy. He's got a little boy waiting for him at home," she declared, "Besides, it's getting dark."

Draphen tugged the breeches on, uncomfortable the second he felt the fabric against his skin.

"He needs a bath. He stinks," Rhoa observed, moving away from the man. He tied the front panel shut, and then allowed his blending skin to fade to his natural tone, fearing the reaction of the women. They merely looked at him—no fear, only curiosity.

"By Arak," Rhoa breathed, "he's like any other man." Her voice was filled with wonder.

Tinna's brows rose. She realized he was bigger than Taneth had said he would be. He was as tall as Taneth, maybe more. He had a fine body, hewn to perfection from his lifetime of climbing. His upper body was definitely far more defined than a normal man's. He was dirty, and he had not a spot of hair on his body, except for a small indication of eyebrows. He was actually very pleasant to look at, Tinna decided. Perhaps not as dignified as Taneth's looks, but certainly very manly. She gave him a nod of approval. He had some difficulty pulling on a shirt.

"What do you do in winter if you wear no clothes?"

"We wear clothes. Just not … this." He tugged on the wool. It was scratchy. Not soft like the winter body tunics and leggings made with the fibers of shanshan tree flowers. They hardly moved in winter, anyway. They found their teardrop- shaped hanging homes, curled up and slept most of the winter, rousing only to pass water or such, eat some rich stores of fatty nuts and dried meats and grains, and return to their nests. He wasn't accustomed to clothing being used for anything else but hibernating in. The women perhaps were better suited to wear clothes, but they didn't layer it on like ground-dwellers did.

His society had few complications, no such thing as marriage, and a pecking order based on age and experience, and largely cooperative acquisition of resources, as well as sharing. Nobody went hungry among his people. Children remained glommed to their mothers by their hands and feet from birth to age one, where they first begin to venture out on the trees, and learn to walk on the wide, aged highways of great boughs from the towering giant Karsu trees, where their clans always built their villages. One tree could house an entire community, and with the thick leaves' dense growth and accompanying parasitic plants growing on the massive tree, they were guaranteed not to be seen from below or above, winter or summer. He often wondered what ground-dwellers did during the winter. They obviously moved about, and did not sleep, since their signs of activity could be found all over the forest in spring. He didn't ask.

He walked with the women, wincing as the breeches chafed at his thighs.

He carried the puppy for Rhoa for a while as they moved toward the daunting city, wondering to himself how these people actually thought he looked like normal people. He was hairless. All the men were. The women were not—but they also lacked the blending skin. They rarely ever left the community. The men were gifted with the mechanisms needed to provide for their people. It was a simple way of defining everyone's role in the community. But somehow, Draphen was never very content with that role. He wondered; as he reached down to pull the seam that was rubbing his skin raw from his crotch, if he had made the right decision.

CHAPTER 10

"I don't understand," Rigerd said earnestly. "What quarrel would anyone have with the high throne? Who would be strong enough to take on such a power? I mean, dragons, for Arak's sake! Who can get dragons to reap such destruction for no reason? Dragons never do things like that for no reason."

He and Taneth were sitting in the main dining hall, facing the hearth, which held a roaring fire for the first time in months—the weather had taken a downturn for a few days, and had become rainy and chilly. They built the fire together, simply talking between friends, and now sat to enjoy the warmth as they wound down from a busy day. Taneth had brought in some projects to do while they talked, positioning himself in one of the five large upholstered chairs that hunkered between the table and the hearth facing the fire, where most of the village leaders sat in the evenings to smoke pipes and discuss the day's events and plan the next day. This night, the Holyman was not present, the stable master was bringing a number of horses out to be bred by the stallion of a neighboring clan, and the Militia Chief was meeting with Militia Chiefs of a number of surrounding Araki settlements to discuss possible action if the danger actually were to reach their borders.

"I am assuming there must be a valid reason, Rigerd. As you just said, dragons are very selective about how and where they use their power. If they weren't, there would no humans left in this world. We are no match to them, plainly."

Taneth sorted through some of his medical herbs, carefully cataloguing which of the vials needed to be replenished and what of the new medicines he'd discovered in the area had to be added to the collection.

Rigerd's mind was abuzz after spending the day out with a couple of the other leaders of various nearby villages, discussing the damage to Hildercross and its adjacent town. They had also talked to people from neighboring non-Araki settlements that were untouched, but witness to much of the destruction. His mind was all a-chatter with speculation and concern about the matter. The dragons had long gone, after destroying only a few select areas.

"The schools ... Those are being destroyed systematically, according to the news brought by the relay riders," Rigerd continued.

Taneth only snorted through his nose, showing his indifference on the matter quite plainly. He then paused from his sorting, and looked up. "Those are institutions run by the High Throne," Taneth thought aloud. "You said that the towns supporting the students, or a High Throne's guard were also destroyed?"

Rigerd nodded. "Then they're attacking systems supported by the High Throne, as if destroying a castle by pulling out the foundation."

"I've no quarrel with the High Throne. They don't bother us, we don't bother them," Rigerd said, crossing his ankle over his knee. He reached for his mug that sat on the ground by his comfortable chair, and drank from it, getting some beer-froth on his mustache. He sighed wearily and stared at the flames.

Taneth thought on the matter. Understanding the history of dragons, and their often-praised objectivity, he found himself thinking twice about whom they should fear. He did not voice these thoughts to Rigerd, who seemed relentlessly puzzled.

"Much of the fringe routes of the relay have been suspended for now," Rigerd said. "There is so much fear among the hamlets in the forests, that they are limiting the movement of their people. Some villages have sent volunteers out to scout, and bring news where it can be found, but they don't wish to do anything to attract the attention of the dragons again."

Taneth shook his head, chewing the inside of his cheek. Hanru shuffled, sleepy-eyed, into the community room, rubbing his eyes with his fists. He crawled onto Taneth's lap, obviously having missed him at home, and decided to demand some affection from his adoptive father.

Taneth quickly set down his task at his feet and gathered the assemblage of limbs onto his lap, and rocked the boy unconsciously; his mind locked on thoughts of this strange one-sided war, and the still-missing Tinna and Rhoa. He patted Hanru's unkempt hair down. "Do you think we should be more proactive about this?" he asked Rigerd, looking up from his reverie.

Rigerd gazed at Taneth's concerned face and arched a brow. "What do you suppose we should do?"

"I don't know. I have always thought the High Throne a protective force, Rigerd. But dragons are never reckless about where they declare their loyalties. In truth, they never declare loyalty to anyone; they usually do what is in the best interest of their own kind. They have no willingness to go after humanity, unless they are specifically threatened by them. And it would take all of humanity as a collective to really pose a threat to them. Who would have the means to threaten the dragon-folk enough to cause them to act like this? The High Throne is a great power, Rigerd, but not one the dragons couldn't eliminate in one deep breath of fire, like they did to Hildercross."

"What are you trying to tell me? That we should be rooting for the dragons who are systematically burning down swaths of our life-giving forest?"

"They haven't burnt anything down that wasn't already cut down and filled in with settlements built by the High Throne. The question is, is the High Throne harboring something or someone that is powerful enough to threaten the dragon-folk?"

Rigerd looked upon his new Wiseman, careful to heed what the young fellow said. If Taneth were right, he wondered what role his people had to play in this madness. He watched Taneth stand up, Hanru's little legs dangling down from under Taneth's supporting arm, the boy draped on his shoulder, sound asleep.

Rigerd liked Taneth very much. He rarely met people of such credit and worthiness. What he did for Hanru spoke volumes about his soul. He trusted the man implicitly, and knew that if there was a role for his people to play; Taneth would make the right decisions for his people, even if it is one Rigerd would think irrational.

Taneth shuffled up the corridor to his apartment, standing up on his bed to tuck the boy in. He feared for Hanru, and his people. He feared for Tinna and Rhoa. He felt powerless. He had no access to more information, nor could he abandon the people who depended on his assurances, and the boy who needed his love and care to search for answers he alone would be powerless to act on. He put the toy wolf Indra had sewn for Hanru as an adoption gift under the blanket with the boy. She'd made it out of real wolf hide, and did an amazing job matching colors to the legs and nose, and making him appear very realistic, complete with two shiny black hematite eyes and a glossy nose made of a polished black river stone. She even used some black suede to make the pads on the paws.

Taneth was very impressed with her skill. Taneth knew Indra had some designs on him, and was very attentive to him. She wore revealing clothes, and cooked special dishes for him. She was exceedingly good to him. But he really wasn't attracted to her. Not like he was to Tinna. And even Hanru loved Tinna in her short time with them, and asked about her frequently. "She promised to bring me a new Nibbles," the boy would say. "She's gone very, very far to find me one. I hope she returns soon. It's been a whole week already."

"She will return soon. I'm sure Tinna is not the sort of person to break a promise," Taneth would tell him. Part of him believed that her absence was a sure clue that she was dead, and Rhoa, too. But some instinct deep inside him knew this was not true. Tinna was full of a vitality and strength that would never allow her to submit to death easily. She was lost…captured perhaps…helping people out of the rubble from the destruction. She was not dead. He would not allow himself to believe it.

Hanru wasn't quite as asleep as he thought, when he tucked the wolf doll under the blanket. Taneth climbed up onto the gently swinging bed, and sat next to the boy, caressing his freshly cropped hair. His eyes cracked open, and he exhaled a shuddering sigh. "Taneth?" Hanru asked.

"What is it, boy?"

"Will my mother ever come back?"

"I don't think so. She's been banished, Hanru. I'm sorry. But it is against the rules of our village to harm another of our clan, let alone her own child. Does it sadden you that she is gone, Han?"

"I am frightened, not sad. What if she comes back and is very angry that I don't live in our apartment any more—and that I live with you, and that I shall have a new dog? She hated Nibbles. She'll kill the new dog, just like she killed Nibbles." Hanru began to cry.

Taneth was stunned. He thought the pup had been carried off and dropped by a large raptor. Why would the boy say such a thing?

"Hanru, your puppy was carried off by a large bird—"

"Mother killed him. I was there when she did it. She told me to tell everyone about the bird" Taneth's ears began to turn red, and his jaws rippled. He kept his composure, barely. He had no reason to lose his temper anymore. The woman was gone. But he still had the urge to go after her and beat the bitch senseless. How could anyone be so cruel?

"He was crying. Mother wouldn't let him stay in my bed, so we left him on the floor. He was crying because he was cold and lonely. Mother got very angry, and started shouting at him to be quiet. I wanted to get out of bed and quiet him down, but she shouted that if

I did, she would make me sleep on the floor, too. I would have slept on the floor, just so Nibbles would be quiet. But I was afraid. She had lispy words. When she has lispy words, she's very mean. I was afraid she'd be angry that I would want to sleep on the floor. I should have gotten out of bed and slept on the floor. Nibbles just kept crying, and Mother got so mad. I heard her climb down from her bed, and I heard Nibbles squeal, and then nothing. The next morning he was lying on the floor, dead. Mother told me the bird story and said if I told anyone anything else but that story, she would do the same thing to me that she did to Nibbles." He talked through a veil of snot and tears. Taneth was horrified. He hugged the poor child close to him. "She's going to kill my new doggie, too!" Hanru wailed. "I should have slept on the floor!"

"You were scared, Han. And rightfully so … she was very mean and hurtful. It's not your fault that Nibbles died."

The boy sobbed. "She's going to come back and kill my new Nibbles, too …"

Taneth rocked him and soothed him, hushing his cries down to frequent sniffles and the occasional hiccup, ignoring the slug-trail of mucous the boy was depositing all over his tunic. Taneth didn't care. He could only feel the depth of the boy's sobs and the profound power of his sadness.

"She's going to do no such thing, Hanru. She's gone. And you live with me now. Your new puppy can sleep in your bed anytime he likes, and I shall never, ever let anyone hurt him or you," Taneth whispered, hoping with all his heart that Hanru's puppy, and Tinna would return, not only to heal the boy's hurt, but also to cure Taneth's own worry. He clung to the boy, strangely finding himself having a short but poignant memory of his father. I suppose, he thought to himself, I am doing exactly what my father or mother would have never done. By doing the opposite of what my parents did for me, I am a better parent. He found that amusing, looking down at the boy as he slipped into a troubled sleep. Taneth sat him through to a deep sleep, and then slid him back onto the bed, and tucked him in, gazing down at him for a long time.

I should never feel bad for my own childhood. I had a bed, a room, and an education. My father and mother may have been indifferent and cold to me, but it could have been much, much worse. He picked up the small hand, and looked at it. Even the boy's hands looked like a set of scaled-down adult hands. He'd been aged by his misery. He put the hand down, and sighed. "I shall personally see to it that every horrible thing you've suffered in your life shall be

97

countered with something good. And I will help you make up for your lost childhood, and help you find a balance between your past and your future so you can be happy, Hanru. Maybe even enroll you in a school. A good school. Nothing like the one I went to. I shall visit you there, and be proud of everything you do as I am now."

His eyes smiled at the lost child. Taneth had certainly not thought he'd become a father so soon, but somehow, it seemed to fall right in place with the rest of the unexpected things that had come his way since that fateful day in the lecture hall. It wasn't as if he'd had any plan for himself or his future. Oddly, this one that was forced into his lap seemed to be exactly what he had been preparing for his entire life. He'd never counted upon serving such a simple yet crucial role in a community that accepted him as one of their own. He could have been many greater things than this, but in his heart, this was what he really wanted.

As he slid into his own bed, reassured by the soft breathing of the child hanging above him, he rolled onto his side, looking at the dying embers of the dinner fire fade into the ashes. There was only one thing missing now. And it wasn't Indra.

CHAPTER 11

Rhoa's forehead broke out in a cold sweat. She could barely stand, her knees had gone so weak. Draphen was of no assistance. He was most possibly in worse condition than she, and both were bordering on panic. Tinna had vanished in the crowds ahead, and neither of these people were in any way equipped to deal with the din and chaos of a city so large. Nobody spoke their language, either. Rhoa couldn't even imagine the distance they must have been brought to be in a land where nobody spoke the common Shelval tongue.

Tinna seemed able to communicate in this new language, and got them some directions for an inn. Tinna needed to secure some funds somehow, and seemed so consumed in trying to figure out how to get enough money for supplies that she lost them. She walked fast, and forgot that her friends were so daunted and awed by the sights and sounds that they were slowed by it all. When Rhoa looked up she realized that her only anchor in this alien, terrible, and frightening world, had moved ahead into the crowds.

"Oh gods, where is she?" Rhoa gasped, panic evident in her voice. Draphen clutched Rhoa's hand like a terrified child. They both stood together as if surrounded by rabid and slavering wolves. In reality, the daily madness of market and work, throngs of people, livestock and drays, coursed around them as if they were stones in a stream. Everyone who passed them was indifferent to the stricken duo.

"C-Can we get out of this street?" Draphen stammered through his cold sweat, feeling nauseous.

"Where should we go? Over there? Where? What if she comes back and we're not here? Should we just keep walking?" Rhoa's voice was escalating into hysteria.

Draphen gathered up his wits for a second, and pulled Rhoa into a doorway. She turned and clutched herself to him, burying her face in Draphen's chest. She started to cry, wishing away the roar of the city, and the feeling of the masses around her closing in like the mouth of a great beast. Draphen put his arms around her, and seized her just as tightly, eyes locked on the unending stream of people flowing by. Not a single one looked at them.

Draphen had no idea there were so many ground-dwellers in this world. So many in once place, for that matter, it was inconceivable even while he was witnessing it right then and there. He knew how many communities of his people there were in the great forest, and he knew that they didn't outnumber the people in this city by half. It frightened him. Were his people so insignificant in the greater scheme? He felt as tiny as a grain of soil on the incomprehensibly busy lamp-lit street. He held onto the only familiar thing as if she would vanish at any moment. Tinna looked up, and stopped walking, shaking her head with resignation.

She had to do what had to be done. There were no two ways about it. They needed supplies, and they needed money. She knew Rhoa would disagree with her methods, but frankly Rhoa would have to deal with the notion and that was that. Tinna didn't know why she felt the need to tell Rhoa anything of her activities, but she felt compelled to on most occasions, which annoyed Tinna greatly.

She turned around to confront them with her decision, only to find herself gazing directly into the eyes of a giant plains ox. The animal's moist muzzle wrinkled and it shook its head, rattling the reins chained to loops bored through his expansive horns, and slinging some of his slobber onto the shoulder of a passer-by. His hump was at least a man-and-a-half tall, and secured to the front of it was a large, stuffed leather strap that circled his chest, and attached to it were two leather loops in which the pulling bars of a huge dray rested. The cart was being filled with casks of beer. An equally gigantic operator directed the loading, gazing down at a parchment purchase order, making certain the right number of barrels were being loaded. Tinna forgot about her missing friends for a moment, circling 'round to where the towering, muscular man was.

"Ahem," she said. The huge man turned to look down at the diminutive Thran, surprised to see one so far north. He was too busy to pay her any heed. He turned back 'round and watched the loaders work.

"Ahem," Tinna persisted. The large fellow turned around again, this time looking a bit annoyed. "What do you want? I'm a very busy man!"

"Are you coming from Suthervale?" she asked.

"Aye. Why do you ask?"

"Would you be willing to take on a few paying passengers?"

"And where do you propose to sit?" he asked. The dray had a hard wooden bench stretched out along the front. There were no protections from the elements, or padding for comfort, but she was desperate.

"On top of the barrels, I don't care. We can walk beside the dray during the day. We just don't know where in the world we are, and if I can get back to Suthervale, I can get my bearings there, and go back to where we were taken from."

The man thought for a moment, puzzlement quite plain on his features. He glanced at her dubiously. "How could you be so lost as not to know where you are at all? I don't quite understand—"

"It's difficult to explain. We were brought here without seeing where we went," she said, trying to make some sort of sense of it, but gave up, waving her hand in frustration.

He sighed, pursing his lips thoughtfully. "I suppose I could do with some company," he mused. "It's a long journey. Fine. You may come along. I'm going to be leaving here on the morn. You can meet me here, I suppose. Don't think I'm providing you with anything for the journey besides a means of transportation and directions. You need to provide your own things. Exactly how many of there are you?"

"Three."

"Oh, well, that's not so bad. I imagined at least five. See you at dawn. I will leave without you if you are late." He turned his back again, returning to supervising the barrel-loading. Tinna then moaned tiredly; she had to go back and find the two idiots. She retraced her steps, finding Draphen and Rhoa huddled in the doorway of a private home. They nearly fainted with relief at the sight of her.

"Keep up this time."

"Slow down! This is a new place for both of us!" Draphen snapped. Rhoa's brow furrowed and she nodded in agreement. Tinna shook her head and groaned, rolling her eyes as she spun about, picking her way back up the walk.

She decided they were already too traumatized to tell them she was going to have to rob someone to get some more supplies. She found a room they could cower in, and set off to get the money to pay for it.

"I'm sorry, but this is really necessary," Tinna apologized. She'd done the same for the man she'd robbed for his clothes. She hated doing things like this. But it really was necessary. She untied the

101

heavy pouch of coins from his breeches, and tied them to the thick band of leather to which her little skirt was sewn. She gazed down at the gagged man beneath her with a regretful expression.

"You're a successful merchant; I'm certain this will be but a drop in the bucket for you. This drop will support several people for a long time," she rationalized. She sat up, still straddling him as if making love to the man. She felt his arousal beneath her, straining against his breeches. She pursed her lips at him and arched her brows.

"Really...you should behave. You have a strange sense of timing, not to mention a bizarre notion of what is arousing," she reprimanded him, enjoying her position of power.

She hesitated in rising from her position, a wry smile crossing her lips. *Why not? I am Thran, after all. Have these northerly living folk affected me so much that I have become one of their wilting women?* She looked at him. He was handsome, virile, and obviously very much excited by her. She pulled the hem of his tunic from under her thighs, and slid her hands up onto the man's chest, delighting in the feel of the warm curls of hair tickling her fingers. The man sucked air in through his nose as her fingers found his little nipples. She toyed with them, smiling mischievously. She pushed his shirt up, leaning down to nibble on them. He jerked from the touch of her tongue. She shoved the shirt over his head, leaving it wadded above his head on his arms, which were bound tightly and tied to the leg of a large table.

She lifted her own shirt off. The merchant's eyes seemed to glaze over, and his arm muscles tightened. She felt an instant response in the hardness pressed against her thigh, moving as if it had a life of its own. She slid her hands down, sitting up, giving his manhood a playful squeeze. She half stood for just long enough to untie his breeches and shove them down his legs. She then toyed with him with her hands for a while, scooting down to have a taste or two. The man was making muffled groans into his gag.

She slid her little underpants aside, and sat on him, emitting a delighted moan as she filled herself with this stranger. Her little skirt flounced around her as she bounced on her victim, pinching his nipples as she pleased herself. She used him until she was spent, and he was as well. She then stood up, and looked around his rooms for his washbowl and decanter, taking a moment to freshen herself up.

The man lay there, unmoving, pants pressed down to his knees, tunic bunched up over his head, his chest rising and falling from the exertion. *Not exactly a picture of dignity,* Tinna thought as she left him, locking the latch behind her. She crept down the stairs of the luxurious inn, and like a shadow, passed through the common room past a number of patrons who were sitting about in peace, reading books, or smoking pipes. She reached the street undetected and walked back to her own less opulent rooms, carrying a heavy coin purse on her hip, and showing a definite spring in her step.

"Where have you been? Besides the unending noise keeping me awake, I was worried to bits about you. Does this bloody place never quiet down?" Rhoa yammered. Aitinna sighed and sat down on the bed, unlacing her boots and pulling them off one by one. She pulled her clothes off, and changed into a large, loose tunic, giving herself another thorough wash, and sorting through her little medicine pouch to find her contraceptive mix, using the inn's rusted kettle to heat up water for the important tea. She felt guilty all of a sudden, and this didn't bode well for a woman who was raised to follow her own instincts when it came to sex, and feel no shame for responding to natural urges. She supposed that it was indeed the northerly living that affected her so profoundly. She opened one of her little parchment packets, and dumped the contents into the kettle. Rhoa put the puppy to sleep on her pillow and came to her side.

"Oh, you're making tea. Good. Maybe that will help me sleep." She reached for two of the three small bowls used for hot drinks, and put them on the table.

Tinna sighed, carrying the kettle over when the aroma of the herbs permeated the coils of steam rising from the simmering water. She poured some into each cup, and sat down on one of the rickety chairs.

Rhoa sat down too, picking up the little cup, and blowing on it to cool it down. She took a sip, and then swallowed, gazing at Tinna with disbelief. "This   is osha and pin leaf!" she exclaimed. Tinna glanced up, the guilt evident on her face.

"Is that where you were?"

"I was securing funds."

"Like a whore?" Rhoa shouted.

Tinna's face darkened into a furious glower, and she rapped her hand on the table. "I am not a whore! I robbed a man. What I did to him afterwards I did because I wanted to. He certainly didn't pay me. It was just a highlight for what was probably a frightening experience for the man."

Rhoa's mouth was agape. "You just did it? With a stranger?" Her eyes were wide.

"Yes. Why is that so difficult to believe?"

"That's horrible. Are you always so promiscuous?"

"The Thran do not believe that following one's natural desires to be promiscuity. Do you call men whores? They're veritable pigs when it comes to sex. Even the most humble and moral of men has his dark secrets. My people simply have a more realistic view about these things. Let's face it, your people and my people do exactly the same things, but your people simply pretend it doesn't happen." Rhoa's mouth was still agape. "Come now, Rhoa, don't think you're fooling me one bit: You knew what this tea was from its taste alone…that speaks volumes."

Rhoa's mouth snapped shut, and she leaned back in her chair, her gaze moving away. Tinna liked this reaction; she picked up her tea and took a good smug sip from it. She did not allow her eyes to stray from Rhoa and let her off the hook.

"Well, it's my sister's fault," Rhoa finally muttered, crossing her arms. "I wouldn't have been curious about it, or done anything, if it weren't for her and her husband. They're always at it. Like animals. And having to live with them leaves me little chance to avoid it. Our homes are not like these … there's only one room. One room! You know that! There is no such thing as privacy at home. Every night, they're at it, oohing and ahhing, rutting like swine."

"Well, it can't be so disgusting to you if you were curious enough to try it."

"Come on, with all those moans and groans, you're bound to wonder what the hullabaloo is all about," she reasoned, downing her tea. Tinna smiled at her, pouring her some more and then refilling her own little bowl. "Who was it? Did I meet him?" Tinna asked.

Rhoa shook her head. "No. Every autumn we celebrate harvest with other villages of our kind. We gather at a place known as Turtle Hill. It has some of the oldest lodges in the area, and used to house one of the largest single clans ever. It was so large it was eventually split up into three, and the argument over who would keep Turtle Hill as home became so heated, it was decided nobody would, and that it would be used for clan festivals. Anyway, it was Autumn Festival, and the Ashmont clan, which never comes to large gatherings, showed up." Rhoa's face softened, and her eyes rolled upward as she remembered the day, leaning on the table with her elbows. "They showed because their new leader had a particular wish to marry another leader's son—so she decided to make the event occur during this yearly gathering. It was a very exciting and different festival from the usual ones because of their presence. There were so many new faces.

"Among them was this young man named Ysiph. He was not only newly inducted into a clan we hardly saw at all, but he was originally from another clan two month's travel to the west, of a people like ours who spoke a completely different language. He'd been like you, a traveler, and he found the Ashmont clan and their sophisticated village built out of the black soil and rock of the Ashmont mountain. He decided to stay when he found that his skills were valued, where at his own home, they were commonly available. He's a potter. And he makes the most incredibly beautiful pots out of the black clay from their home. He brought a number of them to trade at the festival." She sighed with a smile.

"He wasn't like most fellows. He has this air about him that artists sometimes do, a sort of rakishness and brooding mystery … He had this beautiful, light-blond hair that curled like yours, and he had this sort of casual, gentle way about him. He always let his beard grow out just a bit, so he had this sort of uncaring ruggedness to him. He was so earthy, and full of depth, he made me mad for him with just one of his radiant smiles. Now that I think about it, I'm sure that smile worked on many girls. He turned out to be quite the sly one with the women. I can say with confidence that he deflowered more than just one girl that festival. But my sister said that I was fortunate that he was such a man, because normally the first time for a girl can be not such a good experience with someone less practiced. It hurt a bit … but after that, it didn't hurt at all. It was amazing. He had sex with me four times during the festival. My sister gave me the 'morning tea' when I confided that I'd had been deflowered, and subsequently, after each other occasion. That's how I knew the tea. It does have a very distinctive taste." She smiled.

Tinna leaned forward, finding her story very pleasing. "What happened to this man, Ysiph?"

"He went back to Ashmont. He left behind evidence of his passing for some girls unlucky enough not to have a thoughtful sister like mine. They all looked like him. The same light-blond hair and brilliant smile." Tinna laughed. Rhoa returned the giggle.

"Tell me, Tinna," Rhoa began, trying to find the words, "how did you go about—doing what you did—with the man you robbed?"

Tinna explained, concluding the night with the two women sharing a hearty laugh about the whole thing. Tinna had grown a bit of respect for the girl, and Rhoa's opinion of Tinna had improved even more, instead of being diminished by what she had thought to be a promiscuous act. She found it rather funny, actually, and she admired the woman's ability to be so confident with her own sexuality.

Tinna rose very early the next day to catch the early merchants and purchase the things they would need. She woke Rhoa, who went to get Draphen from his own small room across the hall. They arrived at the brewery before their transport, taking the extra time before dawn to sort through their new supplies, and figure out what belonged best with who. The puppy was furnished with a thick, soft pelt of lamb's wool to adorn his little bag. Draphen had more clothing of his own; Tinna had been careful to choose things that were not made of scratchy fibers, for his complaints were incessant.

As the sun rose, and the light traffic on the street increased, the lumbering giant ox appeared, hauling on its own a dray full of barrels, as well as a small horseshoe-shaped caravan latched on the back. It looked much like a Gypsy carriage,

Tinna noted, wondering if he'd commissioned one of her father's people to build it for him. It was very short. Perhaps the length of the man, no more. It was high, and the arched top was roofed with thatching, and the windows shuttered up with brightly painted panels. She realized that this was his own little mobile house. She supposed the addition of the second carriage made little difference to his gigantic beast of burden. The animal seemed not even to make much effort of dragging the barrels, let alone both carriages. The impressive trader was at his place on the bench, holding the reins that were looped to the oxen's massive horns. He yanked them very hard on sight of the three people awaiting him, and the ox's head tilted back and it stopped abruptly, grunting out a half moo in protest. He seemed quite inclined to keep moving at his trudging pace, and showed dismay at the unexpected stop.

"Ugly, stop, whoaaaa," the driver bellowed in his deep, rumbly voice. "Hop on, you three. I think there's room enough for all of us here. I had no idea there would be two of you small things …" He scooted over and patted the empty spot beside him, smiling at Rhoa and Tinna, and blatantly ignoring the bald, rugged-looking fellow with the fancy clothes. Rhoa smiled, and accepted his hand up first. He pulled her up as if she were as light as a feather. She settled in, adjusting the puppy's bag so it would rest on her lap. Tinna let Draphen go after, knowing he'd want to be close to Rhoa. She noticed that he had transferred his obsession with her to Rhoa, gaining a deep appreciation for her after he saw how very much the two had in common, and that they shared the same dislike and fear for the environments that were so different from their home, which they both shared: the deep, lush forests of the east.

Tinna was relieved. She had no desire to be obsessed-over by a chameleonic madman. She climbed onto the dray, and squeezed in onto the bench with the rest of them. "Yeah, Ugly!" the driver shouted. The ox grunted, and the carriage and the trailer lurched forward. This was a caravan nobody dared to impede, and he growing crowds parted to the rumbling construct being pulled by an animal obviously not native to this area.

Suthervale was a vast plain that had once been the bed of an inconceivably gigantic river. It receded to a ribbon of water winding peacefully down the center of this vast sea of waving grass. Small villages clustered the riverbanks, and the oversized animals of this isolated world dotted the countryside in massive herds. Moropus, which looked like overgrown sheared sheep with two enormous claws on their front feet could be seen in dun-colored herds peppering the landscape.

Giant ox grazed the grassland, as well as the running birds, which were as tall as a man, and faster than a horse. They were flightless due to their incredible size, but they were elegant nonetheless, with swan-like necks and heads, and thick, muscled bodies with long, graceful, black legs that could race across the grasslands at incredible speed.

The people of this place reflected the lushness and openness of the plains, for they too were also big and hardy creatures, like their kind driver. They were farmers and fishers. Tinna had come to this land via Suthervale, for it bordered the land of her people, separated by an immense range of mountains that fed the river of the plain. She was close to home, she thought, if she could even think of the place as home She'd never belonged. They all saw her common Gypsy blood. Northerners did not, strangely. They saw only the dark hair and eyes of Thran, but not the high cheekbones and slanted eyes of her Gypsy heritage. She had been relieved to see the unmistakably Suthervalian man and his ox.

She knew that by starting at Suthervale, she could find her way back to the village of Thamatoch again. As the ox pulled them from the madness of the city, Rhoa and Draphen emitted a sigh of relief, but the wide open, nearly treeless land beyond brought them little comfort. Tinna realized she had been rude enough to forget to ask the man his name, and even forgotten to discuss terms. She leaned forward to see him.

"I am Aitinna, this is Draphen, and that is Rhoa. What is your name?"

"I am Borc. This is Ugly." He waved his fisted hand loosely toward the ox; the rein that hung from it dangled against the gigantic, swaying ox's behind. Rhoa had never seen one so big before. She had little fear, being brought up amid horses, which were impressive enough. But she could not have imagined that any animal this freakishly huge could exist, until she had actually seen it. Nobody at home would believe her if she told them, that was certain.

As the day wore on, it seemed they had hardly moved at all. The city had receded against the plains, but the few isolated trees that they used as speed indicators passed by very slowly. The ox moved at a consistent pace, the sound of his cloven hooves crushing the dirt beneath them becoming a hypnotic, rhythmic sedative. Rhoa had dozed off and her head leaned on Draphen, who stared blankly out to the open plain to his right. Tinna had climbed down to stretch her legs, keeping up with the great big bovine with a quick, determined pace, chewing the stem of wild wheat. She was glad she could walk unencumbered, happy to have a place to leave her heavy bags as they traveled. She enjoyed the feel of the grass brushing her thighs, and the breeze tousling her hair. The air smelled so fresh.

Borc was not a graceful lover. But it was not terrible at all, and because she had decided to indulge her needs on this particular person, they were losing no more money from their budget. He was a large, clumsy man, but he was a large man, and for Tinna that was a bonus. Tinna also gained the privilege of spending the nights inside the small caravan, leaving the other two and the puppy to take shelter under the dray, in order to avoid being stepped on by the ox, who spent part of the night filling his immense tummy with all the grass that encircled their camp. Come morning, he would have sheared a perfect radius around them, and would be standing nearby, eyes half closed. Then he would spend the day farting and shitting while they sat behind him wrinkling their noses, except for Borc, who seemed quite oblivious to it all. He, like Tinna, preferred not to spend the day chattering. He was a man of depth, strangely, and he pondered a great number of life's mysteries as his beast of burden plodded along.

Tinna was no self-made philosopher like her ungainly sexual partner. She simply wondered about her own life, and contemplated her actions. She'd never felt guilty about things before. Not natural things. She did what she did with Borc for practical reasons, besides her own desires, but she didn't enjoy it very much.

In all truth, she found it rather unbearable sometimes. She never had such problems before. Perhaps it was Rhoa's influence on her. Since their chat in the room before they left that immense city, Rhoa often walked with Tinna, telling her all about her dreams and expectations, and describing her ideal mate. Tinna found that often, a little piece of her liked what she heard. She would chide herself, saying she'd been up north too long, and then she began to realize that she wasn't really a Thran anymore. She'd given up on her own people, finding herself unacceptable to them, and left them. She came here. She'd committed herself to bringing a boy a dog, even it if meant crossing a continent to do it. She knew she wasn't crossing this vast land just for Hanru, and perhaps that's why she was finding herself more and more concerned about her sexual exploits. She realized it was because she didn't want to have to explain her actions to Taneth. He wouldn't understand.

Even Rhoa didn't truly understand, even if she claimed to. There was a sense of acceptance of her ways, but not understanding. She was glad she'd managed to forge a friendship with her, nonetheless. She found her far less annoying. In fact, her increased attentions to Rhoa had made her less likely to say or do stupid things to get her attention.

Today, she chose to walk beside the ox. He'd eaten an especially large circle of standing hay that night, and gave a preview of the day's coming activities by blasting a hot, smelly fart so loud, it actually echoed back to them from the rocky outcroppings of the mountain range that separated Thran land from the north countries. The mountains began as hills, then tall hills, then rocky hills, and then small peaks, until soon, they could see the high walls and ice-adorned crowns. It had been eighteen days of relentless clip-clopping and gaseous cacophonies from their bovine companion. Tinna knew it wouldn't be long before they'd reach the river and Borc's town. They would be back on foot after that. It didn't bother her to be so, but Draphen wasn't a walker, he was a climber. He didn't complain, except about his clothing, which had stopped as his sensitivity to the fabric waned.

They arrived in Borc's village at the sun's zenith the following day. They'd passed by a number of smaller hamlets on the way, as well as a few enormous animals roaming free that made Rhoa gasp in awe. Borc pulled his heavy assemblage over a stone bridge, into a large-ish town. There, he drew to a halt in front of a trade office. Everyone dismounted.

"Gods be blessed!" A large woman shouted, arms akimbo, running toward Borc from the adjacent building. He was assaulted by a shower of kisses and hugs, and then a frantic rattle of words. "I thought you were dead Gods be blessed you are not!" she yammered. "When I heard of Hamacla being destroyed, I could all but keep myself from fainting—"

"What?" Borc boomed.

The woman stepped back, tall and muscular. "You don't know?"

"No ... Hamacla was destroyed?"

"Yes. We thought you were still there. Imagine my relief when a runner from upriver said that you were spotted coming over the rise. Imagine!"

"When was it ... when was it destroyed?"

"Oh, about ten days ago ..." she calculated. "We got word through the Royal

Relay, which itself has been attacked. They say dragons fell from the sky and blasted the great city into cinders before anyone had a chance to escape. It's horrid. Truly horrid!" she wailed, hand clutched to her generous breast.

"What? Is every city we pass through to be destroyed by those dragons?" Rhoa hissed to Tinna under her breath.

Tinna threw the bags down from the dray, and shook her head. "I think our friend Ledroran put us down there to give us a chance to get in and get out before the strike. Had we stayed any longer, we'd be dead. He did tell us to move on quickly. Something is afoot. We simply must get back to the village as soon as possible. The People of the Horse God must be warned. There are too many of groups of Araki across this land not to be considered a power. They can be either a friend or an enemy to whoever is fortunate enough to have the help of the dragons." She jumped down from the cart, landing with at thump. "We need to go now."

CHAPTER 12

It was raining very hard. The drops stung as they pelted the three travelers. "Do you think you can part with some of your precious gold to buy us some inexpensive horses? We would be making far greater progress on this journey if we had some."

"They would not be any help against this rain, Rhoa"

"There is no way in all creation you will ever get me on one of those animals."

"Draphen, do you plan to spend your entire existence living in fear?" Rhoa shouted over the thunder of the rain.

"Excuse me, but aren't you the one who nearly shit her breeches in terror in the city?" he retorted.

The three of them remained quiet for a while.

"Is there nothing in this place?" Rhoa grumbled. "It's a bloody wasteland full of piles of wild, giant ox dung."

"What I would give for a few nice trees," Draphen mumbled.

"Would you two shut up? I'm sick of hearing you complain!" Tinna screamed.

She stomped ahead, lifting her arms higher so that the leather she used as a pad for her bedding shielded her eyes from the rain. She thought she saw a shimmer of light somewhere ahead, and her heart leapt. She squinted, trying to see the lights again. There it was ... another blink. She picked up her pace. She heard Rhoa and Draphen arguing behind her, but the annoyance it would have normally caused was wiped away by a feeling of hope. The land dipped a bit, and she picked up speed as she bounded down the soft incline. The other two complained about her speed, but Rhoa said, "Look...A light!"

The three flew down the hill, surprised to find themselves assaulted by thick growth, albeit a tad unimpressive and shrubby next to the forests they were accustomed to. The light flickered brightly now as they moved among the trees, heading straight for it, taking little care where they tread to do it. Rhoa fell twice, and Tinna slid down a steep embankment, tearing the sleeve of her tunic in the

111

process and losing her leather padding to a sharp, broken tree limb. The only person who was deft at navigating this thick, sometimes thorny vegetation was Draphen, who finally felt a tiny bit of solace. They suddenly broke out of the thickets onto a lawn so manicured, the meager light that caught the raindrops on the grass twinkled with a uniformity that seemed unnatural. They stopped short, pausing for a breath and to see where they'd emerged.

"This isn't a village. It's a manor." A single bright light behind a ground-floor window shined out. Tinna shrugged, and loped around the building until they arrived at the entranceway. She lifted the great iron knocker and rapped two times. The other two climbed the large stairs, and found shelter with Tinna under the massive overhanging stone portico. Tinna felt the warmth of blood dripping down her arm. After a long wait, the door finally opened, and a gaunt little old lady stood there, looking at them. She said nothing; she made no gesture to them, nor opened the door to them. She just stared.

"Leeta." The clatter of hard boots and a grating, mean-sounding voice called. The old woman was pulled away, and a lean, sinewy man in his fifties appeared. He was as bald as a melon. He had a neatly trimmed salt-and-pepper goatee and eyes so light-colored, they seemed like shards of clear glass catching the stray light from the lamplight behind him.

"What?" he asked.

Tinna sighed. "We've been walking a long way; we'd like to know if there is someplace nearby where we can get a room and some shelter from the rain."

He studied her for a painfully long moment. "No. There's nothing or no one for miles. This house is here for that exact reason. But since you're bleeding and all, I suppose you can rest here. I'm not one for chatty visitors, so I hope you will leave early tomorrow."

Tinna nodded. He widened the door and let them pass. The old woman stood there gawking at them with her lips parted; she had not a single tooth in her head. Tinna stopped in the center of the foyer, taking in the sparse furnishings—seeing masculine dominance in this house.

"Leeta, go back to your room," the man snapped at the little old woman. She seemed hardly aware of him at all, but still, she turned like a sleepwalker and shuffled away. The man's glare was hard and penetrating. He studied Tinna again, then Rhoa, and Draphen, returning to Tinna.

"Come," he said. He led them up the wide, stone stairway and into a corridor that smelled of mildew. The carpet was very old, and worn through to the flags in places. He paused at a doorway. "Man, you stay here." He shoved the door open.

Draphen poked his head into the darkened room. "You can get a flame from one of the lamps in the corridor. There should be a candle on the table just inside the door," their host mumbled. "Ladies …" He continued down the hallway, throwing the next door open. "You can stay here," he said to Rhoa. "The same goes for you if you need light. I'll have Sankar come and light some fires for you people."

He then gestured to Tinna, and led her back to the stairs to a door set into a stone arch on the second-floor balcony that encircled the massive iron chandelier that lit the foyer below.

"This is your room," he said, his sparkling eyes studying her again. "I have a great respect for the ways of the Thran. I gave you the finest room besides my own." He offered a stiff smile. He pushed the door open and took a candle-dish from the little table inside and lit it with a lamp ensconced on the wall next to the door. He handed it to her. She took it. "I will have someone come up and see to that wound," he said before turning on his heel and striding away. Tinna rarely feared anything. This man scared her.

* * * *

Morning rose as if the world were reborn after the violent storm. Tinna dressed quickly, eager to get out of the strange fellow's house. She bumped into Rhoa outside her door, who seemed as eager herself to be on her way. She paused beside Tinna before they went downstairs. "He's up already. I came out of my room this morning and he was standing outside my door. It was very odd," she hissed under her breath.

Tinna nodded, following the wary girl down to the foyer. "Is Draphen up?"

"He said he'd meet us outside. I think he's enjoying the cover of the small forest before we leave this little valley for the plains again."

"Good morning," their strange host called, standing behind them as if he'd materialized out of nowhere. "I've taken the liberty of having breakfast made for you." He lifted his hand, gallantly directing them toward the archway to the dining hall.

Tinna shook her head. "It's all right. We need to be on our way as soon as possible."

"Now, you wouldn't deny me the pleasure of sharing a meal with two lovely creatures as yourself, after I allowed you to shelter

113

under my roof? Please," he insisted, his hand still showing them through the arch. Tinna frowned inwardly, but smiled, albeit coolly.

"Of course not. It is very kind of you to offer us breakfast. We simply did not wish to trespass upon your kindness and overstay our welcome," Tinna replied. She strode past him, Rhoa following, not bothering to hide the annoyance in her face. He had indeed furnished them with a breakfast worthy of royalty. The table was bedecked with platter after platter of delicious foods: meats, fruits, breads and cheeses. Draphen had apparently been invited earlier, and was busying himself over a heaping platter of pickings from the buffet before them, which showed little sign of anyone actually making a dent in its contents.

Rhoa put the puppy on the floor to stretch his legs, and sat down. While the man sank down in a seat at the head of the table, Rhoa used the fine linen napkins to wrap up a number of smoked meats, cheeses and even some of the dried cereals waiting to be softened by the steaming pitcher of milk. She stuffed them into her pack, doing so with incredible subtlety, Tinna noted, finding herself quite proud of her. Tinna on the other hand, used the fact that she was the focus of their benefactor's attention, to keep it so Rhoa could steal her fill. The little dog, having been rebuffed by the man's huge wolfhounds who gave him a rumbling growl of warning when he entered the forbidden zone, returned to Rhoa's feet, whimpering. He was so tiny next to those towering dogs. She would take some food for him, too, Rhoa decided. As she stuffed her mouth and her bag, Tinna decided to dispense with the formalities right away, so to have no more reason to be delayed by this strange man.

"It is very kind of you, sir, to allow us into your home, and prepare such a wonderful meal for us," she said.

"I feel I was a bit harsh with you when you arrived. I am merely making amends. How is your arm?"

"Oh, it's much better." The tiny, frightened girl who had come to see to the wound had been very meticulous and gentle. She was like a small bird, aware of every little noise and movement. She scurried in, did her work, and scurried out, never once uttering a word. "Thank you," Tinna said to her host, taking a sip of the warm milk she had poured into her tankard.

"I must say I am bursting with curiosity," he suddenly blurted. "A Thran ... a daughter of Arak, and a Nimrath ... One could not even invent such an unlikely group of companions easily, even with the most incredible of imaginations. Do tell me, I'm enthralled. How in the world did this come about?"

"It's a very long story. Perhaps not as strange as one would imagine, I would think. Well, the Nimrath is a bit of an aberration, that I concede, but Rhoa is a friend I met while visiting her village to take pause from my travels."

He looked at her. "What does a Thran do in the savage lands? Isn't it more common for your people to avoid crossing to the north into the uncivilized world? Then again"—he leaned forward—"your features are very, very remarkable. They betray your Thran blood without question, but there is something other within them. The eyes … your height … the shape of your face …"

"I am not very familiar with my ancestors," she lied.

But this man was like an eagle. His icy eyes picked up even the subtlest of signs. "I've always considered the Thran a noble people. I've always wanted to go to your lands, and explore. I have always liked the idea of traveling the world, learning about new cultures, and so on."

"Uh-huh."

He leaned back in his chair, pressing his steepled fingers against his lips, his arms propped on the arms of his chair, which were fashioned into elegant carved fish. "And the Nimrath? I must say to get one in clothes, let alone on the ground, is a feat, to be sure. He has eyes for the girl."

"I really don't understand your fascination with such little observations."

"I am an observer by nature. It is a part of me that tends to be almost overpowering. If surrounded by too many people, it can assume a life of its own, so to speak."

"What is that supposed to imply? You live out here in the middle of nowhere because you can't stop yourself from observing people?" Tinna was definitely bordering on rude, but it didn't seem to affect him very much. He crossed his leg, his glass eyes locked on Tinna's so strongly it made her uncomfortable. "All right; it's more than just observation."

"You are Chaiva," she suddenly guessed, "the mind-readers." He didn't smile, nod, or affirm her conclusion in any way, but now she knew why he frightened her. She also understood why he kept vacuous servants about…to keep his mind as clear as possible.

"You do not serve anyone?"

"I bartered for my freedom. I performed several particularly questionable tasks that few would accept, far above and beyond the normal call of duty, and as compensation for this work, I was given the right of early retirement. I took the generous reward for my services, and found this old place. Once, this land was its own grant, and the manor was occupied by nobles. In time, the last nobleman died with no successors, and the viceroy, instead of appointing a new nobleman to the position, simply allowed the entire estate to be combined with the adjoining grant. The house was virtually abandoned, and the villagers were relocated to farm other, more productive lands. So here I am, in a manor, surrounded by nothing, next to a ghostly village."

"I see." She didn't want to know what those questionable tasks were. Probably assassinations or something. She didn't want to go down that road with him … she didn't like to think she had anything in common with a Chaiva at all.

"Well, I am not really at liberty to say what I did anyway, so never fear." He smiled.

Tinna was instantly uncomfortable. There was a pause in the conversation as she decided to focus on her breakfast. She wondered what his name was in passing, feeling a bit ashamed to ask, knowing it would seem even worse to ask so late. She then halted her mind, and fumed. She glanced up sheepishly.

"Phenmal," he answered. She lowered her gaze. It was really very, very uncomfortable.

"It is certainly an admirable, albeit strange, quest that brought you into this situation," he said to her. She looked up from her food; a deep red line crossed her face, from her cheekbone over the bridge of her nose to the other cheekbone—a sure sign of anger.

"Please, I didn't squeeze it from your head; you're harder to read than most. Of course, your thoughts are like voices to me, but your memories are very hard to dig out. I got it from the girl. Her mind is much like a berry bush; a network of supple branches that can be pressed aside to get at the fruit within." He smiled devilishly.

"I didn't choose to be where I am right now. I chose to go to the village near Hildercross, and get a puppy. Someone else chose this fate for us."

"I suppose that's true. What do you make of it all?" he asked. She realized it must not be often that this man got news from outside his insular little world. She knew why he'd stood outside Rhoa's door that morning. He was lost inside her head, sucking out everything he could possibly glean about what they'd seen and where they'd been.

"I have no idea." She shook her head. "I've a notion by the trail of destruction that the High Throne is the victim; the next moment, I'm thinking that if dragons are involved it must be something very grave and justified."

He nodded, apparently in agreement. "I've had many dealings with the dragon folk, and I'm not speaking of the lesser dragons. I mean the ones like your new friend. They are a noble race. It makes me wonder why they are so determined to destroy great swaths of land, including the people on it. They're not exactly prone to going about randomly burning entire cities and their residents to cinders."

"My thoughts exactl—" Tinna couldn't finish without a laugh.

"No, those are my own thoughts. And the information I got was not from your head." His smile was so disarming. All her discomfort melted. He shifted in his chair, switching the crossed legs, and clutching his hands thoughtfully. "I can only imagine they're doing something this rash for a good reason. Perhaps something that will ultimately benefit everyone ... or perhaps they're preventing something from occurring."

"I thought of that. At one point I thought they might be trying to quell a resurgence of the worm-skin plague, and the dragons were destroying any location that showed even the smallest number of cases to prevent it being carried out across the world But the fact that the dragon dropped us at a location marked for destruction to get supplies, that would defeat the purpose, considering that we would have carried the plague out with us for certain."

"Yes. A good thought indeed. Preventing the spread of an illness. Very clever." He sighed. "This is an event definitely worth looking into ... No sense in my sitting here and speculating," He cast his gaze upward, showing that he was giving this a great deal of thought.

"This is a disaster. We were flown weeks from our village, and we see signs of the same thing happening everywhere we go ... plumes of smoke, dragons flying in the distance ... It's very disturbing." Tinna shook her head, finding herself quite glad to have someone of some substance to discuss her concerns with.

Draphen and Rhoa were far too concerned with their own complaints to bother with the world being destroyed. Phenmal barked out a chuckle at that thought. The other two glanced up at him quizzically from their spots farther down the table, unaware of the content of the discussion Tinna was having with their host, but curious to see what had made the intimidating character laugh out loud.

"I can guess it's been a challenge," he whispered, leaning toward her with a brow arched and a wry smile on his face. She gave him a nod that expressed her annoyance very well. He smiled. "I'll accompany you to Silver River. I think perhaps I should take myself from my retirement for this. It's not something I could hope to hide from, not with so many being killed. I will see if I can solicit support for others via the relay."

"The relays are being attacked, too," she told him.

He frowned. "I'll figure something out. I think this matter merits a lot of attention. When I get my mind set on something, it's rare than anything gets in my way."

"I deduced that from the fact that you bartered your way out of service to the Keepers. Not a feat accomplished by many," she observed, pleased to have someone interesting along for part of the journey. He smiled, impressed even more by this deceivingly diminutive woman. She was quite a powerful little entity, and had a beast of incredible rage inside her that fueled her strength and resolve. The little boy would get his dog no matter what.

But even the tightly secured brain in her little head could not keep him from seeing that there was a second reason that made her so determined to succeed. It was a singular force that made her defy even the systematic destruction of towns and cities, and continue on unswervingly. And because she was raised never to know such a thing, it made her all the more determined to acquire it. He understood why the dragon found her so interesting.

"How many days has it been?" Rhoa whined. Tinna shrugged, truly bewildered by the question, trying to tick off the actual time they'd been deviated from their original mission. Their newest companion kept out of the situations where Rhoa or Draphen were complaining. He rode his plodding horse ahead of the others. They'd left the plains for a more familiar territory:

They'd entered a large, forested area—riding on a wide road that was cut through the dense growth, dappled with sunlight from the leafy canopy. The forest was not a greatly deciduous one like their own, being comprised mostly of giant pines and the usual complement of parasitic tick-birch clinging to the many exposed roots and knots, and some even to the trunks themselves. There was also a strong presence of raspberries and other forest berries, including a thick cover of strawberry plants. Their peak had already passed, but the raspberries were in season, and Rhoa had taken to vanishing from the path occasionally and returning with a purple-stained mouth. Draphen seemed to find that charming. Tinna and Phenmal simply found her little excursions most irritating—it was slowing them down.

About the third day traveling the endless road and camping on the side of it at night, Draphen began to get fidgety and behave quite oddly. He became distant and tense. As they were strolling along, Phenmal was leading his horse on foot beside Tinna far ahead of the other two, which had become quite common due to their continuous whining; nobody noticed him tearing his clothing off, or saw him blend in with the undergrowth and vanish. Rhoa, who had been out looking for more sweet berries, yelled out in alarm when she saw no Draphen, and a trail of clothes drawn out some ways down the road behind them.

Tinna stopped, and so did Phenmal, turning 'round to look at Rhoa in puzzlement.

"Rhoa, he's been dying for this sort of environment for days. It's as obvious on the nose on my face that he's probably just indulging his sense of comfort in this forest, and finding his identity again."

"Last time he wanted to go into the trees, he folded up his clothes, and gave me his pack. He did not toss it down and leave his clothes all thrown about as if he'd no plan to return!" Rhoa exclaimed, her voice growing closer to weeping with each word. "Phenmal, couldn't you … hear his intentions?"

"Rhoa, not to be rude, but there's simply no way I would have any desire to listen into the mind of someone whose verbal complaints alone are already driving me to the edge of sanity. There are limits of what I'm willing to endure" Phenmal muttered with a touch of acidity in his tone.

"Look, he'll be back. Go and gather his things. He probably threw them all down because you weren't here to take them from him," Tinna assured her.

Rhoa did as she was told. The puppy had been put on the ground to walk a bit. He gamboled at Tinna's feet, his ruddy little coat of fur sticking out in all directions, and a tiny black mushroom nose decorating a very cute muzzle. He was still very small, and could easily fall underfoot. Rhoa had taken to carrying him less and less, fearful of becoming too attached to him. On the other hand, she'd in part grown quite attached to the Nimrath, and was greatly saddened by just the thought of him leaving the party.

Draphen did not return that day or the next, and Rhoa grew increasingly frantic. She even broke into tears after their midday meal stop the next day, walking behind them dragging her feet, sniffling and making occasional little sobs. Tinna felt sorry for her, but was annoyed by the girl's overreaction. She didn't realize how Rhoa had grown close to him based on their commonalties—they both shared a horrid fear of being so far from what was familiar, and a deep love for the same place. She was now alone, and had nobody to lean on when frightened. There was no one left to understand her, and sympathize with her.

By morning of the third day, Rhoa was so depressed she could barely be awakened. Tinna stooped beside her sleeping roll, and poked at her shoulder. "Rhoa, wake up." The puppy found her face, and began to lick her cheek and nose with great enthusiasm, waggling his little tail. Tinna realized just how deep her funk was as soon as she saw Rhoa's hand reach out and shove the little dog away with a touch of meanness. Tinna smacked her shoulder. "How dare you be cruel to the little dog He's as innocent and helpless as the day he was born, and deserves no such treatment! Now get yourself up."

"I'll catch up," Rhoa groaned, pulling her blanket over her head. "Get up now!" Tinna said in the voice that frightened Rhoa. The girl groaned from inside her blanket, and threw it down onto her belly, sitting up with a sour look on her pretty face. Her eyes were puffy and red from crying. "He'll be back. He misses his home."

"He's a fellow countryman to me. His strength and the world we share are a great comfort to me on what is the worst and most frightening experience in my life. I want him back!" She began to cry again. Tinna sighed impatiently, and got up, picking up the slighted puppy. "Get yourself together. We've got a long way to go today." Rhoa did so grudgingly, a frown on her face all the while.

"DRAPHEN!" Rhoa shouted, her voice full of delight. She ran at the figure in the path, reflecting the leaves from which he had come. She threw her arms around him. The figure lifted its arms as if it were being attacked by something distasteful. The man-shaped walking bush was obviously perplexed by this assault. Tinna frowned, glancing at Phenmal, who shook his head.

"It's not him. This one's taller," Tinna whispered. Phenmal nodded in agreement, having felt this difference at once, but had not yet verbalized it. Another figure appeared, and then another, all still camouflaged. Then she recognized the third, shorter, with the same cocky stride. The first was trying to wrench Rhoa free from his torso. Draphen let his skin return to the natural tone standing nude in the path. Rhoa saw him and leapt back, startled, backing away from the first figure. She moved toward Draphen, lifting the handle of his bag over her head and reaching out to give it to him. He stepped away from her, and shook his head.

"I've met these people that are my kind, but of this place. They know the wood-paths that will lead me home. These men come with me to meet my people. They speak another tongue than I do, but we have managed to understand one another. I will go home by my paths."

"You can't leave me!" Rhoa cried, panicked by his assertion.

"I am not one to travel by ground, Rhoa. I can no longer bear to either wear those clothes, or exist in a world where there are no wooden paths to follow. I will go mad," he explained.

"Let me go with you, please!"

"You cannot climb like we do, Rhoa. We move very quickly through the trees. You could not follow."

"I could. Please, Draphen. I am frightened by the same things, and I will be completely alone!" She was blubbering like a girl, latching onto him. He looked at his companions, and began to make sounds to them, the few words he knew of their language. He gestured a great deal, too. The companions seemed to understand, replying in equally strange sounds. When the conference was over, he looked at Rhoa.

"You will come with us today, and travel with us one day. If you can endure our pace, and contend with the heights at which we will be moving, you will remain with me. If you do not, we will return you to Aitinna and the gentleman." Tinna wondered how they would deal with her when they were doing their lizard-climbing thing that they did, crawling up vertical planes as if they were horizontal.

Phenmal stooped to Tinna's ear, and whispered: "The others have volunteered to help. They're quite intrigued with Draphen's relationship with the ground-dwellers, namely, us. They're willing to take on the burden of a ground dweller to carry up and down trees, just so they can learn more about this relationship.

The interesting thing about this whole thing is that Draphen did not have to return. We would have understood, and he knows that. He returned for Rhoa. He has quite the affection for the girl. He once thought himself quite smitten with you, but finds himself more suited to Rhoa's girlish ways, and their common place of birth and needs. I have a feeling he will carry her on his back if he has to, to keep her near. He just wanted to make sure she was willing to go with him, and verifying his own suspicions that she cared for him as much. They will make a good match." Phenmal smiled. He found the events of this journey most entertaining. Rhoa looked at Tinna, who gave her an approving nod. She walked to the Thran, and Tinna took her hands.

"If you have even the slightest problem, you come back here— but something tells me I won't see you until I get back to Thamatoch.

Be careful, and keep moving, always toward home; I am counting seeing you there soon."

"I am counting on finding you there, too," Rhoa said with a smile. "Good luck finding your way home. Take care of the little dog." She lifted the special bag off of her neck and put it 'round Tinna's. She reached into the bag and petted him briefly. Draphen turned back into a likeness of the surroundings. Rhoa lay Draphen's packs down on the ground, and tightened the strap on her own. She then reached out and took Draphen's hand. "If I get back before you do, I'll tell everyone you're all right, and I'll tell Hanru that you're on your way back with his pup."

"Safe travels, Rhoa." Tinna smiled, dubious that she would get there before her. Rhoa would be a very large impediment to the quick-moving tree-folk. Tinna was quite sure nothing could prepare Rhoa for such a journey, but she somehow knew Rhoa would stick with it, and perhaps grow a bit from the experience.

CHAPTER 13

"It was a pleasure knowing you, Phenmal."

"And I you." He bowed. "I shall investigate what this is all about, and if I discover anything of great importance, I shall try to report back to you somehow. I know you are more than interested in the situation, and I'm sure you'll want to know what's behind all this. Even if it is just to have all the information you need to keep your horse-worshipping friends safe. I hope my old friend here behaves for you. He has served me well over the years, and I'm certain you could use a break from all the walking." He patted his horse's neck affectionately. "It would be best that you start to get comfortable with horses anyway," he hinted with a wry little smile, giving her a wink.

He turned while bidding her a final farewell, and walked gracefully up the wide stairway to the elegant old Phanos building. It sat isolated just outside the tree line. It was not bustling with activity like most other institutions of knowledge, for this was no school. It was a repository, one among many dotting the northlands, keeping copies of all works, literature, scientific research, biographies and such. These conservatories were manned by a small group of deeply intelligent and scholarly people who had dedicated their lives to the preservation of knowledge; they were called the Order of Phanos. They were independent of all academies, and above the scrutiny or power of the throne. They were a part of a single entity known as the Keepers. This group was comprised of the order of Phanos, the Mystics, and the Chaiva, of whom Phenmal had been a member.

The three groups functioned above all government. They had neither military nor police power, nor did borders limit them. The High Thrones of the world feared the Keepers, respected their ability to see through them, and understood that they were the true guardians of culture and religion for the world. Tinna wondered again what it was that Phenmal had done to earn his freedom from the Order of Chaiva. It was quite unheard of for one to be independent

123

of the group. Then again, she smiled wanly to herself, so was being a Thran outside her borders. There were very few of those. She shook her head and shrugged.

Here she stood with his horse, her packs, what was left of Draphen's clothing and supplies, and the dog. She began tying these things to Phenmal's horse, wary of the large creature. She secured the dog bag to the pommel so that it hung on the horse's shoulder, put the puppy in it and mounted, giving herself a moment to settle into the comfortable sheep's wool that covered the saddle seat. She gathered the reins, feeling very tall on the creature. She squeezed her thighs just a little, and the animal began to move at a comfortable walk. It took Tinna only a few moments to grow accustomed to the sway and rhythm. She enjoyed her solitude. It was even better for some reason just sitting on this horse, letting him do the walking while she did the thinking. The rhythm also seemed to help her center her thoughts. She began to experiment when she felt more confident with the horse, trying a brief trot, and later, a canter. But she still enjoyed the horse's gentle plodding walk. She could cross her ankle over the front of the saddle and hold the puppy, and the horse would just continue on without guidance.

She rode on like that for two days without event. There were no villages, no farms, nothing. She camped alone, polished her new arrows, and cared for her canine and equine companions, happy to be on her way back to Thamatoch. On the morning of the third day, she rode on a path that cut through a large prairie of standing hay. She lost herself a bit in the sensation of the grass tickling her bare feet. She was startled from her reverie by a dark shadow sliding over her, and moving ahead. She looked up. Above, a fleet of dragons filled the sky. Their wings were almost translucent against the sun. She shielded her eyes and studied them, her heart leaping as she recognized the large crown-like crest on the head of one of the largest ones in the sky.

"LEDRORAN!" She shouted at the top of her lungs, kicking her horse into a canter to keep up. "LEDRORAN! IT IS I, AITINNA!" The dragon's arched his neck and looked down. He then leaned onto his right wing, and bent 'round to turn back. He dove down closer, and she saw recognition in his eyes. With a gust of air, and a graceful loft and ballooning of the membranes of his wings, he landed nearby, walking the rest of the way toward her skittish horse.

"AITINNA. I AM GLADDENED BY THE SIGHT OF YOU. I FEARED YOU WERE NOT FREED FROM THE CITY

124

BEFORE WE HAD TO BURN IT DOWN," he said through a dragon-like smile. Tinna smiled back, dismounting from her horse, and leaving him to graze so she could approach Ledroran. She took the puppy out and put him in the grass to take advantage of the freedom—he never strayed far from her.

"Never fear, I've gotten quite good at getting out of places before dragons level them. What brings you to this land?"

"ORDERS, I FEAR. TRY TO STEER FREE FROM THE ASKALL MOUNTAINS AND SURROUNDING COMMUNITIES."

"Ledroran …" Tinna lowered her gaze for a moment, and clutched her elbows. "I beg you tell me why you are doing this." She looked straight into his left eye. Ledroran glanced up at the fleet of dragons still flying overhead, some looking down at Ledroran with curious eyes. Tinna noticed two drop down from the convoy, and turn back. Ledroran paid them little heed. He looked torn. He then sighed woefully. Tinna studied the play of light on the angled scales, some a flat deep green, others splashed with an opalescence that reflected the light in soft, pastel lines. He seemed to shimmer. His aroma was also intriguing … the smell of warmth and air, if either had an identifiable smell to begin with.

Tinna looked at the eye that focused on her, the orb moving, and the vertical slit of a pupil expanding and contracting with the change of light. Above, the convoy of dragons persisted—long serpent bodies, with impressive, wide chests, curled limbs, slashes across the sky, held aloft by incredibly huge wings of transparent membrane stretched between frail-looking bones. It was almost impossible for Tinna to accept all of a sudden. All her life, she'd seen them in the distance… heard of them, read stories of them. Here she was under an army of flight-dragons, talking to one of immense consequence and rank amongst his kind, and all the more bizarre, he looked at her with what was unmistakably an apologetic cast to his gaze.

" YOU MUST UNDERSTAND, AITINNA, THAT WE ARE NOT DOING THIS OUT OF SPITE. WE HAVE NO CHOICE," he said. The other two dragons landed, and four more were diving and circling. One rather large dragon took notice of the small dog in the grass, and picked him up with her great claw. She sniffed the pup, and then put him down again, keeping him corralled within a circular area walled in by her coiled tail. She showed concern that he may get squashed by the growing number of dragons. The others approached, giving the pup a quick sniff with their huge muzzles before collecting around the leader. Ledroran looked at them, and then at Tinna.

"What do you mean, no choice? You're dragons; it's not as if we can force you into doing anything, unless you're being forced to by your own kind … Are you?" The dragon lowered his head a bit. One of the other two, obviously female, shook her head.

"SOMETIMES IT IS NOT WHO IS STRONGER BUT WHO HAS MORE LEVERAGE," the female who had the puppy in her tail said, obviously comfortable with Ledroran's decision to speak to Aitinna, and therefore, it was acceptable to her. Meanwhile, more and more dragons were falling from the sky to see what the to-do was down on the ground.

"I don't understand," Tinna muttered, confused, but at the same time exhilarated to be surrounded by so many dragons, and the numbers were growing. Ledroran nodded his head as if to tell the others that he would be the one to speak.

"AITINNA, YOU MUST UNDERSTAND … DRAGONS HAVE ALWAYS STRIVEN TO APPEAR ABOVE REPROACH IN THE EYES OF HUMANITY. FOR THERE IS NO DENYING THE CONSTANT DISTRUST HUMANS FEEL TOWARD US. BECAUSE WE ARE LARGER, STRONGER AND MORE POWERFUL. WE ARE AND ALWAYS HAVE BEEN A THREAT. WE ARE NOT PERFECT BY ANY MEANS, BUT WE TRY. HUMAN TRUST IS PARAMOUNT TO OUR COEXISTENCE." Tinna nodded, apparently able to accept this truth. "YOU MUST ALSO PROMISE NEVER TO REPEAT WHAT YOU ARE ABOUT TO BE TOLD. I TRUST YOU NOT TO." She nodded again. All were momentarily distracted by the high-pitched playful yips of the puppy as he had now engaged in a game of "catch the tip of the dragon's tail." It wormed about as if doing so just to challenge the little fellow. Aitinna looked at the large female, and then back to Ledroran, who was about to speak.

"MANY CENTURIES AGO, HUMANITY HAD GROWN SO LARGE AND POPULOUS THAT OUR OWN RESOURCES WERE BEING DEPLETED. THE DRAGON FOLK WERE PERISHING FROM STARVATION. THE TRINITY CAME TO A DECISION. IN ORDER FOR THE RACES TO LIVE SIDE BY SIDE, SOMETHING HAD TO BE DONE TO MAKE HUMANITY UNDERSTAND THAT THEY MUST CONTROL THEIR POPULATION IN ORDER TO BALANCE THE NEEDS OF OUR PEOPLE AND THEIRS. OUR PEOPLE VOICED OUR CONCERNS TO THE LEADERSHIP OF THE

TIME. HUMANITY, HOWEVER, DID NOT RESPOND WELL TO THIS REQUEST. IN FACT, IT WAS TAKEN AS AN INSULT AND OUR PLIGHT ONLY CAUSED PANIC. OUR PEOPLE BECAME THE HUNTED. WE LOST A GOOD PORTION OF OUR POPULATIONS IN THIS PERIOD. WE RETURNED TO OUR LEADERSHIP TO SEE IF WE COULD FIND OTHER SOLUTIONS TO THE PROBLEM. WE DID NOT WANT BY ANY MEANS TO BECOME A GREATER ENEMY TO THE PEOPLE BY ACTING OUT IN THE MANNER THAT COULD CAUSE THEM TO TURN ON US EVEN FURTHER. THE ANCIENT TRINITY CAME UP WITH AN IDEA." The dragon paused. The growing surround of dragons seemed to feel a collective shame.

"THERE IS A PLACE FAR NORTH OF HERE. IT IS A PLACE WHERE FEW PEOPLE DARE TO GO, FOR IT IS A HARSH AND ISOLATED WORLD WITH AN UNINVITING CLIMATE. A PEOPLE DID LIVE THERE ONCE, LONG AGO. THEY BRAVED THE ICE ANDTHE WINDS AND EXISTED—EVEN THRIVED IN THAT ENVIRONMENT. BUT SOMETHING HAPPENED. SOMETHING TERRIBLE, AND THE PEOPLE BEGAN TO TAKE ILL. SOON, THEIR POPULATIONS WERE DEPLETED, AND THE FEW THAT REMAINED MIGRATED TO WARMER LANDS, CARRYING THIS ILLNESS WITH THEM."

The dragon took a moment to breathe, and sigh in such a human-like fashion that Tinna had to stop and appreciate the emotion.

"THESE NORTHERN FOLK LEFT TRAILS OF DEATH BEHIND THEM. THE TRINITY, IN ITS EFFORT TO STOP THE SPREAD OF THIS PLAGUE, MANAGED TO FIND THE SPREADERS OF THE ILLNESS. WE, THE DRAGONS, WERE COMMISSIONED TO TAKE THEM AWAY FROM OTHER HUMAN POPULATIONS, AND TO BRING THEM TO OUR LANDS, FOR WE ARE NOT SUSCEPTIBLE TO THIS ILLNESS. THE TRINITY STUDIED THESE PEOPLE. THEY NO LONGER SEEMED TO DIE OF THIS DISEASE, YET SOMEHOW, IT REMAINED WITH THEM THROUGH LIFE. THE PEOPLE WERE ISOLATED AND PROTECTED BY THE TRINITY. THEN THE TIME CAME WHEN THE HUMAN POPULATIONS GOT TOO HIGH …" He paused again. Tinna saw where it was going, and swallowed harshly, not quite prepared to hear it.

127

"SUFFICE IT TO SAY, THE TRINITY MADE A DECISION. AND THREE QUARTERSOF THE HUMAN POPULATION DIED. OUR PEOPLE WERE SAFE AGAIN, TO LIVE ALONGSIDE HUMANITY. AS THE CENTURIES PASSED, THE TRINITY MADE THIS 'CLEANSING' A PRACTICE WHENEVER HUMANITY GOT TOO LARGE AND THREATENED OUR RESOURCES. THEY KEEP THE CARRIERS, GENERATION AFTER GENERATION, TESTING THEIR INFECTIOUSNESS TO ASCERTAIN IF THE STRENGTH OF THIS PLAGUE REMAINS AS POTENT AS EVER...."

Tinna was utterly shocked. She balked, her hand reaching up to her lips unconsciously, and her stomach turning to ice. A part of her understood their plight and the Trinity's desperate act. There was only one world, after all, and it was completely in the power of these beasts to eradicate humanity completely if they had wanted to; instead, they "culled" the population by removing those susceptible to the worm-skin plague. That's what it was ... this disease Ledroran described. The worm-skin plague ... a scourge that had occurred and occurred again over time, something like a specter that hung over humanity that could be set loose at any time.

Her brain reeled, and for a moment, she thought she was going to faint from the overload of thoughts and questions that exploded in her mind. Why was it that humanity hadn't developed immunities to it over time, as the swine did to the choke-throat disease that ravaged the porcine populations across the world years ago? Why was it that the original carriers developed immunities, and the rest of humanity didn't? Did the people who survived the illness possess immunity from it? And if so, then one would think the disease wouldn't have been successful in its spread after more than two or three uses. The people had many generations to recuperate from this cycle of death—perhaps that had something to do with their susceptibility to the plague...she had no notion. She didn't know ... nor did she really want to understand. Such thoughts were for a man like Taneth—a man of science and knowledge. Her hands trembled.

She looked up at Ledroran, her eyes glassed-over and her face tight and confused. The dragons obviously held great shame for what they were forced to do; in all actuality, the Trinity took on the role of the gods with the use of this disease. Tinna wondered what this had to do with what was happening now...why this had any connection to the acts of destruction the dragons were now inflicting across the middle lands.

"THE TRINITY KEEPS THE POPULATION OF THE INFECTED PEOPLE IN THE LAND OF THE CHAI-OPSE. THEIR WALLS KEEP HUMANITY OUT, AND THE DISEASE CONTAINED. THERE ARE MEASURES TO KEEP THE UNSUSPECTING FROM STUMBLING INTO THIS LITTLE CONTAINED WORLD, AND ALL SORTS OF CURSES AND WARNINGS STREWN ABOUT TO KEEP THE CURIOUS AWAY. THE TRINITY ALSO BUILT AND MAINTAINS A KEEPER'S ARCHIVE NEARBY, AND HAS BIRD-DRAGONS TO MAN THE BORDER OF THIS LAND. IT SO HAPPENS SOMEONE FOUND THEIR WAY INTO THE ACADEMY. SOMEONE GOT IN THERE, AND DISCOVERED THE HISTORY OF THE ACADEMY, OF THE LAND WHERE NO ONE MAY GO. SOMEONE WHO MANAGED TO STEAL TEXTS KEPT BY THE KEEPERS THAT DESCRIBE THE PROCESS … TEXTS EXPLAINING, PERHAPS ATTEMPTING TO EXCUSE IT … AS IF THERE WAS AN EXPECTATION THAT SOMEDAY THIS SECRET WAS TO BE DISCOVERED—THAT THERE WOULD BE SOME EXPLANATION …"

Aitinna's stomach lurched in her body. Would the order of Phanos hide such a great and terrible truth? She didn't understand. If the Keepers had an archive of this information; that would mean that the Keepers knew of these acts. She found that difficult to believe. They were human … would they enable such a thing to be kept from the world? Would they keep it secret and watch it happen again?

"THE SECRET HAS BEEN DISCOVERED, AND IN PART, USED AGAINST US. THE DISCOVERER OF THESE TEXTS DECIDED NOT TO REVEAL OUR MISDOINGS, FOR IT IS TO PROTECT OUR RACE THAT THIS WAS DONE, AND ULTIMATELY, IT IS OUR DOING. INSTEAD, THE KNOWLEDGE IS BEING USED TO MAKE US DO THE BIDDING OF HE WHO POSSESSES THE TEXTS. OUR PEOPLE WOULD RATHER BE THOUGHT OF AS DESTRUCTIVE WARMONGERS FOR THESE ISOLATED ATTACKS, THAN BE KNOWN FOR WHAT WE HAVE ALL ENABLED TO HAPPEN, OVER AND OVER AGAIN. I CANNOT EVEN BEGIN TO IMAGINE HOW THE CREDIBILITY OF THE TRINITY WOULD BE CRUSHED BY THIS SECRET. WE ALL KNOW HOW CRUCIAL THEIR PLACE IS IN THE GREATER SCHEME."

Tinna was struck dumb. What does one say after hearing such a thing? She chewed her lower lip, and looked around at many of the dragon faces peering at her, trying their very hardest to gauge her reaction.

"NOW, DEAR AITINNA, A POWERFUL MAN, WHOSE MALEVOLENCE AND INFLUENCE WERE ALREADY A CONCERN TO THE LEADERSHIP OF BOTH THE HUMAN RACES AND THE DRAGONS, WILL SEIZE POWER. AMBITION WAS HIS VICE AND REMAINS SO. THE PERSON WHO HAD THE FORTUNE TO STUMBLE UPON OUR SECRET TO BEGIN WITH BROUGHT THE TEXTS TO THIS MAN, AND TRADED THEM FOR A SUM OF MONEY AND POWER. THE DELIVERER WAS PAID WITH BETRAYAL, AND WAS MURDERED FOR HIS FAVOR. THIS POWERFUL MAN HAS POSSESSION OF OUR GREATEST SECRET AND OUR GREATEST SHAME. IN HIS SCHEME TO REBUILD A GOVERNMENT FOR HIS OWN EXPLOITATION AND REIGN, HE USES US TO DESTROY ANYTHING OR ANYONE THAT THREATENS TO BLOCK HIS PATH TO ABSOLUTE POWER."

Aitinna shook her head in incredulity, her emotions out of control and sobs fighting to be heard from behind her hand clutched to her mouth. She lowered her hand, and wiped her eyes. "Ledroran, these events, enacted by the Trinity are not yours. Every race has a right to fight for its survival. Every race," she swallowed, as if unable to rationalize it for herself, "and I must be grateful that you respect our race enough not to destroy us once and for all, and have the entire world to yourselves," she said, her thoughts wild, tears coursing down her face.

"I am sad for you, for this bitter work you must do in the name of the Trinity. But nothing can justify… nothing …" she reached out and touched Ledroran's ruddy muzzle, unable to continue for her tears. There was a pensive silence among them all. Ledroran himself seemed almost thankful for even the smallest understanding on her part, despite the noticeable turmoil she was battling. He knew there was a chance she might react badly to the truth, but she was the only one he knew of that could be trusted with the truth and equipped with the ability to help them in their cause. At that thought, he segued into the next point:

"HE HAS PROTECTED HIMSELF AGAINST RETALIATION FROM OUR KIND AND HIDDEN HIMSELF FROM THE TRINITY. WE CANNOT STOP HIM. WE MUST

DO AS HE BIDS, BRING HIM INTO POWER AND HOPE THAT SOMETIME DURING HIS REIGN WE CAN STOP HIM, AND SOMEHOW MAINTAIN OUR INTEGRITY. NO MATTER WHAT HAPPENS NOW, OUR ACTIONS OF LATE HAVE RESIGNED US TO THE IRE OF THE HUMAN RACE. BUT AT LEAST WE CAN TRY TO SALVAGE AND PROTECT THE TRINITY'S REPUTATION SOMEHOW … THAT IS THE MOST IMPORTANT THING."

"If he is intelligent enough to have you all by your balls, I cannot imagine he would ever leave himself vulnerable to you. Ever," Aitinna concluded, almost harshly. But the dragons understood, and agreed. They were powerless—the most powerful of all the races in the world, without a choice. She sighed, shaking her head.

"HE KNOWS THAT WE HAVE NO ALLIES … CERTAINLY HE CAN BE CONFIDENT IN KNOWING NO HUMAN WOULD STOOP TO HELP THE BEASTS THAT ARE AT PRESENT DESTROYING THEIR LIVES AND HOMES. THE TRINITY CANNOT ASK FOR HELP, FOR NONE OF THE OTHER RACES WOULD ACCEPT THIS TRUTH AND STILL BE WILLING TO FIGHT FOR THEM. THERE ARE FEW AMONG YOUR PEOPLE WHO WOULD HAVE THE ABILITY TO UNDERSTAND, LIKE YOU. SO WE ARE BOUND TO DO WHAT WE MUST TO KEEP THIS MAN FROM USING THOSE TEXTS AGAINST OUR RACE AND THE TRINITY. WE HAVE NO OTHER RECOURSE." Ledroran hoped with all his heart that she would hear what he was saying to her. He saw her cast her gaze to the ground, and he watched her step back. He breathed in, a breath of anticipation.

"WE HAVE NO ONE TO HELP US. WE CANNOT STOP UNLESS THE MAN IN QUESTION IS STOPPED AND THE TEXTS RETRIEVED OR DESTROYED. WE CANNOT ASK HELP OF ANYONE WHO WE CANNOT TRUST WITH THIS TRUTH…AND ONLY A HUMAN COULD HAVE ACCESS TO THIS MAN. THE TRINITY'S EFFORTS HAVE FAILED, THEIR OWN AGENTS COMPROMISED. THEY WILL TRY AGAIN, BUT THEY WILL NOT SUCCEED. THEY ARE NOT EQUIPPED, NOR KNOWLEDGEABLE ENOUGH WITH THE REAL WORLD TO KNOW WHERE TO GO AND WHAT TO DO TO FIND THIS MADMAN," he added for good measure.

Tinna turned her back to them and stared at Phenmal's horse, or more accurately, through it. I have a promise to fulfill, she thought. I have a home to return to … a man I can safely say I care for very much. She felt a bit manipulated. They shared with her this great secret, and for what? To give her a sense of ownership to their plight perhaps? What does one do when the burden of an entire race is laid at one's feet? She knew what they were asking of her. Why me? She was torn between walking away from it, but knowing deep down that she couldn't abandon their plight, and live with herself afterward. The man was untouchable to them, this evil creature who threatened to shake down all the fragile lies her world was built upon. And what did this mean for Taneth? And Hanru? And even Rhoa with her Nimrath? That they would be subject to the rule of someone capable of such heinous acts, willing to destroy cities with thousands of lives within them for his own desires. The Trinity was a power of three ancient dragons … how could they even begin to find agents to help them among the people who would hate them for what they had done?

"I am here," Aitinna said. Ledroran's eyes rolled down to look on her with the tiniest glimmer of hope. "I cannot abide more people being killed for such a selfish reason, nor having such noble creatures as you being manipulated like giant marionettes"

"WHAT DO YOU THINK YOU CAN DO?" Ledroran asked, unable to mask the guarded joy in his great voice.

"Something—which is more than any of you are capable of doing. Who is this person? This ambitious swine that uses you so ill?"

"HE IS OVAMAL, THE HIGH MINISTER OF WAR" Aitinna had heard his name before. She knew little of him other than that. Everyone had some inkling of the who's who of the High Throne and the High Court.

"He is where?"

"WE DO NOT KNOW. HE MAKES HIS ORDERS THROUGH THE DUKE OF WHITMONT, WHOM YOU HAVE HAD THE PRIVILEGE OF MEETING BACK WHEN YOU AND I FIRST MET. STRANGELY, I SAW YOUR STRENGTH AND YOUR RESOLVE EVEN THEN; BUT I WASN'T SO SURE AS I AM RIGHT NOW. I KNEW YOU WERE A TRUSTWORTHY SOUL. I COULD ONLY HOPE THAT YOU WOULD OFFER TO ASSIST US," he roared.

"That man was the Duke of Whitmont?"

"YES. HE'S HAVING QUITE A TIME OF COLLECTING ALL THE UNSEATED NOBILITY WHO CAN BE BROUGHT TO HIM, AND LOCKING THEM UP IN HIS DUNGEONS. THESE PEOPLE HAVE ALWAYS DETESTED HIM, AND NOW HE HAS HIS CHANCE TO EXACT REVENGE UPON

THEM. THE MINISTER OF WAR CHOSE HIS ALLIES VERY WELL; HE FOUND ALL THE DISGRUNTLED NOBLES WHO ANSWERED TO THE THRONE, AND SUBVERTED THEM WITH PROMISES OF POWER. AS YOU CAN IMAGINE, THE MINISTER HAS QUITE THE CIRCLE OF FRIENDS TO KEEP HIS LOCATION SECRET FROM US"

"Well, at least I know where to start. And the good thing is, he will be easier to find than you think. He's relying on your inability to share the secret with anyone ...relying on humanity like some perfect shield. I'll find him. I even know where to begin," Aitinna said. She looked at Ledroran and then the others, scanning the many beautifully colored dragons collected in a large half moon around her. "I ask only this: The people of the Horse God are a larger entity than many assume. They are so isolated in their wild-lands, and split up into tiny clan villages, I believe it's hard to imagine they could be any threat to anyone. But anyone keen on watching his own back would eventually notice this. You must do your best to keep the perception of the People of Arak as it is right now. I do not want Ovamal to see them as a threat and to cause you to harm them. Do not to burn down their forests and their fields. I will tell the world the secret myself, if that happens. Do you hear me? I don't care what you do, one village, and that's it." Tinna looked at them with a furious glare. "They are very important to me," she added, her voice breaking a bit. Ledroran nodded. Aitinna sighed. There was a brief exchange of gazes between Aitinna and the leader of the dragons. When she was satisfied he'd seen how serious she really was, she collected herself and spoke again.

"I will go to Loshan, which is a bit northeast of here. There are plenty of people who can tell me what I need to know to get closer to this nemesis of ours. I will do my best for you, Ledroran. I made a promise to a young boy that I would bring this little dog back to him, and I will not fail in that promise. But I can certainly take a detour if I must, to insure that the world that little boy grows up in is not overseen by a tyrant. I need to be able to call upon you; I may need you sometime."

"ASK ANY DRAGON YOU SEE TO FIND ME FOR YOU. I AM KNOWN AMONG ALL MY BRETHREN. I AM THE SECOND LEADER UNDER OUR BRANCH OF THE TRINITY. BUT IF THERE ARE NONE OF US TO BE FOUND, SUMMONERS CAN BE USED TO CALL TO US, HOWEVER RELUCTANT THEY WILL BE TO HELP, CONSIDERING OUR CURRENT REPUTATION."

"I will keep that in mind," Tinna said, crossing her arms. "Now go on and do your thing. But if you can give people a little more warning of your arrival, perhaps it would make us all feel a bit better about these acts."

Ledroran nodded his huge head, and began to move away, running into other dragons. They all began to spread out and lift off, straining with great effort to lift their bulk from the earth. Once airborne, they pumped themselves up into the sky, and used thermals to climb back up to the heights they had attained before they had been detoured.

One of the last dragons to leave was the colorful female who had kept the puppy safe from the thundering feet of the dragons. She reached around and grasped the little animal, which would have been in proportion to Tinna's hand, but a small pea. She reached out her claw and opened it, the puppy growling and tugging on a fold of the soft-looking skin on the small palm area of the talon. "I BELIEVE THIS BELONGS TO YOU," the dragon said. "I AM LAIRA. I AM MATE TO LEDRORAN," she breathed.

"I am honored to make your acquaintance, and I appreciate the care you took in keeping this little fellow safe." Tinna walked between two of the sharply clawed talons, and reached out to pick the puppy up. He was quite unconcerned with the size of his opponent, and quite ready to continue wrestling with a fold of her skin. Tinna tucked him under her arm, and stepped back.

"THE LITTLE THING HAS YOUR SPIRIT," Laira said. "LEDRORAN MENTIONED YOU, DESCRIBING YOUR ABILITIES. I HAVE ALWAYS RESPECTED THE WAYS OF THETHRAN."

"Well, I am sorry for you then. For I do not respect their ways, which is why I am here." The dragon took the sudden, almost hostile exclamation in stride, and stepped back once.

"YOU ARE KIND TO TAKE OUR BURDEN ONTO YOUR SHOULDERS. IT IS A GREAT WEIGHT TO CARRY."

"I will do my best. I offer no guarantees." Laira nodded in understanding. The dragon female lowered her muzzle and touched it to the puppy's tiny wet nose.

"I LIKE THIS LITTLE WINTER WOLF. YOU SHOULD NAME HIM FOR THE DRAGON, SO THAT HE MAY KNOW THAT WE HONOUR HIM AS WE HONOUR YOU."

"He's just a mongrel, not a winter wolf." Tinna laughed. Laira shook her large head.

"I KNOW THE SCENT OF A WINTER WOLF, MY DEAR GIRL. THAT IS WHY HE HAS SUCH SPIRIT LIKE YOU. HE IS A HYBRID, TOO, AND LIKE YOU HE HAS INHERITED ALL THE BEST STRENGTHS OF BOTH HIS SIRE AND HIS DAM, AND AVOIDED MOST OF THE WEAKNESSES." Liana then turned away. "I WISH YOU THE BEST OF FORTUNE, AND SHARE LEDRORAN'S CONFIDENCE IN YOUR ABILITIES. FARE THEE WELL. AND GOODBYE, LITTLE WINTER WOLF."

She moved out far enough to beat her wings without blowing Tinna or her horse over. She took to the sky with the diminishing crowd of dragons. There was a cacophony of roars as they flew away, loud farewells to Aitinna.

Tinna didn't really grasp the gravity of the task she had undertaken. When she did, her knees weakened and she flopped onto the ground in a kneel, head up, eyes following the last of the dragons as they flew eastwards, filling their cheek-sacks with fire-fluid in preparation for their impending destruction of yet another city. Tinna simply lurched forward and vomited.

CHAPTER 14

"So you're a Winter Wolf. How odd that I didn't see it. Then again, you're just small and brownish gray—not exactly extraordinary." She held the dog up. "That dragon is very perceptive. She saw both of our mixed bloods. My Gypsy and Thran blood, and your Mountain and Snow Wolf blood. How rare a thing you are."

She had new admiration for the dog in her hands. How the animal shelter had come upon a winter wolf pup was beyond her. Winter Wolves were revered, and sometimes worshipped. These superior accidents of nature could not mate among themselves; they could only produce pups with wolves that were of either of the parental breeds.

The two kinds of wolf that made a Winter Wolf rarely crossed paths, but when they did, their offspring were very distinct, and ultimately a breed of its own. They had all the qualities that made them adaptable to any environment, and they had superior intelligence and were fiercely loyal to their pack members—which were usually comprised of lone wolves who had also been banished from their own packs for being of strange appearance—as the Winter Wolves would have been banished. Their coloring was distinct, and yet Tinna did not see them in this little whelp. Normally, they would have a white mask on the eyes and a matching white underbelly and paws. The rest of their bodies would be very dark brown or gray. They had blue eyes, sometimes so lightly colored they were white. They had the agility of a rock-climbing hunter, and the stealth and quickness of a snowy-tundra hunter. They were also often a bit larger in size than normal wolves, a trait of the snow wolf. They were given the distinction of their own name and breed instead of being marked up as but a hybrid because of the consistent nature of their traits, and the extremely unique qualities they displayed, qualities even their parents did not possess.

She looked in puzzlement at the fluffy thing, his eyes light-colored, a deep gray-blue, but definitely not the near-white she expected, and his body was naught but a soft pinkish belly with legs and a small awkward tail. He yawned a gust of oatmeal breath into her face. She laughed to herself. "You're no Winter Wolf. Winter Wolves don't have their own smell, do they?" But then again … She saw my hybrid blood, too … how did she see that? She tucked the little whelp back into his little bed bag, where he balled up immediately into a little 'O' shape, and went to sleep. She closed the flap, and sighed, looking ahead at the road she and the horse followed. She had so much on her mind; she had to put aside the trivial things that took up her time. She needed to move as quickly as possible.

Tinna rode faster, following the infrequent signposts she'd passed not so long ago, before she found the forests of the southeast. The signs pointed her to Loshan, a merchant city on the shore of the Northland Sea. It was an unimaginably huge body of water locked quite a ways inland from the eastern coast. The sea bound four individual vice-empires together, and was the trade hub for most of the northeast lands, and was connected to the ocean to the east by a number of man-made canals, which were impressive to say the least. It was a great hub of activity, and as most merchant cities tended to be, they were seedy places. They had no viceroy or High Throne sponsorship, so all enforcement and government was privately operated through the powerful merchants who founded and oversaw the settlement. It was a greedy place. A good place for the outcasts of society to find a home and to thrive.

Tinna had come to this place after she'd passed through Borc's land when she'd crossed the mountains for the first time. She circled the plains area, visiting a number of the cities, until she was sickened by the crowds and noise, and chose to move closer to the coast, and a bit farther south, where she had heard there were some forests so immense and beautiful there were none other with which to compare. She then entered Rhoa and Taneth's territory.

She didn't like having to go back to this dark and dangerous place. People died here by the hands of others on a regular basis, and nobody could be trusted. But she did know people here. Mainly another Thran, and that was enough for her to risk returning to a world she had so very much ashamed to have once been part of. Aitinna frowned at the sight of the city below, lining the shore of the sea. It was night by the time she'd crested the hill to the Northland Sea. The city of Loshan was a mass of tiny lights straining against the crooked shore of the black void that would be the water by day.

She nudged the horse forward onto the path toward Loshan. It took half an hour to reach the city gates, which were wide open and brightly lit with large basin torches at the top of each stone pilaster. She rode through, going up the main street for a few blocks before turning onto a smaller, cobbled alley between a tannery and a shipping office. There were many doorways lining the irregular buildings in this tight alleyway. There were some torches lit outside a few. She passed one that was a gaming house, circling around the grouping of horses tied up while their masters roared with laughter inside, their silhouettes casting shadow puppets on the ground in front of the disgustingly dirty window. Tinna knew where she was going. She turned right onto another wide and very busy throughway. The street was filled with night revelers and those slinking, darkened figures who were out to make the more questionable transactions that occurred within the gates of Loshan.

She looked for the small street she wanted to find, on the right side of the road. She had to really look to find it. It was a narrow alley, far narrower than the first one she'd used to cross to Market Street. She found the entrance, and turned the horse into it, her legs barely clearing the walls of the buildings. She ducked under a low walkway that crossed over the alleyway. One of the buildings had been set back far enough from the long alley to widen it for the length of the building. It was set about middle way in the alley, between Market Street and North Street. When she rode into the larger space in the alley, she dismounted, walking to a large doorway in the building that was set back from the others. She banged on the arched wooden door, stepped back and waited a good long minute or two. The small viewing slot finally opened, and a pair of eyes took in the sight of the woman and her horse.

"Aitinna. You're back," the woman said in a deep, liquid voice—her accent softer than Tinna's.

She tugged the door open, and Tinna led the horse into what was a decent-sized courtyard surrounded by a balcony held up with thick wooden posts. Between them were stalls for horses. A few of them had equine heads sticking out of the half-doors, chewing hay or straining to sniff at the neighboring horse and squeal at one another.

"You ... on a horse? How strange." The woman laughed, her features plainly like Tinna's. Only she was taller, older, leaner, and her face was a bit flatter, with deep, sunken eyes rimmed with thick black lashes. There were dignified little dustings of white curls among the ringlets of her black Thran hair. She smiled at Tinna, who shook her head and chuckled.

"I need to travel quickly. This horse was given to me by a Chaiva."

"No kidding? A Chaiva?" She pretended to shudder. "Did he mess around in your thoughts?"

"He said I had a difficult mind to read," Tinna bragged. "How are you, Na-ailie?"

"Now, I've already told you I hate that Thran title-crud. You can stop that now. Life could always be better, I suppose—but as things are now, I'm good." She helped Tinna loosen the girth and pull the saddle off, and then the bridle, after leading the weary and hungry horse into the stall. Tinna held the bag with the pup in it in her hands, handing it to Ailie, who opened it and smiled. "Did you bring this for me?"

"I'm afraid not. It's for a little boy I met. He's probably hungry, the pup, I mean; that dried meat just doesn't seem enough for him. Do you think you can give him some scraps?"

"Of course. What a cute little baby." She lifted him out of the bag. "I need to feed your horse. Hold onto the little fellow and we'll take him inside and give him a bowl full of shredded pork—we just took one off the spit; he's in for a treat! Doesn't that shound good, you widdle schmoopie?" She made a strange voice as she said these words. Tinna laughed.

Ailie fed the horse a good meal of mixed grains and sticky sugar-beet molasses, and pumped water into his water bucket. Ailie then took Tinna's arm and looped it through hers, patting the girl's hand in a motherly fashion. Tinna gripped the wolf pup in her other hand.

"There is so much madness going around these days what with these inexplicable dragon attacks. Everyone is panicked that the dragons will come here next."

"They won't. They've only attacked cities sponsored by the High Throne," Tinna assured her.

The woman led her through an archway that opened into a well-lit corridor. They emerged in a large room filled with patrons. It was a tavern; a very nice tavern. There were no bawdy revelers here. The tavern maids were dressed respectably, and groomed nicely. The patrons sat and shared civil conversations, all enjoying the wonderful variety of beers Ailie and her mate made in their own small brewery adjacent to the tavern. They also served very good food, and the aroma from the kitchen made Tinna's stomach growl so loudly Ailie noticed.

"My dear child, you're starving. Come and sit down, we'll have a nice talk." Tinna liked how motherly Ailie was. It was bizarre to think of her as a Thran, let alone a Korrithiva; which was one of the most savage of foot soldiers; not when she was doting on Tinna like this. She'd been quite well known back home.

Even where Tinna lived, which was on the fringe of Thran society, she knew of Ailie before she had met her here in Loshan. Ailie had been a master at the scythe-axe. She'd killed many in the Thran civil wars. She had been feared and revered. Now, she was a mother and a wife, a picture of domestic bliss...a living contradiction. No one would ever guess who she had been, and nobody knew except her mate, her children and Tinna. Tinna's hand tightened and squeezed Ailie's, passing through to her a silent surge of respect and love for a woman who had taken such control of her own life, and defied all convention to find happiness. Ailie looked at Tinna, and smiled warmly, understanding Tinna's gesture at once. Ailie dragged her to a secluded table. She waved her arm and pointed to her table, calling a tavern maid over with the gesture. The girl wove through the tables, and gave Ailie a respectful bow of the head.

"Bring my friend here a platter of tonight's special, and get the little dog a dish of some shredded pork. Oh, and bring a pitcher of water and a goblet of the strawberry blend." She turned to look at Tinna. "I know you're not the greatest beer lover, but you will simply love the strawberry blend!" she exclaimed with a great grin on her elegant face.

Tinna admired this expatriated Thran. She had chosen such a different life from what any woman of her kind had ever known. She had chosen to live with a man who loved her beyond words, treated her like a queen, and understood every nuance of her character and her past. He endured the times when Ailie suffered from her conscience, and bore it at her side with benevolence and love. They ran this business together in a place where their union would not be scrutinized. She had two children with this man, a dark-haired, blue-eyed girl of amazing beauty, who at thirteen had captured the admiration of one of the most influential men of Loshan, and he had been staking his claim publicly for the girl, letting any man know that he would be the first and hopefully only man to propose marriage to her when she came of age. Tinna remembered him hanging about the tavern a good deal of time, gawking at her. She was fifteen when Tinna met her, and she realized that Kailine was now of age. Ailie's other child was a strapping young fellow of dark hair and dark eyes, with his father's northern skin. He was also as beautiful as his sister, and had just been wed when Tinna stayed in the city a year before.

"Your children, what news do you have of them?" Tinna asked.

"Oh, so much has occurred since you left. Renath has a young son," she said proudly. "It took me a while to come to terms with being a grandmother, but once I saw the cherubic little thing, I lost any ability to be selfish like that. He looks just like Kailine, strangely, with Thran hair and skin, but with eyes as blue as his aunt's. Oh, and my sweet, beautiful Kailine has wed. After such a long wait and such persistent affections, she could not deny Astlin his proposal, and she had long since been in love with the fool, since he first started visiting here and lavishing her with gifts and such. She's quite spoiled, I dare say. He positively worships her. But then again, who wouldn't? She's really an exotic beauty both inside and out. She loves him so." Ailie sighed in contentment. "Soon I shall be a grandmother again, I'll wager, and my sweet baby girl a mother."

"Is she with child already?"

"Oh, no. They've only been wed for two months. Where have you been traveling, my dear girl?"

Tinna wondered briefly how a woman with such a bloody, hideous past could be so light and loving. It gave Tinna hope. "I went south a bit, into the woodlands."

"Aren't you courageous! What did you find there?"

"Many, many wonderful things, Ailie. Perhaps my own Hadrin, if all goes well, and I have not judged his character erroneously."

"You can do many things, Tinna, but judge someone unwisely? Not possible, my dear. We both know what it's like to be judged. To be cast into a mold and given no chance to prove the world otherwise. Both you and I perceive the world differently because of it," Ailie reassured her, smiling proudly. "Do you think yourself ready for your own Hadrin, Tinna?"

The younger Thran paused and thought for a moment, and then answered honestly. "I'm not sure. But it was you who told me to follow my instincts, and I've found myself questioning all my ways, solely because of this man." Ailie nodded with a wise, gentle gaze.

The tavern maid brought Tinna a beautiful platter of roasted pork and new potatoes with fresh carrots, and likewise, a small dish of meat scraps, well more than the puppy could handle. The girl also brought him a small bowl of water.

Tinna put him on the floor, putting her tunic down there for him to lie down on when he was done. He ate quickly, and drank a great deal, and then decided to wander off to deposit a warm poop and a puddle in some discreet corner for Ailie to find in the morning. Tinna was so preoccupied, she didn't really think of it. Tinna concentrated on her food, tasting the fruit-blend beer, and enjoying it all as much as Ailie had predicted.

A fellow joined them at their table, a head-full of deep blond hair that was also dusted with white. He had the most brilliant blue eyes Tinna had ever seen in her life, and she simply loved to look at them. They were so expressive, and his face so pleasing and gentle. His hand rested affectionately on Ailie's shoulder, and he slung the towel he used to clean the counter with onto his shoulder. "How are you, young thing?" he asked, grinning at her.

"Hadrin, it is so nice to see you again."

"The feeling is utterly mutual, pretty one. How's the food?"

"Excellent, as usual," Tinna said, full to the gills. She leaned back, watching Ailie scoot over so Hadrin could fit a chair in next to her.

"What brings you back this way?"

"A sort of emergency, actually. I came here hoping you could set me on the right path." They both nodded. "I need to get close to someone who is very difficult to get close to, Ailie," Tinna said in that special tone of voice the Thran could glean meaning from.

Ailie's shoulders straightened, and she glanced at Hadrin. "Tinna brought a puppy. He's around here somewhere. Could you find him and bring him outside before he messes on the floor?" Hadrin knew the look, knowing the words were just dressing. He got up, waving to Tinna. He began weaving through the tables, looking down under tables and patrons' legs, whistling in little bursts, and calling:

"Heeeere doggie, doggie …"

With Hadrin out of the way, Ailie leaned forward onto the table, and Tinna did too, their faces close together. "What sort of mess have you gotten yourself involved with, girl?"

"It is a personal assignment, to speak of, but crucial to the greater good."

"Does it have to do with the dragons? You seem confident and in the know about the whole pattern of their destruction."

"Ailie, I cannot risk the Chaiva finding something out and alerting someone. I cannot share the whole story. I can only stress the importance of this job."

"I understand." Ailie smiled, enjoying the old feeling of conspiring with a colleague again. She leaned back a bit. "Who is it you seek to get close to?"

"A certain Minister who's gone missing." Tinna crossed her legs, and draped her arm over the top of the chair.

Ailie pursed her lips thoughtfully. "The only people I can imagine who could help you with finding this person would be those of the most influence in this city. Perhaps Astlin can help you. He is Kailie's new husband, as you know. I'm certain he would be happy to assist you. He is a highly ranked member of this city, and I know that would normally make you doubt his integrity, but I know, and Hadrin will vouch for me, Astlin is a very good soul, and as far as I am concerned, as trustworthy as anyone can be. I trusted him with my daughter." She gazed at Tinna for a reaction.

Tinna knew Ailie was the only person in this land besides her new friends down in the woodlands that could be totally trusted. She was a kindred spirit. Tinna knew she was being honest with her. "Can you arrange a meeting with Astlin?"

"Of course I can. I'll have them come by to dine at midday tomorrow, and you can join them. For now, why don't you take the green room tonight, and rest yourself? You look very tired, Tinna."

"I'm exhausted, and the hard part hasn't even begun," she mumbled to Ailie. The woman nodded understandingly and stood, waiting for Tinna to follow her upstairs to the guest rooms, ignoring her husband and several other patrons who'd joined him in the hunt for the elusive wolf pup.

CHAPTER 15

Rhoa grew up in one day. She had never known hardship like she had that first day with Draphen and his companions. She was so determined to stay with Draphen that she refused to do anything to reveal her suffering. When they moved vertically, she was carried on Draphen's back, or whoever was volunteering at the moment. Her arms atrophied into the hooked position she'd used over the shoulders of her carrier, and when they were actually able to move again, her muscles spasmed, causing her to shake uncontrollably. She did her best to hide those moments, trying to concentrate on keeping her arms from trembling while attempting not to lose her balance while they crossed what Draphen called tree-ways, but to Rhoa were more like tightropes.

The Nimraths moved with such speed and dexterity they often forgot they were trailed by an inexperienced and quite frightened ground-dweller. Rhoa bit back her tears of pain and determination. She realized now, as she forced herself to keep up, why Tinna was often so hard on her. She complained about nothing. Compared to this, traveling with Tinna was really nothing. When she thought her legs and her arms and her brain were about to give in to the impossibility of keeping up with the Nimraths, the men slowed, gesturing to one another and often barking out occasional words. They seemed to be agreeing on something, and then Draphen slipped around them on the branch, letting his colors fade into his real skin, his hands considerately hanging over his private bits in order to spare her any embarrassment.

"Rhoa, are you all right?"

"Yes. Of course I'm fine," she lied—badly.

"Good. These western Nimraths say there is a small settlement about eleven trees from here. We will apply for a night's lodging and perhaps some food there from the occupants. You will create a bit of a stir there, if you can imagine. So we are going to go ahead and make introductions. These Nimrath speak the same tongue as the people of the settlement, and they will explain our circumstances. I will go with them. Tiko will stay with you. Will you be all right here alone with Tiko, until we return?"

"Of course." She exhaled with a pleased grin, reveling in the notion that she'd have a few minutes to straddle the branch she was standing on, and stretch her arms out. They felt flaccid and weak from all the effort of the day. Draphen then slipped away, one of the two companions following him as they disappeared into the foliage. Rhoa sat down and sighed in relief, noticing the collection of scrapes and bruises she had amassed on her arms and hands that one day. She even had a large scrape on her forehead from not being quick enough to see a branch crossing her path.

Tiko watched her, trying to be subtle as she took an accounting of all of her day's wounds. He squatted on the branch several lengths away from her. She had some dried blood on her arm. She shook her pack off her shoulders, and loosened the drawstring. She pulled out a light undershirt, and tore a perfect strip off the bottom, making the shirt a bit shorter. She then tightened the laces, and shouldered the pack again, reaching for her water bottle. She pulled out the stopper with a satisfying pop, and held it in her teeth while she put the rag on the bottle opening and tipped the bottle over. When she dampened her rag enough, she stopped up her bottle, and put it back into its sleeve. She then began to clean her scrapes and cuts methodically. By the time the others returned, she felt respectable again. Tiko helped her to her feet and remained nearby from that point on. He walked behind her, keeping a close eye on her as she followed.

They were welcomed into a settlement that Rhoa could never have imagined if she had tried. She walked from a thick tree limb onto a wooden walkway built of supple, interwoven branches. There were ropes made of wood fiber set as very low railings. The walkway was only one of many above and below, winding or straight, merging into a single platform the size of a village forum stretched between four enormous trunks. The walkways led up to more, smaller platforms, and down to a select few. All around this network of walkways were strange nests shaped like teardrops. They were made of the same woven wood, and the sloped, cone-shaped tops were thatched in thick, leathery leaves. They hung from ropes braided into thicker ropes, braided into even thicker ropes, and looped over the strong branches of these infinitely huge trees. They had lanterns like her own village had in the oak tree hanging all about, and people, partially dressed, milled about to see the ground-dweller arrive.

There were a large number of beautiful female creatures, padding on bare feet toward her with their heads cocked in bird-like fashion. They had their faces and bodies decorated in strange chalky, pale-green stripes, some with bars across the eyes and bridge of the nose, others with their hair matted down with this strange substance, some even had markings on their long, graceful limbs. There were babies, too, and little children. Tiny babies were held in slings on the hips of the curious mothers, and the little ones able to walk clung to the legs of their maternal protectors, gazing in bewilderment at Rhoa.

Apparently the style among these women was very long loincloth ensembles—with panels that reached their ankles, displaying their firm, climber's thighs on each side. Some were decorated with pretty scrolls and figures that were all reminiscent of flora and fauna. The women had little anklets, stacks of them made of the firm white pits of yellow cherries. A few of them wore simple halter-like tops, others wore nothing, leaving their breasts free. Rhoa saw a little boy shimmer with colors and attempted textures at the sight of her, trying in a fledgling-like manner to hide himself from the ground-dweller.

"Kurr a dictamata'tor," one girl said in a singsong voice, a smile cracking her face. Then Rhoa was surprised to see movement where there had been none, males coming out of the trunks and down from branches, blending in so well they had been undetectable even to a girl who had been spending so much time with one of their kind.

"Lora ..." The girl bowed slightly, directing her with her arms toward a walkway, shimmying along a bit with each repetition of the word. "Lora ... loraa ..." she insisted.

Rhoa nodded in obedience and walked past her toward the catwalk. The crowd of residents opened a path for her, all staring in disbelief at the sight of a ground-dweller in their midst. Rhoa was led to one of the hanging huts. It was very, very small, and there was a gap of at least a foot between it and the walkway. She was frightened to try to step into it as the woman encouraged her to do—afraid she'd misstep and plummet down to the impossibly distant earth below, made invisible by layers of undergrowth and smaller trees.

The woman kept insisting. Rhoa smiled uncomfortably and nodded, grasping the sides of the doorway with each hand. She lifted her leg, and put her foot on the bottom of the small doorway, and hoisted herself into the hut. Her movement made it swing. She had however, successfully launched herself into the tiny doorway, coming to an ungraceful stop on her hands and knees, her bottom facing the outdoors. There was only room to crawl about in the swinging house.

She turned around and nodded to the woman, who then vanished with everyone else, moving back toward the center. Rhoa righted herself, kneeling inside the gourd-like habitat. She looked around her hut. The swinging was actually pleasant. There was a little lamp hanging from the conical ceiling built into the roof complete with a small chimney. It had been lit for her. The walls all around her at shoulder height up, were crammed with little pocket baskets of varying sizes.

A number of baskets at eye-level contained some fresh fruits. She looked out again to see if anyone had come back to invite her out again, but she saw not a soul. She wondered where Draphen was. She withdrew into her hanging hut, and pulled down the thick flap of quilted leather that served as a door from its holders, and closed up the opening. She reached up and hung her one pack on a hook under the lamp. She used the hook to hold her bag while she rifled through it for some necessities. She changed out of her clothes, knowing that they stank from her efforts, silently wishing for a bath. She changed into a pair of loose pants Draphen had discarded as too itchy, which seemed perfectly soft to Rhoa. They had been short for him, a commoner's summer work breeches, hanging to just mid-calf. For her, they fell to her ankles. She tied the drawstring loosely around her hips, and pulled off the shirt she'd been wearing. She replaced the sticky, smelly tunic with a small simple camisole she often wore underneath other clothes when it was cooler.

She just wanted comfort. And she found herself quite so as she arranged herself in the small confines of her little suspended home. The floor of the hut was entirely padded, more like upholstered, Rhoa realized, pressing down to see how far the give went. She realized it was probably stuffed from the curved, cup-like bottom all the way up to the door with something very soft and fluffy, down perhaps, and something wooly to give it structure. The unusual upholstery fabric bound it all down, which was an unbelievably soft material she'd never seen nor touched before. She leaned in close to see if there was a weave, and there was indeed, so fine it seemed impossible to have been done by human hands.

All around the perimeter of the wall, except for the short span of the door, was a single snake-like round, long cushion of the same material. Rolled up on top of that was a blanket. Rhoa was exhausted. She was also thirsty and at the same time, she needed to urinate. She lifted up the flap door, and slid the loop onto the hook that held it up. It was only a bit darker outside, the remaining shreds of day still managing to keep hold against the shadowy skies of night. Rhoa moved to the door on her knees, turning to her side, letting her right leg reach out for the walkway. Once she had a somewhat firm footing, she began to transfer her weight onto that leg. She felt confident she could balance herself enough to draw the other leg out of the hut, and did so, nearly falling onto the walkway as she brought the rest of her body over. She felt so undignified and clumsy next to the people of the trees.

She padded back to the center of the tree village, wishing for Draphen but finding only four women congregated around a flat stone that had been balanced on a perfectly level stump of a cut tree limb. It was almost flush with the platform. They were not on the main platform, but on a smaller one higher up—only a short catwalk connecting the two. There was also another hanging gourd-like object, except this one was made of clay. It was an oven, hanging by two loops pierced through the wide bottleneck-like opening at the top that served as the chimney.

The women were crushing some nuts and seeds with river rocks, rounded and smoothed from use. They all looked up at Rhoa and smiled warmly. "Tarno marhika?" the youngest girl asked, scooting aside. Rhoa shook her head, and tried to convey her discomfort. The young girl immediately understood, and jumped to her young, gangly legs. She scurried to Rhoa's side, and took her hand, leading her back down to the main platform, and then across to another walkway. Rhoa estimated the girl's age to be twelve or such; she was just on the cusp of womanhood, and very elegant and willowy for a girl her age. She had long shining black hair, and a very soft, round face. She had some of that strange, pale-green decorative paint following her hairline, and then dotted three times under each eye. She had a half-length panel cloth on, and a single band of the mysterious soft cloth around her undeveloped breasts. Rhoa wondered what the fabric was made of. She knew anything made of a fiber would have more texture. This stuff was smooth and flawless—there was no weave to be seen from where she stood.

The girl led her to a strange construct. It was an A-frame made of loosely bound rough wood. Inside was part of the long, thick tree limb that grew from the nearby massive trunk, and hung parallel to the walkway. The tree-limb served as a sort of bench. It was planed smooth, even though it was living wood. Rhoa realized it was where she was expected to relieve herself. The girl then skipped away, her hair flouncing from left to right as she bounded up the walkway.

Rhoa sighed, and walked into the A-frame. She unlaced her pants, and sat down, scooting back a bit so everything would fall away from the wood. She sighed, finding her need to relieve herself was more than just urinating. In fact, she hadn't realized how much her stomach had been shocked into an uproar with all the nervous bile that was created that day. She had to sit there a long time, glad that everything fell far below. There were no bad odors, or any evidence to speak of that betrayed the purpose of the A-frame. She felt infinitely better as she finished, using, with a shock of regret and annoyance, a square of that mysteriously soft material to clean and dry herself. There was a gigantic stack of them on a shelf on the A-frame wall. To her it just seemed wrong to use such a wonderful cloth for such a dirty task.

As she righted herself and tied up her laces, she now realized she had to communicate a need to have something to drink. She was so tired she felt woozy, and her arms barely responded to her commands. She wanted a drink, and to find her hut and curl up to sleep inside, perhaps partaking of one of those fruits in the pocket baskets.

She turned out of the A-frame and screamed, coming face-to-chest with a towering man.

He looked down at her, standing practically naked before her with only a rudimentary loin-covering made of that same material. He stooped a bit, and without the slightest reservation he buried his nose in her hair and took a deep smell. He then straightened up and grunted, "Mahrouk." He then reached out and touched her face, his eyes devouring her, and then carefully searching her features, examining every bit of her as quickly as he could. She was afraid to move or to say anything in fear of offending what could be some common practice for their culture. Draphen appeared as if out of nowhere, seeming almost small next to this tree of a man. He reached around the man, and took Rhoa's arm, pulling her 'round, and dragged her away. She kept looking back at this pillar, who stared after her, his bald head shining in the final wisps of daylight.

"Draphen, what was that?" Her words were slurred, much like a drunk. Her head was spinning from fatigue.

"Never mind. Come on. I've been looking for you. I heard you scream; it nearly did me in."

"Gods, Draphen, I'm dying of thirst, and I used my water up earlier," she said, stumbling behind him. "What do these people do for baths? Do you think I could get a bath?" she asked, feeling foolish for asking.

Draphen didn't seem to be listening. He led her to Tiko and Juri, their traveling companions. He broke out into a broken, frustrated conversation. Tiko seemed angry, and Juri showed concern. She was so tired. What was going on? Tiko walked off after some more talking and returned with a soft bladder filled with cool water. Rhoa was so grateful she nearly cried, drinking the water with avarice.

"I'd really like to go and rest now, Draphen." She made a move toward her little hut. His hand clamped onto her arm, and held her there, still conversing in gestures and words with his companions. Juri sighed in resignation, and walked to a woman who was overseeing the group who had been preparing the meal. She looked up and shared words with Juri, looking 'round the man at Rhoa, who was swaying on her feet, so exhausted she was practically sleeping standing up, the bladder of water dangling listlessly from her weak hands.

The woman nodded at Juri's words, and Rhoa was suddenly whisked away by a number of women and girls who tugged the bewildered, half-conscious woman to a platform that was covered with a pretty latticework dome. They had jugs and jugs of water there, and they used it to wash her body and hair after removing her clothing. They rubbed fragrant flowers into her skin and hair. Rhoa realized why this was happening … she stank. She probably offended the towering man with her body odor. She was too tired to be embarrassed by that notion, nor by her nakedness, not to mention the cluster of women around her all working to clean her up. She would have to remember to thank Draphen for mentioning her need for a bath to them.

She felt them dry her body, wondering to herself how she could still be standing since she wasn't really able to will it. They dressed her in that soft, mystifying material in a paneled loincloth like theirs, and no top. They painted the green stuff on her. It smelled very good, she discovered. Like freshly cut hay. She felt woozy, and about to pass out, but the women somehow kept her animated. They led her down paths to the platform again when she was finished. She was relieved to see Draphen there.

"Draphen, please tell them I'm very, very tired. I don't think I can stand here anymore," she said in a whispered voice, leaning all of her weight onto him. The woman who'd been overseeing the cooks then moved to the two visitors, smiling at Rhoa who looked like someone in a drugged stupor. The woman touched the top of her head, speaking unintelligible words. Rhoa's eyelids were too heavy to keep open, so she leaned on Draphen, enduring the conversation the woman had with Draphen as long as it lasted, sleeping on her feet.

She was awakened abruptly when Draphen took her shoulders, and led her to her hut. He steadied the thing so she could climb in clumsily, and with little ado, she flopped down from her all-fours position onto her side, and was snoring the moment her head hit the pillow.

CHAPTER 16

Tinna sucked in her breath and sighed so hard out of annoyance, it all but infected those in the room with her. Ailie was there, as well as her exceptionally beautiful daughter, Kailine, who sat in her tall, willowy elegance on a chair, her slender legs crossed as she watched patiently as her lady-in-waiting worked on Tinna.

"She still shouts Thran, doesn't she?" Ailie commented, pinching her chin.

"Are you sure this is necessary?" Tinna asked.

Ailie sighed in frustration, and Kailine rolled her eyes. This was the sixth or seventh time that question had been posed. "I don't doubt a single word Astlin has said, Aitinna, and if you really want to get into Kanmer's court, you cannot go in looking anything less than a creature of elegance. He is a bigoted pig, and simply despises the Thran and everything they stand for, but as Astlin said, he also happens to be the brother of the man you are targeting. So you have to simply swallow your pride and do what is necessary to get where you need to be," Kailine scolded the slightly older woman with a sharpness that sounded exactly like Ailie.

"You are right, though, Mother. She is far too Thran to get by with just wearing a gown."

"What do you suppose we could do?"

They both stood and appraised Tinna as if she were a horse at market. She did look elegant indeed. She wore one of Kailine's finest gowns, and the lady-in-waiting was hemming up the lengthy folds of fabric that crumpled prettily around her feet. The gown was emerald green that had a stunning shimmery undertone of blue, like a peacock's feather. It had a low-cut, very well-tailored bodice that was a tad tight on Tinna, which did nothing more than enhance her feminine curves and press her breasts up out of the low, sweeping neckline, producing a perfect cleavage. It had a long bodice that wrapped her torso down to her hips, and the simple, gathered drapes of fabric cascaded around her legs.

"The hair, to begin with," Ailie suggested, reaching over the servant girl who was on all fours pinning the hem up. She gathered up Tinna's volumes of curls, and lifted them up onto the top of her head, revealing her elegant neck and shoulder line.

"How is it possible that women can voluntarily wear this tripe?" Tinna complained. Kailine, wearing something very similar of a deep wine red, frowned down on Tinna.

"Stop whining, Tinna. We're trying to help you."

Tinna smiled at the girl, proud of her strong character. She was so damned beautiful; she envied the girl. Nothing could stand in the way of anyone so markedly lovely; she imagined that young Kailine was Thran through and through in her home, as well as with any other man—having her own power and will without being shamed for it. Such beauty opened many doors for a woman of the north, who had little other power over her environment. She was fortunate to have a husband who was mad about her, and he refused her nothing.

"She's just so Thran," the girl repeated, clearly frustrated and perplexed. "Perhaps if we did something to her hair. Illia, that woman who gets her hair colored who makes my gowns, can you find out who does that and have her come up here at once?" Kailine asked the girl at Tinna's feet.

Illia looked up, her lips bristling with pins. She nodded, and continued pinning the gown. She was very quick about it. When she was done, she circled Tinna in a hunch to verify the evenness of the hem, and then straightened. She was a rather plain girl, bordering on unattractive, making up for her inability to secure a husband by securing a position with Kailine to support herself. She had mousy brown hair which was tied tightly back into a braided bun. Her gown was common for someone of her status, a simple, solid blue gown with a utilitarian bodice made of worn brown leather. She had her sleeves rolled up in a masculine sort of way, and not a shred of adornment to make herself look pretty, for she had no need to. She had a complexion of ruddy skin, peppered with pimples, a rather large one on the line of her lip which made Tinna want to reach out and pop it because it drove her mad to see it there. She did have beautiful eyes. They were as green as Tinna's gown, and lively with intelligence. "She's coming to do the stitching for the gown in a little while, so I can find out who it is who makes her hair that color."

"You're not going to color my hair," Tinna warned them.

"Perhaps just a little scarlet to give her more the look of someone from Gheraine. Perhaps she can find a way to straighten it, too," Kailine suggested. There was a small pause in the chatter as the group surrounding Tinna realized what a wonderful idea it actually was.

"Yes…that burgundy undertone. Of course. We'll have to give her some jewelry to adorn her ankles and wrists, as well as a few neck rings and earrings. We will also need to paint her eyes. We can only hope that he won't notice the fact that her eyes are dark, instead of the golden brown of the Gheraine."

The women talked of her as if Tinna weren't there. Soon enough they had managed to get the woman who colored hair—the seamstress had offered to go and get her, and left as soon as she arrived. She returned with the strange character, introducing her as Io. She was a very thin creature, nearly emaciated, with hair as white as snow, despite her young age. She was from Hansin, a town very far north, and had a very strange accent. She had also a number of strange skills, including the ability to dye a person's hair as if it were fabric.

"Your hair is so very dark … it won't show color a great deal," the woman muttered, her glistening blue eyes almost white like those of the Winter Wolf. She looked at Tinna with admiration, having heard a great deal of the southern society of women warriors. She liked how Tinna's skin seemed almost golden brown next to her own pale white skin. "If you want it to be a completely different color, you will be sorely disappointed."

"We want her to look Gheraine," Kailine announced.

The seamstress who had collected the hairdresser complimented Illia on her pinning job on the hem, and proceeded to sit on a chair, glad to be part of this little project. She shook out the gown on her knee, and continued stitching, keeping an eye on the activities.

"Oh. That's utterly doable," the white-haired woman said. "I can wash it with some deep red dye. That will tint her hair so that it will reflect light in a wine color. If I straighten it in addition to a color wash, you will get the affect you want."

"That's exactly what we want," Ailie said excitedly.

Tinna, standing in a pair of under-bloomers and a camisole, remained perfectly silent, festering in her frustration as the number of fussing women grew around her. They handled her as if she were inanimate, pulling little skeins of her hair, holding the gown up to her, clucking away like hens. Kailine's plain little handmaid returned from an errand, carrying a box. She began to sort through the piles of jewelry she had in it, stacking rings of silver of varying styles into piles based on size.

Tinna was then led to the wash chamber, and was forced to sit down in a chair while the white-haired Io studied her curls. Sensing Tinna's growing frustration she ordered everyone else out of the room, and closed the door. She looked at Tinna.

"The color will wash out after a month or so," she assured her. "It's not really a change of color; it's more like a change of tone. Your hair doesn't stop being black, it will just have a shimmer of deep red in certain light—just like the people of Gheraine tend to have...It will be a bit darker, but it will still be close enough to the trait of the westerners."

Tinna nodded at her, her mind consumed with concerns far beyond the tone of her hair. The woman was so kind to consider her discomfort with all the fussing, so Tinna offered her a weak smile. The thin creature stooped in front of her box of dyes, sorting through the packets of natural colors she'd collected over the years. She found the one she had in mind, opening the mouth of the drawstring bag, and sniffing the contents. She then began unpacking a number of things, some bottles, a copper bucket, and various other objects. She pumped a small amount of water into the bucket, but only a bit. She then used a deep-bowled spoon to dip into her little pouch of dye. It looked jet-black to Tinna. She watched her drop two large spoonfuls of the substance into the bucket of water. The powder spread out onto the surface at first, but then began to color the water in beautiful little whorls as the water movement settled. The color was almost black, but just shy of it. It was red, the very deepest and darkest of vibrant red.

"What do you use to achieve that color?"

"It's a mix of various plants. The main contributor of this particular shade of red are the stamens of the rock-flower," she explained, pleased that Tinna was taking an interest in her science. "Back in the days when I just dyed fabrics, I spent many a winter experimenting with plants, insects, and even fish scales, to see what colors could be extracted. This color is only made up of plant matter. There is ichibo, which I am certain you know makes things almost black." Tinna nodded.

"There is also gen-gen. I use it in all of my dyes because it helps the colors to set." She grasped a bottle. "This is wine vinegar. That will help, too. I chose red wine because it lends qualities of its color to the dyed fabric," she explained. She told Tinna her name was Io.

156

She had Tinna lean back and tilt her head. The woman began to feel her hair, untangling some of the tube curls, and testing its elasticity.

"You have beautiful, healthy hair. It's true black, too. Not even Ailie's is true black."

"I'm half Gypsy."

"That explains it." Io smiled. "Now, lean your head back so," she directed Tinna. She began to mix the liquid and powder together with a wooden stick. She then reached for another bottle, unstopping it. She poured a very slow-moving white creamy substance into the mix. The stuff automatically began to thicken the dye even more. When it was like mud, she lifted the bottle away and closed it up.

"What is that?"

"I powdered spear-root after drying it, and then mixed it up with just a tiny bit of water. It makes this wonderful creamy mixture that thickens the dyes to keep them on the hair without interfering with the intensity of the color."

"That's very inventive." Tinna smiled. "I use the spear-root myself with tallow and goat's milk as a remedy for winter skin."

"That is also very inventive." Io stood up, and lifted her bucket of dye along with her. She tucked a wadded padding of fabric behind Tinna's neck, and pulled her luxurious head of hair back. She put the bucket on a chair under Tinna's locks, and began to scoop up the gelatinous mixture, now the color of rich blood, and apply it to Tinna's hair in gobs.

She spent a good deal of time massaging it into the strands, making sure it was evenly applied.

"Do you color your own hair?" Tinna asked. "With such a lovely white canvas, you must be able to choose from any color you can make."

"Sometimes. But rarely. I did dye it blue once, on a whim." She laughed easily, her accent somehow comforting to Tinna. It felt good to know she wasn't the only stranger in a strange land. She also liked the feeling of someone playing with her hair. She closed her eyes. "But honestly, having access to these dyes, and doing it so much has tired me of it for my own tastes. I like to do it for other people now, but I do revel in my own white hair now. Besides, for some reason, the colors don't wash out completely for me, and so I often have to cut the faded colored hair off, and grow my hair back."

"What is it like where you're from, Io?"

"Much like your home, Tinna," Io said, "but to be frank, we're a little more equal in our statuses—the men and women."

"I see." Tinna sighed. "What made you come here then, where you became a second-class citizen the moment you set foot in this land?"

"I could ask you the same thing. But with your Gypsy heritage, I can see why you left. Gypsies are not well-respected in your land or even here…but certainly not to the degree they are despised in Thran country."

"Are they where you come from?"

"We are a people descended from nomadic Gypsies. We welcome them when they come. We are so isolated up there, that it is always good to have new faces bringing news from the world south of us."

Tinna sighed. "I came here to escape the bigots. Why did you come here?"

"I came here because I was willing to trade my equality for a chance to meet people like you. And honestly, I wanted to feel a true summer. And maybe enroll in a few classes at a Torach Academy," she whispered, as if she were a girl sharing some great secret.

"I hope you've changed your mind about that now that you've seen what happens to any organization related to, or answerable to, the High Throne," Tinna mumbled.

"Yes, I've thought twice about it. Very strange indeed, what the dragons are up to."

"What is your theory on it all?" Tinna ventured.

"I know that they must be doing what they are doing for a good reason. They are a very honorable people. I only wish I could sneak into a meeting of the Keepers. They would most certainly know what this is all about."

"The Keepers? Why would they have any idea what the dragons are up to?"

"Silly girl … do you forget that the Keepers are part of the Trinity? They are most certainly aware of what the dragons are planning, and probably part of it," Io chided, her stained hands still massaging the dye into her hair.

Tinna chuckled with a patronizing tone. "Io, with all due respect, you are mistaken. The Keepers are not in any way related to the Trinity. The Keepers is an entity created by humans, and the Trinity consists of the leadership of dragon-kind. The three positions are occupied by three of the most ancient dragons. Everyone knows that."

"Tinna … how could you think such a thing? It is common knowledge that one arm of the Trinity is comprised of the Keepers.

The other is a dragon, and the third is Chai-opse." Io's hands fell as if she were too shocked by Tinna's ignorance to continue.

"Chai-opse?" Tinna sat up, half laughing, half puzzled. Io circled 'round her and looked at Tinna. "Tinna, you certainly could not be conveying to me that this is what you believe. It's simply impossible to accept that you are so misled…especially about something that is common knowledge. You are wrong. The Trinity is not all dragons"

"Then you are accusing everyone in this world of being wrong. Nobody would believe what you claim. How is it that you have come across these erroneous notions?"

Io looked confused. She took a moment to think before sinking onto a bolster in front of Tinna, clasping her gooey hands together, thoughtlessly staining her skirts. "My land is where the Trinity meets and lives," she stated.

Tinna gazed at her, quite beside herself…there was another strange deviation to her own version of what she knew: The Trinity convened in Oramath—far northwest in the regions belonging to the dragons. Somehow, she felt that Io was not fibbing, or attempting to mislead her. Besides, there was no reason for Io to do so.

"I know a great deal of it. Where I was born, it is the land where the Trinity serves. My family, my clan … other nearby peoples, we have been privileged to serve the Trinity. This is how I know."

Tinna realized that Io's people were very insular—their reputation for such behavior was well known, much like her own Thran culture. It was rare to see a woman or a man of her kind outside the borders of their cold-weathered empire.

Perhaps that's why Io's truths had never emerged to disprove the world's misperception about the Trinity. Perhaps she was speaking the truth to some degree. But one thing certainly made her doubt Io. "I would be more prone to believe you if you hadn't mentioned the Chai opse. The Chai-opse are dead. How can along dead race stand as one arm of the Trinity?"

"Dead?" Io laughed at first, but it faded as she came to realize that Tinna was serious. Her face expressed pure incredulity that Tinna could actually be so misguided in her facts about what to her people was common knowledge. She'd never talked about it before with anyone of the southern lands, but she suspected suddenly that Tinna's idea of how things were was universal, from here to the lands of the Thran and beyond. She realized she might be doing some great damage by correcting their idea of the truth … creating conflicts that the Trinity had hoped to hide, conceivably. It was too late, though.

And for some reason, she found herself trusting Tinna enough to bestow her with these truths. She felt the woman would do only good with it. She saw something in the woman's eyes, far deeper than the pain and secrets she saw within them.

"Tinna ... my people are the Chai-opse. That is why the Trinity makes its home with us. We are the pure form of the Chai-opse ... as are the nomads." Tinna seemed to hear her voice echo those words for a long moment, the thought resonating in her brain. Then Io said, "You are half Chai-opse."

"How can that be?"

"It astounds me that you do not know this." She laughed in astonishment still.

"Do you know the tale of the Chai-opse?"

"Uh, yes, I remember a bit. They were the people responsible for the Wall of Ten Empires. They built it to separate themselves from the rest of the world. Humanity often wondered about them, and when the great explorer Ilam decided to scale the wall, he discovered their two cities abandoned, and their villages empty and in ruins. They'd vanished. It was thought that the worm-skin plague had killed them all. Most believed their land to be cursed, and it remains largely wilderness now." Tinna did not mention that the land now contained the people who carried the worm-skin plague. That was between her and Ledroran.

"The Chai-opse felt somehow responsible for the worm-skin plague to some extent, because they did not die of it. The whole race is immune to the illness. And you know the history of their closeness to humanity ... their regard for them?" Io asked. Tinna nodded. It seemed appropriate suddenly, that they move the carriers to the land of the Chai-opse. They were in no danger of infecting anyone there. They did not contract it, so they could not spread it. Io continued. "Such a small, wise, and close-knit race could not bear to think that they could ever go on in this world surviving the pestilence unscathed while millions perished. They believed that the loss of humanity was so great, and theirs so little, that they balanced it out by abandoning their claim to their land, leaving it to the Trinity. They then became nomads, living outside of the mainstream, allowing their identity to diminish with their civilization. Some groups mixed with humans as time passed, and others congregated in lands no humans wanted."

Io bent forward and looked at Tinna, whose brow was furrowed and her lips pressed tightly together. Io appeared to be intrigued by Tinna's seriousness about this subject, and appalled by her ignorance of many truths. Io blinked her stunning ice-colored eyes, and smiled wanly. "Why does this interest you so? None of it really has a direct effect on the world anymore. Even the Trinity seems almost obsolete these days," she asked.

Tinna was startled from her musing, and she shook her head as if to shake off all thoughts of the discussion. She seemed to be searching for the right words. "There's a great deal more to my interest in all that than I can share. But I must say it changes little in what I am here to do, but a great deal in what I thought I knew—and sort of makes it a tad easier to justify." Tinna leaned back. Io stood, and finished doing Tinna's hair.

So the Trinity is comprised of the highest leader of the Keepers, a leader of the Chai-opse and a dragon. It made sense. One representative from all the world's greatest races. She was surprised that the Keepers represented the human population, and not the High Throne. Then again, that too made sense. The Keepers were swayed by neither war nor politics. They ingrained their many special groups and brotherhoods into all societies, protecting every wonderful thing humanity created and aspired to.

The Trinity had not only endorsed, but actually started the acts that made the dragons do what they did. The Keepers—humans—and the nomadic Chai-opse—the Gypsies' forefathers—must have agreed to inflict the sickness on the people in order to secure the dragons a chance of survival. She couldn't imagine how difficult a decision that must have been for the person who stood for the Keepers.

Tinna lost all sense of what was going on outside of her body at that moment. All she could do was think of what she had learned, and felt suddenly that she was burdened with the greatest secret ever created, and that despite its terrible weight, she had to keep it that way. The alliance of three races would vanish with the Trinity, obviously. It would not only obliterate the dragons, it would devastate a nomadic people who were already stigmatized. Worst of all, it would destroy one of the only noble organizations mankind ever created. One that rose above all the inanity and trivial things that people thought important, and focused on what made humanity honorable and worthy of its place in the world. If there were no Keepers, Tinna did not wish to imagine what the world would be like.

Hair color didn't quite matter anymore. Neither did having to wear a bloody gown. She had to move, and move quickly. She lay her head back as the woman began to rinse Tinna's hair with warm water.

The warm water, and soft touch of Io's hands did little to sooth Tinna's mind.

CHAPTER 17

Rhoa woke up with a heavy head and a snotty nose. She rolled over, having forgotten for a moment where she was. But the comfortable bed just large enough for her to stretch out in and the texture and softness of the wonderful pillow upon which her head lay suddenly reminded her of where she was. The lamp had burnt out and it was impossible to see. She yawned quite loudly, and lay on her back, propping her legs up so that her knees were bent and her feet flat on the mattress floor. She fumbled in the dark for her water bladder, and drank deeply from it. She had no idea whether it was day or night, and so she sat up, sitting cross-legged as she reached to lift up the soft door. It was pitch-black outside. She closed the flap and lay back down, staring up at the blackness above her.

Had she slept only a few hours? Or was it very early in the morning before sunrise? Or had she slept until the following night? She'd been tired enough. Her arms were flaccid, barely able to lift the bladder, and every muscle in her back, shoulders, and arms hurt. She stretched out her limbs and flopped back down again, suddenly aware of what she was wearing. She became aware of the flaking powder on her face and arms, and the soft material wrapped around one of her legs. She shimmied herself out of the loincloth and scratched the flakes off her body and threw them out the door as she collected them in her hand. When she felt more comfortable, she lay back again, and sighed, too rested to go back to sleep, but too afraid to attempt navigating the walkways in the dark, let alone climbing out of the hut without light to see. She sighed audibly, moving her arms and stretching her back until she worked a little of the soreness out of it. She was startled by a scratch on her little leather door.

"Who is it?" she asked, prepared to feel foolish if it were one of her hosts.

"Me." Draphen's voice filled her instantly with relief. She sat up and pulled the door open, seeing only just the smallest indication of his face in the darkness. He did not ask, but climbed into the hut with her. She was instantly aware and embarrassed by her nakedness. She shrank away from him as far as she could get in the small space. She heard him securing the door behind him.

"What do you want, Draphen?"

"They were worried about you, but I told them that it was a difficult day for you before and that you needed to rest. You must be hungry."

"I'm all right," she lied. "What brings you here?" she asked, slightly annoyed by his brazenness. He didn't reply. "What are you doing in here?" "I heard you yawning, and knew you were awake," he muttered.

"That's not exactly an answer. I'm completely naked here, and you just came   right in, and frankly, I find that very rude of you."

"Well ... it is my right now," he said with a touch of smugness. Rhoa frowned in the blackness. "What? Your right? Who do you think you are?" she bristled.

"Your husband," he snapped. "Or, more precisely by definition of my kind, your master. It is very infrequent that such a binding of two people occurs—it is done when one of our men wishes to stake a claim on a ground-dweller. If he wishes to take her to the trees, and make her his mate, he calls claim on her. Once that is done, the ground-dweller is taken, and declared as his possession, and that is that."

Rhoa lost any ability to speak, let alone comprehend. "You're such a liar." She   laughed suddenly.

"No. We were married last night. You slept through the day, and now it is night again. I did not assume my marital rights last night because you were so exhausted, but here I am. We share a sleeping space now."

"We did not get married—"

"Yes we did! Have you no memory of it?" he snapped, growing quite frustrated with the whole conversation.

"Does the ground-dwelling woman have any say in the matter? Obviously not! The only thing I remember are those women bathing me because I was so smelly, and I certainly don't remember agreeing to marry you!"

"Do you not wish to be married to me?"

"I would have liked to have been consulted," she pouted.

"I thought you knew, what with that towering idiot of a leader there sniffing after you."

"Tower—? Oh, yes, the man who stuck his nose in my hair ..." she said in a faraway sort of voice. "And how does sniffing my hair

164

indicate that I was to be married to you? I find it difficult to make the connection." Her tone was sarcastic.

"He made claim on you," Draphen said, a tinge of anger in his voice.

"Nobody can just decide to own someone ... that's slavery."

"In my culture and in theirs likewise, a leader may certainly choose a ground-dwelling woman and lay claim to her. The only thing that can prevent him from having her is if another of my kind has previous claim upon her."

"And so you married me?" Rhoa's voice softened. "To keep him from taking me away?"

"I had to. I could have just said we were married, but my companions knew otherwise, and they would have been bound to tell the truth. So I had the soothsayer bind us." He fidgeted.

There was a long silence.

"But, it was only for the sake of appearances, wasn't it?" she asked, her voice betraying a little dismay at the thought.

Draphen stiffened his shoulders. "We are married. There is no such thing as maintaining appearances. It is our state and will be our state until one of us dies," he said very seriously.

Rhoa sat up straighter, and pushed her hair behind her ear, looking into the darkness in his general direction. "So that's it. We're married."

"Yes."

"And so you are here."

"Yes. To claim my rights," he said decisively.

What an odd culture, Rhoa thought, her stomach roiling with butterflies. "I see." She cleared her throat. "And what I think, or want, does that matter at all?"

"Of course it does." Draphen's voice broke a bit, and it was definitely softened.

"To me, anyway. According to the ways of my people, it normally would not." He paused. "But I had it in my mind, perhaps I was wrong ... that you might not object to such a thing. I thought I perceived something, and your desire to follow me instead of remaining with the Thran ... it was not a choice a person would make trivially ... not after the abuse your body has suffered just from this short beginning. I thought it meant that ... perhaps ..."

"Of course it did, Draphen," Rhoa interrupted. "Of course it did. I certainly didn't count on us being married before we even acknowledged anything between us, but here we are, and here it is ...

the situation, odd as it can be." She heard him scoot over ever so discreetly, and the house swung a bit.

"Then I shall claim my rights," he declared. With little ado, he reached out for her, and once she was within his grasp, he enveloped himself around her, gathering her diminutive body into his arms, and straddling her legs. His hands moved with an excited urgency, like a young boy getting his first grope of a girl he'd been admiring forever. He seemed to be making an inventory of what was now his. Meanwhile, he'd locked his lips onto hers, and was kissing her like she'd never been kissed before. Soon he pulled her up, and let himself fall backward, pulling Rhoa on top of him.

"Beautiful, soft Rhoa," he whispered as he touched her. In his mind he was convinced that his false love for Aitinna was an act of fate solely to lead him to Rhoa. No woman had ever made him want her so much. It was more than he could have ever hoped to have her in his arms so willingly. He was glad that fool had laid claim on her. Glad he had an excuse to make her belong to him.

Rhoa closed her eyes, the butterflies turning into a passionate yearning—remembering why she had indeed decided to subject herself to the travel in the trees. It was finally happening. He was touching and kissing her. With little gentleness, and much hungry, desperate passion, the newlyweds made love. A ground-dweller, and a chameleonic tree climber—limbs so entwined they were nearly enmeshed into one.

CHAPTER 18

Tinna made her entrance into the society of Alterat on the arm of Astlin's good friend Lord Hilmal. He was an adorable old gentleman with a pear-shaped body, thick muttonchops, bushy eyebrows, and glistening, gray eyes. He was glad to play along with the farce, taking a boyish delight in it. He had been living alone for a long time, and he leapt at the chance at having company for a few days, especially company as beautiful as Aitinna. Their story had been reviewed enough times to remember it off the cuff. Lord Hilmal was Aitinna's great-uncle. Orec Hilmal had a brother who had married a Gheraine woman, and decided to live there. Astlin knew of the connection, and asked the old man for a favor.

Tinna came to stay with him in his cavernous old manor. It looked and felt much like Phenmal's place. Tinna was given a set of roomy apartments to stay in, and she brought Io with her as her companion. She was really along to keep Tinna's hair straight, a process that lasted three hours, and was tedious and painstaking. Io worked her hair with patience, and re-applied the color whenever the red seemed to be fading. Io was also responsible for the care of the collection of gowns Kailine had provided Aitinna.

Tinna had shared her first dinner with the old man, who talked all through it, as if he'd been saving years' worth of conversation for this moment. She listened intently, and ate, enjoying the company of this gentleman a great deal. "We shall be going to a rather large gathering at our neighboring grant. It is a rite of ascension celebration for their daughter. They've invited me, and I have sent word to them stating that you were visiting me from Gheraine—and requested their kind permission to allow you to accompany me," he explained over thick liqueur after dinner.

Tinna had settled in a tall chair beside his in front of the fire, and she felt quite civilized. Part of her could not keep itself from longing for the cruder, perhaps, but warmer comfort of the Summer

Lodge—sitting in one of the five chairs by the community hearth, where Taneth and Rigerd and the other leaders of Thamatoch sat nightly, mumbling over their pipes. She felt a sudden pang of loss. She missed Taneth and Hanru. And she missed Rhoa. She hoped the girl was safe. The next evening, Io helped Tinna dress, and then Io dressed herself. They were accompanied by Orec into an old carriage, and headed to the gathering.

Orec helped them from the carriage, and they walked into the house where crowds of people mingled about. Orec had made it his business to arrive late. The announcement would not just blend in with everyone else's and that would make them all turn and see his so-called grand-niece. His plan was quite effective. The people who mingled outside the great hall moved aside for the proud little man and the elegant woman on his arm. Behind them followed a beautifully dressed woman from Hansin. Io played her role as companion perfectly, her head bowed down and discreet, so as not to take any attention away from her mistress.

"Lord Orec Hilmal and Lady Layache, and Companion Io Ythan," the announcer shouted.

As planned, the faces turned to see them. Their looks and whispers were the desired effect Tinna had hoped for. She held her back as straight as possible, and looked down her nose at every single set of eyes that deigned to meet with hers. Phir Kanmer leaned on the mantle and chuckled. His four companions smoked pipes and shared drinks with him, the usual pack of men that clustered together at such silly events. "I suppose that means the High King is hiding somewhere with his tail tucked between his legs."

They broke out into a roar of laughter, interrupted by one of his friend's appreciative tone.

"Gods, be still my heart—I think I've gone and fallen in love." The tall young man who managed Kanmer's shipping fleets straightened, turning his eyes toward the entrance of the great hall. The other men followed his gaze, all emitting concurring grunts of admiration. Walking into the hall on the arm of Orec Hilmal was a creature of unsurpassed, exotic beauty—a Gheraine woman with a splash of northern traits, just enough to make her more beautiful than any ordinary Gheraine woman would hope to be. She walked and held herself with the posture of someone of great consequence, and had a whitie in tow as her companion. She sailed in her rich gown, drawing the eye of every man in the room.

"Who is she?" Khorin asked. Kanmer shook his head and shrugged. A younger man of about nineteen poked his head into the circle.

"Someone told me she's his grand-niece. Her husband has recently died, and she has decided to return to the place of her grandfather's birth," he whispered.

"I had no idea Orec had family from that region."

"Now that you mention it, I do recall hearing he had a brother with a rather significant estate in that area," someone else muttered.

"She's a widow?"

"Apparently a very rich one."

"By the gods, she's quite the looker," the young man opined with a smile, delighted to have been included in a conversation with his peers.

Kanmer paid little heed to the boy or his companions. He was a renowned wolf among the people of this circle, with a deep taste for beautiful, experienced women. When his attention was called to this newcomer, he immediately began to assess her for potential flirtation, gauging her character from her posture and her expression, getting a general idea of how great a challenge it would be to gain her favor. The music struck up and the couples began to collect on the floor.

Orec was methodically circling the room, responding to the many requests for introductions. Kanmer was not one to let an opportunity slip out of his hands, and he had to stake a claim on her before someone else thought himself worthy of this new, elegant creature. He broke away from his group without excuse, and strode straight through the dancers, causing a bit of a collision between two dancers in doing so. His path led him on a straight line to Orec and his niece, who stood a quite a bit taller than the old man.

"Good evening," he boomed. He was a formidable character, and difficult if not impossible to ignore. He stood a good six and a half feet tall. He had a shaved head and a very neatly trimmed goatee. His eyes were brown and deep, giving the slightest indication to the observant person that there was a great deal going on behind them. He was a handsome fellow by all means, and dressed in the finest of clothing. He did not feel the need to wait for his introduction. Instead he injected his large person between Orec and his grand-niece and the man to whom they were being introduced.

"Honorable Lord Hilmal. You bring a new face into our limited little society." He smiled, eyes on Tinna all the while. "I would hope you'd be kind enough to introduce me to the lovely lady on your arm." Orec bowed politely to Kanmer, and nodded.

169

"I would never even think of depriving anyone of her gentle acquaintance." He smiled, patting her hand with his papery, wrinkled digits.

Tinna gazed directly on the man without the slightest indication of emotion or fear of this intimidating character looming over her. Orec turned to look at her.

"My dear, this is Lord Phir Kanmer—a neighbor of mine of sorts. Our grants border one another. My Lord, may I introduce you to my lovely grand-niece Lady Niara Layache."

Kanmer gave Tinna an elegant bow, reaching for her extended hand and lifting it to his forehead before releasing it to its owner, who seemed unimpressed by the introduction. Such indifference to him fired up his desire for her even more. Tinna had heard of his taste for difficult women, and knew exactly what role to play, for it was her nature as a Thran to play with the desires of men.

"I am hopeful that you would grant me the honor of a dance or two later on this evening." Tinna nodded in assent, and gave him a shallow curtsy, resuming her path around the room with Orec.

"I dare say, lovely Tinna," Orec hissed under his breath as they walked, "you did very well. He gazes after you with the intensity of a predator, and you've baited him wonderfully," he said proudly, grasping her hand on his arm very tightly. "Never have I seen such a deft example of manipulation in my life—and all done without uttering a single syllable." He chuckled warmly, deriving great joy from this little scheme.

As they finished their circuit through the room, Orec began to seek out a decent place for them to sit. Before he could do so, Kanmer appeared again, smiling with a visibly greedy leer as he offered them a place with his friends and himself, casually sending three of his party away so that they could join them. Tinna and Io sank down into the soft, padded chairs, observing with little expression, almost boredom, the dancers filling the floor.

Kanmer stalked off to fetch his newest object of desire and her companion some refreshments, playing his usual repertoire of moves to make himself desirable to elegant ladies. His lowering himself to errand boy did not seem to even cause this woman to notice, and he had to re-think his strategy, going down his lists of experiences with women to find some ideas that would have an effect on this quiet, reserved creature. She had yet to utter a single word to him, thanking him for his errand with only a polite nod. Gentleness was not getting him anywhere; perhaps being completely forthright, and being himself would work, he thought. He remembered her commitment to dance with him. He would begin there.

Tinna maintained her reserve as she moved in step with the other dancers. She did not smile exuberantly, or engage in conversation with her partner. It was fortunate that her need for concentration coincided with the role she was playing.

She had only learned to dance recently, thanks to Orec and Ailie. She still had to count steps in her mind, and it took incredible control to make it look natural and practiced. She veiled all this with an appearance of cool indifference. Kanmer on the other hand seemed to be maddened by the silence. "You don't do much talking, Mrs. Layache."

"Would you have me chatter on about banalities like everyone else? I should hope not," Tinna replied coolly, speaking with a deep Gheraine accent she had to perform for days to perfect with the assistance of a Gheraine man of Ailie's acquaintance.

Kanmer shook his head and concentrated momentarily on what he should do next. The music, however, was working on Tinna's side, and ended in an elegant note. She stepped away, did a feminine curtsy which she'd been forced to practice over and over again with Kailine. Tinna wondered if when she returned for the dog, if he too would be turned into some overly polite, bowing, proud little thing dressed up in fine clothing. She returned to her "great-uncle," and sank down next to him.

"I am growing very tired, Uncle," she announced loudly enough for the surrounding people to hear. The old man nodded.

"Ah, my dear, your announcement gives me great relief in my old age, for I am no longer suited for these great assemblies. Shall we go home then?" Tinna nodded and smiled at him. The old man rose, and took her hand.

Kanmer, who'd been standing by the refreshment table while he had someone make a plate for the mysteriously beautiful woman, tried to run across the floor to stop the three from leaving, but he was impeded by the bodies of young, lively dancers doing a very complicated skipping step that made them fly about the floor. Kanmer was too late when he managed to forge his way through the people, and ran out onto the steps just in time to see the coach swaying as it trundled down the drive.

"Well, well, my girl, you did a wonderful job!" Orec laughed loudly, slapping his knee.

"What could you possibly mean?" Tinna asked with a coy smile, glad to slip out of her Gheraine persona, and back into her own natural accent. She stretched her legs out, lifting her skirts up ungracefully to remove the tight slippers. She winced at the discovery of a painful blister on her heel.

"You did your job most adequately. That fool is rarely given much challenge when it comes to women. Your indifference has only made him even more determined to have you. You've hooked that big ugly fish, and I predict he will be making a casual visit to speak to me about some matter of business or other in the next few days ... even if he's never really set foot on my property except to hunt with a party of friends once. Excellent work, dear girl." He grinned.

Tinna smiled at him, adoring him so much, she was tempted to abduct him when everything was over and take him back to the village with her. He sat quietly across from her, his head bobbing slightly from the carriage's movement. He contented himself in looking out onto the small window, the moonlight's trickery on his old face making an artistic image for Tinna to enjoy.

"I would prefer that I am invited to his home. The only way I am going to find out where his brother is hiding is if I can have access to his private papers. I'm certain that there is some evidence for me to find somewhere ... a letter ... anything."

"Keep playing the game, my dear girl, and we'll cross his threshold soon enough. I'm certain he will attempt to lure you into his own territory."

"How far is this man's estate from your home?"

"Oh, about four hours. Fastest by horse, obviously. By coach or on foot, that's another story," the old fellow replied. Tinna leaned back onto the hard-packed padding of the coach bench, and nodded, eyes drifting up to the ceiling of the swaying coach.

CHAPTER 19

It was the first time Taneth ever asked himself what the horses were actually used for besides the mare's milk he had yet to acquire a taste for. He watched the villagers cart the herd back and forth from pasture almost every day, but he hardly saw them ride the horses, or use them as beasts of burden. They just took care of them. It seemed a great deal of unnecessary work simply to have a stock of odd-tasting milk and cheese, and a religion that could easily be practiced without the need to shovel manure day in and day out. He was fixated on this subject simply because he was looking to be irksome and irritated about something or other, and this puzzle seemed as good as any.

He was in a dark mood this day. He decided to lighten it a bit by joining Hanru on his daily walk to see Nibbles the Tree. He followed the boy, who walked several paces ahead, carrying a little pail with which to water the tree. Taneth was surprised how healthy the tree was, showing even some new growth already, even so late in the season. He imagined that the tree must have been in need of more light to begin with, because it had grown new leaves in such a short time. He sat down on a stone while Hanru ran to the tree, shouting all the new events of the day at it as if he were informing his best friend.

Taneth propped his elbows on his knees and lowered his head, his hands massaging his face and temples as he tried to organize his stressed mind. Rigerd had laid a large project on his back to keep him from being distracted by the situation outside the calm and peace of their village. He didn't understand how Rigerd and the people of the village could go on functioning normally as if nothing were happening outside the safe little region they called home. Hildercross was naught but a pile of ruins and ashes, along with the entire town and population at its feet. But every day, the horses still went back and forth to pasture, and the areas burned by the dragons were already green with plants, as if the foliage needed this destruction to generate healthier growth.

He wondered what Tinna was doing. Strangely, he had no doubt she was alive … she was Thran, and that alone assured him that she could take care of herself. But it didn't mean she wasn't in danger, or suffering…and then there was Rhoa, whose sister was beside herself with worry, asking Taneth every day if he had any news or ideas of what had happened—him being the only person showing any focus on the turmoil in the outside world.

And then this … Rigerd's unbelievably giant project: He wanted Taneth to research the origins of the Araki people, and the history of the region's clans … and then document it all. As if having to teach the children, heal the sick, maintain the breeding and livestock records, raising Hanru and keeping up with what studies he could, despite the tiny library the previous Wiseman kept weren't enough, now the indefatigable Rigerd wanted this. Taneth's sigh could have shaken down the foundations of a fortress.

He lifted his head a bit, steepling his hands over his mouth and chin, eyes on the boy as he sat in front of the thriving sapling, talking with such animation. Taneth looked to the sky, a view he rarely saw anymore because of the canopy of leaves ever present above his head. Autumn was to come soon. That meant that the clans would be meeting to share harvests and celebrate weddings and such.

Rigerd wanted the stupid project done for that meeting so every clan in the region would have that for their own archives. He didn't even know where to begin. He knew there was a Phanos archive a few days or so from the village, but he doubted it would have very much to offer. He imagined an archive in such a remote area would have very little indeed, but at least he could get a better idea of where to begin from there. Conceivably, Rigerd had burdened him with this project simply so Taneth could get away. Maybe he did need a holiday from the day-to-day activities. He looked at Hanru.

"Hey, little brat, come here a moment."

Hanru jumped to his feet. Taneth took a great deal of pride in how good the boy looked of late. His bruises long gone, his frame filled out, a smile on his face.

He loved to look at the boy; it gave him great pride in his ability to care for him. He ran to Taneth, climbing onto his lap.

"How's Nibbles?"

"Fine. He's growing new leaves! Did you see?"

"Yes, he does look in very good shape. Even healthy enough to spare you a day or two."

"Why?" Hanru asked, eyebrows pushing his forehead up into a patch of little wrinkles.

"I have to go to that archive outside of Lemoram ... want to go with me?"

Hanru nodded enthusiastically, writhing from Taneth's lap and running to fill the pail and give Nibbles the Tree some water.

Taneth was surprised to have been given the horses—after all his speculation on their uselessness, he felt a bit foolish when they were offered. Rigerd had them saddled up in tack Taneth didn't even know they had. Rigerd was worrying again, threatening to send someone along to accompany them. Taneth managed to talk him out of it, and was on his way to Lemoram before the tall, intimidating character changed his mind. Taneth only hoped the city still existed. He wasn't sure if the archives fell under High Throne jurisdiction, but he had to see for himself. He felt powerless in the village, as much as his duties were fulfilling, he wanted to be out there, doing something. It was important to him that he keep his mind occupied and keep the worry down to a minimum.

He often thought of himself as a fussy old worrywart what with the way he always kept dwelling on thoughts of Tinna. Even though more than month had come and gone since she and Rhoa left, Taneth still refused to accept that the girls could be dead—although most of the village had already concluded and accepted this as a sad fact. They let him cling to his hope, and respected his refusal to grieve. However, Taneth's responsibility for Hanru was enough to keep his mind level and focused on the most part. It was easier to set his worries aside with a child to mind after.

Hanru had been assigned his own pony. This delighted Taneth. The village had gone out of their way to find a little herd of ponies to add to their stable when Taneth had declared his need to go to Lemoram in order to complete this project of Rigerd's and that he wished the boy to accompany him. There was a sense of joy about the whole thing, as if everyone were fulfilling some secret little desire after years of longing. The arrival of the Phajett clan members, herding the cluster of fat, fuzzy little ponies was an occasion of great celebration, and there was much oohing and ahhing over the diminutive little horses. They were immediately given their own space in the Autumn Lodge of all places, and all inducted into the clan with a laughably somber ceremony. Taneth could scarce keep himself from snickering, as each pony was led up to the Holyman, who chanted and recited holy words while the stalwart little horse stood there, eyes peeking out from its voluminous forelock, switching its tail and stamping its short little legs.

Rigerd made quite the fuss over having Taneth choose one of the ponies for Hanru. He was determined the boy be given something special. And he knew Taneth could be relied upon to make a good choice for the boy. Taneth chose a jet-black pony as round as a ball with four white socks and a mass of mane and tail for which to cling to when Hanru was being jostled like molded jelly while the pony trotted. She was an even-tempered little pony, by the standard of pony behavior, and she took the short riding lessons given to Hanru in stride, hardly ever attempting the usual cheeky tactics to get the child off her back, as most of the other little horses would tend to do.

Rigerd laughed, stating that Taneth's choice was an excellent one. "For they might be small, but when it comes to brains, they are far superior to the full-sized horses. And they're ornery, and obstinate, and will push the limits of every child who chooses to ride them. The good thing is, once Hanru learns to ride on that little thing, he'll be able to ride anything. It takes skill to handle one of these little things, yes, indeed." He crossed his arms on his wide chest, and smiled down at the boy, who rode by on his little pony, who at that very moment decided to grind her side against their legs in an attempt to wipe Hanru off her back.

Hanru was quick to pick up on her infrequent attempts to unseat him, and rarely fell for them anymore and only after a few lessons as well! Raven (as he named her) did however do one trick Hanru had yet to prepare himself for: His little saddle sat on her wide back, and because she had no withers, it would slide easily over her shoulders onto her neck if she stopped and leaned her head forward.

She would do this suddenly; just stop, and lower her head, and poor Hanru would slide onto her neck, saddle and all. He would then, always very slowly, pitch forward and tumble over her head onto the ground. It took a number of times of this happening on the first two days of their journey for Taneth to lose his patience and to fashion a makeshift crupper. He tied each end of some braided twine to two of the four metal pack loops on the back of Hanru's small saddle seat, and then looped it under her tail. The saddle was now prevented from moving forward, and it only took two or three attempts at her stop-and-slide tactic for Raven to realize she'd been outfoxed. As the devious little pony plotted new strategies, they rode on with hardly any more interruption until they reached Lemoram.

CHAPTER 20

Tinna clutched her hands together, feeling a deep, heavy knot growing in her stomach. It had taken her at least four days to squirm her way under Kanmer's roof. She had once sat through an unbearably romantic play with Ailie—and it was what gave her the idea. It seemed Kanmer wasn't so bold as to visit her benefactor out of the blue, probably realizing how obvious such a thing would be. As he huddled by his fire, formulating some strategy to get at the fine woman he couldn't get out of his mind, Tinna was finalizing her preparations, and eagerly awaiting a rainy day. When that day arrived, moist and foggy, a sure sign of a later downpour, she smiled delightfully, let Io dress her for the part, then set off for a long, healthy walk, accompanied by Orec's large, lumbering wolfhound.

She was quite accustomed to walking, perhaps not in such a terrible gown, but she managed, actually finding some enjoyment in it, glad to have a canine walking at her side again. It took almost six hours and the sky had opened up about three hours into her hike. Tinna was truly exhausted when she reached his grounds. She then set herself up in the right position, on a high hill overlooking his estate, a rather ostentatiously large edifice of hideous fortification-like architecture. It was surrounded by cattle whose odor could be detected quite easily even at such a distance. It was barely visible against the sheets of rain. Tinna then marched down toward the little chateau.

Kanmer could barely contain his delight when he saw the bedraggled, and yet still incredibly beautiful woman standing in his very house. The housekeeper had wrapped a blanket around her shoulders, and led her in after she'd greeted the poor woman and her dog at the door. Her host rocketed to his feet at the sight of her, hardly believing the announcement that preceded her. "My goodness! What brings you here, of all places?"

"A small stroll turned into a hike, and when the rains started, I got lost. I followed the first road I found, and it led me here. I'd no idea it was your home. I am so sorry to inconvenience you like this," she said.

"Nonsense!" Kanmer blurted. "You are no inconvenience." He realized she'd spoken more words in this entrance than she had the entire evening at the gathering. He was ever so delighted at such a serendipitous event. He rushed to her side, ushering her toward the fire, being overly doting. Tinna began to milk it, sniffling and clearing her throat.

The housekeeper, when she entered with a tray of hot tea, frowned at Kanmer. "She has to get out of those wet clothes, sire. Listen to her; she's coming down with a cough. Gods." She began to fuss, tugging Tinna from her seat. She was dragged to a room with a fire where she could rest, and given warm soup to fend away the cold she was acting out so well. She lay in the bed and patiently endured the fussing from the housekeeper and an assigned girl. She managed to hide the fact that her hair was drying back into its natural curl by twisting it up into a bun on her head. She had no idea what she would do later on, but she wasn't thinking that far ahead. Kanmer peeked into the room after a gentle knock on the door to bid her goodnight and to get well. He also stated that he sent a rider to the relay to inform her uncle of her situation.

Tinna waited for things to quiet down. The creaking of feet on the wooden floors soon ebbed, and the house fell into some semblance of silence, making only the sounds old houses made when decompressing after a hard day of being lived in.

Tinna threw the blanket aside and tossed her legs over the side of the massive bed, sliding off and landing with a soft thud onto the thick carpet. She padded in bare feet across the floor, lifting the latch to the door. She didn't have time to dally with flirtations and games to get what she needed—and the rainstorm had created an unsolvable problem with her hair. She would find his personal office. She knew it would hold something that would lead her to where his elusive brother hid.

She tread softly down the corridor, finding the stairs. The hall was pitch-black, but she managed to feel her way down the stairs and across the entrance hall floor of cool flagstones. She started in the one room where she'd been—the private parlor and what seemed to be a very badly stocked library. She walked in and closed the heavy door behind her. The room was dimly lit by the dying embers of the fire she'd sat in front of hours before.

She crossed the room, moving toward a discreet door that blended in with the old paneling. She cracked the door and looked in.

There was a small trace of light being cast into the room by the late-arriving moon. She slid through the door, and latched it behind her, looking around the room. Sitting with its back to the large leaded window was a great big desk, ordered and clean, scrolls piled into a neat pyramid, quills in a holder, a tidy row of ink bottles highlighted by the moonlight.

Tinna walked to the desk, ignoring the chairs, the black hearth and the tall bookshelves filled to capacity with scrolls bundled in white ribbons with black writing on the tips—ends sticking out like honeycombs. She slid behind the desk, and searched for a fire-stick, discovering a small cup of them next to the large four-wick candle. She snapped the fire stick in the middle, and the action caused a spark to appear, and the thick oil within caught fire. She folded the ends down so the flame wouldn't burn her, and used it to light the candle, blowing the stick out and disposing of it in its special little pewter pot with a safety lid.

She rifled through the scrolls on the desk, taking no care in keeping things the way they were left. A couple of them rolled onto the floor. Nothing, save for some newly written purchase orders awaiting pickup from the relay. She frowned, looking down at the drawers. She pulled the long, thin one in the center, and it didn't budge. She tugged again, and the drawer remained tightly sealed. Her frown appeared hideous in the strange light of the four-wick candle, and with a decisive and fearless pull, she broke the lock. The force of her tug made the drawer come out completely, and scatter the contents all over the floor.

She knelt there, frantically riffling through the shuffle of things—a few leather folders filled with promissory notes and two satchels of coins, which she stuffed into her shirt for future use. She reached for the side drawer closest to her while she knelt on the floor, and pulled it open. It was the bottom drawer, and it was very deep, made to hold rolled parchments standing on end. It was crammed with them, all tightly curled and pressing together. She pulled a tube up, and read the caption on the ribbon, tossing it aside. She began to pull them out one bone, squinting in the meager light to read the scrolls' ribbons.

She paused, seemingly unaware of the virtual nest of parchments around her knees. It occurred to her that there were several consistencies in the parchments as she threw them aside: There was a constant reoccurrence of purchase orders and receipts for an estate in Muath, they were dated at very regular intervals, and they were not filed among the many business-related papers lining the walls of the office. She began to sort through the scrolls at her knees, throwing the ones that seemed unmatched with the pattern she'd made out into a pile for further study if needed. She then cracked open the seals of each set of scrolls, carefully reading each copy of the purchase orders signed by the seller, the receipt of sale and delivery, even the information in the sigils stamped onto the documents by the relay itself, and all other papers clustered with each individual transaction.

All were very large orders. Orders of food, and livestock, services, slaves, and more. They were all going to this place in Muath, wherever that was. She frowned, reaching for the other scrolls she'd set aside, discovering a similar pattern among them, except these went to Alchar. Some deliveries even continued on to Alchar after taking delivery at Muath. She wasn't familiar with either place. But Alchar seemed the final destination. She stood, and gazed around the room, looking for a map. She realized that if there were a map in this house, it would be in the library.

She slid out of the office to the library, and ran her finger down the thick, leather spines of the books, finding at last a book containing a list of sovereignties under the High Throne, as well as the smaller duchies and such—there was an atlas within that showed the location of each of the houses listed within. She lugged the heavy tome back to the office and closed herself in, letting the book drop onto the desk. She heaved it open, looking for an index, running her finger down the alphabetical list. Her finger came to a halt at Muath; Alchar was not on the list.

She slid her finger along the dotted line that led to the page number, and read it, using her nails to leaf through the stack of pages to the one she wanted, and opened it up to the map before her. Muath was a rather large vice-sovereignty that covered both pages. The first thing that caught her eye was the name Alchar, which was a dot among many, indicating the presence of low noble houses. She chewed her lower lip as she examined the map, trying to place Muath by the surrounding sovereignties. She didn't recognize them, she had to refer back to the index a few times, and finally, by methodical identification of various contiguous vice-empires, she came to one she finally recognized. That was quite a distance from here…far west—near the coast, she realized, daunted by the notion of having to travel that far. There wasn't time for such things. She snapped the tome shut, and straightened, looking at the disarray she'd caused around her. With a sigh, she leaned forward and blew out the candles. She left the office, and closed the door behind her, and was just crossing the hearth when she saw the dark figure of Kanmer standing before her.

"What would bring you down here at this time of night?" he asked, genuinely curious, without suspicion in his voice.

Tinna assumed he hadn't seen her come out of his office, and controlled her relieved sigh as she shifted about in discomfort. She didn't know what to say, let alone what to do. A part of her was hugely conflicted, and it was interfering with the years of training and programming she'd endured for moments exactly like this. She fumbled in her head for words, and finally said:

"I was looking for you." She then let one shoulder of her loose nightgown fall, and then the other. The whole ensemble dropped to the floor in a heap of folds at her delicate ankles, the thunk of the money purses hitting the floor largely unheard by her rapt audience. She heard Kanmer's breath catch in his throat.

CHAPTER 21

Rhoa felt sick. Although over the last couple of weeks her muscles had reached some state that was beyond pain and soreness, thus making her life much more tolerable, and her ability to balance herself had improved greatly, she found her body beginning to rebel in other ways. It didn't take her long to realize what it really was, and she didn't know how to go about explaining it to Draphen. He and the other two had managed to develop their own rudimentary language, and spent most of the day talking among themselves. Almost all the time, they remained uncloaked by their camouflage, and wore loincloths as they moved along around her.

They moved quite quickly along the treetops, even though Rhoa was sure if they were on the ground, they'd be moving much faster. And now that she realized she was pregnant, that became a very big concern. Draphen however, was determined to put the last settlement as far behind them as possible, likely worried about the leader and his desire to stake a claim on his own little ground-dwelling wife. Before they'd left the settlement that day after their first night together, the leader had gotten into a bit of a scuffle with Draphen, and Tiko and Juri ushered Rhoa and her mate out of the settlement quickly while the leader was restrained by some of his own men. Draphen was not likely to slow down … Rhoa was worried.

Rhoa wasn't sure how Draphen would take the suggestion she was about to make, but she knew that in all practicality, they would be better off down on the forest floor. Things suddenly began to work out very advantageously for her as the day wore on, and she found herself thanking Arak again and again to herself because of it.

As the afternoon began to close in around them, they began to descend a bit, because the forest was thinning into smaller species of trees that were not structurally sound enough to hold four people, nor were their branches long and strong enough to inter-link any more. This was a relief to Rhoa; she hoped the forest would continue on so, and force them to take a ground route instead. She saw the change in her companions as they were forced to descend. Tiko and Juri became visibly agitated, their movements going from relaxed and athletic, like tree squirrels, to more jerky and bird-like. When Rhoa's feet felt soil beneath them, she made no effort to disguise her joy, and she collapsed into a cross-legged position, raking up a handful of humus and taking a good sniff of the fragrant mulch.

"Gods, it's nice to know I'm not at risk of falling to my death at any given moment," she murmured to Draphen.

He frowned. "They say that this patch of deciduous small trees is not so great and that we should be back into the tree-ways within a few days."

He perhaps thought this was reassuring to Rhoa, but instead, her stomach sank. Part of her was willing to go through with it. She was becoming quite decent at keeping up with the three, and her embarrassment from the occasional moment where she required carrying had managed to dissipate after a while. But now, she was afraid. Some switch had been turned on inside her that made her concerns shift over to the new life inside her, and she could not quiet that voice in her head that shouted at her to be more protective of the tiny life within her. She needed to tell him, and she knew she was only delaying it for her own selfish apprehensiveness. She looked up at his face; it was so handsome and attentive. He stooped, as if sensing by her sudden sag of the shoulders and furrow of the brow, that she was about to say something that required his full attention.

"Draphen … I think I should stay down here from now on. You fellows can travel up there. I think I need to stay down here," she articulated.

"You said you were doing fine. We all thought you were greatly improved."

"It's not that." She swallowed hard. "It's that, well, in the time with the others in that settlement … we started something." She lowered her eyes, and chewed her lip. "I think I'm carrying a baby now. It's been only a two weeks, but the signs are there. And I don't trust my body anymore, my equilibrium for one, and I'm always feeling sick to the stomach. I don't want to put the little thing in danger because I feel like larking through the trees. I can follow down here and keep up without a problem, and I won't be putting myself or the baby at risk." She spilled the last bit out in a flow of words that took a moment for Draphen to register and digest. He stood there, hunched in front of her, his brow slanting down in confusion, his mouth open in bewilderment.

* * * *

Tinna clutched her hands together, feeling a deep, heavy tug on her soul—a sensation that was fairly new to her, but something she was growing to understand and respect. It was a feeling of restraint. She looked at Kanmer, who'd stepped forward into the light of the glowing embers. He devoured her with his eyes, his arousal very evident in his loose leggings.

"I walked here to see you," she said, her voice cracking as if even her body was in congress with her defiant mind. "I feigned the illness," she declared.

Kanmer's lip was twisted into a delighted leer as his eyes roved over her body.

Tinna didn't want to do this. She couldn't believe she was hearing herself think this, this was a symptom of being up north too long—being willing to give up her sexual freedom to be with one man. And every time she thought of using her old tricks to get through certain situations, the feeling of resistance and protest came screaming to the front of her head. She clenched and unclenched her hands, feeling her skin go ten degrees cooler with every centimeter Kanmer closed between them. What was the alternative? she thought.

Her heart sank and she fought to hide the dark scowl that wanted to overtake her expression when she thought of it. She saw his hands begin to reach up, opening up in perfect unison into cups. As if time slowed down, Tinna watched his hands speed toward her breasts, and her eyes then moved up to his face, which was fully absorbed in the task of reaching for her. Fortunately, she wasn't left with the decision. Her instincts took control. With almost equal slowness, she saw herself, as if standing beside her own body, reach up, and grasp his head in her strong arms, twisting his head so that his shoulders would follow. She saw his arms flay out in surprise as she got a solid grip on his head, and he was now standing away from her and with a decisive and violent jerk, she snapped his neck.

The body crumpled at her feet on top of her pile of nightgown, and she was suddenly back inside herself, her fingertips and feet tingling with pins and needles, and her heart racing faster than any heart should. She controlled her breathing, and calmed her body down. She collected herself as she always had in the past, shaking off the emotional turmoil along with the chills and the usual goose bumps. She stooped and fished her money pouches from the nightgown.

187

She calmly stepped over the body, padded out of the room and, after climbing the stairs, she found Kanmer's room. She stole a pair of his woolen leggings, and one of his enormous loose tunics, which she belted around her hips. She grasped one of his cloaks, and gave the room a final scan for possible information sources; saw nothing except his old furniture. She was beyond caring about consequences now. By the time anyone found Kanmer's corpse, she'd be long gone.

She whistled for Orec's dog, and exited the house, the faithful hound at her heels. She walked barefoot to the stable and took his horse. She bothered only to furnish it with a bridle, and swung up onto its bareback. She kicked it into a trot, and then a canter, hoping to reach Orec's home before dawn.

* * * *

"Are you sure you want to do this?" Ailie's eyes were wide and stricken. Io clutched the puppy in her hands. He was very neat-looking, the stray fur had been trimmed, and his nails sanded down. Kailine had even made a little red-ribbon collar for him. Obviously he'd been well pampered while Tinna was away at Orec's house.

Tinna nodded, crossing her arms. "I need you to care for the little fellow a little while longer. I'll also need some more gold. I'm afraid I'm not as rich as I was a few days ago, and even with the coins I managed to take from Kanmer's, I won't be sufficiently supplemented." She tightened the strap over her shoulder, and adjusted the bag.

Kailine smiled nervously, seemingly unable to get off the subject that occupied her fears at that moment. "They're really friendly?"

"Yes, they are to me. And it's the only way I can get there as fast as possible. So to Ichru I must go, as your own mother suggested to me herself. Now about the gold—" a pouch of money was casually pressed into her palm before she could finish her sentence by Astlin, who smiled at her kindly. She returned the smile gratefully, and pocketed it. She looked at the group once more.

"All right then. We'll be here waiting for you," Orec assured Tinna. She turned to face him full on, a regretful look on her pretty features.

"Orec, I hope my actions do not bring consequences to your door—people will make the connection between you and me eventually—the other me, that is" she smiled warmly. He mirrored her gentle smile and shook his head reassuringly.

"Tinna, that horrible, murderous woman who claimed to be my long-lost niece was an imposter, using me to get to Kanmer. There was no way for me to know this and I'm such a trusting soul, starving for good company—" he feigned a helpless, dramatic sigh. "—what's an old man to do? I don't know what she did; I only know that she disappeared suddenly. Until someone tells me otherwise, that is."

She bent forward and embraced him tightly. She absolutely adored this man. The thought of leaving him—all of her friends made tears burn into her eyes. Tinna's small circle of concerned friends warmed her heart. She may not have shared everything with them, but they seemed to know something needed to be done and they trusted Tinna to do the right thing, putting their own lives in the balance to help her.

CHAPTER 22

Lemoram, where the Phanos archive was located, was a small city. It was occupied by the more bookish crowd, mostly supporters of the Archive and its acolytes and those who thought themselves part of that multitude. In part, it was a fair place, very manicured, and meticulously trimmed of any blemishes that might make it appear anything less than the perfect settlement. It was much larger and more imposing than Taneth had imagined, and it encouraged him to see that he might indeed find plenty of information in this archive.

Taneth was instantly made to feel savage-like in his appearance. He had lost the look of the scholar in his time with the people of the Arak. He'd grown his goatee out a bit, so that it looked more rugged, less trimmed and the lines less defined. He'd chopped off the longish hair he had and made it very short and close to the scalp, which seemed the appropriate hair to have when among the Araki men. He realized he was trying to look like Rigerd to some measure. All he needed was a silver loop in his ear, plait his beard, and he'd be his twin; albeit a bit less imposing in stature.

He wore the common clothing of a village Wiseman. Here, he rode through crowds of archivists from the Phanos library, scholars, and highbred seekers of knowledge. Those who were part of some order or other were garbed in richly detailed uniforms and chasubles. They were all as scrupulously groomed as their pristine community. They looked at him on the mare that was Taphenus Fox's dam, with a black pony and an exhausted-looking child in oversized clothing behind him. The people did not bother to hide their disdain at this newest blemish to appear in their perfect city. He hoped to find an inn as quickly as possible, and a livery for the horses so he could clean himself up and get started on this stupid project.

The inn, he discovered, was a very plush place. Thankfully, Rigerd had given him a good budget, probably familiar with the costliness of this pretentious city. Taneth stood in the foyer of this very fine-looking inn, fidgeting with his pack, while the proprietor looked him over like he was a piece of meat at the butcher's.

"Welcome to the Forest Wind," the flamboyant character declared with a dramatic wave of the arms.

Taneth suppressed an amused smirk. All his life, he'd been a magnet for such men. In school, he'd been flirted with to no end. One of his roommates in the eleventh year was madly in love with him. They'd been such good friends; it was difficult not to forgive him his eager efforts to win Taneth over. Taneth constantly had to remind the poor young man that he had no such desires. But he never actually did get the point, in the end, and it was just easier for him to not be Taneth's friend anymore—so he decided to tell Taneth he wished no more of his company. It made Taneth sad to think of him all of a sudden.

"And is this your son? Isn't he just adooooorable?" The man reached out a finely manicured hand and ruffled Hanru's already unkempt hair, causing the boy to slide behind Taneth's legs and hide. "I see you have horses out there; we don't usually like to leave them there…you know what sorts of things they leave behind and all. I'll have my assistant go and have them brought to the stable for you. In the meantime, perhaps you would like to see your room?" Taneth nodded, following the thin, handsome fellow with the effeminate stride. He found a door just off the elegant foyer, and threw it open with panache. "It's not our best, I dare say, but it's one of the better rooms. We have a rather well-to-do—and dare I mention rather handsome as well—gentleman staying. But I'm sure you're not the sort to fuss about such things. You look very rugged." Again, the young man's eyes took in Taneth from head to toe. "Anyway, how long do you plan to stay?"

"I'm not sure. I've got a large research project to complete. Never fear, the clan's chieftain has furnished me with the gold I need to insure my boy and I have suitable lodging."

The proprietor nodded gravely. "Well, that's good news. In that case, make yourself at home. We will notify you when meals are being served, and if you are not in, we will set something aside for you unless we are notified otherwise. Is there anything I can get for you directly? A bath perhaps? A shave?"

"A bath would be very nice. Actually, enough hot water for two; Hanru here is pretty dirty from the trip, aren't you, brat?" Hanru clung to Taneth's leg still, looking up at him with wide, stricken eyes. "Then we'd like to just relax until dinner. I think the research can wait until morning. It's been a long journey."

Suppertime came an hour or so after Taneth and Hanru were bathed and made presentable. Taneth took a little time redefining the lines of his beard and trimming it down. His short hair could not be remedied, but at this point, he did not care so much. He was a village Wiseman, after all. There was no shame in that. He'd finally acquired the corresponding markings of a Wiseman—they'd been done by one of the women who'd come with the clan who'd delivered the ponies. She'd tattooed a series of markings right along the underside of his existing tattoos from Hildercross. It was impossible for anyone to mistake what and who he was now. He found he liked the look of the insignia on his face. It made him feel a bit better about being in this posh city. He belonged there as much as any member of the order of Phanos.

He dressed in common clothes made for him by some of the young women of the village, mainly Indra. Most of the people were convinced both Rhoa and Tinna were dead. Indra did not give up hope that Taneth would admit it too, one day. She catered to his needs, and provided all sorts of little things for him, making sure that when the day did come that Taneth's hope was gone, she'd be the first one he'd be reminded of, by all the things she furnished his life with. She had a good eye for clothing, and he appreciated how well he looked in her fine linen tunic and three-quarter-length trousers of such rich brown. He slid on the simple sandals he wore around the lodge sometimes, and took Hanru's hand, leading him to the inn's community room where they would wait for dinner to be announced.

There were four other people in the room when they entered. In one corner, a young woman of exceptional beauty sat with her legs crossed in an elegant yet casual gown, reading from a thick book. By the hearth, a tall, lanky gentleman sat in long leather boots and a waistcoat the same blue color the sky got in late summer just before the darkness took over. Sitting in the bay window was another beautiful woman, but this one of a different beauty than the willowy creature in the corner. She was a rounded, healthy woman, with large breasts and soft curves. On her lap sat a little girl with gold ringlets and eyes that were periwinkle blue.

Her chubby mother had the same gold hair and eyes, and lips that were full and smiling. She had been showing the girl pictures in an elaborate picture book, but lost the child's attention to Hanru, instantly intrigued with the presence of another child close to her age. Taneth and Hanru had drawn the attention of all the occupants in the room, who looked up to see the newest faces among them.

He smiled at everyone, and let go of Hanru's hand, finding the chair across the hearth from the gentleman.

The gentleman's gaze remained locked on Taneth. He had eyes so light in color they appeared almost unnatural. His intent gaze made Taneth uncomfortable. Taneth grabbed the first book from the pile on the mantel, and sat down. The bald gentleman stirred, and uncrossed his legs, switched the dominant one, and then resumed staring. Taneth was about to get up and walk away when he spoke.

"I'm always struck dumb by recognition based on residual memories of others," he said, which sounded like utter nonsense to Taneth. He looked up at him to make sure he was indeed addressing Taneth. "It's just so rare to begin with, but to actually recognize someone from another person's mind ... that's just shy of miraculous." The man's piercing gaze was very much locked onto Taneth, his chin leaning on two fingers, his elbows propped on the armrest most casually.

"I beg your pardon, but is that supposed to make sense to me or something?" Taneth asked.

The man smiled. "You are Taneth. That child there ... that's Hanru." He turned to look at the boy, who was busy getting the little girl's attention by putting another picture book on the floor near her, and sitting in front of it as he leafed through the pages.

Taneth's brow furrowed up into a patch of confused wrinkles and he frowned.

"How did you—"

"As I said, it's a residual memory from a mind that was extremely difficult to penetrate, dare say. What an unusual creature she is. If I had not found her thoughts of you in there, I probably would have made a move on her myself. But I am a man of honor," he laid his pale, long-fingered hands on his royal-blue clad chest.

The little hairs on Taneth's spine stood up, and he straightened, leaning in toward the gentleman. "I'm not exactly sure what you're going on about, but I think you should elaborate." His voice was tense and angry, but betrayed just the slightest hope.

The gentleman's brow rose and he leaned in, narrowing his eyes as he peered at Taneth searchingly. He then seemed surprised by something and leaned back.

"I just assumed ... So she hasn't returned yet," he said. "I'm sorry ... I'm sure she's fine. She's very self-sufficient. And without being burdened by the other girl, she's probably moving much faster and will be on her way home soon."

"All right, no more games. Who are you referring to?" Taneth's skin tingled, and his heart was in his mouth.

"Oh, come on, one doesn't have to be a Chaiva to realize we're talking about Aitinna," the gentleman grunted in disgust.

Taneth leapt to his feet, sat, and then leapt to his feet again, bending down in front of the gentleman and pushing his face right up into Phenmal's. "I don't know what game you're playing—"

"Young man, I have no motivation to play any games with anyone. I'm not the playful sort. Now please step away; I'm not comfortable with people in my personal space."

Taneth's heart thundered in his chest, and he reluctantly sank down into the chair, realizing that his behavior wasn't going to get him any answers. When he was settled, the gentleman leaned forward a bit. "You are here looking for her?"

"No. She's supposed to be dead."

"Please, I am a Chaiva, young man; you don't believe she's dead for a second. I see right into that overactive brain of yours." He brushed Taneth off with a wave of the hand.

"When did you see her?"

"My goodness, two weeks back, possibly a few days more. Came to my house by chance, hurt from something, but—No, no, don't panic; it was nothing. She's probably decided to follow her desire to know what is going on with the dragons. She might have accepted it as another mission; aside from the little dog for the boy."

"The wh—?"

"Yes, she has a little dog for the boy."

"She's crazy," Taneth surmised. "She's miles and miles from where she should have been, and she's still worried about the dog for Hanru?"

"I don't think it's crazy; I think it's honorable. It shows an exceptional loyalty and affection for those she loves. Her distance from her original location is not of her doing, please be assured. She and the other girl were taken to someplace remarkably far-off from here. But she'll make her way back back—there's no doubt. If I am here, from where we left one another, it means she can't be too far."

"What's this other mission?"

"Well, the way her mind was working, I'm sure it has to do with the dragons, boy."

"She's taking on the dragons? She is mad!"

"Well, it wouldn't be exactly taking them on, if she is indeed doing what I think she is. It's more like an investigation; something more benign than coming face-to-face with them, I'm sure. Just rest assured it's nothing she can't handle. She'll be home with the dog soon. She's not someone to break a promise, especially to a child. That boy is very special to her. And you, you are extremely important to her, as well. She does what she is doing surely in an effort to protect you, the boy, and your people, because she has come to love all of you."

Taneth sat as still as possible, afraid that if he moved even the slightest bit, the man would stop talking. He did not utter a word until he was sure Phenmal was finished. "I knew she was alive. And Rhoa?"

"Oh yes, that girl. What a character, eh? She and the Nimrath chose their own direction; poor thing couldn't bear to be outside of the trees. And Rhoa had grown much attached to him. Lost contact with them almost at once…too bad, really. Rhoa has a very sexy mind, albeit a little bit erratic and noisy at times." A smile curled up on Phenmal's lip.

"She's on her way home with the Nimrath?" Taneth hissed, trying to keep the volume down as to not bother the other patrons. The moment was temporarily enhanced by the joyful giggle of the little girl and Hanru as they found a particularly amusing image in the book they were looking at.

"Right. The Nimrath … you never really met him, did you? Yes, he somehow managed to be transported with the ladies to the part of the world closer to my home. He became one of the party, so to speak."

Taneth was struck dumb. He couldn't even envision what a Nimrath looked like, let alone imagine it being part of a party that included his Tinna and Rhoa. It was beyond bizarre. But here it was, right before him, the definitive proof that Tinna was alive … at least she had been two or three weeks ago. And she had a dog for Hanru. "Why are you here?"

"For the Phanos archive," the gentleman responded. "Tinna's visit inspired me to get involved. I found nothing of consequence in the first place, so I've decided to visit some other archives 'round the region, see if there's anything I can find to further the suppositions we came up with."

"You're in contact with her?"

"No," he said flatly, seeming a bit disappointed. "I had hoped I'd be able to use the relay to get information to her, but as you know, the relay has been targeted as well. I think however, that she doesn't need me to send her any information. She's very resourceful. Her need for my assistance was probably unnecessary the moment we parted ways at the first Phanos archive. I must admit, I have just proven myself to be of some measure of usefulness by running into you. I have just calmed a tempest of worry. At least that's something."

Phenmal reached into his waistcoat and removed a pipe; tamping out the old stuff, he dipped into a little pocket for his pouch of filler, stuffing the elegant little bowl, and lighting it thoughtfully with a small stick lit with the flames of the fire in the hearth.

Taneth could not disagree with what Phenmal had just said. He had indeed been very useful. He had proven at last that Taneth's hopes were not wasted; and for that, he was never more grateful to a single person in his entire life as he was at that very instant.

"Thank you. That is very gratifying to know," the gentleman said, smiling. Taneth looked up at him in amazement at first, and then just started to laugh.

CHAPTER 23

Seashells were a commodity where Tinna was born; the ocean, a thing people described but never saw. Her country was landlocked, walled in by mountains to the east and north, and plains to the west, and bordered by the far southern land of Kytrine, a harsh, desert land inhabited by a dark-skinned, resilient people who guarded their territory and their privacy jealously.

Tinna knew a great deal about many peoples, and traveled to many wonderful places, but she had yet to see an ocean. She'd once purchased some lovely little nautilus shells and a few lovely clamshells with fascinating mother-of-pearl lining the insides. They were carefully tucked into a small purse among her things back with Ailie. But not even that minute preview of the ocean's beauty could prepare her for her first viewing of it. She'd never seen a body of water large enough that she couldn't see the opposite shore.

As she rode her horse on the coastal road she had been told to follow, she climbed up over a hill. She pulled her horse to a stop, hardly believing what she was seeing. Below her, the land sprawled out to the sea, still a ways from where she sat on horseback. But there it was, the vast grayish-blue plain beyond the thick grassy hills, and the wetlands, which at current high tide, looked like a field of green laced with silver filigree. Huge white birds glided about on the wind, which smelled of iodine and lifted Tinna's loose curls off her shoulders. She was suddenly overwhelmed with a feeling of smallness as she gazed out at the horizon that blended with the sky like a watercolor painting. The birds cried, the ocean breeze blew, and Tinna's eyes teared-up, for both the blessing of what she was witnessing, and for the longing for home. She found it in herself to nudge her horse onto the road, never once allowing her gaze to stray from the immense ocean at her side.

As she neared the ocean, she began to hear it. She'd ridden around the wetlands on roads painstakingly marked where people should or should not stray. It smelled of old shellfish, and the reedy wetlands were alive with birds, soaring above the vermicular streams that rose and fell with the tide. She followed the road to a rocky outcropping where the road led her upward. The higher she rode, the louder the thunder. She only realized it was the ocean's song she'd been hearing when she was riding within a few meters of the cliff-side. She stopped to observe the ocean battering the smooth boulders littering the foot of the cliff below her.

She was awestruck by the power of it. No description could in any way instill the true sense of amazement as the real thing could. It took her longer to reach Ichru than she had planned because she had to stop occasionally to take in the unbelievable views the road to Ichru offered. Gigantic rock formations shaped like haystacks protruded from the hissing surf just off the cliff-line, like lonely sentinels each—growing paler against the ocean mists the farther out they were from the land. Fishing ships rode along the horizon, followed by clouds of gulls. Tinna wondered what it would be like to live in such a place as she moved on. She was annoyed that she'd been only a few days away from the coast through most of her travels and never thought to actually veer off her aimless path to see it.

Ichru itself was a picture of beauty. The small fishing town was nestled in a cranny between two high fjord-like hills, split by a glimmering river. The village straddled the river, connected by a number of bridges of varying styles. The water's rocky edge bristled with docks and other protrusions to which many boats were tied. They bobbed gently with the water movement.

It was the last place one would imagine finding a dragon-summoner. Such a title created a far more sinister image of a place in the Tinna's mind—not a charming little seaside berg under the late summer sun. She thought perhaps Ailie had given her the wrong directions or town or something, but it turned out that this was indeed the summoner's home. Tinna found him in a quaint little cottage nestled on a walled-in plot of land wedged between a number of similar stone huts along a very small lane just on the periphery of the picturesque little village. It seemed it was a morning of surprises for her. The summoner himself was also the opposite of what one would picture a dragon-summoner to be.

When she rapped on the door, she could hear shuffling feet, amplified with every step closer to the entrance. It cracked open and a pair of deep brown eyes looked up at her, shaded by a set of the fuzziest eyebrows she'd ever seen. His unassuming brown eyes were encased in the folds of skin, lines, and wrinkles of a man who had laughed and smiled a good deal in his lifetime. He was a sack of loose bones, his skin papery and fragile-looking, some of it almost transparent, revealing old, tired veins pumping blue blood back to his heart. His face was a collection of wrinkles and angles, enhanced by only the two huge caterpillar eyebrows, and a tuft of white hair like a hare's tail protruding from a very pointed, decisive-looking chin.

"I can't imagine good fortune would be so good as to bring a lovely woman like you to my door just as a reward for my years of service to this world. So I'll go ahead and assume that you're here for dragons."

Tinna nodded. She had no idea what it was, but she had only just realized she had a little "thing" for diminutive old men. Her kind host Orec, and now this old fellow … they inspired a very strong sense of softness within her; they made her want to tuck them under her arm and take them with her, fuss over them, give them as many treats and little pleasures she could afford to give them. Why, she did not know. She just realized that she liked little old men, and that was that. He widened the door, and waved his hand to indicate that she should enter.

Now, Tinna was a petite creature, despite her being a powerhouse of muscles and strength. She was surprised that she had to duck through the doorway when she was invited in—an action she could never recall doing before in all her days. She ducked under the low doorway, somewhat pleased for once to be taller than someone else for a change.

"I'm surprised I haven't had a crowd outside my door of late, with all the burning and destruction going on," he lamented, latching the door behind her. He shuffled in his leather slippers across the small space, reaching for an iron kettle, which he filled with water from a spigot protruding from a collection barrel cleverly placed over the sink. "But I'm not as popular as I used to be. There are younger, more dashing summoners around these days. No need for me anymore. Either way, it doesn't matter; we only summon them, we don't have all the answers. But don't leave right away, I'm making tea." He closed off the spigot and carried the kettle to the hearth, hanging it on the hook over the small fire. He shuffled to his small cupboard, and removed a couple of tiny tea-bowls, placing them on a tray he probably rarely used.

"I'm not here to find out why the dragons are doing what they are doing … I need to contact Ledroran. He told me I could at any time. I need to now."

The old man paused, and looked at her. "A dragon gave you his name, and not just a dragon, but Ledroran, nonetheless. You are indeed blessed." He smiled, albeit a tad stiffly. He reached for a tea-urn, and lifted off the little domed lid, sniffing the contents, changing his mind, and choosing another urn. Content with the aroma of this blend, he took out a tiny silver spoon and dropped exactly one heaping teaspoon into each of the teacups. He put the tea urn back in its place among the others on the shelf, and then shuffled to another cupboard that served as a small pantry. He opened the pastry box, and studied its contents, and having chosen, he went to fetch a little plate to put his choices on.

"I'll call him for you. How can I not? But candidly, my dear, the way the dragons have been behaving lately, I'm finding it very hard to feel good about what I am anymore," he declared, putting two tired-looking pastry puffs onto the plate. He put that onto the tray, and closed up the pantry, now waiting for the water to boil. He stood there, in all his fading dignity, studying Tinna with his old, wizened eyes.

"Come now, old man, you should know dragon-kind well enough to be sure they would never commit such acts without a perfectly justifiable reason."

"There is nothing justifiable in life, things just happen. It is we who presume ourselves so superior as to decide such things, we who determine what is, and what is not justified. We hold even nature to those standards, as if we have the right to dictate. So what they might deem justified could be entirely different by our own standards. It's all horse crap if you ask me, all of it!" he suddenly snarled with a passion dredged up from sometime back in the days of his youth. The sudden burst of energy faded, and he looked tired again, his ancient hand lowering from its gesture of conviction, his eyes going distant.

"Perhaps that is so. Perhaps their point of view would certainly differ from the rest of the world and humanity, but that's the point." Tinna sighed. "Humanity will not understand. Ever. Even if they know the truth behind it all, or they continue to live in ignorance, they will always have this destruction to hold against the dragons ..." She paused, sighing wearily. Tinna was tired of this debate, not from this particular exchange, but from the same arguments going back and forth in her own mind. And she dreaded to consider what Taneth would think of it all. She diligently avoided that thought, and looked up at her present companion, who looked at her with great intensity.

"It is only through the eyes of certain people—those who understand the world, the dragons, and the bigger picture—who would believe the dragons should be given the benefit of the doubt. Their fate relies entirely on the hope of people like us, old man. I would have thought someone born with your gift would at least maintain the slightest reservation about the current and universal opinion on the matter. They have shown so much trustworthiness in the past, I think they deserve at least that. Are you not placing yourself into the category of those who judge unfairly, with this newfound shame for who and what you are?"

He gazed at her, his frame wavering slightly on his tired feet. His eyes fell a bit, and he sighed. "My shame is indeed reprehensible. But it is because of what I am ... where I live ... the community I serve, that this shame exists. I face judgment every day from those around me. They think I keep truths from them; their trust is long gone. And whatever one might say about honor and ethics, the thing that really matters is what and where you are at this very moment. The past is the past, the future just speculation. You exist in the present, and where I am in the present is what I am concerned with. It doesn't matter if the dragons are right or wrong, it only matters that an old man is being shunned and mistreated by a community he was once an integral part of. Even by his own children. There is my shame. In the here and now." He frowned.

The water was boiling, a little plume of steam puffing from the swan-like spout. Tinna stood and used a frayed felted wool potholder to lift it off the fire. She put it on the thick table-top in front of his little tray. He looked at it blankly for a moment, and then reached for it, carefully filling each cup.

"Then your reputation must be restored," Tinna declared. "And perhaps that is treading into the speculative future in saying so, but it solves the problem in the here and now."

"Is that why you are here? To restore the world's faith in the goodness of dragon-kind and in part, making me an acceptable member of the human community again? Do you think they will ever be trusted the same way, or fully forgiven for all the death they have caused?" He frowned darkly, and lifted the tray, waiting for Tinna to sit in the musty old chair—one of two, facing the hearth.

She glanced around the tiny cottage, taking in the single little bed, the practical use of the small space, and the signs of a man with little money to spend on the little pleasures old people deserved after a lifetime of giving to others. He was right. Tinna had thought about it endlessly. Even if the world were to discover that the dragons were being manipulated like great marionettes by a human hand, there would always be an undercurrent of distrust and anger for their actions. It didn't matter, though. She had to do what she could to stop them in the here and now. Let the past become the past, and let the future contend with the issues of forgiveness and healing. She realized, with a touch of sadness, that the people would never really hear the truth. The dragons would just stop attacking, and the perpetrator of the real manipulation quietly disposed of, and nobody would really know why the dragons did what they did. They would forever be stigmatized for this bizarre set of events. But at least they'd be given a chance to redeem themselves. And the Trinity would remain unscathed—even though at this point in time, she wondered if it deserved to be.

The old man put the tray onto a table made especially to hold it. He lifted up a teacup and handed it to Tinna, and then took his own, sinking with a bit of a tired groan into his own chair, the upholstery flat and hard from years of his bottom pressing into it. "I can see you have been burdened with the truth of all this madness," he said. "Your eyes and face speak of the turmoil that goes on inside your head. Cheer up. My faith in the scaled-ones has not faded, as you might think it has. I'm just a bitter, lonely old man, who receives no more visitors, and whose children are ashamed to be related to him. I see a world where people make judgments on things they really never truly understand simply to make themselves feel like they have some degree of control. Look at me ... look at this place. A far cry from the pride I lived with years ago. I suppose my optimism shrank along with my desire to be anything more than what I have become."

He sipped his tea, his eyes gazing at the flames of his meager little fire. Tinna smiled at him. "I suppose I should be happy you came to me, and not to one of those upstarts who understands nothing of the art of summoning, and will never be held to any standard when it comes to this gift—nobody really knows quality any more. It's a dying art. The world changes so. People expect less of one another with each passing year. I had a wonderful relationship with the dragons. The new ones, they don't really care. It's all about showmanship now. Oh, it's all going to pot. The whole world is going to pot. Maybe the dragons had the right idea to begin with." His dug his bony fingers into one of the pastries, and he tore off a piece, popping it into his toothless mouth, and chewed noisily. "What did make you choose me?"

"A friend of mine suggested your services. There were summoners much closer to where I was, but I trusted her decision. They have a good idea what the situation is, too ... enough to know how to help me move forward in the most efficient and stealthy manner as possible. She knew of you through others; she is well known for knowing the right people; people trust her enough to learn from her, as well as impart their own helpful secrets." She smiled. The old man's eyes glistened. He seemed to like the idea of being embroiled in something that involved the words "stealth" and "secrets."

"Very well then. We'll begin after you eat your sticky bun," he declared. Tinna glanced down at the sad-looking baked goods, and sighed, picking it up with a look of resignation on her face.

CHAPTER 24

Draphen had been insistent on keeping Rhoa in his sights pretty much all day, except to scout out what was going on up above them and to make sure he followed the same direction as their guides. Tiko and Juri still accompanied them, but always took to the trees. At this moment, he had left her for a while to join his friends up in the trees. Rhoa was walking idly along, heading where he had told her to go. She was emotionally drained. Draphen had been acting strange since she declared herself with child, and she was afraid it would drive him away. Part of her wasn't afraid of being alone, but the other part of her wanted him to be with her always. She was his wife, after all.

As she strode along, the limbs above her cracked and shook with great noise, and leaves began to rain down. She stepped out of the way, and looked up. Someone would have had to have been moving very quickly through the trees to make such a racket, and before she could even think of what it could be, something tangible and invisible broke through the canopy and fell with a horrid crack onto the root system in front of her. She screamed. The camouflage was scraped with blood from lacerations from what was obviously a fall from very, very high. As the camouflage dissipated, she was horrified to see Juri lying there with his eyes wide open, his naked form twisted and mauled from the fall. Then she heard the clear, unmistakable voice of her husband.

"RHOA! RUN!"

The trees began to thrash again, and she did not hesitate. She broke into a sprint. Run, she could do. Running, she was very good at. She'd jogged next to horses her entire life. This was her forte. She wanted to stay, to wait for Draphen, but she did not question his command. She knew to trust him implicitly. She was afraid. Terrified. She wanted to know where he was, what was happening, and who killed Juri, but she ran. Not just for her, but for their child.

"MAHROUK!"

Rhoa knew that voice and that word. It took a moment of rustling through her memory to recall exactly the circumstances where she'd heard that before ... but it came back to her. She stopped momentarily, and twisted around, her eyes wide and frantic, looking for shifting light and movement in the surrounding landscape. The voice seemed to be coming from everywhere. It occurred for her to look up and she saw him, clinging upside down to a heavy branch like a squirrel—some oversized, chameleonic squirrel.

"MahROUK!" it muttered again.

"Mahrouk? What in the name of Arak is that supposed to mean? Is that the only word you know, you big lumbering testicle? Where is Draphen? DRAY-FENNNN. What did you do to him, you big piece of shit?" she screamed up at him.

The figure only hung there staring at her in his invisibility.

It occurred to Rhoa to run again. Her legs hurt and her lungs were about to give in on her. She leaned her hands on her knees for a moment to catch her breath, gazing at the strange shadow on the ground this invisible obstruction made. She shot into a run without warning, leaping over roots and fallen flora, praying for Arak to bless her with his spirit, endurance, and speed—but He blessed her with something better: She broke from the trees and stumbled smack into the middle of a Gypsy camp.

* * * *

Taneth did not shirk his original mission to Lemoram. The very next morning after breakfasting with Phenmal, dressed in the only decent robe he owned, he left the inn with Hanru and made his way to the Phanos archive. He was greeted by one of the members of the order, who was just opening up the door to allow the public inside.

"Welcome." She was a woman in her sixties, perhaps, with a sweet, docile expression. Her eyes were alight with intelligence, and her cheeks flushed at the sight of this handsome young Wiseman who stared so intently into her eyes. "I am sister Marolose," she introduced herself with a curt bow. "Have you come from far?"

"A few days south of here. I'm here to do some research for my village. About the origins of the people of Arak, in particular."

"A noble project." The woman grinned. Her eyes then moved down to Hanru, who was gazing up at her with his hand latched to Taneth's sleeve. "It seems a dull and uneventful sort of activity to involve a child in."

"I don't know what else to do with him."

"Well, I suppose he can participate in the school during the day. He will be with other children, and he can draw, and read stories. You have taught him such things, I presume?"

"Yes, of course. I've been schooling all the village children. I'm sure they're all relieved to be given this unforeseen break from their studies while I'm away. Except for Hanru here. He doesn't get a break." Taneth smiled down at the child, who sighed.

"Do I have to go to school?" the boy asked, his face pouting.

"You don't have to, but your other choice is to sit quietly for the day while I study some texts."

The boy made up his mind almost instantly. "Do they have paints?"

"I'm sure they do," Sister Marolose replied with a big smile. The cowl that covered her head and hid her hair, made her face seem amplified in all of its expression. She reached out her hand for Hanru to take. "I'll take you to the school, then. When your father's done, he will come for you. All right?" Hanru nodded.

"Perhaps Ulai will be there, too," Taneth added. He spoke of the friend he'd made at the inn, the little blonde girl. Hanru seemed even more decided to go.

"Go on inside. You should meet another of my order who would be glad to help you set up a little area to do your work. I will be back to help you find the documents you need."

"All right then. Off you go, Han." Taneth sent the boy along with the sister, and he walked into the main hall of the archive.

Libraries and archives always had that particular smell he loved. It was a combination of leather, old paper and sometimes the ink itself, depending on what type of ink each institution preferred to use. It permeated the building like a perfume. He was instantly brought back to Hildercross, and the solemn halls, to his corner of the library in the section where the least desired books were kept, which had been his sanctuary for many a day. He felt a loss, all of a sudden, for the place that had been burnt to ruins. He wondered if any of the students had gotten out, or his professors, like Professor Nelnath whom he loved to torment so, or the headmaster. It was like he'd delayed thinking about it until that very moment.

He pushed the thoughts out of his mind, and looked around in the darkened hall for some assistance. He found it in the form of a teenage boy, an initiate, and the most uncoordinated, gawky, spotty-faced kid he'd ever seen in his life.

"Good morning. I am Taneth, Wiseman of the Clan Thamatoch," he said, realizing that this was the first time he'd ever heard himself say that to anyone. It made him feel fortunate and important. He realized how lucky he was that Rigerd was such a good man to overlook that Taneth had never graduated from the academy, and to give him the title regardless. "I have come to do some research. I was told you would help me find a good spot and assist me in preparing for my work here."

"I am Novice Irith," the gawky boy replied, squinting at Taneth with his huge eyes. "I would be happy to help you." His voice broke a couple of times in that short sentence. Poor thing, Taneth thought. Reminded him of himself to some extent, but he hadn't been as unfortunate as the boy; he'd never suffered from so many pimples, nor was he so nearsighted that he had to squint to see, but the boy's awkwardness was familiar. Not just to himself, but it reminded him of the other students he'd walked out on that day. They were all probably dead now.

Novice Irith helped him find a suitable table by a window, set him up with parchments, ink, and several quills, brought Taneth a special lamp that reflected the light back onto the desk, and a pitcher of water with a thick, bubbled-glass goblet. When Sister Marolose returned, Irith scurried off. She took down a list of Taneth's needs and went off to find some texts to begin with. An hour later, when Taneth had already accumulated a stack of reading material, and was poring over a particularly confusing historical text, Phenmal arrived, accompanied by the awkward boy, who set him up on the table adjacent to Taneth's. He waited for his own assistant to arrive after that.

"Hello again, young Wiseman. How's research?"

"Tedious. I hate research."

"Yes. Not exactly exciting, is it?"

Someone from another table shushed at them.

Phenmal rolled his eyes and smiled. There were perhaps six or seven other researchers in the hall, and the peace was marred only by the occasional member of the Phanos order moving in and out of the archives—bringing the researchers their desired information.

"Tell you what, why don't you do my research and I'll do yours? It would make a pleasant change … and perhaps also lend a fresher view on it for one another."

Taneth thought about this for a second. "And what exactly are you researching?"

"Oh, this is the hard part—it's fairly vague. I'm trying to figure out what is going on presently with the dragons by looking for similar patterns in the past."

"There is no history of such things," Taneth muttered. Someone else shushed them.

"No. But when I was talking to Aitinna, she mentioned one of her theories—and it got me thinking. She said perhaps the dragons were preventing the spread of a plague by burning out places where there were signs of it. Mind you, it doesn't explain why they're only flattening places that are ruled by the High Throne, but perhaps that too has something to do with it—the major cities are all the main relay points—a plague could easily travel and very quickly, I dare say, if a single relay rider were to contract it."

"That is good thinking." Taneth's brows rose.

"So, I'm going back to look at the patterns of other plagues, mainly the worm-skin plague, which has recurred a number of times throughout history and every time, nearly taken out the entire human population. I want to see how that spread, and if that somehow correlates with where the dragons have been going to burn off any creeping limbs of the illness."

"Sounds like a good start. But why would the dragons feel any need to stop the worm-skin plague? They never have in the past, and candidly, they were probably glad of our numbers being diminished so greatly. We are, after all, their greatest competitors for resources. I even thought during my younger years back at the academy, that perhaps they encouraged that disease to spread." Taneth laughed at the foolishness of his words, waving his comment away. Phenmal on the other hand, did not laugh. Taneth's gaze locked on him, and he let his jocularity fade.

They were interrupted by a new face, a member of the order, who poked his head in between their tables and smiled in an insincere sort of manner. "I'm afraid the other people in the research room have voiced some complaints about your incessant chatter. Perhaps you could take it outside?"

"No. They can live with it. Get out of my face this instant or I'll tell your

Father Superior what you've been doing with Sister Fayne in the archives at night," Phenmal growled, glaring the brother down.

The Phanos archivist withdrew as if Phenmal's gaze burnt him, and scuttled away. Taneth blushed.

"What if they did?" Phenmal asked Taneth.

"I'm sorry?" Taneth shook his head, snapping out of his embarrassment for the poor archivist Phenmal had scared out of his robes.

"Hypothetically speaking … what if they did encourage the spread of the plague?"

"What would that have to do with what they're doing now?"

"Just answer the question."

"Gods, I'd imagine there wouldn't be a dragon left in the world after the general population found out. I'm surprised there hasn't been a rebellion yet, just over this last bit of bad behavior."

"That's because on the scheme of things, we're more informed than everyone else in the world. The rest of the world is just beginning to realize that this destruction is proliferating not only locally, but everywhere under the High Throne. But by then, what forces will be left to fight them? The strength of the Empire has been destroyed, along with the relay and the lines of nobility and government. The dragons have thrown the world into chaos. All places except here, the places that are under the Keepers."

"All right, so that's possible. But what does this have to do with now? They're destroying everything related to the High Throne. Their leaving the archives, and the other institutions created by the highest order of the Keepers, alone. What does that mean?"

"Well, perhaps the Keepers have something to do with it. The High Throne is no match for the Keepers. To them, it is but an obstacle to creating the perfect world where all races live with the common desire to attain betterment and knowledge."

"Sounds crazy."

"Perhaps, but what I'm thinking is: The dragons don't care for human-kind in general. We cut down forests, we till the soil until it's as fertile as a desert, we kill one another constantly, and we reproduce indiscriminately; the only entity of our race that the dragons acknowledge as worthy is the Keepers. Perhaps they're in collusion to destroy the High Throne and render the race powerless to fight back so they can take over at last and set things right."

"Phenmal, that all sounds … feasible; but the High Throne only rules the empires within Oromoii. The rest of the world doesn't answer to them."

"Who do their empires answer to?"

"They don't answer to the Keepers, Phenmal. They cooperate with them perhaps, but answer to them, no. Besides, they've had thousands of years to do that before, why now?"

212

"That's why I brought it up. What if the occurrence of the worm-skin plague, which has been somewhat consistent over the centuries, was the perfect opportunity for the Keepers and the Trinity to rein in the human race, and to cut back on the power of the High Throne, or its equivalent of the day?"

"The Trinity, now? Sounds like quite the conspiracy between two of the world's most incredible powers. But why leave it at that, Phenmal, why not just go the extra step and say that the Trinity and the Keepers initiated and spread the plague, and be done with it." He chuckled. "No thanks, I'll stick to researching the Araki people."

Phenmal's eyes narrowed even more, and he sat back in his chair, remaining deafeningly silent for a good ten minutes. He then turned his chair to face Taneth. "That's brilliant. Bloody genius."

"What are you going on about now?" Taneth let his hands fall with two thumps onto his tome, and he sighed.

"What if they did? What if they have been culling the race with this disease?"

"Then why just burn things down, now? Why didn't they just go and throw some of the plague riddled corpse into some water supply somewhere and be done with it?" Taneth's tone was bored with the whole festival of speculation they were having.

"Because it's not the time. We're still recovering from the last plague … it wasn't so long ago, in proportion to its previous occurrences."

"Phenmal, what's your point?"

"Why would dragons do anything to make their reputation with the humans worse than it already is?"

"I dunno. Arrogance?"

"No, Taneth. They could live with people hating them for destroying a few cities; they're definitely not taking out three quarters of the population, as the disease would normally do. What would be worse? Having people despise you for one, or for the other? Again and again, over the centuries, killing hundreds of millions of humans? Or going berserk and destroying the entire system of government for one generation?"

Taneth said nothing; beginning to understand what Phenmal was getting at. "What if they're being made to do it? By some power or entity that wants to destroy the government and remake it in its own image, so to speak? What if this power knows of some past transgressions of the dragons that he/she or it can use to coerce them into doing all the dirty work for him? What if, Taneth?"

"You're as mad as a starling."

"Is it impossible?" he asked Taneth.

The Wiseman leaned back in his chair to think about it, knowing full well it wasn't at all impossible. "I suppose, to a point, yes, it's possible," he conceded.

"But even so, you'd have to prove it, and what could a single person do about it if it were true?"

"I don't know. But I'll wager if we look into it, we will find clues to prove this theory truer and truer."

"And then what? We find out who or what this power is, and stop him or her or it ... or whatever?"

"Yes."

"I'm sorry, Phenmal, but first of all, it's the shakiest theory I've heard of or thought of yet ... not exactly enough to prove such a thing to a whole world which is happy to go on just blaming the dragons for what they're doing and probably won't be interested in hearing anything that implicates human involvement. You forget how ignorance is sometimes bliss for the masses. And so much so, they will actually fight to maintain their ignorance. Secondly, as I said before, let's say this is all true—and Arak forbid such a possibility—we cannot count on the masses to rally together; and face it, there isn't a single thing one person could do to stop it."

CHAPTER 25

Tinna had never gotten the old man's first name. She felt badly about not asking, and mulled over such things while she tried to ignore the pitch and roll of her stomach with the movement of her new steed. The summoner been so helpless and little, but transformed into such a powerful thing after she had finished her pastry and he decided to begin his work.

His little cottage was the last place one would imagine such a thing to occur, let alone by a hearth with a tiny fire, a kettle heating up more water and a tray with two empty teacups littered with old tea leaves and a plate full of pastry crumbs. But he had done it there. Laid out a little hand-embroidered mat and knelt on it; his little hare's-tail beard bobbing up and down as he chanted and sang. As he felt himself connecting into whatever consciousness it was that allowed him to speak to dragons, his weak little voice seemed to become stronger ... and soon, he seemed larger, and more powerful.

Tinna sat as still as possible, focusing on the seriousness in the slant of his fuzzy brows, which somehow seemed more dignified all of a sudden, and the timber of his voice. When it was done, he looked at her, and all that inherited power drained out of him like water from a sponge. He shrank back into the little old man that he was, and he got back to his feet with the same groan he made when he sat down. The water was boiling by then, and Tinna took the opportunity to pour the tea and she used the same type he'd chosen before, swishing the old dregs out of the cup before serving it again.

"They were receptive the moment they felt it was for you," he declared at last. Tinna nodded, and served the tea. "They shall be sending someone for you by late morning tomorrow." She nodded again. "You may stay the night, my dear. I'll sleep on a pad by the fire."

"Nonsense. I'll sleep by the fire," she insisted. "I need to go and sell my horse.

I'll return as soon as possible." She left the cottage, and walked into the quiet town, leading Phenmal's horse along with her. She found the local stable, and let the animal go for a hideously low price. But it was enough to supplement her money to purchase some more supplies, and more importantly, some goods to fill the old man's pantry and home.

He was napping in his chair when she got back that afternoon. She took the opportunity to cram her purchases into his pantry and pepper them around the house, as well. She bought him a pillow to put behind his head on his chair, and some warm blankets. She bought him a slew of fresh and preserved foods that she put into his pantry, including pastries that looked much healthier than the ones he'd served her earlier. She even got him a new pair of slippers made of thick brocade and lined inside with padded lamb's wool. She made a thick stew of beef, probably too expensive and rare a treat for him, and served it with slices of thick bread slathered in creamy butter. He awoke from the smells of cooking and looked delighted to be eating a meal cooked just for him.

"You shouldn't have …"

"Of course I should have. I owe you for your services."

"What's this?" he asked, reaching for some small sacks bundled together.

"Different varieties of tea. I see how you like having a choice," she said.

He grinned. He sat up and ate his meal with relish, tearing off bits of bread in small pieces as if to make the experience last as long as possible. She took the remaining gold and put it into one of his tea urns. A little surprise, she thought, so he could have beef, and fresh butter again after she was gone. Come morning, she made them both breakfast, another rich and lavish meal by his lean standards, and walked up the hill away from the town carrying her pack on her shoulder. There, standing on the cliff side overlooking the quaint seaside town, was a majestic young dragon. Shouts of alarm could be heard below as citizens became aware of the dragon above them.

"I AM ILONO; I AM SON OF LEDRORAN."

"Excellent, Ilono. Lower your head …" She clambered onto him, taking a seat behind his crest, which was significantly smaller than his father's.

"WHERE ARE WE TO FLY?"

"Oh, it's quite a ways, Ilono. It's a place called Alchar … a noble house inside the empire of Muath. He is there."

"ARE YOU CERTAIN?"

216

"Quite. But before you call in the hordes of dragons, I need to make sure for myself. We don't want to spook him into hiding forever." She bobbed up and down as he nodded his assent.

"TO MUATH, THEN." The dragon walked to the cliff's edge, and went over, falling before spreading his wings and catching air, skimming the rooftops of the town and causing a panic in the assembled people before going out to sea to use the strong ocean winds. He needed to gain as much height as possible before heading inland. Muath was far. Almost to the opposite coast.

* * * *

"And you are with child?"

"From a Nimrath?"

"And he chases you?"

"No ... I am chased by a Nimrath, yes. But not the one who has sired this child."

"Was the conception of this child a willing act? Or were you among those who have been taken by force?"

"Willing. He is my friend. My husband." There was a moment of quiet. Then the leader, a tall, lanky-looking fellow of middle-age named Pheri, said,

"And you say one is pursuing you now? He is just outside this camp?"

"He's not very far. A sprint perhaps."

"Rhoa ... what a strange name. Is she an Araki?"

"I told you all—I heard someone shouting angrily near the camp. None of you would believe me," one of the tribe members uttered with a pouting air about her. She was duly ignored by the mass of beautiful faces surrounding Rhoa.

"What of your mate?"

"I don't know." Rhoa suddenly felt weak. She could be, now that she was safe among others. Her eyes brimmed with tears, and her knees gave way. She was caught by Pheri's son Pishta. He lowered her down onto one of the very fancy cushions that surrounded the main fire pit. The crowd dispersed to give her some air. Rhoa wiped her tears away with the ball of her fist, taking the opportunity to look at the camp.

The temporary settlement was in a large clearing, probably used over hundreds of years by the continually circling nomads who followed the seasons from land to land. Surrounding most of the site, positioned in a semi-circle around the fire pit, were the caravans.

Much like Borc's little one, they were very tall, very handsomely created things, colorful cottages on wheels covered with little ginger bread designs and stylized artwork in carved wood and paint. These were significantly longer than Borc's little carriage. They were too big for a single horse to pull. She looked around and found three of the same great oxen as Borc had and four huge draught horses standing with lids half closed, the bovines chewing their cud, the horses switching what was left of their tails, small puffs of hair in some automatic response to the occasional forest fly that annoyed them. Draught horses were a rare sight for Rhoa. Like ponies, they were products of different clans. She was quite fascinated by the size and bulk of the animals. They were huge, yet they seemed to have the same proportions as their tiniest counterpart, the pony, with the same unkempt manes and forelocks and barrel bodies.

These Gypsies had never come through her village. The ones who came through there were a much smaller group, and they had only two caravans pulled by two tired-looking Moropuses. This group was more of a village. There were at least five separate families, judging by the five caravans, and each one had at least four to five members, perhaps more. Everyone had gone to perform some duty, leaving Rhoa to herself for a moment. She petted an amorous little cat that purred and rubbed up against her for a while, and then noticed that the men were gathering up weapons from a locker under one of the caravans. She was distracted by a hand offering her water in a vessel made of cobalt blue glass. She was instantly intrigued by that, and accepted it, looking up at the woman who provided it.

"Poor thing. You can stay in my caravan. There aren't too many of us in there."

Rhoa found she enjoyed their rich accents. They rolled their R's and made V sounds with their W's. It was all very exotic-sounding. And it made her name sound oh so pretty. R-r-r-ro—wah.

"I need to keep going. I need to go home."

"Where is home?" the girl asked.

Rhoa was weeping again, and her hands trembled. "I don't know!" she blurted. "The Nimrath knew ... He knew," she cried.

"Now, now, Rhoa, don't cry," Another, older woman arrived, putting an expertly woven blanket over her shoulders and sinking down onto the cushions next to her. "What is the name of your settlement?"

"Thamatoch," she said through some snot and tears. Some more of the dark-haired women surrounded her. Rhoa began to see Tinna in them. The angle of the eyes and cheekbones, the very dense and beautiful black hair. She missed Tinna. She missed her strength. She knew that if that woman been there, she'd have disposed of the Mahrouk Nimrath and helped her find not only Draphen but also the way home. "It's about three days from one of those academies—Hildercross. But that doesn't exist anymore; it's been burned to a crisp."

"I know where that is," the leader said, arriving to join the cluster of people around Rhoa. He was carrying a strange-looking device, like a horn, with a flared end. He stooped, and laid the long thing across his knees. "We're to pass within a few days of there. We'll take a little detour, and drop you off," he decided. "You're not so far from home as you think. Another nine or ten days, if we leave tomorrow."

"I'm so sorry to throw your routine into uproar," she said. "But your kindness shall not go unnoticed … not by myself or my clan."

The Gypsies exchanged knowing looks among themselves, quite sure they knew better on the matter. They were accustomed to being treated like garbage. It was a given that they would expect such treatment from any native settlement they wandered into. But they didn't argue, nor treat Rhoa with any less care or respect because of it. She was guided to one of the caravans, and given one of the soft hammocks within to lie down in. She slept in fits and starts, tuned-in to the community around her going about their business.

Come evening, she was awakened by the aroma of cooking food. She stepped out of the caravan and was welcomed with bright smiles.

"You feeling better?" the swarthy Pheri asked, a fatherly expression on his handsome face. "Go and sit with Pishta. He's resolved to keep you safe…doesn't care for Nimrath very much."

Rhoa noticed they were almost all equipped with the strange horns. She actually saw someone filling one with what looked like black mud. She sat next to Pishta, who patted her knee with a comforting smile and reached for a plate to offer her food. She took the pewter plate, and watched it be filled with all sorts of delicious food by her hosts. She ate with her hands, and watched the tribe around the fire, all smiling, and eating, children running around the perimeter of light created by the blazing fire.

"What brings you to this part of the woods? And frankly, the question that is on all of our minds, is how did you end up mating with a Nimrath?" Pishta asked boldly.

Rhoa picked up a little shred of chicken, and nibbled on it. "I was with another woman going to the town near Hildercross. We were caught by the explosions of fire caused by the dragons that were destroying the city. We ended up with someone the enemy wanted, and when he was captured, so were we. We were brought very far from here. Past the flatlands where those oxen of yours come from. We've been working our way back ever since … Tinna has taken another route and I stayed with Draphen—he's my mate. He wasn't comfortable traveling outside of the protection of the forest. So here I am."

"And the Nimrath who follows you? Where does he come into this strange tale?"

"We stopped to rest at a settlement very soon into our journey, after we split up with Tinna. It seems the leader of this settlement had wished to stake claim on me for some reason. He's been following since, I guess. We didn't know he was, there were four of us then: my mate and I, and two other Nimraths Draphen had met before we left Tinna. Mahrouk killed one of those fellows for sure; I saw him. But I don't know about Tiko, or Draphen." Her voice became a bit somber. There was a collective silence as if to empathize with her loss, until one of the draught horses made a snort and a half-whinny. Two of the strange, gangly dogs that were tethered to a couple of the caravans stood up and their hackles rose, deep growls rumbling in their throats.

"Koorrati, Pishta," Pheri grunted, and his son stood.

Everyone remained still while slowly, the men began to rise, and twist around, their bizarre horns in their hands. The dogs growled some more, one of which bared his teeth most frighteningly. Everyone was being exceedingly wary of their movements and they whispered back and forth to one another in their native tongue.

Rhoa watched as an elderly gentleman lifted the horn to his lips and took a deep breath, exhaling in a great wheeze. The black substance shot out in a spray, speckling just about everything within its range. His actions caused everyone with one of those horns to spray them in the direction the old man had shot, and to Rhoa's surprise, a figure was suddenly spray-painted into existence by these fans of black sooty stuff. It was very odd, like a figure made of smoke. He looked at his arms, and then his legs, suddenly realizing his invisibility had been compromised, and before he could react, eleven Gypsy men were on him, pinning him to the ground and tying his hands up.

Rhoa knew instantly from the shape that it wasn't Draphen. Besides, he would have uncloaked his skin before entering the camp. It was either Tiko or the Mahrouk one … she severely doubted it was

220

Tiko. She realized she was standing and moving toward the struggling Nimrath as if her anger itself had developed a life of its own. She found herself stooping before the figure. His struggle had further covered him with soil and humus in addition to the candy-coating of whatever that stuff was they'd sprayed on him. He squirmed on the ground in the grip of his captors.

"Is this your mate?" Pishta asked, his brow very tightly furrowed, and his jaw rippling. Rhoa shook her head. "Draphen would have announced himself. And secondly, this fellow is much taller. He's the one who stalked me … the leader of that settlement. The one who probably killed Juri."

"You're sure he killed this Juri fellow?"

"What are the odds that a Nimrath would fall from a tree by accident?" she asked, her brow arched in skepticism.

The group fell into a cacophony of nods and grunts of agreement, and lifted their newfound prisoner to his feet.

"What do you think we should do with this thing?" Pishta asked, clearly disgusted with its sheer existence.

"Don't kill him. I think if Tiko or Draphen are still out there, they may want that pleasure." She narrowed her eyes and glared at the man. "Are they? Are they still out there, you piece of crap?" She lost control and threw herself at him, pummeling his head with her fists, kicking at his shins and his genitals with all her strength until her concerned friends pulled her away.

"I'm not sure what to do with him, but having him around will prove unhealthy for you and your unborn child," Pheri decided.

He turned to his men, barking out a set of commands in the rolling Gypsy tongue, and they dragged the struggling Nimrath out of the circle of caravans and into the darkness. The others only released Rhoa when the men had cleared the small area lit by the fire and lanterns, and they felt she was at no risk of following. She tore her arms from their grasp and stood there, eyes burning a hole into the spot where they had vanished. She understood Tinna now. She understood the rage that fueled her and her quiet but understated fury with the world and its unfairness. She turned around and walked back to the caravan where she'd been staying, and crawled into her hammock, fighting back tears and the misery she'd been keeping at bay for hours. She lay down, listening to the community outside go back to some semblance of normal, gathering around to finish their interrupted meal and quietly discussing these new events that had brought such excitement to their quiet life.

Rhoa could not sleep. She was divided. She could stay with the Gypsies and go home, or she could strike out and find Draphen. She didn't know how she would take finding his body, if she did. And she realized that if he were out there, he'd either be following, or heading toward home as well, knowing that's where she'd be going. She had no idea where to begin to look, but she knew that he would know where to find her. She felt cowardly, somehow, deciding to stay with the caravan. But her sensibilities told her that Draphen would have been with her now if he were able to, and if he were still somehow alive and mobile, he loved her enough to find her. All she could think of was how he had told her to run. What had happened up in those bloody trees? She felt so alone and powerless, her sadness took over, and she began to weep. She did not wonder where they'd taken the Nimrath, or what they were doing to him, she just hoped he'd be made to suffer all at once what she would have to suffer the rest of her days if it turned out that Draphen had indeed been killed. She turned onto her side with some difficulty and tried to sleep, all the while wishing over and over again that Draphen would appear, safe and sound.

* * * *

Taneth held Raven's little reins while Hanru adjusted himself in the saddle. The boy was getting quite expert at the whole riding thing, but Taneth realized he was of the horse people after all, and so it probably came natural to him. Phenmal had tried to keep Taneth from leaving, asking him to remain and help him with his research. He was still fully convinced of his theory, and Taneth, deep down, was beginning to see the sense and truth in it. He had to leave before he allowed himself to believe it outright. It was just too much to know, too much truth to carry on one's own. He saw the research backing up Phenmal's theory with every new day he remained at the Phanos archive, and he didn't want to be there when he found something to make it real to Taneth. He finished his research on the people of Arak, glad he'd had that to pour himself into, finding the project to be more interesting than he'd thought initially.

He'd discovered that the very roots of the Araki came from the race known as the Chai-opse. They came from a group of Chai-opse that had moved from their homeland and had taken up residence in the great central plains, where they became one with the land, learning in the harsh winds of the flatlands to build their homes beneath the ground and to sod the roofs. The people spread south from there, and eventually moved their fragmented society of remote tribes out of the grasslands, submitting it to the newer immigrants who originated from the Kalso regions far north. They were a heavier and stronger people, and they adapted well to the plains. The people of Arak, now fully disassociated with their origins with the Chai-opse, became forest-dwellers, keeping their beliefs, their horses, and their norms. The concentration of Araki clans was unknown, for the forests were too large and too difficult to map in detail, or to create a census of the clan populations. Taneth saw one text that projected that the number of clans were in the tens of thousands. It made him wonder.

He even copied a map of the spread of the Araki people, and also got an acolyte from the archives to write copies of the complicated spread the larger clans had divided up and into over the years, and who they became. His report was extensive. He would be very much revered for his work, for certain. It took him a long time to find the connection between the plains folk they used to be and the original ancestors of the Araki, the ever-mystifying Chai-opse. Taneth resolved upon his next research mission that he would take some time to learn more about the race of Chai-opse. It was a very intriguing subject. As he mounted his own horse, he saw a huge shadow crawl along the street toward him, and he looked up at the thing that cast it. As it passed overhead, casting its shadow upon him, he frowned. A single dragon, riding high on the currents, moving west.

CHAPTER 26

Tinna and Ilono cruised over the landscape; having passed through a patch of rough air, they were pleased for this respite from the harder parts of this long journey. They passed over Lemoram in the blink of an eye, and over the small range of volcanic hills surrounding the foot of Mount Jewel, whose very tip always smoked. They passed through the sulfuric cloud as through a curtain and hit the drier air of the plains. Here, Ilono climbed higher, using the winds blowing up the side of the range to lift his bulk up into the clouds. The air here was frigid, and Tinna found her head spinning a bit. She crouched under the dragon's small shield and huddled there, pulling her things around her to keep warm.

She slept for a while, until she felt herself falling, and awoke, realizing it wasn't she who had fallen, but both her and the dragon. He was descending, and her ears suddenly began to hurt beyond belief. She was too busy trying to pop them to actually realize what was happening. Out of the corner of her eyes, against the deep dark blue, she saw the shape of another dragon meeting up with Ilono: Ledroran. She hadn't heard them cry out for one another. She was amazed they actually found one another in the darkness. Ledroran's wide eye turned to look upon her as she squeezed out from under his son's bony crest.

"COME," he growled.

She glanced down, the wind whipping her hair about, and nodded nervously. But without hesitation, she strapped her bag to her shoulder, and moved to the very edge of Ilono's crest, onto his neck. She gingerly ran down the spiny part until she reached the area between his pumping wings; there, she balanced herself precariously. Ledroran pumped his wings and got above Ilono and lowered his head down over his son's smaller form. He opened his mouth and snapped her up like a bird taking a parasite off another, and banked away, diving hundreds of feet before leveling out and opening his teeth enough for Tinna to repeat the route she took the first time she and Rhoa had traveled in this manner. Once she was installed underneath his far more accommodating crest, she watched Ilono drop like a stone, and then right himself again about three hundred feet above them, bank into a tight curve, and turn back the way they had come.

"HE WILL REST." The dragon's grating voice was mostly lost to the wind. She picked most of it up through the vibrations running through his immense head. She closed her eyes again, glad that Ledroran enjoyed warmer air and lower altitudes. She felt warmth against the soft scale-free skin behind his striking armored shield. Here, she could get some sleep.

Morning came and she found herself wondering where she was for a moment. Then it came to her, perhaps clued in by the view from where she slept. She'd fallen asleep draped across the back of Ledroran's neck, her head resting on a pillow made from her own clothing. As soon as she opened her eyes she could see a bit of Ledroran's opalescent neck scales, and then the land below, a checkerboard of rolling pastures dotted with livestock. This land was not familiar to her. She stirred and sat up, alerting her transport that she was among the conscious again. "ALMOST THERE," Ledroran announced. She stood up and shimmied out, grasping the many horns sun-bursting from the top edge of his shield. She held on tight and leaned out a bit, observing this lush, beautiful landscape.

"Where are we?" she shouted.

The dragon blinked. "MUATH ... AS MY SON TOLD ME YOU WISHED TO GO."

"Yes. Excellent. I think we should keep ourselves out of sight for now. We don't want anyone to know there's a dragon lurking about here. This is land not under the High Throne. No reason for you to be flying about here unless it's one of your usual routes," she shouted at his little ear hole.

"MANY DRAGONS FLY WEST. THE WESTERN OCEAN HAS WARM CLIFFS TO BREED. IT IS WHERE ILONO AND HIS SISTERS WERE HATCHED. DRAGONS OVERHEAD AREN'T ANYTHING UNUSUAL. BUT, PERHAPS MY SILHOUETTE MIGHT BE CONSIDERED CURIOUS, SEEING HOW RECOGNIZABLE I AM. I WILL BE DISCREET."

"Good," she smiled. "Are we close to Alchar?"

"YES. I WILL LEAVE YOU OUTSIDE OF THE VILLAGE...YOU CAN WALK TO YOUR DESTINATION FROM THERE"

"That's reasonable. How will I find you again?"

"I WILL WAIT FOR YOU. THIS IS TOO IMPORTANT FOR ME TO LEAVE, EVEN IF IT IS A DEAD END."

"I have a strong suspicion our man is here. His brother has been supplying him with his needs with such secrecy there can only be one explanation. I just hope he hasn't found out about his brother's death just yet. We might lose track of him if he took flight."

"AND IF IT IS HIM AND HE IS THERE?"

"I'll take care of it. And If I can't do it alone, I'll come for you. I cannot guarantee how long it will be, a day, two days … but if it's beyond three, I think you need to just incinerate the house itself if you don't hear from me." Tinna paused, and then leaned on Ledroran's head. "Great one … I am wondering what you shall do when this is all over? You cannot expect your people will be forgiven for what they have done, nor can you hope that the truth would in any way absolve you … it would do only worse to implicate your people for countless more deaths."

"PERHAPS, PERHAPS THE TRUTH ABOUT THE TRINITY COULD BE TOLD AS WELL."

"But …" Tinna knew that wasn't realistic. She realized that he was being facetious. Both she and the dragon knew that the world owed its stability to the Trinity and its allies, the Keepers. Three great races would never coexist without it.

"BUT … INDEED. SO WE SHALL LIVE WITH OUR STIGMA FOR A FEW GENERATIONS. BLAME IT ON A DISEASE OR SOME MADNESS. WE WILL SURVIVE THROUGH IT, SOMEHOW. ANYTHING IS BETTER THAN THE WORLD KNOWING THE TRUTH."

Tinna nodded, as if he could actually see her doing it. She sat down again, shielding herself from the wind, and watched the landscape recede behind them. She sighed, running through strategies in her head, trying to figure out how she was going to catch and kill Ovamal so she could go back and get the puppy before he was too grown up to be cute and appealing to Hanru.

Another thing nagged at the back of her mind as Ledroran fell another few hundred feet toward the earth. Would Taneth understand what she was doing? Or would he stand in defense of the human race, and despise her for supporting the faction that had had a hand in systematically wiping out millions of them over generations? Deep down she knew the right thing was only really true in the heart of the person who thought it right. Perhaps she wasn't doing the right thing. Perhaps the dragons had had their time in this world, and like the Chai-opse, it was their turn to fade away. Who was she to decide this? Who was she to be deciding the fate of millions? But would they ever learn? If they could not learn after generations and generations of making the same mistakes, perhaps there was no hope that humanity would ever learn to rein itself in. Perhaps the

Trinity was there for that purpose alone, with one of their own kind among them, deciding whether or not humanity should be taught a lesson.

All she knew was that every form of life had its right to fight for survival.

Humanity had proven itself to be a nuisance again and again, and was always given a rather harsh slap on the wrist, and left to grow and earn another chance toward reaching some level of harmony with other life. It could have been much worse. There could have been no Taneth, or Hanru, anymore. No Rhoa or Draphen. No Borc or Ailie or her gorgeous children. But they were there. A small miracle. A blessing. When all powers had the chance to just rid themselves of a parasite, they did not. There was no wrong or right anywhere in this history. Only a tenuous balance between three strong races, which was continually tipped by an aggressive, populous, locust-like group whose few good qualities alone earned them the right to exist a few more generations. The Trinity had hope in humanity and knew one day they might just reach that harmony.

Tinna watched the dots become sheep, the lines become trails and lanes, the patches become mature crops, and in her heart, she knew she risked losing the only person who'd come to matter to her so much. She knew in her soul she was doing what was right for humanity, for the dragons, for the few remaining Chai-opse. There were three races in this world ... and three there would always be. The truth would remain a secret, the government would be replaced, and perhaps, just maybe, this time, they'd get it right.

CHAPTER 27

Rhoa had had enough. She'd reached the very limit of her patience with this journey, and its tribulations, and she did not care for the fact that on top of everything else, she was feeling hideously nauseous and having a yearning at the exact same moment for some steamed river mussels. She'd woken up to the sound of shouts and orders. The caravan was preparing to leave. She was pleased they were headed south for the warmer countries now that autumn had begun, pleased she would be home soon, and pleased by their kindness to her. She'd hoped, in some quiet way so as not to give the mischievous gods who persistently challenged the followers of the Horse God, any ideas; that the worst was over, and she would find Draphen alive and well at the end of her trail.

But such would not be the case. They found Draphen not half a mile away from the clearing as the caravan squeezed through some unbelievably narrow wildlife paths, sometimes having to cut away vegetation. They also found Tiko. Both had been thrown off the trees from a great height, both within only feet from one another, mangled and still—camouflage faded, revealing the indignity of their death and their nudity.

The Gypsies were kind enough to protect Rhoa from these things. They covered the bodies with two of their fine blankets, and let Rhoa identify Draphen's strangely peaceful face. She appreciated the two silver coins the Gypsies had laid upon their eyes to keep the lids closed and to help them pay their way into the next world, as their beliefs required. She did not cry at first. She simply swallowed hard, and tried to ignore the heavy lump in her stomach. She was led back to the caravan by an old woman with snow-white hair, with tiny braids twisted throughout her scalp, much like Tinna, except she had little pierced coins dangling from the ends instead of feathers.

The old woman laid her down on a bench instead of in her cot, and covered her, humming something to Rhoa as she patted down

229

Rhoa's hair. She then went to prepare some tea on the small stove whose chimney poked out of the strange roof of this swaying home. Rhoa stared into the void beyond the realities surrounding her. She sat up for the tea, and drank, not tasting it, not even realizing that she was actually doing it, her movements automated and listless. "Now, now, don't lose yourself in there." A bony finger tapped her temple. The old woman was making her a meat porridge ... the aroma of which reminded Rhoa of her home. "You have a little one now to think of."

"What did they do with that Nimrath?" Rhoa asked.

"I don't really know. The men like to keep their activities to themselves and I think most of us here would rather not know." She cackled while she shuffled about in the narrow space, working on the porridge.

"He threw them from the trees. What a horrible way to kill someone."

"Some men become irrational with the desire for a woman. Some will do anything to take possession of her. In my life, I've seen many things, little girl. I've seen such men many a time. Some become so obsessed they'd rather see a woman dead than alive and not loving him back. I've seen women like that, too."

"It doesn't make me feel better about how Draphen and Tiko died."

"They died fighting him ... saving you. They died honorably." She slapped some of the concoction into a bowl, and jabbed a spoon into it. "Now eat. You need to nourish your body."

Rhoa ate, paying no heed to the strong flavors. No sooner had she finished than her head began to loll, and her eyes drooped. She became conscious, too late to do anything about it, that she'd been sedated. Her angry mind raged as someone came and lifted her into her hammock. She realized this was a good summation of her experience. People all around her were making decisions for her, manipulating her, and doing things without ever bothering to ask her what she wanted. First the bird-dragons dragging her from home, then Draphen marrying her and impregnating her without her really giving either thing any thought, and some bizarre man-creature deciding he had to have her like some common object, and deciding for her that she no longer had need for Draphen anymore. Now, even with their good intentions, these Gypsies had drugged her, probably thinking it would keep her from becoming overwrought and stressed.

She'd had enough. No more. She had to take control of her life from that moment on or she would go mad. She thought of Tinna, who'd always been distant enough to let Rhoa make her own decisions … she let Rhoa stand on her own even when sometimes Rhoa didn't want to. She forced her eyes open, and looked around. I will have to remember to thank that woman when I see her again, she thought.

The occupants of the caravan were outside, clearing the narrow road so that the slowly moving train of mobile homes could make it through the forest. She found enough strength to roll herself out of the hammock, and fell ungracefully onto the floor with a thump. She crawled to where her things were laid out, and stuffed them back into her bag with little concern about order. She pulled the drawstring tight, with limp muscles and all, and tried to stand, finding it harder already from the movement of the coach, let alone the influence of the herbs she'd been given. She managed on her knees, and opened the door. The ox pulling the cart pretty much obscured any view of the community striding along up ahead. Nobody drove the cart, the ox followed by the tether that attached him to the cart ahead. She turned around and crawled to the opposite side of the coach where the door opened out to another small stepping rail. The ox tethered to this cart simply lumbered on, ignoring the pale, desperate face that appeared suddenly before him.

She scooted out onto the rail, and then shimmied her bottom over to the left side. Once she was facing sideways, she let herself slide off, and rolled out into the bracken. She wormed her way into the foliage to hide from the caravan as the remaining two coaches rolled by in a slow trudge. The trail of children and other Gypsies that followed did not see her lying still as the dead on the ground under the leafy flora. They simply kept going. Rhoa allowed herself to sleep only then … letting the drug take its course so she could move on.

By the next morning, Rhoa had found her hunger sated by the profusion of autumn food growing in the forest. She was back in a familiar environment after all. She'd retraced the path of destruction from the caravans to the clearing, and then went out in search of the Nimrath. She was angry. Angrier than she could have ever imagine herself being. She listened, and searched, getting increasingly worried that Pishta, in all his disgust with the tree people, had killed the towering Nimrath, sparing her the chance to do it herself. She was pleased in a very dark way when she found they had not killed him. They had tied him to a tree to die. And he was not dead. He was not camouflaged, either. He did not cry out, or react very much at the sight of his most desired object appearing out of nowhere.

Rhoa moved directly in front of the lanky man, and put her pack down slowly, eyes never leaving the narrow, strange face that gazed at her longingly. She walked toward the Nimrath. His dark eyes followed her, angled face like stone. She saw extensive bruising on his body from the rough treatment by the Gypsies.

"I should kill you this second. But that would be too easy. I have something more dramatic in mind for you."

"Kalastin eh mo-hrooatan'et," he whispered, with a half smile on his face.

Rhoa saw the desire. The madness. Perhaps she recognized that part of it because she had a bit of madness in her own eyes. She bit down on her teeth, and set her jaw; reaching out, she began to undo the network of knots the men had so diligently tied to make sure this Nimrath would never escape his bonds without the assistance of another. The Nimrath was smiling, and laughing, speaking his foreign words, his head following her as she moved around his body and undid the work of those who had beaten and subdued him. He was still covered in the black substance and grime, which had dried into crumbles that fell away as she unbound him.

He began to struggle when there was some slack in the rope, and soon he was free, standing before her tall and sinewy. Rhoa reached for her bag, and slung it over her shoulder, waiting for him to do something. He stepped forward, and reached out to touch her. For a moment, she panicked, feeling the icy tendrils of fear grip her. She slapped his hand away, and shoved him. Her fear was fleeting; her panic suppressed. She had to keep control. His brow furrowed suddenly, and the anger at her reaction was instantly evident. He bent down, and hoisted her onto his shoulder, and without further ado, began to climb. Rhoa did not struggle. She watched the ground recede below her, and she felt his powerful muscles carry them both up into the trees. Higher, she said in her angry head, take me much, much higher.

He'd worked hard to get them up into the tree-ways, and was winded and tired when they reached a place wide enough to rest. Rhoa sat against the trunk of a tree while he crouched and stared at her. She stared back, cool and calculating. Either he wondered why she'd come back and decided to be with him, or he was so deluded he actually believed she wanted him as he did her. Either way, she could not read trust or mistrust in his wild eyes. He just took her in, occasionally moving one or two inches closer. She did not move and she did not draw away. She let him reach out his hand and caress her cheekbone and draw the line of her lips with his thumb. He hunched toward her a bit more, close enough to smell her hair again, to just brush his lips against hers as he took in her aroma and felt the contours of her face. Just these acts alone made him lose himself in desire … his eyes closed, his breath hot on her face.

Rhoa closed her eyes, and drew her mouth to his, parting her lips enough to suck his bottom lip into a warm, brief, sensual kiss. His breath gusted out at this act, and he came even closer, demanding more of the same, his hands growing bolder. He reached for her wrists and held them against the trunk of the tree while he covered her mouth with his, and kissed her deeply. She went along with it, a tear falling from the corner of her eye as she felt his mouth move to her neck, and then grasp her wrists with one hand while he began to grope and feel with the other. His desperation was powerful, and he was losing control to it. Rhoa prayed he would remain focused and deliberate long enough that she would have the time she needed without having to suffer the indignity of being invaded by him.

He began to fumble a bit, desperate to get her tunic and her breeches off. He let go of her wrists, needing both hands to lift her shirt off, and to feel the desired contents within. Rhoa lowered her hands and braced them on the wide branch she sat on, her back firmly against the trunk where the two intersected. The Nimrath had begun to focus on her breasts. She opened her eyes to see his bald head working away below her chin, his hands working at the tie of her breeches. She slowly began to draw her legs up, in a manner which he interpreted as her being receptive, which made him all the more frantic in his movements. Her knees were pulled up tightly, her legs open. He moved between them, even though she still wore her breeches, and he hiked her up onto his lap, leaning over to worship her firm little breasts some more.

Rhoa counted to herself … one … she ignored the feel of his lips on her breasts; two … ignored his hands and body rubbing against her. Three … she counted, and drew herself up into a tight ball, four … she sucked in her breath; feigning a sigh of ecstasy; and while doing so, she drew her feet up and without the slightest hesitation she cried out "FIVE!" and planted her feet in his chest and, using her curled-up body as the springboard, she straightened herself out with a surge of furious energy. She catapulted him from the tree limb…and saw his hands reach out as he fell, and catch the bark with his rough fingers. She wasted no time, she knew their speed and agility, and she hung her legs over the edge so that his hands were between them, and she began to pummel them with her fists and scratch at them with her nails.

"Let GO you disgusting piece of garbage I HATE YOU, YOU MURDERING SICK PUTRID SACK OF BILE!" she sobbed and blubbered, bludgeoning his hands with all her might, and then using her heels to kick at his head. One hand gave way, and he dangled precariously from the thick branch, not close enough to the trunk to take hold. "JUST FALL AND DIE, so you can KNOW WHAT THEY FELT … I HATE YOU! DIE!" His second hand gave way and there was the sound of branches snapping and cracking as he plummeted, taking vegetation out as he fell. She prayed he would not catch anything with his sticky hands or feet, and he did not. She heard a satisfying crash seconds later.

She sat there, staring down at the vertical tunnel his fall had cut through the layers of branches and growth. She saw a pair of pale legs, tiny and insignificant down at the foot of the tree, still and lifeless. Her entire body trembled, and there was a look of irrationality in her eyes. She pulled her clothes back on, and then began to look for ways to get down again, barely able to control the tremors in her limbs. She needed to see her handiwork before she resumed her trek home. She did not want to lose the trail of the Gypsies. She wanted to get back to their caravan before it was too late to take the detour to Thamatoch.

CHAPTER 28

"She's alive … and so is Rhoa," Taneth announced to Rigerd the moment he arrived from Lemoram. The leader arched his brow, wrinkling up his expansive forehead, and looked most dubious. "I met someone who met them. They were not killed at Hildercross. They were abducted along with some nobleman, and then released when they were found to be of no danger to anyone. They are on their way home."

"You're certain of this? Seems an amazing coincidence that you run into someone who's seen them in, of all places, Lemoram."

"First of all, who cares if it's coincidence? And for a man of spiritual beliefs as you are, I'm surprised you're so skeptical of such at thing. Perhaps Arak brought us to him. Did you think of that? Secondly, the man who met them was doing the circuit of Phanos archives because of his encounter with Aitinna. He also happens to be a Chaiva, and he actually recognized me from her memories of me."

"Or he invented it all from riffling about inside your head."

"To what end, Rigerd? What joy would he derive from misleading me? Besides … I believe him. There's no reason for me not to "

"I suppose you're right, there is no reason not to believe him." Rigerd sighed.

"I shall give him the benefit of the doubt, then. I think we could all use some hope around here."

"Yes. Hope." Taneth handed the reins of his horse off to a clansman, and helped Hanru down from Raven. Someone took care of her as well, leaving them to carry their things in and follow Rigerd into the lodge. Taneth found himself glad to be home. He sat down with Hanru and enjoyed a cold meal of leftovers, while Rigerd quietly read Taneth's research report.

He joined the elders at the community hearth, sitting with a sense of relief in his own chair. Rigerd smiled at him. "This is quite the report you made, Taneth. It's fascinating." He read for a long time, often referring back to the maps and the clan structures. He sighed. "It's a pity I can't share it with the clans this autumn."

Taneth looked up, puzzled. "Why? Is it not satisfactory?" He took it defensively, feeling some pride in the work he'd put into the report. He remembered how haphazardly he'd done projects back at the academy, never applying himself, never trying and now that he really did try, and put so much of himself into this report, he had a sense of pride and ownership of it, and was dismayed by Rigerd's statement. He sat up and glared at the man.

Rigerd laughed, and shook his head. "No, you dolt. The work is incredible… more than I had hoped for; you went far deeper than I had expected, and this is something that should be shared with the clans. But there will be no gathering this autumn. The council of regional clan leaders decided while you were away, that with all the bizarre occurrences happening with the dragons, they should play it safe, and keep their people scattered and innocuous until the threat is no more. Only after there is some resolution to the wars with the dragons can we gather as a people again."

Taneth's face blanched a bit. It was no war. A war required two or more parties agreeing to face one another aggressively. This was a massacre. The dragons would just appear, without warning because of the crippled relay, and destroy cities and towns. Nobody had a chance to fight back … no armies were ever amassed.

"People don't see us as much of an entity because the Araki clans are so spread out, but your report here, it speaks volumes of that misperception. And when we gather—all of us in our respective regions, it is very evident how large our numbers are. It could be construed as a threat to whatever power it is that controls the dragons. So all clans are 'staying in' this autumn. We will partake of only our own harvests, and not enjoy the variety of trade. Some clans have set up some regular trade routes to compensate, but the volume will be less, that is certain," he lamented. "You have yet to experience an Araki gathering. It's something all of our people look forward to all year, some working on projects and wares the entire year just to bring to this event. There is great disappointment among our folk, Taneth. Among all the clans."

"But everyone understands, I'm sure," Taneth said.

"Yes, of course. I just wish I knew more about what was going on, and if there was some foreseeable end to it."

"I don't see an end coming. There's probably nobody able enough to stop it." He thought of Tinna, and frowned inwardly. How could she hope to do anything about it? One person?

Taneth had the length of the journey home to think about all the things he'd watched Phenmal pull from the wealth of information at the archive. He had the entire journey home to lose hope … not in Tinna … not in Hanru, or Rhoa … to lose hope for mankind. If Phenmal's theory was right, they were doomed no matter what … Either to be grown and pruned like a grapevine, or to be the destroyers of the only place that sustains them, and to have the annihilation of two noble races added to their list of greatest misdeeds. He didn't know what to believe any more. All he knew, is that somewhere out there, Tinna was alone, a Thran force—she-warrior, bringer of small dogs—facing the dragons.

CHAPTER 29

Tinna slinked. The darkness was like pitch, the sky a carpet of stars above her head. She'd quieted the two dogs quickly, feeling bad for knocking them out, but knowing they'd be all right. She smiled to herself at the notion that she actually felt more sorry for temporarily rendering a dog unconscious than she did killing a man outright. What a strange world it is in my head. She slid along the outside of the building, testing windows as she moved, being as careful as possible.

She'd done the entire perimeter of the immense structure, and found herself still outside. There were guards here. Not very vigilant guards … perhaps the occupant Ovamal thought himself very safe and well hidden here. She moved back 'round the front of the house, taking a huge risk as she slid up the steps in the dark, and tested the latch. It lifted, and the door opened as quietly as butter being spread on bread. She smiled, and sidled through, closing the door with much care while she took in the layout of the foyer. It was decidedly darker inside; the places where there would be any light would be the servant's passages so they could move without obstruction to serve whatever late night needs the home's occupants would desire.

It was late. He must be sleeping. Good, I can murder him in his bed, she mused. Of course I have to make sure this is the right man … can't leave here thinking I've done my work, only to discover I killed his first cousin or something. She dashed across the barren floor to the immense stairway cascading down from the balcony above, flaring out ostentatiously onto the marble floor under her feet. She looked up the steps, straining her eyes for the tiniest shred of light to follow.

Nothing. She then moved toward a set of great doors off the foyer and opened them—knowing from looking in from outside, they were dark and vacant as well. She slipped into a formal parlor, and closed the door, assessing the room. It was gaudy, as most northern noble houses were decorated, with lots of gold leafing glinting from the meager light from the dying fire. She walked along the paneled walls, tapping along with her fingers, too blinded by the dark to make out which panels were actually hidden doors leading to more private parts of the house. She found a door that like the others was made to look like paneling, and opened it, peeking through into pure darkness before moving farther. She was in a narrow hall, flanked by two doors, and facing one. She looked at the foot of each door to check for light, and saw none, poking her head into each of the rooms at both sides.

The room to the left contained an ornate collection of antique weapons. This seemed poetic and intriguing to the intruder. She slipped inside and lit a candle to see better. She liked this room. She found and unhooked a elegant old sword from the wall, sliding it into the belt that held her tunic to her hips. She took a couple of the scrupulously polished old daggers as well, slipping one into the belt on the opposite side of the sword, and another into the tall calf of her boot. She blew out the candle, let her eyes readjust, and looked into the room across from this one.

There was nothing there but stacks upon stacks of paintings, all leaning against one another on shelves. The higher shelves stored the largest paintings, facing outward, two and three deep. It seemed strange to her that someone would wish to possess such artwork without a desire to display it. She closed the door, and turned to face the door on the end of the corridor. She pushed it open and found herself facing a small courtyard.

The perimeter of it was sheltered by a balcony that served an array of windowed doors from the second floor of the building wherein this courtyard was nested. Underneath the balcony was a walkway, also connecting more doors that opened out into this courtyard from other parts of the house. A fountain sang in the center, and symmetrical gardens of roses and lower growing flowers dissected the space open to the weather, leaving a series of diagonal and circular paths to wander through them. The moonless night gave it all a very bizarre appearance. She did not like it at all.

What she did see was a light. On the second floor, across from her on her right, in the very corner was a large set of windowed doors. There were curtains drawn, but not fully, revealing the steady light of a lamp burning away. She looked around, and frowned with thought as she studied the place. The walkway was supported by columns, which had a stone railing connecting them. Occasionally, every fifth or sixth column, the railing was absent to allow people access to the garden paths. The railing contained planters, all filled to capacity with late-blooming plants. All was made of stone, the pilasters squat and densely lined up, holding up the heavy stone slabs that served as the base for the planters. It was solid. She turned left, and moved down the walkway, staying close to the wall in the shadows, following the edge of the courtyard until she reached the corner to the left, facing where she'd emerged from the hall. It was directly down the same wall as the window. There seemed to be the best place to remain out of sight from the window with the light in it.

She ripped out a plant from the rectangular planter, and tamped down the soil, giving herself a good strong base to stand on. She then lifted her leg up. Her dagger nearly slid out of her boot, but she caught it just before it fell free. She swallowed hard and stuffed it down into the leg of her boot, hilt and all, feeling her heart race at the close call. Metal hitting stone in such a closed area would alert everyone around like a clarion call. She took a deep breath and grasped the column, pulling her body onto the planter. There, she stood straight, and successfully reached for the floor of the upper balcony. It too had its own railing, of the same densely packed stiles that mimicked the curves of a hugely obese woman, but this railing didn't have the benefit of breaks in it, as the one on the ground floor. She hopped up, and tried to get her hands 'round the base of the pilasters. They were too wide for a firm grip. She needed more height to get over the railing. She looked around her at the ground floor again, and spotted a large marble urn standing on a small columnar base tucked into the corner under the walkway. She got down from the planter, and as quietly as possible, removed the urn. She lifted the heavy stone column stand, and staggered ungracefully to the railing, where she managed to slide it onto the lip of the planter with minimal noise.

She ripped out more plants, tamped down the soil, and climbed back up, stepping onto the column. It was definitely a lot more manageable now. She could easily hook her hands over the top of the railing, which was serendipitously free of planters. Once she had a grip, she heaved herself up until she could catch her toe between two of the fat-lady stiles, and lift herself up. She threw one leg over the railing, and then the other, and slid off, tiptoeing toward the window with the light.

She peeked in. She saw a part of what was a set of personal apartments. This room was the sitting room, and she could actually see the corner of a bed through an archway to the right. There was no activity … except for the fire in the hearth and the lamp burning on the table next to an overstuffed, badly upholstered chair. She tested the latch, and to her surprise, it turned. She felt her heart racing, and she had to move away against the wall and catch her breath. A shiver of fear ran through her, but then she set her jaw, removed the dagger from her belt, and with a highly controlled, trembling sigh, she was sliding back along the wall to the window, where she gave the scene within a good look before opening the door inward, slowly pushing it open, senses keen. She heard someone humming. A girl. She slid into the room, behind the thick velvet swag, and closed the window without the slightest noise.

She sidled to the frame of the window, and with her finger, she pushed the heavy material away from the stone just a crack to see into the doorway where the humming was originating. It was a small washroom. The woman humming was standing in her undergarments scrubbing herself with a wet towel under the arms, and rinsing the cloth in a copper basin. What drew Tinna's attention was the barely visible mark on the woman's neck. It was a tattoo, ringing her swan-like neck like a permanent necklace.

She's a Breen. Tinna smiled. She sneaked out from behind the curtain and boldly walked into the washroom, clamping her hand over the delicate creature's mouth, and laying the dagger's edge on the woman's perfect collarbone. The woman tensed up, a gust of warm air squeezing through the cracks of Tinna's fingers. Tinna leaned in toward her ear.

"Listen, Breen. I'm here for someone in this house. You're here to provide services, am I correct?" The woman's head nodded frantically. "Good. Listen to me carefully. I trust the Breen. I always have. I trust that if I let go of you, you will not scream because you know I am not here for you. You must know, if you jeopardize the secrecy of my presence, I will slit your throat faster than you can blink your eyes. I am Thran. I have been trained to do what I do from childhood, just like you." Again, more nods. The muscles were relaxing. Tinna took a risk and let go, turning her around and pushing the dagger up against her throat, just under her chin. "Can I trust you?"

"Of course." The woman was beyond beautiful. She was finely chiseled like a perfect statue. Her hair like gold, even fastened on top of her head with a shaved quill, looked amazing. Her eyes were green like emeralds, her skin pure and milky. She was magnificent. She arched her carefully maintained eyebrows at Tinna, and then reached up and pushed the dagger away. "Don't worry," she said, her voice flat and bored. "It's not like I'm carrying some great loyalty to anyone in this house. It's a job like all the others." She circled 'round Tinna and reached for an elegant robe, which she pulled onto her arms, and belted at the waist, studying Tinna with a practiced eye.

"You're not bad for a Thran. Most of you are scary things ... more masculine than most of the men I service." She turned around and went back into the sitting room, casually opening a small box that reminded Tinna of the one she carried for Taneth, containing his fine quill and ink. She took out some small tubes, and connected them end to end, finishing one end with a small delicate flower-shaped bowl. She stuffed it with an herb, and lit it, taking an extensive drag from the long pipe. She clutched the front of her robe, and sat down, smoking from her delicate pipe.

"You could be a Breen. Easily," she said, quite the compliment coming from a woman who was bred for her beauty and sexuality much like horses were bred for speed, to be raised and trained to be very expensive, highly desired companions. They were whores in short ... serving their guild, except they were expected to do more long-term services in most cases, and were taught many other skills aside from the basics. All Breen were incredibly well-educated, always talented in some form of art or two, and trained to be as eloquent in the art of conversation as possible. They kept up with all the trends, news and gossip, and knew exactly what they needed to know to relax, pamper, and please those they serviced.

Tinna had been a close friend to a Breen male for some years as a teen. It was with him that she had enjoyed her first sexual experiences, and had many subsequent encounters with him over the years. She smiled at the woman. "I was fortunate to be guided into my sexuality by a Breen," she told the elegant woman, who smiled gently. "He and his kind hold a very special place in my heart."

"The people of the south certainly have a better respect for our kind down there. Here, it's another story." She sighed. "So who are you here for? I assume m'lord, considering he's the only person here of any importance, despite his efforts to hide it."

"I'm looking for a man called Ovamal. Minister of War for the High Throne."

"There's nobody here by that name ... officially. But he's here. He is unofficially Lord Alrec of Alchar. But I've seen some communications from a sibling he has back east. I've seen the name you spoke of used on various occasions."

"You are here to serve him?"

The woman nodded and rolled her eyes. "Yes, and for four months, with option to renew, can you believe it? It's a bloody nightmare." She stood and refilled her pipe, lighting it up again. "He's got the grace of a pig, and the endurance to match. It's a rare thing for me not to enjoy the act, I tell you. I have always taken great joy in my work ... but this man ..." She rolled her eyes again, and sucked on her pipe, leaning her head back and exhaling the smoke in a great sigh. "He's too distracted. It's hard to get him to focus on the pleasure."

"I'll take your word for it." It wasn't exactly what Tinna wanted to fill her mind with. "Where is he?"

"Oh, out in the east wing. I was just getting ready to ..." She paused, sitting up. "Why don't you come with me? Stand outside his door, I'll get him all distracted ... you come in, take over, I'll leave."

"Excellent."

"I'm thankful you're here. I've been simply dying for a reassignment since my third day here." She sat down in the overstuffed chair for a moment and tamped her pipe out. She tugged on some stockings that had been discarded in front of the chair, and stood again. "Come on." She smiled.

She opened the door leading out to the corridor, and waited for Tinna to follow. They padded boldly down the center of the unlit corridor, heading straight along the back of the wing, passing the balcony with the main staircase that led down to the foyer. She turned to the right into another wide corridor and paused at a huge set of doors. "Wait here. Listen for it—you'll know when it's safe to come in," she whispered. She opened the door and stepped inside, closing it behind her.

Tinna leaned up against the door, and heard her low voice announce herself. There was no sound loud enough to penetrate the door for a while, until there began a soft thumping, which began to increase in volume ... and then came her moans. Tinna knew this was perfect. She turned the latch and went in.

The Breen was nude, standing in a pile of her own clothes by the bed, her top half leaning over the mattress, her arms braced in front of her. A well-built man was standing behind her, thrusting into her with great intensity. The Breen was crying out encouragement that made Tinna blush, using language that was almost impossible to imagine coming out of such a fine, perfectly hewn set of angelic lips. Tinna looked around ... this was a large man. A powerful body. She was stealthy as she sneaked 'round and tugged a tieback for a decorative wall swag from its hook. She crept up behind the man as he literally pounded the Breen, taking a moment to admire the curve of his behind against his well-toned back and narrow hips before throwing the loop around his neck and jerking him to the floor.

He was obviously surprised, but he was also quick. Tinna had to punch him twice before he let go of her arms. She knelt on his arms to pin them down, and she pressed her dagger up to his neck.

"Ovamal," she hissed. "Where is it?" He was exceptionally good-looking, that Tinna could not deny. He was perhaps in his mid-forties, but in the best condition she'd ever seen for a man of that age, not a drop of fat or sag on his frame.

"Where is what?" he murmured, with what could only be interpreted as confidence. Tinna should have taken a warning from that, but instead marked it up as part of his natural arrogance, being a villain and all.

"The proof ... the leverage that you hold against the dragons."

"It's where it is safe from the likes of you. I think that this is going to hurt," he said.

Before Tinna realized what he was saying, she felt something strike her on the side of the head, and she fell to the side, stunned. She felt herself being bound up, her wrists behind her back, her ankles, and then lifted and thrown onto the bed.

"Imagine that. Walking right into my room," the Breen whispered.

"You're right. She's gorgeous," Ovamal sighed, running his hand down Tinna's thigh.

"What are you going to do with her?"

"Oh, I don't know. What do you think?"

"Don't kill her. She's too pretty and sweet. She was exceptionally nice to me. Has a soft spot for Breen. And I admit, I like the Thran."

"Not as much as you like the idea of being mine, isn't that so?" Ovamal gripped the Breen's hair, and pulled it very hard toward him, making her gasp in delight.

"No ... I like that more," she conceded breathlessly.

"You're my good girl," the powerful man growled through gritted teeth. "You have pleased me. What do you want? I shall make you a gift."

"I want you to take me again, and then take her." The Breen's lost gaze locked onto Tinna's glazed eyes.

Tinna still had some awareness as she fought to keep her eyes from rolling into the back of her head, and she felt oddly detached from her own body. She was aware of the strange, misplaced look the woman gave her as Ovamal moved up behind her and wrapped his arms around the Breen's shoulders, smiling with a god-like

245

benevolence upon Tinna. She then lost her fight with consciousness and let everything around her blend into darkness.

CHAPTER 30

"Gods be blessed, where have you been?" Rhoa was scooped up by Pishta as she stumbled into their newest site. It had taken a full day to catch up with them, and she'd jogged most of the way. She was half dead. Her body was covered in scrapes and bruises from her harrowing climb down from the trees, and the effort of catching up to the Gypsy tribe was traumatic and much harder than she'd assumed. She thought they moved so slow she'd have plenty of time to do her thing and then come back. But they were much farther ahead than she had planned, and it took everything out of her to make it back to them in time. At least their trail wasn't too hard to follow. They had to cut back a lot of wild growth that overtook the ancient road during the year, and following the trail amounted simply to finding and following the leafy tunnel the Gypsies had sliced through the forest.

She'd made it, however. She did not pretend not to be angry with the people of this tribe for their efforts to subdue her. But they had no guilt, either; they knew what they'd done was for her own good. It was evident to Rhoa that they had been worried about her. But Pheri seemed to know in his deep, black eyes where Rhoa had gone.

He directed her to her hammock in the caravan, and helped her into it, shaking his head in disbelief. "You went to where we'd tied that thing up, didn't you?" he asked, sitting on a wall bench next to her head. She twisted to look at him, and then nodded, relaxing her muscles and gazing blankly at the ceiling, which was crammed with objects either hanging, stuffed in wall baskets, or shelves. "That was very brazen of you. A bit brave, too, perhaps." He half smiled.

"Do you feel better? Avenged perhaps?"

"No," Rhoa muttered. "Part of me thought in doing what I did, would bring Draphen back. But as reality takes back my mind, I am

247

just sad. Part of me feels forever stained by his blood. Another part wants to dance on his carcass."

"Yes." The Gypsy leader sighed, nodding thoughtfully. "But it did accomplish one thing." He waited for her to turn her head up to see him again. "You took control of your life. I doubt you'll ever feel powerless, or helpless again."

"I feel powerless now."

"Not when you need to be strong. Not when you have no other choice but to act … you now know for certain, that given the situation, you will act instead of buckle. Once you've taken such a task into hand, and followed through with it, no matter how grisly or wrong it was, I doubt very little will ever stand in your way again. I can imagine that child you carry will always be safe and provided for, with or without a father." Pheri stood and stretched. "You go to sleep, and relax … I think you've had quite enough activity for a while. We'll have you home in no time." He stepped out of the stationary caravan, the whole thing lurching as he jumped off the little porch to the ground. He left the door open so Rhoa could hear the sounds of the group, and be comforted perhaps by them. All Tinna could hear was the sound of her own heart beating in her ears. She closed her eyes, pressing tears out as she did, and sighed. Home. Finally…home.

* * * *

Taneth was drawn from his little apartment by a little bit of an uproar … by the standards of this quiet settlement, anyway. He could hear doors opening and closing, and voices chattering as people surged from the lodge out to the little forum. He put down the book he was reading, looked for Hanru, who had apparently gone outside without him noticing, and then decided to see what the ruckus was about. He made up the tail end of the miniature exodus, and found himself pushing his way through the crowd of villagers toward whatever or whoever it was they were crowding around, his heart in his throat. He found himself face to face with Rhoa. At least, it looked like Rhoa, but leaner, more muscular, wise in her expression, perhaps even a bit weary behind her bright eyes. She hugged everyone in succession, ignoring Taneth until last. When everyone had dispersed, and she'd shouted out her promise to her sister she'd be right in, she turned to Taneth and hugged him.

"She's all right, I'm sure of it. If I made it back all by myself, I'm sure she will. Better yet, she'll probably make some great entrance, with her usual panache. And she'll have a puppy, albeit a rather grown one, for the boy as she promised."

"How did you get back?"

"By some miracle, I suppose."

"And the Nimrath? I heard you went with him?"

"How did you hear that?"

"A fellow called Phenmal; I met him at the Phanos archives some days north of here."

She smiled through her tired eyes. "Yes, Phenmal. The Nimrath is dead." Her shoulders tensed and her brow tightened when she said it. "I'm going to go spend some time with my sister now ... she's been worried sick."

"Yes, of course," Taneth watched Rhoa turn on her heel and walk toward her lodge. It seemed wrong for her all of a sudden to be headed there, with all the hope and happiness of newly wedded young folk. She seemed out of place. Perhaps Rigerd would give her the former room belonging to Hanru's mother. She looked like she could use privacy. Her own space. She'd outgrown her sister in her time away from home. Earned her spot with the experienced souls. Taneth shook his head and sighed, taking a moment to watch his people filter back into the lodges, abuzz with this new development. "It's your turn to come home now, Tinna. Where are you?"

CHAPTER 31

This world is cruel and sick. This was the first thing that Tinna managed to shape in her mind as she came to. She took in her surroundings, and suddenly became nauseated. She saw her state, and realized she'd been molested by her captors. She tried to sit up, but a sharp pain shot up her neck and into her temple, and she found herself lying on her own hair, too. Her hands and feet were bound and she'd been thrown unceremoniously onto the floor of a sparsely filled room.

It's a sick world that needs to be cured, she thought, tears forming in her eyes. She used her heels to push herself up against a wall, and then wormed her way into the sitting position, sore, hurting, and humiliated. She let herself cry. She was angry with herself for allowing herself to come to this. To have trusted the Breen ... How could she have known? Breens never form attachments. It was unheard of, but obviously not impossible. Why didn't she even think it even the slightest possibility? Now look at me. She began to sob, looking at her scratched thighs, and her body marked from whatever activities she'd thankfully mentally been absent for. She felt soreness, and knew what happened to her. But no more. No. She would have given up, perhaps, if this were another time. If she didn't have a puppy growing up too fast, and someone who'd managed to become incredibly important to her along the way, waiting for her to come home. She'd been outcast all her life ... she'd been wandering in search of something, perhaps a home, and an identity, someone who'd accept her for who she was and what she was. She'd found that. And she wasn't about to let that go to pot. Not while she still had some strength left in her to fight. She didn't care much about the world any more... or about the dragons. It had become personal, between her, Ovamal and his Breen.

She took a deep breath and sucked in all her soreness, and her pain. She made it all numb. She tapped into all the dogma and practice she'd endured as a Thran child, and felt it come alive in her, like a dormant, furious entity. It had been a long time since she'd let it out to play. She'd given the world some previews of it; some small examples of what one with the blood of a Thran woman could accomplish when provoked. Now, her bitterness, her anger, her eagerness for this mess to come to some conclusion all culminated into a single dark mass which acted as food for her furious inner beast. The beast within consumed this mass voraciously, and began to awaken.

She tested her bindings. They were rope, which was a definite advantage … she wouldn't have grown so optimistic if she'd been manacled in iron. She began to fidget with her hands, twisting and turning her wrists, ignoring the occasional burning sensation, focusing her eyes on the door in front of her. She worked for a couple of hours, feeling the fibers loosening with her movement, and her hands wriggling their way free, millimeter by millimeter. Finally, she had managed to get the thickest part of her hand past the tightest part, and once that hand slipped free, the rope fell away from both. She didn't take her hands from behind her back, however, and chose to remain seated for a while, thinking with her Thran mind.

Suddenly the door opened, and Tinna reacted, slumping her shoulders instantly, and giving herself a defeated appearance. It was her Breen friend. She carried a bowl of soup on a tray. She smiled at Tinna as if she were a friend, nursing Tinna back to health. She stooped beside her and cocked her head a bit. She really was incredibly attractive; Tinna found herself thinking: too bad I'm going to have to push that face in.

"Well … you're awake … and you've managed to sit yourself up and find some comfort too, I'm glad. It's not a bad room, is it? Ovamal had it cleared of all furniture—I think he too has a good idea of what a Thran could do with a chair. But we figured the rug could stay. You deserve some comfort for all the pleasure you have brought us."

"You are both complete imbeciles," Tinna mumbled.

The Breen reached for the spoon and stirred the soup, filling up the silver bowl with broth and lifting it to Tinna's mouth. Tinna ignored it. "Why the two of you are still here is beyond me … even the village idiot would have thought twice about sticking around."

"Why's that?"

"How do you think I got here?" Tinna barked, eyes glaring furiously at the woman's vapid face.

"What do you mean?"

252

Tinna rolled her eyes and groaned, hardly able to believe how idiotic this woman was. She realized, only a second later, that this lack of intelligence or proper thought was most advantageous to her, though. It was her salvation, ultimately. Arrogance and stupidity were a dangerous combination. And her captors lacked neither.

"I flew. On the back of a dragon," Tinna finally said, shaking her head incredulously, wondering how they could possibly have not thought it a possibility. The Breen's hand fell, the soup dribbling onto Tinna's torn tunic, searing the curve of her breast.

She didn't feel it. "I told them if they didn't hear from me in three days, they were to come and burn this place down in a column of fire, just as Ovamal has had them do to all those cities and all those people." The Breen's benevolence faded … her sheen of beauty seemed to vaporize, and she stood, hurling the soup across the room.

"Then you shall die here! ALONE, you stupid woman for telling us that. Did you think we'd take you with us so you would be spared being sacrificed to the flames? I think not!" she hollered.

Tinna simply watched. She carefully slid her foot up, around the Breen's right foot, and then between her legs. Without further ado, Tinna lifted up her legs, and locked them around her calf, twisting her whole body in a crocodile roll. The woman fell like a sack of potatoes, her knee snapping. Tinna climbed onto the Breen's back and pinned her down, locking her hand over her mouth while she twisted the woman's arm painfully behind her back.

"No. I shall not die here at all, but you—you shall." Tinna's voice was low and gravelly from pain and fury. She pinned the woman's wrists under her knee, against her own spine, and lifted her other hand to the woman's head. "I sort of wish Ovamal were here. He would see how I killed his brother. A pity." Tinna wrenched, and the woman's neck cracked noisily. Tinna then stood, glanced down at her torn clothes, and then the woman's gorgeous attire. Tinna shrugged and began to strip what was left of the garb from her own body, before tugging the clothes off the Breen. She heard a delightful ring as the dagger she'd forgotten about, wedged inside her boot came tumbling out when she kicked the footwear off. They hadn't even bothered to take her shoes off to rape her. Her fury deepened; she glowered and took the Breen's clothes.

The Breen had been wearing a nice linen tunic with a plunging neckline, and a pair of loose, drawstring pants. The legs were a bit long on Tinna, but she took care of that problem by cutting off a sizable length off each leg with her dagger before sliding it into the waist of her drawstring pants. She tied her hair back with a strip from the discarded hem, and then left the room, closing the door behind her.

The place was empty ... void of life, it looked like. Tinna's senses were extremely sensitive—spurred on by her violent beast within, and the pain of every step she took. She wiped her nose on her sleeve, annoyed to see she had stained it with old, grainy dried blood in doing so. She hunkered in the house... listening.

It didn't take her too long to find him. He was not being very quiet. He was humming to himself, in some mad arrogance, as he worked as some normal landlord would, poring over some scrolls at his desk in his little office overlooking the courtyard she'd passed through so recently. She came through the courtyard again, noting that her destruction of the planters had been repaired, and the large pedestal replaced and the urn put back on top of it. She didn't waste time with sneaking or stalking. Once she saw him through the window, she moved for it.

She kicked it just where the doors came together and snapped the latch, making the windows burst inward and knock the back of his chair. She walked in, and grasped him by the neck with her arm, yanking him from his chair and sticking the dagger into his back, cutting through the skin, and coming to a stop against one of his rib bones.

"Oh! Dear me! Misjudged that cut...Let's see if I can get between the ribs this time." She laughed, her face a mad grimace. She withdrew her hand and plunged the knife again. This time, it scraped the edge of a rib and slid in between. Ovamal's noises were restricted by her tight grip on his neck, but the shock of the stabbing had pretty much taken away any chance that he'd retaliate strongly enough to overtake her now. She kicked his knees out, and watched him fall, letting him go as he did. She then turned him over and straddled his chest, her legs locked over his arms. His legs struggled and kicked, but the rib injury made it incredibly painful to lift them. She used the knife then to scrape some of the dirt from under her fingernails.

"Like my outfit? I do. I think it's more becoming on me, don't you? Well, she doesn't need it anymore, that's for sure. Her neck made a more satisfying snapping noise than Kanmer's did." Tinna guffawed. She laughed happily for a moment, and then let it taper, returning to cleaning her nails with his antique dagger.

"I'm going to ask you again, and this time, there will be no Breen to save you from answering it. Where is it?"

"You cannot have it. It is my power to wield," he hissed. "Mine."

"The Trinity has the right to that knowledge, and nobody else. Where is it? Is it safely tucked somewhere far away from here?"

"Like I would leave it to chance that anyone could find it…I don't think so," he sputtered.

"So it's in this house," Tinna surmised.

"I'm not telling you where it is. You can spend forever searching; you'll never find it."

"You're too much of a controlling lunatic to leave it to chance … so it is here somewhere, isn't it? In this house," she said. He remained tightlipped and infuriated.

"I don't need to go looking for it, though. I know a way to dispose of it quickly, without wasting any time looking for your secret ferret holes. I could leave you here … but I think you need to come with me, instead. I haven't the energy or inclination to deal with your resistance right now—sorry, but this might smart a bit." Tinna reached onto the desk and picked up a large marble bust. She lifted it up over her head and grinned at him before everything went black for Ovamal.

Ledroran circled like a vulture, smiling in a way only a dragon could smile. Somehow other dragons had gotten wind of the situation, perhaps Ledroran had called them in preparation for having to destroy the house, no telling, but there were many. Nine or ten, easily. Tinna looked at them, all circling with him in a lazy spiral.

"Are you sure? He could have it somewhere secure; someplace that could survive the heat. A network of basement rooms, perhaps—"

"YOU HAVE SEEN FIRSTHAND THE LEVEL OF DESTRUCTION OUR FLAMES CAN WREAK UPON A HUMAN STRUCTURE. WITH ALL OF US HERE, THERE WILL BE NOTHING LEFT BUT ASH AND EARTH."

Tinna leaned back, bracing her foot on Ovamal, who lay across the dragon's neck. Ledroran dove, making a low-grade grunt that instructed the other dragons to follow. The house grew large quickly. She heard him suck in a huge breath, and she could hear the sound of liquids squirting into the pink membrane cheek sacs that contained the flammable venom. There was a decisive click, like two rounded river pebbles being hit together, and then there was a release of breath and the spray of the liquid in the cheek sacs. The effect was unbelievable from the ground, let alone from sitting atop the instrument of destruction. But then, to make it all the more incredible, the other dragons spit as well, the billows of liquid fire pelting the house like a storm from angry gods. The sprays of volatile liquid were far-reaching and shot out with incredible pressure, breaking through windows and burning searing holes into the roof and walls. In no time at all, the dragons had the house blazing like it had been built on the mouth of a volcano, and they continued to spray and burn until it was no more than a blackened collection of sticks in a smoking pit several acres across.

Ovamal wasn't pleased to awake and realize he was still alive. The blow to the head had also been ineffective in its potential to cause loss of memory … so he was instantly and keenly aware the moment he came to of what had last happened to him, and understood that he was about to experience even more consequences.

He awoke as if it were the next instant after she'd hit him, and knew that he'd have been better off being dead the moment he opened his eyes. He was weakened from the loss of blood…Tinna's well-placed stabs were not instantly fatal, only calculated to keep him from overpowering her. It was something she'd been trained to do with great efficiency. She was a small thing, but he realized, probably one of the most dangerous creatures he'd ever known. She weakened her prey before she killed them; played with them. Like a cat with some poor, ill-fated mouse.

Now he saw where he was, and he knew she was planning a final game for him. He saw the tops of the clouds below him for the first time in his life, and knew instantly where he was. He then felt the rough, scaled skin of the dragon he rode, and realized by its crest it was Ledroran himself. Tinna was sitting under that crest, staring at him while drinking from a water bladder. When she saw that he was awake, she leaned out from under the crest and yelled into Ledroran's ear. "We can find a clear spot now. He's awake."

The dragon bobbed his head, causing her roof to rise and fall. He dove a bit, making Ovamal's stomach turn, and they broke from the clouds into a swath of clear sky. Down below, the land sprawled for miles, the landmarks that were normally huge and dominating from the ground naught but little bumps and nubs from here. He could see the roads below, cutting through the landscape, some villages dotting the countryside, and livestock grazing on the lush prairies. He took a moment to appreciate the way the neat rows of cultivated land looked before he felt Tinna lift him onto his knees. She cut the rope from his hands and his feet, and then knelt beside him, hand firmly gripping one of the horns protruding from Ledroran's shield.

"I thought this would be a good way for you to go. Fitting and all, having done what you did to the dragons. I enjoyed killing Kanmer, and your whore, but I think this will be my most enjoyable experience so far." Tinna smiled at him. He saw how beautiful she was, underneath all the cuts and bruises she'd accumulated during this quest to destroy him. She gave him a kiss on the forehead, and then shoved him off Ledroran's neck. "Goodbye," she said.

Ovamal fell, head over heels, the landscape spinning and the horizon turning. One moment the sky was down and the ground up, the next the opposite. It was confusing to keep track of it, but it wasn't hard to see how fast the ground approached. He clamped his arms over his face, and grit his teeth. He never knew when he hit, nor did he scream. There was a strange sense of resignation and acceptance that had overtaken him in his final seconds; perhaps even a sense of justice as his body was dashed across the side of a hill.

CHAPTER 32

The Winter Wolf was bigger, and fatter. But he was still a puppy, much to Tinna's relief. He had been very little when she found him, thankfully, and the nearly two months since she'd gotten him had done little except expand his proportions, and he'd lost nothing of his charm and affability.

Ailie and her daughter were reluctant to part with him, but they understood that Tinna had made a promise, and she had to fulfill it. They backed away from the dragon as it lifted off again, hearts smiling. The destruction had stopped, the dragons had retreated, and a strange stillness had overtaken their world. Everyone waited for the Trinity to fill the void of leadership and to help people rebuild their lives. Only a small group of people knew to whom the world should be thankful for this, and none of them except Tinna really understood the bulk of it—for as promised to Ledroran, she'd not shared the truth with anyone. Ailie was stricken by the state of her fellow Thran. Tinna was in terrible shape to say the least, and insisted she rest for two nights at a minimum before setting off for Thamatoch. She was cleaned up, her wounds dressed, at least the physical ones, her belongings restored to her, and her friendship with Ailie and her family reinforced.

She gathered up her dog, and Ledroran himself appeared to take her home, the second time he'd surprised her and honored her with his willingness to assist her. She left the merchant city at night, so not to alarm the residents. Ailie, Kailine, and Astlin were at her side, riding in the coach to the surrounding cropland—where the soft silhouette of a large, crested dragon stood patiently against the royal-blue night sky.

"Travel well, Tinna," Ailie said, taking Tinna in her arms. Kailine hugged her too, and Tinna bade Astlin a grateful farewell.

"Send my regards to Orec; he was such a dear to help me."

"He will be glad to hear from you. He has been very concerned," Kailine said. Tinna nodded, and walked to Ledroran, who lowered his head so she could climb up to the spot behind his shield as usual. She waved to them, barely seeing them in the darkness. She was glad, because she didn't really want them to see how sad she was to be parting from the again. Ledroran took wing only a moment later, and in no time, he rode the warm air that escaped the land at night up into the heavens, bringing Tinna closer to the stars than she had ever been.

Taneth was sound asleep. Most of the lodge was asleep when Tinna got there. Ledroran had found a good landing place in the small break in the trees over the horse pasture, and left her there. She reached out and wrapped her arms around his snout, her hands trembling. When she withdrew the dragon gave her a dragon smile … naught but a slight part in the lips to reveal the wicked rows of teeth.

"WE ARE FOREVER IN YOUR DEBT, NOBLE AITINNA," he said, in a strange attempt at a whisper. "TELL ANY SUMMONER OF YOUR NAME IF YOU HAVE NEED OF US, AND WE SHALL BE THERE—NO MATTER HOW MANY TIMES."

"What are you to do now?"

"FIRST WE WILL FIND THOSE TRAITORS WHO REMAIN, AND WE WILL DO WHAT WE MUST WITH THEM. AND PERHAPS, IF THOSE WHO PARTICIPATED ARE NOT AS HEARTLESS AS WE FEAR, THERE WILL BE LIVES TO BE SAVED. THOSE THAT WERE TAKEN AND IMPRISONED FOR THEIR LOYALTY TO THE HIGH THRONE, FOR INSTANCE. THEN WE WILL RETREAT TO THE FREE EMPIRES FOR NOW … LET THE MEMORIES SOFTEN A BIT. BUT WE WILL NEVER BE COMPLETELY GONE FROM HERE, SO DO NOT HESITATE TO CALL FOR US IF YOU HAVE NEED OF US."

"I will not … but I do not foresee a need to do so. I do not plan to do anything like this again. I think it's time I plant my toes in this earth and let them grow roots. Perhaps become a mother …"

"NONETHELESS, WE ARE HERE IF YOU NEED US," he insisted. "WE WILL BE SURE THAT YOUR PEOPLE OF THAMATOCH ARE ALSO PROTECTED AND THE PEOPLE OF ARAK ARE WATCHED OVER BY OUR KIND. IT IS THE LEAST WE CAN DO FOR YOU."

My people of Thamatoch. Will they have me? "Thank you for bringing me home, Ledoran. I do hope to see you again one day. Ride up in the clouds perhaps, one more time." He nodded, his yellow-green eye catching a ray of moonlight, giving it an eerie glow. "Goodbye, honorable one." Tinna kissed his muzzle and turned away, heading toward the worn path the horses made when they returned to be stabled.

She didn't look back as the dragon took to the sky again; she only heard the sound of his wings beating, and actually felt the pressure of the wind created from it. She was tired, and excited all at once. Part of her felt used and ashamed of the things she'd had to do … but she decided long ago that she was going to change her life from this point on. And whatever happened with Taneth, she would not let anything she did in the past affect her choice to remain with the people of Thamatoch, or with Taneth, even if it meant keeping it from him if she had to. But she hoped she would not … she hoped she could eventually explain it all to him, and that he would be the kind of man she knew he was, and he would understand and appreciate her honesty. She hoped.

When she reached the village, the lamps were mostly burnt out—the sky was growing lighter, for she'd been in flight for many hours. She pushed open the door of the main lodge, and padded down the hall, coming face to face with Rigerd, who was just coming back from using the waste chamber.

"By Arak!" he grunted, groggily. "Our boy was right—I figured after Rhoa returned, corroborating most of his wild tale, there was a chance, but I'm still amazed you're alive."

"Rhoa made it home?" Tinna's eyes glassed over and she felt shudders of relief ripple through her. She'd tried again and again to put the girl out of her mind, and trusted Draphen would take care of her. I guess he did…

"Yes. She's changed quite a bit because of the experience … but she's home, been home for a few days, recuperating. Taneth insisted I give her one of the apartments in the lodge, says she earned it. I couldn't argue … with the child coming and all."

"She's pregnant?"

"Oh, right. You don't know. Yes, she's pregnant." Rigerd stifled a yawn, and shook his head incredulously. "It's amazing that you're back. I hope you stick around, girl. Our Wiseman has been distracted with worry for you, and I don't think I would like to see him go through that again."

"Taneth," Tinna whispered.

"Yes. Go on then…go to him. I think he should know you're home right this second. I'll let everyone know during first meal in the morning, but I suggest you both sleep in … take a break from the madness. Keep in mind Hanru is living with him now … so try not to wake him," Rigerd said matter-of-factly. He turned to his door and went in without so much as a goodnight or good morning. Tinna shook her head and walked to Taneth's door, lifting the latch and letting herself in. She put her bag down, puppy and all, and crept to the bed where he slept.

He was so beautiful to her. He was all spread out on his bed, arms all thrown out, and one foot sticking off the bed. He wore only a pair of drawstring leggings, and nothing else. In the meager light she could make out his very lean, beautiful body. His shoulders straight, tapering down to his narrow hips ... He was all a-tousle and his mouth hung half open; he was breathing loudly, breaking into a soft snore on occasion. He looked more natural than he had when she had left... he'd let his closely cropped beard take on a softer shape, and stopped trimming it into harsh little lines—and his hair was so short! His covers were balled up under one of his arms and his pillow was on the floor.

Tinna picked it up and sat on the edge of the bed, overwhelmed suddenly by the culmination of this journey ... and her single-most desire to come back to him. She feared he wasn't going to feel the same for her, despite what she saw in him before she departed. She just wanted to hold him, and to be healed by him, both body and soul. She hugged the pillow to her with one hand and wiped away her tears with the other, glancing up at the suspended bed above him containing the innocent boy for whom this whole thing had transpired.

How wonderful he looked. So rounded and whole. His wizened angles gone from his face, the bruises and blemishes—vanished. He slept so peacefully, his little hand curled up under his chin. She reached up and touched his cheek, which was warm and sweaty from sleep, and she wanted to cry again. She looked at Taneth, and reached over to trace the markings on his face, taking note of the new lines added to them, brushing his skin delicately with her rough and injured fingers.

Taneth stirred, swatting at her hand as if she were an insect. When he came into contact with her hand, he seemed to assess it in his sleeping state and he shifted, reaching up to rub his eyes with the heel of his hands. When they fell away, he opened them a bit, and turned his head languidly toward Tinna. As soon as he registered what he was seeing, he shot into a sitting up position, hitting his head very hard on the suspended bed above. Fortunately he did not wake Hanru.

"By Arak!" He hissed loudly, rubbing his head, and then without any warning, he lunged forward and gathered her up into his arms, and pulled her to him. "By the gods … Gods …"

Tinna let herself go at that moment; it was just too much. Too strong a response, and too much the one she had so desperately hoped for; she cried, reaching 'round to clutch him to her.

"Tinna … Gods, you're here … at last," he whispered.

They held one another for a long time, until he pulled away to look at her face, his own expressing the concern and sadness at the sight of her injuries. "I don't even want to know what you've been through; it pains me to see you so."

"I'm all right. I'm a Thran. This is child's play for me." She smiled.

"Gods, I didn't think I'd miss you as much as I did," he confessed.

"Nor did I."

"When did you get home? Just now?"

"The dragon dropped me at the pasture. It only took me a few minutes to get here … I ran into Rigerd in the corridor, and then came directly here."

"Dragon … a dragon?"

"Yes," Tinna said, eyes downcast.

There was a moment of silence, and then Taneth asked, "What happened?"

"The dragons will no longer be burning down the towns and relays anymore. They've been stopped … well, more precisely, someone who had a great deal of power over them has been stopped."

Taneth did not want to hear it. He didn't. It was what Phenmal was saying all along, and it made him sick to the stomach to think of it. "The person you speak of … he knew that the dragons were responsible for the recurrences of the worm-skin plague, didn't he?"

Tinna's stomach twisted … she didn't know how he'd found out, and she wasn't prepared for this. She thought explaining it to him slowly would make it more palatable for him. She knew the moment she committed to helping Ledroran that she risked losing Taneth's respect. She was afraid he would not understand both sides of this tale…and Tinna's upbringing and her divided soul made her uniquely able to. Now he would learn what she has just done, and she knew it could go one way or the other. She looked away, at the pile by the door, her bag, and then the other bag where the puppy quietly slept.

"Sort of. But it wasn't a thing of the dragon's doing … they happened to be the instrument…the weapon, perhaps. But the one who wielded them—I killed him."

He remained tightlipped for a second or two and then he burst into a rapid rattle of whispers. "You helped them. You helped the dragons? They who have killed hundreds of thousands of people over hundreds of years?"

"They had reason, Taneth, whether you care to admit it or not. Just as we thought we had reason when we hunted them. Besides, it wasn't them, really—"

"How can they presume to discipline humanity as if we were all collectively a single naughty child?" he snapped, not listening.

"They want us to succeed, Taneth. They want us to grow and evolve. The Gods gave them the ability to make such decisions and for good reason, obviously. If they wanted us to fail, they could make us fail; they want us to live, Taneth. They do! But you have to understand, it's not just the dragons. It's not just them. It's the Trinity—"

"That's one and the same." He waved her off callously.

"No, it's not. The Trinity is not made up of three dragons … It's made up of a dragon, a human and a Chai-opse" He stared at her in skepticism, unable to formulate words for this claim. But before he could say anything she continued "The Chai-opse are not dead; they are nomadic; they are the Gypsies. The human representative is of the Keepers, Taneth. A human took part in that decision to do what was done. A human, Taneth … and not just any human … an elder of the Keepers." He lowered his gaze to the floor, his mouth agape in shock, and his eyes moving in twitches as he processed this information in his already overwhelmed brain.

"That doesn't make it right," he managed to say.

"No. It does not. Nor does it make what I did right, Taneth." He paused again…and then looked up at her accusingly.

"How could you do that, Tinna? How could you open the door for these madmen and dragons to continue controlling and culling our numbers like we were livestock?"

"I had to, Taneth. I think of your people, and the worm-skin plague, and which peoples have been 'culled' and I think you too, a thinking man, could see what has been happening to our kind … we've been improving. The Trinity is not deciding who dies, nature is. Those equipped with the skills and strength to survive are what continue on."

"How can you say such things, justifying the deaths of millions?"

"Could you justify the death of the dragon-folk? Both races are responsible for them. Both! Every period of overpopulation takes nearly half of the dragon folk before the Trinity acts."

Silence.

"I knew you would react in such a way. I had to believe what I chose to do was right, Taneth. I had to believe in it. I believed in it so much I was willing to give up the only good thing I've ever known." Tinna lost control again, and felt the tears come. She began to weep, fighting it all the way.

"What do you mean?"

"I knew you would hate me for this. I knew it. I could have looked away and kept your respect, but I could not, Taneth. I could not let anything happen to the dragons if it was in my power to prevent it. As much as the Trinity seems the beast right now, I still believe it must be protected. Not just the entity itself, but the Trinity of races, Taneth. We are selfish to think we deserve this world more than they. They were willing to become hunted and despised for this destruction rather than let the truth be told, not just to protect themselves, but to protect the Trinity, don't you see?" She tried to stop crying but could not. Taneth remained silent, watching her intently in the darkness. "They weren't just protecting themselves… they were protecting the Trinity," she repeated.

"I cannot sit here and try to convince you of something you refuse to be convinced of. I just have to go on knowing I've done the decent thing, and helped keep the sanctity of the Trinity alive in the hearts of the people, so that they can help rebuild this world and help humanity do the right thing for a change. I am not asking you to agree … I'm asking you to understand.

"I discovered how much I love you on this journey, Taneth, and I also had to come to terms with the fact that I may never know what it is to love you, and be with you and the boy." She was sobbing like a little girl.

Taneth stared at his hands for a moment, and then at her face. He saw the injuries she had sustained in this quest of hers, and he remembered how it all started, and why she had come back: to fulfill a promise to a little boy for one, and to allow herself the smallest hope that he could open his mind enough to understand what she had done and why she had done it. She was willing to put it all out before him and let him judge her, and that alone was an act of such strength and courage, it engulfed him. After all that pain, and all that danger and sorrow, here she was, lying down before him and begging his understanding. He knew he was being an ass.

He knew he could never know exactly what went on—or understand why at that moment she decided to do what she did, nor could he ever firmly say he wouldn't have done the same in the same circumstances. And he saw her. His beautiful Thran Tinna, here before him, after all this waiting and all the worry and he could not for another second hold anything against her. He loved her. He had loved her from the moment she shyly stepped into the little courtyard of his beloved new home. He wanted her here, to stay. He wanted a woman who'd carry through with a promise even through the hardest of trials, and here she was.

"Tinna," he whispered. She sniffed-in noisily, and held her breath, as if afraid of what she was about to hear next. "It doesn't matter if I think what you did is right or wrong. I'm not really qualified to judge such a thing. Perhaps Arak is, if he indeed exists— don't let Rigerd hear that I've said that … Anyway, what matters to me right now is that you're home. And you're safe. And that I love you. Hanru and I, we need you. We've missed you."

Tinna burst into tears all afresh, tears that were filled with release and happiness. She then reached out and hugged herself to him, crying on his neck.

"Oh, Taneth, you've no idea how happy you've just made me," she sobbed. He hugged her to him, taking in the smell of clean morning air and dew in her hair, and trying not to touch all the tender and wounded spots all over her body. Someday, he would ask her what happened, but he suspected she'd been through enough and didn't need to talk about it until she was ready.

"I hear you carried a pup with you for Hanru," he said. "Did it make it all the way home?" She pulled away, nodding with a smile. "I had friends care for him while I was out west. But I wasn't gone so long. He's grown a bit though, since I got him at the town near your school. Did Rhoa tell you?"

"No. A gentleman named Phenmal told me." Taneth liked the look of surprise on her face and then the shift to a tender smile. He'd forgotten how much he loved her face and her exotic accent, and how much he had missed both.

"Gods. How is he? Where did you meet him?"

"At the Phanos Archive in Lemoram. He was fine, quite well, actually."

"He's still researching? Oh dear." Tinna frowned.

"He's the one who figured it out. I knew about the dragons because of his research. I didn't want to believe it, to be honest with you. But part of me couldn't keep myself from believing it. Do you think he'll go and tell people about it?"

"I think he would understand the dragons enough not to. Did he know about the Trinity?"

"No. How did you find that out?"

"From a northern woman; her people serve the Trinity. She thought that it was common knowledge that there were three races represented in the Trinity. Her people are related to the Chai-opse … as my Gypsy blood is—"

"As are the Horse people. They got around, these Chai-opse." He chuckled.

"I'm just an ordinary human, I dare say. Is that still good enough for you?" Tinna smiled and laughed softly.

"I'm glad it's over, Taneth."

"It's not completely over, Aitinna," he said with a stern voice. "There's a certain young boy who has been waiting for a long time for a certain animal. Fifty-four days to be exact." His voice wavered when he said the number.

"Should I wake him?" she asked with a wistful smile. "He's quite the sound sleeper."

"Yes. It's a huge contrast from when I first had him. He was plagued with nightmares, poor thing."

"How'd he come to live with you, anyway?"

"Oh, it's a long story, to sum it up, his mother had just gone too far. It was time to stop it." Tinna nodded, and stood up. She padded to her things and stooped, picking up the dog bag. She thought about the gift she had for Taneth, and decided to save it for later on. She took the little sack with the dog and opened it up, lifting out the drowsy, soft, and floppy little dog. She carried him over to Taneth, who took him to give him a quick inspection.

"Fine little thing. What sort of animal is it?"

"The dragons said it's a Winter Wolf. Would you believe that?"

"Hardly," Taneth laughed. "But dragons do have keen senses. I have never seen a Winter Wolf-pup before. I suppose it's possible. I hope Rigerd doesn't mind having a full grown Winter Wolf roaming about the village."

"They're renowned for being protective of their pack; he will be an asset. Isn't he adorable? I think he and Hanru will get along grandly." The little dog yawned and rolled himself up into a ball right on Taneth's arm .

"Here. Put him in with Hanru. Let him wake up to the little fellow in the morning … it will be a great surprise. Then I think you should come and get some sleep." Taneth scooted over to the wall, and freed up space for Tinna. She found herself blushing in the dark. Blushing. She knew this was the man for her … Her own Hadrin, if she was actually blushing. She had no desire for sex—not after what Ovamal and the Breen did to her—she would need some time yet. But she knew Taneth wasn't hoping for it. He was just showing her she had a place in his home and that it was right next to him. She picked up the little dog and laid him in front of the boy's little belly. The dog slipped right back into his heavy slumber, as if he hadn't just traveled hundreds of miles by ground and air to take his place next to this particular boy. He took his spot as if it were always his, snuggling down against the boy's sweaty, sleepy warmth.

Tinna thought that was a great idea. She stripped down to her under-tunic and shorts, and climbed into the bed next to Taneth. He welcomed her into his arms, where he caressed her hair. She closed her eyes and let herself fall away, finally in a place where she could rest completely. It was all done now, and she was home. Hanru had his puppy as promised, and she had Taneth and a place among a people she loved. This was the life she was sure now that she wanted, and knew deep inside it held great promise for her as well. She curled up next to Taneth's warm chest, and finally fell asleep.

END OF BOOK 1

BOOK 2

TINNA'S MIGHT

MIRANDA MAYER

Dedications:

To my husband—whatever the world throws at us, I cannot imagine my life without you.

To Stephanie – I may be a strange kind of friend; but I am your friend nonetheless, like it or not. Your support, encouragement and enthusiasm about my work, our shared passions, and all of the endeavors that we pursue as a team, are of more value to me than you can imagine. I am truly humbled by your friendship.

To the Oregon Regency Society and its amazing leadership, for giving me the excuse to play dress-up and to feel like a girl, and for all the wonderful moments and memories your organizers and members have given me.

To Ien, whose dogged efforts helped shape the product you see here today, and whose gentle counsel helped me polish it into something to be proud of; thank you.

To my sisters, who are always there for inspiration and positive feedback whenever I truly need it. I love you guys.

To my departed Papa. Your glistening baby-blues and your gravelly voice are missed every single day.

And finally as always, I dedicate a part of everything I write to Wendy Pamay, the best teacher any young fifth-grader could ever hope for. During many years Wendy diligently provided an enriching classroom environment that fostered imagination and creativity; she inspired countless souls to grow into adulthood pursuing the creative arts. I believe every person should take the opportunity whenever possible to acknowledge and appreciate the special teachers that touch our lives and continue to influence us in our lifelong pursuits.

CHAPTER ONE – CHILDHOOD'S END

Jestin fell hard. He crumpled into a tangle of limbs onto the hard gravely path, skinning his palms and elbows and one of his knees. He chewed his lower lip and hid his face as he waited for the initial smart to ebb away. At nineteen, he didn't want to betray that his eyes felt hot with stinging tears. His horse circled him, the reins still looped on her neck. The other riders came to a stop. "Are you alright?" Avria asked breathlessly. He could hear the amusement in her voice, badly hidden in her sincere expression of concern for his well-being. Hanru was less diplomatic and simply laughed;

"What an idiot." They'd been racing along the deer paths with their horses, letting their mounts negotiate the many obstacles such as fallen logs and gullies on their own. Jestin's riding skills were not quite up to par with the others, and the course they chose was beyond his capability, resulting in his taking a hard spill.

"Han... stop it," another male voice muttered with a tone of impatience. That was Drashun, who rode an energetic two-year old that never stopped dancing. The hollow sound of the hoofs beat like musical drums on the hard-packed earth as they waited for Jestin to put himself back together.

"Who doesn't know how to ride a horse at his age?—any run-of-the-mill city dweller knows how to ride a bloody horse." Hanru was belligerent in his tone.

"He can ride. He rides very well. We all fall, Han. I seem to recall you taking a bit of a tumble out on Kettle Hill just this spring. You cannot deny that. It's part of the process. He just needs to learn how to fall. He'll get used to it." Avria was the voice of reason. She was the only girl among them.

Jestin finally rolled onto his backside, cupping his elbows and gritting his teeth. His prim and proper clothing was marred by a layer of fine gravel, conifer needles, pitch and dirt. The right knee of his tan breeches had a round coin-sized blot of blood on it, and it was growing. He hissed, and clenched his eyes shut, the sting was not passing as quickly as he'd hoped.

He heard boots hit the ground and he opened his eyes, unable to contain the sense of warmth that looking at Avria gave him. She walked to him and stooped, moving like a breeze, her soft curls picked up by her graceful gestures. She took his scraped hands into hers, clucking her tongue sympathetically.

Fair and dark all at once; tumbles of black curls down past her shoulders, skin like peaches, bright, dark-grey eyes rimmed in thick black lashes, and full, beautiful lips; Avria was a vision. Jestin could not look at her without experiencing guilt for the way she made him feel. She was supposedly his cousin. They were all supposed to be his cousins, but none of them were even remotely related—not even the ones who called themselves brother and sister. They'd been forcefully given family connections by the determined efforts of their parents and in his case, grandmother. The three who were with him were a very close-knit little group. There was Hanru, the eldest by five years; the one with the irreverent tone. He was smart, well on his way to becoming a Wiseman like his adoptive father—and he made sure everyone was aware that he was intellectually superior to them all with cutting remarks and righteous indignation. He also didn't like Jestin very much; but made an effort on the most part to get along with him. The only young person he treated with any true respect was his younger sister. That was Avria; beautiful Avria, a vision, tiny and fleet, a rider like he'd never seen, with glistening eyes and a bright, stunning smile. Lastly there was Drashun, the son of a close family friend to the duo, a very light ginger-haired mass of muscle with a sweet face and freckles.

They were People of Arak; children of the wandering people called the Chai-Opse; worshippers of the very same hard-headed beast that had just thrown him to the hard ground. Arak was their mighty equine god. Jestin was not Araki. He was human and came from Loshan, a city to the north, the son of a man some called a criminal overlord, and of a mother who was considered by many, the Great Lady of Loshan. He knew a life of great privilege and it was important to his mother and even more so to his grandmother that he experience a humbler existence through his false-cousins.

It took him some years to realize these were not his real cousins. His family had made him believe that they were and insisted he call them such. His real cousins were back in Loshan, a set of twins and an older boy, with whom he spent some time here and there. His horsy cousins on the other hand spent more time with

272

him than his own relatives. He spent every summer at Thamatoc, three months, sometimes four, and they came to see him for a few weeks during the thick of winter. He was divided in his feelings about the whole arrangement. In his mind, they definitely got the better end of the deal. For him, visitation meant roughing it in a primitive, rustic lodge-village. For them, it meant basking in an environment of luxury they were unaccustomed to, and therefore completely unable to take for granted like Jestin could.

His visits to Thamatoc offered a good thing here and there, for instance, from the time he turned fourteen, he was allowed to stay in his own apartment in the Spring Lodge. He felt very adult and independent with his own little space—at home he had a governess and teacher lodged in an adjoining room to his small apartments, and servants came and went all day. Here, he was responsible for himself. The others spent a lot of time in his little space with him, just being silly and playing games. On the other hand, his visits to Thamatoc meant he had to live very coarsely and to resign himself to feeling unclean and uncivilized, smelling of wood smoke and horses all day. But the worst thing about it was the forest. The forest unnerved him. Trees here, trees there, trees, trees everywhere. They crowded against the border of the settlement like a fjord of leaves and pins, the trees unbelievably tall. They huddled, jostled against the patches of open pastureland meant for the horses, and even the 'open' pasture had copses and oaks that cluttered the open space, and darkened the earth below them. He felt like it would suffocate him one day.

The dense cover of trees made everything green with algae and mosses. Rocks were slick, old-man's beard and hag's hair drooped from branches, the forest floor was often like a sponge, always sopping wet and full of slimy creeping things. It always felt colder because of the humidity, and it rained too much, even in summer.

Then there was the forest of giants several miles from the village where Avria and Drashun loved to go, and Jestin and Hanru inevitably followed. The Karsu trees; with trunks that were wider than the summer lodge, wider than the front of the temple of Atrulath back in Loshan, too big to be a living tree, he thought, unnaturally large; larger in circumference than the village forum where the founder's tree grew... he hated those trees the most.

Drashun explained that his father had come from a forest of giants like this one—Jestin knew that Drashun's father was long dead, part of some story that all of their parents shared before he, Drashun and Avria were born. Drashun claimed that these great trees

273

were where the Nimrath lived, high up in the canopy. His father was Nimrath, a creature much feared by humans. Jestin could never quite put aside his sense of fear from knowing that he was inside the territory of the Nimrath; nor could he dispel from his mind, that tiny undercurrent of mistrust towards Drashun and his mixed blood. It tainted how he perceived the forest and how he looked at the fair-haired, innocent looking young man who supposedly had the blood of some strange race of people that could blend into the environment at will.

The ambience beneath the Karsus, under their massive limbs was frightening and bizarre in his eyes. It was a forest floor that was perpetually darkened by layers of branches that rose up to unbelievable heights, growing leaves in some cases, bigger than a tabletop. Mixed among the limbs were the parasitic plants and small trees that grew on the wide branches of the behemoths. Hardly anything grew on the forest floor, and one could stand and look out at this green-tinted darkness, studded with trunks more massive than the next, like sage-green-marbled, smooth-barked columns in a temple of giants, receding into the darkness under a ceiling of wild growth. Creatures stirred in there; some known, others not. The birdsong was always different in the Karsu forest. The birds louder, their song grating and harsh, no twittering or warbling, just caws and hoots. Jestin really didn't like those trees.

The Araki also buried their dead under trees, and their cemeteries consumed hundreds of acres around the settlement, felling the towering conifers, and replacing them with their blessed great oaks. It had been done for centuries, so there was hardly a time when out riding when you didn't find yourself riding through, or near a place of death; a forest of oaks, with tinker-toys, mobiles and all manner of other junk dangling from the branches. Jestin did not like these things about Thamatoc; but they were things Avria, Hanru and Drashun felt comfortable with. He learned to bear it, but deep down, he never felt at home in Thamatoc, and sometimes dreaded these things as summer approached. And when he was home, he couldn't look at a tree without feeling oppressed.

He glanced at Avria, and in his mind's eye, he saw her as he did first thing that morning when he'd arrived, doing martial exercises with her mother. Both women were lithe and beautiful, their curls catching the golden morning sun like a halo, their concentration on each elegant move of their artful dance. Perhaps, he mused, there are some things that make my time in Thamatoc worth my while.

Avria's mother's qualities were much like those of his mother and grandmother. That was their connection; their heritage. Tinna, Avria's mother was a Thran; a foreigner from a matriarchal empire south of Oromoii, and his grandmother Ailie was one as well. Both had been warriors, and both had a created an unbreakable bond of friendship, one that eventually included his mother, Kailine, when she came to know Tinna as a peer. Tinna was older than his mother, but not by too much. They'd become pregnant at almost the exact same time, and were delighted to discover motherhood together, spending much time traveling back and forth between Thamatoc and Loshan to share the experience as friends. They lived in such different worlds, but always found time to visit one another, and when Avria and Jestin were born, they had them go through the traditional Thran naming ceremony together, marking their babies' right shoulder blades with tiny tattooed pictograms that legitimized their place in the world.

Tinna was wife of the Wiseman Taneth. He was an odd fellow, warm and awkward, with a tender voice, and a gentle way about him. He cooked astonishingly well, and had little problem with the idea of doing this domestic task instead of his wife. She was a free spirit, but she respected the Araki ways as far as she could allow. The people adored them both so much, nobody made issue of her training women and men in her weapons and her martial arts, or not at all partaking in the crafts that most women did; except for occasionally sewing, tanning suede, or helping someone to learn how to spin with a drop-spindle. The people felt more fortunate for the new ideas and skills she'd brought them, and they respected Tinna as much as Taneth. Last winter, there was talk that the village leader was considering naming Tinna his successor, since his own children had gone to lead their own clans. Jestin wondered in passing as he tried to overcome his pain, if anything came of it.

The pair of a temperate scholar and a fiery warrior did not appear peculiar to Jestin. It was a mirror of his grandparents' marriage; the same even-tempered man and barely stable woman. Tinna and Taneth made things feel familiar to him because of it; he felt most at home because of them. Tinna and Taneth were happy together. Jestin's parents were too; but it was a different dynamic; Astlin had the appearance of being the dominant person in the marriage, but that was not the case. Kailine ruled behind the scenes. Tinna and Ailie defied the northern conventions by being who they were; Kailine hid her dominance, and his father let it happen, despite her being far from an even-tempered, stable person. This circle of strange adults were Jestin's world; virtually his parents, all six; and their children, sort of his siblings.

Jestin couldn't deny that he loved this strange not-really-a-family. What bothered him was that he always felt like the outsider. Rhoa's son Drashun, who wasn't even part of the Wiseman's family, was closer to Avria and Hanru than Jestin felt. He was slightly jealous of this. Drashun was not much older than Avria, less than eight months, and they all grew up together, Hanru the ever watchful older child.

Jestin looked up at Hanru. He was a fairly plain young man, not as dashing as people said Jestin was. He had cropped unkempt hair and a pair of oddly tidy muttonchops down his angular face. He was fair-skinned and his hair was a chestnut brown with a hint of red in it. He wasn't overly muscular like Drashun, who looked like a chiseled statue with wide shoulders and a heavy brow. Hanru was long and lean, and easy on his horse, a chestnut stallion with a blaze that covered the whole top of his long head. Hanru's pale gray eyes looked bored and annoyed with Jestin. The younger man knew that deep down, Jestin's conceit was an object of disgust to Hanru, and he figured after nineteen years of spending part of his year with the Araki, that perhaps he could step down from his high horse. Hanru seemed quietly pleased that Jestin had been thrown down from the high horse instead and was now looking more like the frightened little rich boy he'd always been.

Jestin finally got to his feet, brushing his clothes off defiantly, challenging Hanru's gaze. Avria led him his ornery mare, and he took the reins, muttering something under his breath about being able to do it himself. He remounted, hiding his humiliation badly. Avria shook her head and mounted her nimble little horse, a fine-limbed little powerhouse with the color and shine of raven's feathers. She had four white socks, and a steel gray mane that tapered to white on the ends. The horse matched Avria's dark features, her deep, dense black curls of hair, and her dark, brooding gray-black eyes. She looked very much like her mother, with a touch of Taneth in her smile and her mannerisms. She was much softer than her unflappable mother; more Araki than Thran; girlish and sweet. Jestin had been a slave to her from the time they were toddlers. He had fond memories of ambling about the Wiseman's apartment with the large dog Roog while Tinna and Kailine studied the fine fabrics she'd brought from the city for Tinna. There was no one more important to Jestin than Avria. He endured his time at Thamatoc, and saw it as a sacrifice to be close to her.

Drashun cantered past them all, and rode ahead on his restless horse, his dirty blond hair flouncing with each stride. Hanru followed, and then Jestin. Avria took the rear. "We won't do any more jumps until you're more confident," Avria assured him, riding up alongside. He frowned, and shook his head. There were few people in the world he could regard with as much trust and respect as he did Avria. He probably would not have been willing to bear such humiliation with anyone else. He offered her a half-smile, and suspired.

"You really like to patronize me, don't you?" She looked at him in puzzlement, and then frowned.

"Jestin, I can't help being the way I am around you. We've been such close friends for so long." His response was a despondent sigh.

"I've only been here for three hours and I've already been embarrassed in front of them," he jutted his chin towards the two boys who always made him feel like an idiot because he couldn't ride as well as they could, or he wasn't as scrappy or as witty as they were.

"Who cares what they think?" Avria snorted. "You always care what they think." Again, his response was expressed with a dejected sigh;

"Avria, I'm not like you, or them. I love coming here for you, but I'm not a horseman, I'm not an Araki, I'll never be an Araki. I hate having to go through this every time I come here. It's not my idea of fun; it's an Araki idea of fun."

"The only real Araki here is Hanru. Well, Drashe is half-Araki," she conceded with a shrug and a smirk. "You always have this unease when you first arrive, then you get out of your stupid fashionable clothes, and you start wearing normal things, you start to relax. We just need to all sit down and eat something, and get back to normal. You'll see." She reached out her hand and laid it on his arm, her brow bunching up into sympathetic wrinkles. Ahead, the two boys chose an alternate path that looped up a steep rise, over a wooded hill with lots of obstacles for their horses to negotiate. Avria smirked and shook her head, riding with Jestin along the even path towards Thamatoc.

They rode into the forum just at the cusp of noon. People were clearing up the items from their outdoor crafts and filing into their respective apartments for a nice cool siesta. They were enjoying the ebbing days of summer, and soon the rains would come. The leader Rigerd nodded at them when they rode in, appraising Jestin with a critical eye. "Rub them down if you haven't walked them," he shouted in a gravelly, tired voice. He was a towering man, his hair cropped close to his head and a silver plaited beard hanging from his chin. He'd been leader of Thamatoc for more than thirty-five years. He was also Taneth's closest friend. The two of them would sit by the hearth in the leaders' council chairs for whole evenings, chewing on pipes and mumbling to one another.

The village common was a circular space of large dimensions that looked as if it were sunken into the earth. The road led in down a gentle incline between an avenue of trees, and opened up to the common. In the center of the common was a massive oak tree, the huge leafy dome shading the better part of the common's partially cobbled ground. This was the founder's tree, and there was no Araki village that did not have one, except a brand new settlement where its founder still lived.

Enclosing the space in an arc were the faces of the massive earth lodges that made up the village of Thamatoc. The four main lodges faced the entrance road, as well as the stable lodge where the horses were kept. Over the towering nested doors of the lodges, the forest grew, root systems sometimes dropping down over the edge of the roof and twisting onto the sides and face of the lodge building. Inside each lodge, rows of apartments and common rooms housed about three hundred people. The people cared for and bred about sixty Dedrahour Warm bloods, a horse that was valued for its elegant lines and hardy frame; however a few horses of exotic breeds were kept about to breed in some unusual traits that could add more value. They also had nine ponies and four draught horses. This was a moderately sized clan with a small breeding operation, but they did well enough to keep their lodges in order, to pay for necessary trade goods and keep seeds and other livestock coming in for the sustenance of the people.

The people of Thamatoc grew several small crops and maintained a few acres of vegetables. They also harvested the bounty of the surrounding forests and rivers, and hunted the fauna that lived in the woods.

This quiet community went about its business in the most peaceful way, and on days like these, they were taking advantage of the sun and the warmth to do their daily tasks… but when the sun got too warm starting at noon, they migrated into the cool interiors of their underground lodges and the common would grow ghostly quiet. The young people arrived just before the daily summer

278

desertion, and Tinna appeared before they led the horses into the stable. She looked relaxed in some common day-clothes; a long, well-fitted ivory tunic that hung onto her hips with sleeves that covered her knuckles, and rust colored skirts that draped down the length of her legs, and puddled into a short train behind her. She had a dog at each side, and she paused as she strode along to lay her hand on Jestin's smooth cheek.

"You look more like your father every day," she said, her eyes full of adoration for the boy. She was so attractive; and her daughter looked just like her. She and her daughter shared the same head-full of black tube curls that tumbled down against their back and shoulders. She had olive skin, darker than her daughter's peachier tone, but they shared the playful tilt of the eyes, that little dash of gypsy loveliness, thick lashes and dark, arched eyebrows. There were some strands of silver woven into the curls framing her face, and the youthful bloom that Avria had wasn't quite so bright on her mother's cheeks. She had soft hands from all that tallow she used. Like Jestin, she wasn't an avid horsewoman. She rode them to get around, something she only learned to do out of necessity. Her attachment to Thamatoc was Taneth and their children—she wasn't raised to worship horses, and so she did not—she respected them.

"I'm so glad you're back. It's too bad Kailine couldn't be here too. I'll have to accompany the children this winter and stay too." He smiled at her earnest face. His mother once told him that he should never let her face fool him; that she was more dangerous than he could imagine. He couldn't see how this middle-aged woman could pose a danger to anyone. The dogs had followed Tinna and were standing there, gazing up at Jestin, both panting and pleased to see the young people returned. They were too old to join them on the ride, and there were no new puppies in the Wiseman's home now.

It would be more accurate to call them wolves, but Jestin saw them as big, loving dogs. These were members of his extended family he could easily say he was unabashedly in love with. Jestin looked forward to having them around every year. There had been only one at first; Roog. Jestin warmly recalled the huge, sweet dog from his early childhood visits to Thamatoc; he remembered running his tiny hands through his dense silver-gray fur, and lying across the dog's barrel body with Avria, the three of them wrestling by the community hearth while Hanru looked on, keeping a careful eye on his wolf while the small children tormented him. Roog was their companion for years, and as he grew older, Tinna became concerned that there would be no more Roog to warm Hanru's feet at night or to delight her adorable daughter any more.

So she and her dearest friend, Rhoa, who she called her adopted sister, set off to find another wolf one early spring. Her departure had marked a legendary argument between Taneth and Tinna, one people talked of to this day. Such shouting was never heard in the lodge before. There was much throwing of things, and slamming of doors. After Tinna left, Taneth proceeded to declare that this was a wasted trip—and that his wife was insane and that wolves were not so easily found, and that she is undertaking another impossible task. But she returned two weeks later with two puppies, one forest wolf, the other a mountain wolf, humbling the all-knowing Taneth. Finally everyone was happy, for there was peace in the Wiseman's household again.

The wolves were two females. They named one Reega and the other Therta. Roog wasted no time in making several batches of puppies from each bitch before his days ended. The puppies were distributed around the village and to some other clans during the autumn festivals. And in the ensuing years, the clans adopted their own wolves, and bred them with Roog's line. The Araki people now had wolves aplenty; it was all the rage among the clans, spreading out into the deep forests and westwards towards the plains. But the matriarchs, Reega and Therta, now gray-faced and slowed with age still lived with the Wiseman's family; Roog long since passed away, buried under a tree in a glade next to another puppy Hanru once owned.

"I'm glad you've come. You are a bit late for your summer visit, Jestin, but that's good, because maybe you will be here long enough to join us for the autumn festival meeting at Umatoch," she told him. Jestin hoped not. He could barely tolerate one clan, being subjected to many clans of Araki made him feel nauseous. "Come to our apartments for dinner, Jestin. In the meantime, I took the liberty of leaving some lunch for the four of you in your apartment in the Spring Lodge. Eat, talk, catch up with the others, and then sleep a bit. I'll see you this evening. Take the girls with you too;" she patted Reega's head, "they've missed the lot of you. They wish their youthful days were back so that they could run with the horses." She padded away, the train of her skirts catching a dry oak leaf as she moved towards the lodge. Jestin led his horse into the airy stable, his stomach growling at the thought of a nice lunch. He liked the food here. It was fresh and simple.

The dogs' nails clicked on the clean slate floor of the stable as they followed Jestin and the horse inside. He heard Avria giggling and caught her just as she turned to look at him coming in. Her smile was radiant. She makes everything worthwhile, he thought. He wondered if he would be permitted one day to marry his false-cousin. He should be the first consideration. They had the same Thran blood in their veins.

The dogs waited patiently while the young people unsaddled their horses and lovingly brushed them down. The caretaker Elemar shooed them all out when they'd lingered too long, and they crossed the large round courtyard, the centermost part shaded by the founder's tree. Jestin had to admit he was feeling better. He still had grit imbedded under his skin on his hands and elbows, his knee hurt whenever he bent it, and his brand-new fresh-from-the-tailor drath-suede breeches had a fist-sized bloodstain blossom on it, still red in the center; a dried up ugly brown around the edges.

They entered the spring lodge, Avria and Drashun joking boisterously, and then shoving Jestin playfully so that he slammed into the door of someone's apartment. Behind them, the dogs followed. The young people were happy Jestin was back into the fold, even the taciturn Hanru, despite his outward appearance of dislike towards his city 'cousin'. Jestin just had to figure that out somewhere along the line. They all teased each other, and they picked on him the most, but they were all the best of friends.

* * * *

Jestin was awoken by jostling. It was Avria and Drashun jumping on the bed. As soon as they saw him crack his eyes a bit, take them in, and furrow his brow in silent disapproval, they broke into snickers, still jumping up and down next to him. He groaned and pulled his covers over his head, turning onto his side. Avria jumped and then dropped to her knees beside him, and tore the covers from his head, leaning down so that her mouth was right next to his ear.

"GET UP JESSY!" she screamed at the top of her lungs. Jestin twisted away in agony, clapping his hand over his ear. Without any warning he grunted;

"That's it! I've had it with these wake-up assaults!" He wrapped his arm around her waist and whipped her onto her back, and then straddled her chest facing her feet, her arms pinned under his legs. He scooted his posterior towards her face. She squealed, laughed, whined, screamed and kicked, crying "No!" Drashun punched Jestin's upper arm quite painfully, and bounced around them, their collective laughter loud and obnoxious. The dogs barked at the hilarity and excitement. The noise was deafening. "Oh dear! Uh-oh! I think there's a rumble in the basement!" he warned, scooting his bum even closer to her reddened face. His head twisted 'round with an evil grin. Avria screamed out in horror, laughing so hard tears were running down her cheeks, begging him to release her. Drashun was wheezing with laughter. "Help me! Get her feet!" Drashun transferred his loyalties immediately, and grabbed Avria's feet.

"You are all a pack of half-wits," Hanru grunted, walking into the small apartment. They froze and looked at him; there was a pause in the commotion. "Everyone's complaining about the noise you're making. Ave, not everyone wakes up at the crack of dawn, you know. It's really inconsiderate." As soon as his last word tumbled out of his lips, the racket resumed with more energy.

"Oooh, I think it's bubbling down the chute!" Jestin blurted, wiggling his bottom threateningly, and Avria started struggling and squealing again. Hanru shook his head and sighed dramatically, leaving them to their wrestling match. He left with an unnoticed click of the latch. He was simply above such behavior. He always had been.

Avria exercised some of her Thran training—the threat of having Jestin pass gas in her face was simply too dire to waste time giggling. She wrenched her feet out of Drashun's soft grip, and kicked him away, and then lifted her leg up. She locked Jestin's head behind her knee, clamping him between her calf and thigh. With an arch of her torso, he was flipped forward off the bed with a clatter. Drashun guffawed, pointing at him, and then dead-dropped on top of him. Jestin roared as the air was knocked out of him and then loudly gasped to breathe. He shouted out war-cries as he punched Drashun's ribs with his fist. Someone started banging on the door, and it was flung open by a perturbed looking Taneth.

"That is quite enough! There are people with small children living in this lodge, did you forget that? Don't you hear the infants crying from being awoken by this uproar?" Taneth was trying to appear as angry as he sounded, but he could not hide the telling twitch of his mouth as he fought a grin. Drashun was on top of Jestin at an angle, his upper body across his stomach, and barefooted Avria was about to drop on him too. They were all grinning like they did when they were eleven and driving the village insane, rushing through the lodges with the dogs in tow, a rumbling cloud of bedlam.

282

It warmed his heart to see them playing like children. It made him wish he and Tinna had been fortunate to have more children so such joy would not leave his home so soon. They were growing up too quickly. Oh, blast, they are already grown. Look at my little Avria. His eyes misted up suddenly, and he cleared his throat, no longer seeing the nineteen year old woman before him, but the three-year-old Avria, clutching Roog's scruff and nuzzling his soft face, and then looking up at him with her huge, innocent eyes. He wanted to scoop her up and hold her on his shoulders like he used to. Now he had all these plans for her, and for Hanru. He sighed.

They had gotten to their feet while he lamented the loss of their childhood. He studied Jestin, who had a bruise on his upper arm, and he was scraped up from a fall yesterday. Jestin seems so strange, that boy... always so uptight when he arrives from Loshan, and then the next day, he's right back into pattern, being toughened up by his rough-edged cousins, so obviously smitten by my beautiful daughter—Taneth mused. I'll have to nip that in the bud, he thought. We can't have that.

"Come with me, the three of you," he turned into the corridor. Jestin looked down at his drawstring trousers and his sleeping shirt, and was about to protest, but Taneth barked:

"Now!"

CHAPTER TWO – SHENANIGANS

"How many?"

"Sixteen. And Elemar is going to need your help."

"I can't see how I can be of any help. You all know how badly I ride." Jestin sighed intolerantly and raked his dark hair back from his forehead. While everyone else preferred to cut their hair short round these parts, it was fashionable in Loshan to keep the hair on top of the head cut long, to the middle of the ear and trimmed close to the scalp around the sides and back of the head. Avria groaned in annoyance.

"Not that song again!" She lifted her leg up and kicked the back of his shoulder. He rocked forward, and then fell back against the chair, his arms still crossed, acting as if he hadn't felt it.

"Look. You're not children any more. Adults just don't recreate day and night."

"I hear lots of adult recreation going on at night," Drashun muttered boyishly. There were the expected snickers. Taneth duly ignored him and looked directly at Jestin, lifting his hand to point at him.

"You may see your visits to Thamatoc as a vacation of sorts; we see it as an extra hand now. You have to earn your keep to remain here."

Jestin did not think of visiting Thamatoc as anything like a vacation. More like a prison. It certainly wasn't something he wanted to work for, except to be near Avria. Taneth paused and looked at all of them. "You are all overdue for your rites of passage ceremonies; I think it's time to do that. Then you're going to help Elemar take horses east to Darachar. It's not far, only a day or two past Hildercross."

"Hildercross! Isn't that where you were schooled?" Jestin asked.

"Hildercrushed, more like it," Hanru muttered under his breath with a raised brow and a smirk. The others looked at him, amazed that he'd attempted a joke.

"Yes, Hildercross is a ruin. Tell us something we don't know!" Taneth continued without missing a beat.

"Why haven't you had your rites yet?" Jestin asked Avria all of a sudden. She held a long stick sparkling with amber clusters of crystallized syrup from a sugar tree. He had no idea where she'd gotten it between the spring lodge and the summer lodge, but he could smell the sweet syrup from where he sat. She stuck it into her mouth and twirled it and finally answered.

"The Holyman died while we were in Loshan this winter. We haven't had a replacement yet." She bit into the end of the candy-stick, crackling it between her glossy white teeth. She slumped in her chair in the most unladylike fashion, breech-clad legs open, free arm hooked over the back of her chair. Crunch, crunch, crunch. More of the candy-stick disappeared.

"Oh."

"You're getting the rites too, Jestin," Taneth declared. Jestin's black brows shot up.

"I'm what? I don't need the rites. I'm not from Thamatoc, I'm not Araki." He sat up rigidly and furrowed his brow. "Why do you people insist on forcing all your silly little cultural norms on me? I never asked for this!" His sky-blue eyes glistened with defiance.

"Your mother did, actually." Taneth had a talent for stating things so that they sounded final.

Jestin slumped back into his chair. Even he knew that what Kailine wanted, Kailine got. She was the law in his world. Why she insisted on his taking the rites, he did not know, but he suspected that she didn't want him to get stuck in Loshan and become part of the system in which his father thrived. Elevation to adulthood by the Araki would make him Araki. Once they marked him, they would own him.

Kailine hoped to steer him towards a better future than leading a criminal empire. Taneth rubbed the back of his neck for a moment and crossed his leg over his knee. They all sat around the community hearth in the chairs the village elders used for meetings. Avria loudly crunched another few centimeters of her candy-stick, revealing the thin twig within.

"There are going to be some changes around this village in the next few days, starting with a new Holyman. However it's going to be different this time. He's not going to be the traditional Araki

286

Holyman—we're going to become home to a Zshathri Druidic Soothsayer. Then Rigerd is going to retire, and Tinna will take the position of Chieftain here." Hanru, Avria and Drashun's mouths dropped open at Taneth's words. Only a true Araki could understand the weight of these declarations.

This sort of thing simply didn't happen. Female leaders were not unusual among the Araki; there were many. But Tinna had not been born Araki. The idea of a Druid from some unknown, far-off place seemed alien. First the wolves, now this.

The fateful arrival of Taneth and Tinna, two decades ago, now threatened to make Thamatoc the wild stepchild of the Araki clans. Rigerd liked Taneth so much, he put up with just about anything the man did, and he forgave too many of Tinna's infringements on Araki tradition. Rhoa had given birth to the half-Nimrath child Drashun. Tinna taught able Araki women the martial arts that made her a force to be reckoned with. The village of Thamatoc, by diverging from the norm, had become its own strange little aberration of a community among a vast network of rigid traditionalists. So far, the adoption of the wolf-dogs was about as far as many of the other villages and clans were willing to go. At gatherings, the older folk of the more conservative clans distanced themselves from the people of Thamatoc for fear of catching Thamatoc's disease of change.

"What do these changes have to do with delivering horses?" Drashun asked innocently. Taneth rolled his eyes and then massaged his eye sockets with one hand.

"Nothing, you dunce!" Avria reached out and batted her cousin on the head with her the back of her hand. "But it's the reason why we're getting our rites. We're getting a new Holyman or Druid or soothsayer or whatever he is. That's why he told us. He doesn't want us leaving here to another clan without proper markings."

Drashun swatted back at her, snatched the rest of her candy stick and chucked it unceremoniously into the ashes of the main hearth. She protested with a woeful 'Oh! My sugar-stick!'

Jestin chuckled mockingly at her, raised his fists to his eyes and twisted them, pretending to cry like a baby.

"Wah, wah!" Drashun laughed at this with great alacrity, mimicking Jestin.

"Will you half-wits please cease your ridiculous antics?" Hanru grunted. "I can't believe what a lot of children you still are. None of you deserve the rites of passage—you're all still completely infantile.

"Oh, hang yourself, Mr. High and Mighty!" Avria snapped. "When are you leaving, anyway?"

"Not soon enough!" he huffed, crossing his arms and glowering darkly.

"He's leaving around the same time; he's headed north, you're headed east," Taneth interjected. Avria suddenly realized that her brother was going away, and her brow furrowed. Hanru had been allowed to study mostly at home and had left for Lemoram for a month at a time every three months since he was nine. Hanru liked the archives full of dusty books and the new Lemoram Conservatory, founded by Taneth and others of the Keepers to fill the void left by the destruction of Hildercross

The decade after the Dragon Burnings was rife with renewal. After all the destruction and death, a surprising sense of optimism emerged, motivating the Araki not just to resurrect the broken systems, but to create new and better ones and to restore the strength of what was left of the human population. They had dwindled to small numbers in clustered communities, trying hard to recuperate from the devastation. The southern lands below Thran, the Thran themselves, and the Gheraine of the west were the only human settlements left untouched by the dragons, but none of them had significant populations; their isolation had saved them. The core of their race had occupied Oromoii. The Dragon Burnings had left humanity on the precipice of extinction, but over the last two decades, they had begun, slowly, to recover. Taneth worked tirelessly with many of the upper-ups of the Human contingent to help rebuild some of the institutions that had been destroyed. He traveled much to Lemoram during that time, taking the growing Hanru with him on every occasion.

Hanru's days of living divided between two worlds had come to an end. He would attend the Conservatory for two years, full time to complete his education. He was already twenty-five, almost six years older than Avria. It seemed too old to be finishing his education. But Taneth had wanted Hanru to enjoy family life as well as school, something Taneth had wished for very much in his youth, having grown up literally within the walls of Hildercross. He wanted Hanru to know love and family and still get a good education. Hanru already had a possible place as Wiseman in Wye, a small, fledgling Araki clan that was establishing itself on the rocky coast near the mountains, where one could look across the waters and see the Isle of Gales. Avria felt a twinge of jealousy; she had always wished to see the ocean. Her mother described her single experience of it with such reverence; she could scarce keep from leaving to see it for herself. With Han living at Wye, she would have an excuse to go visit.

"So when do we all leave?"

"The Soothsayer is due to arrive any day now. He was traveling by coach from the northwest—the new east road leading to Klatna and points beyond is not quite finished yet, and there's no bridge over the Ashlan River yet. The post-coaches won't travel the gypsy roads. He would have left the road and coach at Hildercross. So he's probably on foot with Veeru now on the Gypsy and Araki paths. Veeru was sent out to Klatna to meet him with pack horses as soon as the relay notified us that he was near. It could take some time, depending on what he's carrying."

The ruin of Hildercross hunkered high on Mount Klatna. The town that had once ringed the foot of this hill was all but grown over with young trees and understory shrubs; save for a small area some enterprising Araki had taken over. They moved in on the destroyed city, and began to restore the better buildings for their own use. They took up what the destruction had left behind and determined to make the best possible use of the only road that connected the northlands with the southern coastal region and the Isle of Gales. The non-Araki had abandoned the region since the burning. The High Throne had all but toppled—the King still ruled, but the system he ruled was no more. No nobles remained in the region to stake claim, and the Araki had retaken the forests. Klatna had once enjoyed a thriving commerce because of the trade road before. The new owners hoped to restore Klatna's glory, but after their own style as horse-worshippers.

"A Druidic Soothsayer brought into an Araki village—and he does not worship the horse. There is something fundamentally wrong about that," Hanru opined.

"They do worship horses, through their reverence for Life and Nature. We need spiritual guidance for the people, and frankly his knowledge and education will take a burden off my shoulders. I've got a growing community to educate, people to heal, problems to solve, projects to start—large, daunting projects, like adding that new lodge to the circle. I need help, and since you are headed eastward after school, I need to make sure I'm covered," Taneth ranted. "With the vast shortages of spiritually educated people, we have to make do." The High Throne's institutions had largely been responsible for molding the Wisemen and scholars, but the Dragon Burnings destroyed the communities, decimated almost all human settlements and undermined the infrastructure. Twenty years on, and they still had not recovered. The Araki enjoyed a boon, their worlds untouched by the dragons. They were slowly expanding into the vacuum left behind by the humans.

Hanru smiled wanly and looked at the black hearth, where Avria's ash-coated candy stick lay dejected. Tinna said that Taneth had once hated anything that referred to spirituality. He'd rejected all ideologies and had mocked the religious. But when he came to Thamatoc, things changed. Somehow, his view about faith had softened. It must seem strange to Tinna to see him bring a Druidic Soothsayer into the fold. The soothsayers supposedly wielded magical powers. Hanru smirked. Magis, Mystics... The Druids... What a crock! He shifted in his chair and shook his head. What next? Talking horses?

"I'm telling you all this because it's high time you got involved in what goes on around here. We have too many horses, and a visit to Darachar gives us an excellent opportunity to get better acquainted with the eastern groups, especially those who will maintain heavy trade through Klatna and the trade road. Once the East Road is complete, we will be connected to all this. We could stand to benefit from it greatly. It's a young clan of young people. So we've decided you would be the best choice. As soon as the Soothsayer gets here, we mark you as responsible adults; which is laughable at this point, and then you're to go," Taneth concluded, watching his girl closely. She seemed quite aloof about the whole matter. She nodded and stood, leaning down to peck her father on the cheek. She turned to Jestin and Drashun and smiled.

"Well, if these are to be our last hours of unadulterated puerility, let's go live it up! I suggest we go to Silver Lake, to the old settlement, and make as much noise as possible," she suggested.

Taneth pursed his lips and arched one brow, standing and rustling away from the hearth in his olive-green chasuble robe, leaving them to themselves. Jestin smiled. He liked Silver Lake, an abandoned Araki settlement with no more space for the dead. The forests crowded against the small pastureland, making it too small and too old for use by a large clan. It was left to a large extended family who maintained the space. They had no herds for breeding, and only kept a few goats and some quorti to keep brambles from overtaking the forest floor. The village was now a sort of community of inns. They allowed guests to stay; Araki for free, and strangers for a low fee. Part of the Spring Lodge was turned into a small tavern, and the stable-lodge was used as a livery for visitors. People would come to swim in the warm lake and to relax on the way from one destination to the next. It was fairly near the trade-road, so it had always seen a steady stream of non-Araki visitors until the burning. Now it was growing again—and like the Araki at Klatna, they hoped to profit. They'd spent much time retrofitting the lodges to meet the needs of visitors.

The four of them slept a fitful night, got up before the sun, packed up their horses, and left. Reega and Therta followed them as far as the gypsy road, and then sat and watched them until the swaying rumps of the horses were well out of sight.

* * * *

The High King had survived the Burnings, but the noble families and lines of Viceroys, whole dynasties that had been in power for more than two-thousand years, were erased from existence, decimated by one evil man who knew a secret so awful, so terrible, that the dragons had to do as he demanded, even destroy every royal city, every royal institution, anything that was connected to the high-monarchy, rather than allow the human race to learn this terrible truth.

That secret had been forced upon Tinna. Nobody else except Taneth and one other older man by the name of Phenmal knew. Tinna had encountered Phenmal during this difficult period of the dragon attacks, and he had become a close friend of the family since. He was bonded to Tinna and Taneth by the secret they all shared. Phenmal had been the connection Taneth needed to the Keepers, that helped Taneth in building the Academy in Lemoram and to spearhead the reconstruction of other academies around the eastern side of Oromoii, over the years, he became a sort of strange, detached member of Avria's family. Phenmal also happened to be a Chaiva; a member of the Keepers, or an associated ex-member of this secretive organization, and he had the ability to read the thoughts of others. He walked in circles far above any that Tinna or any of her kind knew of; since the fall of the human rule, he'd become very active with the Keepers again, in addition to other related groups.

An odd duck, Phenmal intimidated Avria. He seemed to have that effect on many people. He lived in a lonely old manse about half a day on horse from Thamatoc. Tinna said he'd moved from an isolated manor on the northern tip of the forest-peninsula to this new home, just to be close to Lemoram, and apparently to Tinna and Taneth, whom he counted among his only friends. He visited on occasion, claiming that he could tolerate the simple-minded folks of

291

Thamatoc–something that irked Avria and made Tinna laugh. Avria had grown up with this figure in her life.

As much as he unsettled her, Avria had one particular memory of Phenmal that she treasured—and this memory alone caused her to accept this odd creature as a sort of second father in her life, and to see past his quirks to the substance of who he really was. He was a strange man, but she learned from this special moment that he really was a good man—and he had been the one to administer her one of the most important life-lessons she had ever learned.

Phenmal had accompanied Avria and her family to Loshan—he sometimes did. Hanru was at school that particular time. Phenmal needed something from the city and offered the use of his opulent coach if he could accompany them. Tinna agreed whole-heartedly, assuring her reticent fourteen-year-old daughter that he was not evil, that his glacial winter-blue eyes did not bore into her soul, and that being chilled by their companion for a day or two could not outweigh a ride in the comfort of a fine coach, as opposed to riding exposed to the weather, clinging to a sidesaddle in a habit gown. Because they were entering a human city, this was expected of them; even Tinna wore these things and rode aside. Araki manners, astride riding ladies and Araki style clothing were not acceptable among the human upper-ups. Avria was left with little choice but to agree with her mother about the coach, it was a fair trade. It also felt nice to arrive at Loshan looking less disheveled.

The five of them stayed as guests at Kailine and Astlin's palatial home in the city of Loshan, as they always had on these frequent visits. Whenever they came to visit Jestin at his home, he behaved differently than when he was at Thamatoc. A willful, demanding boy, he treated everyone around him with snotty disdain. Avria had some sense, however, that the more time she spent in Jestin's company, the more like him she behaved. Avria didn't see it then, but she could see it clearly now, looking back. Seeing it through Phenmal's eyes, she couldn't help but feel embarrassed.

An evening during that visit, everyone had assembled in the spacious but slightly cluttered private parlor that the family used regularly, Phenmal came in and sat by himself by the fire, near the three youths. The rest of the great house was meticulously kept, with fresh flowers tidily arranged, and gilt picture frames holding oils of Jestin's ancestors; high echoing ceilings and polished marble floors. This room, however, remained informal, the furniture worn, books stacked here and there; lace-making pillows bristled with pins, unfinished skeins of lace hanging from them, hunkered unheeded by the side of the bookshelf; Jestin's model stick-bridge project left in mid-construction on the worktable. The homey shuffle in this room put everyone at ease.

Phenmal settled into his usual spot. He reached into the pocket of his frock coat, withdrawing a suede pouch where he kept his pipe and herbs. He was a creature of habit and his favorite place when visiting the family was by the hearth where he could sit quietly and puff on his long pipe. Avria was used to seeing him there, sitting apart from everyone, quietly assembling the pipe, pressing some fragrant herbs into the little cup with his thumb, and lighting it with a flame stolen from the fire. He was quite content to sit and listen to the children while they played a lively card game. Avria paid little heed to him.

Avria wore gowns that were fashionable whenever she visited Loshan. She didn't hate them as her mother did; Tinna protested ardently every time. However, she told Avria that she preferred the fashions now. Fifteen years ago, she said, gowns had tight corset-like bodices that went as low as the hip. Avria was fourteen, and the styles had changed. A small bodice and stays hugged the breasts and upper back, and the skirts started just under them, loose and flowing, creating columnar, long lines. Avria had to admit, when she was trussed up into her little short corset, and her budding breasts were heaved up into twin mounds in her embroidered bodice, she felt very womanly, that for those moments, deep down, she wished she could dress this way more often. Kailine always assigned Avria her own servant girl who put her long curls up into an elegant mound with strings of pearls wound through it, up off her shoulders in a curly bun, carefully parted down the center and pulled tightly against her head. Two pearl drop earrings, a silver necklace, long sleeves flared over her knuckles, and she looked and felt like an elegant lady. She secretly looked forward to those times; being fussed over by the servant girl, and rustling about in fine silk voiles and muslins.

But part of donning the costume also brought a darker facet to her that was not so pleasant, and the memory of it filled Avria with shame. It was as if once she put these clothes on, she became part of the world of privilege and self-absorption; she and Drashun both. Wrapped up in a fine pair of breeches, stockings, waistcoat and a frock coat, Drashun would strut about like a little cockerel, following Jestin's lead. And Jestin was a rude and selfish fool. He treated servants like rubbish and made sure that he acted as if they were born not only to serve him, but to endure his constant censure, maliciousness and abuse. His personal servant was a paragon of

293

tolerance, barely showing the slightest reaction to the constant barrage of insults, mockery, unreasonable and impossible commands and acid-laced criticism.

Avria and the boys made a game of humiliating this person as they played cards, laughing and snickering as they made unworkable demands, throwing insults and making sure that the servant understood his place. The young boy, an unkempt creature in the ill-fitting uniform of a personal servant stood by stoically, absorbing it, doing as he was asked and swallowing his humiliation. Their actions had drawn the attention of the grave and silent Phenmal, who looked up at them and tamped out his pipe on his boot over the fender on the hearth.

"Avria, can I have a word?" he asked, sounding much like Taneth when he was about to lecture her for doing something naughty. She laid down her cards, stood up from the table, and rustled over to him in her fine snow-white gown, glancing nervously at her mother, who wasn't looking in their direction at all. She sank down into the chair across from him in the most ladylike fashion possible. She folded her hands delicately in her lap and looked at him warily.

Even Avria's physical mannerisms changed; her tomboyish ways vanished and in their place she conjured the manners of a fine lady. Although her elegant manners were something that could be considered commendable, they came with such a cruel and selfish lack of consideration that Phenmal felt obliged to bring it to her attention. He leaned forward so that he could speak softly.

"I want you to remember this, Avria. The people who work the hardest, and do the dirtiest, most humiliating, debasing work are the ones who earn the least. They are poor and all they have is their pride. How would it make you feel to not only humble yourself into the service of others every day, for little money or dignity, but in addition to be treated with meanness such as you and your little friends show? This behavior would not be acceptable in Thamatoc, so you should know that it is unacceptable here as well. You shame your mother every moment you belittle this person who honors you and serves you. He deserves your gratitude and your respect, Avria. Respect." Phenmal leaned back, his face grave, his uncanny eyes shining like two chips of glass under his sharp brow. He always dressed flawlessly, his beard perfectly trimmed. Keeping an unbroken, critical gaze on her, he stuffed his pipe again and lit it.

Avria's cheeks flushed with shame and she bowed her head in immediate contrition. The family friend took in the way her eyes clouded, and her shoulders sagged. She took a deep sigh, a sheen of moisture slid into the bottoms of her eyelids. If he was made uncomfortable by her emotional response to this dressing-down, he did not show it. He cleared his throat, and leaned forward a bit more, pointing the pipe at her as he spoke.

"The reason why I tell you, and not them, is because I know you are a bright girl, Avria, like your mother. And I also know that no matter how Jestin behaves, your example is the one he will be most likely to follow. Everything you do, he is watching. You are enabling him to behave like a willful child by doing it as well. You should know better; you were raised better than that," he reprimanded her in a harsh whisper. "Now, no crying! You get back there and you show that person some respect, and those boys will follow your lead. If you censor them, they will listen. Go on, back to your games!" He shooed her away with the wave of a hand, and sat back, puffing at his pipe a few times.

Avria would never forget that night. He had humbled her, and showed her a truth that she was mature enough to accept. It changed her view of Phenmal; so much so, she began to look forward to his visits to Thamatoc. She had come to love the strange man as one of the family. The moment they shared that night instilled a powerful respect for Phenmal and in part, respect for herself for ultimately setting a better example for Drashun, and even Jestin to some degree. He didn't reform entirely, but showed significantly more consideration and politeness to his family's staff, at least in Avria's presence. It didn't mean he was gracious or even thankful, he was still stiff and superior to them; but at least the games of humiliation and debasement ended when he realized it didn't impress Avria. For Avria, it changed how she behaved with everyone in her life, from the poorest, unskilled member of the clan, to the many scholarly, wealthy people from Lemoram that came to visit Taneth at Thamatoc. It also painted Jestin in a color that would never fade in her eyes.

As Avria watched Jestin riding ahead of her, she thought again of those times when she saw that side of him, and she felt that cool, sorrowful pain she preferred not to feel in the pit of her stomach. She had always excused his actions one way or another, but even now, as he spoke casually to Drashun, his raven hair blowing into his cool blue eyes, his white teeth flashing with a handsome smile, that feeling remained with Avria. She shook it off and sighed, looking out instead to the dappled sunlight cutting through the trees. She had grown as a person since that day, many times over. Jestin might seem on the surface a grown young man, but she knew just below his veneer, he was still the same willful boy. And that saddened her.

* * * *

The fire in the apartment had burned low. Taneth knelt down to jab at the coals with the steel poker, prodding the embers to life, shaking them up. He placed a few pieces of thin kindling on the hot coals, and their wafer-thin edges blackened and popped into flame. He added more, his mind absorbed in the task. Tinna entered the room, pushing through the doorway with dogs at her heels. She backed up to shut the door using her bum, her hand sliding up to close the latch when the door was resting in its heavy frame. Taneth glanced up and smiled at her. She stood in front of the door for a second, returning his smile in a strange, faraway sort of way. She then walked forward, moving behind him, running her fingers along Taneth's shoulders and back as she made her way to the large chest of drawers sitting under one of the slot windows. Here she pulled out a very old sweater, drawing it over her tunic. It hung halfway down the length of her full skirts. She stood there, clutching her elbow of her right arm with her left hand, her fingers covered by the loose knit of the sweater. The dogs settled in on each side of Taneth, hoping to benefit from the warmth Taneth coaxed from the fire. He added a larger piece of wood, and perched it on the burning kindling.

"Taneth…" Tinna said, her voice velvety, her accent, now a bit softened from the years with the Araki; "I need a word…" He stood and wiped his hands on the front of his breeches. His brow furrowed with concern. She is wearing the sweater, he mused. She must be in need of comfort…

"Of course, what is it, my beautiful wife?" She shook her head and laughed gently, always amused by his often-shared terms of endearment. She loved him for that. He never let her forget that he loved her. She slid her hands down and laid them on her belly.

"I'm forty years old…" Tinna muttered, furrowing her brow and pursing her lips. She looked like she was about to cry.

"Almost… but not quite." The lanky, tall man reached up with his large hand and scratched his head with his long fingers, puzzled by Tinna's sudden sadness about her advancement to middle age. She seldom cared about those things.

"I'm old."

296

"No, you are not," he laughed. "If forty is old… what does that make me? Decrepit?"

"I'm too old to carry a child…" Tinna interjected. Taneth laughed and then froze.

"What?" he said; his voice a blend of both a whisper and a shout. Tinna kept him hanging for a long moment, then sighed, her breath wavering as her lip trembled, tears looming.

"Avria is nineteen—nineteen years, Taneth! Nothing. We tried and tried. Nothing. I think I am with child, Taneth." She swallowed his name because it was coming out as a sob. The man balked and grew pale, stepping forward and gripping her hands. He crouched down before her and lay his ear on her belly as if this tiny new life within would share a secret with him. "I suspected it a few weeks ago, just the way I feel. But I've spent the last four mornings with a chamber pot on my lap while you do your rounds before first classes. And my breasts are so sore!" she said through her tears. Taneth suddenly laughed, his face full of emotion, and slid his arms around her hips, hugging her. She laced her arms down around his neck and bent forward to kiss the top of his head, her hair cascading around his face. She leaned to his ear and whispered: "I'm frightened!" Taneth leaned back and put his hands on her cheeks, gazing moist-eyed into her beautiful face.

"Frightened? A woman who rides dragons—frightened," he chuckled. He wrinkled his chin and smiled up at her. "You are married to a healer, Tinna. I will not let you come to harm. You are not the first woman of forty to have a wonderful surprise like this one." His hand rested on her tummy. "You certainly won't be the last. I will monitor you as carefully as I possibly can. You will be fine. Both of you," he said, his voice wavering as the joy of this revelation filled him, "will be fine."

* * * *

Silver lake was a long day's ride, from the edge of morning to a late, lamp-lit arrival south of the Thamatoc settlement. Much of the way followed known Araki and gypsy trails and roads, passing briefly through a narrow corridor of karsu forest. Even in the golden light of afternoon, the behemoth karsu trees blocked out most of the light. The forest of smaller trees pressed up against the five or six monstrosities that extended out over the Araki Road, creating a curtain of filtered yellow light around a deep, greenish, shadowy cavern. At this edge of the forest of giants, wildlife was still quite active, and some understory plants prevailed, not completely given over to karsu yet. But it unsettled Jestin. Avria kept her eyes wide for abnormalities—any sign of a Nimrath among them, blended in with the environment—but she saw none. They emerged from the karsu trees into a dense deciduous region with large maples and cheerful, flickering-leaf birch trees. The yellowy golden light dappled the leafy road, and all was well again for the group.

They circled 'round the end of a towering, flat wall of a natural formation called Parapet Hill, named so because it resembled a massive curtain wall. Its sides rose perilously steep, covered in dark pines and other conifers. The road led round the sheer incline of the hillsides. On some of the rocky outcrops overhanging the road, rock sheep clung to impossible angles and vertical lengths on tiny leathery hoofs. They bounded from minuscule ledge to lump to oddly angled tree trunk, barely stirring a pebble, nibbling at the wild blackberry bushes that grew from the cracks of the sheerest walls. The road circled behind Parapet Hill into a deep valley where the Araki road merged with the main trade road. They followed the curtain wall of Parapet Hill for an hour, and another hill that dominated the area south of the wall tapered a bit to reveal a swath of oaks. As the afternoon bled into evening, they drifted off the main trade road through a part of ancient cemeteries and eventually, just as the sun set, they arrived at Silver Lake Town. The lake for which it was named shimmered to the right of the road, a mirror for the starry night sky with steam curling up off of its surface. On the opposite shore, the twin torches of the settlement gates flickered against the night. They circled the lake at an expectant trot on the well-travelled road and arrived twenty minutes later.

A number of guests had already arrived. Several horses occupied the stable, along with a Moropus and a Dreerdru, the latter a strange southern creature with grey, leathery skin and curled tusks. Intrigued, Avria hurried through Shade's unsaddling so she could get a closer look at it. The group gathered 'round the stall, studying first the animal, then the unusual tack that sat on the bars and hooks in front of its stall. The beast had a barrel body, wider and thicker than a horse's body by far. From it, a deep, low-slung belly hung, held off the floor by four trunk-like legs. Yellow nails capped two large toes and a third thumb-like toe about halfway up his leg. He was grayish brown, with wrinkly skin, and had a blunt, oval head with small, pink rounded ears. Two yellow tusks curled over themselves on each side of his wide, floppy-lipped mouth, and two tiny eyes blinked at them in curiosity, both heavily adorned in thick lashes. Bristly hairs tipped a short whip-like tail.

"Gods! What is that thing?" Jestin muttered. Drashun shrugged, and Avria reached out to pet its equine-like muzzle, which the animal seemed to like. As always, Hanru knew the answer.

"That's a Dreerdru. From the land below Thran. The most common draught animal used by the people there. Never seen a real one before. Only woodcuts. It's bigger than I thought it would be," he confessed, taking a moment to soberly study it. It towered over all the other horses by at least half again their height. Avria examined the wedge-shaped saddle formed for its sloping back. The quilted sides, made of thick brocade, hung from a padded red leather tree. The bridle had no mouthpiece but instead two metal rings that would be looped onto the tusks. Colorful fringe and tassels hung from everything; bridle, brow band, and the stirrups and saddle as well. The animal turned laboriously and began to eat from the pile of hay mounded by the wall.

The group soon lost interest. They gathered their packs and ambled into the forum, where the leaves of an ancient founder's tree shivered as if in greeting. None of them had ever seen one so old, so twisted. The townsfolk had braced its massive lower limbs with elegant iron arches.

The lodges of Silver Lake, with their finely sculpted stone faces, showed their age. Old, long-established forests grew upon the lodges. Recent modifications to some of them served the settlement's new purpose. The tavern and inn now had windows cut into its facade. The wider door had been bricked in, and only a man-sized door occupied the wide face between the windows. Elegantly carved signs, like those of human settlements, indicated each building's use. Large shepherd's hooks held lanterns all about the slate-paved common and hung from the arches that supported the founder's tree.

They entered "The Silver Lake Serpent," a lodge whose name reflected the legend of a water beast that lived in the bottomless, heated depths of the lake. They entered a space much changed. A lodge usually had a large anteroom inside the entrance, a common space where tenants stored outdoor wear and shoes and such. Archways opened onto two large corridors that led into the lodge, past the various apartments, store rooms and corridors to other lodges, then ended at the considerable common space where that lodge's community ate, learned, met and worked on projects. An enormous hearth usually capped the end of a lodge. A main lodge had a series of chairs around the fire where the settlement leadership met and discussed matters. Every Araki settlement held to this general design.

The Silver Lake Serpent's remodelers had torn out the back wall of the anteroom and lengthened the space by at least a third of the length of the lodge. Three fireplaces occupied the center of the room, with large cone-shaped flues hanging over each circular hearth. Chairs and settees of all shapes, styles and sizes encircled these huge hearths. Much of this furniture had been salvaged from Hildercross and Klatna after the burnings. Some still had the telltale scorch marks on the wood but had long since been reupholstered. On each side, dining and gaming tables lined the walls. Long tapestry panels, suspended from the ceiling and drawn along the curve of the side walls warmed the heavy, lofty space of timber and cold stone.

A kitchen and service counter separated the two archways. Two ginger-haired ladies worked in that space, one preparing a pot of something fragrant, a soup or stew, while another wiped down bottles of various spirited drinks. A peppering of people occupied the space. A group of four young men sat at a table playing a game of dice and cards. Two older, dark-clad men that sat in comfortable chairs by the fire closest to the service counter, sipped from wine goblets and spoke in low voices. A group of old men met at a large table on the left side opposite the young fellows, a very exotic dark man among them. A few other folks either stood or sat in various other spots alone. The entrance of the four young people attracted nearly all the eyes and paused conversations, but only briefly; the low murmur of voices resumed, and the group was ignored.

Avria did attract the attention of the gaming table. A low, approving whistle escaped someone's lips, and the gamers shared a few bawdy mumblings, capped by some good-natured chuckles. Jestin's shoulders tensed. He bristled, glaring down the approving gazes of the young men as they watched Avria stride by. The younger, ginger-haired girl behind the counter looked up, and a grimace spread across her face.

"Avria!" she shouted, silencing the room again. She wended her way around the counter and ran to Avria, throwing her arms around her neck. The two girls squealed in delight. "Avria, it's so good to see you! And Hanru!" The girl hugged Hanru, then Drashun and gave Jestin a stiff, hesitant welcome with an uncomfortable smile on her face. "How are you, Jestin?" she asked with civility. He nodded and smiled.

"I am well, Illi. It's been a while."

"Since last summer," Illi said, turning to Avria, taking her hand. "Tell me news! What's wonderful? What's changed since we last saw one another? We get away from here so infrequently; I'm always dying to know what's been going on with my friends since the great meeting."

"Nothing new, really. We're about to be given our rites of ascension..." Avria told her. The girl led them to the middle fireplace and she sat down with Avria at one of the large old settees, still holding her hands. She wore the typical trappings of an Araki woman, a heel-length sleeveless shift over leggings and a cream-toned tunic with wide, floppy sleeves. A bodiced jerkin cinched it all up against her narrow frame. She was a pretty girl, her strawberry blonde hair a mass of curls, her eyes bright and green. The boys in their group, excepting Jestin, both smiled awkwardly at her, their eyes shining. She was keen on hearing from the girl she'd known for most of her childhood, exotic-looking Avria, from the most exciting of Araki settlements, whose mother did the most outrageous things.

"I heard your holyman died. My condolences." She paused, looking morose very briefly. Within seconds, her face brightened and she exclaimed, "It's high time you got your rites, though. Here to celebrate?"

"Exactly!" Drashun exclaimed. She looked square at him with her vivid gaze, and he flushed.

"Good. Then I'll get you some drinks, and you're all probably starving after that ride. I'll get those things and we can all sit down and talk." She stood and wiped her hands on the little apron she had pinned to her front. "I'll be right back!" Illi rustled off. Jestin flopped down on the chair next to Avria where Illi had been, and Hanru and Drashun sank into chairs nearby, scooting them closer. They were all four tired from the long ride. Illi's sister Gheree came over to say hello. Closer to Hanru's age and married, she ignored the goings-on with the Thamatoc group. She knew them well enough but had little in common with them anymore. She brought them drinks, gave them a kind welcome and went back to cooking. She and Illi, two of fourteen members of the family that cared for Silver Lake, were like extended family to Avria, Hanru and Drashun; they had visited the lake countless times and had known them from every autumn festival meeting since they were very small. Coming to Silver Lake was much like visiting an extension of their home.

They passed the drinks around. Avria kicked off her boots, pushed back the sides of her split riding gown and drew her feet, cross-legged, onto the chair. She wore simple, tight leggings beneath the gown. Normally, when out and about in Thamatoc's immediate area, she would just wear breeches, but when traveling, it was appropriate to adorn oneself in the cumbersome skirts. At least she didn't have to ride side-saddle, as the women of human settlements did. She knew how to ride in that manner, but she preferred the Araki way. But at Silver Lake, she felt comfortable enough to push the skirts back and to reveal her worn breeches beneath, sitting in the most unladylike fashion. One of the young men from the card table made his way to their group and insinuated himself into Avria's space. He leaned on the back of the chaise, his back to Jestin, his body angled to Avria. She looked up at him, her eyes large and unassuming.

"Hello. I am Damreth." He reached out his hand. He was a decent-looking man of about twenty five. He sported a clean-shaven head and face, with a tattoo coiled at the back of his skull, the markings of a Kanreth Knight; a cavalry soldier—something rarely seen these days, since few enclaves of human warriors remained, especially those of the Monarchy's forces. Skilled riders, these old-style knights often sought additional horsemanship training from Araki communities. His friends bore the same markings.

Avria smiled. "I am Avria," she replied, accepting his hand and shaking it. "This is my brother Hanru, that is Drashun, and that's Jestin."

"Respected Arakis!" He nodded in acknowledgement. "I come to ask if you'd like to join us. We are tiring of Blood-letter. Arius there wishes to play Alehouse, but we need at least six for a playing set." Avria's mouth turned into a little 'o' of delight. She loved Alehouse. She nodded and stood up.

"Excellent! Come on Drashe! You'll mop the floor with these boys." She grabbed her blackberry wine and climbed over the sofa back in a flutter of skirt panels, following the victorious warrior, who led her back to the table with a triumphant smile on his face. He made room for Avria between himself and his friend, and Drashun and Hanru took seats across from her. Last to arrive, Jestin squeezed into a corner.

"Eight players—a perfect set!" one of the warriors declared in happiness. He shuffled the cards and handed Avria the dice. "Touch them for good luck! Every pretty lady is obliged to." Avria giggled and did as he asked. He doled out the cards as Illi replenished their drinks. Red-cheeked and jolly, they played and laughed as the night wore on.

Damreth waxed bolder with Avria with each passing moment, and she showed no aversion to his advances. She found him handsome and witty, and he made her laugh to no end. First he gave her gentle touches on the arm, and then slid his arm around her shoulders whenever they won. Then he began to kiss her cheek with every victorious hand. They raised their hands and shouted when the winning team slapped down their cards. It was raucous and fun and Avria delighted in the attentions she received. Illi joined them in the revelry, much to Drashun's enchantment, and as the card game became less interesting than just plain merrymaking, the group moved from the table to the fireplace, where Damreth found a place next to Avria, and his boldness increased by tenfold.

At one point in the evening, everyone's attention was focused on Hanru as he pantomimed a humorous tale, his cheeks splotched with red from drink and his eyes bright; infinitely more relaxed than usual. Damreth took Avria's chin in his fingers, swiveled her head towards him and planted a sloppy kiss on her lips—a long, voracious kiss. Jestin noticed, and his face darkened. As they all stumbled to their respective apartments for the night, Jestin diverted Damreth from his path at Avria's heels.

The following morning, Avria was determined to go swimming after they breakfasted. Everyone else was hideously hung-over, but she seemed almost annoyingly chipper and vivacious. Neither quite so chipper as Avria nor quite as smashed as the others, Illi joined them for breakfast and decided to also go swimming. The warriors appeared during breakfast, Damreth with them. His face lit up at the sight of Avria. Jestin glowered balefully and glared at him as he circled the table to sit beside her; however, the warrior was too focused on his prize to notice Jestin's childish behavior. "How are you this morning," he asked groggily. Avria rubbed the top of his head and grinned at the sensation of the fine fuzz of hair growing in.

"We're going swimming."

"Oh, Gods! The water in the lake must be frigid."

"Never. It steams on cool days," Illi asserted.

"You should swim, too. The warm water will make you feel better." Avria patted his head again, and he gave her a charming smile. He reached out and touched her cheek, and she blushed.

"Eat! Hurry! I want to go!" she complained. The group complied with Avria's wishes, some shoveling in their breakfast, a few pushing the food aside due to queasy stomachs. She and Illi vanished to find appropriate swim clothes and agreed to meet the boys at the bathing place.

Natural forces heated Silver Lake's spring-fed waters from below near the center. By the time its currents cycled to the shore, however, the water was neither piping hot nor icy cold. A host of interesting creatures existed at the water's edge, and very few could be fished from the center. But it had no sulfurs, no sourness. The rivers it sourced were alive with fish and health, and the warmth of its waters was deemed to have healing qualities. If one climbed the stone steps between the main lodge and the Winter Lodge and followed the stone-paved path over top the lodges, one emerged at a specially built bathing place. Slabs of textured rock had been laid far out into the lake, well into the hotter areas, paving an underwater road. Huge columns of stacked stone disks along this underwater road served as seats upon which swimmers could climb and rest. The construction was old, and the texture had worn down to a slicker surface, the elegant carvings eroded to little more than weak impressions. Avria and her friends had for many years used the shallowly submerged column seats as places to stand and ambush one another, as jumping points, as traps for those unfortunate enough to be caught wading along the road at the wrong time.

The lake attracted many visitors, but this day, only the nine of them appeared at the shore. The ladies wore swimming shifts and short pants and carried long towels with them. They waded into to the tepid edges of the lake first and forged towards the warmer waters. They swam out to the columns. When they found a column upon which to stand in nicely warmed water, Avria and Illi stood up, ankle deep in water, and beckoned to the boys to follow. Their young, beautiful, curvy bodies, enhanced by the sparse, clinging wet fabric, got the whole lot of boys charging into the water at top speed. Soon a violent game of horseplay erupted, with the ladies the center of it all, standing on their column giggling as the young men splashed, dunked, pushed, kicked and cavorted to gain a foothold on the column with the girls.

The horseplay started to get rough. Neither Illi nor Avria knew exactly when it happened, but at some point in all the chaos of flying limbs and water, Jestin and Damreth started exchanging real blows. They worked themselves back towards the shallower areas, where the fight escalated. It quickly became apparent that this was not an equal fight. No match for the strapping warrior, Jestin nevertheless refused to back down. Damreth planted himself in ankle-deep water, his legs stanced, his fists gripped into tight balls. Jestin would lunge at him with his fists wildly flying and Damreth would just punch him down. The boy fell down with a skid and a splash and then he got to his feet, pushed the long hairs from his eyes and ran at Damreth again as if begging for punishment. As the others struggled to get ashore, the cycle continued, until blood from his nose spattered his bare chest. His eyes went dark and furious. No matter how many times Damreth cast him to the shallow water with blow after blow of hard knuckles; Jestin staggered back to his feet and ran at him roaring, only to meet the inevitable wet smack of a fist. It was starting to look rather pathetic. Avria gasped and cried out, but the pack of men was already swimming after them. By the time the girls reached the shore, sopping and confused, the knights had pulled Damreth away from Jestin. Drashun, strapping and strong, clutched Jestin around the neck and held him against his broad chest, soaked and sullen, with watery blood dripping from his nose.

"What happened?" Avria asked, wading clumsily to the group. Jestin's baleful eyes fell on Avria, and he looked away in embarrassment. He wrenched himself from Drashun's grasp and stalked away, yanking a towel from the stone where they'd been placed. "What happened?" Avria asked again.

"I think he mistook some roughness as aggression. He's not used to this level of rough play," Hanru mumbled, pushing back the soaked hair from his forehead. "He's so defensive sometimes!"

"I don't think it had anything to do with misunderstanding play from fighting," Illi said matter-of-factly, looking wryly at Avria. "He's jealous." She waded out of the water and picked up a towel, shivering a bit when the cool morning air bit her skin. Coils of steam rose off of them all. Damreth went to get Avria a towel and one for himself. He helped her drape it over her shoulders and arms.

Avria glanced at Damreth and back at Jestin's receding form as he climbed the steps towards the lodges. She shook her head and gripped the edges of her towel under her chin; gazing after Jestin. She excused herself and made sopping wet footprints all the way back to the lodge. The fight was not mentioned on the way back to Thamatoc, and the conversation was awkward and monosyllabic. Avria could not have felt more relieved to be home again.

Chapter Three – Mother Dearest

Avria's mother drew her aside the moment they returned from Silver Lake, yanked her through the door of a storage room. It frightened Avria, because her mother looked desperate, stricken, with a sheen of perspiration on her brow, strained in the flickering lamplight, and pale. It worried Avria. Nothing ever unsettled Tinna. Nothing made her nervous or upset. Angry, yes; but nothing distressed her. Not like this. "Avria, I need to tell you something before you get settled in." Avria had never seen her mother so chagrined.

"What's wrong, Mother?" She felt her stomach go cold from the magnitude of her mother's unease. She briefly worried that Tinna had heard about Avria's lack of restraint with the warrior at Silver Lake, or the fight between him and Jestin.

"Avria, I told you my history, you know most of it. But I never told you about your grandmother. I never told you what she was like. I never..." Avria dropped her shoulders and smiled, both in relief and in concern.

"Mum..." Avria took her mother's hands.

"She's here. She's here!" Tinna hissed in a strained whisper. "She came today, with a massive cortege. She managed to find the gypsy road and has her own caravan which is out there, in the pasture."

"Oh, how wonderf—"

"No it's not. No. I'm not happy, Avria. I'm livid. Livid. You must be warned, you must be warned; she is horrible. She is a horrible, horrible person." Avria was shocked. This was so unlike Tinna to be so fearful and unnerved. It gave the girl a sense of dread just seeing her mother so unlike herself. Avria knew this was serious. She knew to listen to every word her mother said, by this reaction alone. If this woman made her mother so upset, she must be formidable indeed. She hadn't mentioned her to Avria in all her life, but Avria knew. Offhand remarks about bad mothers during conversations with family and clan members had clued her in.

"How did she find you?" Avria asked, dumbfounded.

"A bloody Diviner!" Tinna spat, her black eyes growing darker. "She said she searched specifically for me, but I'm not stupid, that's not how it works. Diviners find the significance–the importance of a person's effect on others. She's here because of what I did before. She found out about me and now she's here. Why now and not ten years ago, fifteen years ago? I don't know! It's something noteworthy. I know it is. Just please, please, please, promise me you won't let her draw you in! Please!" Avria stepped forward and reached her arms around Tinna's shoulders, embracing her lovingly. She had finally reached her mother's height. Tinna's anxiety fueled her. Her daughter gripped her tightly and rocked her for a moment; genuinely distressed to see her indefatigable mother so wracked with worry.

"Mother, you needn't fret. I'm a reasonably sharp person. No matter what she does, I'll be sure to see it through your eyes." Tinna nodded and touched her daughter's cheek, sighing woefully. Avria tried to soften the subject a bit. "How's father contending with her arrival?" She actually felt her mother relax a bit in her grip, and Tinna laughed softly, shaking her head. Her state stunned Avria. What caused it all—this horrible fear? Her mother feared nothing. She'd faced down a bloody rock-panther without a second thought, staring it down and challenging it until it fled. Avria withdrew and clasped her hands again, looking into Tinna's fretful eyes.

"She's ignoring him, of course. She ignores men. My aunt told me once she got worse after your grandfather entered and exited her life. Taneth—well, you know your father. He's all a-twitter about the accoutrements of the cortege and the markings and military decorations and such. He's tried to ask questions, but assertive, curious men are not exactly smiled upon, and when he addresses the men, they shrink away in fear of rebuke from the Thran. He's about to explode trying to get information. Poor man," she laughed nervously. "He can't stand to have anything keep him from learning new things. He's obsessed."

"Oh, Hanru will delight in this too." Avria giggled. Tinna laughed again, her eyes filling with relief.

"Hanru will be the same. He is like Taneth, but more measured about it. They'll have their day; it looks like mother is organizing a special performance of dance for the village tonight. It will enact the history of the Thran, the making of the woman warrior and all that," she rambled. "She is doing it in your honor, it seems; excited to meet her heiress."

"Her what?"

"Well, for obvious reasons; like my being an unwanted product of an indiscretion with a lowly gypsy, and my running away from her; she's overlooked me as the recipient of any of her worldly goods or titles, but apparently the moment she discovered that you exist, she's been determined to meet the new heiress of her estate and title."

"She has a title?"

"Yes. Yes she does." Tinna wrung her hands together. "She's a Baroness. A favorite of the throne; and that's the only reason why she was given Ymnoth when she had to hide with me in shame. It was only that preference that saved her from being cast out completely and my being killed at birth. She was once Baroness of Diurtreth—an honored place. Ymnoth is a fringe community... many mixed bloods there... but it's still large and important for trade..." Tinna said absentmindedly, her wandering eyes looking into her past. Avria sighed and then resolved to speak to her mother about Jestin... and her actions. She tilted her head, looking most uncomfortable before she finally spoke.

"Mother... before you learn about it from someone else..." Avria started, scratching the back of her head. "I kissed someone down at Silver Lake... it was just in fun, and we were a little bit tipsy... but I don't want it blown out of proportion."

"Oh, fiddlesticks, Avria... What does this have to do with your grandmother?"

"Nothing... I felt I should tell you..."

"Do you have any idea how many young men I kissed in my day?" she interrupted her daughter, "...or worse for that matter...before I settled down and found Taneth? I won't even tell you." Tinna waved her hand dismissively and sighed. "You were there to have fun; why do you think it's even worth mentioning to me?"

"I don't know. There was some strange stuff that happened. Jestin got into a fight with the fellow, assuming he's protecting my honor or such... it was really awkward. We haven't spoken since. Illi said it was because he was jealous, which is silly..."

"Not silly at all. Illi is an observant and clever girl. Jestin is fostering some strong feelings for you Avria. It's quite obvious."

"I don't want him to foster those kinds of feelings for me, Mum... he's like my brother..."

309

"I know. He'll be hurt to learn it someday… but he will heal and adjust." Avria suspired heavily and shook her head. It was too much to deal with. With her grandmother here, and her mother so concerned, she needed to focus on that, and not Jestin's crush.

"Well then. I have to get into to my apartment and get ready to greet my grandmother… and earn my inheritance," Avria smirked. "Come and get me when it's time." She opened the door to the storeroom to exit into the corridor.

"Of course darling," Tinna paused. "Avria… promise me you will not believe a word she says. I could never have you endure the pain I have. You must trust me in my warnings."

With a meaningful nod, and an assuring caress of her mother's pallid cheek, Avria left Tinna in the storeroom, and dashed up the corridor only two doors. After a childhood of sharing a single space with three other people; at seventeen, Rigerd agreed to give Avria her own space. Her small apartment was meant for a single resident, not much bigger than a storeroom. Drashun had his own apartment in the Spring Lodge, since empty apartments were a premium in the Summer Lodge. Avria felt privileged to have this tidy little place with its small hearth nestled in the corner on the outside wall, sharing a flue with the adjoining apartment. A thick quilt of sheep's wool padded the slate floor. A large chest of drawers hunkered under the slot windows, and a table and two chairs took up a little space across from the hearth. A set of thick armchairs occupied the space in front of the hearth; a small round table in between the chairs held a lamp and a dirty cup. Her bed occupied a little niche. A thick, padded partition like the one on her floor created a curtain in front of it for privacy if needed. When she lived in her parents' apartment, she had to make do with just that niche for her personal space. This whole apartment spelled luxury to her; even if Jestin made fun of it. "It's smaller than my bathing chamber," he mocked. She wondered, since he hated it so much, why he spent so much time in it. Then she sighed, and her cheeks flushed with regret for Jestin.

Never mind that, she thought. I've a grandmother to meet. She plunked down into one of the large comfortable sofa chairs and pulled off her muddy boots, a wry, mischievous smile on her face.

Avria knew that her mother was special in many ways beyond the exotic ideas she brought to the Araki people. She knew by the visitors that came to Thamatoc in search of Tinna that something exceptional and mysterious hung about her mother. This impromptu visit by her grandmother made her wonder. According to Rhoa, more visitors came in the years that Tinna and Taneth were members of the village than in the village's entire history. Perhaps Rhoa exaggerated, but she was not known for hyperbole—quite the opposite. Once full of dreams, according to Tinna, life had tempered her, turned her into a level-headed, pragmatic sort of creature. Avria wondered what Rhoa thought of this grandmother's arrival and what conjectures she might have about this strange visitor.

The visitors—a subject of much contemplation by Avria—consisted of all sorts of characters who came and went. Her grandmother was no exception. Avria could not help but wonder what brought so many unusual and noteworthy visitors to the door of their family apartment. She began to suspect that her mother and father were more significant to Oromoii than their humble life portrayed. She just wasn't quite sure how. She'd never been privy to the secrets that bound them to their visitors and of course to Phenmal.

She suspected Phenmal had a lot to do with their secret, since so many representatives of the Keepers came and went, and he was connected to them. Anyone of consequence in Oromoii could be identified by their markings or garments, and Keepers stood out. They communicated through agents known as Driva, less kindly referred to as the 'letter-heads' by her mother. They came at least twice a year, occasionally more than that, to sit with Tinna and sometimes Taneth. They met in their apartment, with the door closed; even Hanru was cast out during these times. The whole clan went still and tentative during their visits; the chilling faces of the Driva too unsettling to them, too eerie.

They arrived at night, on foot, by the death road from the west through the largest swath of the oak forest. The tall, looming characters, always one male and one female, both completely bald, frightened Avria as a child and still as a young adult. They had fine tattooed lines of text circling again and again around their skulls in a language Avria had never seen before. The lines crossed each other and left strange wedges of clean, stubbly skin in between. One line came down in front of the ear, swooped down to the corner of the mouth and resumed on the other corner, and back up the top of the other ear, suggesting the permanent grimace of a skull-bone. They wore long black voluminous trousers that looked more like long skirts, and a crew-necked tunic that hung to their knees of the same black linen fabric. The ends of a single steel-grey rope hung down the left hip to the knee, tipped in a silver orb the size of an eyeball, embossed all over its surface with lettering like that of the Keepers' tattooed faces.

They didn't speak to anyone except Tinna.

"Are they even human?" Avria asked her mother after one visit the prior winter, after the strange duo had finally gone and Avria was permitted to return to the apartments.

Tinna stood by the hearth, absentmindedly nibbling bits of the night's leftovers from the proofing shelf. She smiled wanly. "No. They're like walking archives."

What business she had with the Keepers, Avria did not know. If Hanru knew anything, he didn't share. He never spoke of the strange goings-on with the Keepers, nor of the other young man who showed up on occasion wearing the sigil of a dragon summoner—an unpopular occupation, considering what the dragons had done. Avria sensed that her mother and father were privy to something massive and clandestine. Nobody else in her world knew the secret that Tinna, Phenmal and Taneth shared—not even Jestin's family, surprisingly, who knew and resented the fact that information was withheld from them but offered only an occasional passive-aggressive comment about Tinna's distrust of them.

"Diviners find the significance–the importance of a person's effect on others," Tinna had said in passing. "She's here because of what I did before. She found out about me and now she's here." For that brief moment, Avria thought her mother would reveal something to her. It felt like being teased with food when starving. She frowned, and continued disrobing, puzzled by the whole thing. Why was her grandmother here? Did it have to do with Keepers?

* * * *

Tinna tapped on the heavy lumber door of her daughter's apartment, feeling that familiar sting she felt when she thought of her daughter growing up. Avria called to her to come in. She bit her lip, pushed the door open and entered. The moment she saw Avria, she shut the door with her back and clapped her hand to her mouth. She started to laugh and cry at the same time.

Avria appeared in full splendor—attired in the high fashions of the northern human cities. She wore a gown of solid white with a pale, creamy peach, gauzy overdress, her hair done up as the fashion required, adorned with the requisite pearls and trimmings. She presented herself in as feminine a manner as possible, in accordance with well-to-do, mainstream, Northern standards. In Thamatoc, long dresses and skirts predominated, but of a more utilitarian cut and fabric than the fine materials Avria had chosen. Styles had changed since Tinna had become a clansperson of Thamatoc, and those styles had spread to other clans. Women wore breeches more often, even in the company of clansmen.

The gown that Avria wore was an intentional slap in the face to her grandmother, whose matriarchal culture frowned heavily on any clothing that they believed represented Northern oppressive fashions. They believed that the gowns and accoutrements were meant to shroud a woman from the world; the focus on shallow beauty; meant to steal her power. "Do you think I'm being rash?" Avria asked, turning elegantly in her gown. Tinna smiled radiantly and gently laughed.

"I think you're pure evil. I couldn't be more proud. You have erased so much of my anxiety just with this act. It will be a triumph. She's going to be holding a great extravagant show to expound the virtues of Thran matriarchy. I mean there's a place for equality, don't get me wrong, but what they do, down there, it's wrong. But showing up in the finery of an oppressed Northern woman... well, it's just poetic." Avria grimaced playfully and gave a wiggle of the bum.

"All right then. Let's do this." Tinna reached out her hand and Avria took it, the laced edge of her sleeve covering her mother's fingers. They both walked down the corridor to the entrance as if in a funeral procession. With a quick glance at her daughter, she opened the main door into bright daylight.

A lot had happened in the two hours between her return and this moment. The forum had changed from its normal comforting calm to a festival-like atmosphere. The whole village emerged into the summery evening, all moving towards the entrance gates. The log-stumps that served as stools stood on both sides of the gate, some spanned with boards to accommodate more spectators. The lamps that hung from the founder's tree shone, and mugs of sap-ale passed from hand to hand. Attention gravitated towards the tall, ornately carved stone pillars of the village gate, riddled with depictions of horses in every stylization centuries of artisans could muster. The village folk gathered along the sides of the gates, the viewing area connected by a space in front of the founder's tree, where the town leadership would sit. In the distance, approaching the gates, Avria heard drums. Tinna gestured to her to sit on the bench that circled the base of the founder's tree. Taneth sat there already, looking like an excited boy. He glanced expectantly at the town gateway before him. Tinna never noticed the silver hairs of his beard, or the subtle crow's-feet around his eyes—to her he hadn't changed a bit in twenty years. He still looked like an overzealous, awkward, egghead student to her.

Jestin, Hanru and Drashun sat on log-stools next to Rigerd and his family. Avria glanced over and caught Jestin looking at her with a strange look on his face—a reaction, perhaps, to seeing her in her gown—or one of shame over the fight? But Jestin never showed remorse for his actions; he merely found ways to justify them. He sported some faint bruises on his cheek and eye. She surmised it was the gown that did it. In Thamatoc, she would not normally dress like this. She received a number of curious glances from her fellow clansmen as she walked behind her mother to the benches; Jestin was just one among many. She made a face at him, and he looked away, feigning aloofness. She smiled at her mother as she slid in between her father and Tinna. Taneth glanced at her with an arched brow.

"I'd ask what your motivation would be for dressing like that, but I suppose I know. Not exactly the best idea to wear that when meeting your Thran grandmother for the first time," he muttered with a bemused smile. She snickered and shook her head.

"I think it's the perfect thing to wear when meeting my Thran grandmother for the first time," she replied flippantly. He patted the seat next to him, shaking his head in bewilderment.

No sooner did she sink down elegantly in her finery, Na-AiSennal of Ymnoth arrived. When Tinna saw her, she squeezed Avria's hand, her lips tight. Avria's concerned eyes left her grandmother, her biting curiosity overtaken by the concern she felt for her overwrought mother; one so unflappable and strong now gripping her fingers so tightly they turned white at the tips.

She leaned to her mother's ear and whispered: "Look at her mother! Look!"

Na-AiSennal of Ymnoth stood tall, thin and formidable, but age had not escaped her. Her legs looked like sticks coming from a skirt too short for a mature woman, even a Thran. A network of blue veins inked her papery skin. She had the same dense curls as Tinna and Avria, but hers had grown almost white, a rainy-gray, like the color of clouds before a dark storm. Her black eyes carried in them a darkness beyond the tone of the iris or the depth of her pupils. She locked onto Avria with the intensity of a predator, her reaction so immediate, yet so contained that only one looking for it would see it. Her mandibles rippled at the sight of her granddaughter, and her glower darkened at the small, self-satisfied smile that Avria beamed at her.

314

"She's a bitter one! Look at her face!" Avria told her mother, smiling easily. "She's weak now; old, and she looks ill, even. Perhaps that's why she's here, because she has little time left to make a mark. But she cannot hurt you, Mother. Look at her! She's as brittle as a dried leaf. She glares and challenges our gaze to divert our attention from her frailty."

"Never underestimate a Thran, even one that old!" Tinna muttered. For but a second, Avria heard the old accent. Somehow, the presence of these Thran brought back the realization that her mother wasn't native to Thamatoc. Her accent, much softened over the years, remained present and distinct. "But I do see her anger. Her bitterness is distilled. Her rage is worse than ever. She cannot speak a word to me that isn't swimming in hatred and bile; and I cannot stop feeling this pure fury just being in her presence."

Avria clutched her mother's hand and sat up straight, continuing to challenge her grandmother's gaze, her fervor fueled by Tinna's unusual emotional state. It never faltered as the old woman walked towards them at a ceremonial pace.

Na-AiSennal of Ymnoth wore the fully traditional Thran formal garb: a skirt of soft material with a wide strap along the hip, sitting low and fluttering, white as fresh snow; a bare midriff adorned with chains of gold and various dangling pendants; long, flared sleeves and a floor-length flowing robe of white. She carried the staff of a Warrior Priestess. The robe and staff indicated her ranking in the religious and aristocratic hierarchy.

Extinguishing her challenging gaze, she turned to her right as a manservant appeared, carrying a spindly wooden chair with a padded seat. He was a eunuch and, like most Drunar, sallow and pudgy, with frightened, beady eyes set in dark purple hollows. He put her chair down. The legs in the front and the back crossed over one another in an X. The feet curled upwards into graceful coils. The top of each X also coiled downwards and formed the ends of the low armrests. A lady warrior took her staff, and stood beside her, a large creature, too chubby for her uniform. Her soft physique suggested that she was no longer an active soldier of Thran. The Priestess took her seat with an affected regal air, gripping her curled armrests. The lady-warrior at her side stamped the end of the staff on the ground four times, which quieted the buzz of the curious Araki, who sensed Tinna's quiet anxiety and in part shared the same distrust of these strangers among them.

The Diviner appeared, a wiry, young looking man with greasy strands of black hair falling into his eyes, and the browbeaten appearance common to Thran men, among whom the small and retiring outnumbered the strong, the strapping and the tall. The Diviner scurried to his place behind the indefatigable Baroness, his eyes darting about to take in the men who seemed so much healthier and happier than he. "Ve are gratevul for the 'ospital-letee ov jur peepell. Baronees Na'AiSennal offeers a geeft of cultooral preesentachun," the chubby guard announced. Tinna rolled her eyes and glanced at her daughter.

"Oh, joy. Here it comes." Her sarcasm oozed from every pore.

The drums intensified, and a crowd of dancers came bounding into the forum.

"Who travels with dancers?" Avria asked, her brow arched, "especially so many? There must be at least five and thirty people there!"

"They're Jeethu. The foot militia. Our morning exercises, the dance of martial arts we do together—they do it too; only ours is a bit different. Thran Jeethu are ceremonial dancers and fighters alike. They are my mother's personal guard."

Avria looked at her mother incredulously and then turned her attention back to the group of dancers. They entered through the village gates in a neat line two by two in full, graceful run, and then spread out, falling to the ground in little fetal heaps. Then the orchestra came, a pack of women carrying instruments, garbed in flowing gossamer robes. They played a joyful tune. The dancers in light colors arose, about a third of them elegant males. While they danced and cavorted to the music, the ones in dark costumes remained hunkered down.

"There are male Jeethu?" Avria asked.

Tinna nodded.

Taneth nodded too, providing the explanation. "Some men are permitted to be foot soldiers but nothing higher. They are good fighters, but not like the elite forces. They are usually the front-line," he said regretfully.

The music turned grave. The happy dancers stopped prancing around each other and hunched their backs instead, stalking about as if in fear. One of the dark, androgynous figures stood, and put a horn to its lips, pretending to sound out a clarion of war, while a horn-player in the orchestra did the honors. The other dark-clad creatures stood, their clothing ragged as tree-moss, their faces masked to appear horrendous.

"Scourge dragons," Tinna explained.

316

Avria nodded. The scourge dragons had once dominated the Thran countryside. The Thran worshipped Ulai, goddess of war and chaos and a distorted version of the scourge dragon's own goddess Viliai. The Thran structured their entire religion around their intricate military. One served the Goddess by serving a branch guild of the military. Religious rank and government rank were one and the same, and their belief system was intermingled throughout their society's structure. Nobody was born in Thran who did not serve the military in one way or another. Tinna had once served as a Kanindra, an assassin.

Avria recalled that the Thran had named a training school after Ailie, Jestin's grandmother, a berserker famous for her skill with the scythe axe. The sweet, quiet Ailie had apparently killed hundreds in her lifetime. Avria had found it hard to believe, but looking now at the stern entourage of women in leather-mail and skirts, holding razor-sharp weapons, she pictured her own mother dressed as one, and found it completely feasible. It offered a fascinating glimpse into her mother's past, one she'd had a difficult time imagining until now. Now she could see her mother in these women. It filled her with awe.

She turned her attention to the dance and watched as the dragons pulled prop swords from their voluminous costumes and raised them to the sky. They clustered closest to Tinna and Avria. The white-clad dancers froze, and the men put their hands to their ears as if to indicate they heard the call for war, and they too produced their swords. The women grew hysterical, dramatically trying to stop them from advancing by grappling their arms and legs as if begging them not to go, but the men callously cast them aside and forged into the line of dragon-dancers. A battle ensued. A third of the men fell, but the beasts were pressed back. The battle over, the wives rushed in and fell upon the bodies of the dead. They and wept and silently screamed in a dance of melodrama, conveying their grief-filled fury to the gods.

The dead rolled discreetly away, leaving their props, and skulked behind the orchestra. Again, the dragons rallied, another war-clarion sounded, and the men again rose up, raised their swords and fled into battle, once more casting their fearful women behind. This time the battle broke out in a melee of dancing and swords flying. The white-clad men fell like rain. When the battle ended, the remaining dragons retreated for a while, having won the battle. The dragons dropped back into innocuous balls on the ground. The dead dragons rolled away, the actors stripping out of their dark costumes and masks to reveal white garb and feminine faces. They circled 'round and joined the stream of women as they returned in a frantic dance. The wives wove around the space, finding their husbands defeated, the ground littered with their bodies, and they fell upon them, their anger at the injustice evident by their gestures and faces.

One dancer picked up her husband's sword and raised it to the sky. Then another woman did the same, and another, until all the women held the swords of their men. The dragon with the clarion horn had conveniently been killed, so all one woman had to do was to theatrically discover it, and with exaggerated and elegant movements of her arms, pick it up and lift it to her lips. She played the tune that the real horn-player blew from her horn and woke the dragons. The revenge of the women was at hand.

The women raged into battle and slew every last one of the remaining scourge dragons, throwing kerchiefs of scarlet red into the air to represent the dragons' blood. When the battle ended, the women stood motionless with arms sagging, the tips of their swords on the ground. But then one raised her sword laboriously in victory, and the rest did as well. They then ran away through the gates, still brandishing the swords, and vanished. The dragons had vanished as well, only their costumes remained. Avria realized the dragons had shed their costumes during the battle one by one, and become part of the army. It was very cleverly done. It made the army of women seem to grow in power as they battled. The music had swelled when they ran off and now subsided. The orchestra took credit for the applause, and then backed away so the dancers could return to receive their accolade.

The people of Thamatoc were no strangers to dramatic enactments of special events—small communities like these had little else to do during the cold winter months, except hole up in the lodges, and perform entertainment such as this. As children, Avria and her friends had put on many a dramatic presentation for the entertainment of the family and friends. With this dance, however Tinna found their applause restrained, and that pleased her. The glorified enactment, while true, suppressed certain details. The women had indeed fought the war and defeated the scourge dragons, but the men had reduced the dragons' numbers dramatically during the battle of Ortrect, in which nearly every adult Thran man had been killed. The death-toll of the war itself stood in hundreds of thousands. Only enough men survived to teach the Thran women how to defend themselves against the invading force of scourge dragons. The dragons, also dwindling in numbers, could only turn away from the few remaining human soldiers to regroup, confident they would finally beat these humans and regain their ancient lands. This bought the women a few weeks to train, to don their husbands' armor and weapons and to face the small army in battle in numbers far greater than their opponents. The remaining men took the front lines, still hoping to prevent the deaths of as many of their wives and sisters as possible. They fell, but not before they had further reduced the numbers of the scourge dragons. The battle ended with the destruction of their army in its entirety. The remaining dragons, convinced that their patron goddess had abandoned them, declared that Viliai now favored their enemies. Forsaken by their goddess, they cast her likeness to the earth and fled. The Thran women adopted this goddess as their own and celebrated the retreat of the dragons. Their victory established a budding civilization of Thran human women without adult men; a world of women who believed that the Goddess of War favored them and offered this great victory as a gift. Nearly a thousand years had passed since that fated war. Thran culture had grown and spread out in the southern midlands, refining and perfecting its feminine dominance.

As for Thran males, only very old men and small boys remained. Every young boy twelve and over had been conscripted when the numbers began to dwindle. The remaining children grew up knowing only the matriarchal way—with fathers away at war for most of their youth, hardly any of the older children remembered a time when robust men had been about. The ancient cities grew, the Thran claimed more and more of the lands, and the borders expanded and as the great empire swelled, so did the dominance of the women. The men would never again regain the dominant role in society, nor even obtain equality. They had become unimportant subordinates in a single generation. Tinna told Avria and Taneth that she did not disagree with their ideas regarding powerful women; she relished it. Thran women had run away with that power, however, and used it to oppress their men, all the while admonishing the North for oppressing women. Tinna could not abide such hardness and hypocrisy.

She turned and looked at her husband's rapt face as he avidly took in every detail of the Thran cortege as they moved about the area before them. Tinna smiled to herself. She had spent so many hours speaking of her homeland to her husband, but this knowledge she'd given him did not in any way diminish his hunger for more. Enthralled, he absorbed the costumes, the movements, the tale they told. Tinna loved him for his bottomless yearning for knowledge.

She often wondered if he felt stifled in so small a universe as Thamatoc; but he found many ways to fill his expansive mind—especially after the burnings, as he traveled constantly to work to rebuild the academies and to foster the education of more wisemen and holymen. When he wasn't out and about on his mission to salvage the world's knowledge, he was at home ordering books from all corners of the great land. Rigerd had long since given up trying to rein in Taneth's avarice for books, and finally conceded him the use of one of the larger storerooms to turn into a library under the agreement that he would fill this space and then stop when it could fit no more. He would have to ride north if he wished to read more, and seek them out at the Lemoram archive.

Four walls of solid floor-to ceiling bookcases with a niche for the door, another for a small hearth, a central table whereon one could work and read, a few comfortable chairs—and Taneth finally seemed marginally content. He sorted his collection of books, sent a goodly amount of them to the Lemoram archive so he could save shelf-space for the ones he knew he could not live without. They already impinged upon the one remaining shelf reserved for maps and scrolls. Hanru helped his father keep track of his library and tried to weed out the books that could be sent to the archive. Only Taneth, Hanru and a young brown-haired girl named Skye were permitted to enter the library freely. Everyone else required supervision from one of those three to enter the sacred space.

Taneth trained Skye in tandem with Hanru. A plain little thing, she squinted over the pages of a book and snorted when she laughed. She often stammered and lost her sentences, and her freckles nearly disappeared when she blushed. She wanted very much to attend the conservatory with Hanru. When he was away at the conservatory, she spent all her free time in the library. She stood near him now, hanging back. Tinna saw that, for once, Hanru did not command the awkward girl's rapt attention. Skye squinted, fixing her gaze on something curious.

After the production, just as the people started to rise, everyone fell still. Veeru entered the forum, a reedy looking fellow with a shock of red hair, freckled skin, and lashes so light-colored he looked like he had none at all. He was Skye's first cousin. Everyone knew him, a Thamatoc resident and second caretaker to the horses. As he led two draft animals, both piled with packs, into the crowded forum, he looked confused to see everyone out in the forum, and then even more puzzled by the Thran hanging about. When he'd left, everything had been as normal as it could be. Now, there were such strange goings on. He drew the pack horses to a halt and looked about with a furrowed, confused brow. The people, however, paid no heed to Veeru. He did not interest them. The person who followed him caused the stir and drew their eyes. The entire Thran faction, having taken up residence in the pasture, had already created quite a buzz, but now a Druidic Soothsayer appeared.

A soft smile curled on Avria's lips and she felt a tickle of something in her stomach; the same feeling she got just before her horse's hooves left the ground to leap a large obstacle; or when her little mare ran so fast, she could hear the wind whistling past her ears. Her heart rang in her ears, and they turned hot red, and her cheeks flushed. She actually felt faint at the sight of this character.

She had never imagined a man as handsome as the Zshathri. Taller than either Taneth or Rigerd, the two tallest men in the village, and leaner, with wide shoulders, he had an incredible face—not entirely different from everyone else's, but exceptionally well put together. His strong jaw framed a wide mouth with a serious line to the lips, and a strong aquiline nose. He had heavy-lidded eyes of a sharp blue under a solemn, heavy brow like a pair of shining black arches. Avria had never seen markings like his. A series of dark blue, thin lines spiraled along his left temple, tapering into whorls of tiny dots. The lines intertwined and knotted with an order that seemed also beautifully disordered. Thamatoc men preferred the kind of frayed goatee that Taneth sported, but this man shaved his face clean except for a thin strip of whiskers, no wider than a finger, beginning under his bottom lip and running down under his chin. He wore three gold rings in each ear and had a head of dense black hair that he braided down his back, flat-straight.

His arms had the same shamanic designs from the wrist to the shoulder, and some creeping up his neck. He wore a sleeveless tunic of soft, incredibly thin leather and drop-front breeches of similar suede with boots that appeared integrated into the leggings, with bits of fur sticking out from the seams. Leather strips laced up his muscled calves to his knees. He carried a staff with the skull of a raptor lashed to its top, complete with the yellowed bill. The skull had large polished hematite stones for eyes, and feathers decorating it. He led a third horse laden with the rest of his packs. Taneth rose at the sight of him, as did Tinna and Avria. Their honored Thran guest was momentarily forgotten as the village's attention turned to the newcomer. Sennal's glare darkened at the sight of the druid, and she whispered to the Diviner with a sour expression. Taneth gestured for someone to take the Soothsayer's horse.

"Eleran of the Zshathri, I welcome you to Thamatoc," Taneth blurted, bustling forward in his floppy chasuble. The towering Druid appraised Taneth with a careful eye, and bowed, hitting his staff's butt onto the cobbles.

"I accept your welcome. I am honored that you would have me. I beg your pardon for my informal clothing, but these make traveling on foot much more bearable." His voice had a resonant bass quality to it that caused all who whispered to fall silent. His diction was flawless, not a shred of an accent. He could have been born in Thamatoc. Taneth waved off the apology, and shook his free hand with enthusiasm.

"We are greatly pleased to bring you into our fold. May I make introductions?" Taneth glowed. Rigerd sat idly on a log-stool near his wife among the people. He had withdrawn from the hullabaloo of leadership over the past several months, quietly giving way to Tinna, though he had not yet officially resigned. Out of a sense of duty, he stood, joining Tinna and Avria as they moved into the circle to be introduced. The druid eyed the new faces, his sky-blue irises noticeably lingering on Avria. She felt her cheeks heat up.

"This is the leader of Thamatoc, Rigerd," Taneth said. "And this is my wife, Tinna of Ymnoth."

"Yes, the Thran for whom I am to enact a ceremony of succession." He bowed. His deep voice made Avria's skin tingle. No man had ever had this effect on her. "And who is this? She looks remarkably like you, AiTinna. I will assume she is your lovely daughter."

"I beg you; leave the formal Thran appellations aside. They are not useful here," Tinna said with a smile. "Call me Tinna. And yes, you assume correctly. This is Avria." Tinna smiled, maneuvering her daughter by the shoulders, so that she stood before her. He took her in even more boldly this time, assessing her dress and finery with a practiced eye. His bold admiration did not go unnoticed by the Baroness, who stood.

"I must intervene. This is wholly unacceptable! For such a godless creature to address Avria with so little respect and reverence!" she spat. "She is not just Avria. She is Avria of Thamatoch, who shall become Baroness of Ymnoth and High Priestess of the Orr-Sran Sect, as I am." Na'AiSennal shoved herself into the close circle. "She is a creature of superior blood and rank, and you will address her accordingly or you will be punished." Avria shrank back in embarrassment and looked at her mother worriedly. Sennal was frightening up close. Her teeth were yellowed and rotten and her breath stank. Her skin was dry and wrinkled, and her curls storm-grey. She looked fragile, but also feral. Everyone pulled back when she intruded, except one. The Druidic Soothsayer did not take this intrusion lightly. He closed his eyes, his jaw rippling. He spoke in a controlled growl.

"Although I am still but a guest and I know your daughter is to be leader here, I must establish immediately that I will not offer my obedience to someone who is of no consequence to me. Moreover, at risk of offending my new hosts, I will state in earnest that I cannot abide anyone who subjugates members of her own people. I do not agree with your norms, Madame, nor will I abide by them. And I certainly will not tolerate being given commands or intruded upon during my formal welcome. I strongly suggest you step away." Nobody expected him to flare up with such anger in the presence of the Thran. Taneth looked stricken, Tinna smiled, and Avria's cheeks burned red as autumn apples.

"How dare this—this foreign man-pig address me in such a way? Do you allow this, Tinna?" Na'AiSennal barked. Her face blanched in sheer astonishment that anyone would deign to address her in such a manner; let alone a lowly man. She raised her hand to summon her personal guard. "This will not be tolerated!" she shouted, "You will learn your place!"

"I do not believe it is appropriate for you to make such orders when you are a guest of the Araki people. You do them a great dishonor," he warned her.

Sennal's eyes widened and she jerked her hand to quicken the orders to her guards. They grasped their weapons and approached at a jog. The tension about the forum grew prickly.

The Druid raised his staff and muttered some undecipherable words, banging it down onto the cobbles again. This time the strike reverberated through the ground, and the land responded with a rumble that sounded as if the bowels of the earth had shifted. The founder's tree shuddered, the leaves rustling and shivering. The stabled horses whinnied nervously. The tremor lasted a few seconds, rippling outward from the butt of his staff. The people collectively shrank back from him, dead silent. The Thran guards froze. Avria rested her hand on her heart, her skin aflame. Hanru's face went white. Taneth looked as if he might faint.

"You are only here by the good graces of your daughter. You shame her, I can feel it. This is not your country, Thran. You have no power here. You will please make yourself absent from this place and take your entourage with you. You will be allowed back later when your daughter deems it permissible." The ground shivered again. Avria watched a small pebble quiver along the top of the cobbles. Her blood coursed with fear and exhilaration.

"You bring a madman into your village and you allow him to cast me out?"

"Go, mother! I think it best you not make a bad impression on our new Holyman. You may return later." Gasps and mutterings of disbelief rippled among both the Thran contingent and the people of Thamatoc. The guards ushered the belligerent baroness away, taking her musicians and her little throne with her. They resigned to the pastures, where their caravan waited. Tinna could only then feel at ease. Her mother's presence unnerved her to no end.

"I fear I have been too bold, honorable Tinna. I must confess I do harbor a particularly potent aversion to certain members of the Thran culture. Many of my kind do. It is a dissonance of their energies that does not meet well with those who are of the magic-bearing ilk. You, of course, do not fall into this unfortunate category; I perhaps disrespected you by so boldly castigating your mother, but I simply cannot bear a presence seething with such negativity. And her darkness oppresses the living things all around us. There is no good there. Only bleakness."

Tinna examined the bold character that had just dressed-down her mother and decided in that instant that she approved of him. Without a word, she smiled, looped her arm around his, and led him towards his new home. He stopped and handed Taneth his staff. Still shaken, Avria's father took it, examining it closely, too rational to believe the power that had just flowed through it. Eleran reached out for Avria's hand. She placed hers in his, tiny and delicate against his calloused skin and heavy fingers. She could scarce glance into searing eyes without feeling lightheaded. She gave him a bashful smile, and he returned one of masculine confidence, tucking her hand into the crook of his arm. As Avria fell into step with the towering man, she caught Jestin's eye again. He looked positively furious, the brims of his eyes glistening with angry tears.

CHAPTER FOUR – THE BETRAYAL

Avria had heard the legends of those who possessed magical powers. The Chaiva, Mystics and the Magis—these were familiar and somewhat explicable. According to her father, these creatures did not work magics at all; they simply used their common senses. Maybe in some way, the senses were naturally amplified in some, but he dismissed the idea of magic. Taneth had explained that some people had deeply empathic abilities to read a great deal from very little, in subtle ways—even just by careful observation of the body's language—but he had yet to explain how they could have such intuitions about people they'd never met or known.

Avria understood the fundamentals of the Druidic Soothsayers' belief systems and their story. As stewards of nature, custodians of the flora and fauna that sustained the people, they used one of the few types of magic that did not fall under the watchful eye of the Keepers; instead, fabled immortals called the Hevra oversaw them. Avria knew very little else about these mysterious and powerful souls. She had read that they could summon the strengths and powers of nature to serve them, but she assumed that, like most tales of magic-bearing people, their stories were nonsense. She'd had no idea until this moment that magic wielders were real. The trembling earth convinced her. That and the powerful pull she felt, when he came near her. He watched her with his blue eyes, following her movements, a predator watching a willing prey.

They had led him to his new apartments, for which he expressed his gratitude, mentioning that his brethren were accustomed to simple treatments and little space. He seemed to like his apartment. He leaned his staff against the wall, looking about him, his expression favorable. "This is more than any humble servant of the Earth Goddess and her Hevra could hope for. A palace!" He turned to make way for Veeru, who brought in his many packs and belongings. Avria felt awkward standing at the doorway. Even when she looked away, she could feel the heat of his glances. Taneth

325

smiled to himself upon noticing the attraction and smirked at Tinna knowingly.

"Well, I'll leave you to it then. The elders will be meeting at the main hearth after dinner on this day. Some meetings are shorter than others. Sometimes they don't happen at all. But we will be meeting tonight. You, of course, are welcome to decline for now if you'd like; you must be exhausted."

"I'll rest a bit, and perhaps I will attend later," Eleran replied. Taneth bustled out, Tinna followed, and Eleran closed the door behind them, giving Avria a final powerful gaze that bore right into the core of her being, before the latch closed. Her stomach roiled with spiders, and her heart fluttered. She felt like an idiot. She lifted the hem of her skirts and ran to her apartment, shutting herself in and leaning on the door. She wondered if he'd cast some spell on her, for she couldn't close her eyes without seeing his burning gaze, or keep her breath from quickening at the thought of his nearness.

* * * *

Eleran felt her across the lodge, a thrumming beacon of heat. He knew without a doubt that she was the one. No other creature could he picture with such clarity in his mind. Her potent blood would mingle with his; he felt that destiny burn through him already. He had felt her before he entered the forum. Before he reached Hildercross, he had felt the rightness of his decision to join the Araki settlement. He knew it would lead him to her. He could barely contain the power of his attraction to her. So much that it nearly made him open a hole in the earth to swallow the crone that sought to remove her from his world and to take her to Thran. That old woman left a slug-trail of darkness behind her; and she was truly ill-intended in everything she did. He was wary of her.

But the dark woman aside, he felt pleased, blessed to have received the rare gift of finding that perfect one. Now he wasn't sure if he could bear sharing a lodge with her or master the powerful desires that destiny itself had imposed on him.

As he rose from his restless nap and folded his traveling clothes, he took a moment to douse his face with icy water and to lean on his hands over the finely carved cabinet upon which the washbowl and decanter rested. He sometimes hated the keenness of his senses; the power of his perception. It was hard to control, and sometimes unbearable, even for common things; he wasn't prepared for this, no matter how much he welcomed it. To find the match at

326

last, someone to look at him, and touch him. His skin went bumpy and he bridled his passionate thoughts—such emotional upheaval could cause physical effects around him. He dressed in casual clothes. He wanted both comfort and concealment if he ran into her again. A long tunic, some floppy drawstring leggings, and he padded barefoot to the main hearth where the community of the Summer lodge was preparing to eat. Silence fell when he entered the space. Unconsciously, the others withdrew from his presence, every person leaning away from him just a shade, as if the air had been sucked from the room, leaving a sense of expectation. Eyes followed him suspiciously. Children clung to their parents. Only Taneth, the Wiseman, threw up his arms and gestured Eleran over to the place where he sat with his wife, who looked so much like the delicious young Avria.

Eleran concentrated on the food. He'd lived in cities of elegance, and he'd lived in towns of the true North men. He'd enjoyed many luxuries, but this was the epitome of life's pleasures— the array of food, the ambience, the subtle smell of wood smoke from the hearth. Before him, a broad, square, wooden platter occupied his spot at the table. On it, a tidy assortment of foods; a roast duck leg and thigh, some sliced baked tuber root of some sort with ferruginous flesh, a fresh blended salad of rounded leaf vegetables mixed with pine nuts, chopped tomatoes and some unusual-looking beans. A little four-cornered bowl at the top left corner of his platter held a steaming, clear-brothed soup with colorful bits of vegetable, squares of some sort of game meat and some dumplings. Without looking at him, as she chatted away with a pregnant woman, Tinna tore a hunk of bread from a fresh loaf and dropped it on top of Eleran's food. Taneth glanced at him expectantly. Eleran studied his strange, two-tined fork, then speared a tuber wheel and bit into it, closing his eyes in bliss. It was delicious and creamy, with an unusual nutty flavor.

He felt comfort in the press of the warm bodies of others, who slowly relaxed and returned to conversation. Taneth is an odd one, he thought. He could feel the man's powerful knowledge, his softened prejudices, and the hundreds of questions he bit back for the sake of politeness. He could feel Tinna's secrets, sensing pain and something dark and powerful within her. All around him, the community throbbed like a heartbeat, each lodge a core, tendrils of connections reaching between them in brightly lit strands of yellow and green, dominant and pulsing like veins around the blue sunburst that radiated from the founding tree. A soft life-force passively connected each person to it. Nobody saw it but him. In his mind's eye, he saw each person in the settlement as a lighted form, saw clusters of life-forces in each lodge, as they gathered in their respective halls for dinner. He found the one who burned hot orange-red, with a white, streaming aura. A smile curled on his lip as he stared blankly at the delicious food before him.

They were talking, but he didn't hear them. He compartmentalized the words, buffered them, his other mind hearing, processing; while he watched the little, red, burning form move about its small space, leave it, and head towards his own searing white shape.

Avria entered the common hall and, without hesitation, sat next to him. She'd changed into more common clothing; a long black skirt and an ivory tunic. To her, he felt like a stove, the arcs of his aura reaching out in electric strands, making her neck and arm hair stand on end.

"What do you think, Eleran? Is it alright if I call you Eleran?"

"Of course you may; I'm sort of part of the village now. I hope everyone will treat me as such. And yes, I think it would be wonderful to do it right away. Rigerd is eager to visit his sons. But we cannot forget about the rites for the young ones. That should happen first." Eleran's second mind fed him the answer he needed. She needs to become an adult; she must have her rites of passage. He moved his leg, just brushing hers; she straightened her back, and her body pulsed hotter. He was close to eight years her senior. But they were meant to be; he knew it. The reaction, the silent language, the colors of the auras, were exactly as the teachings said. Your perfect mate; the Soothsayer powers can only be continued through the perfect match. Here she sat; the tiny thing with black curls. She smelled like cedar.

Just then, the boy who gazed at her constantly with lustful greed appeared and ungraciously made her scoot over. He sat between them. He glanced at the Soothsayer and smiled wanly. "I'm Jestin."

"Pleased to make your acquaintance, Jestin," he said in a controlled tone, fighting the urge to levitate him and fling him into the large fireplace. He could do it easily. Like a toy. But the powers did not approve of such acts. He would pay a hard price for willfully harming someone. This boy wasn't worth it. He did not like the uneasy feeling he gave off. As with the grandmother, something deeply wrong abided within the soul of this child. His only goodness relied entirely on the girl he coveted. This did not bode well, and it alarmed Eleran and set him to thinking. He ate, Jestin providing him with enough ire to keep him focused on something other than his desire to smother himself in Avria. He then had to endure another two hours by the hearth with Tinna, Taneth, Rigerd and several village elders to discuss matters. His second mind, all the while, dwelt elsewhere.

* * * *

Avria lay on the hill with Reega and Therta, one knee up and the other ankle crossed over it. The dogs stretched out perpendicular to her, side by side, resting their heads on their paws. She'd changed into a comfortable set of skirts and a loose, long-sleeved tunic, over which she'd pulled an enormous sweater that everyone except her mother considered communal property. The rust-colored dye had long since leached out, and the wool smelled of comfort and cedar. The sleeves stretched past her fingers, and she snuggled them under her chin. The dogs stirred. Their shining noses and glistening eyes reflected the pale light cast by the crescent moons and stars.

The hill overlooked the oldest part of the cemetery. The night was cool and dark, but Avria didn't care. The Thran contingent still milled about in the pasture. Apparently, Grandmother was coming back to the lodge for a while.

Jestin and his behavior occupied Avria's mind. She sought peace. Jestin was and always had been her cousin—or even a brother in some ways—at least in her mind. Deep down, she knew that he cared for her in another way. He had since they were young. It made her sad now, as she came to terms with the truth, as it became more and more apparent to her every day. She could never feel that way for him. Phenmal had shown her why by pointing out to her the behaviors Jestin had exhibited and that she had ignorantly mimicked.

Jestin had tried to follow her back to her apartment. She sent him on a fool's errand and then slipped out with the dogs. She didn't want him to think of her in that way anymore and she didn't know how to stop it.

And now this Eleran added to her concerns. Ugh! She could barely breathe just thinking about him. Eleran and his spells! She swallowed hard and took a deep breath of the cold night air. This can't be right! Just thinking about him made her tremble and her entire core to heat up. She propped herself up on her elbows, then sat up. She stretched the sweater over her knees and looped her arms around them, resting her chin and listening to the mobiles sing in the oaks. She knew she was safe from Jestin here. He hated the cemeteries. As she sat there, Reega and Therta lifted their heads and swiveled them towards the top of the hill, moist black noses testing the air, when the unmistakable form of the Soothsayer appeared in silhouette. He tramped down the hill and, without pausing, circled round to face her. She didn't move. Her breath caught in her throat. She wondered for a moment how he could have found her. Then she remembered what he was.

He stooped and took her hands, pulling her to her feet. His large hand cupped her chin, and he lowered his lips to hers. She lost her breath. Stars exploded behind her eyelids. A current from his touch shot out to her extremities, and she thought would die. Eleran and his beautiful spells!

* * * *

Jestin could not deny the looks, the games. His heart thumped in his mouth. As the Soothsayer made preparations for their rites of ascension, something that would apparently take days, Avria hung around nearby, her large, dark-lashed eyes on the intimidating character. She was mad at Jestin, or perhaps made uncomfortable by the events at Silver Lake and she took Jestin's jealous behavior as part of his discomfort from Silver Lake, not seeing that he was now infuriated by her infatuation with this newcomer.

Tinna did not act like this, Jestin thought. His grandmother, his mother—they did not behave like swooning girls. They knew who they loved. They would never have chosen their men with such silly girlish looks and flirtatious smiles. Why did Avria act like this? She was his Avria. I've been her friend for years, I know all the things she loves; I know her world better than anyone! This old interloper cannot have her! He simply cannot! He sat on the floor of the food storage room, the door cracked so he could see into the main hall. They were there, together. He watched and listened, his eyes sunken, his shoulders sagging. His sense of hopelessness was heavy and he dwelled on thoughts of it with obsessive determination until he came to a realization.

It occurred to him then that Avria would forgive him. She always did, no matter how horrible he could be. He was no expert about everything, but one thing he did know through and through was Avria's good and sweet character. That fight had brought forth a little awkwardness on her part; but Jestin knew she would forget it, because that is who she was. What he was also sure of was that she was probably keenly aware of his sulking, his discomfort, and probably responding to it in kind. But he also knew that if he wasn't sulking and wracked in self-pity; if he was warm and happy as he always was with her, she would mirror it. It occurred to Jestin that he could possibly do something about this. He waited until they left, the Soothsayer to the library, Avria to the stable and he emerged from the store room as if stepping out of a fugue. With a wry smile, he stood and sauntered down the corridor after Avria.

Eleran had never been an overly possessive man. But he had never been this much in love either. He found his usual easiness slipping away with each passing hour since his arrival. His confidence of Avria becoming a permanent fixture in his heart and in his future never faltered, however he did not completely trust that Avria fully understood the significance of their connection. She had no magic, no second sight. She did not understand the mandates that guided him—perhaps she didn't know she was fated to be with him from the moment of her birth. It wasn't the sincerity of Avria's devotion that he doubted. Avria gave no indication of a diminishment or fabrication of her regard for the newcomer by any means. In fact it was quite the opposite. Avria swooned and smiled and flirted with him endlessly. She hung about him gazing at him almost constantly. She found every free moment to loll about and engage him in a chat. She was besotted; as was he. He was happiest at those moments, when he had her full attention and he could watch over her.

However there was another factor, an unwelcome one and that was the boy Jestin. Eleran could not deny that there was a history there, a friendship and a familiarity that Jestin shared with Avria that the druid did not. And after a brief period of Jestin casting them baleful stares from afar, something Eleran was able to endure with ease, the boy chose another tack and instead vied to usurp the girl's attentions at any given opportunity. Jestin had used this special connection with Avria with impunity, striving overtly to keep Avria from Eleran. Jestin invented reasons to go riding, to go walking, he would crop up some sorrowful moment of his past that he could only share with Avria; it was never ending and it was irritating to no end to the soothsayer. He was having more and more difficulty with each passing day keeping these seemingly irrational and petty jealousies at bay.

Eleran didn't like feeling this aspect of his character so keenly; a powerful jealousy of a mere boy who had nothing to offer Avria; not even a type of personal decency worth loving. Deep down, he knew Avria's feelings for Jestin weren't even remotely as dear as they were for Eleran. For Avria, Jestin was like a brother; a longtime friend. Eleran knew this, but he still could not kick away that nagging little monster that gnawed at him when they were gone away somewhere together. He simply did not like Jestin on an instinctive level and he did not like him sniffing around his woman. It set his hackles on end just the thought of it—and the boy seemed to be overtly taunting him by being in Avria's face as much as humanly possible.

His resentment of Jestin began to grow and he was finding it increasingly difficult to even look at the boy in the face. Somewhere along the line, the boy had managed to suppress his rivalry with Eleran and instead focused on renewing his relationship with Avria. He redoubled his efforts in the past several days. He had such a smugness about him because he knew Avria had known him for so long, she could scarce say no to him. She also had feelings of guilt for whatever it was that happened between them and was trying to make up for it. And to make it worse, Avria was also even more prone to agree to run off for the day simply to escape her grandmother, who now haunted the place like an old specter.

So Jestin whisked her away and distracted her in a vain attempt to make Avria forget the soothsayer. Avria was utterly without guile or clue of Eleran's insecurities when it came to Jestin nor was she even remotely suspicious of Jestin's motivations. She flowed with it all with a natural ease and her eye never caught the furrowed brow or flicker of jealousy in his glance when she returned from wherever she was with a naïve smile, or the exchange of dark looks between the soothsayer and the younger man. It was getting so, in these past three days, that Eleran could barely keep himself from being cross about it. As he set down his book of study of the holy texts of the Araki people in preparation for the ceremonies of passage and Tinna's succession, he was immediately annoyed that Avria was still absent and it was already getting dark. She'd gone off with the boys to what she called Kettle Hill, where there was a wide expanse of open field on a hilltop several miles northwest of Thamatoc. It was part of Phenmal's rather large swath of land. There, the young people liked to race their horses in open fields and it was something of great excitement. Avria seemed doubly thrilled that Jestin was so excited about going riding with everyone, exclaiming her happiness about it to Eleran that very morning when they breakfasted.

"He's back to normal. I was so afraid things had changed for the worse between us, but he is my friend again!" she exclaimed to him, her sweet smile warming Eleran's heart. He knew not to say what he thought was true, that he was doing it to undermine their connection. He knew she had to find that out for herself. His speaking of it would only make him look the jealous fool.

"When will you be finished and ready to perform the ceremony, Eleran?" she asked.

"Probably tomorrow, I have some additional reading to do, and then I must meditate."

"Oh, good. So you're busy all day then, because we're off to Kettle Hill this morning. Hanru challenged Jestin to a race and word got around about a trip to the hill, so now Laren, Aleeya, Itrell, Enress, and his brother and sister have asked to come along as well. It's a long ride out and a long ride back, so I'll be gone most of the day." He kept his mouth shut and gave her a shallow nod. Since she was not yet an adult in the eyes of the gods, she was not available to claim. It was not his place to tell her she should not go. He chewed his mandibles and tried to hide is irritation. She smiled, downed the rest of her hot tea and squeezed his arm as she rose from the bench. Her movement promoted several other bodies to cast away from the table and they all merged as they walked out. Avria cast an affectionate smile to Eleran over her shoulder as she did, completely blind to the raging jealousy behind his kind eyes.

Eleran could scarce concentrate on his work, but he managed to get through it. He would need only do the meditation required of his faith to perform the rites and then after that he could express his intentions to Avria and become bonded in a promise to her. A promise bond would immediately make roaming about alone with Jestin or any young man inappropriate behavior and nip that little issue in the bud.

This notion pleased Eleran, but the sight of Avria's glowing happiness as she rounded the corner of the corridor and strode up to him made him feel sour all over again. He was fully aware how irrational this feeling was, he knew her happiness was an innocent one, but he did not think that the boy Jestin deserved so much of her time. "Ah, you're finally back..." he snapped angrily, slamming the book shut. She halted in mid stride, the light on her face immediately melted into darkness, her eyes wide with confusion and shock.

"What's wrong Eleran?"

"Don't you think it's a bit unseemly that you go off on all-day jaunts in the company of young men? I thought you were better raised than to do that..." Eleran muttered, regretting every word that seemed to leap out of his mouth against his will. He was further dismayed by the look of disappointment on Avria's face, which was then quickly replaced with anger and determination. She furrowed her brow and cast her irritated gaze upon him.

"Thamatoc is not Loshan or Letrios. We are not human settlements bound by human laws, Eleran. Women here don't live repressed lives that revolve entirely around some ancient notion of decency. Here women are trusted to behave themselves and women can take responsibility for their own actions. I had no idea you doubted my character so," she retorted angrily, her disappointment so evident it actually hurt him to see it.

"That's not what I meant..." he grumbled, shaking his head.

"You're occupied all day. I'm just disturbing you and slowing you down," she added. "They're my friends, Eleran. You should know very well that's all they are. You should not think I would ever..." her eyes glassed over at the thought that he doubted her and questioned her judgment. She turned on her heel and stalked off. Eleran had stood momentarily but now sank back down, shaking his head. He never knew he could behave so stupidly over a young woman. He rubbed his face with the flat of his hand and sighed. Now he had to fix it, and he wasn't quite sure how.

Avria stormed to her room and slammed her door, angry to no end. How could he doubt her? How could he think she was anything but genuine in her feelings? How could he believe she would do anything that would damage her reputation or his? How could he put her personal responsibility into question? After the moment they shared that first night; when he'd kissed her so tenderly on the hill near the old cemetery. After that, how could he doubt her? Avria slumped into her chair and pulled off her boots, her eyes misting over with emotion. She'd lived for that moment, it had meant everything. She thought they had agreed. She thought it was settled. Why would he be so angry at her for going out with her friends? He knew her heart belonged to him. He knew. There was no reason for him to treat her like a child.

She let her foot drop and her eyes fell onto her fire, which was healthily chewing its way through the light fruitwood someone had been thoughtful enough to start for her before she got home. She suspected her mother had something to do with it. She sighed and leaned back into her chair. Her mind went back to the hill that first night.

After her head had stopped spinning from that kiss and she'd regained control of her mind, she had fallen back comfortably onto the soft leaves on that hillside. Eleran was so near she could feel the heat of his body emanating from him. She dwelled on it now in her chair; and on what he had said to her when he'd sat down on the ground next to her and began absentmindedly scratching behind the dogs' ears.

"Avria, have you ever heard of the divided soul?" he asked.

She shook her head and tried to make out as much as she could of his face in the darkness. She could see his profile as he gazed out into the blackness below them, listening quietly to the trees hissing in the wind and to the charms and chimes ringing in their branches. "The Zshathri beliefs reach back to before the times recorded. We believe in the ancient gods, in the ones that are all around us, the essence of our world, our skies, and our heavens. We believe that we were not only made from all this but that we are the stewards of it. The very first creatures put on this firmament were created to care for it. These caretakers are the immortals that hide among us. Our people believe that when the gods conjured the souls to animate their creations, they based them on the vastness of their own souls, but they soon discovered that our tiny Human vessels were too small, too weak to contain the power of the originals. The first caretakers went mad. When they created the mortal people, the gods decided to divide the soul. So each person born to the world thereafter received one half of one soul. Men received the sun-half; women received the moon-half."

He paused and leaned back, propping himself up on his elbows, his right hand still clutching hers. "People spend their entire lives searching for completion. Because lifetime after lifetime, that one half of a soul desperately seeks its other half. The search goes beyond individual lifetimes; each time a soul is reborn, it resumes its search. Sometimes it finds its match, meeting only for a time before it is separated again by the death of its vessel. It is the torture of true love, of true completion, the quest we are all doomed to endure. Many live and die never knowing what it is to be whole." He leaned in towards her a bit, putting his weight on his right elbow.

"We of the magic, the ones who can see and step beyond the veil of this world—we are both blessed and cursed. Few of us wield such extraordinary powers, because we can only pass it on to a child born from parents of the same soul. It is a rare thing, Avria, very rare. But we have the advantage of knowing it, seeing it, when others cannot. For this reason, our kind endures."

"You believe that we are the same soul?" Avria felt her heart reaching out to him, reveling in his tale that confirmed, in her eyes, that they would be together.

"No, I do not merely believe it; Avria. I know it. It is certainty. I see it when I look at you. I felt it before I met you. I am connected to you and you are connected to me. I know that, if you told me you didn't feel it the moment we met, you would be lying. We are destined to be together. It would be an affront to the gods themselves if we ever part."

"We cannot have that, can we—affronted Gods? No. So indeed, we should never part." Avria grinned at him in the darkness and she saw the glint of his glassy irises as he gazed at her.

"Good," he said. "I'm glad we've settled that." He stood and brushed off his breeches. Without another word, he walked away. Avria fell back and threw her arms out, gazing up at the sky, filtered by layers of tree limbs, the silhouettes of oak leaves. She'd never known such a sense of rightness. She took in a deep, long breath of the cool, crisp night air, feeling the residual tingle of his touch on her lips and hand and smiled.

That same wistful smile returned to her mouth as she sat in her chair in the now, reliving that moment as clearly as the night it happened. Then her smile faded as another memory of that night came into her head. She remembered following him back a while later to find Jestin waiting for her by her apartment door, appearing wounded.

"I brought back your novel. It's on your table." He gestured to her door, stiff and uncomfortable. "It was really awful," he tried to laugh.

"Thank you, Jestin." She reached for the latch. He did not move out of the way but lingered as if he wanted to say something, then changed his mind and stormed away. Avria shook her head and entered her room. She had actually bolted the door behind her, something she never did. She'd felt a strange sense of trepidation, something she'd never felt before around Jestin.

It was that memory that made Avria realize what was really going on. She sat up and her anger at Eleran melted away. She understood now. With a sigh, she kicked off her boots and put on her slippers. With a determined line on her lips, she left her room, crossing the lodge towards the apartments assigned to the Soothsayer.

A little while after their tiff, Eleran was laying in his bed, his unfinished book lying open his chest under his chin. The candles and lanterns had burnt out and he was cast in the warm deep orange light of the low-burning fire. He had yet to speak to Avria and he could not think of anything else. He was behaving like a child. A soft knock resonated on his door.

"Come in," he muttered. He did not have his second sight open; he was too tired and defeated by his own emotions to sustain it. He left the identity of the person at his door up to chance. Avria peered into the partly opened door.

"Can I talk to you for a moment?" she asked in a soft voice, adding with a touch of acidity; "although my coming in here unaccompanied might be seen as unseemly." He scoffed and sighed, his eyes gratified by the sight of her. She stepped in and shut the door, walking first to the fire and stooping before it. The darkness had shouldered its way close around the hearth, but she stoked the flames and added some light kindling. The flames popped into life and she added more wood as they grew stronger. At length she stood and turned to look at him. He could only see the most prominent parts of her cheeks and nose, the rest of her was mostly a silhouette against the firelight. She crossed her arms.

"We've only known one another for a few days; that's the reality, Eleran. Regardless of what you told me about our connection that first night, we hardly know each other. I can't know what you are feeling, I don't know you yet. All I know is that we share something unusually powerful; something even I cannot deny exists. I cannot explain away the effects of just being close to you. But Eleran, if you harbored anger at my being away from you, you should have said so."

"It isn't your absence," he interrupted her. "It's..."

"It's Jestin," she finished with a tone of finality. Avria was quite wise and perceptive when she wanted to be. She shifted her weight onto her other hip and then pushed her mane of curls back with a graceful sweep of the hand, which in silhouette looked like an elegant dance. "We have been like brother and sister since we were born. It's hard not to fear losing his friendship forever or to keep myself from feeling compelled to make it all up to him."

"Make what up to him?" he asked, his brow arched. Avria shifted uncomfortably and then sighed.

"His feelings for me... I've come to realize they're not as benign as I thought, or perhaps hoped," she shook her head and looked down at the floor. "I hurt his feelings every time I even look at you, or at anyone else. I feel guilty that I can't return his affections in the way he wants. So I think I'm overcompensating a bit; mostly because you have entered my life and occupy so many of my thoughts and absorb much of my time. I never took your feelings into consideration. For that I am sorry. I am however condemned to upsetting either you or him. So I understand I have to make a choice. There is no hesitation or doubt in me when I say I choose you, Eleran. And if it bothers you that I spend so much time with Jestin, then I won't. I will tell him. He will be hurt by it, but I suppose that's my lot." Avria then angled herself a bit towards the fire, her face now washed in its golden light, her black eyes shining. "Goodnight, Eleran."

"Goodnight Avria," he replied softly. She exited in a whisper, the latch clicking gently behind her.

The hurt in Jestin's eyes was overriding. Avria felt a lump in her throat that seemed to have angles and edges sharp and cutting and she tried to swallow it down and compose herself. She hadn't been fully prepared when she ran into him. It was only moments after her talk with Eleran that she found him sitting in the main hall in her father's chair, his feet drawn up against him, arms locked around his knees. She wondered why he was still in the main lodge, it was late and pretty much everyone had retired to their own apartments for the night. But Jestin was a night-owl and it wasn't unheard of to find him wandering about sometimes. He looked up and saw her and his face brightened momentarily. Then he saw the grave look on her face and his smile melted away.

"Hullo, Avvie. Why so sullen?" She merely smiled wanly and sank down into the chair across from him, gripping her knees and quietly formulating her words. That's when the lump formed in her throat.

"I've come to a decision Jestin," she choked, clearing her throat and recomposing herself. She decided to do it quickly and to be forthright. "You know I like the new Soothsayer, very much."

"Ugh, too much. He's so much older than you, Avria, why...?"

"Jestin, I would not speak so ill of someone you cared about, no matter how much I disagreed with your choice. Please hear me out," she interrupted him. His mouth snapped shut and his brow angled downwards in distress. His eyes were locked hard and almost accusingly on her face. She looked away, her eyes falling fast on the fire. "You know I like him and it's more than just a lark. I like him quite a lot; I can even say that I love..."

"It's FAR too soon for you to be dropping the word 'love' about like that, Avria, you hardly know him!" Jestin's tone was almost frantic. He dropped his legs down so his feet hit the floor and his hands gripped the arms of the chair.

"I know it's hard to understand, but I know what I'm feeling, Jestin," she cut him short again, laying her hand over her heart, "and after the rites, it's likely we will be promised to one another. So I will just come out and say it. I can't hang about with you all day anymore. It's not seemly, and it's not fair to Eleran. You are like family to me, but you aren't really related; so it's not appropriate for be with you all the time. I will also refrain from spending too much time with Drashun and Enress and the like as well. But I thought you deserved to know because you know how much I love you. I trust you'll understand and not take it personally." With that, Avria stood and bent down to kiss Jestin on the cheek. She then walked away so she wasn't forced to witness the pain she had caused him emblazoned so plainly on his face.

* * * *

"Where do you go when you meditate?" Avria asked in a soft voice, rocking on her feet, picking the pine nuts out of a cone and popping them into her mouth, crunching away. Eleran busied himself mixing herbs and sorting through symbolic items and tokens. He paused, a soft smile on his face. He noticed that Avria liked to snack. She was always nibbling on something or other, pine nuts, syrup candy, or one type of berry or other. He found her adorable beyond measure as she intently picked at the scales of a pinecone for its delicious seeds, dropping little bits of residue and broken scales onto the ground. He had never felt more centered or focused than in this moment. Since that first kiss, since he'd felt her essence pour into his heart from that single kiss, she had filled in a part of him he had not known was empty; more so since she had declared her choice to him the night before last. He was in love, without the slightest doubt. He would marry her.

He reached out and pressed one of her curls from her face. She blushed and plucked at the cuff of his sleeve in a playful way. He smiled. "Your old holyman meditated too. Before any ceremony for which he had to obtain the blessing of the horse god," he replied. Avria glanced up and saw her grandmother, the Diviner, and a guard pass through the main Hall with Tinna in the lead, looking tired and morose. Avria had not seen her grandmother for any length of time for several days, nor spent any quantitative time with her mother or father, she'd been so busy entertaining Jestin's insecurities and her own obsession with the new holyman. She sighed and turned her attention back to the Soothsayer.

"What happens when you do?"

"I leave my body. I go into the realms of the gods. I speak to the goddess; ask for her blessings to return to the people. In return, I must make myself absent from this world for a while. It's a small price—"

"Why do we need blessings?"

"Any change in a person's life should be made with the blessing of the gods."

"All changes?"

"Any change that I must minister to, yes. You are full of questions today, aren't you, Avria?"

"It's a bit frightening, the idea that you must leave your body. How can you be sure to come back every time?"

"There is a spiritual tether between my essence and my physical form. I can't get lost. Fear not. Again, your holyman habitually meditated, just as I will."

"He usually did it in the privacy of his apartments, so we never saw much of it. Can I sit with you while you meditate?"

"Of course. But it could be for a long time," he warned her with a bemused expression, touched by her concern. "I like to be out here because it's more central to the community, and I can draw from the village's connections more easily," he explained in a low voice. He wanted to kiss her again and again, to wrap himself around her, but he resisted. He had a job to do. Their union would come in due time.

"Here," he picked up a little pot of salve and a little brush. "I'll start with you since you're here. Then it's the Nimrath boy and Jestin."

Eleran was fully aware of the eavesdropper in the storage room, but he made no indication of it. It wasn't the first time Jestin hid in there to listen in on their interactions. He'd made a habit of it when he first arrived, but had stopped for the duration of his daily excursions with Avria. Now that Avria had spoken to him, his sneaky behavior had resumed. Jestin thought himself perfectly concealed—ignorant, as many were, of the druid's special sight. Avria had told him of her desires, and the boy had from that very night turned sour and bitter. He lingered about like a sullen child, glaring at Eleran. He would sit near them at mealtimes refusing to eat and gazing balefully at them. Avria had made it clear she was not going to fall for his attention-getting behavior. She ignored him on the most part as long as he moped about.

The slighted boy has to learn to resign himself to the idea that Avria is not for him. He has to accept it. Eleran sat on the edge of the table and gestured for her to approach. She did, her body drawn to him, every sense focused on him. He had to center himself to control the trembling of his hands. She brought her face close to his. Even crouched down, half-sitting on the table, he was taller than her. He smiled at that. She was a tiny thing.

Eleran reached up and started to paint the herbal concoction onto her temple with a small brush. "This way there is no pain. No piercing of the skin." She felt his breath on her face, and she leaned forward, touching her cheek to his, brushing the very corner of her mouth to his. He nearly gave in. He pressed her back and shook his head admonishingly.

"You're not an adult in the eyes of the gods, Avria," he whispered, "You know this full-well. But if you stop mucking about, we might get there." She acquiesced, barely. He finished painting the delicate design. A serpentine line down her right temple along her hairline, with a spiraling limb within each curve. "I'll invoke the sheffra, and it will sink into your skin and remain." She nodded, lowering her face, but looking up at him with her great big, alluring eyes. Her magnetism was powerful and she knew it. He smirked at the little temptress, pinching her chin affectionately. He offered her a quick peck on her lips and then withdrew.

"Go find your idiot friends. I need to mark them up before I meditate." He left the hall momentarily so that Jestin could extricate himself from his hiding spot. Eleran returned a few moments later, sure that Jestin had slipped down the other corridor and finished his preparations.

Eleran's feelings about Jestin were growing increasingly bleak as time went on and he remained at Thamatoc. Eleran knew the boy only stayed for a few months at best, but his state of mind, so early in his visit concerned the Soothsayer. It would only get worse from here. The closer Avria came to becoming Eleran's mate, the darker the boy's aura became. It was something that preoccupied the Soothsayer; he was beginning to have a feeling that Jestin could be a danger to Avria, and this filled him with a sense of dread. These thoughts came upon him the day he had come to Thamatoc and witnessed the boy's near-obsessive attachment to Avria. With every day that passed, that bad feeling grew heavier and heavier on the man's shoulders. He was beginning to think it was something he had to take responsibility for before something happened to the woman he wanted to marry. He ruminated on this, trying to figure something out as he made his preparations.

The girl returned with her friends. Jestin looked despondent and depressed; Drashun, oblivious as usual. *Poor thing! A Nimrath trapped in human skin; perhaps I can help him release his ability sometime.* Jestin's body language stood out as clear as day to anyone who knew what he knew. He leaned away, a look of hatred on his face as Eleran painted the design on his skin. He looked close to tears. Eleran's eyes studied the boy's face, his second mind trying to see what the boy was truly capable of while he applied the paint to the boy's head.

"Good. You're all done. Now, do not touch the emulsion for about an hour." He indicated the great clock known as 'Clanker' that stood in a casing by the hearth. Old and clumsy, the noisy clock ticked laboriously along. It was the only clock in the whole settlement. "You'll feel it tingle and once that's done, then you're welcome to remove it." He climbed up on the table before the hearth and crossed his legs, lay his hands open and flat on the table at his sides. He took a deep breath, loosened his neck with a quick roll of the head, and closed his eyes. When they opened again, they were white. Jestin made a noise of disgust and stalked away. Drashun wandered away and Avria climbed up onto the table and sat with him through the morning until he returned, barely aware of the tingling as the painted tattoo made itself permanent on her skin. Eleran transitioned back into himself seamlessly, giving Avria's hand a quick squeeze to let her know he was back.

"All right. I have the words I need for each of you." Avria smiled and reached out, brushing his lips with her thumb.

"You—" She paused, then trailed off. She shook her head, blushed, hopped off the table and padded away. His heart followed her. He sat for a moment and then sighed, shaking his head. Jestin had wiped off an almost unnoticeably small part of the design painted onto his skin; his tattoo was incomplete. It was a stupid way to act out, for it had no adverse effect on anyone except himself. He was still unsure what to do about Jestin. He went to his apartments to contemplate this.

The markings had been made, but the young ones had yet to be blessed. That night, when the common room had cleared of everyone but the three youths, Tinna, Taneth and Rhoa, Drashun's mother, Eleran performed the Zshathri rite of passage; officially declaring the three adults. Jestin felt alone. His mother wasn't there with him. His heart was broken and he wanted to feel that someone cared. He watched with baleful eyes as his rival prepared for a ceremony Jestin wanted no part of. He felt some satisfaction that he'd tampered with the man's work. This Zshathri would not drag him, kicking and screaming, into the Thamatoc culture. He had never belonged here, nor did he want to. He wanted to live in Loshan and he wanted that for Avria, too, to live well and to be beautiful and gentle, not forced to live like a savage among horses.

The markings were subtle on their faces, now a pale blue-grey, fine arcing lines and swirls. Eleran touched each one, whispering in his mysterious language. He brandished some strange relics and painted some invisible words in the air with them, then placed his hand on Drashun's head.

"Karoodin pro'odit mordat. Sigulitant prethos," he chanted.

"Karoodin pro'odit mordat. Sigulitant artitoss," Eleran said when he placed his hand on the reluctant Jestin's head. Jestin winced involuntarily.

Then he came to Avria, who never took her eyes from his beautiful face. Jestin sighed audibly and fidgeted, rolling his eyes obstinately.

"Karoodin pro'odit mordat. Sigulitant pferimitos;" he paused, and glanced fleetingly at Jestin, a frown flashing darkly across his brow. With a look of resolve, Eleran added some more words to his spell; "Averoj pregam dacrtrit meetat minmitul, sevratus ver Jad." His touch felt like fire, stung Avria for some reason. She hissed and flinched, but did not draw away, only lifting her hand and almost touching his. Eleran disengaged from her wordlessly and moved to Drashun again and said his name, touching the spot on his temple and the name marks on his shoulder. He did the same for Jestin, then Avria. His second touch to Avria seemed to quell the sensation, and cool the skin.

"We're finished. You're all counted among the ranks of Araki adults now. Congratulations!" Eleran exclaimed, eyes bright. They fell with no lack of joy on Avria, who grinned at him.

"Why was my spell longer?" she asked, her wide, unassuming eyes full of curiosity, and because of it, looking almost too much like her father for it. Eleran thought on it for a second and smiled.

"It's a sealing spell that was meant for all," he lied. Avria, without guile, merely accepted this answer smiled at him radiantly.

"You never told me there would be markings on my face," Drashun muttered to his mother irritably. She shrugged, looking at Tinna helplessly. Tinna smirked.

"My rites of passage ceremony was entirely different than this, you don't see a tattoo on my head, do you?" his mother replied. She then embraced him. "I'm proud of you, Drashun!" She stepped back, her auburn hair and fair skin still flushed and deceivingly youthful. She'd never married. She was Tinna's right arm. She always looked very sad; except when she looked at Drashun. Then she would smile wistfully. As he got older, she sometimes would look at him and mist up. Avria suspected that Drashun looked very much like his father. She could not ask, for the subject of Draphen was off-limits to all. Drashun however, rebelled against his mother; unspoken anger had festered, and they had a strained relationship. For that moment, he looked vulnerable and child-like again as he gazed at her, seeking the forgiveness in himself for whatever it was he could not set aside.

"I had no idea that would hurt," Avria declared. Drashun and Jestin's brows furrowed, and they both smugly replied in unison; "it didn't for me." Avria looked at Eleran, who merely shrugged.

"It's different for everyone," was his airy reply. He set to organizing the items he had on the table for the ceremony.

Jestin sat there, quietly watching the Soothsayer as he put his paraphernalia away. Tinna and Taneth congratulated Avria and Jestin and then went off to the quiet of their apartment. Jestin knew Avria and the Soothsayer were waiting for Jestin to leave; but he would not give them that.

"We're leaving the day after tomorrow," Jestin declared triumphantly. "Me and Avria and Drashun, we're off to some town past Klatna."

"Yes. I'm aware of that. Be sure to keep safe," Eleran said as he worked; his words short and his mandibles rippling. Granted, he was irritated by the boy's smugness, but he now felt worlds better about Avria being around this boy now. With a sigh of relief, he went about his work, enjoying the peace of mind. He knew he'd done the right thing.

The grandmother-crone walked in, dressed in the casual clothes many of the Araki wore—the same long skirts and tunic—only she wore decorative chains round her waist and had her long, curled hair tied up into a loose puff on the back of her head. Eleran looked up and his eyes narrowed—yet another person he could get no positive feelings from. She felt like a malignancy. She ignored him, walking to

Avria who sat propped on the edge of the table, munching on a carrot. She stopped crunching and froze when her grandmother approached.

"There you are. You've come through the ceremony alive," the old woman tried to sound amused and attempted to jest. Avria nodded blankly. "I wanted a chance to speak to you. You've been so busy of late; I hardly have a chance to get to know you. I would like to learn of you and to tell you a little about me and the family you have back in Thran. Is this a good time?" Avria looked at Eleran, then at Jestin, and heaved a burdensome sigh.

"I suppose it's as good a time as any," she said, making no effort to hide her resignation. She shoved herself upright and moved to an elder's chair, flopping into it unceremoniously, chewing the remaining carrot in her mouth. Eleran took his things and left and the old woman sat down in his chair. Sennal glared at Jestin until he finally got the message and exited.

The young man slowed as she reached the archway to the first corridor. He came to a realization—a powerful one. He turned and looked back at Avria and her awful grandmother and a knowing smile crept up onto his lips. Indeed, he thought, I am not lost.

It was first thing in the morning. The sun had not yet fully risen enough to burn off the mists and dew. Jestin's progress through the pasture-grasses was marked by a darkened line of flattened greenery. He moved quickly towards the encampment where there was still very little activity. He could smell some breakfast foods being prepared. He made his way straight into the center of the circle of tents and caravans, his eyes resting on that one caravan sitting idle and untended on the fringe of the grouping. He knew all of a sudden, what her purpose was to be here, the old woman. He felt like he had gained even more power in this agreement, should she acquiesce.

She was not in her own elaborate caravan, but instead in the largest tent on the edge of the encampment. He could hear her talking to someone in her native Thran, the rolling poetry of her words cutting through the thickness of the morning mists. He scratched on the tent, and a strange woman yanked the door flap open, her eyes quite surprised to see a young man there. She widened the aperture, and stepped aside so Sennal could see him.

"What in the world do you want child?" she snapped.

"I have to speak to you, Jestin muttered. "It's about Avria and that intolerable druid." The old woman shooed out the other lady and barked at Jestin to come in. She directed him to a chair, and her cool gaze fell upon him.

"Speak up," she said. Jestin complied, his mouth opening and a ramble of words spilling forth in desperation.

Sennal barely tolerated listening to him. Her watery, bloodshot eyes scarcely acknowledged him at first. She'd only permitted him to address her because he had told her straight away that he intended to keep Avria from defilement at the hands of the foreign man. Jestin pressed the fact that he was one-quarter Thran and grandson of a famous Thran warrior—careful to skirt around the fact that his ancestress had abandoned her empire in disgust. He spoke of his desire to see the place of his grandmother's heritage and to respect the ways of her people. Sennal did not welcome the platitudes. She was sharp; she saw through them, but she allowed him to have his moment and humored him, so he could move on to the important information.

Then he got to the meat of the matter. She listened with the focus of a predator, keeping her black eyes on him like the beady orbs of a raptor. Appointed in a floor length gown of silver-grey with a plunging neckline that revealed her bony chest, seated inside the beautiful tent lined with crafted rugs and pillows of rich, lovely jewel tones, she drank from a polished silver goblet. Over her shoulders, she wore a robe of a fine, billowing silk, her wild hair caught by a silver diadem. The effect amazed him. She looked twenty years younger than she had just the evening before. She gazed levelly at him over the rim of her goblet, his face reflected in it; the oblong distortion made him look like a misshapen freak.

He couldn't bear her silence, so heavy and expectant that he felt he had to fill it. He told her all about the Druid's meditation. "He protects her, yes. But again, when he's meditating, he's not present. He's gone. I heard them talking about it. It will happen again soon. He will meditate in preparation for Tinna's ceremony of succession."

She snorted at that, as if she found the idea of Tinna as village leader laughable.

Jestin continued cautiously. "So all you have to do is figure out when he starts his meditation and you can get her away from him. She may hate you now, but she will thank you for it once she's away from the Druid and no longer under his spell."

"And why do you think I should care?" she asked with casual boredom, crossing her legs under the shiny material of her gown, revealing a sandal with tiny jewels embedded in its many straps and a set of yellowed, horn-like toenails, ridged, blackened in spots. He cast his gaze back up at her scrutinizing glare and swallowed hard.

"You brought that caravan; you expect her to return to Thran with you. I'm not blind." It was a long shot; that he knew. But his first instinct, when he saw the little caravan parked away from the cortege, nobody making use of it, was that it was for Avria. Sennal had come to Thamatoc for Avria. She studied him for what seemed like an endless moment and sipped from her goblet again.

He took a chance.

"I want to go to Thran. I want to go, too. I want to become a part of your household. I don't care how I'm treated. I don't have any issues with your laws concerning the treatment of males but I have been Avria's companion and friend for many years. In exchange for my coming to you, I want that chance."

"Avria will come with me regardless, boy."

He frowned.

"No, she will not. She hates you. She has followed the influence of her mother and my grandmother her whole life. They have taught her to despise your land and your ways. She will never come voluntarily, I guarantee you; and you know that, too!" he snapped. Jestin glared at her, and then intentionally softened a bit. He bit back his fear. "You know what I told you. It's the only way to get her away from Ai-Tinna. Her mother doesn't trust you as far as she can throw you and she's watching everything you do. You know this is the only way. And it isn't much to ask, to add me to your household."

Her gaze bore into his. For a second he saw something flash through her eyes, a darkness he had not noticed before, a black impulse to do something to him perhaps, quickly quelled; an even darker idea, maybe forming in her impossible mind. No matter what it was, it chilled him.

But she shifted back into a state of bored annoyance.

"Very well then. You are forthcoming. This information has been noted." The woman gathered her robes up and turned away. "You may go." She walked away, the train of her robes rustling behind her.

Jestin had no idea whether or not she planned to act on the information he gave her, but it was vital to him that it work. He paused as he turned to go and spoke out: "I have an idea of how to get her to you."

Sennal stopped. She turned around, her bottomless eyes upon him with unmistakable contempt.

347

He told her quickly, then scurried away to his apartments and waited. He knew how to get Avria into the right position and away from the Druid while he meditated. He would just have to wear her down a bit on her resolve to not spend time alone with him anymore. He knew that in spite of her decision, that her desire for him to be happy was paramount to her. As long as he was mad, she would continue to be distant and resolved. But if he played it another way, he knew he could manipulate her into doing what he needed her to do.

* * * *

Avria's tears were a riddle to Eleran, who thought he understood and could contend with pretty much any emotional condition a person could muster up. However, he was quickly discovering that these things were different when it was someone you loved and it required a great deal of energy and sensitivity to come to an understanding and to calm the loved one down. He had always prided himself on knowing how best to behave around others, but he felt like he was learning from scratch with Avria.

She was upset. She was acting as if she were angry at him, but she was continually claiming it had nothing to do with him; but it was to him she shed her tears and to him she came to for answers.

"I know what I told you, and it doesn't mean I've changed my mind or am backing out on anything but it's just so hard to see him so upset, and to have him mad at me all the time. I wish he would go home," she wept. Eleran had suggested he could speak to Jestin, encourage him to spend less time hanging around looking miserable. Avria became more frustrated by his lack of understanding.

"I don't want you to fix it, Eleran. It would only make things worse! I just want you to listen!" she shouted. Eleran, who'd spent the better part of the dawn hours preparing for this new ceremony, was already stressed because he had to meditate, but Avria was having a crisis and required his attention. He didn't understand why, in all honesty. She had made up her mind, Jestin had been told, and yes he was moping about like a stupid child, because that is exactly what he was. Avria's guilt was evident and seemingly without end, and Eleran wasn't sure what he could offer her to make her feel better. It was wearing on him and he realized he was actually looking forward to his meditation so he could center himself and perhaps even find an answer to make Avria happy again. This whole issue seemed to be raised and dwelled upon for no good reason and it confused him. He was perhaps older than Avria, but he was still naïve in the matters of love and understanding. If I do not find answers in my meditation state, I will have to take counsel with Taneth. He is married to her mother, and surely knows what this is all about.

"Avria, what must I do to make you feel better? I can't stop Jestin from being hurt, not in a way that's permissible by my laws; I can't take away your history and friendship with him, so you don't feel his sadness so keenly, what must I do?"

Avria stopped crying long enough to cast him a frustrated gaze and then she simply walked out bawling. Eleran threw up his hands and gathered his tokens, making his way to the central hall, where he was in the core of the village's energies. He climbed up onto the table just as Taneth stumbled into the room.

"Good morning, Zshathri, how are you?" He stood before the table, watching the holy man collect, fold and arrange his limbs around him.

"Perplexed," he replied, crossing his legs, looking quite as puzzled as he declared himself to be.

"Oh?"

"It's Avria. I'm doing something wrong, but I'm not sure what it is, but she's quite angry with me..."

"Ah. Well, you'll discover that will happen often with these ladies. The trick is to be contrite when they're angry, to comfort them when they're in a tizzy and stop trying to fix things. They aren't coming to us for answers; they're coming to us for love," the older man intoned with a knowing smile. Eleran studied his kind face for a moment and then exhaled a gust of air from his lungs.

"I suppose I'll get started. It might take a while," he said to the Wiseman. Taneth nodded and then walked away, waving his hand in acknowledgement as he did. The Zshathri took a good deep breath of hair, loosened his neck to clear his mind and then closed his eyes. When they opened, he was no longer there.

Avria went to Hanru's tree. It's where he went when he was angry and upset and where she had learned to find comfort too. It was a young oak on the edge of an area where the children often played, a clearing with a stream running through it. Here there were always a scattering of toys, and buckets for splashing water. There was a large boulder stone hunkered conveniently in the shade of the tree's branches. She climbed up onto it and took in a big sigh. All she wanted was for Eleran to hold her and to assure her things would get better. Why was it so hard for him to understand that?

As she pondered this injustice, Jestin's figure appeared from the pathway. He looked tentative and hopeful, but still distant. She gave him a sad smile, to which he responded with a friendly relieved one. Her heart instantly warmed at the sight of that smile. She could not bear that she made Jestin so unhappy. He took her smile as permission to come forward, which he did.

"What are you doing out here?" she asked. Jestin shrugged, offering her a shy smirk.

"Same as you, I'll wager." She nodded and he climbed up to sit beside her.

"You look upset."

"I am upset," she replied. He looked at her thick lashes, all clumped together from the moisture of her tears, her eyes still shining brilliantly with the sheen of their wake. She reached up and rubbed her nose with the back of her hand.

"What's Eleran doing?"

"Meditating," she said, her tone irritated. Jestin nodded.

"I know you're decided against spending time with me now, since we're all grown up and you're practically promised to him; but he's busy and nobody cares, so why not go for a ride? I'm so bored." Jestin had grown comfortable again, his mannerisms loose and welcoming. Avria, still upset and annoyed at not being understood, decided that an act of defiance would make her feel better.

Jestin's sudden ease and friendship thrilled Avria so much that she suspected nothing untoward. He'd been so angry and standoffish since their discussion that to see him smiling and relaxed again pleased her immensely. She overcompensated perhaps, by fostering this sudden openness in his manner. She was glad that he liked her again and welcomed it; they'd been so close for so long, she feared he'd never forgive her. He was almost a brother in her mind, and she feared losing him in that capacity. She didn't notice that his laughter came out forced; that he looked a bit nervous even. She was too happy; she'd found love and now she'd found balance with Jestin. She didn't know what had happened to change his attitude, but she didn't question it.

She obviously should have.

It was a lovely afternoon and despite her guilt over defying Eleran's preferences, she thought it would be nice to spend some special time with Jestin to show him she appreciated his gesture of friendship. She hoped to foster this idea that she could still be close to him, just not in the way he hoped. So she followed Jestin back to the stable. Her grandmother appeared as they were grooming and tacking up their mounts. Avria was utterly oblivious to the knowing look exchanged between her grandmother and her friend. Sennal stayed long enough to say hello and then slipped away.

Jestin gave nothing away as he prepared, but although his outside was calm and smiling, inside his mind was exploding with thoughts, doubts, contingencies, plans and he even allowed himself to fantasize about the future in Thran with Avria. They mounted and set out for a nice, peaceful ride in each other's company. Her little mare danced under her, the sun-spotted light giving her coat little blots of golden sheen.

Avria laughed easily and heartily as Jestin talked. "Drashun put a huge millipede in Hanru's pen case. He'll be in for a surprise when he gets to Lemoram." Jestin shuddered as he told the story. He had always hated millipedes. They scurried all over the place in this forsaken forest, thick as a thumb, as long as an arm, slithering around on those undulating legs! He suddenly pictured the ever-smug Hanru opening the pen case and seeing that bluish gray thing come creeping up his arm, and he chuckled. Hanru had left that morning for Lemoram. Avria had missed his departure.

In that moment, just as he allowed himself to forget what was happening; it happened. Four Thran guards soundlessly appeared from the foliage and tore Avria from her horse. One woman gagged her while another tied her wrists and feet. Avria struggled, screaming with the gag in her mouth, her eyes wide and terrified, full of question and betrayal as she looked to Jestin to help her; utterly bewildered by his inaction and his sad gaze as he watched this all happen impassively from his horse. She yelled muffled, undecipherable words at him, and he simply remained hunched in his saddle, watching. He could hear the questions in her cries, the shock and devastation to see her childhood friend let this thing happen to her. The rangers hoisted her onto her horse over the saddle, and two dark-clothed women appeared on horse, leading two other horses each. The guards mounted, two of which led Avria away. The other dark-garbed women looked at Jestin from their horses. He waited for instruction. Clothed in black leggings with steel grey tunics, their hair tied back in long black braids that hung down their spines, they clutched sharp, shining rapiers in their white-knuckled hands.

"Go," one told him. "Go avay." One of them advanced to an arm's length from Jestin, her eyes narrowed and her face bitterly angry.

"I think I'm supposed to…"

"No. You go." The tip of her rapier flashed suddenly under his chin. "I rrrecommind you do igzackly az Ai zay." Her look struck him cold. He'd seen it before, in the eyes of his grandmother, during a rare verbal altercation between her and Astlin. Kailine, instantly terrified the moment she saw her mother's eyes darken, had resorted to tears, hoping to distract them from their face-off. Jestin had felt that same icy fear in the pit of his stomach when he saw her face. He didn't remember the nature of the argument or what his grandmother had said, but he would never forget her bitter resolve and unforgiving darkness. He understood now, seeing these women, that same look, the same mannerisms, the same determined strength that allowed no one to stand in their way.

He nodded, swallowing loudly and turned his horse back towards Thamatoch. He didn't look back, but he heard one of them spit after him and say something in the Thran tongue with a tone of pure disgust before they retreated in a clatter of hoof-beats.

CHAPTER FIVE – SIMPLY TOO MUCH

"I don't understand," Skye muttered, pinching the bridge of her nose. She had another headache. Taneth looked up from his work and furrowed his brow, not understanding her himself. He shoved the packet of herbs he'd mixed for her headaches towards her with a grumpy frown. She took it and impatiently poured the contents into her mug of water, wrinkling her face as she drank it down obediently.

"I told you to take that every morning before you breakfast. Why aren't you taking them?"

"Because it tastes like a horse's rectum."

"Lovely." Taneth cringed and shook his head. "I dare not think how you could possibly know how a hors—"

"Ugh! I beg you, Master Taneth, don't! It was a figure of speech," Skye interrupted, waving her hand admonishingly at him. Taneth smirked and leaned back, looking at her over his index fingers, which he had steepled over his nose as he thought. He really had to do something about her headaches. He rubbed his eyes with the heels of his hands and frowned.

"Anyway, what do you not understand?"

"Well, we are Chai-Opse. At least, we Araki are," she pointedly added, reminding him that he wasn't among those called the Chai-Opse.

"I may not be Chai-Opse by blood, but I look to you as my people. What's your point, Skye?" he grumbled.

"Well, what makes us different from Humans? We're supposed to be a different race, but we look and act just like Humans. What makes us different, a separate race? Don't the books tell us what the Chai-Opse were?"

"I'm not entirely sure, Skye," Taneth admitted with a tilt of the head. "It's a question I've pondered since I studied the whole thing back when. I suppose it's more about how we live rather than actual physical differences or anything else these days. Perhaps the true race of Chai-Opse bred themselves into oblivion by mixing with

Humanity, and we are simply hybrids. Perhaps we share the same blood as Humans now, but our cultures remain reclusive and insular no matter our type—Araki, Gypsy or Ice People. Our advantage no longer rests in our ancestry but in the fact that we've chosen to continue to live outside of the dominant Human society, that we do not submit to their throne and instead defer to the older rule—that of the Trinity and Keepers. That's why we live in safety today, while the entire Human society is left in shambles. We embrace the world, we do not dominate it. Maybe it's something as simple as that, which makes us different from Humans."

It was early morning. Hanru had gone north the day before, to Lemoram. While Avria, Drashun and Jestin readied themselves to take the horses to Elemar, Eleran meditated, preparing for the ceremony of succession; Tinna's assumption of leadership in Thamatoc. The Druid had monopolized the common room for a ridiculously long time; from the morning before he meditated through the night and still sat hunkered on the table with white eyes.

Skye and Taneth studied alone. Classes would begin in a few hours, Arak willing. Surely Eleran would finish his meditation in time! After that it would be time for the medicinal rounds. As his adept, Skye followed Taneth around when he provided care. He considered buying her a few terms at the conservatory; perhaps she would make a good Wisewoman for someone. The Araki settlements needed more of them.

But she had headaches. She needed spectacles, a rare commodity, hard to match to the eyes. He wasn't sure how to do it himself. Perhaps Phenmal could help find someone to assist him. Next time Phenmal visited, Taneth reminded himself, he would ask. He shifted in his leather upholstered chair and scratched his head. "I'm not sure if anyone has an answer yet. Perhaps someday, we will discover what that difference is, or was. For now, we are the dominant race, aside from the dragons. Lots of Thran survive, and some pockets of Humans. No large populations, though, like those who once thrived here in Oromoii. One group in the south, one out west, the Gheraine—those are the largest populations of Humans anywhere, and I very much doubt that any of those three groups outnumber the Araki people now. We have to resign ourselves to our new place in the world." Skye pursed her lips and arched her brows, cocking her head as if she was thinking on it. A knock at the door startled her.

"Come in."

Rigerd poked his head in. "Avria isn't here?"

Taneth gestured to the small space as if to ask where Avria might be hidden in his little library. "Let's be frank, old man, my girl never was the kind to loll about in a library. She's not here. I haven't seen the girl since yesterday morning."

"Well, I can't find her anywhere else, so I ventured a guess. I wish that girl would stop running off. Everyone is ready to go. They're waiting on her."

"Maybe she's with the Druid," Skye offered with a wry smile. "Since he got here, she hardly leaves his line of sight," she snickered. Taneth furrowed his brow disapprovingly and Rigerd shook his head.

"No. He's in the main hall, meditating."

"Still?" Skye muttered, incredulous.

"He does that apparently and he feels the need to do it in the community hall instead of in the quiet of his own apartment. Why, I cannot say," Rigerd mumbled.

Taneth dismissed his complaint. "Perhaps she went off somewhere with Jestin. He's like her shadow; he will know where she is."

"Jestin doesn't know. Neither does Drashun. They haven't seen her since yesterday afternoon, when she went out riding."

"What of Tinna?" Distress grew in his voice.

"Tinna's out there looking for her. She went to the Thran camp to see if she's possibly there."

"Why would she go there? She despises her grandmother!" Taneth snorted.

"She spent some time with her grandmother the night before last. Maybe she's there."

"I seriously doubt she'd seek her grandmother out." Taneth shook his head. Just then Tinna burst into the room, shoving her way past Rigerd.

"They're gone." Her words had a stony finality to them. Taneth felt his stomach hit the floor.

"What do you mean?"

"The Thran. They've gone. Avria and her mare—gone. I found tracks by pure luck. Thran do not leave tracks. They won't leave any more. They took her, Taneth."

"What?" Taneth leapt to his feet, toppling a pot of ink onto a map. He paid no heed to that. He started for the door when, suddenly, the earth began to tremble. A great shock threw them all off their feet and knocked half the books to the floor. "The Druid!" Taneth scrambled to his feet again and pushed his way past Rigerd, staggering with difficulty over the jostling ground to the common room where the Soothsayer stood, an image of rage.

People ran about frantically, others barreled outdoors in blind panic, screaming. Dirt filtered down from the lodge's root-laden rafters. The horse-master called for someone to get the horses out of the stable.

Betrayal! Taneth felt this word pierce his head. Tinna barked out in pain, gripping her temples, folding herself in half in agony.

"Eleran!" Taneth shouted. The Druid stood on the table, his bulging arms out at his sides, fists clenched tight. Veins protruded grotesquely against his muscles. His eyes stared open but blank, irises and pupils gone. White orbs glowed in the sockets. Tinna got to her feet, stepping over Rigerd, who had fallen down from the power of the man's thoughts. She's gone.

"Eleran!" Tinna moved towards him. She broke into a lurching, stumbling run, vaulting at his legs, tackling him. He fell back from the table and tumbled into the hearth, his eyes rolling back to where they naturally belonged. The tremors stopped immediately. He sat up and instantly went to Tinna, checking her for wounds. She pushed herself up onto her knees, then her feet, shooing him away as she favored her elbow and arm. "I'm in no condition to manage this, Eleran," she muttered, her eyes glossing over with tears. "I can't lose my girl. I can't go through this sort of thing again. I'm over forty years old and I am with child... I haven't even told her that yet," her last words swallowed up in a sob." He reached out and took her arm, squeezing it reassuringly, then swallowed hard and dropped his hand.

He had little success containing his fury. "That crone took her. She took her to Thran. They took advantage of the meditation—that I wasn't present. The Diviner. He would know if I wasn't present—" Then he stopped again, and his face turned slowly to Tinna. "Jestin. That little worm! I knew something wasn't right with that little bastard!" He stalked to his chambers, and the door slammed.

Tinna could not restrain her distress; she succumbed to tears. The thought of sweet, temperate, gentle Avria in the hands of that harridan made her skin go cold. Tinna had been toughened by her hard life with her mother; she'd been conditioned to the verbal and physical abuse. Avria was an innocent, soft like her father. Tinna wiped her furious tears with the back of her hand and walked with resolve to the weapons room, flinging the door open. Old, pregnant, it doesn't matter! I need to get her back! Before she could step in, the door flung shut again and slammed hard, causing more dirt to sift down from the tangle of roots in the rafters. She tried to open it, but it remained snug in its casing, not budging a bit. She spun around in a rage and traced Eleran's steps to his apartments, running into him as he exited his room. He'd donned a long, hooded cloak, his staff and heavy boots. Her ire instantly dissipated at the sight of this huge man, powerful both physically and magically, and the look of vulnerability returned to her beautiful face. She opened her mouth to express her fear for Avria; he lifted his hand to hush her.

"Do not fret, Tinna. I will get her back. I have no connections to that crone. I have no issues that will stand between me and getting Avria back. They will only distract you and put Avria in danger. You need to stay here and put that little bastard right. Rest assured; there is no way anyone will lay a harmful hand on Avria. They can take her away, but they cannot harm her. For that, you have my word. I will get her back." He turned, his cloak flaring out behind him and stalked to the storerooms, supplied himself sparingly and exited the lodge, leaving on foot. Tinna ran back to the common room, where Rigerd was finally sitting up, rubbing his balding head.

Taneth extended a trembling hand to his old friend and helped him up. When Rigerd was on his feet, Taneth sank down into his chair by the hearth and buried his face in his hands. Tinna went to him and wrapped her arms around his shoulders.

"Eleran will get her back, Taneth. He will." Her trembling voice betrayed her fear and did little to reassure Taneth. He simply moved his hands down to hers and gripped them, leaning into her embrace as if he needed to absorb some of her strength. "He'll get her back," she repeated.

She let go of him and straightened. People had begun to return to the lodge, villagers coming over to Tinna and Taneth, concerned and offering help. "Ytro, could you and Ordo find Jestin and lock him up somewhere secure? Alantri, could you get today's relay rider for me?" Each person nodded without question, relieved to be given some use during this crisis. Rigerd sat down and gripped his hands, looking thoughtfully at Tinna.

"We'll send scouts down Gypsy and Death Roads. They can't have gone far. A massive entourage like that can't move quickly." Tinna shrugged her brows to indicate that she knew otherwise.

"Go ahead, then. But it will likely end up a waste of manpower and time," she muttered. "They're gone. It looks like my mother brought rangers to make their trail as discreet as possible. She was prepared. Seeing how many paths there are to the west roads, our only hope of catching them is to get to the main roads before they do." She paused, her eyes moving as she worked the ideas through her head. She thought of the endless possibilities, the number of roads they might have taken, and the network of Gypsy paths. Nine separate trade-roads led to the pass through the mountains. "Go ahead. But I think the Druid has a better chance of finding their trail using his own methods—"

A clatter of heels interrupted her. A young, visibly pregnant woman entered the hall, shoving through the crowd of people who lingered, wanting to assist and support the leaders who sat near the hearth. She held a scroll of parchment and a pot of ink with a quill sticking out of it.

"Ree, are you riding today?" Tinna asked dubiously. The girl nodded, breathless from her short run from the Spring lodge.

"Yes, Tinna. I can still ride. Better than most. I understand you need someone to relay a message?"

Tinna hastily scribbled out a message. She rolled up the parchment and gave it to her. Ree slid it into a leather cylinder and capped it.

"That goes to Loshan—to Astlin and Kailine. It is of the greatest importance. See that your relay point knows that!"

"I will!" The girl nodded seriously. She left. Tinna sighed, crossing her arms and looking at all the people milling about.

"Go back to what you were doing, for the love of Arak! You're not helping, crowding around like this!" she snapped. Taneth stood and glanced at Rigerd before taking Tinna's shoulders and guiding her towards the archway.

"Why don't we go, ourselves? Come on."

She complied reluctantly.

"I wondered what it was that drew the old hag here. I thought perhaps—" her hand slid down to her belly— "that this was what the diviner saw. I worried more about that than I did about Avria. The worst that came to mind about her was that my mother might taint her. But I never thought she would steal her, Taneth!"

"I know. How could you have known?"

"Because she's my mother, that's how! I should have known simply from what she is! I should have driven her out the moment she arrived." Tinna waved her hand dismissively and started to cry.

"Tinna, stop blaming yourself! It accomplishes nothing." Taneth steered her into their apartment and closed the door. He watched his wife, so full of fear and regret, sink down into the worn chair where she'd held Avria as a tiny baby, watched her descent into despair.

* * * *

Avria closed her eyes. Her little mare's steady clip-clopping on the old Gypsy road helped her focus her mind elsewhere, away from the chafing bonds that kept her hands fastened to each side of her saddle, forcing her into an uncomfortable hunch. She had been remitted to the care of the lower servants and eunuchs. Her grandmother rode ahead in another grouping on a connected road in the fine caravan. The whole procession, divided into four sections, took alternate paths, and then merged again periodically. The rangers scouting the roads ahead and choosing the routes. Avria, separated by three quarters of a mile to several miles from the head of the cortege, found it most cowardly that they took her by force and then to hid her away in order to avoid her ire.

Most of the day, she was riding flanked by two female warriors. They often rode so close their legs and sides brushed up against her horse. They kept close to her, riding on their nimble, pretty little desert warhorses. Occasionally, they led her to a small caravan brought especially for her—proof that her grandmother had planned to take her with or without her compliance. She sat inside by the little round window that faced back to watch the rangers, of which there were many, following patiently behind the tail of the caravan, carefully blotting out any mark of their passing. With each turn of the wheel, each clop of the hoof, her heart felt heavier. It seemed fitting, even pat, that she had found happiness like no other, only to have it taken from her.

In the saddle again, she pushed down in her stirrups, stretched her calves, and lowered her head. She closed her eyes and felt the tears squeeze through. Angry at her weakness, her powerlessness, she wished with all her heart that her mother or Eleran would come for her.

Now she understood why Jestin had been so affable and welcoming, why he suddenly was able to set aside his jealousy. Now that she was being drawn ever further away from all that was familiar and good to her, from someone she loved; now she knew why. Selfish, entitled Jestin had sacrificed her happiness to secure his own. And he'd used such a cruel method to draw her out, pretending that he had come to terms with her choice and acting as if he valued her friendship more than anything. And Eleran...would he come for her? Could he? What did Sennal want from her?

359

Sennal had taken a good deal of personal satisfaction telling Avria exactly how her friend had betrayed her. She appeared to savor Avria's tears of disappointment, and used Avria's misery to prove to her that the people around her were never to be trusted. Sennal then left her to the care of her peons, smirking smugly to herself.

Avria opened her eyes and felt the ice of her own tears on her cheeks. The soldier on her left snorted at her and laughed disgustedly: "En emberressment to oll woman, no spine, cry cry bebbee teers."

No, Avria thought, her eyes cast down. She chewed the inside of her cheek. I am no Tinna. I am no Thran. I cry baby tears.

* * * *

Jestin had not a shred of regret when it came to his choice to help the old woman take Avria. He only lamented that the old hag had cut him out of the deal and broken the agreement. But even so, they had separated Avria from the Druid. He felt self-righteous, in spite of being held prisoner while he waited for one of his parents to collect him. It was the most inspired idea he'd ever had, to separate Avria from that lecherous, aging bastard. He paced, dressed—as if to show his defiance—in the finest clothes he'd brought with him. He turned the chair to face the door of his apartment and sat in it, so he would be looking straight at whoever walked in. He stared through the door, his arms crossed. He knew what he had done would incite Tinna's wrath, but he also knew that no other course of action would have achieved his aim. Taneth and Tinna approved too much of Avria's flirtation with the Druid. Neither of them showed the slightest bit of concern.

He leaned back into his chair, putting his mind to work. He wasn't resigned to not getting his way and being parted from Avria. She was the only one who ever really mattered.

* * * *

"We are on the precipice of war." Phenmal paced in front of the small fireplace in the library, hands clamped behind his back. Tall, lanky and completely bald, the pale-faced, sharp-eyed gentlemen wore his consequence as boldly as he did his deep wine-colored frock coat with its astonishingly high-collar. The tails flared out as he walked and turned, swishing from side to side. He looked at the map on the ink-stained table and pointed to Chrotrioth Pass, the one place where a caravan might cross the mountains between Oromoii and Thran. Tinna had first entered Oromoii there. There could be no doubt that the Thran had taken Avria that way, too. "Pridoo said they're massing armies just south of the border. There's been a power vacuum for years. They see it as an opportunity. The Throne is trying to rally troops. Pickings are slim."

Tinna paid little attention. She sat with her elbows on her knees, her temples clamped in her hands. She'd been downcast and distracted since the Soothsayer left. Nine riders had taken the main roads in hopes of finding the caravan as it emerged from the secret roads. So far, the relay did not bring any messages from them, which did not bode well.

"Tinna, this is extremely important. I know you're worried about Avria, but you've got an unstoppable force of nature out there after her. The Thran are planning an invasion of Oromoii, and they will most likely succeed if you don't snap out of it and help us here!" Phenmal barked.

Tinna straightened and nodded but she looked dubious.

"What do you expect of me, Phen?" she asked. Her voice broke. She looked tired.

Taneth grunted, "well, the Human army isn't exactly adequate. They'll suffer the fate of the scourge dragons." His worry lines had deepened. Since Phenmal had arrived that morning with a look of urgency on his face, a new sense of concern had roused the village. He usually arrived like a grumpy relative, pleased to see the soon-to-be leader and her family, hanging around them with a sense of belonging. He loved the family and loved the village in spite of his finding of the simple-mindedness of its residents something worthy of mockery.

"The Human minority," Tinna mused. "To this day, it still seems bizarre to think of it that way." She scratched the back of her head. *If it weren't for me, there might be even fewer of them left,* she thought.

"Well. I know one thing you can do." Phenmal poured himself some brandy and drank from the fine, cut glass goblet, gazing intently at Tinna.

"The dragons?"

He nodded and waved his hand dismissively while he swallowed his drink. "Yes, yes; they could help. And frankly, it would improve their standing in this world, if they did. But I wasn't referring to them in particular." He walked to the map shelf and ran his finger down the cascade of ribbon tabs hanging from the ends of the honeycomb of rolled papers. He found what he wanted and tugged it out of the stack, rested it on top of the one they'd been looking at. With a flourish of velvet cuffs and brass buttons, he rolled it out and pinned the corners down with the bottle of ink, his goblet, and two stone weights.

Taneth gazed down at it. Tinna stood, walking around the table. The map was one of Taneth's making, from about twelve years ago. Based on his prior research and information from a series of scouts, he'd mapped out every Araki settlement he could find in the great forests, all the way west to the plains and a few lingering settlements there as well, where the horse-worshippers had originated.

"Twenty years ago, you wanted to hide this information. Now I think it's time for you to brandish it."

"How do you propose to get everyone to come out and fight?"

"How about telling them what's going on at Chrotrioth?" Phenmal barked impatiently. Tinna groaned and sat down again, laying her head on the table.

"Phen, I don't even know where to start."

"Well, start by getting the summoner to call your old dragon friend. When is he scheduled to come?"

"Not until next month, always before the festival."

"Send someone for him now. And get a message out to the Araki settlements at once," Phenmal suggested.

Taneth pursed his lips and shook his head with uncertainty. "Phen, there are several hundred large settlements, not counting all these fringe ones, here, and here." He gestured over the map at the spray of tiny green horse-heads that indicated individual Araki settlements. "The relay only follows old pre-burning roads. We don't have a fraction of the people we need for an undertaking of this scale."

"You need to find more relay riders, scouts, whatever you need, and you need to get the word out. Work like a web. Send out riders to the nearest settlements and have them send out more riders to more settlements. Continue to branch, out until they've all been notified."

Tinna lifted one thigh onto the tabletop and turned the map so she could see it better. She studied it for a second and then nodded.

"Very well. I think Astlin can help us with the problem of riders for this first stage," she muttered. "He owes me quite the favor, since his idiot son helped them take her. In the meantime, Taneth, we need to make as many copies of this map as possible. Send Skye to Lemoram to the print-press. We're going to need…"

she paused and tried to count in her head, but gave up with a sigh. "We're going to need a lot."

She cast her husband and Phenmal a sidelong glance and slid off the table. "Now if you don't mind, I'm going lie down." Tinna trudged from the room, her hand lying protectively on her tummy; a cloud of fugue seemed to curl in her wake. Phenmal turned to Taneth and frowned in concern. The older man nodded and followed at Tinna's heels. Taneth knew the mind-reader would be more of a comfort to her at this point. Taneth took the lead in getting things rolling.

CHAPTER SIX – THE STAGING

"Oh Tinna…" Kailine sat hunched in the chair near the hearth in the Wiseman's apartment. Astlin stood by the narrow slot window, gazing out the long, stone-lined tunnel beyond the undulating pattern of the sand-cast glass, to the leafy patch of daylight beyond, his arms crossed, his wavy black hair falling into his eyes. He looked incensed and lost all at once. Taneth glowered at Kailine in his large wing-chair, his knuckles white as he gripped the worn arms. Tinna wore no expression; her eyes looked on, unreadable and therefore frightening. She stood by Taneth's chair, her arm resting along the top behind Taneth's cropped head.

Tinna did not trust the criminal Astlin. He worked all manner of shady, questionable deals but kept his distance from any actual crimes, orchestrating everything through others, benefiting without getting his hands dirty. Nobody had ever proven anything against him. Tinna accepted that part of him, but not without a sense of trepidation. She trusted Ailie and her daughter Kailine with whom she had a close, family-like relationship. As the years progressed, the public stigma of Astlin's occupation faded. He had laughed at the threat of prosecution for twenty years and more.

Loshan, the dark and dangerous hub of outlawry and legitimate trade alike, connected everything from the mighty plains valley in the west to the rich coastal regions of the east and the isles beyond by a network of rivers and canals that snaked across the empire, following the rise and fall of the land with the help of complicated lock systems. Barges carried goods from all over Oromoii to Loshan and from there both overland and by canal to the sea to meet the massive vessels bringing goods to the island nations across the oceans. Loshan sat at the nexus of it all.

Now, after the crumbling of the existing system of government, Astlin's fortune and power had grown with the force of wildfire. Loshan, being an independent trade city, had escaped destruction. Astlin's systems had taken over where the government left off. His reach stretched far out along the canals and trade roads now, including a new information relay, six times larger than the Throne's had ever been. Royal enforcement had evaporated. The laws of Loshan; created and enforced by the criminals that ran the city, filled the vacuum. Astlin served as the headpin and imposed his will. Fortunately for the many people of Loshan, his will was not tainted by selfishness or evil. Born to lead, he simply did what felt normal to him. What his style of accomplishment lacked in kindness, it made up for in effectiveness, and he acted always with the intention of improving the reputation and appeal of the city of Loshan and the quality of its citizens' lives.

As he distilled his efforts and enforced his laws, things changed. Slowly, he replaced his darker methods with less questionable ones. Legitimacy and honesty trickled into the lives of people who had never exercised those traits before. Tinna believed that the Throne, in order to extend its own power, would be forced to recognize Astlin's authority. The Lord of the Thieves, she called him, laughing. All that aside, she had never quite allowed him into her own circle of trust. His wife and mother she would keep forever on the outside, where they might speculate interminably about the secrets she kept.

Kailine and Ailie resented Tinna's reticence, but they held no illusions about the importance of Astlin's connection to her, regardless of the varying depths of her trust in certain matters. Tinna's relationship to them lent the Loshan family some legitimacy in the minds of the Araki people, their largest market now. That connection was crucial in these days of human scarcity, as the Araki rose in power. As mother and grandmother to Jestin, they had hoped to derive great benefits from his connections in Thamatoc. But the boy had ruined that. They could only hope to salvage what they could in friendship now.

Kailine had always feared that, because of all the freedoms he had, Jestin would become one of those obnoxious products of good fortune and privilege, that his pervasive sense of personal entitlement had bred in him the wrong notions about people and the world. She hoped Thamatoc would keep him grounded and propel him forward with better opportunities through Taneth. It did help some, for a while. Avria's influence was strong, but he was like two people sometimes—one in Loshan, another at Thamatoc. She knew, without the slightest doubt, that he was happier at Thamatoc. He might find much pleasure at home and greater ease in Loshan, but he only ever experienced real happiness in Avria's company, playing at whatever they played at, wrestling with Drashun, and snapping back retorts at Hanru.

Kailine had hoped, with all her soul, that Avria would save him. The girl had never once thought of herself as a formative element in Jestin's life. And now, Jestin had turned it all upside down. Kailine could only scramble to salvage what trust she could from Tinna and hope that Jestin hadn't destroyed everything for them.   Tinna's friendship was so pivotal in their lives.   Kailine tried to contain her tears. She had no idea what to do to even begin to make up for this.

"Where did we go wrong with that child?   You insisted he come here, you were certain it would make him a better person; and look what he's done!" Astlin suddenly blurted accusingly at his wife. Kailine's hysteria flared and she shook her head, unable to reply.

Tinna   frowned   balefully.   "Astlin,   I   don't   think   it's accomplishing anything to stand there and point fingers.   We all hoped it would be a good thing for Jestin; even you. Frankly, Jestin is and always has been his own person, willful and selfish, no matter how we tried to influence him for the better. Even Avria, who stands at the center of his universe, hasn't permeated that veneer of narcissism. I should have listened to Phenmal. He said that the boy would end up doing something insidious. I should have listened, but I thought Jestin would grow. I thought he was capable of betterment. I thought Avria's influence would be more powerful."

"I am so disappointed," Kailine finally said between sobs. "I am so sorry, Tinna! Please let me tell you how sorry I am! I know how your mother… I know how you have struggled! Oh, Tinna!" She fell into sobs again. "Avria, the poor, poor, sweet girl…" Kailine could not surmount her sorrow.

Tinna had confided to her, as she had confided to few others, the dark truths about the way in which the shrew Sennal had raised her.

"The worst part is that I cannot go after her," Tinna muttered, pushing away from the chair and gripping her elbows. "It seems that the Thran have decided to fill the power vacuum to the north. Almost twenty years after the burnings, they've decided to mount an army against Oromoii. Naturally, it becomes my problem; I still can't figure out how that is. Why does every world-changing issue seem fall on me? In the name of—" She stopped short and shook her head. She sighed, "Our holyman, who hasn't been here more than a week, has gone after Avria. But even with his magic, I cannot imagine he'll ever catch up to them. He can head towards the pass, but the army is there now, and Sennal will have full protection and concealment to go back to Ymnoth, I suppose. One druid versus an army," she shook her head hopelessly. A long spell of silence intervened; then Tinna's voice broke it, quiet and coarsened by the tightness of her throat as she battled her own tears.

"Avria isn't me. I'm not disparaging her, but she is not built like me, outside, inside. She wasn't raised with the smacking and knocking, the toughening that Thran women receive from their instructors and mothers. It hardens us. We learn to bite back our pain and our anger. Any sign of sadness or emotion is weakness." Tinna barely spoke above a hoarse whisper. "Avria is an innocent. I taught her some of the things she needs to know to fight, but she's not hard, unforgiving. She hasn't had hatred beaten into her. She feels everything and wears it plainly. I cannot even begin to imagine how she will survive in such a loveless, distorted environment, Kailine. I raised her for this world, not that horrible place. It is why I left Thran to begin with. And now Avria is going there." She paused, feeling her emotions slipping out of control. "I'm not trying to make you feel worse; I just need to tell you what I fear. I raised her for this world." Tinna's hand moved to her chest and she swallowed a sob. Her voice wavered and her eyes moistened. Taneth stood and took her into his arms. "Taneth, I feel so powerless!" He hushed her and tucked her head under his chin.

"I think there's something you should keep in mind, Tinna." His voice alone soothed her. As she pushed back to look up into the face of the man she loved, she couldn't help but feel loved and secure, even at this moment. His ever-evolving beard, which changed from a neatly trimmed goatee to a patch on his chin to a full faced beard to clean-shaven, had returned to what she thought of as its original state, when she had first met him—a neatly clipped goatee with two narrow strips following his jaw line to his meticulously shaped sideburns. Little strands of silver now streaked the dark mahogany. His luminous eyes, bottomless, curious, saddened and warm all at once, sought hers.

"What's that, Taneth?" she asked, studying him as if she saw him for the first time; taking in the subtle aging around his eyes and mouth and the wrinkles worn into the skin between his thick eyebrows from his constant state of puzzlement and inquisitiveness.

"Rhoa wasn't much different than Avria, when she was that age. In fact, Avria is better equipped than Rhoa, an even temper, a good, calculating mind; her physical abilities are far greater than Rhoa's were, thanks to your training. If Rhoa made it home from your journey twenty years ago, Tinna, all by herself, then the odds are definitely in Avria's favor. And Eleran is going after her as well."

"Yes," Tinna responded with a nod, looking back at Kailine, whose eyes had grown red and puffy, fidgeting with a kerchief with her hands. Tinna embraced Taneth, laying her head on his chest for a moment, focusing only on the sound of his heart.

After a momentary lull, Tinna stepped away from her husband and faced the visitors.

"I need you to help with something, Kailine, Astlin." They both turned to her. "I need your relay—possibly every relay rider in the eastern district."

"They're conscribed by their own towns, Tinna, they're not mi—"

"I need the relay, Astlin. I need the riders." An icy moment hung in the air as Astlin gauged Tinna's resolve. He chewed his lip, trying to imagine the consequences of taking down the regional relay. It would render communication with Loshan nearly impossible. The thought of that alarmed him greatly.

"May I ask why?"

"I need to get a wave of riders out to the surrounding Araki settlements; they can send their own riders out from there to supplement the numbers, but I need word to get out quickly. Your riders are notoriously fast. I need that speed. We only have nine available endurance riders here—not nearly enough. I've got nine valuable people already out riding the roads in search of Avria. I need more."

Taneth stood and walked to the sideboard under the window, picking up a rolled map, a copy of the one they'd looked at before, with his scrupulous record of the Araki settlements among the forests and plains. He gestured for them to approach and rolled it out on the table. Astlin strode over and studied it for a second. Taneth had recently added a fine network of lines in varying tones of ink. Each color represented a leg of the relay, starting with a deep burgundy as the first leg leaving from Thamatoc and spreading out like the limbs of a tree. Each point generated another spray of lines leading to the next collection of settlements, making a strange, organic design. The densest cluster of lines radiated around the horse-head that represented Thamatoc like a red corona.

"There can't be that many settlements!" he joked dismissively. Taneth's serious gaze did not falter. Astlin's half-smile faded. He looked again.

"Gods! I had no idea. And Thamatoc is here?" He pointed to the little dot where the web of lines originated. Tinna nodded. "There are nearly seventeen settlements within a typical relay leg of here, if you go around like the spokes of a wheel. If we plan it correctly and get at least that many riders out to the first leg, then the next group can fan out from each settlement to cover the ones in their immediate area. But some settlements don't keep many endurance riders, so we'll need some extra ones. That's where you come in."

"You'd expect them to do a double-leg?"

"With rest and a fresh horse, if necessary? Why not? What the Araki might lack in modern conveniences, they certainly make up for in horses." Tinna grunted. Astlin shook his head dubiously and grimaced while he pondered. A lean, severe looking man, older than his wife by over two decades, he had shared certain traits with Jestin: the straight line of his brow, the chiseled features and the swarthy tones. He pinched his chin and his fingers rasped against his beard stubble.

"That would leave Loshan without communication from the flatlands and the coast for weeks. I don't know if that can be done."

"It survived the burning well enough with a broken relay, Astlin. It can survive a few weeks without the rider network. You can always set up a skeleton relay using riders from outside the region for a few days; supplement it with some lay folk…"

Astlin shifted on his hip. He was being resistant.

"So eight more riders isn't enough to supplement the nine you have?"

"I was hoping for double riders for each leg, so if one has to go on, he can."

"You want a total of thirty four riders?" Astlin snapped. "That's impossible! Each station has to have at least two riders! That would leave Loshan stripped! Loshan can't function with a skeleton crew. No." Astlin sliced out his hand horizontally and glared at Taneth stubbornly.

"Astlin…" Kailine had risen to her feet during the discourse. She moved in a rustle of fine silks to join them. Kailine always wore the most forward of human fashions, elegant feminine gowns, silken stockings, and lace as light and delicate as the wings of dragonflies. As genteel as she might appear to be to the casual onlooker, Kailine's resolve and personal strength was as much Thran as her mother. She merely hid it better in her guise as a modest, timid, gentle lady.

Her voice cut in with an unexpected starkness. Tears had clumped her lashes into bulky strands, making her blue eyes, still reddened with tears, even more dramatic. She narrowed them to slits, the glassy irises and pupils fixed on her husband's face. She set her jaw and clutched her kerchief in an unwavering grip. She'd gone from downhearted and miserable to angry in the blink of an eye. "This is not a choice. It is our obligation and the least we can do. Not only because of what Jestin has done, but because there's a Thran army about to invade Oromoii. And I'd like to remind you that Loshan is in Oromoii. They won't care whether your loyalties bind you to the throne or only to yourself. They won't make distinctions, they will simply march. Loshan is as vulnerable to attack as any other city that stands in their way.

"Do you think our pitiful city militia can hold off hordes of Thran warriors? If you do, you're deluded. If you do, then you have learned nothing of the Thran. Their entire culture is based on war and battle. Their primary deity is the Goddess of War. Their temples are training grounds; their clergy are assassins and murderers of the highest skill. They churn out products like my mother and Tinna by the tens of thousands. They begin training them when they are six years old. They're more dangerous than you can know.

"Because they're women, and smaller, they train them a hundred times more intensively than our military is trained. You've seen it for yourself. You have. How do you think our militia would fare against an army of young zealous Tinnas and Ailies? They will flatten us. Flatten our city and march on; crush Loshan beneath the heels of their boots. It is your duty to Loshan, to Oromoii as much as it is to Tinna to do whatever you must to help stop this invasion." Astlin gazed at his wife for a good long while and then slumped his shoulders. He knew from the moment he'd seen her as a young girl, that she would rule him. She occupied the center of his universe, then and now. She owned him, this he could not deny.

Her unspoken words rung true as well. To do this for Tinna would be a step towards solidifying his place as leader of Loshan, should the Araki ever take power. This notion was growing increasingly likely with the fading influence of the Human throne. The map before them spoke volumes. It was the Araki people's world now. He understood quite clearly what she had implied without uttering a word. If they did not help, they stood to lose everything because of Jestin's actions. To help would insure that the trust between he and Tinna would remain fast.

"Very well," he conceded and turned to Tinna. "I'll get you twenty five of my best riders. I'll send my personal messenger back to Loshan to order it immediately." Kailine straightened herself regally and turned, moving back to her chair.

"Good," she said, sinking down into it gracefully. "I'm glad you agree. Maybe you should toss in a few extra riders just in case." She dabbed her eyes and glanced at Tinna. She could not mistake the look of gratitude the older woman gave her. While Astlin and Taneth pored over the map, Tinna sat next to Kailine and reached out to squeeze her hand in a quiet gesture of thanks.

"It's going to be alright Tinna. Avria will come home. I will do whatever I can to help." Kailine smiled warmly and apologetically. They sat in silence by the fire while Taneth and Astlin made the arrangements they needed.

Neither of his parents had gone to see or speak to Jestin yet. They were not compelled to rush to his side, either.

* * * *

"What are you doing here, Skye?" Comfortably embedded in one of several thickly upholstered chairs, each with its own table, lamp and plush ottoman, Hanru rested a book in his lap. He seemed perplexed to see her, but the new Conservatory library, annexed to Lemoram's ancient archive building, was the first place Skye had thought to look for him. "Only students are allowed in here."

"I thought I'd catch you up on the goings-on while I'm in town, which isn't for long." He seldom saw her in casual riding clothes. She smelled vaguely of sweaty horse and fresh air. She swiped at her tousled brown hair and squinted at him. "They let me in because of Taneth and all. I've come to purchase loads of parchment and to get some prints made."

"What in heavens for?" Hanru sat up and scratched his head. "I'm surprised. You know what an old curmudgeon Rigerd can be whenever we need supplies for learning. Didn't father just order a bunch—"

"Tinna is sort of leader now, for one, and the parchment isn't for school; it's for something else."

"Right. I forgot that mother is already elevated to the leadership," Hanru smiled widely, proud of his mother. He put his book down and set his feet on the floor. The wrinkled, reddish-brown leather of the ottoman slowly returned to its original shape when he removed the weight of his huge feet. "So what's the big hullabaloo that brings you here? Why do you need loads of parchment? What copies do you need printed?"

"I thought it was important to give you all the news. It turns out that Avria's been stolen by her grandmother, and there's going to be a war. The Thran are staging an invasion at that break in the mountains called Chrotrioth."

Hanru's brows shot up incredulously. He stood.

"Go back for a second! Avria's been stolen?"

"Yes. The magician has gone after her. And Tinna is trying to stage one of the largest relays ever. We need all this parchment to make maps. Taneth asked that I see if you can help make maps, or perhaps know someone at the press who can do an engraving of it, so we can block print it fast." He stood there for a moment, eyes darting about as he put his head into it. Suddenly he shook himself out of his reverie and looked at Skye.

"Well, that's entirely possible. We have a full department dedicated to block printing, woodcut and engravings. Come on, then. Did you bring an original of the map?"

Skye nodded, rolling her eyes to communicate her disgust. How could he even think that she hadn't brought it? She produced a tightly wound tube of paper from her shoulder-bag. He took it and hurried her along, his mind moving at a much greater speed as he tried to process all this news. Both hurried down a wide hallway, Hanru's long school robes and Skye's riding skirts snapping and whooshing as they hurried along.

"She wants one for each settlement that will continue the relay, so she can identify which settlements each Araki group is responsible for notifying. We counted them up; three hundred and sixty-four in total. That leaves out the last stage, but I think they should all have a copy, just in case. And since you have this gentleman to do an engraving, I think we should print four hundred and twenty or so."

"I don't know if an engraving can last for that many printings, Skye," Hanru muttered cautiously.

"Oh, it can." Boros interrupted matter-of-factly. "I won't use wood, we'll use copper. If I take care of it right, I should be able to make that many maps. It may take a while, though, for them all to dry."

"Then we need to get to work. This is an intricate map."

"Trust me." Boros took the map and rolled it out to study. "I can do various stages in different colors like the one here."

"Don't make it too complicated, Boros. We don't have much time."

"I understand, truly. Rely on me; I'll get these done for you. We all will. I think we all understand the importance of what's going on." The young professor gestured behind him at the eighteen students puttering about the printing equipment in the large room. It smelled sharply of metals and other ingredients used to create ink. A blue glass jar the size of a human torso stood half-filled with oak apples. An object of great utility to the Araki people, the oak apple provided tannins and served as fake eyeballs and various other props for acts of silliness. Thick twine stretched from workbench to ceiling, draped with printed papers of all sizes and shapes, some festooned with tiny lettering, others embossed with ornate colored images and giant letters surrounded by little stylized beasts and flora. Large binding presses lined the back wall, jammed with stacks of paper waiting to be sewed or covered in leather, all in various stages of progress on the long work-table on the east wall under the windows.

Boros took the map and walked towards a large drafting table, laying it flat. He called his students, who dropped what they were doing, and gathered around him. One had gold ink smeared all over his thumb and index finger; another's were stained purple. Hanru glanced at Skye. "I suppose you're stuck here for a few days, then." She couldn't hide her smile.

* * * *

"Zhritok." Eleran grunted the word and covered his eyes with one hand while holding his staff horizontally above his head with the other; the eyes on the skull glowed white hot. He circled, humming under his breath. Above him, wings whispered, trees thrashed their limbs. Avian creatures had to work hard to find a way through the dense, deciduous canopy. Eleran felt a large weight press down on the staff and a gust of wind against his cheek that accompanied the papery rustling of feathers. He lowered his hand from his eyes. A large raptor perched on his staff looking down at him, swiveling its head one way and the other as it took him in with each eye.

Bright, aqua-colored feet with yellowish-white talons, sharp and unforgiving, signified the torval eagle. Feathers of blue-grey adorned his proud breast, silvery-white along his wing edges and beautiful tail, and deep copper-stained feathers over the rest of him. A matching aqua surrounded his eyes, bright blue under his noble, serious brow. A huge, fierce, dignified beak of ivory yellow tapered to a black tip.

The bird opened its mouth and a shrill cry blasted out of him, as if the noise were bigger than he was. He flapped his massive wings impatiently, and waited for Eleran to do something.

Eleran reached up and gripped his second hand around the staff; the bird was heavy. He lowered it slowly so they came face to face.

"My greetings to you, Honored One," Eleran whispered.

The bird looked at him with his right eye, then his left, and puffed up the feathers around his neck.

"I have need of your sight, Honored One. I have need of your wings."

The bird watched him, blinking thoughtfully, balancing beautifully before him.

"Help me find what I seek."

The eagle studied him for a second, their gazes meeting, and then he launched himself upwards, his feathers whistling as she took to the air, and found a way free of the forest canopy.

Eleran sighed. It would be difficult for the eagle to see anything below the canopy; he knew it, but he had to do what he could. He needed a wolf. Something with the ability to follow its nose, but he felt none nearby. He lowered his staff, placing the butt on the ground. He closed his eyes for a second and wavered.

From above, the eagle called out its shrill cry.

Eleran opened his eyes and pressed on, following the traces that Avria's soul left behind. The soft, smoky, blood-colored wisps dissipated far too quickly.

* * * *

Tinna could not hide her relief at the sight of the arriving riders. Two hard days had brought a crowd of them from Loshan and its vicinity to the gates of Thamatoc. She clutched a message, rolled up and slightly flattened in her hand. Hanru had sent it to inform her and Taneth that the academy printing department would print the maps. He estimated that they'd have enough copies within a day or two. In the meantime, they had twenty-five souls to house, along with their horses. She watched the villagers swarm around, warmed by the sight of them. The people of Thamatoc had served as an extension of her being these past days, ready to do whatever needed doing. They consolidated store-rooms, hung bed platforms, repaired and re-stuffed mattresses, turned storage spaces into private apartments for guests, whatever it took to make the riders comfortable while they and their horses rested before the first relay. They had a little while to relax before the maps arrived with Skye. Considering the circumstances, Hanru decided he would abandon his studies for the time being and return with her.

Astlin had done as he had promised. Before they left with Jestin in tow, he'd taken Tinna's hands and begged her forgiveness. Kailine had been too ashamed to do it herself and remained on her horse, looking as if she would melt from the guilt. Jestin sat smugly in the saddle, challenging every glance Tinna gave him. She bade Astlin goodbye, then walked up to Jestin, reached up and pulled him down by the collar of his shirt.

"It will be a long, long time before I will be able to look at you without feeling the urge to snap your neck, little boy. You think long and hard on what you've done. And if anything happens to her, the burden of her fate will rest on your shoulders alone. You had better pray to the gods that she stays safe, Jestin. Pray hard! Because if anything does happen to Avria, my face will be the last one you will ever see," she growled. She then shoved him back and, for a second, she saw what she had hoped to see: abject fear in his eyes. She knew what her own fury looked like. It resembled Sennal's—black eyes tinged with madness, lips in a straight, serious line, and ripples of fury that revealed a shade of the beast that lurked inside every Thran. Few had seen Tinna's monster, but those that did rarely lived to speak of it.

She kept her eyes burning on the boy until they'd ridden out of sight.

A day had passed. That part was done. The boy was gone.

The relay riders had come. She focused on that.

Tinna turned and walked towards the main lodge, weaving through the people leading the guest horses into the pony-lodge where they would stay. She felt woozy, her knees still shaking from a particularly brutal session with her face over the chamber pot, reliving her breakfast in the most unpleasant manner. She glimpsed Taneth walking towards her with the pregnant Ree in tow. Ree's large, rounded tummy filled Tinna both with love and dread. She paled... feeling a fresh rush of nausea. When she looked at Taneth's face, she saw that he looked as white and stricken as she, which surprised her, and her sickness was momentarily forgotten.

She pressed through the traffic and the three met by the founder's tree.

Taneth gave her another rolled parchment. "Look at the seal."

Tinna's eyes rested on it. Her skin faded even more, her breath hastened.

"Where did it come from?"

"It arrived at the Whiterock relay stop when I returned from Ethlo. They gave it to me, since I was coming home anyway. Another rider had delivered it. That's all they told me." Ree gripped her elbows over her swollen belly. "I asked questions, I did, I saw the seal and I asked everything I could think of for more information of where it originated or who brought it, but nobody had anything to offer."

Sitting on the bench that surrounded the base of the founder's tree, Tinna furrowed her brow and broke the seal. It seal bore the impression of her mother's ring, the Thran raptor and sword with the Ynmoth winged serpent clutched in its talon. Her eyes darted back and forth over the careful script. No one in Thamatoc read Thran but her—her and Taneth, of course, who'd spent many hours learning the language once Tinna had come into his life. She sometimes spoke to him in Thran, for practice and sometimes to share words she did not wish others present to understand.

She read the letter, and read it again, disbelieving.

"Diviner?" she laughed shortly. "Clearly, the woman is insane," she suddenly crammed the letter into Taneth's hand; "clearly." She stalked off, her rage falling behind her like an aura. Taneth unfurled it and read, much more slowly than she, having a decent but not stellar command of her native language. With a shaky sigh, he followed Tinna into the lodge.

Phenmal had just finished bathing and was quite nude underneath a long, banyan-style robe. Tinna didn't give much thought to his state. She pushed past him into his apartment and waited for him to follow. Taneth apologized to Phenmal, who stood drying his bald head with a soft towel, and handed him the letter as he entered. He closed the door behind them. Phenmal's brow rose as he first belted his robe closed, and then opened the letter and studied the tiny, intricate characters for a moment. "I can't read Thran," he finally concluded, looking bewildered. Curls of steam still rose from the brass tub in which he'd just bathed. The water was milky from the soap; and the scent of lavender still lingered quite strongly.

"Well…allow me." Taneth took it back and sat down by the fireplace. Tinna stood against the hearth, glaring down at the flames. The older man stood in his robe, gazing at them both expectantly.

"Please forgive my less than perfect translation; it doesn't sound as simplistic as I am going to read it, I just do—"

"Just read the bloody thing!" Tinna snapped impatiently. Taneth nodded and looked at it.

"To Tinna of Ymnoth, etcetera, etcetera… Our Sovereign has been informed by her powerful Diviner that you pose a threat to Thran and its people. Seeing how base your life has become, contenting yourself to live among savages, I am unconvinced by this Diviner's predictions. However the Sovereign takes them quite seriously. She has used my connection to you to force my hand. I have orders to forestall your pursuit of power. This is the reason that I found you, and the reason why I have taken Avria. I must clip your wings, daughter. Any sign that you choose to defy the Sovereign's demands, and I will kill Avria." Taneth read haltingly. "If you remain insignificant, then Avria will be safe. I will include her in my household and instruct her in the ways of civilized beings."

"Pursuing power?" Tinna said incredulously, interrupting Taneth again. She shook her head in perplexity. "The woman is mad, I tell you, bloody stark raving mad!" She threw her hands up and made a great noise of exasperation, letting her hands fall hard against her legs. Taneth frowned with thought. With Tinna expecting, he was concerned about her. The arrival of her mother had raised her anxiety levels to something he'd never seen in his wife before. Now that Sennal had gone, and taken Avria with her, Taneth worried about the pregnancy. Tinna's powerful emotional state could not be good for their developing child.

Phenmal remained pointedly silent for a moment and then blurted with excessively dramatic flair: "What could the Diviner have seen, I wonder?" He took the letter and stared at it, as if in doing so, it would become clearer to him. His performance seemed almost affected. Tinna wasn't sure if he was serious in his curiosity or he was mocking the diviner. He was so difficult to understand sometimes.

"He saw enough for them to feel threatened. I can't imagine what threat Tinna could pose; she's a leader of a small clan of horse-worshippers. How could she threaten an entire people?" Phenmal's theatrical air dissipated into seriousness and he lifted his finger and shook it, nodding.

"Ahh, but she has also just broadened her influence. The visiting riders might remind you of that. Plus the Keepers have made a point of remaining in close touch with her and with you. Not to mention the summoner on his way."

"So I stand to possibly stop the Thran invasion. That is pursuing power?"

"The Diviner saw that. That you might succeed in stopping them, and so they chose to stop you."

"That explains why Sennal came here. The interest in Avria as a successor was a lie. Her intentions were ill from the moment she arrived. Avria could be in greater danger than I possibly imagined. Had you been here, Phenmal, you'd have known my mother's intentions right away. But it never works out that way, does it? It always has to be difficult. Avria is in real trouble!"

"I wouldn't jump to that conclusion. Sennal would expect you to, so there is no doubt in her mind that you believe her threat. But Avria could be safe in her hands, safer than in the hands of anyone else. She is still her granddaughter, still blood, and no matter how small a connection she might feel towards Avria, it's a connection nonetheless," Phenmal said quickly before Tinna could run away with her imagination.

"What should I do, Phenmal? Call off the riders?"

"No!" Phenmal snapped. "You cannot allow this invasion to occur!"

"What of Avria?" Tinna shouted. "I cannot allow her to harm Avria." Taneth remained tight-lipped, almost in a state of shock.

"I don't know. I don't know, but you cannot stop the riders. The invasion must be curbed immediately! The human armies are gathering. The Thran will crush them. Decimate them. All your efforts of twenty years ago will be for naught!"

"What of Avria!?" Tinna asked again. "Am I to write her off for this? Let her die at the hands of my mother? And regardless of what you say, I know what my mother is capable of. She is capable of doing exactly as she said; mark my words!" A pall hung over them. Tinna glared at Phenmal, her arms rigid at her sides, her lips tight, her brow a mass of wrinkles. Taneth stared at the flames from his chair, his leg shaking nervously. Phenmal put one hand on his lean hip, and massaged his temple with the other.

"I know you will hate me for saying this Tinna, Taneth, but you must put Avria's fate into her own hands. Into the hands of the Druid. You cannot control what happens to her now; you cannot foresee anything that your mother will do, good or bad, whether it's now or later. You need to confine your energies to what is right in front of you! Focus on what the Diviner saw to begin with." Tinna's hand was on his throat before he could say another word. She charged him against the wall. The back of his legs ran into the small dining table that stood by the wall, upsetting some items that had been resting on the tabletop. She pinned him to the wall by his neck. He sat on the table, his hands flat on the heavy stone that divided this apartment from the next. Tinna was petite, but her power was immeasurable; especially when she got angry. She pressed hard into his neck, her fingers white from the pressure. She slid up to him, angled her face close to his.

"How dare you! How dare you!" she seethed. Taneth stood, walked to her, and took her shoulders.

"Let him go, Tinna. Phenmal has been our friend for a long time now." The tone of misery in his voice was as plain as the pallid tone of his skin.

"What sort of friend would ask me to sacrifice my own child?" she hissed, pressing against his throat again. Taneth noticed the tears then, slipping down her furious face. He reached up and wiped one away with his hand, and rested his chin on top of her head. He reached out and placed his hand on top of the one she had on Phenmal's neck. He squeezed it gently, and he felt her muscles slacken. He carefully pulled her hand away, and then folded her into his embrace, her back against his chest, while guiding her away from Phenmal, who'd patiently stood and waited for this anger to peter out. He slumped his weight onto the table and rubbed his neck, shaking his head in defeat.

"I know I could have phrased that differently, Tinna, but I've always been honest with you. Always. It is what I truly believe to be right. I know it's not what you want to hear, and I could feel you resisting it before I even said it. But it had to be said. It had to be said because it's the only thing you can do. You must move forward and prevent this invasion, Tinna. You simply must."

A tortured sob escaped her. Phenmal watched her crumple in Taneth's arms. Her husband held her up by her waist and slid her into the chair he'd occupied only moments before. He knelt before her and took her hands, letting her rest her forehead on his shoulder and weep.

"My poor Avria! She must be so lost and afraid!" Tinna bawled. She looked up over Taneth's shoulder at Phenmal; the man who'd somehow managed to insinuate himself deeply into their lives and family, and a wash of regret coursed over her. "I am sorry, my concubine..." she whispered. He smiled gently at the private joke, and shook his head. They referred to him as such because he spent so much time with the family. He was like a second husband to Tinna and a second father to Avria.

"I cannot blame you for that, Tinna. It was a terrible thing to say, but it had to be said." Phenmal admitted. He sighed and looked at her lovingly. She turned her face back into Taneth's chest. Taneth kissed the top of her head and let his mouth rest there, his eyes beset with worry.

Phenmal moved to sit across from them, resting his elbows on his knees. He waited for Tinna's grief and sadness to play out. He knew that she'd made up her mind, that her tears were tears of guilt and resignation now. He sat back and crossed his legs, pinching his chin with his fingers. Phenmal adored Avria. He did not express his feelings for her openly, as her parents could, but he, too, worried. But his connection to the girl was just as strong, if not stronger. He had been there when she'd had her first broken heart, and he helped her construct her special imaginary place where she could retreat when she was upset, and often joined her inside this illusion to play games with her, and cheer her up when she was down. He'd taught her to play the swan-harp, and they exchanged books and letters via relay whenever he was back at his estate. She sometimes rode there just to spend time with him, and to wear her dresses and feel civilized on occasion. Avria was the daughter he'd never had. He loved her. He feared for her safety, for her life. But he had to convince himself that the Druid would find her and protect her. He, like Tinna, did not have the luxury of succumbing to sorrow or weakness. Tinna was already in a tender emotional state because of her pregnancy. He had to make her strong again, and find the strength in himself to soldier on.

How else could they move forward? How else could they mobilize the Araki people?

CHAPTER SEVEN – THE SCATTERING

Avria gazed balefully at the sour face of her grandmother, not touching her own food, though she was hungry and it smelled wonderful. She found the way the old woman ate reprehensible; the noise of it, the way she moved her lips. Avria's caravan had graduated up the line of the procession until it now followed her grandmother's. Today, they took their first meal together. Sennal did not ride alongside but remained in her caravan, reading and writing by her window. Avria rode most of the day on her own mare, as she had from the beginning, a mount far superior to any of the little pure-blood desert horses the Thran women rode. Theirs were durable enough, and sure-footed in the sand, but never bred for the forest environment, where Araki horses proved as fleet as deer. Avria calculated her advantages. Even with her hands bound to the saddle, she knew that, given the opportunity, she could do something. She'd mulled on it for days.

"Did you know that you're eighteenth in the line of succession? Your grandfather's blood raises questions, but that's a minor issue, really. The male line is ultimately irrelevant. Seventeen royals will not likely drop dead all at once, but I thought I'd make you aware of how close to true royalty you stand." Sennal rambled, speaking fluidly in Avria's language, her inflection soft, almost undetectable compared to Tinna's distinctive speech, which had desensitized Avria to the Thran accent. She watched her grandmother bite into a cake-ball covered in a sweet and fragrant spice the color of powdered rust. It peppered her chin and lips. She wiped it with the back of her hand.

"You should be grateful I extracted you from that horrible peasant hole you lived in. Even that boy couldn't stand it there; he knew you were too good for it."

Jestin. She's talking about Jestin. That boy. Avria wondered what he was doing now. Back at Loshan, she wagered, smugly ordering his servants about, a devious smile on his insipid face. Traitor.

"He would make a decent concubine for you, Avria. He's very devoted. Not the smartest I've seen, but that's a good thing when it comes to men. The dim ones make more compliant partners, easier to control. They think with their sticks, you see; control the stick, and you control them. Always watch out for the smart ones. They're schemers. But we find if we give them projects to figure out, bridges to build, they usually stay quiet. But never trust a smart man!" She wagged her finger at Avria. "Ahh...but you think they should all be smart, like the one who fathered you. Smug, intrusive creature your father is. At least he's not a gypsy. Tinna did one better than me in that aspect. She was always a prime manipulator, that one. She could get a man to do anything she wanted. She used her sexuality like a weapon." Sennal drank from her silver wine-goblet, her thoughts rambling like her mouth.

Don't you all? Don't you teach the stealthy assassins the use of such weapons? Avria wondered.

Sennal had not bothered to dress herself for the day. Her sleeping gown, with its low neckline and no waist, hung straight as a column, her hair tied back in a bun. Looking up from her meal at last, she noticed the look of disgust on Avria's face.

"Oh, come now! Do I shock you with my description of men and their sticks?" she laughed easily, amused by Avria's arched brows and pursed lips. "Your mother raised you as a northern prude! I thought she would at least instill a little sense in you when it comes to natural things. Oh, that's so discouraging!" She threw her napkin down and stood, the caravan rocking as she moved around in it. Avria watched the heavy napkin unfurl and settle on the table.

"You'll figure it all out sooner or later. And once you do, you'll realize that you were meant to be a Thran. Your mother is just bitter—bitter at her own half-bloodedness—and too weak for a true Thran. No spine. No strength." She reached for a long pipe with a tiny bowl and stuffed it with fragrant herbs, lit it with a thin, tapered candle and took two thoughtful puffs from it. She then glanced at Avria.

"You not eating? Nor do you speak. I see. You are a stubborn thing, aren't you? Well, then, go without!" She knocked on the door to the exterior. The guards who stood outside opened it. "Get her out of here, and let's get the caravan moving again!"

They both nodded. One entered the caravan and took Avria by the upper arm, pulling her out of her chair. She led her through the door, down the steps to the ground and let her mount, quickly fastening one hand to her saddle.

As the guard circled behind her to fasten the other hand, Avria squeezed her legs around her mare's barrel and lunged forward into the guard holding the bridle, knocking the plump woman off her feet. Shade bolted. Avria leaned into her neck and found her stirrups, standing in them, her body hunched forward over her mare's shoulders. With a careful lean and a squeeze of her calves, she directed the mare to veer agilely to the right, onto the road the caravan followed. Pressing her body close to the mare, her knees absorbing the shock of the movement, she squeezed hard, feeling Shade's power explode into a sprinting gallop. She steered her into the thick of the trees, a command the mare followed on pure faith, leaping through thick undergrowth and vanishing into a wall of foliage. Mare and rider crashed through the understory plants as one beast, weaving around the young saplings that populated the forest. Avria's free hand grappled at the buckle to free her other wrist. Steering her mare with her legs and knees, she moved her upper body to avoid the many obstacles Shade flew under and around, taking low jumps over fallen logs and dips, lunging up steep embankments, banking hard around tree trunks. She raced as she had a hundred times before, with Hanru and Drashun at her heels. She leaned into the next curve and then ducked to avoid a low-hanging branch, her free hand never stopping until she felt the clasp give way and her other hand fall free at last.

A raptor's cry cut through the chaotic shouts of the Thran cortege—a full and welling eagle's call made as if in jubilation. The bird tucked its wings against its body and fell like a stone, spreading them again to level out only feet above the forest floor. A deft twist of the wing and tail, and it wove between the trees, trying with all its might to keep up with the girl on her speeding black mare.

* * * *

Taneth and Phenmal studied a map tacked onto the wall with square horse-shoe nails. They'd colored it, showing the directions of the relay web and the subsequent movements of the riders to a common meeting point. The two men bickered about meeting places. Tinna had grown depressed over the past two days. She was sleeping again. Phenmal insisted they let her be for a while. Her early pregnancy made her fragile, and her emotional state teetered as if at a precipice. When Skye arrived with the maps, they set the riders to rolling them up, sliding them into hastily-made leather tubes and writing destinations on them while they discussed the final decisions.

"They should meet here," Phenmal pointed to an area near the pass, "only a few leagues from Chrotrioth."

"No," Taneth argued. "They will be seen. The one advantage we have is surprise. They should meet here, by the foothills of Mount Jewel, halfway between the range and Jewel, at a town there called Iromi. It used to be a large settlement. A large trade road leads from Iromi over the great river; we can turn south there, and then come up behind the human ar—"

"Strategizing?" Tinna asked, walking into the room. She looked exhausted. She gave Phenmal an apologetic look. She could not avoid looking at the four dark bruises under his chin and jaw. She looked her forty years this day, her curls tied back in a frizzy tail, flyaway hairs sun-bursting from her hairline, eyes puffy. She wore one of Taneth's tunics, which looked huge on her, a pair of leggings, and no shoes. She sighed and sat down with a tired plunk at the table to look at their map.

"Yes." Taneth reached for a cut-glass goblet and filled it with water from the pitcher. He walked around the table and handed it to her, touching her cheek with his fingers. The rumpled bed linens had embossed her face. She took the water and drank it absentmindedly. "We're running short on time. We got word this morning that the army is gathering south of Suthervale. They will move on Chrotrioth soon. We need to get our riders out, Tinna; otherwise, they'll arrive too late."

"Let's do it then." She sighed. "Send out the riders."

"To Iromi then," Taneth concluded. "They will meet at Iromi in ten days."

"You can do that?" Tinna asked.

"The relay will move fast. Once they do, the settlements will get as many people as they can on horse and on their way to Iromi. Each settlement will present their map as they arrive, so we can account for them. We'll let the horses rest a few hours if they need it, have a smith check shoes and such, then we ride to Chrotrioth."

"We will have to mark Iromi on the maps," Taneth muttered in annoyance. Phenmal shrugged.

"It won't take much to make a little inkblot to them. We can have the riders help."

"I should get ready and head out to Iromi at once. I should be there as the Araki arrive."

"I would offer my coach, but it's too slow," Phenmal muttered. "If you ride hard for a week, you'll get there." Tinna sighed and shook her head.

"Oh, no. The summoner arrives today. I will have much faster transportation than a horse. And the two of you are coming with me."

"Hanru can go in my stead. He wants to go with Skye anyway, to help account for the arrivals. I'm not sure what help I could be," Taneth muttered. Tinna smiled softly at her husband, the homebody. She shook her head.

"This time, you're coming with me." He hesitated, she knew, because he had never quite overcome his fear of the dragons, but she would not take no for an answer. He would have to learn to trust the dragons, as she had. She stood and stretched, looking at the two men who stared at her expectantly. "Well? Are you going to dispatch the riders, or do I have to do it?"

Rhoa was only a bit younger than Tinna. A clumsy, awkward girl in her youth, she'd grown into a strong, hardened character over the years since her return to Thamatoc, after Tinna had whisked her away. Tinna still looked upon Rhoa as the innocent and sweet thing she'd been before their trials, regardless of her now-wizened gaze. Her ginger-red hair had softened to a chestnut brown; her curved, youthful shape had shrunk to a thinner, bonier frame; her rounded cheeks into gaunt angles. Her freckles no longer seemed sweet and charming, they were just freckles. Rhoa stood among the best riders in the village, as did her son, Drashun. When the call went out for relay riders, she appeared with Ree and the others, with Drashun at her side. Tinna knew better than to argue. She only looked at her friend and shook her head with a sigh. Rhoa challenged her gaze, and looked deflated when Tinna did not try to dissuade her.

The riders of Thamatoc gathered at the community dining table. Taneth, Phenmal and the others sat by the hearth, their chairs turned to face the crowd. Tinna, freshly bathed and put together, looked more herself now. She wearily clapped her hands and shouted at the gathering to quiet down and find places to sit if possible. Hanru and Skye appeared behind the group of riders. They carried stacks of map tubes just re-rolled after having hasty dots put on them to represent the final destination. Behind them, the riders from Loshan began to filter in. Nearly fifty people crammed into the communal hall, making it warm and uncomfortable. Taneth hung his master map over the mantel and helped his son and Skye spread out the tubes on a smaller sideboard that hunkered by the huge fireplace.

Tinna cleared her throat and pointed to the map. "You start here and ride to your first relay point. Some of you may ride on;

others may return home, depending on how well each settlement is supplied with riders. The human army is massing here, according to the updates from the relay. Our groups meet outside Iromi. Some of you will follow and join our mounted army. We won't force you, but our numbers are questionable, and we need every last rider we can get." As Tinna spoke, a youthful man with a round face and a peppering of freckles entered. Behind him, two pale, unsettling faces appeared from the darkened corridor. Their strange glyph-like smiles chilled her. She had no idea why the Driva had come, but if the Keepers sent them, it signaled something important. Each one carried a bulky carpet-bag, straining against the weight of it. They rarely carried anything—a fact that had always struck her as bizarre, considering that they traveled on foot and surely needed clothes and food like everyone else. Those who served the Keepers always proved enigmatic. She acknowledged the young man and the Driva with a nod and continued.

"It's nighttime. I've heard your complaints, but we have everything in place and we need to move now—immediately. Take your maps. Your relay points are marked. You'll ride out in twos for the first leg. You may ride together again, for how many legs cannot be known, so choose your mate well." She watched the riders look at one another and slowly filter into pairs. Rhoa chose a stranger from Loshan; Drashun, a young man his own age.

She handed Rhoa and her team-mate their set of maps. "You'll ride east to Klatna and Darachar, covering most of the coastal settlements. Another group," she said, passing three more tubes to Ree and her partner, "will take the relay down the coast to the mountains. Next?" Hanru handed her another set of tubes. "Drashun, your leg fans out southward to the range. Ride hard!"

Half an hour later, as the last set of hooves clattered off through the town gates, Tinna sank into the chair next to Taneth and looked at him gravely. The lodge seemed eerily quiet without the bustle and anxiety that had shrouded it for the past days.

"I hope we can muster enough Araki fighters to make this worthwhile. I'm afraid we're going to be wiped out along with the humans."

"Not with the dragons on your side," said the summoner who had arrived with the Driva. He sat down with Tinna and the others by the fireplace, accepted a goblet and sipped, smiling at the flavor of the special beer the Araki made from sugary tree-sap. Tinna glanced down at her goblet of wine, nodded, and sighed.

"Dragons will help, yes. But we need ground forces to keep the Thran from simply turning their arrows and pole arms skyward. In mixed battle, dragons have a limited role at best. Perhaps taking out the archery clusters…" She shook her head dubiously. "If we don't provide ground distraction, they will destroy the dragons."

"We will work with what we have!" Taneth blurted. "We have no other option but to make do!" He looked to the two Driva hanging back by the right entrance to the hall, awaiting Tinna still. "What brings them here?"

Tinna ignored them. "I'm not sure. No doubt the Keepers have gotten wind of the situation near Chrotrioth. I cannot imagine what they think they could learn from me. Unless they somehow heard about what we're doing."

At last, Tinna stood and walked over to the Driva. The female smiled wanly at her, the permanent grimace of her tattoo simply too bizarre as it contorted with her facial movement. "Shall we talk in private?"

The woman nodded, and Tinna vanished with the dark couple.

Skye frowned, her eyes squinted together tightly. "Those people just give me the willies," she mumbled. Hanru nodded. He was familiar with them; they'd been visiting the town for years. Their presence put him ill at ease. He glanced at his father, then at Skye. "Maybe they're offering help," he suggested.

Taneth simply started laughing. "The Keepers, the Trinity— they may have our best interest at heart, but they are not proactive, boy. They sit back and let things happen. If they do wish to accomplish anything, they let others do it for them. Trust me; the Keepers will not offer any real help—they will try to influence what happens, yes, but do something helpful, like sending a legion of their magi or such?" He laughed again. He stood and shook his head bitterly. With a sigh, he looked at Hanru and said, "By the way, my boy, you're going to be a big brother again." He turned and exited. Hanru and Skye looked at one another in bewilderment.

"Your mother is with child?" Skye asked.

"I guess that's what he was saying. By Arak! That was the last thing I ever expected him to say. I should see mother…"

"You should wait. She's worn out. She probably wanted to tell you herself, but, with all due respect, Taneth isn't very keen on social niceties. Talk to her about it later." Hanru nodded and slumped down in his chair. Skye shook her head. "Everything is just upside-down. Now we have to go to Iromi?"

"Yes," Hanru smiled, "but on the back of a dragon! That alone makes everything worth it!"

Skye rolled her eyes and got up. She turned away, running into a footstool and nearly tripping over it. Hanru smirked. At the school, he'd forced Skye to sit through a long process of testing lenses on her eyes. This helped him and the eyeglass-maker figure out what type of lenses she needed to see. While Skye spent hours in the printing room, Hanru oversaw the process of her spectacles' construction. He'd given the man a good portion of his year's allowance for them. In his pocket, tucked into a small, velvet-lined box he held her new, fragile spectacles. He planned to unveil them in the morning, when they were about to leave, so she could see the firmament as clearly as he could, from the back of a dragon.

* * * *

Ledroran, an impressive dragon twenty years ago, now inspired awe. The years had added mass to his girth and luster to his tone; his head-shield had grown broader, his horns longer and muted with more ivory hues. He took up a good part of the pasture and moved with a sinuous grace, despite his size. His head alone occupied the space of a small cottage. The sight and distinctive smell of the beast overwhelmed Tinna—feral and fresh, with a metallic edge to it and a touch of what she called 'sky'—a permanent scent that reminded her of the air after a thunderstorm. When he opened his mouth, the acrid aroma of the fire-fluid that filled his cheek-sacks caused her eyes to water. His eyes smiled when she appeared. He waited for her to walk up to him.

"Na-AiTinna, my dear, dear friend." Dragons spoke with dexterous tongues; their gaping, toothy mouths had no articulate lips with which to form sounds. Most of the consonants came clipped, hardly distinguishable from one another; he might have said, "Ai-Pinna" or "Ai-Dinna." Regardless, they managed well enough understand one another.

"Ledroran." Tinna reached out and leaned on his head, laying her arms in a circle around his eye. He had cast and regrown his scales many times since she'd last seen him, a regal blue-green streaked with pearlized jewel-tones and hints of orange. Burgundy edged his soft, sage-green belly-plates. If dragons had a royal hierarchy, Ledroran, an elder and a leader, would have been King. Only those dragons that represented their race in the Trinity stood above him. Tinna and Ledroran shared a secret history. They maintained their friendship by occasional communication through the summoner. He had not seen her since he'd borne her home, two decades past.

"It is so, so good to see you again! You look well."

"I am older, that you cannot deny," she smirked. "But I am as well as can be, considering the circumstances. I have much to explain."

"We have time. It will be a long flight, and I am not trading you off to anyone else. I go to Iromi with you."

"And the others?"

"They come as well, to carry your friends. There are other dragons who will join us along the way."

"How is Ilono, that handsome rogue?" Tinna asked. She spoke of Ledroran's son, who had helped her as well. Ledroran's visible eye darkened.

"Ilono was lost to human hunters eleven years ago. We've lost many because of our role in the burnings." A heavy silence descended between them for a moment. Taneth and the others stood by, not quite understanding what was happening. Tinna dropped her arms and stepped back, placing her hand on the pinkish-yellow plate of Ledroran's cheek.

"I'm sorry," she whispered. He nodded, then he sighed in the way only a massive dragon could sigh—a shuddering, whooshing breath that sounded like a gust whistling into a cave. His eye gazed into hers, and silent understanding bound them. "Let's go." He nodded subtly and lifted his head off the ground, turning to look at the others.

"I am Ledroran. This is Droth, and Rueath. They will carry you. AiTinna, and the mate, Taneth; you come with me. The Chaiva can ride another... I do not like Chaiva." The dragon gave Phenmal a hard glare and lowered his head again. Tinna looked at Phenmal and shrugged. Tinna walked to Rigerd and put her hand on his arm.

"I'm sorry to do this to you, Rigerd, but you are still leader here for the time being,"

"Acting leader," the grizzled, hulk of a man replied. "Watch over Taneth. This is not his way."

"I know. I will."

"I will send out our best riders to meet you at Iromi as soon as I'm finished here. I will only keep a few of our stronger men home. Maybe Frajik and Choron. They both have big families and would probably prefer to stay here."

"As you wish, Rigerd. Don't strip the town. If you send all sixty of our good horses and riders, it'll probably be the biggest group at

391

Iromi, so it should suffice. If any messages come for me here, be sure to relay them to Iromi. I promise you, I will do what I must to get home soon, so you can finally retire."

"Farewell, Tinna. Goodbye, Taneth. Travel safely!" Rigerd shouted. Taneth waved, the regret evident in his face. He did not wish to go. Tinna patted Rigerd's arm and moved towards the dragons. Rigerd backed away and crossed his arms. The five travelers proceeded to climb onto the dragons, others remaining on the ground to hand heavy packs up to them. Tinna grinned at her husband before using the thick, stubby horns protruding from the dragon's jaw to climb up onto the back of Ledroran's neck, ducking under the wide shield that jutted from the back of his skull to provide ample shelter from wind and rain. The wide neck offered the perfect shape for a couple of passengers. It had grown broader than the first time she rode him. She wondered if dragons ever stopped growing.

After hauling her packs up from Taneth, she held out her hand to her husband, who refused it and scrambled up to join her. For the first time in years, Taneth did not wear his floppy chasuble, but normal clothes. It looked strange to Tinna to see him this way. His hands trembled. Tinna nestled their packs into the nook under the dragon's shield and watched as Hanru, dressed in casual clothing and a warm stocking-hat, and Skye, in her standard riding garments, climbed aboard the dragon called Droth. Phenmal would travel alone on Rueath, with most of the packs. He had to wait, while a townsman handed him item after item. He did not look thrilled. He wore a long wool greatcoat, with several stacked shoulder capes, and a hat over his bald head. He gave Tinna a rueful glance before ducking under his steed's shield and sitting down on one of the packs.

Hanru waved to his mother, an excited smile on his face. He then turned to Skye, who knelt on the dragon's neck, tenderly touching the smooth coral-and-green scales with near reverence. She glanced up at Hanru. Tears stood at the brims of her eyes. "Can you believe it?"

"Hardly!" He grinned, stooping next to her. "Are you afraid to fly?"

"No!" Her smile broadened. Hanru laughed and shook his head incredulously. "You and I won't be there for long, but I am so happy we got to go there this way!"

"Close your eyes! I have a surprise for you," Hanru blurted.

Skye blinked and furrowed her brow quizzically. She was so delighted to be with Hanru. Getting to spend so much time with her crush already exceeded all expectations. Now she was about to take to the clouds on a dragon! What could Hanru possibly have that would improve upon this moment?

"Go on," Hanru insisted. She complied and clamped her eyes shut. Hanru reached into his pocket, took the little spectacles out of the container and spread them open over the bridge of her nose. He let them relax and pinch together.

"There." Skye's eyes popped open and for a second. She wavered. She blinked, then sat back onto her bum, reaching up to touch her glasses. Then she squealed in delight and lowered her hand, looking at it through her glasses. Then she gazed around her, looking up at the trees that ringed the pasture, and at Ledroran, and at the smaller dragon on which Phenmal had settled. Her mouth stood agape. Her eyes watered. She stood, then staggered, steadying herself by grabbing the spiky rim of the dragon's crest.

"Bless Arak! I feel ten feet tall! Look at the branches! I can actually see individual branches! And leaves! I can see leaves! Look! I can see the hay on the ground, too!" Forgetting herself, she hugged Hanru tightly, the delight in her expression warming his soul. As she gazed in awe around her, the dragons began to move. Hanru secured their belongings and came to stand next to Skye as the dragons lumbered to the end of the pasture. One at a time, they unfurled their massive pairs of wings, which had been folded so tidily against the barrels of their bodies a moment ago. Impossible expanses of membrane peeled away from their natural pleats and stretched across the thick, trunk-like bones of forearms and fingers, seeming, even as they rose, too thin to carry such massive creatures aloft.

The riders held on tight as first Ledroran, then Droth and then Rueath, broke into a gauche lope and began to work their wings. One pump, two, and the talons were off the ground; three, four; they rose arduously, but the higher they got, the easier it felt, and soon, the forest looked like a mat of soft moss below them. Above, the mare's tails in the sky appeared so much closer. The air cooled bit by bit, with each beat of the colossal wings. Skye hugged herself, and Hanru gestured to her to sit under the shield of their mount, much smaller than the ample shelter Tinna and Taneth enjoyed. They settled in, both silently riveted to the vistas all around them.

"Skye," Hanru shouted over the buffeting wind, "I think after I complete my studies, that perhaps we should marry."

The girl's eyes widened and she swiveled her head to gaze at him with incredulity. "I beg your pardon?"

"Marry...you know...wed," he elaborated.

393

Skye's mouth hung open. She gazed at him speechless for a moment, her hair waving wildly as the gusts of air flowed behind the dragon's head-shield. Then she said, "Hanru... We have never even acknowledged any feelings between us, let alone kissed or shared any romantic gestures. Well, except for these..." Her hand touched the flimsy little spectacles pinched on the bridge of her nose. "These are thoughtful and romantic."

Hanru laughed, and waved his hand dismissively;

"Skye, don't be obtuse! We've been friends and companions from the moment you started taking father's reading classes. Then he discovered your aptitude for so many subjects and took you into his tutelage along with me. We've been coexisting for years. I knew by the time I was seventeen that you were the best suited for me. But you were just fourteen and still young. As I was just riding to Lemoram for my final two years, it occurred to me how much I would miss you; knowing that I wouldn't be coming home after a month like I normally would. I thought perhaps you might come to Lemoram to attend the conservatory eventually, but that wouldn't happen immediately. Then I thought, if I go to Wye as a Wiseman I'd be without you indefinitely. It came to me that I did not wish to go to Wye to live without you. So logically, it meant that I should marry you, so you would join me at Wye. I know this isn't the best way to do this, perhaps I should start courting you properly and all those things, but I cannot. I go back to Lemoram to finish my education as soon as we finish the preparations at Iromi. I needed you to know my intentions so you could have time to think about it."

"I don't need time to think about it, Hanru," Skye laughed. "I will gladly marry you. I will gladly wait for you to complete your education at Lemoram and happily accompany you to Wye as your wife. However, I would hope that I could continue my studies as best I can, and perhaps serve beside you at Wye. Taneth can formalize my education."

"I don't have any ideas of changing who you are, or what you do, Skye, I just want to be with you."

"Understood," she replied. She then turned her head to look down at the miniaturized firmament below and sighed a happy sigh. Gently, she reached out her hand and found Hanru's fingers waiting to wrap around hers.

Tinna pulled on her old, ugly sweater. Taneth sat under the shield, trying his hardest not to let his eyes wander down the side of the dragon's wide neck. Tinna looked over at Droth, who flew a bit lower to Ledroran's left, and saw the small faces of Hanru and Skye, filled with wonder, smiles bright and innocent. She saw their hands clutched together, Hanru staring at Skye's awed face while she gazed out below, using the spectacles for which Hanru had saved his allowance. It warmed Tinna's heart to finally see some gesture of bonding between the two. It was about time. Hanru chose a nice moment to acknowledge his feelings for her. Skye's happy glow was almost blinding from where Tinna sat.

"I think Hanru has finally told Skye how he feels," Tinna told her husband loudly. "They're holding hands. And look at her face!" Taneth leaned forward and looked down. A smile crept over his lips. He laughed through his nose and shook his head.

"That boy is so much like me, it's a wonder he's adopted!"

Tinna chuckled and nodded broadly. It was hard, sometimes, to remember that Hanru was not a product of their marriage. He integrated so well into their pairing. He brought them together. She sometimes forgot that he wasn't really her son. She thought of Avria and wondered if she was all right. She knew Avria would have loved flying with them, standing behind the shield, letting the wind toss her hair about. She would have squealed in delight to see Hanru finally fulfilling Skye's hopes. She would be over the moon about the prospect of a little sibling—something she'd asked for all through her childhood but that her parents could not supply, until now.

Tinna clutched her elbows in her threadbare sweater and found a nice spot under the higher edge of the shield where she could gaze out. The dragon's wings pumped and glided a short ways off to her left. Such a massive creature! What a miracle that it could hang from such fragile-seeming wings and not drop from the sky like a stone. She pushed her sweater up, so that the ruddy yarn covered her nose and chin. She breathed through it. This sweater had seen her through the hardest parts of her life. It had traveled with her from Thran, at seventeen, and accompanied her to her new home, when she discovered Thamatoc. It had kept Rhoa warm on her first ride on a dragon, and it had stayed with her until she'd come home to Taneth with baby Roog in her pack. Hanru had been so small then, tiny and vulnerable.

Tears filled Tinna's eyes as she thought of Hanru and of Avria. She smiled under the sweater as she thought of Avria in the sweater as a tot. She stole it constantly, as if she drew strength from it, just as Tinna did. The long, distended sleeves hung far past Tinna's hands. When Avria wore it, she looked comical.

The sweater had once belonged to Tinna's father. It was the only thing she had that had belonged to him, that connected her to him. When she wore it, she felt wrapped in his affection; she felt loved, cherished. She had no idea what kind of man her father was, but if his sweater said anything about him, he was gentle and soft, comforting and reliable. He likely possessed none of those qualities, but she needed to believe that he did, since her mother clearly did not. The sweater, of all things, had taught her how to be a good mother to her own children. Tinna clutched the sleeves to her chest and sighed.

Taneth found the courage to stand and move to her side, his face waxen and fearful.

"You still looking at Hanru?" he intoned over the wind.

Tinna nodded, tilting her head so that it leaned on his shoulder. Her hair tickled his face.

"He's so grown up."

"Handsome thing, isn't he?"

"I was just thinking that the last time I did this, I was coming home to you two. He was barely five."

"Yes. Avria came soon after, didn't she?"

Taneth smiled nostalgically, relaxing a bit as he wrapped his arms around Tinna's waist and clutched her tight. "I love you so very much, Tinna. I always have."

She reached up and placed her sweater-covered hand on the left side of his face. "Oh, Taneth," she sighed, her voice shaky. "I feel so weak and ineffective. It's not who I am! But I feel like the situation with Avria has hit my very core—as if my mother has stolen my might from me."

"That old hag has taken none of your power, Tinna. She's only made you stronger and more resolved. I know you, Tinna. I know you better than anyone else and nothing defeats you; it only pushes you, makes you even more determined. Avria is fine. She's more like you than you think. And with that beast of a druid on her heels, I feel even more assured that she's going to be safe at home someday soon. This war—you will turn the tide. You move mountains, Tinna. You've done it once, and you'll do it again. It's who you are. Nobody in this world is strong enough to stop you or to sap your power."

Tinna watched the world slide by, the forest seemingly endless below. She leaned back against Taneth and sighed. Her rock, the only one that would never judge her or doubt her for having a weak moment, held her close. He was worth every change she had made in her life in order to be with him. Every choice, every decision that brought her to this moment, was worth it. Again, she had found a place where she felt she had to fight to maintain the status quo. Taneth was right. She felt it inside her—that sense of determination, that power that she thought she had lost. She realized that this threat to her happiness only made her stronger.

She pushed Taneth away and ducked under Ledroran's shield. Taneth followed, and they both settled in against the soft, rubbery skin that stretched across the back of his skull. It was quieter here, they could speak without needing to shout, and the whorls of wind did not reach so far back. She scratched the dragon's head lovingly, glad to her soul to see him again after so long. She then lay down, her head on Taneth's lap. She felt that familiar tickle inside her brain, the smoky, black monster that occupied a place in her soul, tiny and hidden, but still there, squirming inside her. She hadn't let it out in many years. She didn't need to. She didn't want to. Her beast was a force to be reckoned with, a darkness that could lead her to kill without blinking an eye, to perform brutal acts with a fearsome grimace. She could slay with no regard for the humanity she destroyed. She allowed herself to be comforted by that dark presence, to be glad of it. She feared it, but she also respected it. She held onto the Thran side of her past for the sake of keeping the life she had now. She closed her eyes and sighed. Given time and the proper motivation, she could get it back in full force. At Iromi, if I need to let it out, I will control it. She opened her eyes and looked up at the cloud base above them. For the sake of our lives, and the wonderful hope of this new child, if I need it, I will have it, I will use it, I will control it.

Her eyes wandered to the side, to one of the large bags the Driva had brought. She sat up and reached for it, heaving it toward her. She unbuttoned the opening. It chilled her just to look at it. She reached down and touched the silver sheen of the metal, somehow expecting her fingers to sink into its depths instead of stopping at a cool surface. Taneth shook his head incredulously.

"How did they know?"

"I suppose somehow they just do. With their Chaiva and their Driva and the mystics and Magi, nobody really knows what they do. But they know. It is so strange."

"For years now, they've come. They've discussed using Araki resources to maintain and restore what the dragons damaged or destroyed. They've talked to you about nothing, really. Infrastructure, restoration, the movements of the High Throne and its ridiculous aristocracy—all manner of details pertaining to the dragon burnings—but nothing of value, nothing really of great consequence. Yes, they and the Trinity funded the building of the Academy and helped me to begin rebuilding other academies, and they gave me the people and funds I needed to take the census of the Araki groups. I took it for an interest in rebuilding, in restoring what we lost, in making reparations for the mistake they made. But frankly, now that I see this, I'm starting to think they helped to do all those things for this event alone."

"Taneth, that is ridiculous. The Keepers cannot control the direction of events that haven't occurred. If they could, they would have done something to prevent the need for wormskin plague, to stop the dragon burni—"

"Unless it suited their desired end," he interrupted.

"The Trinity would never stand for that," Tinna muttered. "Would they? Would they do that at such a cost?" Her voice trailed off as she realized the inanity of her words. They'd paid that cost many times over and obviously would do it again.

"The Keepers and the Trinity are one and the same. One is the head, the other the hands. You know how odd the whole thing is. Barely comprehensible," Taneth muttered. The entire idea had baffled him for years.

The common misconception held that "Trinity" meant a triumvirate of ancient dragons. Taneth, like most other humans, had been raised to believe this. The Trinity, one of two such organizations, functioned at a level above whatever government stood at any given time, persisting for centuries behind a veil of secrecy. Many people refused to believe in the Trinity's existence; very few knew anything about it; however, throne after throne had bowed to the pressures of the mysterious Trinity and to the other faction, the Keepers, a human-driven organization that served the will of the Trinity. The Keepers purported to stand for knowledge, not power. They kept Humanity's legacy—its histories, its innovations, its creations—all of its intellectual advancements. They had a network of archives around the world, maintained by brotherhoods and sisterhoods who served knowledge as others served their gods, dedicating their lives to it in study and reflection, maintaining the texts and documents that came through their doors. The Keepers also fostered and helped to promote artisan guilds, artists, educational organizations and, of course, the mystical arts, keeping a tight rein on anyone born with special abilities.

They fostered the people with powers; humans who could wield magic, speak into or read minds, foresee the future, gaze into the past. The Mystics, the Chaiva, the Driva, the Drathar demons, the Fyrloe—these were known as the 'children' of the Keepers. Few mystical types avoided the oversight of the Keepers, who collected them as soon as they revealed their talents, and brought them to academies to be molded and shaped to Keeper standards—including those like Taneth, who displayed exceptional intelligence. Bright children were scuttled off to the local throne-sponsored academies to learn the knowledge necessary in order to serve the common good. They served out their lifetimes in payment, doing whatever the Keepers and their respective rulers required of them.

Phenmal had come from this system. A Chaiva mind-reader, and a powerful one, he had served the Keepers for much of his life. However, he bought himself out of further servitude by performing a task that he had yet to disclose to Tinna. It must have been something of great significance, for it earned him his freedom and enough resources to afford an old manor on a secluded plot of land, far from cities and relays and roads, with only empty-minded servants to assist him. There, he sought peace in his mind. And he had obtained it, until Tinna stumbled onto his land. She had opened his eyes to the dragon burnings and to the turmoil that humanity suffered. He had left his home to find out more.

He eventually moved to a residence, similarly isolated, but set closer to the woman who'd changed his life, where, by his own silent consent, he found himself absorbed into her strange family. He served as perhaps a father-figure to bring sense and perspective to Hanru and Avria, and a close friend to Tinna. Lastly, he befriended and mentored Taneth, who found the older man both unsettling and comforting at the same time, someone to whom he could speak of his dull subjects and find himself rewarded, for a change, with an animated response. Moreover, Phenmal supported his endeavors to rebuild a broken education system.

He knew greater things about the Keepers, even the Trinity, but he did not speak of them. His connection to them had been renewed after the burnings, and it had subtly changed. Now, Tinna and Taneth wondered if Phenmal knew what they were up to.

Tinna had learned that the Trinity was not an association of dragons only, but of all three dominant races—the Humans, the Dragons and the Chai-Opse, the last of whom Tinna, like everyone else, had assumed for most of her life, to be a long-dead race. Once from a land far in the northwest, they had simply vanished. But

Tinna had discovered (as Taneth had, upon researching the matter) that the Chai-Opse had simply become a nomadic people. After the first devastation of the wormskin plague had taken much of humanity, centuries past, the Chai-Opse, immune to the disease, had relinquished their land—perhaps out of guilt—and had traveled to all corners of the known world. A number of them still traveled as gypsies; others settled in the cold lands, where they served the Trinity; and others migrated to the plains and eventually became the Araki people; giving up the plains for the forest as Humanity pushed them out.

Taneth had yet to discover how the Chai-Opse differed from humans. They resembled humans in almost every respect. The differences were subtle: an uncanny ability to tame and understand animals, for instance, and a closeness to, and respect for nature that Humanity did not possess. They presented as great a mystery, in Taneth's opinion, as were the two organizations that seemed almost omnipresent in his life.

The two entities, the Keepers and the Trinity, were not defined by any government and did not exercise power in that capacity; despite the obvious influence they had on thrones and sometimes on who occupied them. They strove to preserve the interests of the three races, and especially those of Humanity, who obviously needed the extra help, since they seemed bent on conquering their environment without the slightest regard for the other races. During difficult times, when Human populations had swelled, the Dragons tended to remain passive, despite repeated periods of near-extinction brought about by shortages of food and resources. With each resurgence of the virulent wormskin plague, however, which decimated a good part of humanity every few hundred years, the Dragons tended to recover.

The Chai-Opse made themselves scarce. They once dominated the plains but had migrated slowly to the forests and settled there. The race now occupied primarily the forests of Oromoii. Some continued to live as nomads, but they were few and far between. Humanity had remained the most prevalent race, bouncing back from the plagues stronger and more determined each time. Taneth joked that the purpose of the Keepers was to preserve Humanity's constructive achievements, which they wanted to make sure that, in the event of their own extinction, the Humans would leave something positive in their wake. However, the wormskin plague never quite got rid of them all.

This time, only the humans in the Empire of Oromoii, where they were most concentrated, had been decimated—and by dragons, no less. Thousands of settlements under the throne were burned to the ground, and people died by the hundreds of thousands. Only Tinna, Taneth, Phenmal and a few unfortunate others knew why.

Since the burnings, the Keepers had kept in close touch with Tinna through the Driva. They showed up to discuss goings on with her, to bring news, to talk to Taneth about rebuilding projects and the sharing of the archives with the new schools—mostly benign subjects. Tinna thought they wanted to remind her that they were still there, and still strong, in spite of the catastrophic destruction of most human settlements inside the borders of Oromoii. Sometimes they discussed the dragons and Tinna's relationship with them; other times, they simply wanted to make sure that Tinna kept her promise to remain silent about the truth she'd learned so long ago and about her actions in that instance, which had saved what remained of humanity in Oromoii.

Taneth suspected that their visits meant more than that now. "They had a full harness of armor made for you." His hand indicated the tidy bundle in the bag. "That alone took months of planning and work. It looks to have been cast from your very body!"

Atop a great many other items in the bag rested a gleaming breastplate fashioned of shining metal with filigreed designs, shaped to resemble Tinna's curves. Underneath, folded neatly into two heavy rectangles, lay a long-sleeved hauberk and leggings of chain mail lined in linen of red—the finest mail she'd ever seen, each link smaller than her pinkie nail. Scaled knee and elbow copes were tucked in to one side, along with a pair of full gauntlets and vambraces to protect her lower arms. On the other side, two greaves, curved to the shapes of her calves, snugged up against the folds of the chain mail leggings, as well as two plates for her thighs. There were pauldrons, a chain mail coif hood to protect her head and a helm to go over that. Armors of this style were used in profusion two centuries prior by northern warriors. Of course, the common foot soldiers wore lighter, less cumbersome gambesons, reinforced around the shoulder and neck with mail, but the higher bloods who battled wore full armors; the mounted knights, entire suits of it.

War hadn't broken out since the line of Brithelle took the throne, and the old armors fell out of fashion. Lighter, better options took their place. The old kind was stored as displays in great houses, considered archaic and too unwieldy to wear in battle anymore. This one wasn't quite a full, traditional harness, but a blend of the old and

401

the older—which made it oddly modern. Neither an armor of plates gusseted together with mail, nor a suit of mail alone, like some of the older armors, it felt, despite its archaic appearance, forward-thinking in a way that Tinna couldn't put her finger on, though she marveled at it. Unique in its assembly, with interesting and clever ways to hinge and fasten the pieces together, the mail so fine it fell and rumpled like heavy velvet, as if knitted, with decorative designs worked into the pattern of the links. The metal, a light alloy, shone like silver of the highest quality. The sheer artistry took her breath away; the mechanics of it boggled her mind. It amazed her even more that they'd brought an entire harness of armor for a horse as well, and had even thought to include plumes of white and red to insert in the little holders atop two simple helms—one for her head and one for the head of her horse.

"It's a fine piece of work," Taneth muttered. She nodded, still struck by the idea of it. The entire harness sat atop the back side of a shield, which lay face down in the bag.

"They said they would be at Iromi. For what, I do not know. I suppose I'll have to wear this, just to please them. I can't see myself waddling about clanking and ringing like a monster made of cooking pots."

"It's not as awkward as the old armors. The chain is so exceptional! And the surcoat is very handsome. They even gave you your own insignia. That's something, isn't it?"

"It's disturbing." Tinna reached into the bag and removed the sleeveless, knee-length robe that went over the armor. The outer garments included a wide, dyed-leather belt and scabbard for a sword that would rest low on her hip. One half of the surcoat was red, the other white. She would be bisected by color. In the center of the chest and back, an insignia was deftly sewn onto the fabric. The artist had cut a rearing horse and a rearing dragon in each color and laid them opposite one another on the center seam, their tails entwined. On the white half, a red dragon; on the red, a white horse; each divergently rampant yet still connected. Below them, two green sprigs of oak leaves with acorns. The same design had been painted onto the shield. Tinna let it fall into her lap. The wind made the hem flap against her leg.

"This is insane."

"Indeed. I'm on the back of a dragon, looking at armor made for you to wear for a future battle nobody could possibly have known would occur. Insane doesn't quite cover it, my Dear." He sat back and took the surcoat from her, folding it carefully and placing it back into the bag, closing it. "I won't even go into the mechanics of flight—how the very fact that we are flying ought to be impossible— that dragons have four arms, in essence, and—" he paused, taking in Tinna's arched brow and amused smile. He sighed. "All I have to say is that I cannot wait to see you in that armor." He smirked playfully. Tinna laughed and shook her head. Their shared gaze was interrupted by the massive roar of the dragon upon which they rode, as he called out to his brethren to climb higher.

CHAPTER EIGHT – THE FIRST SACRIFICE

Eleran sprinted sure-footedly across uneven terrain, keeping his eyes closed, the better to trail a creature infinitely more proficient than he in this environment. The doe's fleet, fragile-looking legs covered far more ground, and in more graceful bounds, than he. He felt the heat of her breath, the beat of her heart, as she moved with little noise and disruption through the leafy forest on delicate, cloven hooves. He saw the forest through her eyes. Ahead, the eagle called, unseen.

The doe came upon a mare, standing exhausted, its head hung low. It barely moved at the arrival of the deer. Eleran slowed as the deer slowed, froze when she froze. At a small movement, she lifted her front left leg, ears forward, her muzzle moist and twitching. The horse heaved a deep sigh through its wide nostrils. Eleran approached and spooked the deer. She bolted away, zigzagging in bounds, flying over underbrush as if made of air, disappearing in a flash of white tail and spindly legs. Eleran scanned the area. Avria's mare, unfazed by his approach, allowed him to move to her side and rest a hand on her hot, moist neck. Sweat foamed around her saddle and girth, as well as under the bridle. Spittle had flown from her mouth and landed in dingy, greenish lumps on her shoulders and chest. Perspiration slicked her coat, making it curl and wave in a pretty pattern. She still breathed heavily. Avria was nowhere within eyeshot.

"Where is she?" Eleran asked the exhausted horse. She only twitched her ear and stamped a large blue-bottle away from her belly with her hind foot. He stepped back and closed his eyes, listening for Avria's essence, seeking, detecting the whorls of life that trailed behind her. He found the source, faint and hidden by the powerful life-force of a lone Karsu tree, a mere juvenile, its trunk only as twice as wide as the mare was long. It had yet to create the canopy that would block out the growth beneath it. Smaller trees, shrubs and saplings still surrounded it, vying for the light that the Karsu would soon obliterate, thereby dooming them all. The growth underneath it had concealed her.

Avria. Seems natural harm is exempt from the protection I put upon her, he mused. "Lucky girl," he said in a low voice.

A large knot distorted her forehead; a deep scrape ran alongside it and continued to her temple. A pool of blood had congealed in her left eye socket. A dried smear of it streaked her face.

Eleran felt his heart finally rest. He stooped beside her form. She lay on a bed of humus and leaf-litter, partially hidden beneath the leaves of a wild berry bush, its thorny limbs caught in her clothing. She lay on her back, her head turned slightly to the right, completely unconscious, her skin pale. He slid one hand under her back and the other under her knees, catching the thorns as he did. He lifted her up. The thorny tendrils clung to them both as he extricated her from the tangle. He carried her limp form to the clearing where her mare stood on dry, clear ground. He laid her down and sat with her, pulling her head and shoulders onto his lap. He rested his hand over her heart and closed his eyes. When his lids cracked open, the orbs within shone white.

Avria rested inside a makeshift tent made of a blanket covered in large fern-fronds. Eleran's connection to the energies had weakened from his exertions. He relied on his basic senses to monitor her while he puttered about outside, making a fire. She had awoken for a fleeting moment when he returned to the physical plane and looked down upon her. She had been barely coherent, her eyes glassy. He had seen her recognize him, a half-smile form on her lips. After a sore attempt at uttering his name in a gusty sigh of relief, she had slipped into a peaceful, heavy slumber. He heard soft snores emanating from the tent and smiled; the momentary image of her happiness at seeing his face still fresh on his mind.

He put a pile of sticks and twigs he'd gathered down in the spot he'd cleared for a fire. He'd found some rocks to encircle the pit. He piled up the pine-cones and dried leaves and twigs he'd gathered earlier, and used a quick summoning of his tired powers to bring them to flame. As the new fire sizzled and snapped, he started feeding it the thicker pieces of wood, concentrating on the task. He'd taken the saddle and bridle from Avria's horse and curried Shade down with handfuls of leaves and grass. The horse now stood quietly to the side of Avria's tent, chewing on dried wild grasses Eleran had gathered for her. She didn't try to move away, or wander. She stayed close to her bonded rider, who rested nearby.

Eleran was grateful for Shade and her blind trust in Avria, and he had stood by her for a good long moment, his hands on her crested neck, telling her in his own way, how thankful he was to her. The mare's eye studied him intently, the long lashes flickering, the orb taking in the form of the tall man. With that silent acknowledgement, Shade then turned her head and snorted out a long, relaxed breath, flicking her tail.

Eleran put together a stew from the dried food he'd grabbed from the storage room before he left the main lodge. He'd hardly eaten since he'd gone after her. After all the work and all the magic he had performed, he was spent. He needed energy, and so did Avria. He'd used some of his dwindling strength to conjure a deep trough into a large river stone for something to cook with and put it on the fire. He had fetched his water-bladder to fill up the depression with water.

He sat cross-legged and began adding in pieces of the dried stores, some venison jerky, a dried cake of made of autumn vegetables, and anything else he had left. The dried goods blossomed into a fragrant soup as the rock heated up. To the soup, he added more water and some pine nuts and mushrooms he'd found. He let the rock heat up just enough and then knocked down the fire to embers. He did not wish to advertise their location with a light and a pillar of smoke. The residual heat in the stone would cook the soup well enough.

Eleran sat against a tree and glanced at Avria, whose feet protruded from under the low tent. He was so tired. He leaned his head back and gazed up at the darkening sky. He felt his eyelids droop. He was too tired to fight it.

It came as a nagging feeling. His slowly returning strength perhaps helped him awake in time. It was pitch black around the camp when he opened his eyes. The embers had burned out, and the pit was black, but the stew steamed. It smelled good.

The horse snorted and raised its head; only the shine of her eyes, the points of her ears and part of her muzzle were visible to him in the light cast from the diffused and meager light from the stars. Her ears perked towards the darkness ahead, eyes following, nostrils flared. He could feel the horse's muscles tense, but she did not move. She merely observed. Eleran stood immediately, his neck and back sore from falling asleep as he had. He looked at the horse and then out to the blackness. Avria slept still, her breathing quiet and regular. A strange call sounded in the darkness, and another responded from the opposite direction. Eleran's hair stood up on the back of his neck. He stiffened, closed his eyes and took a deep breath.

As a steward of nature, Eleran knew, even in his current weakened state, to listen when it spoke to him. He knew by instinct that the call was not created by any creature of the wild. He reached for his staff and twisted the bottom into the leaf-litter and humus of the forest floor.

Tendrils of power immediately wicked into his staff, drawn from the soil, from the earth, the bedrock, from deep in the very core where stone boiled hot red. He felt it infuse his hand and travel through his body, up into his head, beaming from his eyes, through his fingers, down into his feet and out through his toes in an invisible web that illuminated the living things around him in varying tones of gold. They shimmered like the embers of a fire. The larger the creature, the more complicated the form of life, the hotter it glowed. Like a ripple in a pond, his fire extended outward, bringing into his awareness every creature, from tiny sleeping chipmunks to the cooler tones of a Karsu Owl, huge and still, eyes like two moons.

Then they appeared. One to his right, several hundred meters away, hunched behind a large stand of shrub trees. Then another, further away, standing directly in front of him by a large tree. And a third, slightly to the left and behind the second. Women, their shapes aptly revealed, strange glowing facsimiles, hollow-looking. They moved stealthily through the trees towards their campsite. In their hands, they carried the unmistakable shapes of wooden longbows. One woman was crouched, preparing to aim into the darkness, an arrow nocked.

"Erimus," Eleran whispered. "Vradimatu erimus ki." He felt physical pain as the earth taxed him for his purchase. He bit down on his inner cheek and held fast, whispering pained chants between gritted teeth. The ache was unbelievable. Again, the staff drew from the earth, but also from his being. More power traveled up into his hand, while his own essence seemed to be sucked into the staff and into the earth. The power traveled up to the raptor skull, the hematite eyes glowing suddenly like a lantern. The revealing spell changed now with the utterance of his words. The tone of power tapped by the staff glowed a hot, icy blue and shot through him so violently that his whole body jerked, his fingers and limbs tensed up like he was seizing. The power found its way to his feet and exploded along the earth, following the path of the previous ripple, devouring the soft gold and leaving pitch black in its wake. The circle of blue energy widened. The chipmunk bolted out of its nest, and the owl went reeling into the sky. The trees shuddered; the leaves trembled as the wave of power passed through them. Eleran screamed in agony, biting his lip so hard it began to bleed. He half-heard, half-felt the shriek of one in terrible pain, then another, and a third. They escalated to desperate screams of suffering, carrying across the night. The trees stilled themselves in order to hear the outcries, almost inhuman, hideous and raw. Then abrupt silence fell. The eyes of the staff went black. Not a creature stirred or called. None dared disturb the stillness. Shade had not stirred. She was alert, but remained close to Avria, her ears pointed towards the screams until they stopped.

Eleran lifted his staff out of the earth and fell to his knees, wheezing. He'd bitten through the skin of his cheek until he bled from his mouth. His hands trembled. He shuddered from weakness. With a final lurch forward, he fell onto his shoulder. His staff tipped and clattered over the fire pit, and everything fell into a stony silence.

* * * *

The sky opened up halfway home. Jestin's parents rode ahead; neither of them had spoken to him since they had come to Thamatoc for him. He looked up at the raindrops as they splotted down from the forest cover, happy to know that they would soon emerge from the trees to the more pastoral lands around Loshan. He was sick of trees, sick of his life. Sick of his righteous parents, who followed at the heels of a country bumpkin like Tinna, taking her side over that of their own son. They disappointed him bitterly, but he bit back his anger, conceding the truth at last to himself, finally, that the witch grandmother had dealt him out of her own plans completely. His eyes stung. He was humiliated. As the rain drenched him, he stewed.

As they always did, his parents veered eastward a bit to the town of Escel, a small farming village with a comfortable inn. The horses slogged through roads that flowed now like twin rivers of muck. His mother, looking tired and sodden, announced that she was looking forward to the dry heat of a fireplace. It was growing late. Twilight had finally given way to night as they entered the village. Mud caked the horses' bellies, the legs and hems of the riders' clothes. Astlin helped his wife down onto the wooden decking before the inn and waited for Jestin to get down on his own. Their personal servant took the horses to the livery. Jestin's guardian and servant followed him into the building.

The five of them pushed through the heavy door of the large, grey stone building and stepped into a common room, where the warmth from a central fireplace welcomed them. Kailine moved straight to the fire and pulled off her wet cape, draping it on the back of one of the many heavy chairs that circled the hearth. She sat down in the chair and sighed, her blue eyes reflective and distant. Jestin quietly slid into a chair nearby and glanced at her.

"Honors of honors, you are all back!" the innkeeper declared in a lyrical, girlish voice. A lithe blonde thing, willowy and beautiful, glided into the room, her arms akimbo. A stunning creature, golden and youthful, she knew these guests all too well; they stayed at least four times a year and spent a lot of gold to stay in the most comfortable apartments. "The weather is most dreary and wet; you must be chilled to the bone! We'll get you all set up with warm drinks and some towels to dry off your hair while I have Varini prepare your apartments. We will be serving dinner soon as well," she said. She gestured to the servant that accompanied them. He followed her as she sailed out in a rustle of layered ivory muslins. Astlin shook off his great coat and sat next to his wife, who stared blankly into the fire.

"Jestin," he muttered, "we haven't said much to you since we left Thamatoc, but I think it's time we talked about consequences."

"Ugh!" Jestin rolled his eyes and shifted in his chair. His mother's lips formed a tight, straight line. She glared into the fire.

"Don't scoff, young man! You have no idea what you've done."

"Yes I do. I'm quite clear on what I did, and I know it was the right thing."

"Supposing Avria makes it home again, can you expect her to forgive you for what you've done?"

"I don't need her forgiveness. I know I may never see her again. I just want to keep her away from that…peasant of a druid that dares to think himself worthy of her."

"Avria had a right to choose for herself, boy. It wasn't up to you to change her mind or her path."

"Oh, hang her path! What was her path except to live in that squalor among the horses and trees? You speak as if she had something desirable in her life and her future, being some nonsense wife to a weird freak from goodness knows where? She's a girl. So at least among the Thran she'll have respect! She'll gain rank and influence someday. I've guaranteed her a better future—certainly less bleak than the old one, imprisoned among the damned trees!"

"That's not your decision, Jestin," Kailine said between gritted teeth. "She does not perceive her world as you do. She loves

Thamatoc, loves her life. Now that horrible woman has her in her clutches. A creature so hideous she nearly broke Tinna's spirit—and seeing that Tinna's spirit is pretty much unbreakable, I must imagine that Avria's grandmother to be little shy of a monster! The stories Tinna told me!" Kailine shook her head and sat up straighter, her eyes glassy. Biting back tears, she turned and glared icily at her son. "You've delivered the girl you love to a future of brutal discipline, cruelty and a life without a shred of love. I hope you are happy with that decision Jestin!" she hissed. Rising with an icy glare, she stalked out of the common room, bustling in papery, damp silks to the stairs that led to their usual apartments. Astlin sighed and gripped his hands on his knees, blowing out through his lips and puffing out his cheeks. He then reached up and massaged the back of his neck. Outside, lightning flashed and thunder rumbled. Rain pelted the windows. They had arrived just in time.

"It'll be a while before your mother will be able to look at you or even speak to you with any civility, Jestin. If you're half the man I hope you are, you'll suffer through it and somehow try to make up for what you've done. Maybe one day, your mother will forgive you."

"What of you, Father? What of your forgiveness?" Jestin asked, his words tinted with derision.

Astlin stood. He paused and sighed, gazing down at his son, his face unreadable. Without a word, he simply turned away and followed Kailine.

Jestin sat in his chair for a while longer, until a servant brought him a thick glass goblet of hot cider infused with fragrant cloves, which he sipped absentmindedly, his eyes locked somewhere beyond the fire and the inn. Lightning lit the leaded glass, turning it a hot blue. A moment later, thunder boomed. It shuddered Jestin to the marrow.

The silence of the common room amplified the ticking of the large cabinet clock, like a mallet hitting a log. The pendulum swung languidly, lazily, as if it didn't have enough momentum to make each swing, but inevitably, it clicked and swung back. It mesmerized Jestin for a moment, until the mysterious cogs and workings began to whirr and rattle in the casing, and the clock bellowed out a deafening single chime to mark the half-hour.

His guard had fallen sound asleep, and so had everyone else. He moved quietly through the main room to the inn's library, which supplied guests with books and information if needed. He lit a candle and used it to search the shelves. There, he found a map. A vague

411

one, but it demarcated some of the local settlements. Those that had been destroyed years ago someone had crossed out with big red Xs. Then he found what he was looking for—a road south. He couldn't think of anywhere else to go. He knew nobody outside of Loshan except for the people at Thamatoc, and he had worn out his welcome there. The only other place to go was where Avria's grandmother was taking her. At least, if he went there, Avria could advocate for him. Which she would do, as soon as she realized that she had no other friends there.

He needed to get to the border of Thran, and then find his way to Ymnoth. A good library would have a broader map. He gazed at the one he had and saw Araki settlements marked on it. He thought of Taneth and of the other wisemen he met with sometimes from other clan villages. Some of those settlements had very good libraries. This was the opportunity he sought. He rolled up the map and put it in his coat. With a puff, he blew out the candle. Thunder still crashed and rumbled like great boulders colliding, and the rain hissed against the roof and pelted the windows. With a reluctant sigh, he strode to the door, and with a tightening of the lips and a determined frown, he opened it and stalked outside.

The livery was shut down for the night, the horses tucked into their respective stalls. No lamps burned inside. He slogged through the muck at the entrance and opened the door, ducking into the stable. The coach horses were tied in a tidy row along one wall; each one occupied a narrow slot. Many of the rumps tilted to one side, a back hoof cocked, all relaxed and sleeping. The livery smelled fresh and pleasant. Straw crunched beneath his feet. Most of the time, the Araki used dried mosses to line their horse stalls, only using expensive straw for foaling stalls. He liked the way straw smelled. His movement awoke a few of the horses, and he heard some tentative snorts. In the darkness, he could make out the faint shapes of curious ears perking forward at him.

He had no horse of his own. He had ridden a variety of creatures at Thamatoc and he had three of his own at home, none of which he really cared much about. All he had to do was pick a horse out of the ones in the loose boxes. He unhooked its bridle from the side of the stall door and put it on the horse. He then slung the thin Araki-style saddle onto its back. He tugged on the girth quickly and led the horse out of the stall and into the corridor, squeezing the tired animal out through the inset man-door. He mounted in the rain and turned the horse to the road that led out of the village. He would have to take the same road they had come in on for a while, watching diligently in the darkness for the turn that his map indicated on his right, leading southwest. He would have to do some creative navigating, but he knew if he watched carefully and kept his head, he would find his way to Brehrach, an Araki settlement northwest of Thamatoc. From there, he would find his way to Thran.

* * * *

In the early moments of dawn, when the birds had returned in full song, Avria found Eleran as he lay. She used her strength to roll him onto his side. She covered him with his cloak and balled up her blanket under his head, then ate some of the tepid soup that remained waiting in the stone bowl. She felt strangely well, despite the crusted scab on her temple. She was so happy to see Eleran. Upon waking, she had faintly recollected seeing his face, but she couldn't have said whether that was real or not; she knew now that it was. She stooped at his side and placed her hand on his face. He felt feverish. He twitched and groaned.

"Eleran," she whispered. He turned onto his back and cracked his eyes at her, a soft smile appearing on his face before transforming into a grimace of pain. She waited as he dealt with his discomfort and woke up some more. He sighed.

"We need to get out of here," he grunted, sitting up with concerted effort.

"I found your staff on the ground. I put over with the tack. Thank you Eleran, for coming after me."

"We need to move out of here," he repeated. "I had to use a forbidden power last night to dispatch three Thran rangers. Their equipment is still out there; we need to collect it and get back on the road again. Your path of escape was far from discreet."

"I didn't have time for stealth," Avria laughed uneasily.

"I know. When the first group of rangers does not report back, a second will follow. We need to go."

"You need a horse."

"I cannot summon one. I've depleted my powers." He got to his feet laboriously and stretched his back. Neither had taken the time to greet one another in the way they wanted to. Eleran was so preoccupied with getting them out of there, and Avria feared for his state. His hands shook. Only his desire to protect her from being taken away propelled him forward. Otherwise, she had no idea where he drew his strength from; he looked drawn and pale, older even.

413

"We can find one. Ride behind me for now. I'll go and fetch the things you mentioned. Where are they?" Eleran reached out and wrapped his arms around her suddenly, gathering her in. She gasped and fell into his embrace. He leaned on her heavily and wavered on his feet.

"I'm so glad you're here," she confessed, tears filling her eyes.

"I am glad I found you." They held one another for a long moment, breathing in one another's warmth, clutching each other in relief. Avria pushed away from him, and he winced.

"My muscles feel like I've been stampeded by moropus," he laughed uncomfortably. "You'll have to content yourself with being in love with an ordinary man for a day or so, until I recover my strength to reconnect with the powers. I may have angered someone by doing what I did... it may take a while for me to return to normal."

Avria snorted and shook her head. "Where do I find those things?"

Avria's spine tingled as she approached the site. She felt it before she saw it. The hairs on her arms and neck rose as if a lightning storm threatened. A distinct aroma hung in the air, like burnt flesh. She found the first ranger, a pile of blackened ash with fragments of bone. A jawbone rested atop the second. Their clothing, bows and other weapons remained intact. She shivered as she picked up the items, taking most of the clothes and covering the rest along with the ashes under some dead vegetation, as Eleran had instructed her. She swallowed hard as she picked her way through the trees, dreading the next pile. It was barely imaginable that these little heaps of blackened ash and bone had been living women only hours ago. She carried her armload back to camp and threw them down. Her face expressed her shock and her horror to Eleran.

His eyes darkened, and he shook his head, his face waxen, and his eyes sunken.

"I had no strength to offer a drawn-out, fair fight, Avria. I had enough in me to summon a magical immolation spell. It nearly took me with it." She heard shame in his tone.

She shook her head and looked down at the items. She picked through them, taking some of the clothing. The rangers wore leggings over a pair of thin breeches. Avria couldn't bring herself to take any of the undergarments like the breeches or the shifts. She took a set of leggings and one heavy knit tunic of itchy wool, folding the spare ones and packing them away into the rangers' supply packs.

414

These she tied to the front of her saddle. Then she pulled the leggings over her own black breeches, removing the riding skirt she'd worn for days and folding it into one of the packs. The woolen tunic hung to her knees, so she had to belt it with a piece of rope. While she packed up everything she could find, Eleran ate the rest of the soup and drank all of their water. He was listless and heavy, and he fell asleep against her back as they rode away. Her horse was small but stalwart, and she managed to carry the extra weight, but Avria knew she couldn't for long.

They walked as much as they could, but Eleran grew weaker and weaker. His efforts to save her had drained him of everything. He had barely eaten since, and Avria became the primary provider and caretaker for the following days as they rode along an unknown path. She found berries and other foods she recognized in the forest, saving the dried goods she'd taken from the rangers. She hoped to find a village or settlement somewhere. Eleran needed real rest and real food. And they needed a fresh horse. She could trade the crossbows for one, but only if they could find people. They simply had to reach a settlement.

* * * *

If living amongst the horse-folk had provided any advantage for Jestin, it had taught him to ride. He had to concede that even if he hadn't achieved the mastery in the saddle of his so-called cousins, he had learned enough to navigate questionable terrain and slick conditions with some measure of skill. He took pride in knowing how to let his horse negotiate the forest but at the same time keeping the animal engaged and paying attention to what he needed him to do. He suffered only minor scratches from low-hanging branches and a scrape on his leg from skirting too close to a broken tree limb that jutted out into the narrow path. He'd veered off the main roads to find the Araki horse-path that would lead him to the settlement.

His horse skidded down a steep hill, causing a mudslide; however, they managed to ride it down to the bottom without incident. There he found the telltale horse path he sought. He steered his horse back southward, hunching forward over the neck. Rainwater rolled off of his sodden greatcoat in sheets. By the time the downpour tapered to a misty sprinkle, it was almost morning. His horse had acquired a subtle hitch in its gait, a minor limp in the front left leg. He'd stayed inside the oaks for half an hour, riding between two cemeteries. He knew he was near. He rode into an Araki settlement at the crack of dawn and dismounted under the founder's tree.

Brehrach looked very much like Thamatoc; however, it had many of its own distinguishing characteristics—different gates, different carvings on the faces of the lodges, bigger lodges, and a larger circle of them. He was met by a lean fellow who seemed to take his arrival in stride. Glancing at Jestin over his shoulder as he walked from the stable to the main lodge, he said: "The relay has already come through. All able riders were dispatched and maps sent to at least eleven settlements west of here." He stepped through the inset door of the main lodge and shut it behind him. Jestin frowned and left his horse standing in the forum. Exhausted, it didn't budge. Rain dripped from its muzzle. Its sopping mane plastered its neck. Jestin crossed to the lodge and battered the door. A woman of about sixty opened it and twisted her lip at him.

"Who're you?" she asked.

"Jestin… of Thamatoc." The woman immediately did a head-to-toe appraisal of the drenched, disheveled creature at their door and arched her brow dubiously.

"Thamatoc? Indeed…"

"I was visiting Arthrios. I'm sort of a relative to Tinna, part of her extended family."

"What are you doing here then?"

Her attitude puzzled him. Why wouldn't he be here? It was a logical stop if he had been coming from Arthrios. He'd thought this through. Little did Jestin know that his mother and father had kept any knowledge they had of this situation to themselves, and did not tell him any of it. He was utterly mystified.

"Well for one, my horse is gone lame. And I was looking for directions from here. A map perhaps."

"You were given no map? How can you join the Araki army if you have no map?" she asked, her brow furrowed.

He fell speechless, not knowing how to respond to this seemingly randomly cobbled conclusion. He opened his mouth to let whatever came to his mind first spill over his lips, but she interrupted him. "They're a long way ahead. The Thamatoc people. Tinna and Taneth are probably already there. From what I understand, they went on the backs of dragons! Imagine that! You being a relative, maybe it's not so surprising to you, but to us—well, it's more than strange! Most of our leadership left to join them, too, but on the backs of horses. Nothing quite as extraordinary as your village leader—but she isn't exactly conventional, is she? You've got some

416

riding to do. You'll need a new horse. I'm not sure if we have any good ones left, honestly. Well, either way, once you have a horse, you should find them, no problem. And you have no map, correct?"

Jestin's head spun. He furrowed his brow and mustered up a response as vague as he could possibly make it in hopes of getting more details from this woman;

"I have a map, not the map. I've been away. I've missed most of the…events. They must have been in quite a hurry to leave without me," he laughed uncomfortably.

"Oh. Well, I am confident our Wiseman knows where you're supposed to go. Get your map and come into the main hall." She shut the door in his face. Jestin hated how simple these people were sometimes—how rude and coarse—but he had to suffer with it if he wanted to find out what was going on. He walked to his exhausted horse and pulled the map he'd taken from the inn's limited library from his saddle packs—a rudimentary, outdated thing that showed a peppering of human and Araki settlements around the northern edge of the forestlands. The human ones mostly didn't exist anymore.

He strode to the door and pushed it open, feeling for a moment that he'd entered the main lodge at Thamatoc, half expecting to see Rigerd's grizzled face or to glimpse Taneth with his expression of permanent puzzlement, bustling to the main hall to teach the little ones to read letters. He felt a painful sensation of regret in the center of his chest, but it passed quickly. He closed the door and looked for a short moment at the most familiar sight of an Araki lodge. Above him, the massive wooden rafters held up a latticework of thick wooden poles that held a load of shale and a huge pack of earth. Root systems had winnowed their way through the dense construction, but caused little damage. He knew that above him, the forest floor still grew, and anyone riding along would see the earth suddenly end in a steep drop, exposing a village sunken into the ground below, the dome of the founder's tree covering nearly the whole circle. The rider would realize they stood on the roof of the main village lodge, or in the case of this village, one of a circle of seven lodges, with a wide path between two of them leading out into the trees. The lodge-fronts all faced the circle, each lodge covered in forest floor, partially underground, all connected by tunnels—the chimneys cleverly concealed amid the riot of forest growth.

Jestin headed down one of the two long corridors, past the succession of doors to private apartments, connecting tunnels to other lodges and store rooms. He headed to the very back of the lodge, where he would inevitably find a huge community hall furnished with clumsy furniture—long tables and benches for dining, the immense hearth. He knew he was in the main lodge because the huge fireplace was surrounded by ugly, old-fashioned, heavy upholstered chairs, where leaders met over pipes after dinner amid the never-fading reek of wood-smoke and venison drippings.

There he found a young man of nineteen or so who held his left arm, scaled for the body of a child, curled up against his chest. He wore robes like Taneth's. This is their Wiseman? A boy his age? He is younger than Hanru.

Jestin realized that this young man must have recently graduated from Taneth's academy of Lemoram. He had completed his schooling faster because he did not have the option to prolong it, as Hanru had. Jestin shook his head and handed the fellow his map. The boy accepted it with his good hand and shook it open, looking bewildered. "Drethi says you need to go to Iromi to meet the others. And that you are family to Tinna?"

"Yes," Jestin muttered, speaking without any idea what he was doing. The boy nodded.

"Good. Well, your map isn't quite the right scale--too small an area. We need to broaden it. Luckily, I was paying attention when the relay riders arrived, and I got a good look at the maps before they went off to the next leg. I can show you exactly where you need to go. Let me get my atlas. I'll draw you something crude but accurate. It'll get you there. In the meantime make yourself comfortable. Drethi is looking into getting you a mount with good legs; yours will heal well enough here in the care of the horse-master."

Jestin wanted to ask so many questions but instead sat down in one of the leaders' chairs, his mind ablaze with speculation. He tried to understand what his plan was, or what it had been; but he had none. He didn't even know why he wanted to go back south. Did he expect to find Avria? He did not know. He did know that something was going on, that Tinna was involved and that, possibly, so was Avria. He could think of no reason that Tinna would leave Thamatoc now, with Avria in the custody of her grandmother, unless she intended to go after her and try to take her back again. He leaned back in his chair and pinched his chin, impatient for the young Wiseman to make him his new map, anxious to be on his way—but glad to be, for the moment, dry.

CHAPTER NINE – THE SECOND SACRIFICE

Iromi, once a rather large human settlement and, unfortunately, the capitol of a small duchy, had earned itself a quick and devastating burning from fleets of dragons twenty years prior. The burning had reduced the city to an independent community with non-aristocratic leadership and a toughened population. A neat patchwork of crops had replaced the booming population of the outer settlements, and the leadership of the town had knocked down the sprawling ruins of the burnt manor and built for themselves a smaller set of fine residences to occupy the center of the town. As the dragons descended through the graying clouds, Tinna could make out the old footprint of the city carved into the land, probably invisible from the ground but quite clear from the air. What remained of the city was now reduced to an eighth of its original size. Despite all the new growth and rebuilding, the old roads and city boundaries had etched the city's past into the landscape like an old set of runes.

The dragons did not bother to hide themselves. Skye's squeal of delight cut through the thundering gusts of wind when they folded in their wings and dropped. Stretching them out again, ballooning the membranes, they slowed their descent with a stomach-curdling lurch and leveled out only meters above undulant fields of golden wheat. The air disturbed by the dragons created a pattern of whorls in the crops, causing the heavy-topped wheat to sway and bend in a beautiful dance. The dragons found footing just at the edge of a sheep pasture. They landed surprisingly smoothly, gliding into a run, and then to a stop. They walked energetically towards the town and stopped at the city gates. Tinna slid down first. Taneth handed down the packs. The others dismounted and thanked their steeds.

The dragons bade them a quick farewell and turned back towards the pasture, scattering a flock of sheep as they took to the air. They did so just in time to avoid a group of militia that poured from the main gate only moments after they'd turned around. The men ran at full tilt, dragon-pikes ready to fly. A large man approached

419

the dismounted riders sporting a shaved head, a grizzle of a beard, wide shoulders and a palpable rage.

"Who brings those murderous dragons into our midst?"

The group of men turned their weapons on the Araki. Tinna merely sighed and hoisted a pack onto her shoulder.

"Oh, the five of us have come here to burn down your city of course, to decimate your population and bring you ruination," she muttered, overtly bored with their alarm. She pushed her way through the militiamen.

The leader turned and shouted at her. "You bring them back to destroy us all again!"

"For twenty peaceful years, they have harmed not a soul, even though people still hunt them. If they wanted to, they could reduce every human being in the world to cinders, rid the world of us forever—yet they haven't." She paused, and made a puzzled face. "Hmm," she pondered deliberately. She then rolled her eyes intolerantly and turned away again and started walking, shouting, "They have left us here and gone. You have nothing to fear."

Taneth followed, as well as Phenmal and the two young people. Tinna had proceeded quite a ways up the main road before the militia followed. They turned and looked skywards before lowering their pikes and straggling back into the small city.

The new buildings were obviously not made for style but for utility. The Iromians had attempted to restore some of the older buildings that managed to survive the burnings, but for the most part, they'd lined the streets with simple daub and wattle edifices to which they had applied a variety of paints and roofing material salvaged from other buildings. A party of outsiders stood at the top of the main street before the City Master's manor. They did not fit in this busy place. It was a place for decent, hardworking farmers and tradesman. These people were not such.

Tinna stopped short, and Taneth let the heavy harness of mail fall to the ground. The nine people stood at the gate of the small compound, all garbed in black robes. Chaiva, it seemed, or some other type of mystic. Not Keepers but of the Keepers. They bowed shallowly at Tinna. Then one of them, a lanky woman of young age, stepped aside and gestured for Tinna to pass through the gate. The small contingency of Araki picked up their heavy charges and struggled past the silent reception committee, outnumbered. The nine followed them inside, where the City Master stood, a man of about forty years with a large belly and two thin little legs. He had a long beard and tied his graying hair back in a tail. He wore common clothes, in spite of his elevated status. He bowed to Tinna, eyes glancing nervously at the company of nine that stood behind them.

"Na-Ai-Tinna of Thamatoc, we have been expecting you." Tinna glanced back at her husband and shook her head subtly before facing the City Master again.

"I thank you for welcoming me—but please dispense with the Thran appellations. Tinna will do. We have appointed this town to be the meeting place for our mounted army. I am not s—"

"Yes, so our other guests have informed me," the City Master said nervously. "They warned us about your arrival on dragons, but frankly my militia captain would not trust the dragons to behave and defied my orders to stand down. I hope his actions did not offend."

"Master, I understand the Captain's concern. We all do. But you must trust our word that the dragons only mean to assist us in this crisis."

"I understand. I cannot say I can am fully comfortable with the idea, but I will take your word, Madame." He straightened himself and gestured for her to follow. "Leave your bags there. I will have someone bring them to your rooms." Behind her were two muffled clanks and relieved sighs. He led them inside. Tinna gave Phenmal a curious glance and walked on. Phenmal merely shrugged and followed.

To Tinna's astonishment, the City Master had already assigned areas for the riders to gather and had set aside space for Tinna and Taneth to spread out and plan. He had arranged for a set of offices in one of the four surviving stone fortification's drum bastion towers overlooking the lower croplands, where the riders would arrive. The sleeping accommodations for her group were precise in number and fully prepared to receive a married couple, two single gentlemen and a young lady. This puzzled Tinna utterly. She had given no prior notice of her arrival. None. The Iromians even provided heavy, warm outerwear for the group in consideration of the cooler temperatures at these higher elevations.

Tinna took little time to appreciate the quality of her and Taneth's rooms, but she noted that the sitting area overlooked the edge of town and part of the field where the riders would lodge. She turned to the City Master, who showed them in like a common servant, and asked if she could see the offices. As they walked behind him through the waxing evening, which had turned rainy and cold, Tinna turned to Taneth and shook her head. "Did you by chance send anything to Iromi to announce that we were coming?" she asked in a strained whisper.

He shrugged. "No. But I think the presence of the Keeper-mystics might have something to do with it," he replied with a touch of sarcasm.

"We never told them, either."

"Did you?" Taneth turned and looked over his shoulder where Phenmal quietly followed, gazing thoughtfully at the slick, shining cobbles as he walked. His pale head turned upwards and his glassy eyes blinked.

"I certainly did not. You keep looking at me, but I have had nothing to do with this. However, it doesn't surprise me to see them here. The Keepers know what goes on in the world. They obviously approve of our presence here, and have provided us with support in their own way." Tinna glanced back at Phenmal, then at Taneth. Droplets of rain soaked into her curls. Taneth nodded and pursed his lips. She faced forward just in time to climb the steps to an old fort.

Phenmal wasted no time in setting to work unpacking and unfurling his maps and setting up his desk area. He sat down to pore over his strategies. The round room featured a semi-circle of curved cabinetry and desks built right up against the wall, a fireplace and a round woven carpet on the floor depicting an old knight on destrier in full gallop, sword aloft. A round table occupied the center, which Phenmal and Taneth immediately would cover in papers and maps. Soft chairs hunkered on the wall opposite the desks. During the day, light would pour in from the narrow meurtriere windows that ringed the wall. Enclosed now in leaded glass, they presented but a series of narrow, black slits in the walls. The stairs led down and up on the near wall, centered between the chairs. It was a large, comfortable space, and all theirs.

"The stairs lead up to the wall-walk, which is still sound, and you can climb the back of the tower steps to the top for a clear view," the host explained. They thanked him kindly, and he left them to their devices.

At midnight, candles still burned in the sconces in the tower. A short night of sleep for everyone, and come morning they were at it again. Tinna sat with Phenmal a good part of the day, talking in mumbles and whispers, while Taneth tried to find some usefulness in the nine Keepers. They surprised him with the many ideas and unexpected resources they offered, and Taneth found himself directing them with logistics—having tents set up, temporary shelters and fenced areas for the horses, looking for places to store the unexpected supplies that arrived by dray from seemingly nowhere. Hanru and Skye acted as helpers to the adults and kept busy running to and fro with messages, directions and other, more mundane errands like asking for food or refreshment. Tinna planned for a moderately sized force. She imagined three to four thousand at most, assuming ten or so riders from each settlement. They began to work based on this assumption, giving them something to do while they waited for the first of the riders to arrive.

The Keeper nine hovered about in general silence in their black robes. They followed Tinna wherever she went, for the most part, one or two occasionally splitting away to arrange something with Taneth. They whispered to one another but hardly spoke a word to Tinna or her retinue. Even when dealing with Taneth, they let him do most of the talking, while they communicated in gestures and actions with a sporadic, soft-spoken word or two.

The second day after their arrival found Tinna in her most frequented spot in the tower offices looking at Phenmal's updated map of the human army's position. The dragons continued to reconnoiter along the great valley, watching the progress of the armies from on high. They reported their findings to Phenmal by making low, sweeping passes within range of Phenmal's keen mind during the night, when they were less likely to be seen by Iromi's people. Their flight patterns appeared innocuous and random to the growing forces of Thran, as they arrived. The dragons subtly took stock of the arrivals.

The human army moved slowly, led by a grizzled old Duke and infamous dragon-hunter from the north countries, who attempted to boost his numbers by recruiting among the farming towns he passed through on his way across the plains. According to intelligence from the dragons, the Thran army remained close to Chrotrioth for now, while more troops arrived from various parts of the country. Tinna wondered what the King was doing, if anything at all. It seemed odd to her that in this crisis, he had been utterly absent—not even a mention by the Keeper nine.

None of the nine had bothered to follow her into the room today; Tinna enjoyed the respite, until the door opened and the long female walked up to her and produced a parchment. Tinna took it, and unrolled it.

The woman exited without uttering a word.

"It turns out the Keepers will provide arms and supplies for the riders as well. Uniforms, weapons, new tack, packs, food, carts and draught beasts," she mumbled in astonishment. "They say they will begin to arrive as the riders do."

Taneth shook his head in bewilderment and took the parchment. "Who are these people?" he blurted.

Hanru shrugged.

Skye arched her brows matter-of-factly. "I don't care who they are, they're helping. That's all that is important."

Tinna couldn't argue with Skye.

* * * *

Jestin did not enjoy cooperative weather or riding conditions. The rains, the relay traffic and the riders that followed had beaten the road to muck, nearly obliterating the thin strip of grass and pebbles that ran along the center of the road between the ruts, where cart wheels had churned the puddles to a quagmire. Jestin's horse yanked a hoof from the sucking mud and retrieved it with a glop. He steered her towards the side of the road to rest. She was a small thing, as horses went. Her slender, narrow frame and high withers left him sore in the inner thighs. The deep, sunken areas above her eyes and the graying around her muzzle and forehead spoke of her age. He dismounted and tied her to a tree, sat down on a road marker and tucked his hands under his arms. A trio of riders blasted by at full gallop, sending clods of muck flying through the air. One struck Jestin's shoulder with a painful thud. He slid his face into his hands and felt the burn of reality in his eyes. His frustration, his anger, his regret, his pain, his jealousy…

He swallowed his feelings and straightened himself. He needed a break. He needed to think. He needed to plan. He stood up and stretched, turning to see a sign in the road. He studied the granite slab; read the figures carved in its surface.

ESRU
DEVORELL PRIMARY ACADEMY
2 Dreths
SOUTH ROAD AFTER CLIFF.

The prospect of a non-Araki human community appealed to him. Esru was an old town, Devorell a children's academy. He hoped it still stood. He led his horse on, trying to balance himself on the ruined center strip. Two more fast riders passed him as he trudged along. Their horses seemed to fly over the sludgy terrain, while he and his horse skidded and stumbled. He saw a tall granite cliff that jutted from a steep hillside and crowded the edge of the road. Across

424

from it, another road split off to the left. It looked a little less traveled than the main road, still in active use but not beset with traffic. He led his horse onto that road, where he found solid earth underfoot. He mounted and rode.

A few miles down this drier road, he came to Esru. Behind it, a massive hulk of stone and mortar dominated the side of a large, steep hill. Tall, cantilevered houses of stone and lumber and brick huddled together around the main market square, from which radiated a series of dark, narrow streets, where covered walkways connected the upper floors of the houses, and the streets simply tunneled their way through. The square itself was in full market. A cluster of ramshackle kiosks cluttered the pavement, offering goods from surrounding towns and farms. The villagers dressed warmly against the weather, the women's gowns heavy, quilted things hemmed in mud. They paid little heed to Jestin, as he rode up. His feet hit the cobbles with a thump. He tied his mare to a hitching post near the market entrance, in an annex where other horses and ponies were tied. He stepped into the street and looked about, taking in the busy scene. A small herd of sheep jostled him on their way to a pen at the edge of the square. Their wool, laden with lanolin-scented rain water, soaked the legs of his breeches like woolen sponges as they brushed up against him. Their loud bleating and sharp smell proved almost too much for him to bear.

He followed the shepherd into the thick of the crowd, weaving through the townspeople, looking for the source of a savory aroma that had set his stomach roaring. He found himself drawn to a large kiosk with a leather-covered awning. Underneath it, several men gathered in front of the service counter where they bought and imbibed warm spirited cider and ate pretty, half-moon-shaped meat pies. He went to the counter, ordered the like and paid, nodding his head awkwardly in greeting to the gruff traders, who barely acknowledged him. They resumed a conversation his arrival had interrupted.

"Zibran says that the army's marched halfway down past Quonath, not far south of Suthervale. They'll come close to the border soon enough."

"And then what?" another interjected with a dubious laugh. "They say the Thran have at least two legions at Chrotrioth. Ten thousand, at least."

"The Araki have been going out in waves to a town near the smoking mountain."

425

"Hah! Araki! So send a few hundred riders to save Oromoii? Hedge your bets, my friends! We'll see ourselves occupied by those savage creatures, no doubt."

"I saw more than a few hundred ride by Avrell only three days ago. So I venture we'll have a decently sized force. If we packed our bags and left today, I'll wager, we could stand with the Araki before they march to Chrotrioth. I'd rather die in battle than fall subject to their rule," another man bellowed, downing his cup of ale.

"You're going?" the eldest said, his face shocked beneath the stubble and road-grime.

"Aye," the younger one said decisively. "No man able to carry a blade should sit by and wait for the inevitable. Our army is not large, and we are capable. It is our obligation to stand with our fellow countrymen. I and several of the hands from Losleth logging farms have decided to go. We have the blessing of the landlord. He and his own son are leaving as well."

"Indeed?"

Jestin eavesdropped with care, keeping his face lowered over his hot cider, his ears open.

The young man nodded, and the eight men fell into pensive silence for a moment.

"When do you embark?" Jestin suddenly asked the young fellow. The others gazed at him in puzzlement.

"Sometime tomorrow. We're waiting for a few more fellows from the farm to join us."

"I will ride with you if I may," Jestin blurted. "I have a map to the town where they are gathering, it is called Iromi. I also have some funds."

The kiosk owner's hand reached over the counter, holding the meat pie Jestin had ordered, still steaming from the pan. Jestin took the plate, picked the pie up by its light cloth wrapping and bit into it, hissing at the explosion of juicy, tasty lava that filled his mouth.

The boy nodded at him. "Why not? The more the merrier, I say."

A moment of quiet contemplation passed, while the men ate and drank.

Discussion resumed when another pair of men appeared to purchase the fare and learned that the young man intended to follow the Araki into battle. Jestin's volunteerism inspired more. Soon five of the original eight and both newcomers spoke of riding out.

Jestin followed the boy back to a large empty barn where they met two more boys, both young and idealistic. They welcomed Jestin with immediate camaraderie. Since he carried no weapons and little money and rode an old horse, he wondered how they thought him sincere in any way, but as more poor farm workers began to arrive with nothing but the clothes on their backs, he reasoned that if they could leave their homes and jobs at moment's notice, then his own behavior must not seem odd to them. Pleased to find a way to get where he needed to go safely and in the company of others, he fell into his role.

* * * *

Avria worried about Eleran. He had sunk into a strange, feverish state, which made traveling nigh impossible. She had belted him to her waist so he wouldn't slide off, and poor Shade grew more and more exhausted. Finding a narrow trade path marked by stone plinths that indicated a settlement nearby, she sighed with relief. "I've never heard of Taruttee. What an odd name!"

As they approached the town, she dismounted and held Eleran's leg, letting Shade lead the way through the farmland that edged the settlement. Two young ladies and a young man working in a field spotted her. Only their heads and shoulders appeared above the swaying wheat. Avria slowed, offering them a meek smile. They stood and watched her, implements frozen, eyes following her distrustfully. She couldn't tear her eyes from them. They were so small, like children.

Taneth had told her the story years ago, how for centuries, whenever a human gave birth to a small one, the child was taken and delivered to an Auberge town to be raised among their own 'kind'. Taneth grew visibly angry as he told the story. If the small ones were of a certain 'kind' why were they born to average-sized people?

"You mean to say that if I had been born little, they would have carted me off to live with strangers?"

"Well, if we lived in Loshan, perhaps, or another human settlement. I don't think Araki do that, though I've never seen little people among us, now that you mention it." Taneth shook his head and frowned. "Of course, things have changed quite a bit since the burnings. Who's to say if it's still done?" He shrugged, returning to his work.

Avria nodded in greeting, forcing her eyes forward to the town. At her approach, the people paused in their daily routines to watch as she walked Shade and Eleran into the town center, a lovely oval space with a central fountain, the only thing that made any sound

427

besides the clippety-clop of her horse's hooves on the cobbles. She stopped, feeling strange. She turned to look at the people staring at her, and for a moment, she forgot about Eleran, until he slipped from the saddle and fell in a groaning heap on the ground. She gasped and dropped to her knees.

"Oh, Arak! I am so sorry, Eleran! Gods! What's wrong with you?" She forgot the little people now, seeing Eleran's pallid skin and sunken eyes. She clasped his face in her hands, realizing at this moment that perhaps his state was graver than she had imagined. A sheen of cold sweat slicked his face.

A shadow fell across him. She looked up to see a late-aged gentleman and a young woman who slid up next to him. They looked at her quizzically.

"I don't know what's wrong with him. He's been getting worse for days. I don't know what to do!" She felt tears filling up her eyes as helplessness consumed her.

"He's a seer? Nay. A bearer. Borne himself sick it seems," the gentleman sighed with an air of resignation. "I have no idea where we'll put him. We have no beds for ungainly big people."

"He can stay at the inn, Father. Stop being dramatic!"

"He needs a sheltered space, Manehra. He's consumed by the essences, paying back a debt he could not afford. What sort of magic has this man performed?" Avria stood, unable to answer the man's question. The older man gestured to a group of four strapping young men who had been loading barrels onto a cart. Like everyone else, they had stopped to watch. Now they hopped down and swaggered over.

A serious-looking young fellow led them. He appraised Avria with an appreciative gaze before turning his attention to the older man.

"Master Gavorre, what need do you have of us? My father expects his barrels delivered within the hour. Then I have to get back to the barracks."

The older man looked up at the taller fellow and smiled. Master Gavorre had silvery white hair and a long face that reminded Avria of her father. He wore a pair of leather breeches and a fine, quilted vest over a tunic of cream linen. He seemed an ordinary citizen. In Thamatoc, one could identify a person's role by garb and markings. Here, everyone dressed casually, ambiguously.

"Offrin, pick this lummox up and bring him into the stockroom of the shop for me, then you may return to your task. I'm certain your father will understand."

428

The young man nodded. He and the others positioned themselves around Eleran and managed to lift his listless form off the ground.

"Manehra, run over and make up a bed for him if you would, Dear—on the bay table; that would be best."

The girl took off running on her short legs, her golden hair flouncing as she circled the slow-moving group that hauled Eleran towards what looked like an Apothecary's shop. The man turned to Avria.

"Give your horse to Ilvo and join me at the shop."

"Who's Ilvo?"

The Apothecary pointed to a building directly across from them; a livery stable. The doors stood open. "Go on."

Avria nodded and took her horse's reins. Her horse followed, tired and hungry.

The stable master looked displeased to have a full-sized horse appear at his door. "You expect me to fit that in here?" he gestured behind him where a few ponies peered out over half-doors, munching hay.

"She's not that big. As our horses go, she's on the smaller side. She's got a bit of the Thran desert horse in her. You can put her in your paddock, if need be. She won't wander."

Ilvo eyeballed her for a moment, and then sighed. "You're Araki, right?"

Avria nodded. "I suppose it'll be a good horse, then. It is your horse? It did come from your town?"

"Yes, of course. My chosen horse. Birth bonded."

Ilvo pursed his lips and sighed.

"I'll stable her. I can add a rope across the doorway to keep her from going over the door." He reached up for the reins.

She gave them to him, then took her packs off the saddle. Laden with the bows and five packs, she sighed. "I'll be at Master Gav…"

"I've got eyes, dear. Besides, it's not as if I would have any problem finding you, when you tower over most of us by two heads." He furrowed his brow and shuffled away.

Avria watched as Shade ducked her head under the low doorway. Then she jogged at a noisy rattle across the way, back towards the town entrance. The small door of the apothecary's shop had a bell on it that jingled when she entered. She ducked through, her bags giving her some trouble. She managed to pull everything through, then shut the door behind her with another cheerful jingle.

429

A long counter stretched across the front of the shop, with a low desk facing the door and a large bay window to the left.

Master Gavorre stood on a ladder behind the long counter between two of the four shelves that butted up against a narrow walkway. He reached for one of the hundreds of clay urns of myriad sizes and shapes that filled the shelves. Each one had a neat label on it. He selected a jar and climbed down, rounded the corner into the area behind the desk, where more shelves, filled with books and scrolls and other clutter, lined the walls. He gestured for her to follow him and disappeared through a doorway in the back wall. Avria ducked low behind him, clattering through the doorway with her encumbrances.

She entered a narrow kitchen just in time to see him disappear down an even narrower corridor, passing a staircase. The ceiling brushed her head. He took a right through a doorway under the stairs. Avria squeezed through. They emerged in what looked like a stockroom and workshop. How they got Eleran in here was beyond her. He lay on a large worktable built into the back wall, between two tall shelves in front of a double window. The young lady tucked a blanket around him. The master put his jar on a large central worktable and looked up at Avria.

She set her packs down near the doorway, grateful for the higher ceilings in this room, where a huge wooden rack, suspended from the beams, held drying herbs. Jars and canisters littered still more shelves, along with boxes and bunches of dried plants. Two tall windows flanked Eleran, one on either wall, but six large lanterns suspended from the ceiling provided most of the light. She went to Eleran's side.

"No time for you to fuss over him, girl. Get me the large mortar and pestle from the shelf over there, and that clay jar beside them."

Avria nodded and scurried over to the area he indicated, locating the marble mortar with the matching tool sticking out of it. She brought it and the clay jar to the master apothecary, who filled it with an herb mixture and pushed it back to her.

"Pulverize it, dear."

He moved to Eleran and placed his little hand on the seer's sweaty forehead, whispering. Manehra returned with a bowl of water and a rag. She swabbed his feverish head.

Avria set to work, mashing up the herbs, her eyes worriedly locked on Eleran.

"He's taken lives," the Master said gravely. Manehra withdrew with a gasp as if she'd touched something tainted. The master turned to glower at Avria, whose hands fell still. She nodded, eyes filling with tears.

"He had no choice. Look what he's done to himself! He did what he had to."

"I won't ask what sort of trouble you've gotten yourselves into, but he has tapped into a forbidden place, and he has given almost every shred of his being to use it. He could even die. He pays a hard price for what he has done."

"Don't you think we both know that?" Avria snapped. "If he could have given a fairer fight, he would have, but he was already weakened, trying to save me!"

The Master frowned and shook his head.

"I don't know if I can save him, girl."

"Please try!" Avria's voice broke. The second word came out in a sob. She had to lean on the table. "Please..." The Master looked poignantly at Manehra, who shook her head.

"Go get Baruld."

Manehra nodded, and left. The Apothecary looked back to Avria, who wept.

"Stop blubbering and finish what I gave you to do, girl!"

"It's Avria. My name is Avria."

He arched his brows and pursed his lips and returned to his whispering over Eleran's tortured face.

Baruld arrived clad in all black, a severe creature with a straight, heavy brow, and a hard frosty gray glare. Exceptionally short, no bigger than a two- or three-year-old, he had a powerful presence nevertheless. Silver rings studded his short fingers, and his ears and lip dangled silver loops. Dark tattoos covered the left side of his face and the back of his pate.

"Violator of the laws," he pronounced the moment he set eyes on Eleran. "He deserves none of my help."

"We don't know the circumstances. I do not doubt the sincerity of the girl. Besides, if his intentions were bad, he would not have lived this long; you know that."

The apothecary had not intended for Avria to hear this debate; he'd sent her to the kitchen to heat some water. She heard them talking as she returned. She made a deliberate noise as she entered, and both men turned to look at her. She brought the water and put it on the table, then moved to the side of the apothecary. Baruld, she now understood to be a powerful mage like Eleran, although the people of the Auberge called mages and seers 'bearers'.

"What happened? I must know if I am to risk sullying my powers with those of a tainted bearer."

"I was injured. He used himself up healing me. When our pursuers came, he was too weak, so he did what he did. He had to take three lives."

"What pursuers?"

"Thran rangers. It's a long story," she said dismissively, unsure if she had the wherewithal to tell them all of the circumstances.

"This far into the forests already?" Baruld muttered.

"Why did they pursue you?" the Master asked without missing a beat.

"They took me from my village, against my will. My grandmother, a Thran woman, took me from my family. Eleran came for me." She looked directly into Baruld's cool eyes. "Have you been expecting them here?"

The Master answered. "They've gathered at the pass in Chrotrioth. Baruld here thinks they're staging an invasion. We had no idea they had penetrated the forestlands. I wonder if they're scouting."

"Invasion?" Avria frowned, then shook her head. "No, they weren't scouting. At least these ones weren't. They only came because of me." Avria turned, her face blank and confused. She sat on the table, and shook her head. Invasion.

"Well, then we don't have to worry about the Thran yet. What of this bearer, Baruld?"

The small mage frowned in thought, then turned to Avria. "Come here."

She hesitated, then walked over and stooped in front of him. His jeweled finger came up and rested on the side of her face. His sharp gaze bore into her soul, and for a moment, she forgot herself. She seemed to leave her senses. Then suddenly, she popped back into awareness, only to find the powerful mage's eyes boring into hers.

He lowered his hand and nodded. "Alright then." He turned to the apothecary. "Have you prepared a drooth?"

"We started it. Avria, can you keep working on the mixture please? It needs to be crushed very fine."

Avria nodded and went back to work pulverizing the contents of the mortar. The two men stood over Eleran and stripped the blanket away.

"Let's get started then," Baruld muttered.

* * * *

Four days after the dragons had left Tinna and her family at Iromi, the Araki riders began to arrive. The first group came in close to midnight. A servant woke Tinna and Taneth from their bed. Tinna pulled on a long flowing robe and padded barefoot down the corridor of the Magistrate's villa, following at the heels of the servant who'd awoken her. Taneth followed, slower and grumpier. Tinna walked to the bastion and climbed the old stone steps to the planning room. She saw the lights of the first arrivals as they entered the field below, where a large circle of braziers revealed at least fifty riders. She turned to Taneth, who came to the top of the steps wheezing.

"Gods, why does this room have to be all the way up here?"

"Don't be silly, Taneth. This is why." Tinna directed him to the narrow window. He looked out at the scene, brows arched in surprise.

"I wonder how many settlements this first group represents."

"I don't know. I hope not too many. This gives me hope. But if they come from many different settlements, we won't make a very sizable force."

"Don't fret over what you cannot control."

"I suppose you're right. What else can I do at this point? We've done everything in our power. We'll just have to rely on the dragons to balance us."

* * * *

Eleran awoke from his stupor in the morning, still pale and frail. Both the master and the other mage insisted that he rest and refrain from doing anything that required magic. His body felt tender, he said, his muscles sore and spent. But the fire in his eyes when he looked at Avria burned as fervently as before. He held her tightly the moment he was strong enough to sit up, and he kissed her tears of relief from her cheeks. A young man by the name of Offrin, who had helped to carry Eleran in from the square the day before, had been conscripted to help Eleran get around. The four of them, including Avria and the master, spent much of the day in close quarters together.

"I can do it myself! There's barely room for both of us in this hallway, just move ahead!" Eleran snapped at Offrin.

433

Avria helped the master in the apothecary shop, writing on labels and affixing them to urns, jars, pots and bottles, while he filled them with fresh product and organized them on the shelves. They looked at one another and then to the door as Offrin steamed into the room, looking cross. He was extremely well proportioned for his stature. He shaved his head, as all their militiamen did, and wore a tidy goatee, like Taneth's. He belted his simple linen tunic around a pair of leather broadfall breeches. His ankle boots were finely made. When he glanced up to see Avria looking at him, his anger washed away into an admiring smile.

"Your man's a handful. Doesn't like help from anyone." Avria shrugged and raised her brows as if to say; what can one do? Eleran bumbled into the room through the tiny door, his huge frame filling it and then some. He barely managed to straighten himself in the shop, his head brushing the box-beams of the ceiling.

"I know herbs. I can be of use here."

The Master glowered at him.

"You're supposed to be resting, you lumbering buffoon. Go back to your attic or the workroom! Leave us alone!"

Eleran looked to Avria as if hoping she'd plead his case, but she simply looked up at him with her huge eyes and shrugged her brows again.

Eleran sighed intolerantly and huffed back through the doorway, Offrin at his heels.

"I said, go away! I can get through here on my own!" Their noise faded into the back of the building. Avria glanced at the older man questioningly.

"How long before he gets better, Master?"

"Oh, hard to tell. Baruld had to work very hard to bargain him back from wherever he'd gone. The powers were angry with him indeed. Such actions traumatize not only the physical being, but also the essence of a magic-bearer. His pain and his wounds are more spiritual than physical. Who knows how long such a thing will take to heal?"

"It is the penance the mage spoke of?"

"Yes. He tapped into forbidden energies to do what he did, and he took lives. Baruld thinks your friend may suffer longer than usual."

Avria frowned in thought as she scratched "Milk Thistle" on a label, blotted it, then swabbed the back with rubbery glue and pressed it onto a light-blue glass bottle. The apothecary scrutinized her work before taking the bottle and shoving it onto a shelf with other liver remedies. There was approval when he saw her careful hand. There were benefits to being the daughter of a Wiseman. Perfect penmanship was only one of many.

Avria's countenance, from the moment she arrived at Taruttee had been gloomy and depressed. Even now, with Eleran awake, her spirits had not lifted much. Master Gavorre rummaged through the many small drawers that occupied the lower half of the front desk, barked an exclamation of success, and withdrew a tiny paper packet. He went to the kettle, which sat on the kitchen hearth behind them, and poured hot water into a mug. He dumped the contents of the packet into the water and gave it to Avria. She took it questioningly.

"To brighten your spirits, girl! Eleran is well. He is going to recover, perhaps at length, but recovery is at the end of it all."

Avria nursed the bitter tea while she continued labeling.

* * * *

Eleran shuffled about the confines of the Master's upstairs living space during the day and shared the attic with Avria at night. Their feet poked out from the end of the short bed, but their host had set a large chest at the end of it and laid a stack of soft linens on it. Eleran, sore and listless most of the time, grew friskier when in such close quarters with Avria. Gavorre shouted at them a number of times for making too much noise over his own sleeping chambers.

The nighttime activities caused Eleran even more soreness and misery the next day. Avria could not hide her mirth at his pained expression as he ducked low, tilting his shoulders and grunting like an old man, to squeeze through the doorway into a small parlor where everyone sat in the evening after dinner. He eyed a small wingback chair warily, wondering if he'd be able to extricate himself from it. With a burdened groan, he resigned himself to his fate, and sank down into it. His weight made the floor and chair creak ominously.

Mrs. Efnam had brought a thick stew and crusty, light bread still hot from her oven across the square, where she lived with her husband, four of her own children and two adopted. The two youngest, having come by way of the relay post coaches, proved that people continued to shove their little children into the hands of the Auberge villages. The little ones had taken to Avria right away. The moment they set eyes upon her—whenever she went out to see to her horse or to take some sun and stretch herself after too many hours in the cramped apothecary shop, assisting Master Gavorre— the children poured out of the woodwork and crowded around her, a sea of bobbing red and blonde heads, giggling and squealing and asking a hundred thousand questions. The eldest of them, a boy of eleven, carried the tiniest baby as if it were a doll.

Avria wasn't used to so many children. Thamatoc had a few, but nowhere near as many as Taruttee. She found them extra adorable, owing to their unusual smallness and their wide, curious eyes. She delighted in the sheer mass of them, as they followed her about her chores—especially the little girl called Dree, who stood not much taller than Avria's knees, a tiny shock of bright red hair and a spray of freckles across the bridge of a snub-nose. All the Efnam children, except the adopted ones, had ginger hair and freckles like their mother's. The adopted ones, the tiny baby and a four-year-old girl of unsurpassed prettiness, had blonde, almost white, locks with golden strands shooting through their perfect curls. They didn't seem to feel out of place with the Efnam pack and were always with them as they charged about the place. Dree was nine years old, and Avria's favorite, a serious sort of girl, and most curious about Avria, her horse and everything else about her, including her black, curly hair.

Mrs. Efnam took care of the apothecary. Gavorre's own sweet daughter lived several miles away in a fledgling Auberge town where she had recently married and now, being pregnant, could no longer look after her father. The old man's gastronomical care was duly remitted to the hands of Mrs. Efnam when Manhera left. She cooked his evening meals and brought him treats from their bakery nearly every morning. When she could not, Dree or one of the other children appeared at his door holding a basket covered in a square of cheerfully woven fabric with food hidden underneath. On these occasions, a rare enthusiasm and pleasure played across the face of the habitually grumpy apothecary. When he spotted an Efnam coming across the square, he came clomping down the ladder, rushing through the gap between the desk and the counter to greet them with a smile. He grasped the basket and ferreted it into the kitchen immediately, where he rustled and fussed for a moment or two, most likely having a little taste or a good sniff of Mrs. Efnam's excellent cooking before returning the basket and slipping a coin into the deliverer's hand.

Tonight's delivery of stew had been a heavier package than usual, to accommodate the guests now staying with the Apothecary. Avria, Eleran, the Master and Offrin had eaten together, hunched around the tiny table in the small dining room. Nary a crumb remained of Mrs. Efnam's cooking. Offrin went back to his barracks after dinner, and little Dree came back for the serving dishes, strategically bringing her older brother, sending him home with the items so she could sit, uninvited, with Avria and ask her more questions. She now sat on a small bolster next to Avria's knees, her hands working furiously over a knitting project she conveniently had brought with her, while she enjoyed the fire and a moment of rare and pensive silence. Eleran entered and took Avria's attention from her momentarily. She started chattering again when the big man settled in.

"Your grandmamma was probably bad in doing what she did, but it brought you here, so I can't says that I am sad for it," she rattled. Avria's eyes locked with Eleran, and she smirked. "You're so pretty, even though you're all tall and gangerly and all those things, but mother says that you can't help it and that you're fortunate to find someone who is tall and gangerly to love you." Her little head tilted back and forth as she chatted, fingers knitting all the while. The Master opened his mouth to ask the girl why she made a nuisance of herself here, so close to bed-time, when a commotion coming from the direction of the square distracted him. He shuffled in his quilted tapestry slippers to the window and peered out, his fuzzy brows closing together.

"Oh, dear!" Avria stood and came up behind him. He pushed her away. "Both of you, get to the work room, right away! Eleran, move as quickly as you can possibly move! Go on! And keep your voices down!" The urgency in his voice rose with every word. "Go!" He didn't shout, but spoke in a raspy, loud whisper. "Dree, please take the back door and run to Baruld's home right away and tell him to come to the shop at once! It is important; go!"

The tiny girl dropped her knitting on the floor and dashed in front of Avria's legs through the doorway before the tall woman could duck through, with Eleran at her heels. The apothecary followed, trying to hurry Eleran along. The stairs rattled as the tiny girl raced down them.

"Master Gavorre... what is it?"

"Those rangers you spoke of? I think they're here. Women in uniforms, in the square as we speak. Go, go, go!" He nearly shoved them down the precipitous stairwell. Avria clattered down the steps and turned immediately to the workshop door, glancing back for Eleran who still moved slowly. She pulled him along, the moment he stepped down, and dragged him into the stockroom where the master closed and locked the door behind them.

"All right, this way!" The Master led them to a large shelf, which he easily pulled out and slid aside. Behind it, a passageway opened into a short corridor. "This leads to the shared yard. You can go straight into the back of the alehouse from here and come out on cottage lane. Take the lane west! Stay low! I'll stall them. Go to Caspin's place—a rust-colored cottage with about thirty dogs in the yard. You can't miss it. Just listen for barking. Tell him I sent you, he won't question you."

Gavorre shoved the tall ones through the door and closed the shelf behind them. Straightening his robes, he unlocked the stockroom. He then went to a shelf unit and pulled down two bottles. A quick riffle through a drawer and he withdrew a scarf, which he wrapped around his face. With look of fearful resignation he unstopped the bottles and poured each one into a stone bowl. A noxious smell ensued, so horrible that it made him retch. He staggered to another set of jars and filled his arms with them.

Baruld entered and glanced behind him quickly. "The child told me to come. I can see why. They're asking Foth where the tall people are. Foth is no liar; they'll be here any minute. Gods, what a pong?" The mage wrinkled his face and gagged.

"Anything to distract them. I sent the two to Caspin. Mind following them?" Master Gavorre's scarf muffled his voice.

"Anything to get away from this reek." The magician circled around him and slid out the back shelf-door, closing it behind himself. A few moments later, Foth peered around the corner of the workshop door, looking in from the corridor.

"Master Gavorre."

The apothecary squinted at him. "What is it, Foth? My hands are full right now."

"There's some...er...ladies askin' for ya."

"Eh?"

"Ladies. They're asking to see you, and you didn't answer the knocking."

"I'm back here. I can't hear anything, and the shop's closed, anyway. If it's not urgent, tell the ladies to come back tomorrow morning. I'm busy and this is not a pleasant task." He poured more of the substance into the bowl and activated it with the contents of the other bottle. A fresh cloud of disgusting aroma rolled out through the door to the corridor. Foth was yanked from the doorway, and two towering, lithe women ducked in, both stunningly beautiful, with the same black hair that Avria had, but with skin of muted tan and luminous black eyes. They wore the garb of Thran rangers. They looked like they meant business. To the Master's delight, however, he saw an immediate reaction to the stink. Their noses wrinkled, and one covered her nose and mouth with her hand, turning her head as if to fight off the urge to vomit.

"Ahh…tall ladies, I see. I'm sorry, but the shop is closed. You'd best cover your faces. This isn't good to breathe straight in like that, stink or no stink. It can burn your lungs."

One of the women coughed and gagged. The other took the rumpled neck of her shirt and lifted it over her nose, and the first did likewise. It did little to filter the stench. He watched their lovely eyes water.

"We don't get tall ones around here much. What brings you to Taruttee? What can I do for you? I suppose I can mix up some herbs for you when I'm done here."

"Ve ave bean told dat a girl like us eez here."

He paused, and pondered a moment.

"Yes, I did have a lovely guest like you. Same hair and eyes. Lots paler though." He gestured to his scarf-covered face. Another dollop of some other substance and the mixture hissed, jetting more little puffs of reek into the air.

"Vat is dat? Eeeuugh!" the second Thran complained.

"It's a work in progress. When it is finished, it will dry out and won't smell quite so horribly. It's a poultice for wounds. With our militia training sessions beginning soon for new recruits, we'll need a lot of it." He stirred it up some more.

"Verre is she?"

"Oh, right. The girl, Avria. She and her friend left this morning. She traded her horse for a larger one that can carry two people, and they left at first light. Said she was going to a place called Chrotrioth. Heard of it?"

The Thran both glowered under the necks of their tunics.

"Nobeddy sedd dey leff…"

"Oh, they were very careful to do it with discretion. We wondered why they were so secretive, but we don't ask questions. We just wanted them out. They take up too much room! No offense, of course, but our towns aren't meant for the big folk."

The women recoiled and exchanged foreign words. The first one gagged, and they both ducked out of the room, leaving the apothecary with a slam of the door.

The Master reached for a jar and dumped a powder into the stinking, roiling mess that neutralized the smell almost immediately. He lowered his scarf and sighed. "That helped a bit, I dare say." He opened a window to air out the rest of the smell and shook off his powdery housecoat, hissing in annoyance.

"Where is that Offrin when you need him?"

The rangers weren't stupid, and they knew their quarry was nearby. They were bright enough to realize that the apothecary's stinking display was but a distraction, and they immediately exited the building to confer briefly. They decided that if anyone would be escaping, it would be through a back door. They jogged along the front of the shop and the adjoining buildings until they found an alleyway to the back lane. They found one between a yard full of huge pigs that adjoined a butchery, and the flat side-wall of the saddler's shop. The pigs oinked in alarm and schlocked about in the mire of muck, spattering the rangers' breeches in the reeking stuff as they pressed against the wobbling wooden fence. The sickeningly sweet smell of their feces seemed to pale against the substance the apothecary had mixed.

A gate at the end of the alleyway opened with a lift of the latch and they emerged on a dry, well-traveled lane behind the town center's buildings. They looked right first, and saw nothing, and then left, and there they saw the retreating forms of Avria and a large man quite a distance down the road, and a very small man running at his fastest behind them. They could only assume that the tall man was the very devil who'd transformed their sister rangers into piles of ash back in the forest. He looked worse for wear and he was slowing the girl down.

"Let's go," the older one snapped in Thran. They broke into a run towards the slow-moving couple.

Eleran lost strength quickly. His breath was short, and he struggled to make it to Caspin's home. His fatigue slowed them tremendously, and Avria grew increasingly alarmed. She let him lean on her slight frame as she watched the narrow lane behind them. She saw Baruld following at a distance, huffing and puffing from the effort. She heard a flurry of pig squeals, and when she glanced in that direction, her breath caught in her throat. What she saw filled her with terror.

"Hurry, Eleran!" The desperation in her voice caused him to look, too, and he groaned.

"Stop, Avria! Stop!" Eleran muttered. "I can take them."

"No!" She felt tears starting to burn in her eyes, a sense of hopelessness overtaking her. For some odd reason, her brain decided to conjure a vivid image of her mother's face just at that moment. It gave her pause. She suddenly stopped and carefully helped Eleran to the ground, leaning him against a stone wall. Behind it, a multitude of dogs barked anxiously. Eleran worked to keep himself upright. He started whispering in tongues. Eleran knew they would not harm Avria, it was not their mission. The only way to stop them from taking Avria was to stop them himself.

"Don't you dare! Stay here and shut your mouth!" Avria hissed at him. She straightened herself and moved to the middle of the lane. The running Thran skidded abruptly to a cautious, wary walk as they both eyed her distrustfully. They wove around Baruld, who was almost too tired to move any more, wheezing, sweaty and leaning on his knees as he caught his breath. Tinna appeared again in the back of Avria's mind, the murmur of her careful instruction, morning after morning, practice after practice, replaying the graceful moves of the fighting dance. Avria had no weapons. It doesn't matter. Stop thinking about what you don't have; think of what you do.

Avria's glassy eyes followed the two rangers. She felt a lump in her throat and wondered if they could see how close she was to collapsing into tears and begging for them to leave her be. She heard Eleran whispering again.

"I am not going with you," she said firmly, hiding the waver in her voice as best she could.

The two rangers looked like vipers ready to strike, their muscles tense, their eyes locked on her menacingly. One began to circle her.

They are rangers, not fighters. Rangers have only basic skills.

"Eet iz nott a choice, eh? Not for me, not for joo." the older one said with a smirk. Avria kept her knees bent and sank down, taking her weight in her calves. She held her arms away from her sides. As the younger one attempted to circle her, she squatted more and leapt into the air, twirling with one leg out straight. The arch of her foot caught the woman in the temple. Avria landed deftly, ducking to avoid a hand strike. A tiny smile took the corner of her mouth as practice and theory fell into place. She'd never looked at fighting as a dance before. She danced as an exercise in concentration and discipline. She had scrimmaged with her mother, but always softly, gently. She learned to respond gracefully and instinctively to certain attacks. If she saw an upper body movement from her opponent, she responded almost choreographically. She feints that way, I respond this way. Simple as that. But when she came into contact with the ranger's head, she felt power well up through her, as

441

if from the figures of the dance. A potent heat rose up from her core, a sudden confidence.

She rose from her crouch and twirled downwards, sweeping, hooking her leg around her opponent's, then rolled away from a kick, leaped back to her feet in a fluid movement. She attacked with a series of powerful kicks, turned and landed a final elbow to the woman's face that rocked her backwards.

Stunned, the ranger retreated, pressing her hand against her cheekbone, fury in her black eyes.

"Vausar bassum arute-ay agnama cretamusar…" Eleran's whispered chanting rose above the din of the barking dogs.

Avria determined to end this before he did something stupid, did something unwise as well. She charged the ranger like a bull and knocked her flat, pinned the woman's arms with her knees and sat on her chest while she pummeled her face, until the ranger rolled to one side, bucked and flung her off.

Avria landed at the feet of the older ranger. From between the woman's laced boots, she saw the master emerge from a gate with Offrin at his heels.

The ranger's heel connected with Avria's throat. She tried to roll away, but a weight fell on her side and a boot struck her in the ribcage. She rolled onto her belly to protect herself, and one of the women pinned her.

Eleran quietly wished one of them would lose her temper and just try to harm her. To knock her out, to strangle her. Then he would not be consigned to do what he was about to do.

"Shavra mooneel reh bassum vausar."

Eleran's voice strengthened. He planted his hands in the earth. Far away, he heard the little mage chant something as well.

Vines sprouted from the dry soil and grappled at the legs of the rangers.

The women, both strong and quick, snapped the vines and wrenched them out of the earth with little effort. One ranger, kneeling on Avria's back, resorted to her weapon. Detaching the crossbow from her belt, she pointed it at Baruld. He fell silent.

Avria kicked and fought, but she had two rangers holding her down. The older one with the crossbow knelt on her back; the other sat on Avria's legs and pressed the sharp point of an arrow bolt against the back of her neck, limiting her ability to struggle.

Draw blood. Please… harm her, Eleran wished in silence.

"Diss iz note joor matter," the older Thran warned the little mage menacingly. Eleran's eyes widened. "And joo weel stop da magique!" She waved her crossbow at Eleran, who simply smiled.

"You can't kill me. You can't kill me. You can't hurt me. It's not your mission," Avria cried triumphantly to the woman holding the arrow bolt to her neck. She wanted Eleran to stop, he knew. He also knew that they could and would kill him.

"Baraneti Bassum HATH!" he uttered, stressing the last word like a barked command. His fingertips dug further into the soil as he pressed his back against the stone. The crossbow pointed at him. The frenzied barking of the dogs behind the wall abruptly stopped, followed by a cacophony of frightened whimpers and the scratching and pattering of fast-retreating paws. Then silence. Eleran sat against the wall, his back arched, his head back, teeth clenched together. A tormented groan erupted from his mouth. Veins in his neck and temples bulged.

"Joo stop now or joo die!" the ranger screamed.

Eleran merely lifted his head and grimaced wickedly in return, his bloodshot eyes narrowing at her. Too late, his eyes informed her.

Baruld whispered something, and she turned her arrow to him.

"Joo both die!" Panic crept into her voice.

"One or the other, go ahead and choose. You'll still be killed," Offrin shouted with a smug tone.

The earth began to seethe. The fine, sandy grains started to churn as if they had life in them.

The ranger's eyes went wide, her lips a straight, hard line. She squeezed against the tension in the trigger of her crossbow and kept swinging it from Eleran to Baruld and back again.

"Get off her!" Eleran warned her, straining his words through gritted teeth. "Get off her or you will be killed, like your sisters were killed!" His eyes bore into hers. In spite of his physical frailty and pain, he saw that the power of his glare unnerved her. She squeezed the trigger, the arrow flew.

It did not travel far.

A vine whipped up from the ground and snatched it from the air too quickly for the eye to see. The mage smirked through his straining face and began to whisper words again. His fingers dug further into the earth.

The slow-hissing sand began to pick up speed, and then everything blew out of control. The sand and dirt around Avria unexpectedly exploded upwards in great curtains and formed a swirling vortex that shrouded her. The rangers immediately drew their arms over their eyes. The sand swirled faster and faster, the glistening grains turning into countless tiny projectiles, scratching the women's exposed skin.

Baruld realized what was happening and screamed for Eleran to stop. He began to work a counter-spell, but Eleran had already tapped into the forbidden energies. His head rocked back as he gripped the undulating pulse of the earth and wielded it to create the vortex surrounding Avria where she lay under the struggling, screaming Thran.

A dome had woven itself around her, an invisible shield against which soil and sand and pebbles simply glanced aside, even as they whipped around the two women, filling their eyes and nostrils, searing their skin. They stood in a panic and tried to flee, but the vortex followed them, moving faster and faster, gathering more material from the road as it spun along, until it completely obscured them, choking off their screams with dirt.

With a sudden, strange finality, they fell still. The earth that swirled around them rained down atop their slumped bodies and covered them in a blanket of bloodied soil.

Avria staggered to her feet and then to him, weeping. "Why did you do that? Why?" she sobbed.

"I had to. They would never have just walked away. Get out of here, Avria. More will come," he said weakly. "Remember that they cannot harm you, be bold in that knowledge. They still have the power to take you away, and you must force their hand if they ever get hold of you again. Understand?"

She did not. She merely nodded stoically, not sure what he was saying.

His eyes rolled back into his head, and he drooped limply to the side. Avria's cry came hoarse and terrified to his ears as she fell on him, weeping.

The three little people gathered around her, looking at one another with expressions of great regret.

CHAPTER TEN – THE APOGEE

Avria could not deny Offrin's skill as a rider. Even on his leggy but significantly smaller pony, he managed to keep up with her. She pushed Shade down a steep ravine, leaning far back in her saddle. Behind her, Offrin's pony snorted with effort and slid down the incline behind her, hooves sinking into the soft dirt and causing small cascades of moss and mud to roll down in front of her. Shade leapt down the last length to the bottom of the ravine. With a hop over the small brook that followed the ravine's vermiculate path, her sharp hooves grabbed the opposite slope and bounded powerfully to the top. Avria turned to wait for Offrin, who appeared over the edge only seconds later. They paused and looked down the ravine.

"It's so strange, riding so far around without coming upon an oak grove."

"We don't honor our dead the way you do. We prefer to leave the forest to grow what it likes to grow." He gestured towards the towering conifers. This close to the mountain range, the forest grew lush and green, with garlands of old man's beard adorning the lower branches of the evergreens. Moss covered everything. 'Don't stand still for too long, or it'll grow on you,' Master Gavorre had told her a few days before, when she'd slipped on a slick mossy step at the back of the apothecary shop. She loved it. The river roared boisterously as they approached it, no longer the mellow, quiet thing that slid behind the village.

The brook in the ravine joined it a short way round the bend. Offrin rode there, his eyes glistening as he watched Avria. He knew she'd lodged her heart somewhere else and he had no idea how she thought of the small people, but the more time he spent with her the more attached he became. She came up alongside him, her mind temporarily distracted from the sleeping man that occupied her soul. "How do you honor your dead then?" she finally asked.

Offrin looked up at her and smiled. "We bury them as well, but in special burial gardens."

"No trees?"

"Oh, rarely. Some people choose to plant something that flowers over them, but most graves are marked with a simple stone cairn. Important folk, leaders and what-not, get a stone menhir."

Avria nodded. It seemed such a waste to her, not to let a living plant of some kind absorb their essences. Where did they go then? Into the earth? She knew Taneth would be most accepting of this practice, a firm believer that the Araki performed their burial practices for the benefit of the folks who survived rather than for the deceased. He did not believe in souls or essences, but he was always very moved by the oak forests when he attended ceremonies and he treated the practice with quiet respect. She glanced at Offrin, his admiration of her quite plain on his handsome features. She smiled wanly. She was used to men gawking at her. Since she had turned thirteen or so, she had noticed them ogling. Her mother said they looked at her because she was so pretty, but Avria had never seen herself as pretty; she thought herself dark and plain next to her fairer friends. She figured they stared because she had such pale skin against such dark hair.

"Thanks for taking me out for a while. I think I needed to get away. I've been in that dark storeroom for days. I'm afraid I'll start growing mushrooms if I stay in there much longer."

"I like to get out too sometimes. We train a lot and stay in the company of the same men for weeks. I get out to help father with his brewery on occasion, but not often enough. It's refreshing to be in new company these days. Taking care of Eleran, and spending time around you folks these past days has been a nice diversion."

Avria smiled at him. They crossed a stone bridge over the rocky river. It led them onto a wider road.

"This isn't the road I came on," Avria observed.

"Oh, no; this is the south road. It follows the river, which goes all the way out to the huge river there at the plains."

"Indeed! Your people didn't make it, then?"

"No, it's an old empire road." Offrin pointed to one of the telltale stone plinth markers with directional symbols on it. "Jepnath used to be that way, it's but a ruin now—" he pointed west, then turned east— "and what's left of the city of Tamnat the other. The road has fallen into disrepair in some places because of the lack of workmen to fix it these days, but it persists, and we maintain what we can of it, since it connects three of our Auberge towns. This road supposedly goes all the way from the great river to the coast, following the foot of the range. From this one, we'll catch the village road south of town and follow the river for a while; it's a pleasant route." He turned his horse westward and they walked quietly along, the mounts cooling off after the hard run through the forest. To their left, the pines scaled the steep foothills and obscured the peaks of the mountain range.

As they rode, the sound of thundering hooves came from behind them.

"Gods! The relay traffic these days has surpassed anything in my prior experience!" Offrin muttered. "They've been racing the roads for days!"

Avria nodded blankly. Having spent the past few days inside the storeroom with Eleran, she had no idea what was going on around the town. She watched Offrin as he pulled his pony in front of hers to make room for the riders, who careened around the bend and blasted by them at a full gallop—two riders, one on a nimble relay-branded horse, the other on a towering chestnut that looked familiar. Before she could think about it, the rider leaned abruptly back in his saddle and pulled hard on the reins of his mount. The chestnut skidded to a halt. Avria's eyes went wide with disbelief. "Drashun!"

He wheeled his horse and cantered over, leapt from the saddle in mid-stride and ran to her. Avria slid off her horse into his arms. He wrapped her in a tight and desperate embrace and turned with Avria in his arms.

"By the gods, I thought—! Blast, I had no idea what to think!" he exclaimed, tears in his eyes, his voice wavering. "You're well, that is so good. And you are free, are you not?" he rambled. Avria nodded while she sobbed, clutching her best friend with all of her soul. Offrin sat on his pony, quiet, watchful and wholly confused.

"Drashe, what are you doing way down here? You haven't come looking for me, have you?" Avria asked through her tears, her syllables clipped by a blocked nose. She had not released him from her hug yet.

"No offense, Avria, but we had to put your fate in Eleran's hands, much to your mother's regret. We're facing a massive war. We're rallying the Araki riders." Drashun pushed her away and wiped his eyes with the back of his hand.

"The Thran, right?" Avria speculated.

Drashun nodded. "How'd you know?"

"The Adrei know of the army gathering at the pass. They mentioned it when I told them about my grandmother."

Drashun glanced at Offrin and finally thought to greet him with a nod. Offrin, still mounted, bowed more graciously from the waist. The second rider, having realized that Drashun had stopped, now returned for him, the approaching hoof-beats on the edge of everyone's awareness.

"Where's Eleran? Did he find you?"

Avria's heavy lashes fell. She furrowed her brow.

"He found me. He's very, very ill. Offrin's people have been caring for him. We've spent the last week or so with them."

"Your mother is on her way to Iromi. She is probably there already by now." He rubbed his forehead and laughed through his nose. "She's definitely got to be there already, I just forget how many days I've been on the road..."

"Where is Iromi?"

"Just north of Chrotrioth, where the Thran army is massing."

"What's she doing there?"

"Waiting for the Araki. The human army is slipshod to say the least; they don't have enough men to keep the Thran at bay. Your mother is trying to get the Araki to supplement them."

"Makes sense." Avria did not hide her disappointment that her mother had written her off so easily.

Drashun merely shook his head. He knew that she would not accept his explanation. She did not understand the magnitude of recent events.

"What's the hold-up?" the second rider shouted rudely. "We have to go."

"Here." Drashun reached down and opened a tube that tied to the front of his saddle, withdrawing one of the many maps rolled together inside it. "Take this. Iromi is on there, where your mother has gone for now. You can see more clearly what's been going on by the markings on it. Perhaps you can meet us there when Eleran gets better. I'm on one of the last legs of notifications, and then we're heading to Iromi."

"Strider lost weight," Avria pointed out, looking at his horse.

"He's run countless miles since this began, but he is tireless. We'll fatten him up again when we get home. For now, we both must work to get the word out to the settlements."

Avria took the map and blinked her teary eyes at him. They studied one another for a moment.

"She fought for you, but everything is against her right now. This is really dire, Avria. You have to understand. She didn't just dismiss you, she never would. My mother would, but Tinna, never."

"Nonsense, Rhoa loves you more than any—"

"Look. I have a job to finish, and then I'm off to Iromi with the last leg of riders. Get on your horse and go there if you can. Maybe if you see it for yourself, you'll understand." Drashun reached over and put his hand on her cheek. "I'm so glad to see you well, Avria." He gave her a final glance and a kiss on the forehead before flinging himself up into his saddle, wheeling his mount around and kicking his sweaty, lean horse into a canter. Before long, he and the other rider had reached full gallop again and were gone from sight.

Avria stood for a moment with the map in her hand, eyes full of tears. Offrin approached on his mount, his expression questioning.

"I won't even pretend I understood what just happened."

"My cousin. Drashun. War. The Thran are about to crush the humans." She proffered the map. Offrin took it and unrolled it. "They're calling all Araki riders to help because there are so few human troops. It sounds quite hopeless," her voice wavered.

Offrin's expression grew serious as he studied the map. "We should get back to town. I think the elders ought to see this." He rolled it up and tucked it into his knitted tunic.

Avria climbed back onto Shade and gathered her reins. Offrin broke into a canter, and she followed.

* * * *

It had taken a small tantrum to get some answers. While she could not frown on the inexplicable deliveries of armor and armaments, considering the situation, Tinna found the Keepers' secretiveness inexcusable. What did they know and how did they know it? What did they expected of her, of Taneth and of the Araki? She'd reached the end of her rope the night before, when another group of Araki arrived—three hundred riders in one fell swoop, a column of bobbing horse heads and bedraggled riders.

No precedent could have prepared the Thamatoc group for the sheer magnitude of the mounted army already camped at Iromi and still growing. Every day brought new hordes of riders. The fields around the city had been trampled to a quagmire teeming with muddy-legged bodies. People poured constantly from the town of Iromi to the temporary corrals, to the first, ordered lines of camps surrounded by hastier, more ramshackle shelters thrown up for later

449

arrivals. Taneth referred to his map to mark off the settlements already represented by riders and saw that those from more than half the Araki settlements had yet to arrive—mostly those of the eastern regions of the great forestlands. The plains clans had arrived first on their dun-colored, short horses; the clans of the Darthrell forest peninsula, the northernmost arm of Araki territory, arrived soon after on their impossibly huge draft horses. With those groups in place, others from the southern regions had begun to trickle in; by the eighth day, a deluge of new riders had opened up. Nobody seemed to care any longer about the languid dragons patrolling from the skies for any Thran scout who might learn of the massing army and ruin the element of surprise the Araki expected to enjoy. The fear of dragons had passed in this place; more important things were afoot.

Tinna fretted at first about having sufficient supplies and stated her fears to Phenmal, who simply admonished her. "Tinna, things will fall in place. Just concentrate on organizing these people, the rest of it will work its way out." Like magic, supplies began to arrive by dray from the north in the timeliest fashion, along with better tents, arms and armors, blankets, clan flags and surcoats all in matching red-and-white, like Tinna's.

Quickly assembled wooden walkways laid across the muck made camps more tolerable. Waterproof tents arrived, and rich blends of sticky molasses and grain and fresh-smelling hay for the horses brought from Suthervale farms on towering carts pulled by moropus and great plains oxen. Tinna kept her mouth shut, but Phenmal's cavalier attitude toward these timely gifts annoyed her. He knew so much and had not confided in her. Considering that the role of lynchpin in this scheme had been bestowed upon her, whether she wanted it or not, she believed she deserved an explanation.

After giving directives to a group of Iromi citizens conscripted to assist in organizing the arriving forces, Tinna filed out of the room with them. "Be sure to put the Bareet Clan in the west fields, away from the Devronat Clan!" she called after them as they left. "They don't see eye to eye." She shot out her arm and locked her hand on the door frame, creating a barrier for Phenmal as he idly strolled to the door, trailing behind the others.

"You aren't finished here."

He looked at her sharply. Then, sensing the all-too-familiar jumble of questions in her mind emitted a sigh of annoyance. "Ai'Tinn—"

"Don't Ai'Tinna me! And stop shuffling off my questions! I want answers."

450

"I don't have any," he lied with a supplicating thrust of his hands.

She frowned darkly and pointed to the chair he'd vacated only moments before.

He groaned and complied, moving to the chair and falling into it with the obstinate look of a child. Tinna crossed her arms. She glared at him. She realized that somehow, he seemed to be getting younger instead of aging; at least he looked more youthful than she was used to. She let the thought pass, annoyed that she was thinking of how attractive he was. She pursed her lips and moved her head as if to say: Well? He remained tightlipped, gazing at her with his brows raised expectantly and his legs crossed, taking an arrogant posture.

That set her off.

"I've suffered this silence long enough!"

"I am not in a position to provide you—"

"That's a pile of manure and you know it! Every time a bloody dray shows up, weighed down by supplies from the gods know where, you stand there with that smug glint in your eye!"

"The origin of the supplies is no mys—"

"Oh, stop! You know what I mean. Who sends them, Phenmal?"

"The Keepers. You know that. Their nine representatives are here, it's no secret..."

"Be more specific!"

"But I honestly do not know the specifics. The Keepers are not led by one or two individuals. You know this. They are a collective. I am not privy to their identities or to how they divide themselves into what groups and hierarchies." Tinna could not know this was a blatant lie.

"Then tell me what they know. How do they order all these supplies? How do they time them to arrive so conveniently? So perfectly? How did they prepare all that armor? All those blankets and swords and lances and pole arms? The surcoats and the crest of the dragon and the horse? What do they know?"

"They are the Keepers, after all. You know all too well how so many of the members of this group can do such extraordinary things."

"Yes, yes, yes! But I don't understand all the secrecy. And why me? Why did they pick me to manage all of this? Don't I have more personal concerns? I'm growing a child inside me! And I'm not a spring chicken! I should be out looking for Avria! I don't need to be here! Any clan chieftain could do this! Why me?"

451

"Do you really need to ask this, Tinna?"

"Because I stopped the burnings? That's why? That was years ago! In the scheme of my life, it's one thing. One thing that's long past. I live a simple life. I'm happy living a simple life. Is that it? The burnings?"

"Yes. And also no. It's complicated. I don't know exactly why, Tinna. They don't tell me things, just as they don't tell you everything. They choose people because they see a destiny...like your mother's diviner, they—"

Tinna threw her hands up in exasperation. "For twenty years I've endured their useless visits! They sit there and drone on to me, for no real reason, about the status of the human populations, the unending litany of mind-numbing minutiae. The empire's movements. Political decisions, the spread of sicknesses, the movements of the noble houses. Year after year, they bring this useless information to me and insist I sit through it! What's it all for?" she shouted. "What?"

Phenmal sighed and pinched his chin.

"There is an obvious answer here, Tinna."

"Oh, is there? Then why don't I see it?"

"Perhaps you refuse to see it. Perhaps they have been preparing you all along, giving you a background, a foundation upon which you will have to lead—"

"Really?" she snapped. She narrowed her eyes and glared at him in utter incredulity, "I needed to learn about the human aristocracy? The politics of the throne? Details of the royal decisions and mandates? In order to ride in front of any army?" She laughed. She shook her head. She sighed. "That makes no sense. They have more in store for me. You know it and I know it. I don't want it. I want my life at Thamatoc."

"I don't know what to tell you," he muttered with a shred of regret, "but I can promise you that what is meant to happen will happen and that things will work themselves out."

"That can mean anything! I wish you'd stop saying it," she muttered. "They insist that I retain the services of a summoner, that I keep contact with Ledroran and the dragons. That makes sense to me now. But the rest doesn't make sense. Or if it does make sense in the way I suspect it does, it frightens me. Beyond measure."

He gazed at her in a frank and friendly manner and stood, putting his hands on her shoulders.

452

"Tinna, I know you suspect they expect more from you, and you are probably right. But right now, you need to focus on what is right before you."

"It's taking care of itself, really. I feel useless organizing arrivals, giving directions to people who could just as easily make the same decisions themselves."

"You are far from useless," he whispered. "Just flow with it. You cannot fight the tide." He leaned forward and planted a kiss on her forehead. "I knew from the moment I met you that you'd bring out the best in me, as you do in anyone who knows you. I am, as always, honored to be shouted at by you."

Tinna shook her head and laughed gently.

Phenmal studied her for a moment. "It looks like we're getting close to sending troops forward. It's timely; the human army is nearly there, and the Thran sects that have yet to arrive are also close by. It's time."

Tinna nodded and leaned her backside on the desk, crossing her arms. A veil of grey clouds muted the sunlight, giving the room a gloomy feel this morning. Even the brightly colored glass in the meurtriere windows couldn't make it cheerier.

"Then we should send out a messenger to the leader of the human army... Darakoor, right?"

"Adracoor," Phenmal corrected her. "A grizzled character, but worthy as anyone can be."

"Then we should let this Adracoor know we're on our way. He is desperately recruiting, he needn't anymore," Tinna muttered. Phenmal remained starkly silent for a moment and then shook his head.

"There's no time for messages."

"Dragons can carry them," she replied, her brow arched incredulously. "He needs to know that there's a supplemental army at his disposal. He won't have to practically abduct every young man he comes across."

"We cannot be bothered by that, Tinna," Phenmal insisted; a sternness took over his voice, an insistence like a silent command for Tinna to let it rest. But he knew Tinna too well to imagine she would let it rest. "Besides, the Duke of Adracoor is a notorious dragon-killer. It wouldn't be advisable to send a dragon down to issue a message. It won't come back. All we need is for the humans to kill a dragon and create an enemy of a most valuable ally." Tinna's brow shot up, and as if his resistance spurred her forward, she set her jaw stubbornly.

"We can spare a rider, Phenmal. Why are you so insistent on not sending a message to the human army?" Phenmal frowned.

"Because the Keepers forbid it," he finally blurted. "Let it rest!"

"To bullocks with the bloody Keepers!" she screamed. She was steaming. "They need to know!"

"Things need to play out as they are meant to, Tinna, and forewarning the human army isn't part of the plan. They have a reason for everything. Just stick to what is happening here and now." Tinna simmered for a few moments and then cooled—once again cowing to the will of the Keepers, no matter how mad it seemed. The only explanation that seemed even marginally acceptable as to why they didn't want the human army to know what was going on, was simply to fortify the story in the end; boosting the heroism of the Araki people as they arrive last-minute to save humankind. She kept her thoughts to herself, but she was sure Phenmal heard them regardless, for he had a knowing smirk on his face.

"Fine," she grunted. "It seems trite, honestly, to control whether or not the Duke knows of our army coming to his aid. But we will be there regardless. Right now we need to focus on what's happening here."

So what's the plan?" he asked. She looked at him contritely and rubbed her temples.

"Taneth is gone, so I haven't been able to sit down with him. The Keepers summoned him north for a brief visit. They promised not to keep him long and he went by dragon, believe it or not. But I've studied the map, and there aren't really that many people missing that we can't afford to just start marching very soon; we won't travel so fast that they cannot catch up, especially with the supply drays and such. But yes, I want to get going. Soon. Possibly in a few days if Taneth gets back."

Phenmal nodded in agreement and walked to the desk of open maps, looking intently at them.

"You and Taneth are going with the army, decidedly?"

"Of course."

"I am not. I leave for home very soon. I will see you when you get back to Thamatoc."

"Why?"

"I have some obligations to see to. My purpose here is complete."

"What was your purpose here exactly?" she asked, reaching for a cup of water. She sipped while Phenmal shrugged and smiled at her enigmatically. She wanted to ask him what her purpose was, but she knew she'd get the same vagaries—either that, or the truth, which she did not want to hear.

"What of the young ones?"

"Hanru will return to Thamatoc with Skye when we leave. They won't be useful on the battlefield. They were of a great assistance here, but the people still at home require oversight and Hanru needs to focus on his education. They'll take horses home. Even the Annoying Nine are talking about leaving."

Phenmal nodded, and then gave her a long, meaningful look. With a smile, he closed the door and left. Tinna crossed her arms and stared at the door for a few moments after he left. She thought of Phenmal's dedication, his loyalty and his unchecked love for her and her family. She loved him too in many ways, in spite of his secretive ways. Even Taneth understood there was something more there. She tilted her head in bemusement, and then sighed. Alone, she sat down to study the map again to see who was still missing.

* * * *

Shade's flanks were slick with sweat and foam. Avria stood beside her, gripping her stirrup leather to keep herself from collapsing. Her horse still panted, her chest heaving, and Offrin stood before them with his sword coated in a bloody viscous enamel, at his feet was the body of a Thran soldier. Avria's eyes wandered up to look behind him, where more bodies lay splayed on the ground amid the confusion; horses and soldiers.

Three days prior, after running into Drashun, Avria and Offrin returned to Master Gavorre's carrying the map. The map was snatched from their hands the moment Offrin explained what was happening to the west, and Master Gavorre threw a greatcoat over his shoulders and stalked out of the shop without another word. All around the village, as word got 'round by messenger to the village elders, village leaders exited their homes and rushed to the town meeting hall to discuss the matter. Avria and Offrin were left well out of it. They ate dinner alone. Avria tended to Eleran as best she could, and went to bed.

That morning, a flock of pigeons were released to carry messages to all of the Auberge towns—how many, Avria did not know, but there were many pigeons. Master Gavorre had come home late, well after Avria had gone to bed and Offrin had returned to the barracks, and the old man awoke groggy and grumpy. Avria didn't press him with questions, and simply helped serve up their simple breakfast of ham, cheese, bread with butter and jam, and warm, lightly spiced milk. She slid down across from him at his little dining table and shook her napkin out onto her knees.

"You look tired, Master," she whispered. He grunted.

"Eleran has stabilized. He looks," he paused, thinking of a word, but settled on: "better."

"He looks the same to me," Avria muttered.

"He's fine. For what it is," he snorted testily. "Avria, we will be sending the Adrei militia Northwest, to Iromi, to join your mother's forces. Our garrison will be leaving at about noon. The Quarter Master has been issuing the kits, and your friend will be off soon enough with his comrades. I think you should accompany them." Avria looked up from her breakfast and furrowed her brow.

"I can't leave Eleran."

"He's not going anywhere. You should go with them. Your family must be very concerned about your welfare, and honestly, I'm not sure how long it will be before more rangers come looking for you. In spite of our efforts to go back and erase their markings as best we could, they are skilled like no others and they will come. It's not a matter of if; it's a matter of when. It's better that you go to your family wherever they are. You can always come back to visit. The Araki settlements are not so far from here."

"I can bring him home..."

"Until you have someone of magical ability under your lodge's roof, my dear, Eleran isn't going anywhere. He needs not only care, but he needs maintenance from us to keep him tethered to his body, no matter where his spirit has been sent. No, you need to leave Eleran in my care for now, until I can find some answers and assistance. I've sent a letter to the Keepers of Emethral requesting them to advise me." Avria stared at him in puzzlement for a moment and then her expression transformed into something infinitely darker. She was angry to be asked to leave Eleran's side. She remained tightlipped and put down the food she was about to eat. He didn't even look at her as he spoke.

"You will be protected by the soldiers on the voyage, it won't be a long one, Iromi isn't all that far from here. Two or three full days of riding, at best. Pack up your things and go with them. That's an order."

Wordlessly Avria threw down her napkin and she stalked off, her anger almost coming off of her in a black cloud. Gavorre put down his fork and sat back, sighing audibly.

Within the hour, Avria was ready to go. She stood by Eleran's still form for a long, drawn out moment, kissing his inanimate lips and fighting back her tears as she whispered goodbye to his deaf ears. She exited the shop carrying her bags, brushing past Gavorre, offering him only a small, hard-eyed nod before passing through the door. She made her way across the plaza to the livery to fetch Shade, and then rode her up the north road towards the garrison barracks.

She was astonished by the size of this force when she rode up. She really hadn't spent any time at the barracks, she generally knew where they were, but she had no idea there were hordes of ponies and so many men, she could not count. Offrin found her immediately, not a difficult task when her horse towered over every other equine in the area. He waved to her as he loped towards her, the reins of a handsome pony clutched in his hand.

"Good, I was wondering if Gavorre had convinced you..." he said. Avria glanced at him with a flash of anger and glowered.

"He did not give me a choice," she snapped. Then her face softened, knowing it wasn't fair to blame Offrin, who was nothing but kind and affable. She shook her head, and sighed. "I feel awful leaving him behind like this..."

"He will be fine. Master Gavorre will look after him," he said. "Come, we are about to embark. Ride with me. Before we go, allow me to attach some additional supplies to your saddle. You'll need your own tent." She nodded and waited for Offrin to mount his graceful pony, and they rode towards the thick of the growing cluster of Adrei soldiers. They organized themselves into ranks three-riders-wide, and embarked at the height of noon, underneath the white glow of the sun behind the bank of stone-grey clouds.

By the next morning, two more garrisons from different Auberges had joined had them—merging into their ranks as they moved along the roads the evening before. Now, the combined force was stirring. Avria breakfasted with Offrin and his friend Hevrin. They shared a small fire, sitting on small folding chairs. It was completely inexplicable to Avria as to why the rangers would come after her while she was sitting on the edge of a military camp. She tried to suss it out, to understand them; all she could come up with was that they were desperate and lost sight of their caution upon seeing Avria. Either that or they underestimated the strength and skill of the little soldiers. It was accident, not cleverness that brought them to her—and nothing more. They were merely traveling the same road. The Adrei contingent had simply merged onto the main road just between a large gap in the Thran cortege that had stolen Avria to begin with. Thankfully, the Thran soldiers and Sennal herself were already far ahead. There was only the last grouping of Rangers coming up behind, apparently still carefully working to hide the passage of the large contingent.

When the Adrei stopped for the night in a largish meadow by a river, they had no idea there were rangers behind them. But that morning, when Avria was having breakfast near her little tent, set up next to Offrin's and Hevrin's, on the fringe of the Adrei camp, the first three rangers attacked. Avria had gotten up to put on a heavier sweater against the morning chill, when she felt two hands grip over her mouth. She managed to squeak out in shock, alerting Offrin immediately. The soldier jumped to his feet and shouted. He watched as a dark-clad woman pulled Avria, struggling, into the edge of the trees. He saw two more almond-skinned faces waiting there for her.

The soldiers scrambled, swords were drawn and it wasn't long before a great horde of Adrei was in pursuit. The Thran's choice to attack made no sense to anyone in the group. Two of them were thought to have escaped, and they managed to kill the third and free Avria in a violent scuffle. About thirty men in total went in pursuit the other two, who were subsequently stopped before they could get away.

Offrin helped Avria get back to her feet. She was scratched up from being dragged through some dense brush, and a mark of red shaped like a hand still emblazoned on the skin of her face. She was stunned.

"They're still after me!" she barked. Offrin shook his head.

Offrin's eyebrows furrowed and he shook his head in puzzlement. "It's strange they just pulled you away with all of us about. It was not good decision-making by any means." Avria nodded, her brows rising in incredulity. She shook her head and snorted, still astonished by the brazen attack.

"There are lots more of them if the road is telling the truth," Hevrin muttered, walking through the camp to reach them. He pointed ahead of the camp with his sword. "I just walked ahead a little bit to see if there were any tracks of other Thran, and it looks like a small army just came through here. It's not Araki as we assumed yesterday. Too many wheels and feet, and too few hoof-marks."

"It's the cortege!" Avria blurted. "My grandmother's cortege. We must have come up behind it," she said disbelievingly. She stood

458

there, open mouthed, shocked at the odds of this happening. The caravans were slow, but not that slow. Unless the search of Avria had impeded them, she did not know. She pondered it all.

"I think we need to get you to Iromi as soon as possible," he said. "If any one of those women got away to warn the people ahead of us..." he postulated.

"I was just thinking of that. When I was in the column at the beginning, they kept me at the back with the rangers. They rode at least one hour distant from the main cortege, erasing the passage of the contingent. We must have come onto the road just inside that gap. Gods! There were twelve women when I rode with them. Twelve. Eleran killed three, and then two... now three more are dead; there are four left. They could be out there hiding, it's their greatest skill, or they could be riding ahead to alert the soldiers that they'd found me. The whole column could be turning back and coming for us," she said. Offrin again, shook his head.

"Well, maybe we need to get out of here in case they did get away."

"Let's get on the road!" he shouted. The camp was quickly broken down and within the hour, they were on their way.

Following the trail left behind by the Thran horde, they discovered that the grouping took a southerly road long before the road to Iromi appeared. Avria allowed herself to hope in spite of the knowledge that the missing rangers would raise eyebrows, and that someone would be on their way soon to see what happened to them. The soldiers and Avria turned onto the northwest road, angling up towards Iromi, and hoping they'd avoid further conflict. She was ensconced in the fold of a sizable army of Adrei, which had just been supplemented by another garrison from another town that had come up behind them shortly after the first attack. It would take a great deal of arrogance to stage another attack or an attempted abduction in these circumstances.

But as a people who believe themselves divinely appointed to the act of war, they were indeed arrogant, and by late afternoon the bulk of the mounted soldiers that had comprised the cortege appeared behind the Adrei forces at full gallop and immediately engaged the soldiers in a skirmish right on the road. This created sufficient distraction to drive Avria and her protector Offrin to the edge of the fighting, where the remaining rangers and several soldiers awaited. Thankfully, Avria was in her saddle, and without the slightest hesitation, the second she realized what was happening, she kicked her horse into a full run. Her pursuers followed, and Offrin took the rear with some of other Adrei soldiers who were smart enough to know what was going on. Their ponies were not quite able to match the longer strides of the horses, and they got ahead by some lengths quickly

Here there was some forest behind them, but before her the land opened up into great fields, some tilled for agricultural purposes, some enclosed by stone walls and filled with livestock. Avria veered her horse to the north and allowed her to vault over the stone wall, scattering the sheep that grazed inside the pasture, and thundered across towards the next wall, where two horses had been grazing. They now watched her intently as she neared the wall. When Shade sailed over it, they wheeled and whinnied and chased her as well, while the other riders fought to keep up with Avria's speedy little mare. One of the Thran ladies went flying off the horse as it refused to jump the stone wall, and tumbled over it to fall motionless on the ground on the other side. The Thran horses had already been running for some time, and were tiring quickly. Shade was rested and excellent for sprints. Offrin and several Adrei soldiers remained on the main road, riding parallel as best they could, their ponies' sides already growing dark and slick with sweat. They were getting closer because the whole group was slowing. Everyone but Avria.

Shade took the last wall before merging back onto the road, riding ahead of the Thran, seven in total, thundering on their horses. Behind them all were the Adrei. The hills parted before her as she rode up a slight incline to reveal a nice-sized town. On the fringe of the town was a large market area, which contained her salvation. Avria nearly burst into tears of joy at the sight of about sixty Araki riders idling about in their saddles in an open field, drinking beer from mugs being offered by the locals. It took a moment for the jovial pack to notice Avria thundering towards them, but as soon as they did, the mugs were dropped and they were riding towards her in concern.

"Thran!" she cried as she got near enough. "Thran!"

The seven Thran riders saw the pack of riders battering the earth towards them and stood up in their saddles and pulled their horses to a stop, wheeling them around. The Araki riders, with Avria at the back took chase, pulling some old, rusted swords from their scabbards, or in the case of some prairie riders, huge long-bows designed to be used in saddle. "Ride up!" the leader shouted back at her. His name was Dranatoth, and he was the father of one her good friends from the prairie clan of Edrotoch. Avria rode into the gap they made for her, and while the man nocked an arrow, steering his lithe, short-legged, stalwart horse with his legs, he turned and looked at her.

"Just these seven?" he shouted over the din.

"No. I'm with a mounted group from the southern forests, many riders. There is a sizable force of Thran attacking them, keeping them busy. They're after me..."

"Must have something to do with your mother, I'll wager..." the man replied with a knowing grin. "Well, come on then, let's dispatch with this problem already. We're already late to Iromi," he barked. Avria nodded, and she pushed on, all at the heels of the terrified Thran soldiers.

The armies met in a clash. Several Adrei were already injured or dead, but there were as many of the Thran if not more lying in the road as well. The addition of the sixtyish riders was an onslaught, and the arrows flew and the swords fell. Avria was made senseless by the sight of it, and she sat there, slack-jawed for a moment while she took it all in.

The Thran, knowing their numbers were limited now, began to retreat, but the Araki soldiers were merciless, and went after them. They did not want the Thran to carry the news south that riders were armed and gathering. They preferred that the cortege was left to speculate about their disappearance. Offrin had left Avria's side and was into the fray, his sword flying, his face speckled in blood, eyes black with rage. She watched, breathless, drained and exhausted as the Adrei and Araki dispatched with her grandmother's personal guard, one after the next. After a while, the sound of slower horses came up behind her, and the locals from the town were coming, men on foot and on horse, to help finish the last of them.

She slid out of her saddle to the ground, her knees barely able to keep from giving in, her breath ragged. Shade was a mess, slathered in foam and sweat. Offrin approached her, savage like in his bloodied, feral state, and their gazes met. Around them, arms stopped clashing, shouts became silent, and everyone began to realize the skirmish was over. They stood about on their mounts in confusion for a little while. Offrin rode up to Avria and put his hand on her shoulder.

"We can ride to Iromi now, Avria. What's left of your grandmother's guard will surely not be enough to dispatch after you. She will require protection to reach Chrotrioth. I can't imagine

461

you're in danger of being taken or harmed by her now." Avria nodded, still clutching her stirrup leather.

"Can we give the horses some time to rest? Shade needs to rest. She needs water," she said.

"The village will have that. Come, all. Let us go. We can take rest at these people's fine village, and then ride on from there," Dranatoth barked, having been eavesdropping on their discourse. The townspeople nodded and began to filter back, some of the men staying behind to take care of all the dead. Above, the dark, boulder-grey clouds were gathering, booming their threat for a good, soaking rain.

All Avria wanted now was to go home.

*   *   *   *

Tinna leaned back in her chair and looked out the foggy window. It had done little but rain since they'd arrived. The army had grown to an astounding size. She could not account for it. How had the forests produced such a force? She never knew. Nobody had known. Even the extraordinary numbers in Taneth's census couldn't paint an adequate picture that the physical presence of so many soldiers all in one place could. The eastern side of the encampment strained against the edges of the small city. Steady foot traffic flowed in and out of town, where the Araki riders found diversions.

Inside the rooms, the fire snapped and popped in the fireplace, and a cup of hot tea steamed on a little table at Tinna's side. A half-eaten breakfast cooled on a finely hewn platter on the same table. After a morning of violent retching, she had found her appetite again and absently chewed on a piece of dry toast. She could not bring herself to feel optimistic; no matter how well everything fell into place, no matter how beautifully the Keepers equipped her army, no matter how powerful it had grown. She did not worry about winning or losing the war. No matter the outcome, her new view of her future trod her down. She felt trapped in a role created by powers she did not understand. She would never have the life she hoped for. After twenty years of working toward a simple existence, everything had to change. That change, already underway, could not be stopped.

She shifted in her chair. Her movement caused Taneth to look up. She heard him snap shut the book in his lap and cross the sitting room to lower his frame into the chair next to her. "What's on your mind, my beloved?" His hand reached out and wrapped around hers, pulling it down from a reddened patch of skin at her neck that she scratched worriedly. She glanced at him and smiled wanly.

"What isn't?" she laughed softly.

He smiled, and shook his head.

"You're worried about Avria, I know."

She nodded. Her lips tightened. "How could I not be? She's our little girl."

He heard this refrain every day in one form or other. He could only swallow his own concern and reassure her.

"I know…"

A fast rap at the door interrupted them. Without leave, Hanru entered with a rumpled piece of paper in one hand and something bundled under his other arm. He handed the paper to Taneth with a look of complete bewilderment. Taneth scanned the paper and barked out in a surprised laugh. "More armaments? More supplies?

"How is this possible? We already have more than we need! Most of the clans are accounted for—and the ones that haven't arrived yet already have their supplies here waiting. We're about to leave this place. More deliveries?"

"That isn't it. You should see these things! Look!" Hanru let the bundle under his other arm drop into his hand. He handed it to Taneth, who shook it out, holding up a red and white sheet for a steed that looked very much like the others issued to the Araki cavalry, except in size. Taneth glanced up in puzzlement.

"Is this a joke? This is too small."

"Exactly. Everything is too small. Everything is undersized or altered. The horses' and riders' armors, the vestments, the weapons—all shrunk down."

"Why in the world do they send us this? What purpose does it serve to waste resources and time on nonsense like this? Were we supposed to arm our children?"

Tinna got to her feet, turning her back to the men and reached forward to wipe away the condensation on the window, her fingers squeaking against the glass.

"I think you have your answer, gentlemen. Once again, the Keepers have anticipated our needs." She leaned back to let them look through the pane she'd cleared.

"I'll be damned!" Taneth mumbled. He reached up and opened the latch, pushing the windows open so he could see the full view. "It's the little folk—from the Auberges."

"The what?" Tinna asked. She stood and squeezed between him and Hanru, looking down at the neat line of riders joining the encampment from the main road.

"The Auberges. Special towns where they send children born of small stature," Hanru explained.

Tinna watched in fascination as the groups filed in, welcomed by their Araki counterparts. She smiled, and propped her hands on her hips, taking in the ponies and the varying size of the riders. They were interspersed among Araki riders she recognized from the summer meetings. Her eye came to a hard stop at the sight of a familiar black mare and its rider. She leaned forward to get a better look. Her hands gripped the sill. She took in an elated breath—something between a gasp and a sob.

"Oh, gods! Oh, gods!" she whispered. "Avria!" she screamed out the window. "AVRIA!" She turned, eyes wild with happiness, glassy with tears. "It's Avria!"

She clutched the front of her robes and dashed out of the room barefoot, the men at her heels.

CHAPTER ELEVEN – THE MARCH

The din of hundreds of riders drowned out her mother's call. Caught up in the overwhelming welcome that her people showered on the Adrei, Avria's heart swelled. The sight of so many familiar faces from so many clans, all smiling at her and her friends as they rode into camp, elated her. She giggled as the Araki riders reached out to ruff and pet the manes and faces of the hundreds of ponies that filed by, then gripped the wrists and patted the shoulders of the riders. She felt what everyone shared at this moment—a sense of instant brotherhood.

The newcomers were directed to the western edge of the field, where a sizable space remained unclaimed and several drays conveniently awaited them, laden with provisions, including winterized tents and all the armaments they could possibly need. Offrin glanced up at Avria and grinned. "I had no idea we'd be so welcomed!" he said.

Avria smiled back and shook her head in bewilderment. "It's like they knew we were coming! It's so nice to see my own people again! I need to go find my family and my clan." She drew her horse aside, and Offrin remained with her. They let the procession ride past them. Her eyes searched the camp and its countless faces and constant movement. She couldn't see anyone from Thamatoc. She turned Shade into the surge and rode against it, ponies coursing around her. Offrin followed in her wake. Her ears picked out a familiar call that brought an instant sting to her eyes. "Avria! Avria!" Her mother's voice, unmistakable, edged with joy and panic. She searched the chaos for her, but her mother, so petite, disappeared among the bobbing heads, tents, horses, flags, smoke and muck. Then she saw Hanru's red cheeks and glistening eyes and her father's grinning face(they were both tall men) and in front of them, zigzagging like a jackrabbit through the crowds, her mother's dark head and occasional glimpses of her frantic face as she wove towards Avria. The girl dismounted and absentmindedly abandoned Shade, elbowing her way through the crowd towards her family, the tears already flowing.

"Mother! Oh Mother! Father! Han!" A break in the horde, and suddenly they came running at her, her mother barefoot, wearing nothing but a flimsy sleeping gown and a robe, both hemmed in mud. She threw herself at Avria. Their bodies collided with painful force, clutching one another as if each one had to verify the reality of the other. Tinna wept with joy, pressing her daughter's cheek to hers, leaning back to cup her face, then clutching her again. Soon, the arms of the men had enveloped them, both Hanru and Taneth kissing Avria's cheeks and hugging her close, gripping her hands. Her father openly sobbed with joy to see his girl, his nose turning red. Relieved and happy, grieving and joyful, she felt all manner of things as she touched the people she loved and let them wrap her into them. All her anger with her mother vanished. Seeing this army, she lost every trace of selfishness and doubt. She understood.

Feeling herself being pulled away from the camp, she resisted. "Shade...and Offrin," she said, wiping her nose with her sleeve.

"Shade will be taken care of. Who's Offrin?"

"My friend. He's there." She spun around and pointed to a rugged, handsome little fellow sitting on a tall moors pony so well-proportioned that it looked like a little horse. He had thought to snare Shade's reins and lead her along as he tried to follow Avria through the milling crowds of people and horses. He now smiled at them awkwardly.

* * * *

Master Gavorre's cheek twitched. He snorted, breathing deeply and heavily. In the hearth, the fire snapped, and a log split and burst. The fire grew hotter, radiating its comfort and peace. He sat comfortably ensconced in his chair by the fender, a book flat and open on his lap where it had fallen, his pipe burnt out and dangling precariously from a slack hand hanging over the edge of the chair arm. The log popped loudly again, and he startled, his pipe falling to the floor. He opened his eyes a bit and grumbled, straightening himself groggily in his chair. As he leaned down to pick up his pipe, he saw a rather large pair of feet standing in formal slippers on the floor in front of him. His eyes traveled up two pristine white stockings to a pair of fawn, fall front trousers and a gold waistcoat and black frock coat of the most graceful style, above which perched the face of a complete stranger of tremendous size. The man stood as tall as Eleran, but leaner and more angular, with great bony hands and bottomless brown eyes. Another creature blocked the firelight, a willowy creature of the palest complexion, also tall, beautiful in a severe way, with hair like black silk falling straight to the middle of her thigh, the bangs cut in a tidy line just below the line of her eyebrows. Not a hair strayed from its place. Her eyes, a vivid green, gazed down at him from her tilted face, rimmed in shimmering, thick lashes. She, too, wore the most current human fashions, an elegant columnar day gown of red silk with gold trim around a high waistline and embroidered fleurs-de-lis on the bodice front and short sleeves, pinched and decorated with little gold dots, over a longer pair of false sleeves. A fichu filled in the low décolletage made of the sheerest fabric. An elegant velvet redingote and a greatcoat draped across the chair he still thought of as Avria's, with a stylish bonnet and a large feathered bicorn atop them.

The woman stood with her hand resting on the shoulder of the man, who sat, as Eleran had sat so many times, in the chair across from the Master. They both stared at him with strange expressions of patience and benevolence. There was something about them-- something he couldn't place. He did not panic. He barely reacted at all, simply straightened in his chair, marked his page and closed the book and laid it, then the pipe atop it, on the little table by his chair. He checked that his robe was closed, adjusted his cap, and gave them his full attention.

"Might I ask who you are and why you've come to my house?"

"You should not concern yourself with who we are," the man said, his voice deep and resonant. "We only come to find the Soothsayer."

Gavorre studied them more closely. They neither looked nor acted like Thran. They seemed to him more Northwestern in demeanor, possibly even Zshathri, like Eleran. Perhaps they were his patrons; they had the appearance of aristocracy, but of the oldest blood. Master Gavorre cleared his throat and smiled at them stiffly.

"The Druid is here; however, he is also absent."

"Yes, we understand. We would like to see him regardless." The woman's voice had a smooth, velvety quality to it. Gavorre found her most attractive. He considered the two of them for a moment. They had entered his home uninvited and they knew the Druid was here. They could have gone to him at any time, yet they did not simply go up to the attic to see him; they came instead to Gavorre and waited for him to wake.

"Are you his family? His patrons, perhaps?"

They just nodded. For some reason, he could not sense anything to mistrust in them. He was instead drawn to their inexplicably attractive nature. "He is upstairs. Allow me to show you..." He stood, his slippers shuffling from the worn rug to the wooden floor, which creaked under his weight, and led them upstairs to the room that Avria and Eleran had shared.

Eleran lay silent on the bed, as if in state. His chest barely rose and fell. He looked wasted and drawn. The woman made a little whimpering noise and lifted her hands to her extremely full, red lips. She sailed to him, her silken train rustling behind her, and dropped down to sit beside him on the edge of the bed. The man moved around to the other side and sat as well. Gavorre could only look on from the foot of the bed, at Eleran framed by these beautiful strangers. The woman's pale hands reached out and fell upon the Druid's sallow brow. She looked to her companion and her dark, lovely brow furrowed. The man peeled back the blanket that covered Eleran to the chin, and picked up his hands, folding them onto the chest and clasping them both in his own hands. He and the woman began to whisper together in a language that Gavorre recognized, though he did not speak it, a tongue so ancient, so mystical that only a few souls in the world could understand it. At that moment Gavorre knew who and what these creatures were.

With an expression of utter reverence and humility, the Master stepped back against the wall, and the blood drained from his face. He remained deathly still and watched them. While they whispered, Eleran stirred. His torture showed plainly in his face, and he groaned in the most agonizing way. His chest rose, and fell, the agony fading into his former death-like slumber. The man slid his hand behind Eleran's neck and pulled, so that he sat upright. Whispers in unison, and Eleran moved, still unconscious, but somehow present enough to follow their lead. The lady stood, keeping her hands on his forehead, as Eleran's legs slid from the covers and his feet touched the floor. Following their whispers, he moved as if only the contact of their hands animated him.

They grasped each hand, and he stood. Without a word to the Master, they walked with Eleran to the door and led him slowly, arduously down the two flights of stairs. Gavorre gathered their coats and hats from the chair in his sitting room and piled them into his arms, following them out through the shop and into the little square to a large, elaborate coach hitched to two massive Gridgian drafts. Rare creatures in these parts, they dwarfed any horse he'd ever seen, their silver-grey, dappled bodies massive barrels, their hoofs bigger than a person's head. They stamped their hoofs on the cobbles and snorted impatiently. A silent coachman sat facing forward.

Eleran was loaded into the coach, and the lady followed him in to settle him on the rich upholstery. The gentleman turned to Gavorre, taking the coats and hats and handing them into the coach. The footmen, strange quiet creatures, simply waited. The tall man bowed gracefully to the stalwart magician, who gawked up at him in awe.

"We will do what we can to save him, but he has done great wrongs; it will require more than our two voices. He will remain in our care until he is healed."

"His love… she awaits him."

"She will find him when the time is right. For now, he is a coveted child. He must be watched over, and possibly healed. Only we can help him."

Master Gavorre wanted to ask how they had known where to find him, how they had known of his condition…but these were silly questions. They were Hevra, the first of all the kinds. Immortal creatures wise beyond any other. They carried the souls of gods and purportedly they all suffered madness caused by the power of their godly souls. He had no right to question them. He merely allowed them to take the Soothsayer.

The coach lurched under the weight of the man as he climbed in. Did a soothsayer matter so much to the gods that they would seek one out if he were imperiled? It seemed so. Gavorre watched the door close and the coach lunch forward as the draft horses began to move. The clatter of their massive hooves deafened him as they broke into a powerful, earth-battering trot, setting up a din of iron wheels and shoes against the cobbled square, until the coach, rocking softly on its suspension, vanished into the forest cover.

Master Gavorre wrung his hands. "What in the world am I going to tell Avria?" he muttered worriedly. With an apprehensive sigh, he scuttled back into the shop.

* * * *

Avria mounted Shade and turned to look back at Offrin, a silly grin on her face. They both smirked, and he puffed out his chest, showing off the red and white colors emblazoned on his torso. Avria looked down at her own colors and waggled her shoulders, making the dragon and the horse dance. She then lifted up the small, delicate helm and dropped it comically on her head wiggling it so that her plume danced as well. Offrin laughed and did the same, pushing his pony into a trot, making no effort to sit the trot smoothly, instead letting himself bounce in order to maximize the rattling of the armor pieces that bedecked him and his steed. Avria giggled. He trotted around her.

"Avria, a girl of such silliness, it's contagious," Hanru admonished, riding up in a cassock like his father's, with significantly less decoration and a shorter capelet. "I have to say, I won't regret missing this battle. I can't believe that you want to fight, after everything you've been through."

"How can I not?" she snapped.

Offrin had stopped rattling around and had maneuvered his pretty pony parallel to Shade. He looked up at Hanru with a half smile.

"Well, at least mother will be with you, I suppose."

"What are you and Skye going to do?"

"Go back home. That's what we were told to do. Also, I want to set up a nursery in their apartments, as a surprise for when they get home."

Avria smiled at that idea, nodding in enthusiastic support. The news of her mother's pregnancy had given her such joy that she had wept. A little sibling, at last!

"What of Phenmal? Will he come?"

"He left this morning. I think he went home."

Avria snorted at that and arched a brow dubiously. "Gone off to see the Keepers, I suspect!" She sighed and rode up to her brother, throwing out her arms to embrace him from horseback.

"Keep yourself safe Avria, please!" His voice came tremulous and tight.

She rubbed his back and kissed his cheek. "You too, big brother. I love you very much."

"I love you too, Av." He let go and turned his horse away quickly, embarrassed of his watery eyes. He needed to give himself a moment before he rode up the road a bit and said goodbye to his parents.

Avria, less embarrassed by these things, blinked out a tear and smiled at Offrin, who looked on with an empathetic smile on his face. She sighed shakily, and they turned their steeds towards the part of the column where the Adrei were gathering. She watched her brother canter up to the head of the army, where their mother and father had already started to move.

The people of Oromoii had not seen a sight like this in centuries. Thousands of riders--over twelve thousand Araki and an additional eight hundred from the six Auberge towns--each clan having sent every capable rider, including women. No one had heard of such a thing before Tinna had come along. Until now, women had officially ridden only in the relay.

* * * *

Hanru passed clan after clan. They all wore the red and white; their shields differentiated them by clan. All shields had the horse and the dragon emblazoned upon them, as did all surcoats; however, each clan carried its own design on the shield beneath the horse and dragon. His mother's had oak leaves to represent the Araki as a people, but others' bore porpoises, turtles, flowers, walnuts...over three hundred groups, each with its own emblem. The lead rider of each clan carried its heraldic flag, which also bore its emblem.

The column had begun to move, but with lagging slowness. Hanru had to gallop quite a while to reach the front, where he spied his mother looking anxiously about.

"There you are!" she shouted, reining her horse to the side of the road. They did the awkward horseback hug. "Are you going to be all right, traveling home on your own?"

"We should be fine. The resident summoner will arrive in two weeks, according to the relay, so we have to get moving today. I just wanted to say goodbye one more time."

"Oh, I don't know where Avria is in all of this mess."

"I found her. She's riding with the Adrei."

"Good!" said Taneth, grinning as he rode up alongside them. He wore a long cape over his cassock and a strange little box-shaped hat. He hugged his son from the other side and patted his back roughly. "She was afraid she'd miss you in all of this."

"I can't find Drashun anywhere. And where's Rhoa?"

"I don't know, they're somewhere. Hanru, be sure that the dogs are well fed and cared for, and please, please, please don't go to Lemoram until we get back. I need to have someone of sane mind there, watching over everyone. The children haven't had classes since I left, and also, you should start a search, if you have the resources. We're still without a holy man."

Hanru simply shook his head and sighed at his father's rambling. "Don't fret yourself into a frenzy. We'll be fine. Go. I love you both so much."

471

His mother blew him a kiss and kicked her horse into a canter to catch up to the front of the line. Taneth lingered a moment longer. He patted his son's knee and, with pursed lips and a furrowed brow, turned and followed. Hanru stayed there for a long while, observing the rumbling procession. Carts and drays thundered past, horses whinnied and pranced, riders laughed, armor clanked. The people of Iromi lined the side of the road, bidding new friends farewell, handing them bottles of refreshments and packets of food. Hanru finally found both Drashun and his mother. The boy rode with some riders from the Wye clan, and Rhoa cantered by, trying to catch up to the front. She paused long enough to kiss Hanru on the cheek and galloped away.

Hanru sighed and turned his horse back towards Iromi, riding on the side of the road rather than forge against the unstoppable tide of red and white.

* * * *

Jestin and his friends arrived at Iromi just as the last of the procession was leaving. They crested the hill, and the town came into view. "The army is moving!" someone muttered. They kicked their horses into a gallop and left Jestin behind.

He was in no hurry. He watched as the others rode down to merge with the tail end of the army. He dilly-dallied along, looking at the newly ploughed, muddied fields and observing the thin traffic coming towards him. To his surprise, he saw Hanru and Skye riding up the hill in his direction. He quickly tugged his old horse's reins and rode off the road, heading towards a small cottage farm on the hillside. He pulled the hood of his cloak over his head and kept his back to the road as they passed. He could hear Skye's animated voice, and Hanru laughing. When they had safely passed him by, he turned and followed the road for a little while, but just before a great stone bridge, where the column had turned onto the plain, he turned southwards along the river and followed it to Chrotrioth. He looked over his shoulder at the ragged tail-end of the column, which consisted of supply drays and late-arriving riders, those on slower-moving draught animals. He missed entirely the miles of riders moving south along the smooth arc of the road ahead, beyond the forest. The few small groups that he did see straggling along only amused him. Counting no more than two hundred people among them, he thought: They have no chance against the Thran.

472

* * * *

"Look!" Avria shouted. A new column merged onto the road from another lane that led from a small village.

Tinna glanced ahead where she pointed. "Kanreth Knights!" she said. "Look at their black uniforms."

"A dying breed," Taneth muttered, his tone curious at first, gradually turning professorial. "They ride such huge black destriers—every one of them! And look at the knee boots? Notice how much thicker the leather is over the shin?"

Tinna admired the tight black breeches that wrapped their thighs, their bodies layered in black tunics, sleeveless black gambesons and black leather plate armor.

"And the chest plates!" Taneth went on, "See the embossed silver? Can you make it out? It's a skull sitting on crossed swords. They pride themselves on their swordsmanship. See? Each one carries two massive swords, one hanging from each side of the saddle, behind the leg, where they pull easily from the scabbard. The angle of the hilt allows it to rest on the upper thigh, and the blade hangs diagonally down the length of the horse. The end of the scabbard hangs by a strap from the crupper of the saddle."

"Such ornate saddles!" Tinna marveled.

"Yes, and deep! These knights can steer a horse by the legs alone. And those swords—anyone else would use one as a two-handed sword--they're extremely light and thin, but long enough to reach a foot soldier. They can swing one in each hand and cut down an enemy on either side. Each pair is matched and unique in design to its owner."

The silver hilts shone like jewels against the black backdrop of horse and rider. All had their helms propped on the tall horns of their saddles.

"The Kanreth are one of the most ancient knight's guilds in Oromoii. Only a few remain. Their training academies were among the first to fall during the burnings, so now they come to Araki clans for--"

Avria cut his lecture short. "Damreth!" she shouted, waving at the company of Kanreth Knights, her smile radiant.

A great whopping grin of recognition lit up the grave features of a young knight, who kicked his horse to a canter to meet the approaching horde. He looked downright ecstatic to see Avria.

473

"Avria! Imagine that! What on earth are you doing out here? And dressed like that?" His eyes took in the girl in her armor and heraldic surcoat, then he took in the rest of the group leading the column. Eventually his eyes traveled beyond, to the long procession that followed.

"We're on our way to Chrotrioth," she declared.

Damreth fell in step with her, listening carefully.

"We are, too. Word is a battle is brewing down there, so we've come to lend a hand. We stopped by Yreth to find a few more of our brothers, but it turns out they've already gone south. So we're off to follow. I take it you are on your way to help?"

"The human army is very small; from our intelligence, only about five thousand. The Thran army has swollen to fifteen thousand and growing. They've already started moving their camp north, which means they have reached their desired size and are ready to stage an invasion."

"Gods! Fifteen thousand!"

"We are more than evenly matched now," Taneth interjected, indicating with his chin to look behind him.

Damreth smiled, then focused on pretty Avria again. "It really is good to see a familiar face. It seems like forever since Silver Lake."

"Tell me about it!" Avria chuckled with a blush. "A lot has happened since then."

"Then we shall ride with you, if that is acceptable?" he asked, turning to Tinna.

She nodded and smiled at him, knowing by his admiring gaze and Avria's flushed face that he was the fellow from whom Avria had stolen kisses at the lake. She smiled inwardly and gazed benevolently upon this young man.

"I am Damreth," he said.

Avria introduced the others. Damreth recognized Drashun.

The Kanreth column filed in comfortably between the Thamatoc and Ilmeth Clans, a patch of black among a riot of red and white, gladly taking their place among the Araki army.

* * * *

Jestin reached up and tenderly touched the side of his mouth, which throbbed with sharp pain. His fingers came away slick with bright scarlet blood. He stretched his jaw, wincing as fresh pain shot through his face. He pushed himself up onto his other arm and got to his feet. He'd gotten into some scraps before--at Silver Lake, in

474

muss-ups with his so-called cousins--but this was different. Something hard and brutal announced itself in what had just happened. There was darkness in it. The blow to his head had been calibrated to inflict pain, to cause him injury. Neither anger nor passion had driven it, but something much more calculated and malicious.

Linar glared at him, his fist still clenched behind his ear, ready to strike again. His eyes burned with an inexplicably cold fire, his lips curled in a cruel smile. At his side, Eria looked on impassively. She twirled a skein of wheaten hair on her index finger. Her face and body contradicted the manner of her dress. She boasted the yielding curves of a Northern woman, her countenance fair and bright, with eyes of forget-me-not blue and lips like the pink petals of a rose, full and parted, her sensuality soft and stunning; yet the hard Thran cut of her uniform dissected her, rendered her crisp and uninviting; the contrast disconcerted Jestin.

She took him in: his rakish hair, his angled, brooding, handsome face, his baleful blue eyes, his lean body. Changing her demeanor from indifferent to sultry, she appraised him from head to toe, while he relived the regrettable events that had brought him to her mother's tent.

Because his horse had refused to set hoof on the ferry, working itself up into an anxious sweat and fighting him when he tried to get it to board, he'd left the animal in the care of the ferryman's son and boarded the flat boat on foot. The ferryman had taken forever to pole his way across the water. Jestin disembarked on the pier of a small warehouse at a silo-ridden village. The place looked to have been abandoned since, as the ferryman told him, it lay only a few miles from the Thran. "Their camp's south," he said, "over the great hill."

Jestin had started walking. Before long, he'd spotted a Thran scout. Not long after that, two Thran cavalrywomen approached him. He lifted his hands and said: "I am Jestin of Loshan. I've come to serve Na'AiSennal."

Now--thanks to Avria for spurning him and to the Druid for appearing at just the wrong moment and ruining his chances with her--he stood wiping blood from his chin.

Eria finally reached up and pulled Linar's fist down to his side. "I'm bored," she muttered.

Linar glanced at her acidly and turned away, forgetting Jestin immediately.

Eria smiled seductively and sighed. Moving quietly to the opening of her tent, she brushed past Jestin, deliberately grazing his hand with hers. She gripped her elbows and looked out at the camp. "I will be happy when this thing finally comes to a head. It's high time a righteous people ruled over the North. These Northerners err in all that they do. Their treatment of women--so reprehensible!"

Jestin, touching his hand to his mouth again, sank down warily into a chair. Eria saw this out of the corner of her eye and spun on him. "Don't bleed on my chair, you useless pig!" she shrieked.

He stood and rushed past her, leaving the tent before Linar decided to act on his mistress' anger again. Jestin took several strides out of the tent but stopped short. Below, he saw Thran forces on the move. Eria's mother's tent perched on a high hill among the other tents of the upper echelons of the religious order, overlooking the main encampment: round tents with spire-like pinnacles, heavy, flapping canvases in tones of grey and brown, their bottoms muddy. Flags snapped and curled from the center poles in various colors, representing the many Thran warrior sects. He saw Sennal standing below, among a cadre of other highly-ranked women, her arms crossed and her face stern.

It had nonplused her to see him again, but Jestin's presence gave her the hope she needed that Avria was still attainable. She resisted her first impulse--to kill the boy. Instead, she thought that keeping him alive might inspire her granddaughter to trust her a little. For more than anything, Sennal wanted Avria at her side. She wanted a successor, someone to fill the place in her heart that Tinna could not. She admired Avria's spirit, her strength, the boldness she had shown in making her escape. She found these qualities commendable and desirable in a successor. When she first saw her scouts dragging Jestin to her, it filled her with rage, but that quickly dissipated. She began, instead, to hope. After the invasion, she would find Avria again and show her that she had taken her wishes into consideration by allowing her friend to live.

She remanded him into the care of a direct subordinate, a Northern woman by the name of Vara who had a tent of her own among those of the hierarchy and a daughter of Avria's age. Vara could communicate easily with Jestin, having been born at Suthervale, and the daughter could keep him in check. She was sure that Jestin was best placed in their custody for the time being.

Everything had happened so fast. Jestin hardly believed that he was here. It had devastated him at first to learn that Avria had not yet arrived. Sennal indicated that she had escaped but assured him that she'd get her back. It was only a matter of time. With a force like this, the Thran would storm the pathetic Araki and flatten them. Avria would be captured and brought here, where he would be waiting for her.

He'd told Sennal what he'd seen of the rag-tag Araki forces. What quick work the Thran would make of them! She seemed certain that Avria would have joined with their riders by now, a fact that pleased her greatly. Her glee informed him that he had done very well.

Now that he stood watching the Thran troops coalesce into huge masses, he knew that he and Avria would soon be reunited. Warriors filed out of their sect encampments into a single wide column, chaos trickling toward orderly ranks. With amazing clarity, the soldiers sang a battle hymn in unison, their thousands of voices rising up the hill in a harmony that seemed impossible, as if made up of only a few voices. The High Priestess of each sect blessed the warriors as they passed, then fell in stride with their sects towards Chrotrioth, their soprano voices riding along the crest of the hymn, ululating in harmonious song.

Jestin found himself mesmerized by the flocks of soldiers: feathered helms and bristling spears and voulge pole-arms, the bobbing, feather-adorned heads of the small cavalry of tiny desert horses, the glint of armor and the flutter of hundreds upon hundreds of little white skirts. For a moment, he felt the icy tendrils of fear creep up into his stomach and chest as he watched the hordes move towards the hills of Chrotrioth. He realized what devastation this war would wreak, and for a second, he thought of his mother and his grandmother, of his father and of Avria's family. But he set all that aside and stretched his painful jaw again, feeling the dried blood crack and crumble away. It would be worth it. Everything that he had originally intended would come to pass. Avria's grandmother--the old harridan--did not seem averse to his unexpected arrival. She seemed, at worst, ambivalent, and had remanded him to this tent, sequestered him with the horrible creature, Eria, and her first chosen husband, Linar, a deeply disturbed young man.

A Northern woman, Eria's mother had run away to Thran after only a few months of marriage to a man who had beaten her. She had carried his child, and that child had grown into the scornful, mean little thing in the tent. Eria's mother stood now among the clergy of this religious army, near Sennal. She had a head of hair like her daughter's, wheaten and bold among the dark heads of the Thran women. All five of the high-ranked priestesses overlooked the exodus. Eria burst out of the tent, elbowed her way past Jestin and tramped down the hill towards her mother, her golden hair flouncing on her shoulders, her skirt lifting up with each step to expose the short pants underneath and the swell of her rounded buttocks. Jestin could not stop staring at her, despite his dislike of the little beast. He didn't care, he refused to be bound to her, anyway; but as long as he had to stay with her, he was subject to her assault via proxy, battered by her stupid dog of a husband, who obeyed her commands. He liked to hit Jestin for his insolence. He did so with a sick pleasure. Eria did not like that Jestin spoke his mind. She seemed worse than any Thran woman he'd ever met, and she wasn't even Thran by blood.

He watched her boldly join the hierarchy, who all but ignored her, except her mother, who glanced at her as she prattled on, her voice competing in volume with the marching hymn.

"I find," Eria said to her mother, "that this ridiculous creature that came for Na-AiSennal's granddaughter has some interesting features."

Her mother arched her brow quizzically in response.

"Yes, he is insipid and weak and polluted by Northern ways, but that's nothing that a few months under Linar's tutelage couldn't improve. He's not the type to offer much resistance when told what to do, especially with a good example to show him the way."

"What are you saying, Eria?" her mother blurted, a strange smile on her face.

"I think that if that granddaughter doesn't claim him, I would like to consider taking him as a concubine. I like the dark hair and the blue eyes. I find it attractive, different from the dark-eyed Thran fellows. I think it would make for an attractive and unusual look in a daughter. The fact that he is part Thran also has its appeal. And I am fortunate enough to have a well-mannered first-husband to show him the proper way to comport himself."

"Well, if I don't find Avria," Sennal interjected, "then I have no use for him. Honestly, I have no use for him, anyway; however, I do think I should at least give her the chance to choose. She might want something familiar from home to make her feel better about the change. However, if she does not make it back with us, or she does not want him, you may do with him as you please." She graciously waved her hand.

478

Eria smiled broadly and nodded to her mother. None of them even glanced back at Jestin, who stood a ways off, watching them and the army.

"I thank you, honored Na-AiSennal! I am most grateful."

"Just be wary of that one, Eria. He might look reedy and weak, but that boy is as insidious as they come. A sneaky little backstabber. He will probably give you more trouble than he's worth."

"Well, I think Linar can keep him in check. But I will heed your wise warnings, honored Na-AiSennal."

"See that you do! If it backfires, I take no responsibility for your choice."

"Of course, Ma'am." Eria muttered, glancing sidelong at her mother, whose inferior rank made her bite her tongue.

* * * *

Jestin focused on the visual interest the movement of the troops offered, and on the power of their battle song. Soon, he would be traveling south to make amends with Avria and to plan his future with her.

Before long, the song followed the warriors over the hill, fading to no more than a faint hum carried by the winds. The leaders walked back up the hill. Vara, Eria's mother, barked something in accented Thran. The daughter sighed loudly and stalked away towards the nearly empty camps below. Linar, who'd come to stand a ways off from Jestin, followed, now dressed in his uniform. Vara glanced at Jestin, then to Sennal, asking her something. Sennal nodded, and Vara glowered.

"I suppose I must resign myself to having you as part of my household for now. I don't know why Sennal doesn't just kill you; you serve no purpose. But you should stop standing about like some entitled Northern boy; we don't tolerate that here. You make yourself useful or you make yourself scarce. Go and see to the tent. Help the eerand break it down and pack it onto the dray. We are moving to the final camp now."

He watched her weave around him. Beyond her tent, in the little enclosure with the main fire pit, the fine horses of the high priestesses waited. Their slaves helped them onto their steeds. Once mounted, they reined their horses around the tents and pushed them towards the tail end of the columns. Only the eerand remained--the lowest of low. Jestin found himself among these castoffs of Thran society, captured foreign men, slaves. He glanced at the slave master, a huge Thran male carrying a crossbow, and set to work on Vara's family tent. After today, he hoped, his circumstances would improve.

CHAPTER TWELVE – A WAR IN ONE DAY

Adracoor, Duke of the Zadrudas Isle and one of the few remaining nobles of the old rule, had been taken into custody by the usurpers twenty years ago. Once a gentleman connoisseur of regional wines, well-bred, with soft hands and superior brocades, he had enjoyed the finer things in life and had particularly relished his apple brandies. But prison, torture and starvation had hardened him. The dense, closely trimmed beard of silver-black that now carpeted his cheeks did little to disguise two reminders of his ordeal in the dungeons of those who had conspired with the man who had misused the dragons. A deep-rutted scar divided the top of his right forehead, cutting through his eyebrow and slicing the apple of his cheek before it disappeared into the forest of his beard. His captors had also branded him with his own brass button, leaving the red shape of an eagle embossed in the skin of his left temple forever. Over that eye, which they had burned out of his head, he wore a patch.

His days of refined foppery were over now. Transformed into an angry warrior, he drank cheap ale and lived in the barracks with his men, his manners and gentlemanly airs erased completely and replaced with a brash forcefulness. He had gained bulk, acquiring the frame and muscles of a man who trained constantly with other fighters. He organized hunting parties to take down any dragon foolish enough to stray into his land, and he had amassed an army larger than any other seat in Oromoii. Adracoor declared to all those in his charge that he would die before he would allow devastation and war to come to his world again.

Now he sat his horse, scrutinizing the sprawled formation of his own troops, occupying the sharp ridge that tapered off the rocky outcroppings of the southern range. Here, to the northeast of Chrotrioth, the Thran had started to move; they neared the source of the plains river, in view of Mount Jewel to the northeast. Directly east of them stretched the range of mountains that separated Thran from Oromoii. The majority of the fighters Adracoor had gathered fresh from the crop fields, stocky plains people, farmers and laborers recruited as his army made its way southward to Chrotrioth. Shabbily equipped and hastily trained, their numbers swelled his small, powerful army but diluted its experience and discipline.

His brown cape flapped noisily in the wind, as he let his good eye wander across the valley to the next rise, where the Thran Army, in its magnitude and orderly ranks, silently mocked him. He never knew there could be so many soldiers in one place. Mostly women too, lovely in a menacing way, with tall armored boots, white skirts, armored plates on their chests and white, long-sleeved tunics with plates belted around the shoulders and arms. They all wore feathered helms of metal covered in black leather, with plumes of pure white dancing as if in jubilant anticipation of certain victory, as the strong breezes toyed with them.

He bit his lip and rode forward a bit, his agitated horse sensing his tension. The wind blew blustery and cold, the sky overcast and the air prickling with expectation and fear.

"Gods! We're about to step into eternity, every one of us!" the nervous voice of the High King's primary counsel muttered next to him, sent by the monarch to assist the highest-ranked nobleman in this hopeless battle. "It's the end of Oromoii!" the young fellow concluded with a tremor in his voice.

"Would you turn and run back over the hill? And then what? Run from your towns? Your villages? I'd rather die here than die running, Portnan," Adracoor grumbled gruffly, his voice like a horse's iron-clad hoof on gravel. "We've seen enough slaughter. At least this time, we can die fighting." The younger man, silenced, studied the older, grizzled, ruined nobleman for the hundredth time and frowned. The duke looked nothing like he had twenty five years before. Portnan had seen a portrait of him and his long-dead wife in the great gallery of the High King's summer palace. He'd been an impressive figure, elegant and handsome, and his wife a creature of unsurpassed grace and beauty.

Now, his wife gone, the Duke wore common black, quilted linen under ancient, nicked and dented armor, undoubtedly taken from one of the corridors of his recently restored great house where he displayed ancient harnesses. His chain-mail had rusted in spots; his sword, also ferruginous, gleamed along its edge, having been recently sharpened.

The counsel, too young counsel anyone, let alone the High King, was dressed for royal court; no armor, just his elaborately decorated robes of office over a soft muslin collar-shirt and his favorite goat's wool breeches. His hands shone white and soft. The sword hanging from the front of his saddle looked out of place. He'd ridden south in a coach that now sat abandoned in the ghostly camp over the ridge, by the river behind them. There, crows had cried out as they broke camp, picking at leftover foods, tossing through rumpled clothing and other gear the men had simply tossed aside, as if none of it would matter in a few hours.

Adracoor heard the boy swallow his terror. "Well then," he said sharply, a strange smile on his face. Portnan's lips tensed and he gripped his reins tightly, his eyes going glassy and wide, nostrils flared. Adracoor wondered in passing how old he was. "I suppose now's a good a time as any. I'd rather not wait for them to start it. Won't make as good a story if they do." He glanced up at the dense clouds in the sky and sighed with resignation. It seems oddly appropriate to die under a sky like this one, he thought. "No need to draw this out any longer than we should."

He pulled his sword from the scabbard and lifted it high in the air. In response, the trumpeter, sitting on his horse a distance away, raised the horn to his trembling lips and blew.

The blast came shrill and cold. Two tones, one low, the next high, sliced through the windy jangle of armor and weapons. It carried across the valley to the Thran who blanketed the far hill, spears and pole arms waving like a field of wheat in the breeze. The horn lowered, the frayed flag moving gently in the wind, the human army drew its weapons and, in a roar that swept across its mass like a wave, began to surge forward, the dense pack suddenly looking less fearsome as foot soldiers distanced one another, loping down the hill towards the Thran army.

The enemy hesitated, then began to move in a more orderly charge, phalanxes bundled together in domes of shields, bristling with razor-edged spears. Adracoor watched as the first row of archers ran to take their places in preparation for the leading volley.

The ground began to rumble, a rolling thunder building underfoot--the din of the Thran army on the move, Adracoor thought at first, but he soon realized it originated behind him. His stomach rose to his throat. Had the Thran found a way to flank him? Had they got behind his forces? Portnan heard it too, the alarm evident on his young face. Before either had time to react, a line of horses exploded from the rise of the hill and sailed over it, running full tilt in fluttering red-and white colors, a river of equines cascading over the ridge. The riders shone in their new armor, weapons held aloft, struck with a sinister gleam as if they yearned for the bite of flesh. The iron-shod deluge surged around Adracoor and flooded the ranks of the Human army, weaving through the now thoroughly confused foot-soldiers and surpassing them in great strides. Woven into the stream of powerful mounts came a current of smaller horses and ponies elegantly outfitted in the same colors and heraldry, the small riders equipped with large weapons and armors made to fit.

Out of the clouds a massive column of flame vaporized the mist and fell like a burning house on the archery line, moving like the great fiery hand of a god, burning a swath through the astonished Thran before they had a chance to react to the mounted charge. A cacophony of roars erupted as scores of dragons dropped from the bottoms of the clouds. Spiraling downward on massive wings, they blasted scorching torrents of fire at the ground, scattering the Thran charge and driving the neat lines of archers backward in chaos, answering the dragons' roars with screams of panic, rage and pain.

Grounded, lines of biped dragons arrived amid the horses, sprinting past them with smoking nostrils. Jaws agape and roaring fiercely, they covered great tracts of ground with each stride. The human soldiers cowered at first, as the bobbing dragon-heads made their way towards them among the stampede; but the dragons kept running past the humans towards the Thran, growling and hissing with dog-like focus.

The leading edge of the red-and-white army of running dragons, horses and ponies collided with the Thran line. Weapons rang out as still more riders surged over the hill and dragons continued to drop out of the sky. Portnan wept openly, unable speak for his tears of joy and confusion. Adracoor laughed, his tears also falling. As they watched, a small cortege, led by two riders, split away from the coursing deluge and slowed to a leisurely pace. They turned towards Adracoor and Portnan. One of the lead riders was an awkward-looking fellow with the markings of an Araki Wiseman and the robes of high-office. The other, a small curly-haired Thran woman, with the largest, blackest eyes Adracoor had ever seen, bore into his soul with them.

"You are a welcome sight!" was all he could say for a second, astonished as he realized that Araki riders made up most of the army that had come to his rescue; as he realized this, a massive, seemingly endless shadow slid over them. The dragon that cast it skimmed over the hillside and sailed out across the battlefield, blasting a firestorm at a group of Thran archers trying to reassemble in the madness. Adracoor lowered his eyes to the face of the dark-eyed woman. Behind him, a younger version of herself sat on a lithe black horse with silver-tipped mane that danced with the grace of a swan.

"I don't know how you got the dragons to help, but Gods! I cannot say I am not happy to see them too!"

The older woman rode up to his side and looked out over the field below, which was now a strange mass of red and white, silver scales and blood. "The dragons have always had our best interests at heart, Duke Adracoor; even when they got tangled up in events far greater than we are."

Across the valley, the blackened hillside teemed with skirted Thran, avoiding the fires that still burned, shooting arrows and hurling spears at the dragons that kept dropping from above. As they watched, a dragon took one spear to the neck and another in its side. It faltered and plummeted, breathing out a great ball of fire over itself as it crashed into a huge phalanx of foot soldiers. Tinna's eyes filled with tears. A collective roar of fury filled the sky and stilled the fighting for but a moment. Then a new rain of fire fell upon the Thran as the dragons, infuriated by the loss of their brother, exacted a flaming revenge.

The Thran, already defeated, continued to fight. The mounted Araki and Adrei, with the help of the ground-dragons, like a horde of giant, rabid dogs, had the advantage of numbers now. They suffered few losses, despite the superior fighting methods of the Thran. The overwhelming might of the Araki army, with the added advantage of the smaller, more dexterous Adrei and their ponies, only made the combined force deadlier. A few horses lay immobile in the field, their blankets of red and white mounded among the bedlam, their riders splayed beside them. Some Araki, some Adrei, a ground dragon or two had been lost, but the rest continued to fight valiantly.

Tinna saw an Araki rider raise a lance and skewer a Thran woman with it, piercing her through the soft midriff. She fell back onto it, and then slid down the shaft, her face a grisly mask of death. An Adrei warrior steered his pony around an unsuspecting Thran and poised his sword, jabbing it through a thick jerkin into her back. Embedded in her ribcage, it wrenched free of his grasp as she fell. He had to circle round and yank it from her back. A ground dragon leapt impossibly high into the air and fell jaws-first on a screaming Thran. Tinna tore her gaze from the turmoil, moving them back to the hills of Chrotrioth. There, her eyes widened.

"The berserkers!" She scoured the sky. "Get the attention of the dragons!"

Avria dug her heels into Shade's flanks and pushed her to a gallop, speeding to the trumpeter and shouting over the din.

Across the battlefield, a new group arrived. Dressed in ivory and grey, they wore little armor and carried heavy weapons, large, fierce-looking voulges, pole-weapons with nasty, long-bladed heads. Some had points and barbs artfully cut into the design; blade-hooks adorned the tips of others. The shrill cry of the trumpet caught the ears of several dragons, who refocused on this new scourge. Once a Thran berserker set her rage free, nothing within the reach of her voulge would live. They had to be stopped before they joined the fray.

The dragons responded. Columns of flame passed over the berserkers. Now that the archers and spear bearers no longer posed a threat, several dragons swooped in. Avria's face wrinkled in disgust as a dragon snatched a berserker off the ground in mid-flight, flung her up into the sky like a rag-doll and caught her with a loud snap of the jaw. The dragon's open-mouthed chewing revealed more than Avria wanted to see, before he sent the berserker to his stomach with a gulp. Horrifying screams erupted from the liquid flames that several dragons poured out all at once on the remaining troop, consuming them as they scattered. Tinna knew it couldn't be long before the Thran would sound retreat. This fate was too brutal to withstand much longer. No more legions appeared from behind their hill to save them. Too many were burnt to death or killed in the stampede, too many others eaten by dragons who hadn't tasted human flesh in centuries. In the valley and on the hill, where they knew they would not risk catching an allied soldier in the flames, the dragons burned relentlessly. Between breaths of fire, they belted out celebratory roars.

The sound they all waited for fell upon them at last, the clarion of retreat. The Thran warriors ignored the first low bellow of the horn and fought doggedly on. At the second blast, however, they all stopped. One by one, they lowered their weapons and began to back away, unpursued.

Araki and Adrei reined in their steeds and stilled their weapons. The ground dragons, called to halt by their airborne cousins, obeyed, albeit with a reluctant, bloodthirsty gnashing of their voracious jaws. The Araki army stood aside, a fluttering bastion of strength and victory, while the Thran wove through them towards their burnt hillside. The dragons circled once and arched up into the clouds, their roars muffled by the coils of moisture that engulfed them.

Adracoor turned on Tinna. "I wish you'd sent us word! Something, at least, to let us know you were coming! It would have saved us having to wash several hundred pairs of breeches, I'd wager!" The battered nobleman laughed uncomfortably, but his eyes burned with banked rage.

Tinna nodded, unwilling--in fact, unable—to answer his complaint. She turned her gaze to the opposite hill, where a contingent of Thran officers sat astride their horses, watching her, the white feathers of their helms twisting it he wind. Without ado, one of the officers broke into a canter, threading around her own retreating soldiers in Tinna's direction. Adracoor drew his sword as the Priestess approached. She was of Tinna's age, much like her, except harder; her hands scarred from battle, her muscles sinewy and stringy underneath the fluttering hem of her ivory skirts. She reined her horse a short distance away and bowed her head shortly to Tinna.

"Ve ver not prepared forr such defense. Vee err not sure verre dis horse arrmy come from; vee spint jeers assessing jer forces. And ze drageens verre an enemee, no?" She paused, her brow furrowed in confusion, casting her glassy, tear-brimmed eyes away for a moment as if she needed time to grasp what had gone wrong with their planning. She shook her head and looked at Tinna again, resignation washing over her fine Thran features. Tears threatened her eyes; her voice came choked. "I ghave been told to annunce owar deefeet to you. Ve vill retreat to ower borders and deefand zem shood joo and de drageens come."

Tinna noted the young woman's rank and smiled. Fearing for their own lives, this girl's command had sent the lowest ranked priestess to declare defeat. Cowards. She looked at the two Priestess Generals who watched the proceeding from a safe distance as their drastically reduced numbers flowed past them back towards the Thran borders. She wondered where her mother had hidden herself.

"We have no interest in what happens beyond the border, Daj Mouhreni." Tinna's command of the Thran language and the use of the Priestess's formal title visibly shocked the emissary. "Just be sure you stay behind it from now on! We have eyes in the sky now, Daj Mouhreni, and we are watching. Any further attempts at invasion will be met with the same as you witnessed today—and next time, we won't respect the border anymore. We'll take the battle into Thran."

The priestess nodded in respect, wheeled her horse around and cantered back to her superiors.

"Avria!" Tinna called to her daughter, pale and frightened beside the trumpeter, watching the Araki army gather up their weapons and assess the damage. Avria smiled nervously. For a moment, Tinna reveled in the pride she felt in looking at her girl and in realizing that this was the measure of her success, this daughter. Avria knew what her mother wanted. She nudged the trumpeter, who once more lifted the horn to his lips and sounded a heart-swelling call of victory for the humans and the Araki. The horse army turned heel and headed towards camp, and the human farmer-soldiers followed, still alive. From above, the faint cry of Ledroran reached Tinna's ears. The Human and Araki army exploded into roars of victory, grins and laughter spreading across the battlefield.

"Thank you my friend!" Tinna whispered to Ledroran. She looked at the Duke, at Taneth, at the frightened boy charged with advising a King.

"Thirsty?" she asked brightly. "I know I am."

* * * *

A strange sense of rightness settled over Tinna as she leaned back in a creaky camp chair and propped her armored legs on her saddle. Her mail hissed as it slithered with the movement. She gazed past her tent flap at the untold numbers of horses being groomed, wounds tended to, unsaddled, fed, watered and doted upon. Even Taneth, writing in his journal behind her, could not account for the massive numbers of Araki riders. His census had never made the size of the population real to him. Perhaps their time had come now--the time of the Araki, and of the Adrei, whose quiet, hidden lives could no longer remain a secret to the rest of the world. Perhaps the humans would have to step back and let their castoffs and the Chai-Opse have a go at it now. Who knew?

Nobody had imagined that so many small humans hid in the Araki forests, nor that they made such fierce and efficient fighters, willing to throw themselves into a battle on behalf of the very people who ostracized them. She watched two of these small people walk by, leading a fat, squat highland pony and two leaner, more well-proportioned ponies of the steppe and moor varieties, all three soaked from a scrubbing at the river. The young men wore only breeches and the padded gambesons normally worn under mail hauberks, gear that the Keepers had prepared long before Tinna even knew these small people existed. Most of the riders had strung up their red and white surcoats like flags around the camp.

The ground-dragons were a welcome surprise, merging with the army only a few miles before they reached the battlefield. More than a thousand of the small, fierce fighters were commanded by Ledroran to fight beside the Araki. Now, they we already gone, on their way back to wherever they hailed from; running off into the distance without a backward glance like a flock of great big birds, their tails sticking out awkwardly behind them. They flowed like a river into the westlands towards the mountains, back to where they'd come from, leaving a battered trail of taloned footprints behind them.

Tinna righted herself and put her elbows on her knees, shaking her head in disbelief. Behind her, Taneth seemed to sense what she was thinking. He snorted and went back to his scribbling.

"Taking a moment to take it all in, I see." Adracoor's gravelly voice startled her.

Adracoor's presence gave Tinna a sense of worth and justice, knowing that she had been the reason that he had regained his freedom, after the torture that had scarred him so badly. He knew nothing of that. He seemed to feel quite comfortable around her now, his gratitude outweighing his consternation over her lack of communication prior to the battle. He'd excused her with a passing joke as they rode back.

"You should have told me you were coming," he lamented, giving her a sidelong look. Tinna's regretful glance took him aback, and he chuckled. "But if you had, then it surely would not be as remarkable a story to tell, would it?" She offered him a stiff laugh, and nodded, unsure how to tell him she had been forbidden to give him hope. He seemed to accept her after he made his joke.

Now, Adracoor shouldered his way into the tent carrying four leather mugs of ale. He handed one off to Tinna, then ducked behind her to give one to Taneth. "Where's your stunning daughter? I was hoping to catch a few more glimpses of that one before we all went our separate ways."

"Oh, who knows where she is? Out there somewhere, looking for her friends, I'll wager, or tending to Shade."

He nodded, tightlipped, eyes a bit guilty when he realized he might have offended Tinna by speaking so gruffly. Tinna showed no offense. She eyed him good-humoredly.

"Why are you asking after her anyway, you dirty old man? You're twice her age, you scarred mess, and as old as dirt! You haven't the slightest chance!"

"Give me time," he smirked smugly. He sipped from his ale, gazing at Tinna intently over the edge of his cup. "No offense, Bookworm," he said to Taneth, "but if you weren't an issue, this woman would be my first choice. The sight of those two riding up in full harness will stay with me for years to come!"

Taneth put his pen down and laughed softly. "I can't argue with that." His eyes fell on his wife, whose own dark orbs smiled upon him in return. "I've never been more in love with her than at this moment, nor more proud of my daughter."

Another body pushed into the tent. "Speaking of your daughter, where is she?" A hand instantly reached out, proffering a leather mug of ale to Offrin, who accepted it, glancing up at Adracoor with an arched, curious brow. Offrin looked dignified in his harness of the upper ranks, which he hadn't bothered to take off. He carried his helm tucked under his arm; his hood of mail lay draped down his back between his shoulders.

Tinna smiled at him. "She's very popular, it seems."

Offrin nodded.

"She could be anywhere. She'll find her way here sooner or later."

"I know, I know," the younger fellow scoffed, waving his free hand at Tinna. "Baruld wonders if she might want to come and stay in Taruttee for a while. Until she feels better. We'll start organizing our people for the ride home soon. I wonder if she might join us."

"You do realize you aren't obligated to return to your towns anymore?" Taneth asked.

"Where do you expect us to go? Back to the families we haven't seen since we were born? And a greater part of us were born in our towns. Despite being forced into the auberges, this war just taught us that we're stronger together as a people. Perhaps little people who are born from now on will choose to live where they like; with us or among the big humans. Meanwhile, I don't imagine we'll dismantle the auberge towns any time soon. They're nice towns, built by us, for us, and in spite of the circumstances that brought many of us to them, they are our homes."

"Fair enough."

"If you see Avria, do tell her to go see Baruld. You wouldn't mind, would you, if she chose to go back to Taruttee?"

"Avria's a big girl. She can go where she likes. If it's Taruttee, then so be it. It's not that far from Thamatoc; we can always visit," Tinna said. "But let your superiors know that we will be starting out in column on the Vayre road, come morning—your people can ride with us until you find a suitable southern road."

490

Offrin nodded, drained his ale, put the cup down on Tinna's little table and bowed deeply to Tinna, then brusquely to Taneth and Adracoor, who sipped thoughtfully from his mug.

"Offrin?" Tinna stood and moved to him, stooping before him so that she could look him evenly in the eye. He stepped back, as if uncomfortable that she would do this. "Thank you. Thank you and all of your people. On behalf of the Araki, I offer my gratitude, and I am proud to call the Adrei my brothers and sisters." She reached out her arm, and he his. She gripped his wrist, and he did likewise.

"It was an honor to serve beside the Araki. We would do it again without the slightest hesitation." He bowed again and marched out in a jangle of armor.

Adracoor laughed softly. "A whole world has been living under my nose all these years, and I knew absolutely nothing about it!"

"All sorts of worlds rest hidden in our own; that's a lesson I've learned many times over since I was a young man." Taneth chuckled, finally taking some a deep gulp of ale. Tinna chuckled.

Avria sat on Shade's bare back. She had ridden her into the shallows of the great river, where she watched the movement of a herd of Moropus on the far shore, dun-colored dots at this distance. A small river-fishing scow struggled against the powerful current of the Plains River. She could make out the white cap of Mount Jewel, its angled rock face hunched alone, comfortably nested among the forested hills, A good way off marched the fading procession of peaks that divided Thran from the forests of the Araki. She felt small. Turning, she looked at the Fureen Range, to which the ground-dragons had retreated, which cut from south to north, chopping Oromoii in half. She had never seen such majesty before. Her life had been confined to the less spectacular fields and forests between Thamatoc and Loshan. She felt a tightness in her throat, wishing she could share her sudden sense of awe with Eleran.

Behind her, a soft, buffered sound of hooves approached. She turned to see her Aunt Rhoa riding up, also bareback, comfortably appointed in a long ivory tunic and floppy, wide-legged drawstring pants. Her hair swung loose in a mass of ginger waves.

Avria felt close to Rhoa. She always had. But it felt strange to see how bright the eyes and smile of such a morose soul had recently become. She seemed different from the woman Avria had known in Thamatoc, still grave, but in a different way. She had greeted Avria warmly enough at Iromi, upon her sudden arrival among the Adrei, but the enthusiasm of that greeting had quickly passed. Avria had been too wrapped up to pay attention. Drashun arrived only shortly after with the very last leg of the Araki riders. The whole family had ridden and camped together since, but Avria hadn't spent much time with Rhoa.

She approached on a lumbering draught horse. The animal splashed into the shallow water and stopped beside Shade, lowered his muzzle to the water and drank. Rhoa shook her head and patted the huge horse's neck. He made Shade look like a pony, he was so massive. He was not her bonded horse. This was a new horse she'd gotten somewhere in the camp; her own horse was made lame from infections on his feet from the prolific mud of the Iromi camp, and remained at a livery at Iromi to heal. Someone would probably have to fetch it to bring back to Thamatoc.

"It's nice to be out of the armor. I thought we'd come away from the crowds for a while and cool down."

Avria nodded with a smile. She wondered at her mother's description of Rhoa as a girl: silly, clumsy, awkward, eager, a homebody. She saw none of these things in the older version. Shifting a bit on her horse's soft back, she followed Shade's line of sight. The little mare's ears perked forward as she gazed out over the water. The moropus had moved to the river's edge on the opposite shore. Shade snorted in an attempt to take in the smell of these odd beasts. She watched them intently. Avria's hand slid down to her soft neck and patted her, fussing with the silvery strands of her mane.

"Well, child. Lots of goings on and it feels like nothing makes a lick of sense."

"Exactly!" Avria chuckled.

Rhoa's eyes smiled, and then she relaxed her face into a neutral mask and broached her subject. "Your man... Drashun said he's dead." A sympathetic patch of creases crossed her brow, and her eyes filled with sorrow.

Avria replied hurriedly. "No, not dead. But something like it, I suppose. The Adrei mage thinks he may never wake again."

Rhoa nodded, reaching out and touching Avria's cheek lightly with her knuckles.

"I'm sorry." Rhoa's eyes misted. Avria knew that her aunt was reliving her own pain. She'd been close to Avria's age when Drashun's father died. Most people found ways to live with grief; Rhoa had never let go. Perhaps that explained why Drashun felt so abandoned. Rhoa acted as if the loss had been hers alone; she'd never let him share it, nor was she willing to let it go. He competed with her grief. Rhoa wasn't a bad mother; she just let Draphen's death

492

consume her, never allowing her son to share that part of her that lived in grief.

"I'll be all right, Rhoa. I cling to that hope. I know I'm probably setting myself up for disappointment, but it's all I have right now. I'll suss it out somewhere along the way—find the right path, I suppose."

Rhoa looked at her from her tall horse, her expression unreadable. They gazed at one another in a silent exchange until, suddenly, Rhoa dipped down and squealed. Her horse, intending to lie down in the shallow water, lowered himself to his front knees. Then his rear followed, the bulk of his body falling with a huge splash, casting Rhoa into the river with a second splash.

Avria burst out laughing.

Rhoa sat up, soaked, hair matted in front of her eyes. She pushed it back and sat watching her large horse roll in the water, soaking his itchy body. She laughed openly.

A voice called out to Avria, and she turned to see Offrin, with the large battered-looking duke at his heels. They both grinned at the scene. Rhoa turned too, curious.

"We found you, Avria! We've just been pestering your mother in search of you."

"Never mind! Tinna needs a good pestering now and again," Rhoa joked softly, getting to her feet and sloshing to her mount, who climbed back to his feet as well. She took advantage and hopped onto his back as he rose, holding onto his soaked form as he righted himself. Water dribbled from them in a shower. Rhoa's eyes fell on the grizzled, scarred atrocity of Adracoor and froze on his face. Something behind all that destruction, in the gentleness and the hurt in his gaze, held her. He was a tragic figure, much like Rhoa. She glanced at Avria, then back to Adracoor, in a silent request for an introduction. Avria caught the hint, mildly surprised that Rhoa would show an interest in anyone. She didn't care for strangers and usually remained silent.

"This very wet lady is my Aunt-of-sorts, Rhoa of Thamatoc. Rhoa, my friend Offrin from the Adrei. And this gentleman is Duke Adracoor of Zadrudas. He led the human contingent."

Both men stood on the shore and bowed. Rhoa nodded to each of them in turn.

"I was part of the fray, so I missed the formal introductions on the hill."

"Ah. I have to confess, I am still having a hard time getting used to the idea that women rode among that army. I had no idea the Araki were so liberal," Adracoor said to Rhoa, his eye sparkling.

"Tinna's presence in our culture has had more of an effect than we know, I think. Women have always ridden our relay routes. It was probably just a natural progression for them to be part of the groups sent from the clans, considering the urgent need for mounted fighters. Our women fought well, notwithstanding the limited training most of them had.

"I was looking to formally thank you, as I did your mother and father, for your presence. And to express my delight in meeting you," the Duke said to Avria, who seemed taken aback by his declaration.

"You're welcome, I suppose. But I had nothing to do with all that, I am just a bystander," she replied. "No thanks are necessary to me." She could not understand the Duke's true motivation, and that was to befriend the whole family that he truly believed would rule Oromoii someday.

A moment of strained silence intervened, before Offrin spoke with a sheepish smile. "Baruld wants to speak with you, Avria."

Avria nodded. "I should go, then. A ride, Offrin?" She approached the shore and lowered her hand, which he took, yanking him up behind her. He vaulted fluidly into place and put his arm around her waist as soon as he settled in behind her. She glanced at Rhoa, who silently gave her leave. Avria nodded to her and then to Adracoor, clippety-clopping back towards the camp with her passenger.

"Well, then. I suppose you would be kind enough accompany me to my tent, Adracoor of Zadrudas?"

The man looked at Rhoa for a spell as, soaking wet, she smiled at him. He seemed bewildered by the request, but then complied with a bow, letting her ride her horse up to his side. He put his scarred hand on her horse's damp neck. She rode; he walked alongside.

"So you have known Tinna for how long?" he asked.

"About twenty years. She is my good friend. Almost a sister."

"Indeed," he smiled. "I've decided that I like her very much."

"That's most everyone's reaction. She's a worthy sort of person."

"And what sort of person are you, Rhoa, aunt of Avria?" Adracoor asked with a bit of a smirk.

Rhoa smiled and laughed. "As flawed as any other, I imagine."

They wound around the campsite of a group of rowdy Adrei, that fell silent as they passed by and resumed their noise the moment they were out of their camp.

"Do you miss your home? Many of the horse worshippers speak of feeling exposed in this place and long for the intimacy of the forests."

"Strangely, no, I don't miss home right now. When I was younger, I'd surely have cried for home, but now I feel oddly liberated. I think I need a change. The forests I once loved so, they bring me too much heartache. I think I may seek some new places to explore." She looked down from her horse, water still dripping from her hair, and gazed at the rough, world-weary man beside her. A wry smile crossed her lips. "So where exactly is this Zadrudas Duchy of yours?"

Tinna sensed them by the tension they created before she actually saw them. She'd been expecting her mother. And she knew that she would come with at least a small group of soldiers. She'd been washing the grime from her face and stood in her chain mail and surcoat, her plate armor removed. She'd also removed the armor from her legs and wore only the black breech underpants. Her face hung over the clean, hammered-copper bowl, her muted, warped reflection gazing back at her tiredly. Gods how things change, she thought. Then the air seemed to change. She reached for the towel, straightening herself while patting her neck and face down. By instinct, she turned and looked out the flap of her spacious tent.

Many of the Araki riders had settled down for the evening around her tent, their densely arranged campsites surrounded her. Directly outside the front of her tent, she could see at least nine separate fires. She could also see her people standing up and looking towards the battlefield, their bodies stiffening; and the air seemed to thicken.

Sennal's plain clothes and those of her accompanying drunar and soldiers had allowed them open passage through the enemy camp unimpeded so far—the enemy watched her with a wary eye as she passed, but nobody moved. Sennal's drunar carried a weapon and a shield. Her four soldiers were also armed. They moved with birdlike timidity on the most part, aware of the hordes of armed enemies that surrounded them, watching them like raptors about to strike. They were poised to attack should the intruders even indicate the slightest aggression. Hands slowly reached for swords, muscles tightened, noses flared, eyes locked on them as they passed. Sennal seemed quite unaffected herself, unarmed, old, and determined, her gaze remained locked on Tinna the moment she sighted her and never wavered as she approached. It was a challenging gaze.

The Araki looked to Tinna immediately, to gauge her reaction so they knew how to act accordingly. Tinna knew Sennal and her group couldn't get away with much, being surrounded by their enemy. She had six soldiers with her and the drunar of course, her personal eunuch manservant; who shrank beside her, quite evidently discomforted by all the empowered males that surrounded him. He clutched Sennal's weapon and shield tightly to his chest, watching the army around him as their collective hackles bristled.

Tinna toweled her hands off and tossed the rag aside, standing at the entrance of her tent. Sennal gazed directly at her and stopped, the hatred plain in her eyes.

"You have a lot of nerve, coming right into our camp," Tinna said in Thrani, her eyes blazing. Movement a distance away revealed Avria idly riding along, with Offrin sitting behind her. They wove their way through the dense encampments, smiling and stopping to chat here and there as they made their way towards Baruld's tent. Tinna returned her attention to her mother, whose soundless assault of dagger-glares was impossible to ignore.

"I've come for Avria. You will give her to me. She belongs in Thran."

Tinna laughed out loud and shook her head, mouth agape in disbelief. "You do have a lot of nerve, don't you mother? We made a mockery of your 'holy army'. We served them their own heads on our shields. And you dare to come here to make demands?"

Several riders, sensing the tension, rose from their fires and wandered calmly towards the confrontation.

"Call it nerve, whatever you like, Tinna!" Sennal spat. "I am merely ensuring Avria's birthright."

"She doesn't want it!" Tinna screamed. "What are you not understanding here? You can't force her to do anything she doesn't want! You couldn't force me, and you cannot force her!" Her fury set loose by her mother's gall, she felt the heat of it in the pit of her stomach. Her fists tightened into stones. She turned suddenly into her tent and grabbed her sword and shield, the bright red and white of the coat of arms catching the late afternoon light as she pushed her way out of the tent. Sennal's eyes dropped to the arms, then jumped back to Tinna's face.

"It's this you want, isn't it, mother? You don't care about Avria. You just want to beat me!" Tinna brandished her weapons. "It would be too easy to just tell these people to finish the lot of you off, wouldn't it? But it's not what you're hoping for. You want this! You would not have brought your arms if you didn't." Tinna's glare seared into her mother's eyes. "Is it what you seek?"

"I think having a fair fight for custody of Avria seems reasonable."

"Fair, eh?" Tinna scoffed.

"Oh, come now, Tinna! These young fighters are green! A mere exercise. And only fair for you to expend some of your strength on them to make it fair between you and I. I am sixty-two years old now. Hardly an equal opponent!"

"Fine. Let's have at it, then." Tinna slapped her blade against her shield and took her stance, her bare feet flexing in the dirt. Sennal and her people stood in hesitation for but a moment. With a resolved set of her jaw, she gestured them forward. Six fighters closed on Tinna, drawing their swords from their scabbards.

CHAPTER THIRTEEN – THE INEVITABLE END

The commotion called Avria's attention. She turned and looked worriedly over her shoulder at Offrin before kicking her horse into a canter. As she wove through the various campsites and came to a trot, then a walk, pushing her way through a crescent-shaped crowd of onlookers, a hand gripped her thigh and reached for her reins, tugging her horse to a stop. She glanced down and saw her father's hard and worried face. He shook his head at her and kept hold of her horse's reins. Avria watched as six warriors circled her mother.

She'd never seen her mother fight—not for real. Tinna had always made a dancing game of their training together, full of laughter and smiling. Now she wore her own face like a mask, something that Avria had never seen before in her mother. It was a feral, predatory face like that of a wolf. Her lHHHerHips parted, her teeth gritted together, her eyes scanned each of the fighters in turn, watching for any sign that would imply attack.

She remained calm on the surface, but Avria saw the fire burning within, the wildness of her eyes. "Father, she needs help…"

"She would not accept help, Avria, you know that. She needs to do this. It needs to come to a head, no matter the outcome. Nothing too terrible can happen, Avria. She is surrounded by her people, and every one of them is holding a sword."

Avria frowned and put her hand on his shoulder, squeezing it hard.

"What of the baby? She shouldn't be exerting herself like this!"

Taneth's sad, tense gaze silenced her.

Tinna waited for the first strike. It came from a fighter at her shoulder. She slapped the woman's arm away with the flat of her sword and sidestepped at the same time, taking a powerful swing at the offender. Seizing on the opening, the other five approached her all at once. Tinna fended off two blows with her shield while back-kicking one warrior and jabbing her sword at another. Avria watched in disbelief as her mother used her shield to push back against three. Then, with a hard sweep of her sword, she sliced across the cheekbone of one woman and lodged her blade in the side of another's neck. The second woman fell like a stone in a clatter of weapons, blood spraying high into the air and beading on the sandy soil.

Tinna did not stop or even falter; she moved liquidly from one attack to the next, throwing an elbow into the chest of one woman, twisting and jabbing, sinking her sword deep into the abdomen of another with a deep and nasty grate of the blade against a hip bone. She yanked her sword free, as the woman fell back, and gouged the pommel into the face of another, while slicing her shield horizontally to knock a sword out of her way. She planted and kicked sideways at the fighter. Four remained, one slow and in pain, blinded by the blood gushing from a cut to her brow. Tinna took advantage of that blindness and, in the middle of a turn, swiped her sword across the woman's shoulder and chest, scoring her leather breastplate. Then, with another backward thrust of the sword, knocked her off her feet.

The remaining three fighters persisted, but more warily, all now quite aware of Tinna's strength and skill. She fought brutally, using little of the finesse that Rhoa had once described. Blood spattered her calves, bare feet, her sword hand and the mail on both upper arms. Several large, red blots smeared the front of her white surcoat now. Blood streaked across her cheek and chin and sopped her curls. She gritted her teeth and snarled as she fought, her brow pinched and furious. She lunged with a primal scream, waved her sword over her head and brought it down against her quarry's blade with a loud clash. The crowd looked on in cooled silence as Tinna disposed of the younger women one after the next. A full turn, and she caught the arm of one who shrieked and recoiled in pain. The one who had been thrust down struggled to get back to her feet, but Tinna would not allow it. A deft kick to the head sent her flat on the ground again. Tinna raised her arm, and jabbed her sword downwards so powerfully that it pierced the woman's breast plate and sank into her chest like a hot knife through wax. The other attackers balked, and Tinna took the time to brace her foot on the dead Thran's breastplate to wrench her sword out. When she swung it free, the woman's blood sprayed in a perfect arc over her shoulder, spattering the onlookers.

The remaining two fighters assessed her and saw that she was barely breathing hard. The rabid look, the hunger for more blood evident in her eyes, chilled them.

Even her daughter sat on her horse with her mouth agape, her cheeks wet with tears she didn't know she had shed.

The Thran did not attack again. They stepped back and looked at their superior in alarm. Sennal glared at them expectantly. One shook her head.

"We've lost. I won't die fighting an enemy we already surrendered to," the young woman muttered fearfully in Thran. "Not for anyone. You can try me for defying orders, I don't care. I won't die for this." The other one simply nodded, and they both stepped back, joining the spectators. Tinna lowered the bloody sword and swiveled to look at her mother.

"I suppose you're next," she whispered loudly, her throat raw from her primal cries.

Sennal hesitated. Seeing the burning hatred rise up in her daughter, she realized that the swordplay so far had not tired her; it had only whetted her appetite. Her hatred, her rage over Sennal's attempts to restore Avria to her own, rightful people only fueled Tinna further. But Sennal saw that she had no way out now. She could not turn and flee like the girls she'd ordered to die. She let her eyes flicker to the four souls that lay around her--three dead, one too badly wounded to be of any help. With a resolved set of her jaw, she straightened herself and hardened her posture. She reached for her own sword and shield, yanking them from the hands of her meek drunar. He cowered at the power of her glare. She took them and stepped into the circle of soil stained with blood.

A dark smile curled onto Tinna's lips. She twirled her sword and then swung it into a perfect figure eight before positioning herself again.

No dance, no taunting, no conversation--they simply engaged.

A sinewy grace overtook Sennal as she swung her sword at her daughter, letting her resentment carry it forward. Tinna blocked the blow with her own weapon, punching her shield out and bashing it into her mother's. The older woman leaned into the blow and jabbed her sword at Tinna, who swiveled sideways to avoid the blade and jumped back. As her mother stumbled forward, Tinna planted her sword firmly into the ground and used it to vault into the air, planting both feet in her mother's shield, propelling the old woman back against the circle of onlookers. Sennal hit the ground and scrambled to her feet again, screaming out her anger and running back at Tinna with her sword aloft.

Tinna ducked and tripped her, but Sennal managed, as she fell, to move her sword just at the right moment to catch Tinna's thigh.

Tinna barked out in pain and drew back. Sennal slid along the ground on her shoulder, then got to her feet, grabbing her sword. She attacked Tinna full on, her anger flaring. She rained down blow after blow upon her daughter, which Tinna fended off with her sword and shield. Turning her shield flat as her mother pulled back for another blow, she jabbed the pointed bottom of her shield into her mother's gut. The old woman grunted out her breath and fell back hard on her bottom, the wind knocked out of her. Tinna smiled darkly and stepped forward, tossing her shield aside. She twirled her sword, licking her lips and gazing down victoriously at her mother, whose gray curls lay strewn on her shoulders, her elbows in the dirt.

"It's time," Tinna sang, her voice edged with a touch of madness, eyes wild.

"MOTHER!" Avria cried. "Mother, no!" Avria jumped off her horse and shoved her father's restraining hand aside, shouldering her way through the crowd.

Tinna lifted her weapon and raised it over Sennal's head.

"Mother! Please, no!" Desperate to be heard, Avria's scream rose in pitch from mere terror to a nearly child-like shriek that pierced the air, a squeal so plaintive that it wrenched the eyes of the onlookers away from her mother and grandmother. Her mother's fury immediately dissipated, like a mist in the sun. Her arms fell, the sword singing as the tip imbedded itself in the ground. Avria pushed her way into the clearing, crying as she did when she was a little thing, her tears cutting paths through the dust on her face. She shook her head, unable at first to form words. "Mother…please…you cannot do this. It won't accomplish anything. Send her away but don't kill her. You will have to live on knowing that she won, that she turned you into the pariah she wanted you to be…don't you see?"

Sennal looked on, seething with indignation.

"She's not worth this, Mother. She's not worth your soul."

Tinna's shoulders fell, a sudden pallor falling over her features, as if the consequences of her actions only now occurred to her.

Avria stepped in front of her and pulled her sword out of the ground, throwing it aside. She gripped her mother's arms. "Just let her leave."

Tinna's eyes studied the beautiful, sweet face of her daughter, the pride of her life, the sweet, innocence she'd toiled so hard to protect. Then they darkened and fell upon her mother behind her, widening in horror as she watched Sennal take her weapon and jab it with a malevolent grin into Avria's back. Tinna sprang forward, but she knew it was too late. She wrapped her arms around Avria to catch her as she fell.

Avria only looked at her in bewilderment, her puzzlement deepening as Tinna yanked her forward. She stumbled the few steps and turned to see where her mother was staring so desperately. She saw her grandmother on the ground holding half a sword.

The other half had puddled on the ground, a red-hot pool of metal, hardening quickly. The old woman glared, bewildered and infuriated. She stood, and threw the half-sword aside. Reaching for Tinna's Sword now, she heaved it into the air and swung again. The sword should have sunk into Avria's arm. Instead, it simply melted. A perfectly curved, shimmering wall appeared as soon as the sword came within a few inches of Avria's body, a translucent light concentrating around the blade where contacted the magical field. Red strands of light arced around the blade like a wildly flailing web of miniaturized lightning. The sword sank into the bright mass of writhing light and melted like a piece of wax on a searing hot pan. The molten alloy dolloped onto the ground and hardened in a beautiful sunburst splatter, glowing hot red. Sennal's rage grew with her frustration. She cast the second sword aside and reached to strangle Avria only to recoil in agony, her scream hoarse and furious, as twin patches of red energy seared her skin only a few centimeters from Avria's body.

"Eleran!" Avria whispered. Her huge eyes filled with tears, and she staggered back, looking with shame and shock upon her grandmother, who hunched, curled around her clawed, burned hands, weeping.

Sennal gritted her teeth and got up again, coming at Avria, who did not move, but only stood there, weeping for her grandmother's hatred.

Tinna stood aghast, watching her mother try again and again to kill her own grandchild. Everyone stood frozen in shocked silence while the old woman clawed her hands at Avria again and again, only to cry out as the arcs of light burned her.

Tinna had seen enough. With a sad shake of the head, she stepped forward and kicked her mother to the ground. She turned to the two remaining guards and indicated with a jab of her chin for them to take the old woman away. They approached the crying Sennal and lifted her to her feet. She wrenched herself from their hands and staggered away, still weeping.

Tinna turned to her daughter and reached out, laying her hand on her daughter's face. She stepped forward and pressed her cheek against Avria's, a gentle, loving gesture. She withdrew and looked at her daughter's wide, moist eyes and smiled at her, tilting her head. "You are my soul, Avria."

The girl hiccupped out a sob and wiped her eyes with the back of her hand.

"Eleran put a protection spell on me. I don't know when. It worked before with the rangers, and I didn't even know it."

"I think he might have done it long ago, before Jestin betrayed you—a spell to keep harmful hands from falling upon you. He said something of the like to me, and now I understand. He foresaw something and planned for it."

"Yes. Yes, he kept saying things like that; I didn't understand what he meant. Before he left me, he told me that nobody could harm me; that I should be bold in that knowledge. But if I was protected...why did he sacrifice himself, Mother?"

"If they didn't act to harm you, they could still take you away. He feared you would be lost to Thran, as I did."

Avria nodded and frowned. Tinna watched her mother move unsteadily through the crowd of onlookers, who stepped back to let her pass, silent, curious, and piteous. The Araki guards now followed at a discreet distance, the drunar taking up the rear only after picking up Sennal's ruined sword and shield.

Tinna turned to look at Avria again. "I knew Eleran was a good man the moment he arrived at Thamatoc. I knew he would take care of you, and he did, even when he couldn't be with you."

"I must go back to him."

Tinna's eyes softened and she cupped her daughter's chin in her hand. "Then go back to him, my sweet girl. Be there beside him if you must. You know where home is when you need it. If you want, bring him back to Thamatoc, and we will see if we can find someone to help him."

Avria nodded.

Tinna turned to the onlookers. "Swaddle the dead and prepare them for the trip home," she ordered. "No Araki will be buried in these empty lands. They will return home to the oak forests where their ancestors await. Someone take a travois and bring these bodies to the battlefield, and let their Thran sisters do with them what they may."

Forty-eight dead--nine Adrei, seventeen humans, an even twenty Araki. Only two dragons. Next to the Thran, their losses were minimal. It was time to clean up the mess and prepare for the trip home.

* * * *

Sennal had barely stumbled to the edge of the camp before she fell to her knees, catching herself on the burnt balls of her fists. There she wept and blubbered until she had nothing left in her to give. When she was done, she got to her feet and tried to muster a modicum of dignity before she stalked to her waiting steed and managed to mount the tired beast. Her guards had long since returned to the Thran camp. The drunar remained with her, standing confused with her shield as she wept. He remained to tie the other four remaining horses to his saddle in order to lead them back to the Thran encampment. Only then did he affix Sennal's shield to one of them, and mount his own animal, following far behind Sennal.

Sennal rode back alone across the field of battle, where slaves dragged the bodies of the Thran dead and laid them out in circles, pointing their feet towards the center to form the traditional flower petal configurations that would mark the landscape for years. Covered in stones, the strange daisies would leave a lasting mark and homage to Ulai's chosen children. Wherever Thran sects clashed in battle, daisies like these appeared, large and small. The rolling hills of the Thran country had many such graveyards. This time, thousands died on their side. Thousands cut and mauled by blades, thousands charred by the columns of flame that blasted from the sky. Sennal felt cold and empty.

The others had suffered hardly any fatalities. Mostly horses, two large dragons and a few of the running ones--a few dozen people at best. She frowned. Not even the berserkers had had their chance to even things out a bit. She would kill the Sovereign's diviner, she decided. Kill him for not foreseeing this, for not warning her that the Thran would have no chance to achieve their ends and expand their great empire. She would kill Jestin, too, for telling her such lies about the size of the Araki army.

The camp stood half-dismantled, much of the remaining forces had already left, certain sects already fully absent except for their slave groups, who managed their dead and the breakdown of the camp. The leadership tents remained at the new site by the river. She entered her tent and collapsed into the fine chair, rubbing her face with her burned and blistered hands.

"They let you live!" a voice said.

The High Priestess General stood at the entrance, her hand on the flap. She looked weary. "We are fortunate that so many of us still have our lives. They could have done much worse. Had those dragons followed us to camp, they could have destroyed every last one of us. They showed mercy when they could have obliterated the entire Thran army. There's something to be said for your daughter, Na-AiSennal. Merciful, yes; but also powerful. The Diviner had that much right. If she had considered us a threat, she would have followed us. Finished us off."

"I have no words to share about my daughter at the moment," Sennal grunted, "nor that insipid creature that calls herself my granddaughter. I am ashamed that such creatures came from my line!"

"I think you underestimate your line, Sennal. We thought we had control of her, the way she kept to her little village, living so simply and humbly. Someone like that, who befriends the dragon race, one who can muster an army so great and inspire the loyalty of a people wholly unconnected to her and so different from her—she's to be admired! I cannot imagine that her daughter would be that much less of a person."

"You praise her?" Sennal blurted in astonishment.

"The Goddess Ulai teaches us to honor a valiant and victorious enemy, Sennal. Have you lost your path so that you no longer find solace in our sacred warrior doctrine? We should take the compliment, perhaps, that Thran blood courses through the veins of the enemy whose army laid waste to our mighty forces. We can be proud of that much—to be bested by our own."

"Half-Thran!" Sennal spat.

"If only half, then even more impressive," the High Priestess General retorted gently. She dropped her hand and approached. "You have always regretted her, Sennal. It is time you let her go."

"Do not tell me how to--"

"I will speak! I am not only your superior in rank, but also in faith. You will heed me now! Your rage and your regrets have made you old. They have withered you. Your sense of loss and abandonment has made you abandon your sense. It is time for you to set aside your anger with your daughter. You should return to Ymnoth, choose a successor from your sister's line, and retire in peace. No more. I will ride out to their camp before they depart and speak to her. I will assure her that she has nothing more to be concerned with from us. That includes you. You will do nothing further to provoke this woman. She can easily destroy us all."

CHAPTER FOURTEEN – FEALTY

Morning arose with a strange calm. Outside the laced tent flaps, in spite of the deafening noise, an odd peace reigned. Tinna had slept in, huddled up against her husband in their large cot, bundled in blankets. His warmth and soft snores made her want to melt into him and forget the world outside. Instead, she rolled onto her back and stared up at the tent top. *So much has happened! Now it's time to go home, to peace, at Thamatoc.* A scratch at the tent entrance distracted her.

"What is it?" she barked, annoyed by the interruption. Taneth awoke to the abrupt voice with a start and sat up with blinking, little eyes. She smiled at the sight of him.

Rhoa spoke. "The chieftains wish to address you."

Tinna sighed audibly. "Tell them we're leaving soon. Sorry! I was tired."

"No, they want to address you formally…if you would."

Tinna glanced at Taneth, who yawned and rubbed one of his eyes with the heel of his hand. He dropped it tiredly and shrugged at her. She got to her feet.

"Very well. I will dress and meet them in a few moments."

Rhoa's silhouette slid away.

Tinna moved to the washbasin and poured out some fresh water. "You get up too, old man! I'm not addressing the chieftains without my man beside me. Make yourself pretty," she smirked, looking at the bed-wrinkled skin of his face, his unkempt hair. He glowered at her playfully and groaned as he got up.

She washed down her face and body, then her hair, combing it out and ruffling the curls to give them more volume. She shook out her freshly washed but still faintly blood-stained surcoat and sighed. It would have to do. She began the slow and arduous process of getting into her harness, adjusting the soft under-layers, the incredibly light and slinky chain-mail, and finally the plate mail. She ended with the surcoat and belted on her new sword. Taneth grunted and smiled, one side of his mouth curled into an admiring grin.

"Gods! You are a beautiful woman!" he muttered. He had washed and dressed as well, in his fine cassock—one of many new cassocks he received when he was awarded a promotion by the Keepers just before the army left Iromi. He was now what was known as a Keradreth, the highest form of Wiseman. He donned his capelet and began unlacing the tent flaps. Tinna stepped out into the morning, shield in hand, to find herself confronted by a crowd of faces. As her eyes took in many familiar and far more unfamiliar ones, she realized each one was a chieftain. Nearly four hundred of them, clustered together in their formal armors, similar to hers. Some wore their helms, plumes dancing in the morning breeze. When Rhoa had said "the chieftains," Tinna hadn't quite realized what she meant. Before her, the leadership of the entire Araki people stood with all eyes on her.

They had chosen Rothro to speak for them, a chieftain from the northernmost group and a man she knew fairly well from the yearly gatherings. He moved forward and gave Tinna a formal bow. "Long ago, before the High Throne existed, the Araki were a united people. Our gatherings unified us all, as we stand united today. Once, an Ashru; a great Chieftain, ruled over all. We no longer have such a person. And our gatherings are fractured and separate, restricted to regions. This marks the first time in over four hundred years that our clans have come together as a whole. Every settlement is represented here. Our numbers have grown astonishing. I think we all needed to see this for ourselves in order to understand the state of the world. We have you to thank for that."

"Thank?" Tinna laughed. "We came together to fight a war!"

"Yes, but you called us together. Your reputation among our people left more to be desired among some of the more traditional and conservative clans—those who have the greatest oak forests, mostly--the oldest ones. Your influence spread beyond your own clan and ruffled the feathers of some, perhaps; but I see, and the rest of us see now, the good that you have done.

"You are not Araki by blood. But today, we know that you are pure Araki in spirit. And we cannot let this day pass without acknowledging it. We realize that perhaps our separate ways do not serve us well in these new times and that perhaps you have shown us that we must live as a unified people. So we have come to a consensus—all the chieftains of the Araki people. We have decided to name the one who unified us again, Ashru. The Chieftain of All. Ruler of the Araki people."

As Rothro's words fell away, Tinna gazed at him with an expression of incredulity. She muttered incoherently, "But I didn't... Phenmal was..." She shook her head and blathered for a few awkward seconds. Then behind her, Taneth spoke in a gentle voice under his breath.

"They would not have followed Phenmal, Tinna."

"I am not worthy of this appointment, Rothro. You know this. I live simply--"

"We were told of what you did twenty years ago, when the dragons destroyed all that the human throne touched. We know through the words of your Keepers. We know what you did for this empire and for humanity. Please do not dismiss these achievements as unworthy. You have earned your place as our Queen. We have decided." Rothro approached and took her hands and bowed, touching the tops of her fingers to his forehead. "I, Rothro, Chieftain of Clans Bakratoon and Darthrell, honor you, Ashru." He dropped her hands and rejoined the crowd.

Another chieftain, whom Tinna did not know, approached and took her hands, mimicking the movements Rothro had made. "I, Fadrick, Chieftain of Clan Gadroc, honor you, Ashru."

"I, Reddria, Chieftain of the Clan Tethrine, honor you, Ashru."

Tinna's hands trembled. Humble tears dripped from her eyes and chin, but she stood rigid and determined in her armor, gazing at the face of each and every Araki leader as each one formally welcomed her as a member of their people and as their highest leader.

"I, Eron, Chieftain of the Clan Avratelle, honor you, Ashru."

Beyond the crowd, her daughter, her friend Rhoa, her sweet son, Drashun, her newfound friend, Adracoor, and the leadership of the Adrei army looked on. Phenmal had remained at Iromi; how she wished he were here. She suspected that, somehow, he had known this would happen. The Keepers had been aiming for this. They had shared her secret. The Keepers. They told the Araki what she'd done. They had diligently kept her current with human politics. Since the Araki numbers now dominated Oromoii, her position as Ashru made her, in essence, the Throne of the empire. What does this mean?

"I, Kitmer-Avroush, Chieftain of Clans Dresh, Eld and Fillou, honor you, Ashru."

Fading humanity's king had little relevance any longer.

"I, Hurtu, Chieftain of the Clan Darachar, honor you, Ashru."

This realization made her stomach go cold. She had no idea what it would mean. She would go home. She could hope that nothing much would change. She could only hope.

"I, Nella, Chieftain of Clan Eratoch, honor you, Ashru."

The tents dropped one by one as the supply corps began to dismantle the camp. Where they intended to take all the implements and incidentals of the campaign mystified Tinna. She assumed the clans would claim their own supplies for possible future use. She hardly cared. Instead, she looked at her new horse and smiled at Adracoor, who sat on another steed with Rhoa at his side. "Are you sure, Rhoa?"

"I am."

Tinna handed the reins to Taneth momentarily and walked to Rhoa, reaching up to take the woman's shoulders as she leaned down to her. They embraced in this awkward way, Tinna unable to hide her regretful tears.

"I am going to miss you!" she grumbled in Rhoa's ear, biting back a sob.

"You'll surely see me now and again. At events that involve royalty and aristocrats and all that sort."

"I doubt I'll be part of those things. I think our lives won't change too much. The yearly meetings might change. Maybe a trip north to the palace of Miranne to speak with the High Throne? Nonetheless, you have always been near me, and I'm not sure how well I'll do without you, Rhoa."

"You'll do fine. I'll do fine. Adracoor and I, we understand one another well, and I think I would very much like to know about his land and his people. I think I need this change."

"I can't argue with that. I think change is good for you, too. What of Drashun?"

"He will stay at Thamatoc. He's happy there. I'll see him sometimes, I'm sure. He is a grown man now."

Tinna nodded and sighed. "Then off you go. North to Zadrudas... I hope you'll write me."

"I will."

"You too, Adracoor. Tell me how you fare with this troublesome creature."

"I am no scribe, but I will try. I look forward to seeing you again, honored Tinna."

They wheeled their horses 'round, and Tinna watched them rejoin the human army, swallowed by the milling crowd of riders and soldiers. Soon, the mass began moving north along the river towards Suthervale. Tinna mounted her horse and looked about. Taneth had mounted, and her group was assembling.

A disturbance caught her attention on the southern edge of the camp. She saw riders and soldiers gather, creating a corridor for a Thran High Priestess General and four guards, who rode toward her. Tinna reined her horse to face the priestess and frowned. What now?

"We accepted your surrender. There is no need for further discussion," Tinna called out the moment the priestess came within earshot. The woman looked up at her, and Tinna was surprised to see admiration in her eyes.

"Na'AiTinna."

"Do not use your ridiculous Thran appellations on me! I am Ashru now. Ruler of all clans. You will show me the proper respect and address me as my people do!" Tinna snapped before she realized it. She laughed inwardly at how arrogant she sounded.

"I greet you with honor and humility, Ashru."

Tinna jutted out her chin and gazed at the woman questioningly. "What is it you want?"

"I come to you as representative of the Thran people. I come to offer assurances that we pose no threat to you any longer."

"I think that's been proven most succinctly," Tinna smirked.

The priestess continued. "I come to you to assure you that…that past transgressions of certain members of our people should not speak for the rest of our countrymen. I come to assure you that these members of our people will no longer present you with any problems—that our brief war has earned you the humility and respect of the Thran people, and because of your heritage, I would like to declare that, if needed, we would stand beside you."

The declaration shocked Tinna beyond words.

"We wish only peace with this new power of Oromoii. Had we known it existed, we would not have provoked it. We instead would declare that as long as your line rules the North, you have only our alliance and respect." Without another word, the woman and her guard wheeled about and rode away. Tinna turned slack-jawed to Taneth, and they once more shared a bewildered and awed gaze.

"This is just getting too strange! Let's get out of here!" she mumbled. With that, she turned her horse east, heading for the river crossing, and hopefully, without further impediments, for home.

CHAPTER FIFTEEN – HOMEWARD BOUND

In succession, the clans dropped away, veering southwards. Every branching road that pointed south took a clan or two with it, quietly heading back to the obscurity of the forests. Tinna and her family chose to take the traditional way home--by horse rather than dragon--riding near the head of a massive column that clogged a large road bordering the forest. Tinna sat on a horse, a rare occasion, her quiet husband beside her on his beautiful stallion, Taphenus. Taneth had grown into the saddle in his years among the Araki and looked as natural in it as they did, his hips swaying gracefully with the stride of his horse, his hand resting on the smooth cantle of the thin, simple Araki saddle, the reins loose and swaying as his horse clip-clopped along.

Tinna's horse, thick and feathery-legged, a jet-black, large-hoofed draft-destrier mix, snorted and turned his head and ears as the he gazed about with casual curiosity; the roached mane on his dense, crested neck standing up like a raven-colored bristle brush. His huge hoofs clattered above the din of the column of cavalry all around. Tinna was saddle sore, but she appreciated the soft, cloudy gait of this great, stamping horse, a gift from Duke Adracoor. She found the animal's size and grace greatly to her liking and had fallen in love the first time she'd ridden him—something she thought she'd never do with a horse. But Beast was well-tempered for a stud, and easy to handle, even for someone who hadn't been born to the saddle and she knew her horse-master would also trip over himself to breed some of the Thamatoc mares to this graceful stallion.

The Duke had seen the glow in her face when Beast had lipped her hands and buried his huge muzzle in her mass of curls, and he could not resist giving him to this beautiful creature as a gift for simply showing up. Now she rode him in the full red-and-white blanket she'd transferred from her other horse, leaving the armor pieces in a large carriage that followed far behind. She wore casual clothes, her own fine surcoat and armor tucked safely away as well. The war was over; she had no need of them now.

A cloudless sky graced their passage home, after too many grey, overcast days--a blue so vivid that the dragons' silhouettes wavered against it stark and out-of-place. Autumn was upon them. A crisp edge to the air portended cooler times to come. Tinna glanced up. The dragons flew with the column, following along at a languid glide, hundreds of them suspended like fixtures, unmoving except for an occasional subtle shiver of a wing membrane as they ballooned on the powerful winds or an intermittent flap of the wings to regain lost altitude. They occasionally turned back in lazy circles when they got too far ahead of the riders. The multitude of horses had long since calmed from the unnerving presence of the scaled ones, and the whinnies and spooked dancing had quieted down soon after they were underway. Over the din of hoofs and rattling arms and whinnies and snorts reigned an odd peace that nobody could deny.

For the first time in weeks, Tinna had felt no sickness that morning. Instead, she now craved river mussels cooked in ale and blue onions, and some of Hetra's beer-bread. Her eyes sought out her daughter, who rode ahead.

As if by providence, a shout from the group of pony riders drew her attention. Avria, the one tall rider among the group directly ahead, twisted in her saddle and looked back at her parents, her heart-shaped face bright and vivid, eyes almost too large to be natural. She smiled, lifting her hand to wave farewell. The front group of Adrei then split away on yet another of the many southbound roads and veered off, with Avria in the thick of them. Tinna watched her form retreat into the tunnel of evergreens. She tried to keep her eye on her for as long as possible, but when she lost sight of her, she looked up. A few dragons, diverging from the main group, subtly banked to the right, just enough to change course and follow the Adrei. Watch over them! Tinna thought. She dropped her gaze to her husband, who looked at her with glassy eyes.

"Everything changes so quickly!" he muttered.

She gazed at him, the love evident in her eyes.

"We had some time...the times that matter most, when she was growing up, when she had a tiny voice and she sang songs of made-up words and she first rode Hanru's pony..." Tinna's whimsical smile gradually vanished. "We still have Hanru for a little while."

"And the little creature taking shape inside your belly," Taneth added.

Tinna looked down at her tummy, then looked up at him again, smiling as if she'd only just remembered.

Taneth laughed to himself and looked at his wife. "It's strange how Hanru is like me, a homebody, and Avria turned out to be so much like you."

"I wonder who the little one will take after." Tinna wondered.

"Who is to say? Let's hope with all our hearts that he or she will not turn out like Jestin," Taneth said with sadness in his voice.

Tinna nodded grimly and sighed. She'd gotten word through the relay from Kailine and Astlin that Jestin had abandoned them. Where he had gone, nobody knew. Avria would fare better at Taruttee than she would at home, where Jestin would be free to do as he wished. She could only imagine what the boy was capable of. He'd already shown a very dark and selfish side in betraying Avria.

"Let's hope that boy finds his own path and doesn't cling to elements of his old life, because I was not kidding when I told him I'd kill him if I saw him again," Tinna said icily.

Taneth saw the set of her brow and the darkness that fed her words. He sighed and reached out to take Tinna's hand.

"Avria is fine. I would say, no harm done, but you'd know that for a lie. We can only hope that providence will do with him as he deserves. I doubt he will return to Thamatoc. He will remember your words. His bridges are burned."

* * * *

Jestin ran, his breath ragged, his hair plastered to his head with sweat. In the pitch of night, he ran. Behind him, receding into the darkness, the pale lights of Vara's estate cast their glow onto the carefully maintained grounds. The large, plain-looking manor sat in the center of a leafy forest, in the unbearable heat. Even at night, it sweltered. Everything was built of a strange black brick, the architecture heavy and imposing, with rooftops of hot red tiles. Almost all of the decorative art he'd seen bore war-related themes. Even the portraits of ancestors, women posed in full military regalia, their subordinate male concubines standing demurely behind them in the ever-evolving fashions of the time.

Jestin had determined from the moment he arrived that he would escape. At this moment, mother and daughter sat at the large round table, enjoying a quiet meal. It was the best time. The servants would be occupied with serving the meal, while the men got to wander about on their own. He hated staying so close to Linar all the time. He was such a ridiculously stupid fellow, with a temper beyond the pale. Jestin had already suffered a tremendous beating that laid him out for days, after the war had ended so badly and Sennal had demanded his head. Jestin had to be thankful for the indulgence Vara showed her daughter. She had prevented his execution, because Eria was so set on having him as her first concubine. Sennal, already defeated, already broken, did not resist. She simply gave in and walked away, wavering in her step a bit, her eyes distant and lost.

Jestin was alive. For how long, he wasn't sure. His pace grew sluggish in this heat. They would find him missing soon enough and would surely chase him down. But he had to try. He refused to give in, to end here.

He would not endure this life, not without Avria. Only her presence might have made living with the Thran tolerable. With resolve, he moved east, traveling away from the routes they would search first. His lungs burned, and his legs hurt, but he ran. For the first time in his life, Jestin wished for a horse.

END OF BOOK 2

BOOK 3

TINNA'S REIGN

MIRANDA MAYER

Dedications:

To my first uber-fan, Jathia. Thank you for your beautiful enthusiasm. It is the sort of thing that makes writing worthwhile.

To Alex, Dan, Nee, Hellie, S2, Molly, No-no, Charlie, Heather & Aelfgyva. You guys are lifeblood.
And to Wendy Pamay—as always.

CHAPTER ONE – MARRIAGE

Offrin gazed up at his bride and he could barely contain his joy. He could not believe his fortune. He wanted the ceremony to be completed immediately, so nothing could disrupt the union. Two years of solid longing, hoping and striving to earn her affections all culminated into this moment, where she stood beside him as his bride. The ceremony seemed to go on forever, but it proceeded uninterrupted, and Offrin's fast-beating heart swelled when she said "I take him to me," and he saw her pale arm reach out to receive the binding bracelet.

She was resplendent, a good head and a half taller than he, Avria wore a gown of snowy white; of fine, sheer, wispy fabric over an emerald green under-dress with a high waist and elegant draping skirts. The short train of the white over-dress fanned out gracefully behind her. Her long sleeves, sheer white and fitted to her arms had gathered lace cuffs that flared slightly out over her knuckles. Her hair was a shock of black curls decorated with a circlet of stylized silver knots of the Adrei style; and freshwater pearls nested in woven bands of silver adorned her neck and ears. She knelt beside Offrin at the altar of the great temple, where Master Baruld stood in his ceremonial robes, shorter by far than Offrin, but still powerful and grave in presence.

Offrin knew Avria did not love him as he loved her. She cared for him deeply; she did love him, but not in the way she loved Eleran. Her love for Offrin was sweet, and sedate, trusting and gentle; her love for Eleran was one of burning passion that would remain locked away inside her heart. Eleran was gone—time had softened her grief, and Offrin's doting attentions soon won her heart; at least most of it. He was content to have that much; he loved her so. When her fingers slid into his, and Baruld sealed the binding bracelets, he thought his heart would explode it was so full. He looked up at her beautiful, serene face, her dark eyes taking in his happiness, and he kissed her tender lips, still unbelieving that he had been so lucky as to be wed to her.

He had loved her the moment he first set eyes upon her. She had led her horse into the Taruttee village square, Eleran was hunched, pale and weak on the graceful equine and as soon as the she stopped, he keeled sideways and fell from the horse. Offrin recalled seeing her, kneeling with terrified eyes over the still form of his rival when he'd slid out of the saddle, and crumpled to the ground. He'd been called to her side then, and had remained there since. Through the war, and after, he was there, comforting her when she wept for Eleran, cheering her up when she was moping, following her between Taruttee and Thamatoc, and helping her as much as he could in her work with Master Gavorre. It was inevitable that she would come to love Offrin. Now here she was leaning down to kiss him for the first time as his wife.

The spectators exploded into applause when they kissed, and Baruld gestured for them to stand and to face their community and family as the wedded couple. And with that, the ceremony was over and the celebration would begin.

It was a mixed crowd; people of Taruttee, quite short in stature, mingled in with the taller Araki people, all jubilant and merry. They stood from the long stone benches facing the grand altar, and flowed into the aisle behind the newly married couple. The ceremony was being held at old human settlement of Klatna so that they could make use of the restored temple there. It was big enough to hold the extraordinary number of guests that expressed a wish to be present for this binding.

Klatna was a second home for Avria's family now—the city had become such a gathering place for the regional peoples, it was inevitable that they choose it as a venue for this momentous occasion. The crowd poured out onto the street, cascading from the forest of columns of the temple, and following the new couple up the hill in a euphoric procession, throwing handfuls of pine nuts up the road towards the couple, and showering them in blessings and on several occasions, stinging pain from particularly fast flying pine-nut projectiles. The crowd moved with festive purpose towards an old manor where a banquet and musicians awaited them.

Above them, the stones of the academy were being replaced, the broken walls being resurrected, the towers under reconstruction. The old academy of Hildercross had once dominated the crest of Mt. Klatna like a crenellated crown, the town once spiraling up the hillside towards it. However the destruction had decimated the better part of the small city, and killed nearly all of its human inhabitants, rendering this ancient academy into rubble, leaving only a few walls standing. It was a long time coming for this academy to receive such special attention. Klatna's placement on a crucial trade-road made the town important, so the Araki took it over and went about rebuilding the things they thought necessary for the city to thrive. The Academy was never high on the list, but after the One-Day War, priorities were shifted. The balance of the decisions now rested largely on the will of two people alone; Taneth; Avria's father, and Tinna; Avria's mother.

Both of Avria's parent's were trailing quietly behind the wedding crowd, holding hands. On Tinna's free arm, propped on her hip was a little baby boy of just shy of a year of age who was avidly chewing on his little fist. He was a wide-eyed, handsome little creature with silver-grey eyes and a thick thatch of dark hair. This was Avria's new sibling Istvan; an already well-established personality even at so young an age. He was also already attempting to toddle about and was most curious by nature, much like his father.

Tinna smiled when Avria looked down the hill for her, breaking into a brilliant grin and waving when she finally caught her mother's gaze. Tinna marveled at how beautiful her daughter was, and what a wonderful person she had become. Both she and Taneth adored Offrin, and thought them to be an excellent match. They loved him greatly, and cared only that he make their daughter happy after all the trauma she'd endured.

It took Drashun and a few of Avria's closest friends at home to get used to the idea that she was marrying a little person, but since the war, the auberge communities opened up to the Araki, and they had begun to function more like a single community; both little people and the irrevocably average Araki horse-worshippers. In fact, Taneth, who was a highly ranked Wiseman, had become particularly close to the Adrei apothecary with whom Avria had lived and trained with for some time. His was known as Master Gavorre. Both he and Taneth now traveled often together to the archive town of Lemoram, and Master Gavorre contributed a great number of ideas to the reformation of the educational Academies, including Hildercross, working to include a place for his people in the plan. It had been a busy time since they returned from the One-Day War.

The couple climbed the wide steps to the old-style brown-brick manor house, and threw open the doors. The wedding attendees flowed in behind them, the last to enter; the manor's actual residents. Once but a shell of masonry walls, the manor that was to host them was a home away from home of sorts for Tinna and her family. Tinna had refused to move north and leave the forests as the Keepers had requested. She was however, the Ashru of the Araki, the chosen Queen of sorts for the largest group of people in the world now—and the Keepers were pushing her to become more than that. The human leadership was laughable at best; non-effective and not even useful as an inspirational figurehead. The High King, a young man recently crowned in place of his aging father, was an insolent, useless youth, and he represented a population that was dwindling into insignificance instead of growing strong again.

The manor was a compromise. She would take residence here for some times during the year, and then return to the humbler abode at her clan village of Thamatoc when she'd had enough. Being a new mother after forty was taxing as it was; adding the responsibility of a struggling empire was another matter altogether. Mix in the marriage of her daughter and the planning for a wedding, and Tinna was looking forward to leaving Klatna in the morning and spending a good, long, quiet winter at Thamatoc. Taneth predicted that the bright sun and crisp dry skies would abate, and the snows were soon to arrive. So soon, she could smell the sharp scent of it in the air before she entered the manor. Winters in the forestlands were known to be harsh. She hoped it would be a heinous, snowy, icy winter; that it would hinder travel even for dragons and give her some peace.

This day it was cold, but it was clear and bright, and the afternoon was giving way to a raw night of flawless skies filled with myriad stars. The manor sported fires in its recently restored hearths that bellowed out warmth and welcome into its two connected assembly rooms. The whole manor still smelled of the new wood and fresh lacquer they'd used to treat the new paneling on the walls.

The guests gathered around two great tables stacked with platters containing a variety of foods. Each table had a mountain of tiers topped by an elegant hart of made of bronze. The tiers boasted platters of foods, from freshly roasted slices of venison heaped into a cone to tiny cakes in snow-white icing topped with sweet winterberries of salmon pink. The spaces between the platters were decorated with evergreen boughs and sprigs of holly bright with berries, and fragrant branches of juniper with their subtle blue berries. The tall ceilings were hung with a row of swags made of conifer sprigs, evergreens and berries, filling the rooms with the scent of pine. Between each window, massive standing candelabras brandishing branches full of thick candles shed warm light into the darkening space as the afternoon gave way to evening. Behind these were mirrors hung to reflect even more of that light back into the festive space.

Draperies of rich fabrics, and portraits both new and salvaged adorned the newly paneled walls—one particular portrait of Tinna and Taneth in stately pose and costume dominated the wall above the main hearth in the great hall. Tinna hated it, Taneth couldn't help but puff his chest out and smirk when he saw the image of himself in his fine formal robes of office standing over his wife, who was seated in an stylish chair in a gown of midnight-blue velvet with silver embroidered hems. They looked downright royal, and Taneth thought the depiction of his wife was masterful, and marveled at how her black eyes seemed to follow the viewer wherever they went in the room. Whenever he had the chance, he would boast of this, and make visitors join him in his experiment, navigating about the room and exclaiming: "See? She's still got you in her sights!"

This evening, Tinna was dressed like royalty again; a true lady. Like her daughter, she wore a trained gown, hers a sapphire blue silk as light as air, her hair up, jewelry on and dainty silken slippers. She removed her heavy black cloak and a servant seemed to materialize out of the ether and took it. She switched carrying arms for the boy, glanced at her husband, who smiled down at her from his lofty height, and entered the great hall at her side. The baby was immediately yanked from her arms by his elder sister, who twirled him and made him squeal in delight. She hugged him to her chest and kissed his nose and cheeks, lifting his little tunic to blow raspberries on his belly. His laughter rang out in peals of enchantment.

"Well then, little brother, what think you of all of this?" she asked. "What think you of your new brother? He cuts a fine figure does he not?" Avria danced around Offrin who laughed merrily. All the while, the child produced the most brilliant dimpled smiles he could muster; simply tickled to see his sister he adored so. His face always lit up when he saw her. Tinna laughed gently and found a free seat. In the back of the second hall, the musicians were plucking their instruments and tuning them up; passively summoning the dancers to the floor. Offrin grasped his wife's hand and dragged her away, baby and all. Taneth went to retrieve the boy so they could head the dance as a proper couple. He returned toting his young son, and sat next to his wife, plopping the child on his knee. Istvan was entranced by all the people in their bright and sparkling clothing. The music made him squeal again and he kicked his feet as if dancing himself. The dancing began and immediately, the noise level escalated, and the festive mood intensified.

Couples wove about the space as the dance began, gowns flaring out, smiles flashing while the vaulted ceiling was filled with music. Rigerd danced with his wife; even Rhoa had come from the north to join them for the wedding, guiding her gruff ungainly Duke through the steps. "You mock me now," he shouted, "but in my day, I was quite light of foot, with the grace of a buck!" he shouted over the music, a smile looking odd on his badly scarred face. Tinna laughed, and Taneth chuckled. Avria was radiant, her husband even more so, his face aglow. Offrin looked fine in his elegant blue frock coat and snow-white stockings. Master Gavorre appeared quietly at Tinna's side, and he glanced up at her.

"They are good together."

"Indeed," she sighed. Master Gavorre had become a sort of uncle to Avria. When she was at Taruttee, she stayed with him. She studied what he did in his apothecary shop. It was a good enough reason for her to stay at Taruttee. With Jestin; a young man who could potentially bring her to harm; still theoretically about and dangerous, they thought it would be good for her to remain at the Adrei community, in spite of the fact that the person she'd returned there to be with was no longer present. Eleran had been taken away before the war ended, but Avria remained on the most part. At first she remained in the hopes that Eleran would return, but eventually, she stayed simply because she had grown to love it there and to love Offrin too.

"Offrin; he has a curative effect on her. She has forgotten her loss, it seems."

"Oh, Tinna, do not be fooled by her smile, that girl's heart is still broken. But she put that part of it away for now. She is living a life that isn't entirely hers. She plays a role," the apothecary muttered gravely. Tinna's brows rose in concern.

"Is that what you believe? That she is unhappy?" Her eyes wandered back to her daughter, who at that moment danced around Offrin, and stole as kiss as she passed him by, her grey eyes sparkling.

"No, I do not doubt her happiness; but her complete happiness is forever lost. She isn't whole anymore. She never will be." Tinna frowned deeply and she turned to look at Taneth. Her eyes looked worried. Before Taneth could open his mouth, another person joined the conversation.

"Sorry I'm so late." Tinna looked up to take in a tall, lanky gentleman of later years, with hauntingly light blue eyes, a shaved head and a pointed, meticulously trimmed beard of grey. He was dashingly handsome and he never seemed to get older in the years she'd known him.

"I won't brook excuses, Phenmal, Avria looks to you like a second father. You should have been here for the ceremony," Tinna immediately admonished, quite serious in her dressing-down.

"I apologize with all my soul, I…"

"You chose to travel by coach, when Leya offered to fly you here herself in place of Igro!" Tinna snapped.

"I am not comfortable with dragons. Mind you it's not always a personal level—they're mostly tolerably kind and affable as individuals. Igro and I, we tolerate one another well enough, and I've come to trust his flight over time, and we can partake in reasonable discussions about reasonable things. Other dragons? No. Igro can be trusted not to purposefully shake me about or drop like a stone from the without warning for laughs. The others seem to delight in doing things like this to me for their amusement. What bothers me most is the whole being suspended in the sky thing. It's being huddled behind a head-shield does nothing to protect a rider from the gusts of wind and the cold. I do not like being at the mercy of these beasts." Taneth nodded emphatically in agreement beside his wife, he was no great fan of flying on dragons himself.

"The dragons offer to take me hither and thither, yes. They do. But truth be told, they don't really like me because I am Chaiva. They make sport of playing with my apprehensions about flight and torment me. With Igro, we've come to a sort of mutual respect; he is decent and does not do stupid things like his brethren. If I am to travel on wing, it is with Igro alone," he retorted with more animation than any of them had seen out of this gentleman in a long time.

"Not to mention that Igro and I share many hours on the wing as it is, so when I have the opportunity for respite from the blowing, cold air in exchange for the comfort of a plush, upholstered coach, I will take it. And Igro gets a rest to boot." They listened to him with amused expressions, taking in the impassioned light in his remarkably clear and strikingly blue eyes.

It was good to see Phenmal, and unusual to see him in a city. He didn't like the voices of a thousand people filling his head and avoided it as much as he could. However Tinna had to concede that he was here, facing a houseful of people after all; a huge sacrifice for a sensitive mind-reader.

"If Rhoa could swallow her fear and pride, so could you," she snorted, half smiling. "Now go and apologize to Avria, she was disappointed not to see you before the ceremony," Tinna grumbled. Taneth looked to his friend and shrugged as if to say: what are you going to do? Argue with her? Phenmal knew better, and bowed curtly, striding elegantly towards the dance area, where the quickstepping jig was just ending and the introductory notes of a more sedate dance were being played.

Phenmal caught Avria's hand before she was claimed by anyone else, and led her onto the floor, bowing elegantly to her. Everyone could see the reverence and adoration in her eyes at seeing Phenmal. She once feared this icy man, now; her respect for him was unmatchable. The couples lined up, and the music began in earnest, and away they went, into spins and turns, bows and curtsies, setting and casting in stylish figures. Phenmal moved with liquid grace, one hand clutched formally behind his back, the other handing her off and turning her, his chest out, his steps smooth. He did cut a fine, dignified figure, Tinna could not deny it. He seemed even more handsome every time she saw him.

Offrin came to Tinna to ask her to dance, but she declined before he had a chance to open his mouth.

"Don't even bother, Offrin, I do not dance," she said good-humouredly, waving her hand. "Even Taneth must go and find a partnerless woman when he desires to dance, for he knows I will refuse him." Tinna's Thran accent was still quite evident, and Offrin found it quite pleasant.

"There is still plenty of time to join the bottom of the set, Lady Tinna. I wish you would…"

"Offrin, I thank you, but no, truly no. I do not plan to dance at all this evening. Please go and choose a willing partner, it would be a waste to spend the entire dance trying to convince me to do something I am most certain to refuse." Offrin gave up and bowed in concession, offering her a smile as he turned to find someone else to pester.

They rarely danced at Thamatoc. Just making room in the main hall was such a task; moving the massive tables and the benches, it just wasn't much worth it. They did dance in the summer sometimes, out in the village common under the founder's tree. At the annual clan meetings, they performed dances almost every night. Everyone knew these individual dances by heart. They were old dances. In the few remaining human settlements, these dances had gone out of fashion long ago; however, since human fashions and pastimes were no longer the trend, these old dances were enjoying a new life as the markedly old-fashioned Araki influence spread out from the isolation of the forests.

It was a glorious sound; the music. The festive colours and food was also delightful. Tinna was beside herself simply sitting with Istvan in her lap, and taking in the ambience. In the past two decades, she had yet to experience a celebration this lavish and grand, but here she was, acting like a true blue-blood, lording over a crowd of her beloved villagers from Thamatoc, a large group of Avria's friends, Offrin's family from Taruttee, and some of the closer clan chieftains and their families from other Araki towns. It was a great affair by Araki standards, and extremely high-brow; servants and manors were not the norm. But with the shift of power between peoples, things were gradually altering, and so was the lifestyle the Araki were accustomed to. Everything was changing.

Towns were being taken over by Araki clans. Chieftains were becoming mayors and governors. The trends were changing from insular communities to more human-like settlements infused with Araki culture.

Tinna took a moment to hover about the table to find some choice treats to sate her mild hunger, and then wandered back to the area where she'd been sitting before where the men still sat in discussion in the circle of settees and chairs. Tinna sank down next to her husband who scarce noticed she'd left in the first place.

"How do they plan to do that?"

"I am not sure, truth be told. Those sorts of mechanics are not my specialty, but it is a good way to start including the dragons into things; making things accessible to them," Taneth replied to Master Gavorre, who held the baby's arms while he stomped about in circles and then used the chair to sidle to his mother. Tinna scooped him right up and propped him on her lap again. They were discussing the dragon rookeries that Taneth wanted to install at the various new and restored towns and settlements, including here at Klatna. "Towers with narrow bases, no great footprint is required if it's built and balanced well. They're proposing a byre of sorts to top the towers; with high, vaulted rooftops and doors to close out the cold. They are also discussing some sort of oven below-floors that can heat the byre from below, for when they come in winter…" Tinna's mind faded out immediately. Since the war it was nothing but talk about building this or changing that. She was exhausted by it all. Her husband was either gone on some trip to plan these projects, or at home rattling on and on incessantly about them. With a subtle sigh, she turned her attention to the dancing; but the realization crept up on her that she was extremely tired.

All the talking and activity, as exhilarating and sophisticated as it felt, exhausted Tinna quite quickly; and Istvan grew weary as well as babies do when the hour grows late. When he began to fuss, Tinna excused herself and climbed the great stairway, carrying the boy to the private apartments; which were ten times the size of their apartments at home. Here, she lived like true royalty. The rooms were all tall ceilings, detailed woodwork, delicate architecture of the human style, towering windows, paneled walls and woven rugs of rich colours.

Istvan's room by comparison was small, but it was cozy, snug against the back of the fireplace chimney, which generated a nice passive heat. She changed him into his night-clothes and tucked him into his cradle, and sat with him, rocking his ornate cradle until he went to sleep. He was an even tempered, calm child, not restless and endlessly active like Avria had been. When he finally dozed off, Tinna shucked her formal gown, and dressed in something more appropriate for Thamatoc; loose floor-length skirts with a slight train, and a wide V-necked fitted tunic sweater that ended at her thighs.

She sank down into the comfortable chair and stared at her baby boy. With a sigh, she leaned back into the tall seat, and within a few moments, Tinna was sleeping soundly.

It was well past the midnight hour when the last of the guests exited the house. Taneth had retired for the evening hours before— rousing his wife from her chair to guide her to her sleeping clothes and bed. Phenmal was snoring lightly in one of the soft chairs in the private drawing room where he'd retreated to smoke his pipe and escape the chatter of the guests. As close to a member of their family as one could be, Phenmal had his own rooms set aside upstairs, but he hadn't quite made it that far. Offrin was eager to go to bed, and went upstairs ahead of Avria to stoke the fire in their apartments.

"Are you sure you won't stay?" Avria took her cousin's arm and gave him a worried look. "It's so late already, and you will be riding in the dark. It's really quite cold out here…"

"We will be fine. We have a room at The Saddle. It's only a short ride down the hill. We won't leave for Thamatoc until morning, I promise," he assured her. "It's likely we will be ahead of your party well before sunrise," he said.

Avria bade her cousin Drashun and his young wife Ynn goodnight, and watched them climb onto their horses, which had been saddled and brought forth from the manor's stable and tethered to the gate only moments before they left the house. Ynn mounted sideways on her traditional astride saddle, grinning awkwardly at Avria. She was Araki; she would be fine with a knee crossed over the flat pommel of the thin Araki saddle. With the fine gown she had made for this occasion, she did not want to tear its delicate seams by riding astride, nor did she want to gather it up and ride with her stockings and pantaloons exposed. Araki women did not generally own sidesaddles, they rode astride with split skirts and under-breeches; although Avria and Tinna did own sidesaddles for their jaunts to Loshan and points north into the human settlements, where sidesaddle was considered proper and more practical for the long-skirted, voluminous habits that were the fashion.

Ynn waved at Avria, as did her husband, whose endearing smile warmed Avria's heart. "Goodnight, Drashe, bye Ynn. See you two soon." She watched them fade into the darkness until they were nothing more but the retreating rhythm of hooves on cobbles.

Below her, the lights of the small city sparkled between the swaying branches of the young evergreens that grew where many of the old buildings used to be. Klatna had once been a densely packed city with hardly any greenery. Now, much of what grew in after the destruction was left undisturbed, and new construction was built around most of the new trees. Most Araki felt comfortable where there were trees. It was only natural.

It was exceedingly cold. Avria clasped her elbows and watched her breath turn into steam. She could see yellow glow of lamplight behind some windows in the houses below, and the many arcs of chimney smoke rising up into the darkness at the same slow angle from the rooftops of the houses. Some lanterns had been placed on the curbs to shed light onto darkened streets for the late-night revelers like her cousin and the remaining guests who'd left only moments before. Most of the guests chose to travel through the night to avoid the possibility of being caught in bad weather. Rhoa and her husband for instance left on dragon hours ago, flying north towards Zadrudas. Neither Avria nor her mother had spent much time with them. Avria felt bad. Others chose to lodge at Klatna, betting the weather would hold out long enough for their trip home. It was their bet too. The prospect of a warm bed seemed much more appealing than the idea of saddling up and leaving at that moment.

Avria sighed, standing on the wide stairway alone, the double doors wide-open behind her. She clutched a shawl around her shoulders, and looked out into the night with sad eyes. Her head snapped in the direction of the uphill road for a moment, for she thought she heard something stir. But the wind blew and hissed through the evergreens, and nothing moved that she could see; except a single, minuscule snowflake that meandered down from the sky. It gusted before her, catching the light from the doorway. With a little sigh, a passing shadow of sorrow and resignation crossed her eyes. Avria turned back into the house, and closed the night behind her.

* * * *

Eleran took her in. His beauty. His love. He'd watched through the tall windows all night, as she twirled and danced the evening through, until the curls around her face sagged and clung from perspiration, and she could dance no more. He watched her chat spiritedly to old friends, throw her head back and laugh heartily at a joke. She drank dark wine, and bent down to kiss her new husband now and again, who stood beside her as much as possible, his arm possessively draped around her waist.

How beautiful she was in those gowns, they flattered her form. He recalled the first moment he saw her, upon entering the small village common. She was a lily in white amid a garden of muted nothings. She wore a gown like the one she wore tonight. She was fully innocent then, wide-eyed and idealistic, barely more than a girl. Now, she looked like a woman. She looked tired, and he felt her sense of... he paused for a moment, trying to place it. Resignation, perhaps, he was not certain. None of that matters now, thought he. He moved but a shade, but she sensed it and for a moment he thought he was discovered. He felt his heart swell at the idea of seeing her face to face. Alas, she did not see him. It is for the better. For now. He watched her go back inside, and tried not to think about the fact that she was going upstairs to another man. The trees suddenly began to shiver all around him, as his eyes turned baleful.

Two hours before dawn, Offrin was awoken by the movement of the bed. He turned to see his new wife bathed in sweat, squirming and twitching in the throes of a nightmare. He reached out and touched her face. Her eyes shot open, she pulled away and screamed. It seemed to take her a moment to recognize that she was looking at Offrin and she then collapsed back onto her side, plopping her head on her pillow. In the waning light of the fire, she looked weary and frightened.

"What is it, Avria?" Offrin asked, patting down her wild hair and soothing her. She sighed heavily, her bare shoulder rising and falling, and she shook her head clumsily on her pillow.

"Nothing but a silly dream; I can barely remember it," she lied—her voice broken and groggy. She scooted closer to him, and huddled against his body. She was still trembling. He wrapped his arms around her and kissed the top of her head. Soon, she was sleeping again.

That little snowflake had been the first of many, for come morning, there was a layer of snow eight fingers thick blanketing the mountain. It thinned out significantly as the group of riders descended Mt. Klatna and left the city, but the snow showed no sign of stopping. They turned onto the main trade road, and followed it south for a bit before turning onto the gypsy roads towards Thamatoc.

"I had a strange dream last night, mother," Avria muttered this as the two women rode ahead of the group. "I can't get it out of my head." Tinna huddled around Istvan, who was propped in front of her on the saddle, held fast to her torso by a sling. He didn't seem much bothered by the snow that still fell, and waved his chubby fingers about and grasped hunks of Beast's mane. Avria did not respond to his giggles of delight as he took in all these things. Offrin mentioned her little nightmare to Tinna that morning while they breakfasted, and pointed out how morose Avria seemed. She told Offrin that it would pass, and thought nothing more of it. Tinna glanced at her and frowned with thought, waiting for Avria to elaborate.

"It was strange and horrible," she continued. "I was walking... or maybe riding, I don't remember. And it's dark, and out of the darkness comes Eleran. I think it's Eleran at least, but he's so disfigured I can hardly recognize him. He is different," Tinna saw Avria shudder and her brows furrowed deeply.

"How do you mean, different, Avie?"

"He's all wrong. He's still there, I can feel him in here..." she clutched her hand to her heart, "but there's something deeply wrong. He is chasing me. I am afraid of him and I am running. He finds me and then he comes for me, but my response is terror, not happiness... that's when Offrin woke me."

"And you don't think it's just a bad dream?" Tinna asked without admonishment. Avria shook her head, her eyes glassy, and her throat tight.

531

"How often do your dreams stay with you? Less than an hour after you're awake, you normally don't remember them…"

"That's true," Tinna conceded, "but still, what do you think it could be otherwise? Eleran is gone. He may not be dead, but Gavorre said his essence was no longer connected to his body. What remains of Eleran is a shell, Avria, and wherever that shell is, it cannot harm you."

"It didn't feel like a dream, mother," Avria said, her eyes wide and scared. "It felt like… him." There was a stony silence as Tinna took in what Avria was saying.

"You think Eleran could return? That his essence has been reunited with his body?"

"I'm not sure…"

"Why would you feel fear of that, Avria? He loved you beyond measure. Surely this dream is connected to your feelings for Eleran; perhaps you sense that you somehow betray him by moving on with your life? You should not feel guilty for finding love again. I am certain, if Eleran could, he would wish this for you as well. He would not wish you to continue on pining for his existence until your death,"

"No. It's not guilt. I know what I have chosen is right, I love Offrin. Eleran is gone. But this dream, it was different. Eleran was something other than what he was. He felt… evil."

"Eleran loved you so much. So much so, he sacrificed his soul to save you," Tinna said, her eyes filled with concern. "He would never harm you. He loved you."

"And I, he. But again… I don't know," she whispered. She was stricken, her eyes sunken and her lips a hard, tight line of worry. In her mind, she thought of Eleran's tale; of his people's beliefs that people only carried half a soul and that the other half was always out there inside someone else. He said if they were lucky enough to meet during a lifetime, that there was no mistaking that connection. He could see it because he was gifted with powers. She only knew that the moment she saw him she was drawn to him like a moth to a flame. She wondered if that same connection was what caused her nightmare. She shifted in her saddle and smiled wanly at her mother, who still gazed at her with worry. Snow drifted down and settled into her curls. "It's nothing I'm sure, mother. I am probably still suffering some residual stress from the wedding. I'm looking forward to wintering at Thamatoc. It will be good to feel truly at home."

532

CHAPTER TWO – FORESHADOWING

Tinna sighed in contentment and reached for the kettle with a rag protecting her hand. She lifted it off the hook and carried it to the table where a pot full of tea leaves awaited. She poured it into the pot and then took the kettle back, where she put it in one of the many nooks built into the façade of the hearth. She turned to look at Avria, who was wearing informal Araki style skirts of dark brown with a droopy black tunic. Tinna was dressed just as casually, a similar long set of layered skirts of black and grey, an ivory undershirt, and the most threadbare, shapeless sweater made of knitted wool. It had once been a vibrant orangey-red colour, but most of the dye had faded away. The colour wasn't even, leaving it looking less than fashionable. The shape it once held was now gone, and the neckline barely caught Tinna's shoulders, one side sliding down onto her arm. The sleeves were too long now, and Tinna bunched them up on her arm to keep the cuffs from dipping into the tea.

No matter how old and ugly that sweater had become, it was still the most valued piece of clothing amid the immediate family. It was the only artifact of Tinna's past that she held onto—it had belonged to her father. She knew nothing of him at all, except that he was a gypsy; but somehow when Tinna needed comfort and peace, she found it wearing his sweater. Avria loved it because it was soothing to be in, because she saw how much comfort it gave her mother. They treated it like it was spun of gold. Tinna knew how to knit and fixed it as best she could when a piece of the yarn snapped, but its days were nearing an end, and soon it would be too fragile, too spindly to wear anymore. It was irreplaceable, but Tinna could not keep from wrapping herself in it.

Tinna sank down in her chair, and poured the tea into the tiny cups, looking at Avria with a motherly glance. She handed Avria a cup and she took it. The girl smirked and said: "Gods, it's good to be home."

"I second that declaration my dear. No offense against you my sweet girl, but I am glad your wedding is done. I'm glad you chose to come here instead of going back to Taruttee. It's nice to have you home."

"Staying with Master Gavorre with a new husband isn't appropriate, and Offrin lived at the barracks, so we were want for a place to go. I confess only to you how strange it would be to continue to live and work in a home where everything is scaled to the uses of the Adrei... I'm no giant of a woman, but it's still close quarters for me much of the time. It's good to walk through wide doorways and sit in reasonably sized chairs," she smiled easily.

Tinna had never heard of the Adrei until the One Day War. She learned that human communities sent babies and children born with small bodies to what were called Auberge communities; places of shelter, where they could be among their own 'kind'. The humans believed that the little people that were born to them were something other than human.

They were misguided, but she imagined it was far more humane than what she knew her own people, the Thran would do to imperfect babies. Her being a half-blood gypsy alone nearly marked her for death. The only reason she still lived is because her mother was nobility, and had the favour of the ruler. But surviving this still exposed her to a childhood of abuse and cruelty far beyond the norm for Thran girls.

The practice of sending imperfect, small-statured children to the Auberges had mostly ended since the war, Taneth made sure of that. The law was now that the little children would remain at home until they are old enough to choose their own way; and the Adrei, the little people of this northern world, would remain in their communities as they pleased; always offering an option to those who wished to live in a world built to suit them. Many humans still resisted this edict, still holding on to the idea that their child was not human and not meant for their world. The Adrei were always there to receive the unwanted and to make them welcome—and the adoptees still arrived with a fair regularity. Master Gavorre's daughter had just taken in a new baby only a few months before. It would be a difficult task, to educate the ignorant on the matter, Taneth declared to Master Gavorre on the subject. "There are so few humans remaining the practice will surely fade anyway."

Avria explained to Tinna that sometimes the Adrei couples would produce a child of average size. But they did not send them away, most did stay but some children would go off to seek out the greater world. Most of them stayed at the auberges with their families, married and lived their lives, hunching under doorways and squatting in tiny chairs.

"Almost two years I've been in and out of there, and I still hit my head on Master Gavorre's door frame in the kitchen," she shook her head laughing. There was a light rap on the door, and Taneth poked his head in.

"Snow's getting hideous out there. We have a small band of visitors asking for shelter..." he added, looking concerned. Taneth was a lanky, awkardish sort of fellow with a unique handsomeness that Tinna found quite appealing. He had a long face with strong angles softened by a trimmed goatee and a thick mat of short hair that was graying at the temples. His whiskers also had a silver dusting. He looked at his women with his stormy grey eyes and rubbed his nose with the back of his hand, sniffling a bit. He wore a pair of tiny spectacles pinched to the bridge of his nose, something he'd just acquired from the city of Lemoram only a few weeks ago to help him see things close to him—but he often forgot he had them on and looked at everyone else over the top of them. He was dressed quite informally this day. Taneth was a high-ranked Wiseman, one of consequence, and had the robes to suit his office, however, whenever at home on the most part, he stuck to comfortable clothes and bare feet as much as he could get away with it. He was bundled up against the snow this day, and his cheeks and nose were rosy from the chill. He plucked his spectacles off of his nose and put them carefully on a small table in a box where he usually stored them.

"Visitors?" Tinna asked, wondering who in their right mind would be traveling in this weather voluntarily. For a moment she dreaded it would be someone from the Keepers; but she knew Taneth would mention this if it were.

"Gypsies," he elaborated. It wasn't unusual to have a band pass through. They had a network of circuitous routes through the forests that they traveled on, constantly moving along in and out of the forests, to the far north and then south again. The Araki used and often helped maintain the roads when they cut through clan territory. The nomads passed through once or twice a year, traded their unusual goods collected from around the land, and then were on their way fairly quickly. It was unusual to have them at winter, and even more unusual for them to seek shelter. Their caravans were well equipped and they were set up to survive the hard seasons unaided. The snow had been coming down quite hard when they got home that afternoon. They were relieved upon entering the lodges, which were comfortably underground and warm from constant fires. After two and a half solid days of riding, it was a welcoming feeling. This storm was particularly wicked; with powerful winds that brought limbs and branches down, and hurled the snow into stinging projectiles, even underneath the canopy where the winds were usually more subdued by the protection of trees.

"Well… They can go into the worship lodge, without a doubt. It's not as cozy as the residences, but it's a nice series of broad spaces and the open hearths ought to serve them well. They can stable their horses and draught animals in the back," Tinna replied. She stood and so did Avria, and they both tugged on their soft hide fur-lined boots. It took only a moment for them to grasp cloaks, and they followed Taneth out of the apartments and down the long corridor to the entrance hall, where he opened the door and was pushed back by a powerful wind that showered the floor of the antechamber in tiny crystals of snow. The women stepped into the gusting wind, and the flakes of snow felt like needles on their faces. They all three forged out into the common after Taneth pulled the door closed with all his might.

"By Arak, this is awful," Tinna shouted over the whistling wind. She had no idea it had gotten this bad in only a few hours. "Some of the wedding guests are probably traveling in this … I hope they're alright. Perhaps I should ask Ledroran to send out a dragon or two to scout them out and see if they need help..." she yelled. Taneth shook his head, picking up most of what she said.

"I can't imagine even dragons would fly in this."

"Or see anything…" she added. Most of her words were eaten up by gusts of wind and buffered by the volume of snow blowing around them. "They can only fly above it."

He led them to a figure against the curtains of blowing flakes and gestured for him to follow. Tinna then noticed several other figures behind the first one, all clutching fur-lined hoods closed around their faces, she sensed more people, but they were obscured by the snow. Taneth led them to the rarely-used temple hall, one of the smaller lodges but still sizable enough to accommodate the travelers. "You can probably bring your caravans right in if you need to. The door here opens wide enough," he shouted at the man-but he gestured that he couldn't hear. Taneth opened the man-door that was nested into the larger door, and they all stepped in out of the storm. Suddenly, as the heavy door was shut, the silence became as deafening as the din of the storm. The gypsies threw back their hoods and looked to Taneth and then Tinna. There were eight men and six women. Five children clung to various adults... Tinna hadn't seen them all because of the horrible visibility. Two mid-sized dogs also accompanied them.

"Get your animals in here. We can open the main door and you can have them drive your caravans inside. They can snug them up against the side wall here and fit nicely. This storm is terrible... they should not be out there in it any longer than they need to," Taneth instructed the swarthy, severe-looking people.

"We only have three caravans... six pullers; two draught horses, four Moropus. We normally don't do this..."

"This isn't normal. This storm is the worst I've seen since I've been here. Please... I will help you."

Taneth and the men went out and Tinna and Avria closed the inset door and then lifted the bars that kept the larger door secured against the weather. They heaved it open and snow blew right into the large space. Tinna took off her cloak and draped it on a half wall, and then went back to light torches and brighten the darkened, little-used lodge. A few minutes later, the shadow of the first caravan filled the opening, and the two moropus pulling it widened their sheep-like nostrils and warily stepped inside, pulling the rumbling house behind them. The man that led the animals pulled them deep into the lodge, and soon the second and third of the caravans arrived. The men shoved the great door closed. The gypsies set to removing the harness from the pulling beasts, and then led them to the stall enclosures in the back of the lodge where newborn foals were kept with the mares for the first few weeks of their lives. Here the stalls were spacious and comfortable. There was already a good stock of bedding moss and hay stored there taken fresh from the fields in the waning days of summer. The animals were settled in and fires were lit in the three central hearths.

Tinna and Avria stood by watching the gypsies going about their work, both curious and waiting for Taneth to finish up his business. As they did, one of the gypsy women passed close to Tinna and stopped, tilting her head as she looked at her. She boldly reached out and picked up the hem of Tinna's old, ugly sweater. "Lathlo," she smiled. "Old, but unmistakable. The knit pattern is Garev Clan. When did they come through here? It's not their normal route. They prefer more southerly trails..."

"Pardon?" Tinna asked.

"Gypsy clans, madam. This is the colour and knit pattern of the Lathlo Garev clan. It's worse for wear, but their workmanship has probably made it last a lot longer than any ordinary knit garment would, I'll wager." Her accent was thick and luscious, and her eyes dark and full of kindness.

Tinna's eyes took in the woman's clothes, she wore a shawl, a triangle of knit wool dyed a vibrant but dark blue, barely discernible in the weak light of the lodge. The pattern was pretty, a scaling of V shapes in the knit. She never noticed that before, that they wore the same type of knit wear. The pattern was the same on all the pieces she could see. The men wore similar sweaters to hers, much less damaged, much less stretched, adorned in the same pattern as the woman's shawl. They wore clan colours—it was a revelation. She did not know this of the gypsies. Few probably did.

Tinna's throat tightened and she clutched the sleeves of her sweater to her chest.

"Then my father must have been of this clan," she said to Avria, who looked on with wide eyes. She saw joy in Tinna's face—such a delightful discovery for a woman who always wished to know more about her father.

"So you are of us," the gypsy woman surmised. Avria glanced at her with an arched brow while the woman appraised Tinna carefully. "You are of the Lathlo-Garev, your tunic speaks of this, but now that I look, your features are distinct, I can see the Lathlo family in them; the way your brows are angled, serious it looks; the tilt of your eyes. You look strongly of that family, despite the mix of Thran blood. Your father must have been strongly connected to the Lathlo line to produce such distinctions in a mixed blood. Your Lathlo features are more powerful than your Thran ones. Any of the six Lathlo family clans would know you as one of their own by looking at you. Any one of them."

"I know nothing of my father's family or his clan…" Tinna muttered.

"I know little myself of the Lathlo besides my sister's marriage into that particular clan. It is a large clan, with eleven bands in it alone."

"First family, then clan, then bands," Taneth whispered, appearing as if out of nowhere beside his wife. Anything new, anything interesting, he wanted to be part of it. This was exactly the sort of conversation that would attract Tinna's husband. Tinna's brows rose up and she pursed her lips.

"So you or anyone else, would not know of who my father could be?"

"No. If you must know, you should go to the family gatherings." Tinna nodded, and clutched the front of her tunic. The woman picked up the droopy hem again and shook her head.

"This is so old. It isn't quite dead yet though. If you pass it to me, perhaps I can fix it; re-knit it with some of our wool to give it strength. I can try to match the colour and dye it afresh, and tighten the knit perhaps… give it new life. It looks as if we are to be snowed in a few days. I think I can do this in that time. A small gift for your hospitality." Tinna looked at her apprehensively, and the woman stuck out her hand. "I will return it, I promise."

"She needs to go out in the snow… it's the only lodge that isn't connected," Avria interjected. The woman nodded and took her blue shawl from her shoulders, and proffered it to Tinna.

"A fair trade… we can exchange them again when I am finished. We will not leave until it is finished to your liking. I will respect your heirloom with my soul; I see what it means to you." Tinna lifted the heavy knit work over her head, fully exposing the wide-necked white shirt she wore beneath. The woman took the bundle of yarn, and Tinna lifted the shawl from her hand, and draped it over her shoulders. Avria handed her the cloak she'd left draping on the wall and Tinna put it on over that.

"There. You will see how well I can give this old thing new life and do its first owner justice."

"She is the most skilled artisan among us," a dignified looking elderly gentleman interjected, arriving behind the ladies. Tinna had seen him helping set up the horses for the night and assisting in lighting the fires in the open hearths. He bowed deeply to Tinna, studying her closely, and then looking at Avria.

"I see it as well, your heritage. It is good to know the leader of this village is of our kind. It makes us feel welcomed when most of the time we are not. We know this village has been much welcoming to other bands, they speak well of Thamatoc."

"You are too kind, Elder."

"I am Azrash… the seer of this band."

"Like our holyman?" Avria asked. It was the first time in all her life they actually truly engaged the gypsy passers-by. They usual kept a respectful distance from one another and spoke only in transactions and trade. Rhoa was the only one who had any long-term experience with the gypsies, and she now lived far north.

"In essence, yes," he replied. He then turned to look at Tinna. "We are glad to find shelter among welcoming people. It has not been awfully welcoming anywhere else. The non-Araki settlements outside of the forest have been especially unkind to our people of late," the Azrash told them. Tinna's brow furrowed.

"You mean the human settlements?" He nodded with a regretful look on his face. She turned to Taneth, her brow furrowed. "I can't imagine why they'd act cruelly against them all of a sudden?"

"They have always been leery of us, we are used to that. But we were never completely unwelcome. We bring things to trade, and stories of different places, so we have always found some place to stay near their towns and cities. But there is definitely some tension these past few months; some towns have taken to chasing our caravans off their lands, and refusing to trade with us. This is the reason why we come to you now for shelter. We would have already been at our wintering region by now, but we had to travel farther during summer and autumn to trade for the supplies we needed to bridge the coldest months. We don't understand the sudden change of heart, but we suspect it might have something to do with the war—because it seems to have begun shortly after that." Tinna nodded and sighed in agitation.

"Or perhaps with the coronation," Taneth said knowingly. Tinna huffed again through her nose and shook her head.

"There have been some tidings from the north of the King and his kind making declarations that might incite the human settlements to resentment. They are few and far between to begin with, their world has been shattered nigh twenty years and they have not recovered at all in all that time, in spite of our efforts to assist them. They tried to protect their land from invasion with an army so small; every last soldier would have been massacred. They have much to be sorrowful for. But still... I don't understand. The people of Arak saved them from the Thran. Our armies stood up to keep theirs from being obliterated, and yet they still are able to harbor anger against anyone remotely connected to us," Tinna grumbled.

The understanding of the connection between the wandering people and the horse people had become common knowledge since the war—as did everything else Taneth learned about the shape of the world. He believed it was important that humanity understand who walked among them, so they could be more understanding of them. It had apparently taken the opposite effect and given reason for humanity to further isolate themselves from the other races. Taneth's brow was furrowed, his lips pursed. "There's no good reason for that. I am greatly sorry for that, kind Elder."

"You do not need to apologize for the human race, good lady. It is a challenge we've known before, even when we once believed we all shared the same race; and it will be something we can endure and overcome as we always have." There was a lull as they pondered all this, and Tinna clutched the shawl closed at her neck. Avria's eyes were wide and curious.

"Well then," Tinna said, feeling sudden quite awkward, "we'll be on our way. We'll leave you to your lodge..."

"There is another matter I wish to discuss before you return to your lodge, although I am hesitant to bring it up." The Azrash smiled gently, and then paused. The expression on his face was one that indicated he had something important to say but didn't know how to say it. He looked at Tinna pointedly and cleared his throat. "On the matter of my being Azrash... I wish to tell of something that has raised my concern since my arrival," he paused again, looking as if he was having difficulty putting it into words.

"Please, do feel free to share your concerns, Azrash," Tinna said. He looked uncomfortable, as if he would be mocked for his exertion, but he nodded and spoke.

"I have, since my arrival in your village, been overcome with a sense of something... I don't know..." he sighed, gritting his teeth in frustration. Avria's eyes widened and she clutched her elbows, looking to her mother, who frowned.

"Sir, I beg you not hesitate to speak to us of your concern," Tinna urged him.

"You do not have a spiritual guide here?" he suddenly asked. "Do you have a holy man, as your settlements normally do, or any kind of spiritual leader who uses or senses magic?"

"No. At present we have no such person here," Avria muttered, her voice cracking. Tinna's hand fell on her daughter's shoulder reassuringly, and she glanced at her and then the gypsy seer.

"I suspected as much. There is an absence of something intangible. If you did have such a man present, they would tell you the same as I would say to you Madame. Since our arrival, I've sensed it. I do not like the way it feels. It feels..." his pause was lengthy.

"Wrong," Avria finished. She bit her lip and Tinna glowered. Taneth merely looked confused by the whole discussion but didn't interrupt.

"Yes. Something is amiss. It is difficult to describe without sounding half-mad. But I do sense this, and it looms heavily."

"I have no idea what that could be," Tinna admitted. The gypsy's eyes wandered away from Tinna and onto Avria. The girl's face seemed to drain of colour.

543

"Nor can I identify what the thing is." He looked at Tinna again, and shrugged his shoulders. "However, I assure you, for as long as I am here, I will keep my senses keen Madame Leader, kind Wiseman. This I promise. If anything changes, I will surely let you know the moment it does." Tinna nodded silently, clutched the front of her cloak together. She led her daughter into the snow, leaving her puzzled husband behind. They returned to Tinna's apartments to sit and drink cold tea in a strained silence. Even when Istvan was returned from Jenyk's home, his innocent antics did little to lift the strange quiet gloom.

The gypsies did not take Taneth up on the invitation to share general meal with the tenants of the main lodge. Instead, they kept inside their lodge, avoiding the short but harrowing trek across the village common to the summer lodge. The blizzard was not abating, for a day it continued to howl and blow. The sunken common and the tree cover kept the bulk of the snow from accumulating in the circle where the lodges faced, but the wind made it impossible to see where one was going, and the snow that was accumulating was drifting up against the doors of the lodges.

People traveled through the various connecting tunnels that linked lodge to lodge underground rather than cross the common. The worship hall was the only unconnected lodge, and the gypsies seemed content to remain isolated in there from the curious Araki community. Taneth could not resist making the trip to check in on them here and again during the day, always fascinated with unusual things.

"I'm glad you decided to get married when you did, Avria," her father declared, shaking snow off his shoulders and stamping his feet on the floor of the entrance hall. Avria happened to be passing through the entrance hall in search of Offrin, who'd gone to the library an hour ago and had yet to return. "This is the worst storm I've ever seen in my twenty odd years here. The worst. I'm sure Rigerd would say the same. By Arak, it's hideous out there. We missed that storm by the skin of our teeth coming home. Let's hope the rest of the guests made it to shelter, because this is the kind of winter that kills wisemen and holymen." He traipsed through to the second corridor and left Avria with an odd smirk on her face. He was referring to the village 'curse'. They'd lost a Wiseman and a holyman that way; each had gone out before a storm, never to return. Taneth was the one to replace the lost Wiseman many years ago. The Holyman was lost before the war a little over two years before. Each one was found frozen to death and those winter storms were not half as terrible as this one by far.

Avria moved towards her father's private library and knocked twice and then entered without leave, finding Offrin, Phenmal and Master Gavorre all seated around the central table, feet up on the table-top, smoking pipes and laughing. The fact that they were here without Taneth was astonishing. There was a strict rule when Avria was growing up that nobody was to enter the library without supervision from either Taneth or his senior student adept. But here they were, treating it like their own personal public house; drinking and carousing. What was worse, they were smoking their pipes, something Taneth would normally fly off the handle about in defense of his books against yellowing. The laughter stopped the moment she pushed open the door, and by the time she was able to fully look into the room, they had all managed to drop their feet down and straighten up in their seats. She smirked.

The fire was high and bright in the hearth and a bottle of wine hunkered on the table by an old tome they'd apparently been looking at. It was open, and the cover rested in a way that implied something was hidden beneath it. Avria suspected a deck of cards and some gambling chits. Three thick glass goblets were distributed 'round the table, a fourth one was waiting for the mysterious fourth accomplice on a sideboard under the window with wine in it.

Offrin looked downright guilty. "Eh, Avria, sorry, I sort of became distracted," he muttered. Avria smiled and shook her head. There was something that delighted her in this scene. All these men she loved in different ways came from different worlds, and they were hanging about together like chums, gambling and drinking; including her new husband who had fretted terribly about truly integrating with her clan. Here he was, right in the thick of them with Gavorre as if it were the way things ought to be. It warmed her heart.

"It's nothing, really. I'm glad to see you've found the sanctuary of this library; my father spends much time in here when not abroad," she said in an overly sweet manner, giving Phenmal a quick narrow-eyed glare as he chewed his pipe and gazed at her smugly. "Does he know you're here?"

"Yes," Master Gavorre grunted. "He will be joining us again once he's back from wherever he traipsed off to." Avria's brows rose in mild shock. Perhaps her father was becoming mellower as he aged. She addressed her husband:

"I was going to go and sit with mother and Istvan, if that's alright with you. You needn't get up; I just wanted to let you know where I'd be."

"Of course, that's fine my dear," the young man retorted. He wore a knitted hat that hugged his bald head, and was clothed in far commoner clothing than he'd worn at Klatna; a heavy tunic, some thick breeches and a pair of leather lodge slippers. All three of them were dressed for relaxation. The other two looked on in amusement. Avria ducked out of the room. She heard the conversation and laughter resume as soon as the latch closed, and she laughed through her nose. She then heard the unmistakable snap of the cover of a book being closed. She stayed long enough to hear the whir of cards being shuffled and the click of chits being thrown onto the table. The brats, she thought. With a smile she went to find her mother.

She poked her head in the door of the family apartment. The lamps were lit, a fire was burning, but there was nobody there. Tinna couldn't be far. She thought perhaps to check Jenyk's apartment. She crossed the corridor and knocked on the door. Jenyk opened it, her round face changing from a look of annoyance to happiness when she saw who was at her door. "Avria, good you're here... Could you give me a hand with something?" She opened her door and stepped aside so the girl could enter. Jenyk's apartment was always in disarray. She had two children, and often watched the smaller children for other families in the clan. Istvan was not present. Instead, her children were happily occupied in playing a game of Enemies, but since both of them were too young to understand the complex rules of the board game, they merely took the multitude of beautifully carved pieces and acted out a battle on the inlaid wood board. They ignored Avria completely.

On the large table where Jenyk often did her work was covered in a large swath of lovely snow-white fabric as sheer as a fading mist. She would probably make a garment from it, and then dye it. White was not always an easy colour to maintain in an Araki village. "For the life of me, I've been trying to get an even fold on this to start cutting the skirts for Tinna's summer gowns for Klatna... It's so wide I can't manage it, and there's no way I'd lay it on the floor with those little gremlins running about with sticky hands and grimy feet." Avria laughed. "Help me fold this?" she asked. Avria nodded, and did exactly as she was asked, matching the corners, and stretching the long piece of fabric all the way across the apartment, and then doubling it up and folding it so it could be managed better from her work table.

"Have you seen my mother and Istvan today, Jenyk?"

"I had Istvan for a few hours this morning while she met with the elders, but she came and got him just before luncheon. I have no idea where she is if she isn't in her apartments. She could be in any of the lodges." Avria gave Jenyk her end of the fabric, and sighed. She waved farewell to Jenyk and set out again in search of her mother.

She looked in the main hall, and saw nobody. It occurred to Avria that her mother would likely be at the new lodge, where Tinna was setting up a special work room for crafts which would solve problems like Jenyk's—it was a large space with huge work tables and the carpenter was making a bank of shelves to rival the archives at Lemoram. Thamatoc relied a great deal on goods trading; they did not farm much, they bought the majority of their flours and grains and fresh vegetables from clans with large agricultural land areas. Instead, Thamatoc traded hunted meats when they could, furniture and hand-crafted goods. The village was peppered with a variety of artisans that created a plethora of marketable goods, but there was one common complaint; the lack of workspace and light. So Tinna's solution was to assign a huge segment of the newest lodge to the artisans. She was excited about this project and spent a good deal of time overseeing the construction of it. She was having larger window-slots put in and an array of hanging chandeliers in addition to other wonderful things.

The newest lodge was finished only this summer, and because it was new, it was the one on the farthest end of the arc around the common. Avria sighed with annoyed resignation and walked to the corridor that connected to the autumn lodge. With a groan, she forged into the darkness, making the long circuit to where her mother and brother only might be.

CHAPTER THREE – DEVASTATION

The spring lodge was the last of the old lodges, and the two new corridors to the new lodge were still freshly excavated and dark, they both took a bit of a strange circuitous route around some massive boulders that were found beneath the earth. The front corridor was shorter simply because of the angle at which the lodges were placed, but it was under repair, as one of the newly excavated ceilings had collapsed to create a bit of a sinkhole in the forest floor above. The shortest route was off limits for now, blocked by several lengths of wood, and Avria was most irritated to have to walk the length of the Spring Lodge to the back, where the longer corridor was. Avria made her way without a torch or a lamp, by feel alone.

Her hand slipped along the freshly laid stone walls lining the way. The masonry gave way to the grittier surface of the first of the two massive boulders, both of which were each as big as a human house. She slid along, resuming the wall between the two boulders, when she came to a sudden stop. Her fingers had come up against a something soft that radiated warmth, something wearing a smooth, yielding fabric. Whoever it was, they were leaning on the wall, not moving, not speaking. She held her breath and squinted as if to see in the pitch black.

"Who's there?" she asked, "this isn't really very funny whoever you are. It's not a funny joke," she muttered in annoyance. Then she sighed intolerantly. "Drashe, if that's you I'm going to kill you." In the darkness, something brushed her cheek; cool fingers. Avria jumped back, out of reach of the wall. She turned a few times, feeling frantically about in the pitch black for a wall to guide her. "This is not funny at all." There was an edge of fear in her voice.

"Avria..." the voice froze her. Her breath was locked inside her lungs; she felt heaviness in her stomach and a pain in her heart like she hadn't felt in ages. She blinked in the darkness, listening, her head moving like a bird. She listened hard—in spite of the whooshing in her ears. For a moment she thought someone was playing a game with her; perhaps using some sort of spell to make her think she was hearing him. She could not think of a single person besides Jestin who would be so cruel—but Jestin did not have a proclivity for magic that she knew of and had no means to fool her with this voice she knew all too well. Her mind raced, her heart beat so loudly the blood was rushing in her ears, which seemed deafening in the silence and pitch darkness around her. If it wasn't Jestin, then perhaps it was him…

"Eleran?" she whispered, the incredulity raw and keenly evident in her voice. She remained alert, backing away from any small noise that might indicate his approach. She didn't know why fear filled her instead of abject joy at the possibility of reuniting with her lost love, but she could not control her instincts. She backed into the opposite wall, and clung to it. "Eleran?" she called again, needing to know where he was, or if she had dreamt his voice calling her name. It was unmistakably Eleran's voice. The memory of it was burned irrevocably into her heart. When she heard nothing, she immediately began to feel her way with a frantic air towards the spring lodge again until his voice stopped her cold again.

"My lovely Avria, I could not keep myself from you any longer." All that came in reply to this was a strangled gasp and then a sob. Whoever it was, it moved towards her. Avria was sidling away along the farthest wall.

"Where are you going?" Apparently her attempt to flee upset him, he sounded angry.

"Where have you been?" she whispered accusingly, her throat tight. The tears were palpable in her voice. "Where were you?" she sobbed. She stood with her back to the wall, her hands flat on the surface. Her instincts told her she should run, but her heart needed to know.

"I was lost; out there in the place beyond this world. But the Hevra brought me back, and here I am." She could hear his voice grow louder as he approached her. She imagined his face as she saw it in her dream, misshapen and twisted, and her stomach turned to ice. Suddenly she felt an arm encircling her waist and she stiffened in terror, trying to pull away but his grip was tight.

"Why do you fear me, my Avria," he asked; his breath hot on her face; the disappointment clear in his words. Avria's trepidation compelled her to reach up and lay her hands on his face—to know he was not the monster her dreams had painted him to be. There were no scars or ridges, no hideous deformations as her dream had implied; it felt as it always had, strong and beautiful, and her tears came harder. He bent down and she felt his lips fall upon her tear-soaked mouth, and for a moment, she was lost in his kiss, lost in the man she had loved so surely. But then her instincts started to prickle at her again, and she pushed away, unable to extricate herself from his grip. He pinned up against the wall.

"You were gone... You were..." she stammered. "I am married now, Eleran. Let me go. Things are different now. You should go back to wherever you've been." There was a moment of quiet, and he pressed against her. She felt his shoulders stiffen and her anxiety flared.

"What does a ridiculous gesture of commitment, this empty binding matter in the greater scheme?" He snarled in her face suddenly, his anger raw and powerful. She felt the spittle on her face when he hissed out the words, "our souls are one; marriage in this existence means nothing at all." His words took an edge to them that was feral and wild. "That half-man you chose to give yourself to is nothing at all to me, to existence itself. You will come with me. We will be together. You belong with me." He said the last phrase between gritted teeth. He was bordering on rage. He was all wrong, twisted, deformed. Not his physical form, but his essence, his soul. It was wrong. Her dread turned to panic and she struggled violently against him.

"I will scream!" she yelled. "Scream until someone hears me... and Phenmal will feel you, you are probably discovered already!" she bellowed out hoarsely.

"That Chaiva is easy to block, my dear," his words suddenly chillingly calm, his body barely moving as she writhed and bucked to escape his grasp. "You are with me now. You are my soul, Avria. I will not let you go." She continued to weep and squirm, and the more she resisted the harder he leaned against her, the more firmly he pressed her against the wall. He knew Avria wasn't the wilting flower she seemed to be. He was aware of the training her mother had given her, and he knew the best way to hold her in place to render her helpless. She cried out for help, and screamed for her mother, but the long rough-walled corridor did little to carry her pleas. The Druid had chosen the place well. She felt him lean forward and bury his face in her tumbles of curls, taking a deep breath.

"I have missed your scent," his voice became deeper, and he ground against her. "You have no idea how much I have missed you, my precious Avria," he breathed, the heat of his excitement pouring into her hair and onto her neck. "I have thought of this moment for months, touching you again." His hand slid up and he squeezed each

551

breast in turn. In a move that surprised and terrified Avria, he leaned back enough to grasp the collar of her tunic and in a powerful yank, he tore her tunic open. He grunted to himself as he felt her bare breasts his hands. Then, his free hand started to fumble with the drawstring of her skirts, sliding his fingers against her belly. She blanched, her screams growing increasingly sharp. Her movement made it impossible for him to untie her skirts with one hand, so he simply bent only enough to catch the hem, and he hiked her skirts up. Avria trembled and whimpered now.

"Why are you doing this, Eleran?" she sobbed. "Please! Eleran don't do this!" He did not answer. His mind was focused elsewhere; on the softness of her body, the scent he adored so which hung in his nostrils and fueled his desire, the fire of her resistance. When he'd shimmied up her skirts, his hands found the low-slung waistline of her winter leggings, which did not resist being pulled down. He used his feet to kick them away, tearing off Avria's lodge slippers as he did. Avria's high-pitched whining increased tenfold when he then freed himself from his breeches by opening the flap of his fall-fronts, and breathed heavily upon her as he moved to position her, gripping one of her thighs and yanking one of her legs up against his side.

He covered her screams with his mouth, and with a powerful thrust, he bore into her. With a groan of ecstasy, he buried himself in, and lingered there for a second, his skin trembling. "Ah, yes, this is the Avria I missed..." he breathed onto her face. He kissed her savagely and then began to move again. At first gently, but that faded almost immediately into brutal, unchecked thrusts. No matter how she kicked, no matter how she screamed, he did not cease. Instead, he was fed by her horror, and more determined to do what he wished the more she struggled, to show her who was in control. He forced himself into her with a cruelty Avria had never known, gripping a handful of her hair and pulling it hard to keep her pinned, causing her pain and injury as he repeatedly ground her onto the rough stone. Tears flowed down her face, and her child-like crying was muffled by his vicious kisses. She wrenched her face away from his, hitting her temple hard on the wall, not feeling the hot sticky blood as it coursed down the side of her face.

Avria cried and begged for him to stop, to let her go, pleading to the man that she thought she knew. He only continued until he reached climax, his huge frame dwarfing hers, rendering her helpless against his attack. He drove himself deep into her and then released, pressing her onto the wall with his chest, and shuddering, his breath searing the side of her face. "You will always be mine, Avria," he whispered hoarsely, victoriously; sated by her, his sweaty chest soaking the tatters of her torn tunic and chilling her bare front. "It is not in our power to change what is destined. You will always be mine," he hissed into her ear. She squirmed away, still sobbing, and then he stepped back and she fell into a heap on the ground. "You need to remember that," he added. She heard him fiddling with the fabric of his breeches and then he stooped in front of her.

"This only served to teach you your place, Avria. This is what happens when you defy the fates."

"What happened to you?" she sobbed. "Who are you? The Eleran I loved would never have done this."

"The Eleran you loved was weak... laughable," he spat in disgust. "He was not strong enough to bear the powers that he possessed, and he paid the price. But now, I am stronger than he ever was, and I have returned to claim what was his; to claim the half of my soul that is rightfully mine," he spat. "You will see it in time, Avria. I have been kind, and I have let you live on thinking you have not betrayed me—but now you know the truth. You have betrayed me. But I can no longer bear to see you giving yourself to anyone else. We were fixed for one another; I nearly died to save you. You are obligated to me—you will stand beside me again. You will come now." He reached down to take her arm.

"Onithoth Teghed!" a new voice shouted, and the darkness was suddenly filled with blinding light. For a fleeting second, Avria saw him, the man she'd felt such love for, the man who'd just taken her dignity so barbarically; lit up by the flash of brightness; his hair long and silky, loose against his back, black as night, still wavy from the braiding he often kept it in. His face was still angled and beautiful, not disfigured as she'd dreamt, but the expression was foreign to Avria. She'd never seen such hatred in anyone before, even with his sockets cast into shadows by the hot light, she could see his evil. She weakly lifted her trembling hand to cover her eyes, for the light was searing, and she saw Eleran fly off the ground and fall into a heap meters away before the light faded into blackness.

Eleran could be heard getting immediately back onto his feet, and he hissed an unintelligible word, and a blast of lightning exploded from his chest. The Gypsy Azrash responded with words of power and spread his arms to receive the bolt, absorbing it into him as if it was nothing, and his body glowed from the gift, casting a soft light about the bend of the corridor. He bellowed out two more words, but no sooner than the magic was cast, Eleran vanished in an explosion of light, and just before he disappeared, he looked at Avria and flashed a cold and haunting smile.

Avria, slumped to the ground, bruised and bleeding, tears flowing in a grief and pain she'd never experienced before. She heard boot heels approaching, and she saw the familiar and welcome image of Phenmal's face as he entered the reach of the gypsy's glowing light. She fell into fresh tears, and let the older man stoop before her and cover her with his banyan.

CHAPTER FOUR – CONCEALMENT

Phenmal carried the Avria's huddled form discreetly into her apartments and placed her on the bed. He was visibly upset and shaken, his eyes glassed over and his mouth tight. He kept whispering "I'm sorry, Avria, I'm sorry. I didn't feel it until it was too late." He tucked her under the blankets and sat on the edge of the bed next to her, pressing his hand on her cheek. She winced and he withdrew. The mind-reader was beside himself. "I didn't feel it until it was too late," he told her. She sobbed quietly and she took his hand and rolled onto her side, tucking it under her chin and constricting herself into the fetal position as if to wrap her body around it. He looked at this girl and his anger flared. She was scraped badly; one side of her face there was blood still seeping from cuts, one on the edge of her brow, another the back of her arms, and several on her back and her spine, blood stains peppered what was left of her garments.

He'd sent Offrin to find Tinna immediately simply to give the frantic man some occupation for he was almost out of control at the sight of his wife in the state she was in. The only other person in the room was the Gypsy wizard, who looked so much older and benign than he had when he was in the corridor. He sat down in a chair by the fire, his eyes focused somewhere else. He hummed something under his breath.

Phenmal was rusty at the arts he once performed in his younger days when he was a minion of the Keepers in earnest, and not just a means of supervision and manipulation of the Keepers' new obsession; Tinna. He was once a ruthless invader. But he had not practiced those arts in a long time. It was easy enough to just read someone's thoughts; they were as intrusive and loud to him in his head as they would be if people were holding conversations all around him. But to enter someone's inner mind, to affect healing or inject false memories, or erase the contents of a lifetime, these are things he had not done in some time—and he did not want to damage the mind of a girl he looked upon quite as his own—nor was he willing to erase what just happened to save her the pain, as appealing as the idea was. It was too invasive and with what had just happened to her, he did not want to do that to her. Everyone around her would know—and they would treat her differently, she would always wonder why. He thought about it once more, and then his brow wrinkled in sadness. He had to let her keep the memories, but he would have to find a way to help her live with them.

He loved Avria and Tinna like no one else in his entire life, and he was pained to see what destruction had been done by this horrible rape of her body and her soul. He bent low over her and with his free hand; he cupped the back of her head. She was no longer weeping, but still trembling. His gaze bored into her eyes and her trembling ceased as if someone had shut the door on it. She fell into a strange trance as he looked into her.

"Retreat, Avria. I am there with you. Where you go to when things are hard." He knew that place; it was a fabrication of her past, but with her own improvements to create comfort. The place had evolved over the years to include or exclude things. For a while, it was a hillside overlooking the oak cemeteries, where Eleran awaited her with a loving smile. Phenmal knew she retreated here even during her betrothal period with Offrin. When she was a child, Avria would retreat to her special place when she was upset. It was different when she was little. He would see it when he was visiting, when she thought she'd escaped her parents and was sulking. Today, her retreat world was the one of her childhood, not the hillside. The childhood place was her parent's apartments. They seemed slightly bigger, but Avria was as she always was in this secret place, innocent and small, a little girl, sitting by the fire on the soft sheepskin carpet, leaning on the body of a large male dog. She turned to look at him, her eyes red and puffy.

"Phen..." she whispered, her grown-up mouth never moving in the quiet room of reality. The tall, lanky man, younger in her image of him, stooped beside her and lifted her to her feet. She wrapped her child-like arms around him and nuzzled her face into his neck. Phenmal stood and carried her to the chair, where he sat down and let her cry into his shoulder. He sat there, rubbing her back, feeling her misery and her pain course through him like a river. He always knew the intimate crime like this was one that scarred its victims with a permanence nobody could understand; but he never knew such humiliation or horror, such violation; he never understood that it was such an invasive way to cut into someone's soul. Eleran had stolen her power; he'd stolen her dignity, her control, her sense of self. He had rocked her wellbeing into oblivion. She was a child again, vulnerable to anything, unable to fight back; rendered helpless. If she could not have control of her own being, then what did she have dominion over at all? She was nothing.

He huddled her to his imagined self, and remained with her while the world outside her head went on.

Phenmal heard Tinna long before he saw her; he'd focused almost every part of his essence into Avria's retreat, and was stunted in his awareness of reality—which in terms of a Chaiva, meant he could only see and hear things; he could not read anyone else's thoughts. He could project thoughts and power, but not take in any more, since his head was full of Avria's sorrow. He heard her first with his ears, a cry of such fury; it could be heard by the whole lodge. Her screams of rage grew louder and louder until Tinna exploded into the room with Offrin, Taneth and Master Gavorre at her heels. Phenmal lifted his hand flat and formed a mental barrier between them. Tinna's rage was cut short by the painful twinge in her brain, and she cried out and turned away, gripping her temples. Offrin was the only other one who'd run against it and he roared out in anger.

"Phenmal, find that monster so I can kill him!" Tinna spat between gritted teeth. "The gypsy warned us he felt it. I should have known. I should have known Avria's instincts were spot-on. He was and is here. We need to find him. he needs to die!" Offrin flared up as well.

"Old man, Avria is my wife; you cannot dare to tell me I cannot…" Phenmal turned and glared at him, the force of his gaze silencing him.

"She has been violated, Offrin. By someone she once trusted beyond measure. Her heart is broken. Besides, I've taken her outside of this room right now. I have retreated her."

"Phenmal, where is he? Where is Eleran?" Taneth barked.

"He is nearby," the gypsy spoke. "The displacement spells never bring you too far unless you are a mage of tremendous power, or you are carried by the power of other mages. I did not sense that he has anyone assisting him. I sense him alone. He is powerful, but not so much so that he cannot be stopped. The Zsathri fled me. He sensed imminent defeat if he'd stayed to fight on. But do not take his cowardice for granted. The Zsathri are particularly cunning wielders; they have the power of the Hevra behind them. This one is a true danger. He was a trespasser; he broke sacred bonds, and instead of enduring the punishment in the voids, he was retrieved and freed. To retrieve a punished wielder from the voids is a terrible gamble. Returning them from the voids, the emptiness spawns madness; there are things in there that no soul should see…" he paused as if stricken by the idea. "The only way we will stop this wielder is to kill him or force him to kill with his magic, the latter I would prefer not to do."

"He will return," Tinna flared.

"Not as long as I am here beside her," the gypsy replied. "I sense him. He is distanced now; but I sense his nearness. I felt him when he came. I could not pinpoint him as fast as I would have liked. He was blocking as well, Chaiva. He was casting a spell to keep us blind; it was not your doing that you did not feel him. He only became vulnerable to you when I cast him down the first time; separating him from his spell. It was nothing you did not do that made you unable to sense him."

"I wish to see my daughter, Phenmal," Tinna interrupted. Phenmal shook his head.

"In a while. Let her retreat. I'm in there with her. She is wounded, and humiliated. She feels as if she invited this, and she is afraid that Offrin will no longer love her. She feels like she is no longer the custodian of her own being; that its ownership has been relegated to someone who aims only to harm her; someone who had once meant everything to her. She needs time in there, and I will help her through it."

"You are not her father! Who are you to… to… to just take over like this? She's our daughter! Ours!" Taneth snarled. Tinna put her arm out to block her husband who felt it necessary to advance on Phenmal. Considering that Taneth was the most non-violent man in the world, this was a clear indication to Tinna that he was deeply, deeply upset by this situation. She'd never seen him like this, his rage just boiling under the surface. He looked at her in vehemence and betrayal, pushing against her arm. Tinna locked her eyes on his, and he calmed almost immediately. She shook her head coolly and told him to stand down with just a look. Phenmal watched this with little reaction. When Taneth's anger was marginally under control, he looked at each of them gravely.

"You must go. Everyone must go, except the soothsayer."

Taneth with a jaw set hard and furious, mandibles rippling, guided his wife towards the door and Offrin followed reluctantly. Before they were to the door, the mind-reader called out: "Tinna… in a few hours, can you send a tub with hot water please, and soap too?" She will want to wash him off of her when she awakes. "Pick some of her favorite clothing for her and prepare her some comforting food as well. Taneth, you should make her your sweetcakes. Those always make her happy. She will be feeling hollow and lost; we need to create an arsenal to tempt her back to some normality. Offrin, you will welcome her with love and gentleness. Until you can look at her without that mask of rage on your face, I recommend you stay away. She is already overcome with self-reproach. Keep your wrath and your revenge to yourself. Now is not the time for that." Phenmal then turned back to Avria, who lay still in her fetal coil, her eyes open, but unreadable.

"I will not be here forever, Mind-Reader," the gypsy sorcerer said when the others had retreated. "What then?" Phenmal turned and looked at the old man, and then back to Avria. Indeed, thought he, what then?

Avria opened her eyes and she thought she was alone in her humble apartment. A bit of white daylight was coming in the narrow window. The apartment was still fairly dark, no lamps were lit—only the strong fire in her hearth poured its yellow light into the room, flickering on the folds of Avria's pillow. For a moment she was disoriented, but then it all came flooding back, and she felt an instant hollowness in her chest, and all she wanted to do was sleep it all away. Her eyes felt dry and sandy, and her limbs listless.

She then remembered the quiet bath where she sat, water dripping from her face, staring at the cloudy surface of the water. Her body hurt. Her mother was there. She had lifted her arms and washed them gently with a cloth, her touch as light and feathery as she could manage. Tinna's face was waxen, but she kept offering Avria's distant gaze a wan smile in an attempt to offer comfort. She did not speak; she only focused on helping wash Avria's bruised and battered body.

Phenmal sat with his back to her by the fire next to the sorcerer. Neither of them had left her side at all since the attack. She remembered Phenmal's once-frightening eyes so full of concern and kindness, it nearly made her cry thinking of it. She loved the old man, more than she knew, and she realized that he loved her far more deeply; as if she were his own child and her throat tightened. She thought of how he felt, to see her pained, to feel her pain, she could sense his feelings when he was with her. He hated that he'd been powerless to stop what happened to her. He had been so gentle, and so caring; the memories of his being there felt more like a strange dream—but it somehow had helped. It had blunted the edges of the knives that cut into her heart; it brought her from the deepest of despair and wretchedness to an odd fugue where her feelings, although still keenly present, were not as sharp and prickling. He had given her the ability to function. Had he not helped, she knew she would be in much, much worse pain.

Her mother's ache was another matter altogether. Tinna, always the bastion of strength was barely holding herself together. Avria knew first-hand how much her mother invested in Avria's sense of security and happiness; she knew how much her mother valued the idea of Avria never suffering the indignities and sorrow of her own youth. "You can't save me from everything mother," Avria whispered to Tinna when she was standing and letting her mother wrap her in a towel. Tinna's lips tightened and she shook the words off, helping her daughter step from the tub. Tinna listlessly combed her hair and plaited it in two braids, one over each shoulder. She wordlessly helped Avria dress in her nightgown and robe and sat with her until she fell asleep.

"My little baby girl," she heard Tinna whisper just before she drifted off.

She had no idea how long she'd slept. She merely awoke with a snap of the eyes. She heard something, a subtle noise and lifted her head to see the elderly gypsy squatting by the fire, feeding the flames fresh wood, and gazing at the hungry blaze pensively. She sat up and put her legs over the side of the large bed. She clutched the neck of her robe tightly closed and padded towards the wizard, the rustling train of it following her. Her body was so sore. Every muscle. The skinned patches on her body were already scabbing over, the cut on her temple felt tight and itchy. He turned his head to look at her and offered her a weak smile.

"It has been a difficult time for you," he said. She sat down next to him in Offrin's chair and hunched forward, wedging her elbows against her belly and leaning on them, staring at the fire. "You are fortunate to have the friendship of the Chaiva. They have many special skills." She took a long, silent pause before saying anything to him.

"I used to be so afraid of him; but I realized it wasn't fear, it was respect." Her voice was groggy and faint, and she rocked a bit in the chair. "How long have I been asleep since when I last woke?"

"Two days."

"Two days?" she repeated, incredulous. She rubbed her face, and then toyed with her braids, which were frayed and tight.

"The storm has abated. My people prepare to leave. You will be leaving as well," the old man informed her. Avria looked at him warily and then shook her head incredulously. The old man simply resumed tending to the fire. Avria didn't ask any more questions. She merely hunched forward and continued to watch the fire, her expression one of detachment and disappointment. Avria only then noticed that her small mantel clock was dreadfully loud. It had taken her some time to get used to it when Taneth brought it for her a few months ago when he came to Taruttee. Then she got used to its sound, and eventually found comfort in it. When it stopped and needed winding, her little room seemed too quiet. Now it sounded like a mallet striking an anvil. She glowered at nothing and then flopped back into her chair. She remained there unmoving.

About an hour later, Tinna entered the room. She carried a packet wrapped in rough linen, and laid it on Avria's little dining table. Avria stood and went to her mother and the woman wrapped her in a deep embrace. She felt her daughter trembling in her hold. Tinna's heart hurt for Avria, the idea of what she was suffering was too painful to bear. Tinna allowed herself to weep for her daughter. Avria's tears were dried it seemed. She was depressed and faded— somewhere distant and detached.

"Where is Offrin? Is he disgusted by me now?" Avria asked. Tinna wiped away her tears and shook her head, reaching out to touch Avria's pale, tired face.

"Not at all, Avria, he is so worried. We've sent him to Klatna with Haneet to fetch some herbs and medicines your father requested for your care. It's a fool's errand, but he has been distracted so by his fear for you. Giving him a purpose has kept him focused on helping rather than dwelling and festering on his rage."

"Mother..." Avria suddenly started to cry. She moved back to the fire and flopped into the chair and Tinna knelt in front of her. "What happened to Eleran?" her hoarse voice cracked when she asked this, and her tears ran down her nose. "What happened to him?"

"The sorcerer knows. It's not his fault." Tinna turned to the gypsy man, who was snoring in the chair. "He says it has to do with Eleran's punishment for killing using his powers; being cast out of his body into what is called the voids. It drove him to madness, and when he was retrieved by whatever power, he returned as someone other than the Eleran you knew." Avria wept harder, hunched forward on herself.

"I loved him so much. He has broken me into bits."

561

"I know. And he can hurt you again, Avria. His protection spell that saved you before is no more. When it was taken we do not know, but the gypsy says you have no spells over you now. I was hoping you'd be awake, Avria because I've something to tell you."

"I'm going away?" Avria guessed. She looked with purpose onto the sleeping sorcerer to indicate that he'd told her something of the like. Tinna nodded ruefully and stood up, clutching her elbows. She paced the open space in the center of the room.

"Phenmal told us he knows of a place of safety where you will be shielded from Eleran—so that he would not be able to find you using his magic."

"Why must it be like this? First Jestin, now Eleran... why?" Avria suddenly screamed, rocketing to her feet. The old man was startled into wakefulness just in time to see Avria pick up the sorcerer's clay mug of hot cider, now tepid, and hurl it across the room where it shattered into a mess over her bookshelf. "Why must I be subject to the whims of people like Jestin and Eleran, Mother? Why?" She started crying again. "I don't want to run any more. I want to be happy with my husband," she sobbed. "I just want to be happy—but how can I now with the memory so sharp of Eleran causing me pain?" Avria bawled, "How can I when he stole everything away?"

"It will heal, Avria, this I promise you. Enough so you can find some measure of peace with yourself and with Eleran. Phenmal will help you. And where you are going, you can find help there too, Phenmal says. You will not be gone forever; it's for now, until Phenmal can get to the bottom of this; to find out who retrieved him, and try to track Eleran down somehow. Please, Avria. Just for now…" Tinna approached and took Avria's hands. They were cold, and her fingers hung limp in hers.

"What of Offrin? Does he know of this?" Tinna's eyes dropped and a wash of shame moved over her.

"No. We will tell him when he's returned and you are gone. We do not want to risk him following you and leading Eleran to you. Not even we know where you are going; Phenmal wants to avoid the chance of our knowledge being stolen to find you."

"Such deceit, he will be devastated."

"He will come to understand it and accept it for the sake of your wellbeing. He loves you so, he will understand. But you must prepare to leave now."

"Now?"

"Ledroran has sent Eritrix to take you."

562

"Mother I don't want to go…"

"I don't want you hurt again, Avria!" Tinna said a bit too forcefully. She stopped herself and swallowed her feelings, calming herself. Only then did she look up at her daughter and continue. "I don't want you taken away again." There was a pall and then Tinna added: "if it makes it any more appealing to you, Phenmal let it slip that it is an island in a sea." Tinna knew this would make her pause, even now in her distracted misery. The ocean, much like it had once been for Tinna, was a fantasy of sorts for Avria; something she dreamt of seeing. Her elder brother Hanru had missed her wedding because he was on his way to Wye, an Araki settlement by the ocean, where he would be the new Wiseman. She had lamented her disappointment in not seeing her brother but also her jealousy that he was to live by the sea. It was something she wanted to do all her life, and had yet had the opportunity. Tinna saw it at once; the immediate effect of this idea on her broken daughter—a silly, childhood fancy to hold onto when everything else seemed to be crumbling away. Surrounded by the sea.

"Only for now?"

"Yes my dear. Only for now." Tinna pulled her forward and embraced her again, resting her hand on the back of Avria's head. "I am sorry, my little one. I am so very sorry." Avria's head became heavy on Tinna's shoulder, and she fell into her mother in racking sobs. Tinna stood it through, gently rocking Avria as she wept away her horror. When Avria was wicked dry of her tears, she stood back, empty and waxen, and she took her mother's hands, this time clasping them tightly.

"It is probably best that Offrin is away. I love him, but I fear I could not bear any man close to me or touching me right now."

"Yes. You need time to heal," Tinna agreed. Avria stood silent for a second.

"I don't know how I will do that, mother," she confessed. Tinna could only purse her lips and look at her with sad eyes. Avria nodded and said: "I will dress then."

"Warmly," Tinna warned her. She then crossed the room to the table and opened up the package she'd brought in. She pulled out the contents and turned to show Avria. It was the old sweater. The faded pumpkin orange had been rejuvenated into a vibrant burnt umber-rust, the old, thin fibers were now twisted around fresh, newly spun and dyed yarn, the pattern now raised instead of stretched, the tunic sweater again shaped and blocked like new. She held it up to Avria's front and smiled; her eyes glassy at the sight of it.

"It's so beautiful, like it was when I was a little girl, and he put it on me when I was cold. That is my only memory of him, and I don't remember his face. I remember the warmth that still lingered in it from when he'd taken it off his frame and then put it on me. I remember the tender loving smile, and a gentle laugh at how large it was on my tiny body," Tinna whispered. Avria's pale hands slid up onto the sweater being draped on her front, and she touched it lightly. "I want you to feel that same love when you wear it, to know that I'm here with you—even if we are to be separated again by tragedy." Avria's eyes glassed over again watching her mother suffer through this moment with her. She gathered up her wits, however, and cleared her throat.

"It will keep you warm, until you come home," Tinna said with slightly forced optimism. Avria nodded, and hugged the sweater to her. Hands still clutched to her chest, she simply walked into her mother, and dropped her head on her shoulder again, sighing deeply. Tinna patted down her disheveled curls, and kissed her temple. "Pack up some clothes sweet girl. The dragon will be here soon."

She felt a subtle nod under her chin, and Avria withdrew, moving quietly to her chest of drawers. Tinna slipped out, leaving behind her shattered daughter and the sorcerer, who'd fallen back into his comfortable doze by the fire as if trying to soak up as much of the quiet and warmth before he would be back in the swaying caravan again.

Tinna wrung her hands and moved down the corridor, rapping softly on the door belonging to Cennik's apartments. The young man opened the door. He was looking a bit rough 'round the edges, as if she'd woken him after only just falling asleep. His eyes were puffy and small. He was bare-chested, wearing only a pair of loose legged drawstring pants that looked like they'd been tugged on in haste, for one of his cheeks was barely covered and the front hung tenuously low. His breath smelled of spirits, and behind him, she spied the unmistakable shock of red hair of a certain young Dara in his bed.

"It's a bit late in the morning for you to be just waking up," Tinna intoned with a touch of undue acidity. The extremely comely summoner blushed a bit, and scratched his head of wild hair, which stood up straight, slanted to one side, pillow creases still red on the other side of his face. Cennik had arrived a year ago to reluctantly become the first resident summoner for an Araki community. He was a rake and a sophisticate of the human city of Rida and he was not pleased to be asked by the powers-that-be to live in an isolated somewhat backward community. But when he arrived at Thamatoc, he discovered an entire village full of fresh, beautiful and naïve single ladies all fawning over his worldliness and noble good looks. Suddenly, his inclination to stay was increased. He'd already bruised two hearts in the past year. Tinna knew he'd have a harder time with Dara. She was as fiery and willful as one would imagine a red-haired creature to be, and Tinna knew it was only a matter of time before her rogue of a summoner would learn his first lesson of the heart. She doubted it would slow his roguery down at all; he was young and dashing and was still being led by something other than the brain in his head.

"It was a late night," he admitted groggily. Dara stirred and her arm flopped out of his bed. She continued to slumber deeply, unnoticing of the movements of her own limbs.

"Have you had a chance to…?"

"With all due respect, Madame chieftain; it's fairly obvious I've had no chance to do anything this morning since you know you've only just woken me; but I will do you the favour of calling for the status of the arriving dragon, for I am certain this is what you wish to know."

"A little more respect in your tone, Cennik. Mind yourself," she snapped. Any fondness for humor at this point was not to be found for Tinna. She was about to send her daughter away to some mysterious location, and her little girl had endured the most horrid of experiences and she would not be there to help her through it. Tinna glared at him. Clueless to the chieftain's grave mood, he gave Tinna a blatant appraisal with his golden brown eyes, conscious of how well formed his body was, and how attractive, even in this rumpled, hung-over state, he was. His flirtation was a taunt if anything and Tinna arched her brow and glared dourly up at his smug face, disinterest plain in her burning glare. "Just get hold of the dragon and find out already, so we can get Avria on her way." She sailed away in a rustle of linen skirts and vanished into the main hall. Cennik turned, reminded that he had finally gotten Dara into his bed. With a wry grin, he closed the door and went to wake her.

Eritrix was a young, graceful, swan-like dragon—still fresh from the cliffs of the west, but eager and full of wonder and idealism as most young people were. She seemed almost miniscule to Tinna. Tinna was used to the mass and presence of her dearest Ledroran; the leader of the dragons, and he dwarfed his little grand-daughter by at least ten times. He was the largest dragon Tinna knew of, and he could barely land at Thamatoc anymore because the pastures were barely enough to accommodate his takeoffs and landings. But this lithe, dexterous creature, her scales a mix of ruby red and creamy white moved like a dancer. She came in with the grace of an eagle, landing; hardly disturbing the soft layer of snow. She'd glided into the pasture area, one of the few spaces with open expanses, and then let the cold air balloon on her wings, she stalled upwards just long enough to catch the ground with her delicate talons, and then she let her weight follow them.

She turned her head on her graceful neck, and lowered it. From behind her short crown-like head shield, a person appeared. Tinna was stunned at the sight of her. Garbed entirely in black, in breeches no less; a golden beauty leapt down from the back of the dragon's neck. She wore a thick cloak of black as well, with the hood edged in grey wolf fur. She looked in all respects except her fairer features, like a Thran. She moved like a Thran, with a trained purpose, sinewy, with hidden power. She walked over the snow towards Tinna and Avria, her eyes taking in the mother with a calculated assessing gaze, and then to Avria. When her eyes fell upon the girl, her brow furrowed into a tight patch, and concern filled her azure eyes. When she reached Tinna and Avria, she curtsied, giving Tinna a look of reverence. Then she reached for Avria's hand.

"I am Adrenne. We must haste. I am hiding our arrival as best I can, but this is a Zsathri, from what I understand. They are cunning wielders. I would love to stay and make introductions, but we must go at once." Tinna nodded, her eyes misting over. Avria blankly assented with a nod, and looked to her mother one more time.

"Tell Offrin I am sorry and that I love him."

"I will. Go now, darling."

"Where's father?"

"He isn't happy about this, Avria. He isn't coping well with anything that's happened. I told him it would be best I see you off alone."

"And Phenmal?"

"He's gone already, to find ways to stop Eleran. Go, sweet girl." The sister put her hand on Avria's shoulder and guided her to the sweet, young dragon that lowered her head for them to climb up.

"It's going to be dreadfully cold, Avria. Put on your cloak, and cover your hands. Huddle in there." Tinna heard the sister instructing her. Avria's face appeared 'round the edge of the shining red shield of Eritrix's head and she was crying.

566

"It won't be forever, Avria. We will fix this." With that the dragon spread her wings and began to move them in graceful gusts, lifting herself with little difficulty, blowing snow over her freshly made tracks. In moments, they vanished into the low clouds of the early afternoon sky. And with that, Avria was gone. Tinna swallowed back her sorrow, and made her way back to the village.

Try to find her now, you savage, Tinna seethed, thinking of the creature that claimed to be the honorable and good Eleran. The woman who had come for her looked like a warrior. Magic bearing too. The moment she saw the woman, she felt that Avria was in good hands. In the meantime, she would do what she could with Phenmal to get Eleran out of the quotient so Avria could finally live some semblance of the life she wanted; the life that Tinna herself had wanted; a life of simplicity, of family, of belonging. She would do what she could to insure that for Avria despite recent events. She would do her best to make it work for Avria, despite being resigned that there was little chance of that happening for herself. Things were going to change. They always did.

As she walked down the road towards the gates of Thamatoc, the gypsy caravan was already moving southward towards her, the beasts dragging the tall, lumbering carriages through the thin layer of snow that remained on the roads. Grejnal and Ordran hitched up the heavy draught horses to drag the plough sledge along the main paths around Thamatoc to clear the roads somewhat. Once the Gypsies found the deep forest roads created and managed by their people, the heavier forest cover would hopefully have protected them from heaviest of snowfall, and would be moderately navigable for the caravan. At this point, Tinna did not concern herself about their wellbeing, she was sure they were well equipped to contend with all sorts of situations. She was, however, grateful for providence, which had brought them and their Soothsayer to them when he was needed the most. If they had not come, she had no idea where Avria would be.

She stood by the side of the road when the gypsies passed, and thanked the woman who repaired her sweater, and thanked the sorcerer, and told them that they should always feel welcomed at Thamatoc, and they would always have a place to stay if they wanted it. These were partly her people, after all. She shook their hands and watched them move away. So persecuted they were as a people; misunderstood, and feared for their differences; feared for their incredible bond of brotherhood among their own clans, and their unusual ways—because of this fear, they'd grown insular and shy.

She wished she would have time to learn more of them; to go to the Lathlo family gathering, to know relatives of her father. But she had other things to concern herself with. She hurried through the cold towards Thamatoc to soothe her distraught husband now. Poor man, can't wrap his mind around what's happened to his little Avria. Tinna frowned and walked through the crunching snow into the summer lodge. She was greeted by its warmth, but she didn't notice it. All she saw was her pale husband waiting for her with tears in his eyes

CHAPTER FIVE – THE KEEPERS

Phenmal stepped off the dragon before it had come to a full stop, and landed with a feline grace on the ground, falling immediately into a determined stride, his great-coat flaring out behind him. The dragon, his most frequent flying companion by the name of Igro was used to Phenmal's athletic and premature dismounts and didn't bother to stop. He moved directly into a takeoff while Phenmal strode from the open courtyard into a vaulted covered passageway. The heels of his tall boots clattered on the hard floor. He strode past stone arcs that supported a hefty ceiling. Between each arc stood a soldier, one on each side facing one another like mirror images. Each was clutching a polearm, and they had beautifully hewn feathered helms that closed over their faces. They looked almost like effigies.

Phenmal did not slow. He looked out from under the broad brim of his black hat, keeping his thick black woolen scarf wrapped around his lower-face. The man presented a different aura than he did when he was among his Araki, or haunting the halls of his large empty home on his own. Here, he stood tall and moved lithely without the appearance of age or infirmity. He approached a door flanked by two ornately uniformed soldiers of the human army. They did not impede him; one simply stepped aside and opened the door so he could stride through, bowing his head in respect.

Phenmal walked right into a gathering of elderly men. The room they occupied was rather large but still managed to evoke a welcoming coziness. The tall ceilings were covered elaborately in brilliantly colored frescoes depicting stylized images of the ever-changing calendar of prophesies. These images were animated and alive whenever the old men were in this room, which they were most of the day, every day. So each time Phenmal visited, the ceiling looked different.

Personages of past and future significance languorously moved in a band of graphics around the base of the long, smooth, rounded coffin-like space lofting above them. The images were cast in the golden light of a painted, gold-leafed, and intricately carved medallion of the sun, which dominated the center of the ceiling. The sun's painted rays radiated out to the wide ribbon of images of the events and people. As always, the distinctive black hair and olive skin of Tinna's figure never ceased to haunt Phenmal when he looked up at it. He remembered recognizing her in it the first time just over twenty years ago, when being summoned to see the old men shortly after the destruction of the human settlements by the dragons. Tinna's figure was shadowed by the shape of Ledroran, who now still glided over her image, but higher up into the rays of the sun. Tinna had moved forward since the last time he'd been here and she wore different clothes now; a formal-looking gown with a train that trailed behind her. Before her, an arm was extended and she was holding a sword by the hilt with the blade pointing downwards.

He paused to study this newer placement, his eyes cast upwards. He could never fail to notice the sudden and noticeable absence of images that followed Tinna's figure and circled 'round to connect again with the earliest events on the timeline. Instead of a collection of images showing what was to come, Tinna's figure stood before a band of tangled vines and leaves. It had been like that for years now, the tangle growing longer with each passing year, the older events vanishing one by one behind her, but no new prophesies appearing ahead of her. The vines had once acted as the marker to show where the prophesies began and ended, and the patch was never that large. Now it took up a full third of the whole ribbon of images and with every visit Phenmal made to the Citadel, it was growing larger.

This fresco was created by one of the ancient keepers, long ago. The magic that sustained it was provided by the mere presence of the other Keepers that occupied the great palace now. They paid little heed to the moving images. They seemed quite unconcerned about what could possibly be hidden behind the expanding tangle of greenery and they were quite determined to move forward on what they knew was the only possible course. Their prevailing thought was that the new prophesies would either reveal themselves when Tinna's time passed, or that the fresco's creator's spell was meant to end there. All they knew was that her effigy now wore the crown. The armies she'd rallied marched behind her in their uniforms—two years ago, they were in front of her, and she was bedecked in armor and chain mail. The band of vines was smaller then, but the prophesies were running out, and Tinna had finally put the last of them behind her, except for the crown on her head. Such faith in the steadiness of the ceiling's imagery and their own powerful ability to see what was to come, the old men did not take any message from this tangle of leaves and vines except to look forward to what lay hidden beneath them. They believed that once Tinna wore the crown in earnest, that the vines would reveal what was to come. Phenmal did not see it in the same way they did. It could represent many things—but he had the sense that they weren't all good.

One of the old men looked up when Phenmal entered. He waited for Phenmal to take a moment to study the changes on the fresco and when Phenmal's cool blue eyes fell down upon his face, the old man exclaimed: "We were just talking about you, boy," alerting the others of his presence, all of whom seemed quite unconcerned with his arrival. Phenmal pulled his scarf down from his face, and tugged off his gloves, shoving them into the pocket of his heavy greatcoat.

The room was a simple rectangle with a fireplace centered on the wall directly across from the door. Both of these were placed on the mid-mark of each long wall. The short walls were both comprised mostly of five towering windows on each side. One side overlooked the wintry forest park that sprawled out from the face of the building; the other gave view to the more intimate, white-dusted courtyard around which this massive building was wrapped. There was only one more entrance to the space and that was the hidden servant's door that was blended into the dark paneling on the back wall near the corner.

This citadel was as old as the forest, if not older. Its walls protected the old men, just as they kept it from falling apart. They rarely left the security of the citadel's walls. What they had to fear, Phenmal did not know, but they lived like frightened little mice, puttering about their ancient edifice. They were strange characters, even from Phenmal's perspective. He'd been acquainted with them for many long years—and he still found them odd after all this time. Some had come and some had gone, but they were all, strangely, the same—as if they were all born of the same source. Young or ancient, they were all the same.

Phenmal felt the room's warmth infuse him and the scent of burning wood filled his nostrils. The feel of the thick woolen rug beneath his cold feet was good after freezing himself on that long flight from Thamatoc. The austere portraits of past Keepers circled the room in an oddly ordered scattering on the long, tall paneled walls. There were a few intermittent shelf-nooks here and there, or a

571

sideboard-style piece of furniture holding huge urns exploding with sprays of dried pussy willows, winter-berries, holly and evergreen branches. In the center of the room was the arc of chairs facing the door and on each end of the room, softer chaises and lounging sofas were set in intimate sitting areas along with a few small tables and some lamps. All of the room's occupants however were collected in front of Phenmal, but he only had the attention of one of them.

"I do not have much time, honorable Master. Please make your message quick," Phenmal barked. The other old men were huddled around a table that had been wheeled in by one of the elusive servants, holding a large silver urn, from which they were dispensing a steaming tea into diminutive cups. Next to the urn was a tiered platter holding a luxurious selection of little cakes. They all looked up when Phenmal spoke. Six doddering old men, all of them dressed richly in velvet frock coats in a variety of subdued colours, in sculpted soft leather slippers and the finest silks, seemed reluctant in giving the newcomer his due attention, more focused on securing themselves a cup of hot tea and one or two of the tiny cakes. The man Phenmal had addressed frowned.

"What could possibly be more important than a summons from the Keepers' high-seat, my boy?" he asked sternly. Phenmal glowered.

"I'm hunting a Zsathri and I don't have time to be distracted. I confess I was not happy to receive your summons."

"Hunting a Zsathri you say? Whatever for?" another asked.

"That is personal."

"There are no Zsathris to be seen," one of them muttered, gazing up at the mural.

"Zsathris are irrelevant," another replied. Phenmal took their mutterings in stride, he was used to them.

"So you say it's personal; I see. Well, perhaps, if you sit down and share some tea with us, I will send someone to help you find your Zsathri; someone to help you contain him. Come, come old friend, have some tea and a little cake. We are to be brought freshly roasted chestnuts, right from Gadrin's home. His granddaughter gathered them just before the snowfall; they should be ready soon."

"Your message," Phenmal growled. The old men straightened and then dispersed about the small room, moving to their chairs in a guileless, tottering sort of way. A cacophony of slurping sips followed as each one drank from his small cup, and one or two of them made appreciative little grunts of delight as they popped a cake into their mouths. Phenmal stood patiently and waited for them to settle in. There was no sense in hurrying them, he knew this. They would do as they wished—they did not change.

These seemingly ingenuous little old men were the most highly-ranked leaders of the Keepers. They seemed like dodderers, but Phenmal knew better. Each and every one of these long-lived old men was a force to be reckoned with. Each one wielded tremendous power in one form or another; it was a requisite to being a Keeper. How one became one was a mystery to Phenmal, but they continued to appear, the children's annex always seemed to have fresh young faces there.

The Keeper's control of the world's goings-on was paramount. In spite of their claiming they oversaw only the sacred lands of Oromoii, it was well known that they interfered elsewhere as well. They had a hand in everything in the known world. Their power superseded any throne. This group was overseen by one power alone, and that was the Trinity; a triumvirate of leaders from each most dominant race. The Trinity watched over these old men and their meddlings. The Trinity held court much farther north, in the icy wastelands but agents resided at the Citadel to keep the connection strong between these two ancient organizations.

These particular six old codgers were the top tier of the small army of Keepers, their collective arranged tidily into ranks over which the six ruled. Each of the five ranks had its own residence in the citadel, and its own purpose to follow, and they remained in their isolated groups on the most part. Some managed the pursuit of collecting knowledge, others were responsible for identifying children for tutelage in the academies, others tasked with finding the ones born to magic, and there was even a small group responsible for finding new Keepers as they arrived into the world as babies.

Phenmal dealt mostly with these six, and a few of the ones ranked directly below them. He occasionally saw the little boys slated to become like these old men being led about in neat files around the Citadel's great campus. But he did not interact with any others. The citadel housed many of the strongest bearers of power. Chaiva were not usually privileged to have a place at the citadel, but Phenmal was a special case since he was connected to Tinna.

"Gentlemen, please," Phenmal grunted. A few more sips and one of them muttered:

"Yes, yes, boy. Take your kettle off the fire, please. This is a matter of some importance; I do not believe you should be taking this information in any other way except with the gravity it deserves," Master Heln said in his booming, bass voice. Phenmal felt drained by their energy; he could not read any of them. He could feel the passive restorative powers working on him just by being near them. Anyone who worked closely with them could live an unusually long life. One particularly beloved servant Gadrin was hundreds of years old. His marriages and the families that branched from those over the years were many.

"Dearest boy, it is nice to see you. It's been two months. Last we spoke you said you were to attend a joyous occasion; the wedding of the Ashru's daughter. Has it occurred?" Phenmal did not answer. He did not wish to encourage the idle chatter these little old men lived for. So much time spent in limited company had made them act like a clutch of tittering old ladies sometimes. They seemed to get the point of Phenmal's silence, and one of them took a serious tone.

"You've put yourself in a place where you have become quite crucial to us, Master Phenmal," he said. "I know we say that often, but you must be reminded how important it is you continue your path. It's vital!"

"I've put myself in that place? No, gentlemen; you have put me there. It was naught but a chance encounter that brought me to her. You are the ones that tied me to her irrevocably,"

"Fate is to blame for that, my boy. Fate. However, now you advise the Ashru of the Araki, and she has had significant influence on the world. Even the Thran have dedicated their loyalty to her, to some degree. You must know this."

"I have not been living in a cave these past two years," Phenmal grunted. They ignored his insolence and continued.

"Her influence; it is affecting things among the humans. It is time now to move things forward, time to stop this before it becomes a problem."

"Stop what?"

"The High Throne has been restless since the coronation last year. The father left the son with little to rule, and the over-indulged boy regrets is lack of power most keenly. He is angry. Angry that the race of dragons has been returned to their trusted status among the Araki majority—his father's lingering hatred of them has been carried on in the new King. He is frantic that the greater part of Oromoii's people are Araki, Dragon kind and Adrei and that their armies are unrivaled now, even the Thran have proven no match, and lastly, he is furious about the Ashru. He knows we seek to put her in his place. He has been hard at work undermining the efforts made to bridge the gap between humanity and the Araki, to break down the trust

574

that was created when the Araki came to humanity's salvation against the Thran.

"He does not want to give up the High Throne. He's been gathering people around him; people who do not want to relinquish rule to the majority race. Humanity is languishing but they are too proud to let go. There have been stirrings, Phenmal. He's been careful to keep the scent of revolt quite undetectable in Araki-strong settlements like your Lemoram, or the city of Loshan. But the remaining pure human communities from Suthervale to Gheraine have been infected with this angered entitlement, and people are being made to believe that the motives of the Araki people and their allies are no better than those of the Thran. The High King enjoys his privilege and his power. He is not content to leave well enough alone. The Trinity has asked that we move forward; that we act before there is more war. It is time, Phenmal. It is time to move her up. To establish her leadership, and neutralize the stirrings before they spread beyond our capacity to contain it. We worry it might be too late already. She must don the crown."

"She's not ready," Phenmal grunted. "Your sense of timing, like the last time, is questionable. Something terrible has happened to her daughter…"

"There's no time for these paltry things…" Master Ijka waved his hand dismissively.

"Then make time!" Phenmal barked. He glowered at the old men each in turn. "Why are you so worried if the humans are growing restless? They are so few, how much of a threat could they be? The Araki army could subdue any uprisings with ease; not to mention the how quickly a few of the sky borne dragons could stop something!" Phenmal snarled. The old men shifted about in their chairs. His question was a good one. It seemed simple enough. But their eyes cast upwards to the mural. What they saw there that Phenmal did not see, he did not know. They wanted Tinna at the Seat of High Power at Miranne and that was that.

"You propose to destroy the race your Ashiu fought so hard to save? Twice in her lifetime she's come to the aid of these people. This race could easily disappear into oblivion if they become embroiled in war with the Araki. It would be their end."

"And Tinna could stop this?"

"Without a doubt. She has earned her credibility; she needs only supersede that of the sitting monarch to succeed. The people will respect her. But we need to get that pox of a King out now before his infection spreads and put a hero in place no one can

575

question. He will not stand in the way of prophesy! Nothing stands in the way of the prophesies! You know all this, Phenmal. It is our lot to ensure things happen as they should!" He sighed intolerantly and shook his head, giving them all an impatient look.

"You may go and hunt your magic bearer, Phenmal, but only after you've put things in motion. The High King must be removed from the throne, and the Ashru must become Queen; and her strength, her army, her power must be elevated to the highest position so there is leadership. It is what must be. If there continues to be no leadership and this old-blood royal continues to create problems, we will have another war. Humanity is threatened; we must either unify them with the rest of the population or they will separate themselves. We will insure the transition is smooth with whatever resources she needs, as usual."

"How am I supposed to go about this?"

"We'll take care of the little king. You must get the Ashru to the Palace at Miranne just in the same way you got her to Iromi two years ago," the eldest of the Keepers said gruffly. He paused, looking at Phenmal's angry face. "To make this easier for you, because I know even without personal problems, the Ashru is an obstinate, stubborn, strong-willed sort of creature; we will provide you with a Drathar to hunt your Zsathri." Phenmal's face blanched a bit, and his brow tightened. There was little that struck fear into the heart of a Chaiva; but the mention of this creature sent chills down his spine. He did not protest. If anything was capable of stopping a magic-bearing madman, it would be a Drathar. He nodded subtly and bowed his head in a rare outpouring of gratitude. It would be of tremendous help to him.

"Get some rest; you can fly out tomorrow morning."

"I bloody hate flying," Phenmal grumbled. He turned on his heel and walked out towards the private residences where he had his own small apartments. He did not like coming to the citadel. Although he held a high place in the ranks of Keepers, he was not at home here. He, like Tinna, wished for something simpler, but also like Tinna, he was given little choice for the past twenty or so years. He'd given these little old men over three hundred years of his life already. He'd brokered a deal some decades back with the old men; they would agree to set him free of service in exchange for one particularly questionable job they wanted done. He did it, and they had sent him adrift to age in peace. But then Tinna came along, and the dragons started destroying the world, and everything changed. He was thrown back into their clutches. Enough was enough. He wanted it to be finished; he wanted to age and to die like a normal person, to fade at peace, in the company of people he enjoyed, if any at all. Instead, his relationship with them persisted, and his youth was being returned to him bit by bit.

Phenmal's encounter with Tinna had indeed cut his retirement short and had prolonged his connection to the Keepers. It was a worthy sacrifice in the end, for Tinna and Avria were part of his life and he would not wish that away by any means. But he wanted to be the safe fatherly figure; to remain benign and non-threatening to women he loved; to putter around and grumble about the stupidity of people, and sit and smoke a pipe in the comfort of the lodge at Thamatoc while Tinna spoke in her velvety voice. But that was already changing, and he wouldn't be able to hide it much longer. Soon she would notice the years were taken from his face; no longer interpreting it as his being unchanged. The infirmities he'd worked so hard to acquire were all dissolved away and he spent most of his time pretending to be older than he felt. Tinna would eventually notice it. So would Avria. He couldn't think of a single person who would be so annoyed to be given his youth back.

He moved through the labyrinthine passages and walked through a garden courtyard covered in snow, where he found the door to his apartments. He climbed up a flight of stairs and entered the familiar space. He spent little time here, but it remained his private residence in spite of his frequent and extended absences. It was decorated to his preferences and his servant was always present to anticipate his needs. Fires had been lit, and a warm supper had been laid out at the small table by the window where the snow fell. His servant knew full well that Phenmal liked his privacy, and remained successfully unseen. He sat down and leaned back in his chair, sighing wearily. His eyes looked down through the window to the courtyard. The evergreens were weighed down with snow, the cobbles covered. A few tracks showed that people other than he had come through recently. He picked up a cup of steaming tea and sipped.

Suddenly, his skull began to throb. His eyes locked on the doorway across the courtyard. He squinted and fought the cringe of pain. "Stop…" he hissed through his teeth, spilling a bit of his tea. The pain suddenly subsided to a faint hum and Phenmal's shoulders relaxed a bit. A second later, the doorway opened to the courtyard and a dark shadow of a creature appeared.

Garbed entirely in black, including a sheer black veil over the face, the Drathar stepped out of the door, and paused. He moved with precision, and his face angled immediately upward towards Phenmal in the window. There was somewhere in this citadel where the Keepers housed a handful of these dark creatures. Phenmal was not privy to where. They were rare and excessively powerful—known to be the most powerful bearers of magic of all—rumored to be even more powerful than the magical Keepers themselves. How the Keepers kept them under such a tight rein, Phenmal did not know. But they served quietly, stoically and remained mostly elusive and secret. Phenmal had witnessed first-hand the devastating effects the unveiled gaze of a Drathar can have on a person. He knew their powers were vast and varied.

The older man nodded to the figure, and watched him continue along, crossing into the main building and vanishing under the archway. Phenmal's headache worsened with each approaching step. When he felt like his eyes were going to pop out of his head, the door opened without a knock or an invitation, and the shadow stepped into the room.

"You will take me to where this magician last was seen; where he cast magic." A young-sounding voice mumbled from behind his veil. Eerily white skin could be seen through the sheer fabric and the shine of almost-white irises. He wore a heavily draped black woolen cowl, a cloak of the same material and underneath, a dense, thick felted sweater, and a pair of loose black trousers that bagged down around some crumpled, rather shabby looking leather boots. He carried no weapons, nor did he boast any adornments.

"I will. In the morning. We leave at dawn. You will have to dress warmly—it's a cold ride up with the dragons," he mumbled. "Be forewarned," he said, "dragons do not take kindly to being read or having their heads invaded. They are telepathic, and speak to one another over great distances using it, and that means they are more sensitive to unsolicited invasions into their heads. If you want to stay in the air, I suggest you keep your mind to yourself." He drained his tea and then poured himself a fresh cup. "You did not need to pry about in my head, Drathar. I am trusted among the highest ranks of the Keepers."

"I pry everyone... even the old men," the shadow replied. "You would not suffer a headache if you weren't fighting me. You bring discomfort to yourself," he muttered in a strange, hollow voice. He then turned to walk out, pausing briefly to add: "You keep interesting thoughts, Chaiva. You hold people close; a great liability for one so high; but I can see why you cherish them," he stopped for a moment, as if relishing the images Phenmal's mind showed him.

He then sighed, and said: "I will be here at dawn." Phenmal watched him slink like a wraith across the snow.

Drathar were few, and they operated all from this place where they could be closely monitored by the elderly men. Phenmal had worked with one or two in his time and was somewhat familiar with them. Among all their other powers, they also possessed capabilities as his, and he knew that the Drathar had scoured every corner of his mind and gotten clear, detailed images of everyone Phenmal cared about.

CHAPTER SIX - PURSUIT

This time Tinna did meet Phenmal with defiance when he came bearing bad news. It was as if she knew that was what he was going to do, but she merely shook her head and looked across the room where the baby was napping in his bassinette. "I can't leave. I can't go to a palace where I am not welcome. I can't be expected to do all this, Phenmal. Not now, not ever..." she sighed. "It's already hard enough with just the visits to Klatna; it's already taxing to live this double life." Phenmal, still bundled up from the flight was stripping off his outer garments and looking at her regrettably.

"Then perhaps simplifying as much as you can; moving you and your family where leadership is supposed to be," he watched her shake her head and smirk at his lame attempt at persuasion and he succumbed to laughter too for a moment. "The Keepers are worried about the High King; he still keeps a circle of influence. He is propagating fear among his kind. There are rumours that he is decrying the idea that humanity should relinquish ruling power to the dominant race as they should. He will start a war, Tinna, and the humans will either fall at his side in fear of becoming irrelevant, or they will trust the woman who saved what was left of this empire. You need to step in before this little idea catches fire among a desperate race." At that moment, Taneth entered and seeing Phenmal, he gave him a terse smile and crossed to Tinna, kissing her before asking her what was going on.

Taneth had been focusing on his duties for his village to keep his mind off Avria's absence and the tragedy that had been beset upon her. He looked at Phenmal, his eyes pained.

"I thought you were hunting that animal..."

"I will be. I've brought some help. He is at this moment where..." he paused, surprised at the emotional response he felt speaking of it; "where it happened. I came to deliver a message to Tinna."

"I see," Taneth said tightly, quite keen on his wife's stressed look.

"I will be following the Drathar for a few days…"

"The Drathar? Those actually exist?" Taneth blurted. "Aren't they supposed to be some sort of demon?"

"Not necessarily…"

"You have brought a demon to Thamatoc?" Taneth was a skeptic by nature, but he'd become more open minded this past few years now that a good portion of the types magic bearers and creatures he'd previously believed non-existent had passed through his doors at some point or other. He still believed in the rational, and did not think there was anything unnatural about them, and that their powers or existence could eventually be explained. It was funny to Phenmal to hear him complain about bringing a demon into his community.

"They are not demons. They're not exactly human; but they are not the wild mythical things the books say they are, Taneth. They are powerful, the most powerful magic bearer known to the world; and they are rare, so we are privileged to have one assisting Avria. I do not find pleasure in much of my dealings with the Keepers, my friend, but this is a significant gift they've given me. They've all but guaranteed that Avria will be safe by giving us the service of this so-called demon," Phenmal said strongly. Taneth's mouth snapped shut and he scratched his head, shaking it incredulously.

"A bloody Drathar…" Poor Taneth. A stanch skeptic of the strictest kind, these past years had been difficult for him; an exercise of acceptance, a challenging puzzle. He was a man of facts and science, yet he was now faced with creatures that defied logic; and he spent many an hour trying to wrap his busy mind around it all, trying to find some way to explain it all with science and knowledge. Each time he felt he could explain something, or had a theory, he was presented with something more insane and incredible. Phenmal smirked at Taneth's bemused expression.

"Tinna, when I return, we need to speak in earnest of this. I hope you will think on this while I'm away." As he spoke, the Drathar slid into the room and Tinna and Taneth immediately grunted in pain as the creature invaded their minds.

"Get out of my head!" she roared, her eyes turning feral. The Drathar withdrew from her head, and then assaulted Taneth, who groaned from the discomfort.

"Enough, Drathar; these are my people.

"I seek traces of magic, Chaiva. They leave footprints, if spells had been cast to glean information…" Taneth shook his head,

"The Zsathri can't do that, they are natural wielders, and they can follow auras and…"

"A normal Zsathri respects the laws; this one is tainted. Much tainted. Not just by madness but by something else from the voids. This is no ordinary bearer here. His powers are not incredible; the other magic bearer that chased him off proved that," the Drathar muttered. He moved about the space, running his fingers along the spines of some books on the small shelf by the door, picking up and examining a small carved figurine of a horse; "The place your Chaiva here chose for the girl was an inspired choice, she will be protected there and untraceable using magic. But he already has an idea where she is—if he can read as clearly as I think. Surrounded by the sea, he took that from your head," he turned to Tinna, who frowned and her eyes glassed over.

"There are not too many places one can live fully protected, and magic bearers know them all to begin with; knowing that it is an isle narrows the options significantly. This Zsathri is no longer bound by any laws; something has given him freedom from those. The gypsy magician said he could be incapacitated if he used his magic to kill again; this is not true. He can do as he wishes. And he will. He will find her. For now, I have an impression of him. I have something to follow. Once I know his bearing, I will know if he has found the right place." The man's voice had a strange gentleness to it; which contradicted his appearance and his hidden face. Tinna wondered why he was dressed as he was and wondered what was underneath all the draping folds of black fabric.

"I must follow these signs now, before they fade." Phenmal nodded and turned to Tinna, tugging on his greatcoat and donning his gloves which he'd scarce stripped off. He picked up his scarf;

"I will accompany him for now. I will return in a while. After that, we need to have that talk." He looked at her gravely and then wound the scarf 'round his neck and face. "Come, Drathar; dragons do not like the cold and the snow; our friend must be less than pleased waiting upon us." The Drathar nodded and they both bowed to Tinna and her family. They exited the apartments, striding with single minded purpose down the long corridor to the front of the lodge.

"The Zsathri did not transport himself too far, but he is probably long-gone from there, but if we move quickly, the trail can be found," The Drathar muttered. Phenmal followed, watching the

Drathar wrap himself further in a thicker coat, wondering what sort of person lay beneath the veil. If there was any benefit to traveling with a Drathar, it was that they were unreadable. It was strangely peaceful for Phenmal. They exited in silence and were soon on the wing.

Taneth and Tinna remained quiet for a while after the departure of the two men. Taneth helped himself to a late supper. "Phenmal had that grave look I do not like; it harkens back to before the little one was born."

"Yes, it's that sort of thing," Tinna agreed, taking some more tea. She walked to the fire and stood there. "It's so much and we have yet to face Offrin, who should be returning soon."

* * * *

It will be like it used to be, where she would welcome me, and wrap herself around me with love and bliss. She will moan with pleasure beneath me once more. She will kiss me and touch me in the way she once did. She will look at me as she used to, her eyes so hungry for the sight of me, her body drawn to me, her eyes always on me—as if I were true north and she was a compass. She will. Eleran's eyes were glassed over, the lower lids shining with tears. She is all I see, she is the scent that fills my head. There will no longer be a need to show her, or punish her. He froze, and swallowed, a tear falling onto his hard cheekbone. He bit down on his teeth with determination, and chewed his mandibles. No. No need to punish her. She will understand.

His hands moved quickly as stuffed his items back into his bag. With a strange, faraway look, he threw it over his shoulder. "An island in the sea…" he said to himself. "Dodderer forgets things sometimes when he's around the mother." He is powerless to her. If I ever wanted to hurt that old man, I would just have to hurt Avria's mother. But I will not… because it would hurt Avria. I do not like to hurt my Avria. But sometimes I must be firm, sometimes it is necessary.

The island in the sea. She awaits me there, and all will be as it was. She will be away from the half-man, away from the ones that persuaded her that I am the enemy. She will welcome me again, she will want me again. She will no longer fear me, for how could she fear me? She had loved me once as I loved her. She has to know I was only better than I was before, so she could only love me more. There is no reason for her to fear me. She would surely know this.

584

She is mine. She is my Avria after all. My perfect little dark-haired siren, my love. The other half of my soul. He would go. He had an idea where she was going. It would not be easy, but he could use his powers to make the journey shorter. He would work out the challenges on the way. She must be removed from the influences that harm her. She must be returned to me, where she belongs. Bundled in wintry clothes, the Zsathri fastened his items to the stolen horse. With a smooth movement he swung up onto its back and yanked the rein harshly. His eyes focused forward onto the road ahead. With a flash of light, he gave himself and his mount a good head-start.

CHAPTER SEVEN – THE CORE

Avria's way of contending with the wind, the cold and the pain in her ears was to sink further against the warmth of the dragon's head and into her cloak and hood. She'd heard the short introduction from the woman that had come to collect her. She was a member of the Dreff Sisterhood. That was all she shared for that moment. The sister's body was presently wedged up against hers, and the woman's face was not visible in profile, only the fur of her hood and a few locks of her wheaten hair that hung free and tossed about in the frigid winds. They did not speak. The dragon's short head-shield did not provide enough coverage to keep out the heavy winds, and if they wanted to speak, they had to scream. Avria was in no mind to do so, and she didn't quite know what to say to someone like the sister. She'd learn more about her soon enough. For now, she concentrated on keeping herself warm and keeping her hands and feet wrapped tightly in her thick cloak.

She managed to slip into a strange light sleep through the night, where dreams intermixed with glimpses of starry sky and moonlit cloud. For hours, the dragon carried them on the winds; her wings pumping occasionally, always level, always forward. At dawn, Avria's ears began to hurt horribly again and she felt as if her stomach was moving up into her throat. They entered clouds again, and all she saw was whiteness and grey. With a startling dip down, they broke out from the bottom of a rather thick layer of clouds and Avria found herself looking down at an expanse of water of the like she'd never seen before. For that second, she forgot all that was awful, all that horrified her and all she could see were the tall haystack rocks being pummeled by the white-capped waves. Down the back of the dragon, receding behind her, she could see the mainland; it was barely visible in the mists of early morning, the pink light of the rising sun tinting the faces of the cliff sides.

"Where are we?"

"En route to the Isle of Gales," the Sister replied loudly, her voice nearly lost to the wind. Avria was astonished. She immediately looked back at the cliffs that grew further and further away, and she thought of Hanru, and Wye so nearby.

The Dragon dove a bit more, and then banked slightly towards the south. Her speed was slowing, and the air seemed warmer. Avria looked 'round the edge of the head-shield to see where they were going and she gasped. Before them was what looked like a table of rock; the Isle of Gales. A platform of land rose high above the turbulent waters, it was surrounded entirely by cliffs of stone as black as soot; the land on the isle a thick, lush thatch of green, dense with trees with an undulating landscape. This greenery was currently flocked in a coat of sparkling snow and ice. As they descended in altitude, it grew large, so large she could not see the other end of it. There was a ridge of mountains down the center, the peaks rocky and covered in fresh snow. There were several steep fjords cutting into the island, the one before them massive beyond Avria's imagination. A forest of towering stone pillars carved to look like gods jutted out from the waters in tidy rows, taming the rough seas where they met the waterway, and someone, sometime in history, had sculpted the two rocky cliffs that opened into the fjord to look like a tangle of colossal tree trunks. The dragon dropped down low over the fjord, following the waterway from the thundering waves pummeling the impossible constructs of the pillars, to the place where the water swirled in a heavy, powerful battle with the river meeting the sea, and then inland, where it grew languorous.

A flock of wintry-white cliff-birds had caught the Dragon's tailwind and then began to overtake her, flying parallel to the elegant creature's body, some just over the wings, instinctively rising and falling along with their movement. Avria watched all this with a sense of awe. The sister stood gingerly on the dragon's neck, and holding the edge of the shield, looked out over it. "There is the abbey," she leaned down and shouted. "Take a look, you must. This is the first time a sister has seen it from above. They will all expect you to bear witness and describe it." Avria stood clumsily and moved next to the woman. She was much shorter and could barely see over the tall fan-like shield behind the dragon's head. The wind buffeted her and blew her hood off, but it wasn't so frigid that she couldn't bear it long enough to see the abbey for herself.

Two unimaginably large tapering spires rose up from the forest cover, between them, the angled, snow-covered roof of the stone abbey. The towers bookended the building where the roof gables would have been, and the edifice was covered in hundreds of windows without much order to their location. There were few rows, few columns, they seemed randomly scattered, with a variety of shapes and styles that spanned centuries of architectural trends. Off the back wall, what looked like a glass hot-house clung to its side, the bottom like an elaborate corbel holding a faceted jewel with a dollop of snow upon it. The walls themselves were a mottle of various masonry stones and styles, some areas covered in a smoothened plaster which was old and flaked away. The towers on the other hand each had a line of windows encircling them in lazy rising spirals, connecting fairly regularly spaced horizontal rows of windows. The tiny size and sheer number of the windows bespoke the tremendous mass and dimension of this building. It was bigger than anything Avria knew of; bigger than the palace at Miranne; bigger than Hildercross before it was reduced to rubble, and she realized the height of the towers when they approached them and was completely astonished by them. Avria ducked down, for the cold wind was making her lips blue.

Sister Adrenne followed, grinning. "What a rare gift I've been given in collecting you. To ride in the skies," she said loudly. The sister touched the soft skin of Eritrix's head underneath the shield that protected them from the violent winds. Avria smiled wanly and then squealed as the dragon dropped and banked at the same time, making her stomach lurch. The woman laughed in delight and then leaned out. Avria had ridden dragons before, and she often forgot that most others were not permitted this privilege. She had to take pause from her own thoughts to acknowledge this, and be amused by the Sister's wonder.

"Oh, there's the High Mother, I can see her in her red robes standing in the bailey to receive us," she smiled easily. The dragon had come between the towers and over the roof, and below them a round courtyard surrounded by a wall of smaller buildings hugged up against the face of the main building. The forest surrounded the entire installation. Avria would be comfortable here. The dragon turned sharply and dove again, and the rooftops came into view. Within a few seconds, there was a flap of the wings, and the lurch of her stomach, and they were down safe on the cobbles. The sister was already off the dragon, and reaching up to help Avria down.

Reality returned the moment her feet touched the ground. Standing there, her bag slumped on the thin layer of snow of the courtyard, her fatigue, being surrounded by strangers; she suddenly felt her exhaustion and perhaps a touch of defeat. She was in a place with wonders that she suspected even her father knew little of, but could not find the true wonder in it. She felt alone. A hand clasped her shoulder and she turned. Facing her was a woman almost as tall as Taneth with chestnut hair that fell well below her thighs. She wore a gown of the style Avria wore at her wedding in a soft rose red, and over that a deep red robe with a train that fanned out behind her. Six more women stood behind her, all dressed in black as her travel companion was, all wearing the same ankle-length cloak with the heavy hood with the fur lining. They were all tall, lithe, willowy creatures, all strikingly pretty, and all staring quite adoringly at Eritrix. All except the woman in red, who was focused on Avria's pale face and sunken eyes.

"The ladies wish to know if it is acceptable to greet the dragon with touch?" the High Mother asked. Avria shrugged.

"Ask Eritrix. She can speak for herself." The large creature looked on with dragon-bemusement. She nodded without speaking, comprehending the conversation for herself. Sister Adrenne reached out and touched Eritrix's cheek to show the other sisters, and the women immediately gravitated towards the large red dragon, their hands fanning out on her scales, sounds of wonder and delight mixed into their voices. The High Mother smiled at Avria.

"They've been waiting with great anticipation since Adrenne left us to see the dragon for themselves. We see them so rarely; these cliffs are not warm enough to tempt them here. The Chaiva's message was a great surprise to us, but I am glad you are here, young Avria and I am pleased to be here to assist you. Come." She lifted her hand palm-up, and waited for Avria to take it. Avria hiked her bag onto her shoulder and placed her hand in hers.

The High Mother was an elegant woman of Avria's mother's age, perhaps a few years more. Pretty would be too little a word to describe her mature elegance and grace—her presence was powerful, and overwhelming. They left the dragon and the sisters behind, and she led her towards the main building. "The great abbey is many thousands of years old. We are privileged to have use of it, to care for it. We have been stewards of this great isle for generations, and part of our work is to preserve the great works of the ancient ones who dwelled here long ago… the ones that built the spires and the gates of Dareen, and the sea-breaker gods. It is an ancient land," the woman explained. "It was once part of the greater land that is Oromoii, but the connecting land was washed away in the five floods during the age of Storms."

"I think my father would very much benefit from meeting you."

"Oh?"

"He is a Wiseman, and like my mother says, he wasn't just made a Wiseman by his school, he was born with it in his blood, for he wants to know everything about everything. I thought he knew everything about everything; but seeing this world; he has much more to see and learn."

"Everyone has much to see in learn, even those who have lived long in this world," the High Mother said. She paused by a colossal door and looked back. Avria followed her gaze. The Dragon had broken away from the women, and was following Avria.

"What is it Eritrix?" Avria asked. The dragon stopped several paces away and lowered her head.

"I cannot stay. This cold is not for me. But I will return when it is your time to go home," the dragon hissed between her teeth. Behind her, the sisters huddled together, still entranced by the vision of the beautiful creature among them.

"I understand," Avria replied. "I thank you, Eretrix." The dragon bowed her head.

"I will go now. I bid you and your friends farewell." Eretrix then pivoted on her hind legs, and jumped over the line of women causing a titter of delight and excitement, bounding almost like an exuberant dog, flaring out her wings and leaping up into the air, catching the wind and lifting herself up in powerful pumps of her wings. She spiraled up and then cast herself west, following the river to the fjord, back to the sea-breakers, where she would head to warmer lands until she was needed again.

Meanwhile, the High Mother opened the great door, which swiveled inwards with astonishing ease and led Avria into the great hall. Avria was instantly cowed by a sense of smallness and inadequacy. The great hall was exactly as it was named. It was a chamber of impossible proportions; vaulted ceilings towered high above her, held aloft by great pillars and buttresses arching together to give the ceiling the appearance of a cage of ribs. The floor was a shining white marble. Swagged between the pillars were chains holding massive chandeliers with hundreds of candles shedding weak light into the cavernous space. There was no feature anywhere to be seen except for the pillars and the smooth floor. Three towering windows of leaded glass loomed over the end of the chamber, casting a soft, snowy light into three arched pools of brightness on the floor before them. The sound of heels clacking on marble resonated and then echoed high above Avria, making it impossible to determine where they were originating.

"What was this place, before it became your home?"

"Nobody knows. There were no temple statues, no glyphs, merely what you see. We think it was a palace, for there is indication that there was once a dais over in the head of the nave by the great windows… we think perhaps a throne sat there," she pointed towards the depths of the chamber. Far off, Avria could see two red-garbed figures crossing the main hall. It wasn't heated, it was cold and unwelcoming. The High Mother led her down the center and then turned left, leading her between columns that led to an archway into a vaulted, dark corridor.

"And your order, the Dreff," Avria began. The High Mother launched into a lengthy explanation as they moved down the long corridor, passing other arches into other spaces, and wide stairways spiraling into the darkness.

"We are much like the Zsathri your Chaiva described. We are stewards, but we are not children of the Hevra as the Zsathri Druids are. We are sisters to another higher-order of magic bearer, one that is often reviled and feared. But we possess many of the same qualities. The Drathar are our brothers. Like they, we are gifted with powers that we believe are a divine bequest, and should be used with discipline and discretion—our powers against our brothers' is tempered and much less dangerous, but it comes from the same source, an ancient source. We believe that our gifts and those others who possess them are a danger to others without proper training.

"The powers can regulate themselves to some measure. For example, as in the communication from your Chaiva friend implied, the Zsathri that pursues you was first rendered helpless; his spark and essence extracted into a place called the void where he might harm no one with the gifts he was given. No matter the intention, when powers are used against those without them, that is the price. Sometimes, depending on the situation, the punishment can be lightened; sometimes, when the crimes are too grave, the wielder is doomed to be banished out of his body until it dies," she paused at one of several spiral stairway columns rising up along the corridor, and gestured for Avria to precede her. Avria climbed, and the lady followed, resuming her explanation.

"Your Chaiva thought of us, because he knows our combined powers create a space of peace and restraint—your presence in this world is rendered invisible by your being inside the reach of what we call our core. Our core emanates a cloud of magic that removes the powers of those inside it for as long as they remain, it neutralizes any magic cast upon others and it keeps prying magical eyes from spying within the core. There are several places I can think of that have a similar effect in our world; but ours is the only one created from the powers of a collective," she was breathing a bit harder as they climbed. She continued on. Avria waited for an indication to stop, to veer off into one of the doorways or archways they passed, but she did not. So Avria continued climbing, listening, feeling her bag getting heavier and heavier with every step.

"This cloud does not affect us, but only others who come bearing powers; we are here to heal, to teach discipline; for those who are not raised among these walls find it difficult to control their powers, so our Core assists them and enables us to help them. We help those who sometimes are punished by the powers; but on the most part, our purpose is to be stewards of our gifts and of the gifts of others. Your Chaiva also knows that this core is connected to us; it is part of us; and once you are within our protection, we will know if anything happens to you. He chose the right place for you," The High Mother finally stopped at a doorway facing the wide flight Avria had just crossed. Avria turned back. The High Mother laid her hand on the latch of this heavy wooden door, and smiled kindly and sympathetically, "and if I might add at the risk of touching a sensitive subject… it is also a good place for you to heal from the injury that has been inflicted upon you." Avria blushed and felt a burn of tears almost at once. For a while, she'd forgotten, all this new information, these new sights, for a second, she'd let herself ignore the pain of her body, the humiliation of her memories.

High Mother lifted the latch and pushed the door open, letting Avria pass before she did. Avria found herself walking into another hallway, this one more reasonable in its proportions. The High Mother turned left and followed it, and Avria looked out the intermittent windows that lined the left wall of this corridor. They were above the tall trees, and the morning was rising bright and clear. The forest that grew up against this abbey was coated in ice, each branch, every pin, every tenacious leaf. Lone ravens kited into the sky, riding the icy currents, their grating calls barely audible behind the thick glass and stone mullions. The floor was carpeted in a single long woven rug of intricate design, a weaving pattern in ivory tones against a ruddy red background. There were portraits on the right wall between the occasional doors, portraits of sisters, portraits of elderly high mothers.

They walked the full length of the corridor to its end. There, a set of double doors was imbedded in a large stone archway. She opened one side and ushered Avria in. Avria realized they were in one of the towers. A set of stairs landed just to the right of the doorway and rose up, hugging the curved wall of this large chamber. The stairway, open to one side with no railing, vanished into the ceiling. The wall to the left was straight, and it cut forward and then angled towards the curved wall some ways back. This appeared to be a large parlor of some sort. It was commodious and a warm fire burned in a hearth on the flat wall directly in front of the double doors. Shelves covered the wall to the right, crammed full of books. Avria smiled wanly, thinking of how Taneth would love this room. There were two work tables with work lamps on them, and a number of chairs of varying styles peppered around the room, including one particularly beautiful reclining settee that looked newly made, with beautiful silk upholstery.

"This is one of our many special reading rooms for tower guests. This room is shared by three sets of apartments, but you are the only guest here right now as we rarely get visitors in mid-winter. A fire has been lit in here for your use. Come with me, the High Mother crossed the room, and entered a short hallway through an arch that butted up against the tower wall. There were two doors and a window in this small space, a door directly ahead, one to the right and the window was on the outer wall. It was a larger window that went from the floor up to the ceiling, with large divided lights and wooden framing so it could be opened. It was shut fast and the panes were frosted in the corners. The priestess pointed to the door directly to the front of them; "that is another set of stairs to the other apartments," she said. "Here," High Mother opened the door to the right, and Avria found herself in a set of opulent apartments. Cut from a significant wedge of the tower's area, the space opened up into a welcoming sitting room with cozily appointed chairs and a warm fire sharing the same flue as the fire in the large parlor. There were no windows in this part of the room. A double door of paned glass separated this sitting room from the sleeping room, which was a massive space with a huge bed smack in the center of it facing the three widows looking out of the tower. To the right was an open wash chamber with a large bathing tub made of marble. Avria had never seen anything so beautiful as this room.

"This is much more than I need…"

"It is what you get, my dear. You are royalty, after all." Avria's brow furrowed and she shook her head, confused by the statement, but not quite bothered enough to argue with her about it. Bewildered, she put down her bag and turned to the High Mother.

"I thank you for your hospitality."

"You are welcome. You may go wherever you wish; but be sure to stay close to where there are others; it's easy to find yourself lost in this place. Just please don't walk outside the gates of the abbey; our core only extends as far as the abbey. You will have someone to assist you of course; she will bring you your meals and help you with whatever you require. I would like that you please dine with me the evening after next; I would like to have a nice talk with you. I must go to Nadeem today. The people are restless there and require guidance, but I will be back soon. Sister Adrenne is here, your assistant can help you find her if you need to find someone you know. I just ask that if you come upon the sisters and they are meditating, please do not disturb them."

"Of course. Thank you." With a smile and an elegant sweep of the red train of her robes and she was gone. Avria stood for a long moment in silence, unmoving. The fire was freshly stoked, and the sound of it gave her some comfort. She sighed deeply. She shucked her cloak and her other outer garments and threw them onto one of the chairs, and she sat on the edge of the bed, staring out at the forest below, which from this perspective looked like a silvery green ocean. She felt like someone else. As if she'd stepped out of her nightmare and into someone else's life. Perhaps that was what she needed. She flopped back onto the huge bed, and laughed bitterly to herself. Royalty indeed.

CHAPTER EIGHT – ADMISSION

Offrin stormed out of the family apartments and slammed the door so hard, dirt sifted down from the rafters. Tinna looked at Taneth and shook her head. There was no arguing with him. He decided he would go to Master Gavorre for guidance; in what neither of Avria's parents were sure. They wondered if he was going after Eleran or going to find his wife, or going home; he was so angry, it was difficult to tell what he was communicating except his abject fury. It was unbelievable to Tinna that such a gentle soul could hold such a violent temper. He'd screamed non-stop for at least ten minutes and he punched the furniture, upset the tea table, smashing Tinna's favorite tea pot and the plate of sweet cakes that Taneth had made for his wife that morning. The baby was startled by the noise and crying at the top of his lungs. That instantly dissipated Offrin's violence and he stood there steaming for a moment as if utterly without thought. He then told Tinna that he would go to Gavorre to find the help she was so unwilling to offer, and accused her of being a terrible mother to Avria and then the door was slammed with bravado. Tinna stood stricken, her eyes filled with tears.

Tinna spent the better part of the day concentrating on getting things together for the trip north, arranging for a military Araki rider escort, finding a suitable coach, coming up with an appropriate wardrobe to stand in the presence of the High King. She also had to move Cennik north as well. He was her assigned summoner, and she knew it would be hard to tear him from Thamatoc now that he had grown so accustomed to life here. Phenmal had returned as promised only two days after his departure with the shadow-man and he looked tired and worried.

Phenmal arrived while Tinna was alone. She had just finished bathing the baby, and she was putting on his tiny clothes so he could crawl freely about the apartments while she packed and fussed. She looked up at Phenmal when he strode in, and didn't say anything to him as he stripped off his outer garments and made himself at home. Her eyes smiled at him. His heart melted. If only she weren't married. But she was and to a man he liked quite a bit, so he had to set aside his disappointment for a moment to give her some news.

"The Drathar found a trail. Eleran is cleverer than I gave him credit for. He is headed in the correct direction. But Eleran does not have the benefit of flight and his magic can only carry him so far. Only the most powerful of bearers could bridge great distances and he is not so powerful. It will take him time to travel, even with his powers. The Drathar says it will be impossible to shape out which route he will take at this point, so hunting him is a wasted effort. But the Drathar is certain he will ultimately end up where Avria is hidden. The shadow has gone to greet him there. I've instructed him to remain at Avria's side. As sorcerers and magic-bearers and the like go, there are none more powerful than the Drathar. They are barely human; the magic consumes so much of their being. They have abilities upon abilities. Avria will be safe."

"Then why bother keeping her where she is? Why not move her back?"

"Because if Eleran goes near her, he will have to stand in a place where his powers will be drained and blocked. Drathar is not subject to the effects of this spell that protects Avria. It is the best way."

"To use her as bait?" Tinna asked matter-of-factly, her brow arched. He'd dreaded this moment, because he knew Tinna's concern for her daughter was above all else. He'd already experienced her rage when delivering similar news to her before the war. In her mind, Avria's wellbeing should never be secondary to anything, and Phenmal seemed to always fall into a position where he had to force Tinna to put her concern for Avria aside for more pressing matters. She'd nearly choked him two years ago, he was waiting for her to explode again—and this time Taneth was not in the room to intercede as he had last time.

"In essence. We can waste time and resources hunting down the Zsathri in the forests between here and the coast, or we can just wait for him to come to us." Tinna remained collected and level-headed however, her shoulders tensing up and her jaw setting hard.

"You know it won't be that easy; just capture him as he arrives. You know he will have thought things through," Tinna reminded Phenmal with a hard glare. The older man nodded in resignation. She stooped and picked up little Istvan, who was looking drowsy after his hectic day of play, bathing and toddling about on his own.

She put him in his cradle and gazed down at him with an expression of concern. The child merely turned his head towards the window and stuck his thumb in his mouth, his eyes drooping.

"We will do what we can, Tinna. We have been working on contingencies; she is surrounded by protection. Let it be." She sighed and rubbed her temples. Phenmal took in the stacks of clothes, the empty bags on the bed, the shuffle or papers on her desk.

"I see you've made up your mind..."

"As usual Phenmal, you pretend as if I actually have a choice to begin with." Tinna put her hand on her hip and shook her head. Beautiful Tinna. Like Avria, she had a magnetic presence; she was still ravishing at forty and post-baby; her body still toned to the point of perfection from her daily ritual of martial dances; which she practiced with other village women. She hadn't lifted a weapon since her battle with her mother, but she was always prepared to do so if needed. It was her nature as a Thran; a warrior born. Her softness had come to her over the past two decades; having raised her own daughter and an adopted son. She found a well of nurturing she didn't know she had, and she discovered satisfaction in it like nobody else.

She was happiest here, at Thamatoc with her awkward brainy husband, going about her daily duties as leader, resolving petty conflicts between villagers with an amused smile, planning trade runs with the new foals, appointing new elders, being the mother of an entire community in essence. Phenmal wanted the same for himself, to knock about back and forth between his quiet house and this bustling village of close lodges and tiny apartments; to sit at Tinna's fire with Taneth and discuss the variety of nonsense that interested the intellectual man that was Tinna's spouse; to tease Avria, and watch her grow as a human being and watch the newest one in the family grow up, such potential this dark-haired boy had. Phenmal knew on a personal level what Tinna was giving up as she packed away some of her common skirts he doubted she'd wear where she was going. It was trite, an act of cluelessness, or comfort, he didn't pry into her head to find out. She would hit him if she sensed him in there; that he knew. She hated it when he rummaged her brain.

"Well, my concubine; what other grim things do you bring?" she said, bringing up the private joke between she, Taneth and Phenmal. A discussion had come up when Avria was six or seven, as to what Phenmal truly was to their family. He spent an inordinate amount of time at Thamatoc, specifically in their apartments or with Taneth. He loved her children like his own. For Avria's sake, they appointed him honorary grandfather, since Avria had none. One evening, after a community supper, they retired to the family apartments for a sip of wine and some discussion. Phenmal had been away, and they wanted to catch up. After a few glasses of wine, the conversation strayed to personal things; namely, where Phenmal stood in the family hierarchy. Phenmal responded: "Grandfather, how insulting. I'm more like a second husband if anything.

"You wish you were a second husband," Taneth blurted into his glass, which was tipped up over his nose when Phenmal had spoken. Tinna laughed heartily and got up to get the bottle to pour some more. The wine oddly made her graceful, sensuous, and it made her more flirtatious. Phenmal knew that when she was young and free, she had been a terror to mankind; a temptress and a user. He often pictured her during those days in his imagination. It was the encounter with the strange and pragmatic character of Taneth that tamed her.

"Perhaps a concubine," she suggested, her curls framing her beautiful face, her dark lashes making her black eyes even more striking. "I can have as many of those as I please, is that right?" Phenmal, like every other man who knew her, even the dragon Ledroran, was hopelessly in love with Tinna. She had an almost supernatural attractiveness that Avria had inherited. In Tinna's case, her tough exterior prevented it being an issue; for Avria, it created monsters.

"Ahh, maybe, but I do not enjoy the benefits of that title," Phenmal lamented.

"That's all mine," Taneth said smugly, slapping Tinna's behind as she moved to sit beside him. She shook her head, and smiled at the older man, her eyes shining.

"I'll take the leavings, and that's good enough for me," Phenmal confessed. "As long as I am welcome."

"That you always are, no matter what a strange creature you can be." Tinna's gaze was hot, teasing and flirtatious. Phenmal felt that little minx's powerful affection for him; he even sensed some temptation on her part, which was torturous to know. It made his tired body heat up a bit, and he had to clear his throat and look away from her plump lips, stained with wine, and the cleft of her breasts. He loved Taneth like a brother, he was a good man, but he was the most bizarre match for the former Thran. Despite a vast chasm of differences standing between them, they managed to be quite disgustingly happy together. Phenmal still couldn't figure out what it was that made Tinna choose such a creature, but he'd given up trying.

"Except when he brings bad tidings. Then he's not welcome," Taneth chimed in. Phenmal snorted and crossed his legs, his foot wagging with a touch of irritation. He loved Taneth, he reminded himself. Taneth was like a brother—the simpleton.

"Concubine indeed." One glance at her, and her gaze burned him to the core. He would have to make do with the leavings, he told himself, as he had so many times. He did know one thing; leadership would involve her with the Keepers. She would be around a long time. Perhaps long enough.

Now, her gaze was far from flirtatious, it was tired and confused. She was so comfortable with him, her eyes spoke more clearly than her mind or her mouth could say. Phenmal hated that he was the deliverer of this fate. He wanted more than anyone to free her of this unwanted responsibility; to help her escape the destiny of being someone she did not want to be. He wanted to let her stay here, at Thamatoc, and let her live here in simplicity as she wished until she was old and grey and he was only a warm memory. His selfish wishes aside, he did truly wish this for Tinna.

"Oh, Tinna," Phenmal said with more emotion than he normally expressed. She put her hands down from folding clothes, and looked up at him, her eyes wide and searching. He approached her and put his hands on her shoulders, "I am so sorry about all this. I know I had no control over what they chose for you; but perhaps I could have done something..."

"Phenmal, appointing blame and taking unnecessary responsibility is not going to change anything. You're here with me, and you always have been since the moment our paths crossed. I need you, and I need you to not feel bad for what is being imposed upon me. It's being imposed upon you too," she said, looking up at him. He studied her beautiful face, hardly showing her age since he first met her; a grey hair here and there wound into her curls. He reached up and pinched her chin, smiling at her. How he wanted to kiss her.

"Ah woman, you are everything. You and that maddening daughter of yours."

"I do love you Phenmal. I have for a long time."

"I know."

"Of course you know," she laughed easily. He gave in. He bent down and kissed her lips gently and then withdrew. This was the first time they'd ever shared that sort of affection in more than two decades in one another's company. She leaned against his chest,

601

laying her ear on his heart. Her arms wrapped around his torso, and she let him envelope and comfort her.

Taneth strode into the apartments and took it all in with no concern. "Phen... when did you get back? How goes the hunt?" Phenmal didn't release Tinna, and Tinna did not step away from Phenmal; he simply retold the things he'd told Tinna only moments before, still soaking in her love; wishing to drown in it. Taneth knew this was no betrayal. It was just the way things were. It was family.

CHAPTER NINE – FAMILY

The Drathar watched her for a long time before he made his appearance. He knew there was something indefinable about this young woman that made so many men mad about her. She was singularly... something. She was with child, but she didn't know it yet. A spark of life started from the encounter of violence with a former lover. He felt the power of the little seed already radiating from her belly. It was a power of the likes he'd never seen. The Keepers should be made to know of this, he thought. He did not feel particularly compelled to share it. Especially after he'd assessed and read Avria.

He studied the new mother. He felt her unease with herself, her damaged sense of self and her broken sense of control. The Chaiva had given her a good head-start on healing, softened some of the more painful thoughts, given her a foundation of strength to draw from. But she was still brittle. She was shrunken. But her beauty was not easy to miss; it did not shrink with her. It wasn't just her appearance; it was the light she exuded, the goodness and the kindness; the decency and understanding, the capacity for love and acceptance and even forgiveness was only just beneath the surface, but she was fragile. Too fragile.

He was gentle as he explored her mind; shared her pain, wandered through her childhood, her broken heart over the betrayal by her childhood friend Jestin, her journey with the Zsathri that she still loved in spite of what he had done, and then her sweet affection for the man Offrin who she thought of much of late and feared she would lose. It was her capacity for love, her steadfastness, her hidden power... The Drathar felt it all. He understood why the Zsathri had loved her with his entire being; believing her to be his other half; he understood why Jestin had risked even his own sanity to insure he could keep her, he understood why Offrin had worked so hard to mean something more to her. What the Drathar found even more compelling, was that he sensed that despite all the heartbreak, the devastation, even the resignation, this woman was not defeated. She was floundering a bit, yes, but she was not completely damaged. He felt her healing even as he watched. He felt the influence of the powerful mother, her steadfast father; and the Chaiva who would give his life to keep her safe.

He understood. With a controlled sigh, he approached her. Avria was walking back to her reading room and apartments after having gotten lost several times. She finally found the right floor, the right stairwell, the right corridor, and now she was walking towards a shadow. It took her a moment to realize that it wasn't what she thought; that it had form and substance; that it breathed. She paused, terrified. Her scream was stifled however, it would not escape. She just froze in horror for but a second.

"Do not fear. Phenmal sent me," the figure said. Her face had gone waxen, but the mention of Phenmal's name gave her an immediate sense of security. She clutched the pages she'd gotten down in the scriptorium and nodded stiffly in greeting. The Drathar found that the sight of her eyes struck something deep inside his soul. Dark and wide, still possessing some element of idealism and innocence despite what she'd endured in her short life.

"I see," she muttered. "I need to go through that door you're blocking..." she said nervously. The Drathar stepped aside, and let her pass, following unbidden. She walked into the reading room, and set to lighting one of the table lamps. "One of my favorite things to do with my father is to help him copy texts. I've done it since I was little. I find it soothing," she explained. The Drathar stood in front of the door after closing it, watching her. "I thought, since I'm alone with my thoughts most every day here, I would do some of this work, copy a few books that I know my father would like but might not have; there are many books in here I know he would like," she rambled. She put her paper stack down on the table, and went and got a pot of ink and a stylus. She looked again at the Drathar.

"You should not be alone with your thoughts," he said.

"Why are you garbed so drearily, why do you have your face covered?"

"My gaze can be damaging to people," he replied, still not moving. "Our skin is sensitive to light. So this is our... uniform of sorts."

"Like the Dreff sisters? They wear black too, except the high-ranked ones. They wear red." Avria picked a book from the shelf and took it to the table.

604

"They are the counterparts of sorts, of my kind; a different order perhaps is the best way to describe it. They too have similar restrictions, but they are not so dangerous as to require a veil to shield the world from their gaze. And they are not afflicted with the same physical manifestations as we are; not all of them."

"Are you always so? Always looking through the fabric? Or do you get to take it off in company of each other?"

"There are only eleven of us in this world right now. We don't see one another much if at all after we reach adulthood."

"That's it? Only eleven?" Avria asked, both interested and not.

"More might be born someday, but we are a rare type of bearer. One that many ordinary people fear; one where babies born like us might be killed before they are given a chance. We are too different; too frightening." Avria pondered this as she sat down, holding her book.

"And does the core of the Dreff, does it neutralize you?" He smiled underneath the veil, finding her curiosity charming.

"No. We are the same. When we are here, our essence contributes to the core. We are always welcome among our sisters."

"Why are you here? Why did Phenmal send you?"

"I am here to find him. To stop him." Avria froze and her face grew pale again.

"Is he here?"

"He comes."

"Then I should run again? I do not want to run again," her throat tightened and her eyes immediately misted up. Raggedly, she added, "I'm so tired."

"No, Avria. You have an army of sorceresses here—my sisters; and you have me. You will be safe. But I must remain with you. He cannot perform magic in the core; but he might have tricks up his sleeve. So I am to stay and protect you at all costs."

* * * *

Phenmal was tired, but further exhausted by yet another trip through the icy winds on dragon to the citadel. But he was finally at Thamatoc, and for the moment he had no need to go anywhere yet. He found Tinna packed and irritable, but happy to find him at the door when she opened it. She ushered him in, sliding her arm around his waist and hugging him close.

"Have you any news of Avria?"

"No. The Drathar is with her by now. She is in good hands."

"If you say so," Tinna feigned a shudder and smiled tersely. She was in her usual attire of a trained skirt and long tunic. Her thick hair was tied back in a tail with a metal cuff. The apartment was in an unusual state of disarray. There were toys scattered by the hearth, the bed in the corner and the cradle were a tousle of blankets, clothes were piled high on a chair, the table a shuffle of papers. Tinna looked harassed.

"Where's the little one?"

"With Jenyk, of course. I just got back from a meeting with the elders. The elders are not too pleased that I am leaving this village. They refuse to appoint a new leader in my stead. They will only agree to someone as acting leader. It's simply ridiculous," She stopped and her shoulders sagged. "Phenmal..." she turned to look at him. "I don't want to leave. I don't want to."

"I'm sorry Tinna," he intoned, dropping his gloved hands. Tinna sighed and rolled her misted eyes up to his.

"I miss Avria. She's alone with all this pain and horror; she needs her mother."

"I know she does. It won't be long, Tinna. She will come to Miranne as soon as the situation with Eleran is resolved; and trust me Tinna, it will be resolved." Tinna gazed at Phenmal for a long, poignant moment, her eyes looking deep into his.

"I cannot live at Miranne without you," she said with finality. Phenmal sighed and took off his scarf and hat, shrugging off the capes of his greatcoat and throwing the whole lot on the back of a chair. He felt that was all he was doing of late, taking his damned greatcoat off and shrugging it back on over and over again.

"Taneth will be with you..."

"Taneth is more than a Wiseman. He is Artreth now. He will be traveling to the academy at Adremateen constantly and he disclosed to me today that he wants to start arranging conferences with all the Wisemen serving in Araki villages in addition to those at the human settlements. And all that aside; my husband is not built for the life at Miranne. He will come and he will go, but what I need is you. Your mind. Your support, your ideas, your presence."

"I don't know, Tinna." Phenmal picked up the pile of clothes and threw them on the bed. He sank down into his usual chair and rubbed his face. "I don't know..."

"I can isolate your living quarters so you are separated from the people. The palace at Miranne is not nestled in a great city..."

"I know. It's not that."

"You can escape just as you do now when things get too noisy for you, come back to your manor here…" she spread her hands in bewilderment.

"Tinna, please..." She stopped talking and dropped her hands, her dark, elegantly arched brows furrowing. He looked up at her, and the sight of her guileless expression and the natural beauty of her face just filled him with heartache. She would need him more. Even more than she had during the war; but that was only a brief period of time and he could run away to his home where he could take a break from the torture of being around her. Her expectant look turned to confusion and she faced him fully.

"What is it Phenmal?" He shook his head and sighed.

"I don't know if I can do it."

"Why not? Please, tell me why not? I don't want to be obstinate about it, but honestly, Phenmal, if you're not beside me at Miranne, I will not go." He groaned and put his face into his hands, the anger building at the position she was putting him in. "I won't go, Phenmal."

"How dare you blackmail me, Tinna?" Phenmal shot to his feet and shouted at her. She did not balk or cringe, she stood against it, her brow angry as well.

"Tell me why!" she shouted back at him.

"Because you drive me mad! I can't be around you all the time and not have you! It's hard enough here, but at least I can go, at least Taneth's presence tempers me and brings me back to the reality; but I cannot be at Miranne so close to you all the time, it's bloody torture," he barked. "I can't!" He realized he'd let it all slip and he exhaled in resignation, and let his eyes fall on Tinna's face.

"I love Taneth."

"I know."

"I love you."

"I know," he laughed sardonically, and shook his head. "But Taneth is your husband and he is a good man, and I respect and love him too much. I feel tremendous guilt for harboring these desires because I feel like I am betraying a brother." Tinna's gaze burned into his, and unexpectedly, Tinna moved forward, lifting her hands to grasp the sides of his face, and she pulled him down to her lips. The kiss was not the tender, gentle kiss they'd shared the a few days ago. This was a passionate, burning kiss that seared his lips and set his body ablaze.

They staggered backward towards the bed, lips and tongues entangled all the while. Tinna grappled to undo the front of his heavy woolen waistcoat, and then the removal of the cravat and the crisp white shirt beneath. She and pushed it up, tugging it over his head, interrupting the kiss only for the material to pass over his face. His hands did the same for her tunic. By the time they reached the bed, they were both bare from the waist, up. Phenmal reached around to Tinna's back and pulled the silver cuff from her thick hair, freeing the thick make of raven curls, tossing it to the floor with a clatter. Phenmal stepped back to look and groaned at the sight of her.

He did not live like a monk, by any means, but he did not sleep around too much either. He often simply found someone to bear the brunt of his frustration for Tinna, and then went weeks without. It had been awhile to begin with and now the woman he dreamt of stood before him bare breasted, with fire in her eyes. He was completely incapable of controlling himself. He tore at the lace of Tinna's skirts, shoved down her little winter leggings and the sight of her in the full glory of nudity made his mind reel. He picked her up by the waist and put her on the bed. With a smooth movement, he kicked off his long boots and breeches and under breeches, and crawled onto the bed over her. He could scarce believe he was about to make love to Tinna. He used his arm to swipe away the clothing and wads of blankets and he settled over her. One hand propped him over her, the other found her hip, and then slid up her waist to her breast.

"Gods, this is so wrong…"

"Hush…" Tinna replied huskily. Her eyes were glazed over with passion, her cheeks filled with a youthful pink glow. Her body was a marvel, still a perfectly honed weapon. How a woman who existed in a reasonably sedate life of deskwork, supervision and travel, she still looked like a warrior. He leaned down and kissed her deeply, his tongue twisting with hers. Her breath was heavy and hot, her soft moans sultry. He pulled away and looked down at her flushed face, her glazed, heavy-lidded eyes, and her lips plump and parted. He lowered his face between her breasts, following the subtle ripple of muscles to the flat of her tummy, which showed hardly any sign of her pregnancies. He could barely contain himself, he was painfully aroused, and Tinna was so, so beautiful. He lapped at her hard, erect nipples and then, his thighs trembling, he maneuvered himself fully between her legs. Tinna did not let him drag it out or hesitate; she was never the type to play games. She wanted him, so she reached down and guided him into her.

Phenmal's face dropped to the hollow of her neck and he licked her there, his breath cooling the moisture and making her skin rise into goose bumps. She moaned as he began to stroke into her. "God I've wanted this for twenty years," he groaned, thrusting into her more ardently. Tinna's fingers raked across his shoulders and back, and she writhed sensuously beneath him.

"I love you Phenmal," Tinna said hoarsely, wrapping her powerful legs around him. Phenmal's well-hidden youthful vigor, the gift of the Keepers, surged through him, and any attempt to look his age abandoned him. He brought her to a screaming climax, and then let his own needs satisfy themselves inside the woman he had loved for two decades. When he collapsed, sweating on top of her, she wrapped her arms around him and kissed his face.

"I belong to two worlds these days, Phenmal. There are two of me. One that wants to be here with Taneth, one that needs to be at Miranne, and leading the Araki people with you at my side. I am about to leave the world that Taneth belongs to and expect him to leave it and to take the lead as an Artreth, possibly higher," She said. "I know we joke about the concubine thing, but it isn't a joke," Phenmal rolled off of her and propped himself up on an arm, his face a picture of puzzlement.

"I have discussed this with Taneth." Phenmal's brow creased and his eyes widened.

"You what?"

"I talked about it with Taneth; after our kiss the other day. After you left. I told him what I needed. I explained my feelings. He knows I love him and that will not change. Nothing really will except for some details. He knows he loses nothing." She said matter-of-factly.

"I don't understand…"

"I was going to talk to you about this after we got to Miranne. I know it's selfish, to ask Taneth to sacrifice and share." She paused. "Phenmal… will you marry me?" Tinna asked. "I think I realized I need you more than ever. I have always loved you, perhaps not so much in the beginning, but you grew on me. I need you, not just for practicality, but for your strength and for how crucial you are to our family. Avria needs you, Istvan needs you. I don't want to go to Miranne without you.

"Taneth's attitude towards the palace is ambivalent at best. He wants to focus on his duties as Artreth and he, like me refuses to give Thamatoc up completely, however I will not get my way. His obligations are not so burdensome that he can actually keep a strong

609

connection with Thamatoc..." she paused, her voice breaking. Phenmal knew this was painful for her. She loved Thamatoc like no other. "I asked Taneth what he thought; of my taking a second husband and his reaction, as always was pragmatic and rational. I gave him leave, if he wished, to take a lover, but he did not want that. He loves me, and wants no other. He said his work is his lover; and he feels less guilt focusing more on it knowing he is not leaving me without support. He even seemed relieved and he told me that if it had been anyone other than you, he might have been hurt, but you have always been part of our lives and so it changes things little."

"Except now I finally get the benefits of the title of concubine," Phenmal chuckled. Tinna rolled onto her side and propped her head on her arm. Her face looked so young and lovely. Phenmal could not help but let his admiring gaze slide down to her beautiful breasts. He could hardly believe he finally got her into bed.

"Not concubine... husband. You never answered my proposal."

"Of course, I will marry you, in so much as I can. Is it permitted under the laws? It is for men to take multiple wives, with the regional rule's approval. But this is progressive; and who would approve of it?"

"I am the law now, am I not?" Tinna grinned. Phenmal laughed heartily and pulled her to him, her small, tight frame felt so good against his body. She slid her thigh up his and arched her body against him.

"You are the most beautiful creature ever to grace the earth." Tinna sighed contentedly, and ran her hand along his strong jaw line.

"Why is it you never get old, old man?"

"It's a secret," he replied. Tinna sighed. Her eyes wandered down to his chest, and she noticed some strange little figures and letters drifting on it. They looked like they were partially submerged in milky water, buoyant but not entirely, rising up to clarity and then sinking down into the murk of his skin. It was the strangest thing she'd ever seen. They were sort of like the markings she'd seen on the Driva, but not quite. These moved; these drifted.

"What are these? I've never seen your chest before."

"They are my Chaiva markings," he replied, lifting his head and awkwardly gazing down his nose at them. "They sometimes are faint, other times, they ride the surface and are clear. If I am... excited they tend to surface. Most creatures of powers possess some manner of these letters or other. At least those that I know of." He seemed unimpressed by the letters. Tinna touched his skin where they seemed to float just beneath the surface. As he relaxed, the letters sank down into oblivion.

"I suppose I need to tidy this place up and finish packing everything."

"Where is Taneth anyway?"

"At Adremateen. The Keepers are keeping him busy."

"Yes. They do that," Phenmal grunted.

"They are demanding and suffocating, aren't they?"

"Controlling, sometimes yes," Phenmal agreed.

"It could be worse, I suppose. We can be grateful that they aren't completely mad like the Hevra," she said with a smirk. "If we must be controlled by some powerful faction or other, at least it's not a pack of lunatics. I'm glad of that."

"Who told you the Keepers aren't complete nutters?" he asked, but he paused for a moment. Something came to him. An inspiration. Of course. Phenmal rolled onto his back. He reflected for a moment and then returned to the moment at hand.

"Nobody tells me anything about the bloody Keepers," Tinna muttered. Phenmal turned his face towards her.

"I suppose I need to give you my answer about Miranne?"

"That would be helpful." Tinna raised her brows and smirked.

"Well, you did go through significant lengths to persuade me," he grinned. Tinna smiled and kissed him, a hot, sensual kiss that stirred his desires again. "My answer is yes, if you're wondering," he replied. "But on one condition; that you travel north without me." He had to put his finger on her lips because she was about to protest.

"Wait a moment. I will meet you at Miranne. I need to go northeast to Effring."

"What for?"

"The Hevra. Eleran belongs to them. I think I should go and see that they take some responsibility for their little boy." Her playful face had gone stone serious. Phenmal sighed heavily and groaned.

"What's that about?"

"That's about being away from you again; now that I've finally gotten you where I want you."

"Oh, is that so?" Tinna laughed. He nodded, and she smiled smugly. "So you think this is your doing?" Phenmal arched his brow and nodded again. In a quick move, he threw her onto her back and climbed over her again, a sinister smirk on his face. Tinna sighed contently and relaxed in his grasp; pleased he was happy to take control.

CHAPTER TEN – FAIRY TALES

Igro dove down, and instead of the temperature climbing, it seemed to get colder. Phenmal frowned darkly, imagining himself back in Tinna's bed. The thought of it brought his core body temperature up and he smiled to himself. It was more than he could have hoped for. He thought of the idea of being a second husband and it made him laugh, but it was all silliness in the end. The conventions didn't matter—the root of it was he was able to love Tinna the way he had always wanted, from the moment she arrived at his old manor on that rainy night.

I hope you will not be here long; it is almost too cold for me here. And there's nowhere for me to go

I won't be long, Igro. I suggest you drop let me hop off and then keep circling. I'll call you when I need you. The dragon nodded. Phenmal had one advantage that nobody else shared. He could speak to his dragon companions telepathically. Igro had gotten used to thinking his replies, and projecting deliberate discussions so Phenmal would hear it over other chatter if need be. There was also a much greater advantage of distance. It had served everyone well during the buildup to the One-Day-War. Dragons had scouted the enemy movements and informed Phenmal of them using simple flyovers.

Igro informed Phenmal they were near and he dropped into a plummet, picking up incredible speed before leveling out over a frozen lake, flying at an arrow's swiftness towards a large fortification on the shore. He climbed suddenly to a near stall so he could clear the parapet wall. Phenmal prepared to dismount and Igro managed to fly only a few inches above the ground and he leaned a bit so Phenmal could leap down in his usual fashion. The man landed on the snowy ground with a crunch of the boot heels, sliding a few feet forward in an agile, graceful move. The dragon pulled immediately up and flew vertically up the face of the main building, vanishing over the roof.

Phenmal barely straightened when three guards emerged from the large door carrying large voulges. Phenmal used something he rarely used anymore and he stunned their minds with a painful, searing din. The guards gripped their heads and fell to their knees. Phenmal stepped over one and walked up the steps to the old-style castle.

He entered a rather shabby looking hall flanked by fires. The rest of the guard was inside, gripping their heads and writhing on the floor. The only figures that weren't doing so were the tall, willowy forms of what Phenmal knew to be Hevra.

He wasn't sure how many there were in total, but five stood in this hall. They lived in a collective and rarely separated. They were beautiful creatures; the first of the soul-bearers, made immortal to watch over the world. Legend said they held whole souls, and it was too much for the physical body to bear… the soul drove them mad. It was only then that the gods realized their mistake and instead imbued humans and other creatures with only half-souls, and made them mortal.

Phenmal didn't quite swallow the legends like others did. He knew they were powerful, and old. The Hevra were the most ancient living creatures in the world. But he also knew they were not created by the gods, they were born to the earliest peoples. They were immortal, and they could not make new Hevra. Their branch of peoples had died out eons ago; he knew they could imbue magic into certain mortals, and they did so, creating their 'children' the Zshathri. The Zshathri were not born of magic as others were—and the Hevra were fiercely protective of their children; preventing any of them from falling under the control of the Keepers.

Many centuries ago, there had been a conflict between the human Keepers and the Hevra for control of their children. It was a war nobody could win; and there was a treaty signed that one would leave the other to do as they wished, as long as nothing adversely affected the path defined by the Keepers. A peace had reigned since, but the Keepers were not shy in sharing their low opinion of the Hevra, and did a great deal to undermine their creation of new magic bearers by the Hevra, or allowing the Zshathri from breeding with other magic bearers to produce born-Zsathris.

Phenmal was surprised to see them all dressed in the most modern of finery. He had heard of their strange quirks; their vanity, their preening self-absorption—but he didn't think it was quite so bad. Here they were with their ancient residence crumbling all around them, and they looked like perfection in the latest fashions from the human cities.

Each one looked impassively upon him while their guards suffered. They could have been effigies they were so still.

"Why have you come mind-reader?" asked towering woman with hair cut shorter than he'd ever seen on a woman before. She wore a sapphire blue gown and stood near the fireplace. The massive room was not cozy or comfortable by any means, but they collected there, on a worn rug, sitting on heavy old-fashioned furniture. An ancient tapestry on the far wall hung in moth-eaten tatters.

"I pass through here only to tell you a story. Then I am gone." The five heads tilted in interest, all in unison and he hid his satisfaction. Once during a gathering of the Keepers, he heard one of them mention the penchant the Hevra had for stories.

"Like little children they are, as soon as they hear 'once upon a time' you have their undivided attention. They do get angry if the story ends in tragedy however." he had said gravely, chuckling mockingly afterwards. "Old as the sky but as dense as a brick of lead." Taneth did not believe this was true—but it was worth a shot. But it was, for three more of the graceful creatures entered, soon followed by three more. Phenmal noted the fine wool of the flamboyant frock coats and the shining silks of their waistcoats. The women rustled in silks too precious for ordinary day use… but here they all were, dressed as if about to go to a ball, trimmed in diamonds and gems, feathers and dancing slippers. It was a stark contrast to see these richly; fashionably dressed figures against a backdrop so dilapidated and ragged.

"Not so long ago, there was a Zsathri. A Zsathri who broke the laws of bearers; a Zsathri so besotted, so filled with love and dedication for his chosen woman, he sacrificed his own essence to protect her from danger; casting spells that took lives. The powers punished him, and cut the tether between his being and his body and held it fast in the prisons of the voids." As Phenmal spoke, four more of the willowy creatures sailed in. Perhaps they were planning to have a ball. There was not a single plain one among them. They were all riveted, their strange, beautiful faces almost like dolls. One more and then five more gathered from another archway.

"The Zsathri slept and was lost to those who watched over him. And one afternoon, a handsome pair of Hevra appeared and they carried him away in their coach. His loved one mourned his loss, knowing she would never see him again." One particular woman, with immaculate skeins of raven hair as smooth as silk, dabbed a tear from her emerald eye. Phenmal took a dooming tone, and continued.

"But somehow, the essence of the Zsathri escaped the voids, and returned tainted and twisted. He returned to his world in search of his loved one, but his love was tainted and twisted, and instead he harmed her and caused her terrible pain and he hunts her. He is no longer bound by the laws of the bearers and he can take lives with his magic with no consequence. He runs free, searching for his love, seeking only to harm her." Phenmal stopped abruptly.

The dark haired woman's huge eyes blinked. "Is that the end of the tale?"

"The tale has not ended. He hunts still. He will harm her. He will continue to harm. It is up to the Hevra to bring this story to an end."

"The story is of Eleran," a male uttered. "Our dear child, Eleran." Phenmal stepped back.

"I will release your guard. My dragon comes. I hope you enjoyed my tale." A woman with white hair suddenly intoned in a singsong voice:

"But when does the dancing begin? We must celebrate the comings and goings, the beginnings and the endings," her hand lifted, bound in a white calfskin glove that wrapped her whole arm, circlets of diamond glittering on her wrists. She snapped open a tatty fan in her hand and made it flutter to indicate her excitement. Phenmal heard the approach of his mount and exited the still-open door. The dragon was not about to land, so he simply flew low enough to grasp him with his talons and lift him off the stairs.

Phenmal climbed the leg to the shoulder and managed to get onto the back of the neck.

Were you successful?

Who is to say? It's like speaking to a mob of half-wits. But since they like stories so much, I left them one they can attempt to conclude on their own. Happy endings are always preferable in stories, I'll wager. I don't know if it will help; but it was worth a try.

I don't like the way this place feels or smells.

Neither do I. Let's go to Miranne. There's a warm barn and some fresh mutton in it for you. You certainly have earned it. The dragon's head rose and fell, and Phenmal settled in for the long flight. Phenmal, who was always so grumpy about dragons and flying, was grateful for his friend today. He sat down against his head and patted the soft skin on the back of his skull, scratching it. Igro made a pleasant sound; like a great cat, purring.

He could not read Hevra. They could not read him. He had no idea if this silly venture was worth the effort and the time away from Tinna, especially now; but he had to try. Avria would be safe as long as the Drathar remained with her; but what would happen to Eleran still remained in question; even the Drathar was bound by the rules of the bearer. Would he sacrifice his essence for Avria as Eleran once had if the situation called for it? There was no way to know. If the Hevra came to assist, perhaps there was a chance Eleran could be neutralized forever without requiring such a sacrifice from anyone.

CHAPTER ELEVEN – ATTACHMENT

Her charm was almost magic; almost as powerful as a spell. He watched her toss and turn; his glassy eyes never leaving her fevered sleep. In the middle of the night, her eyes opened and they locked on the dark shape hunkered on a chair by her bed. It was a direct and cutting gaze directly into eyes she could not see. It surprised him.

"You don't sleep?" she asked in a groggy whisper.

"I am not like you. I can go without."

"What do you look like, beneath all that black? I haven't seen you leave me once except when I want to use the chamber pot; which you haven't done as of yet. You haven't eaten, you don't sleep, you don't bathe, but you don't smell… what are you?"

"I am not quite the same as you. I am something other than human."

"Or Araki," she surmised.

"We are more ancient than that."

"But born of humans?"

"Humans were born of us; we are remnants of the old kind. We are born different…"

"Let me see you."

"I cannot show you my face, girl."

"Then cover your eyes; let me see who sits by me day and night." It was never done; not even for the Keepers. It was their secret, their mystery. As children they still had remnants of their humanity; but that faded with age, and now he was something akin to human but not quite. He could not resist her; he did not wish to. He wanted her to see him and to know him. What compelled him to comply with her wishes, he did not know, but he suspected it was her hold over him.

He reached up and shoved back his cowl. "Close your eyes until I say," he instructed her. Avria obeyed. He unwrapped the sheer fabric through which his world was filtered every day, slightly

619

shocked by the brightness of the dark room. He then lifted off his tunic for her to see the markings and then carefully tore a strip off of the sheer fabric, tying it around his head like a blindfold.

"What happens when someone looks into your gaze directly?" she asked while waiting.

"A thrall that does not abate. I empty the mind when I look into the eyes. I steal what's in there. It becomes mine. It is why we have so many abilities." She was silent, her eyes still closed. He could see through his mask and he stared at her in her vulnerable state, innocent and distracted by curiosity. "You may open your eyes."

Avria sat up on the bed and scooted closer to the edge. Her eyes took a moment to adjust; it was dark, but the fire was still shedding a bit of light into the room. She first saw the preternaturally pale glow of his chest, and a shock of snow-white hair that grew long down his back, as straight and as silken as the web of a spider. His face was beautiful, a white marble, with a square, defined jaw and lips like those of an expertly hewn statue. He wore a black blindfold that cut into his pale colours like a knife; his entire torso and arms and hands were covered in text, it wound all the way up to his neck. He reminded her of the Driva, another mysterious creature, but they lacked hair and the text wound around their faces and head. His face and head were clear of markings, and his hair was lush and beautiful. She could not resist and reached out to touch it. She grasped a skein of it, brushing his back with her fingers. He started. It was something he didn't expect and it was the first time in an incredibly long time anyone had ever touched his skin.

"You're too spare, there's not an ounce of fat on you... you should be eating more," she noted casually. "You are beautiful though. Not what I expected," she admitted.

"You expected massive deformities?"

"No. I expected you to be less human looking. Your skin is just skin, but you have the look of one of the old statues, of the old gods. Just a bit more than normal... the text, what does it mean?"

"I don't know. None of us do. The text is unknown and indecipherable. But we are all born with it, and it sometimes changes, words move about, appear, disappear." He felt her fingers touching the letters on his side and he froze, his eyes closing and his lips parting with a small gasp of hot breath; she took back her hand and looked embarrassed.

"I'm sorry. I let my curiosity get the best of me," she smiled timidly. She thought he was beautiful, as Eleran had once been to her—his body was lithe and elegant, wide shoulders, narrow hips, a chest and stomach defined and attractive. His hair was also striking, down to the nape of his back, cut into a perfect straight line across the bottom. His face was almost too perfect in shape; when he didn't move, he was a sculpture. He was like the opposite of everything Eleran had become, yet his presence reminded her of him; the real Eleran. Something deep inside her tugged at her heart and she started to feel the burn of tears.

"I wish I could see your eyes," she suddenly said, her voice tight. She slumped back into her bed. He shook his head, and then began to reassemble his clothing. He put the wrap on his head before removing the strip he'd used, putting it in her hand. She toyed with it, her mind temporarily elsewhere. He put on his tunic and his cowl.

"The light does not like my skin. It burns me sometimes. I must be covered," he said. He paused and looked at her. "I've never done this for anyone before. Nobody sees us as we are after a certain age. Our bodies are our secrets. The text starts to appear in greater and greater volume; we grow paler, our eyes become weapons. It is a difficult life for someone who cannot cope with being alone."

"I imagine," Avria said distantly. She was looking the other way, lying on her back, her fingers twisting around the skein of fabric. He could see, with his mind's eye, the silent tears dripping from her eyes on to her cheeks, pooling on the bridge of her nose before overflowing onto the pillow. He was unsure what to do.

"It isn't unusual for one of my kind to take his life." Avria's head rolled over to look at him, her eyes just watery glints of the meager light in the darkness. Her skin shone where the tears had fallen.

"Have you considered it?"

"A few times," he admitted.

"Me too," she whispered.

I know.

"Much since I've been here. But I cannot help to think of all the people who would be hurt by such a deed…"

"It is good you keep those you love in consideration. It is good you have them to consider. I don't have that to keep me grounded. I have nobody." There was a deeply pained silence that lasted a good long while. Then Avria stirred.

"Drathar… do you have a name?"

"No."

"Drathar," she paused, and then reached out her hand, opening it. He responded by laying his bare hand on it. Avria clasped her fingers around his and he felt her tears give way in earnest. It wasn't loud sobbing, just sniffing and the occasional gasp. Her mind was filled with memories; of moments with the man she had loved with all her soul; of kisses and of making love in a bed too small; making such noise that it roused the owner of the home where they were guests. He saw images of this Zshathri; bathed in the light of her love, short passionate moments, and then he felt her loss at his absence. He relived the rape with her, experiencing the gaping void left behind by the loss and betrayal; her confusion and humiliation that she clung stubbornly to hope that Eleran could still be what he once was-but she knew also that she could not forgive him. Her misery was profound.

She tugged on his hand—she did not ask him with words; only with images.

Without hesitation, the Drathar climbed into the bed next to Avria and lowered himself onto his back. Avria rolled up to his side, and rested her head on his arm. He gently placed his hand on her waist and reveled in the sensation of someone so close. He knew it was selfish what he was doing; providing her comfort was only secondary to his desire to feel her close to him. She toyed with the fingers of his other hand while she sorted through her thoughts. His head bent back, he reveled in the sensation of her skin touching his, her breath stirring the thin veil over his face. His heart raced. She sighed deeply and the movement was like ecstasy, her warmth radiating into him. She talked about her irrational desire to stop feeling as she felt, and she talked about how she wanted things to be normal again. He closed his eyes and focused only on her words. He listened until her sentences faded, and she slipped into a heavy slumber, her head growing a bit heavier on his arm. He reached up and touched her face. He wanted to know what a kiss would feel like; to know it from this broken bird. Instead he turned onto his side and gazed at her through his dark veil, his preternatural eyes seeing her as brightly as he would see her in the day. He arranged her frizzed curls around her face, and traced the line of her jaw and eyebrows with his finger.

He clamped his eyes shut and chewed his mandibles. He could do it...as easily as a game. He toyed with the temptation, to deceive her; to manipulate her. He could transform himself to appear as the man that occupied her mind; to become Eleran; the gentle, loving Eleran she wanted. The Eleran she wanted to forgive. He could make love to her, kiss her, and take on the guise of the man with the shining black hair who captivated her so. To heal her somehow by bringing the man she loved and not the one who pursued her now. The desire to do so was so powerful, the Drathar had to withdraw.

He slid away from her without waking her, and nearly stumbled onto the floor. He stood there for a moment, confused by his feelings. There was some power there, in the attraction, it had to be, for in his two hundred years never once did he succumb to the wiles of any woman as he had with her. He'd never wanted anyone so badly. He straightened himself, and carefully readjusted the state of his clothing until he was tidy and in order again.

He then sat down in the chair and faced forward, mouthing the words of concentration and meditation that he used to hone his powers. By the time morning came 'round, he was back to himself. Avria awoke, and turned to look at him, stiff and stoic in his chair by the bed, his eyes hard and forward. When Avria tried to take his hand, he simply let it fall slack on his leg. Avria's brow furrowed and she first looked confused. She then she glowered. The servant girl appeared with a decanter of hot water and deposited it on the side of the bath-tub. She left to fetch some more. Avria rose wordlessly and padded into the bathing chamber, and with no consideration for her companion, or likely too much consideration of him, she lifted her night gown off of her body and climbed into the tub. The Drathar was immediately aware of not only her body, but the bruises and scrapes that still marked it.

She knelt down and poured a little bit of the hot water over herself and bathed right before him. The Drathar did not turn his eyes away. The servant girl returned several times with urns of heated water and Avria bathed at a leisurely pace, her baleful eyes fixed on the Drathar. He sat in his chair and bore witness to a woman who seemed to be hanging on the precipice. He had no idea what to do.

Avria was pale and despondent. Her silent companion had gone cold on her, and she knew deep down it was probably for the best, but she could not help but feel completely abandoned. She hardly ate. Even the ever-distant Drathar told her she should eat, that she had not only her own welfare to consider. He liked to remind her apparently, that he was without people to care for him and that she was so fortunate. He never left her side, but he had also remained aloof and silent. After touching the person behind the veil, it was difficult for Avria to cope with his silence and distance. It hurt her. She needed comfort, friendship; to be held and to be heard. Her project of transcribing books sat untouched on the desk, and

Avria spent the better part of each day either curled up on the bed or sitting by the window in the chair with her knees drawn up to her chin, lost in her thoughts.

She thought of Eleran. Of his crime against her; of his forceful, willful pursuit. She thought of the man he once was, and she tried to erase the pain he caused her. She tried to think of all of the guidance and caring from figures like Phenmal and Master Gavorre that got her through his vanishing.

The Drathar was in no doubt of Avria's emotional decline. He was at a loss. This was too personal a need, too much to ask of someone whose entire sense of control had been shaken by simply by the nearness of this girl. He watched her as she sat, all day, every day in her chair, or curled in the bed. He listened to her silence, and amused himself by sorting through the memories she wasn't touching; the ones of her childhood, of her brother, of the group of her closest friends, including the now lost Jestin. He observed her memories of playing in the river on a steaming summer day, of idling about on horseback, without saddles, all wearing nothing but short leggings and cool tops—forging across shallow waterways on atop their horses to cool off. She had crisp, untapped memories of hanging about in the deep grass under the sun at Kettle Hill, just talking about nothing while their mounts grazed; tails switching. The Drathar often saw moments like these, moments of what was normality—of what most young people in her world did to occupy their free time and he was envious of her. She was so separated from that part of her now; she could not appreciate the gift of it. He thought it was a terrible shame.

She was dwelling. He could hear it all in her head; the confusion, the memories of her own distress and sadness—her betrayal and her sense of being completely abandoned by everyone who supposedly loved her.

And then he sensed the dangerous thought the moment it appeared; the one where she realized that not everyone who loved her had abandoned her. Not everyone.

The Drathar, who was in the same chair he'd been in for days, rose to his feet and approached Avria. He had no idea what to do, but he had to do something. There was nobody here close to her to guide him.

"That is ridiculous," the Drathar intoned, the hint of disgust coloring his words. Avria was startled from her reverie and she twisted in her chair to glare at him, her brow creased; her chapped lips a heavy frown. Her hair was a frizzy disarray of raven curls, piled into a messy bun on her head. Her nightgown hadn't come off for two days.

"Pardon?"

"To interpret the obsessive, mad pursuit of someone who means only harm to you as something other than what it is; to call it 'caring' or to give him undue credit for being the only one not to abandon you. No matter how alone you feel; do you not see how selfish and self-destructive this thought is? To erase his actions for the sake of feeling loved?" Avria's face blanched and she became furious.

"Stay out of my head!" She screamed, her eyes glossing instantly with tears, her fingers gripping the hair at the sides of her head. "Stay out of my head you bloody savage, how dare you?" She leapt to her feet, sobbing. She stalked to the dresser, and she pulled on her riding breeches and overskirt, throwing her nightgown to the floor and pulling on a thick woolen tunic directly over her bare skin. Still weeping, she pulled on her boots and ran for the door. "Get away from me!" she cried, slamming it in front of him. The Drathar followed at leisure, sure by the misdirection in her head that she would lose herself in the labyrinthine passages of this old place.

True to form, she did get lost. She took the wrong stairwell and the wrong landing, and ended up in a place where the Drathar easily found her. She entered a dark library of low ceilings and shelves that seemed to be holding up the entire room. There was row upon row of them, all filled to capacity with books, paper stacks, scrolls and even jars containing odd looking things suspended in strange fluids. She came to a halt, and frowned through her snot and tears.

The Drathar simply moved from one place to where she was. His transition there was a smooth, subtle thing; his form disappeared from one place in a curling cloud of black smoke, and he reappeared directly in her path the same way. The sight of him appearing invoked her wrath, and she attacked him.

"Get away!" she shrieked, tears still flowing. She grappled at his clothing and in a desperate move, she tore away his veil. The Drathar immediately clamped his eyes shut even in the dimness of the library, and took a step back from the glare of the distant window light. Avria had no notion of the danger she'd subjected herself to by exposing his eyes. She ran away sobbing. Blind, the Drathar used his powers to guide him. The unrest created by Avria's outburst had stirred the core. The sisters were responding at last to her pain.

He found Avria again kneeling on the floor of an old conservatory. Avria had seen part of it on her arrival on the dragon, a faceted glass jewel embedded in the back of the large building. Once upon a time, this construct had surely been impressive. Now it was a sorrowful-looking place. Its age and state of disrepair gave it a sagging, derelict feel. Piles of snow had accumulated on the glass roof. Many panes were cracked, and all of them had years of accumulated dirt etched on the surface, making what should have been a bright, white snowy day seem yellowed and tainted. The wild-growth of plants in the conservatory were osteal, wretched and spare; growing crooked, or spindly, with tendrils and vines shooting out from the rusted, crumbling containers. There was the sign of someone tending to the greenery, but they were doing a dreadful job of it.

Avria had run in and was blinded by the sudden glare of dirty light cast in from the snowy panes. She fell to her knees, shielding her tearful eyes with her arm and wept. She shrugged off the hands that touched her shoulder, only to be grasped by another set of hands and then another. A circle of black wool rustled about her trembling form. Pale faces surrounded her. Small, reassuring whispers calmed her hysterics, and she found herself being lifted off of her feet, the hard chest of her insensitive, cruel guard coming against her side. He hoisted her into his arms and cradled her. The sisters, who continued to appear in whispers of black smoke, gathered around them. Hands fell upon her like gentle snow while the Drathar carried her in his iron-hard arms. His face was exposed, his eyes pinched tightly closed, his skin showing signs of burns from the cold light. A sister draped her shawl around his beautiful, hard stone face and shielded him from the day as the rest of the sisters soothed Avria's pain.

"Fair and Ancient Gods, she is not alone," someone whispered in sheer wonder.

"No, indeed; have you ever touched such power?" another agreed.

"Shh," the Drathar hushed from beneath his facial covering. The sisters obeyed, their whispers of wonder subsided.

"I will tell the Mother Superior," someone said in a rich, velvety voice. "Return her to her chambers. Others will follow." Drathar nodded, and left the conservatory with Avria in his arms. She did not feel or sense the transition except to see the searing dirty light suddenly trade itself into the cave-like darkness of her assigned sitting room. The room then accepted three more forms of concerned sisters. Candles were lit.

"You did not tell us she was this far gone," one of them chastised the Drathar.

"It is not my task to assess her state; I am here to protect her. It's your job to care for her emotional wellbeing," he grunted. "Not a single one of you has visited..."

"We have been distracted by some unrest in some of the local villages. They are acting against those that are not entirely human or that bear powers," the sister explained. "We have been tasked with instilling peace. We cannot leave this place en masse without shrinking her protection in the core, so we must spread our efforts to calm the locals."

The Drathar hadn't been paying attention to his sisters' thoughts or their activities. He'd been too preoccupied with Avria to notice. "It is good you roused her ire when you did. She was in a dark place. You might not have tasked yourself with her emotional wellbeing but you surely must be aware of it on some level to have interceded when you did."

"Stop talking about me like I'm not here," Avria muttered through her tears, her runny nose making all her words sound staccato and child-like. She pushed the hands away as the sisters began to undress her.

"A hot bath will do you good. I've ordered to have the whole tub filled. Wouldn't that be nice?"

"Stop talking to me like I'm an idiot child..." Avria mumbled. She did however cease interfering with the sisters' efforts to disrobe her. The strange, seemingly useless valve on the side of the tub was opened, and hot water began to spill into it from mysterious origins. The water was fresh and scented, the tub filled quickly. She wondered if it was so simple to make the valve actually work, why they bothered making that poor servant girl carry urn after urn of hot water to her. She'd toyed with the strange metal valve before and nothing had come out. Now it was gushing like a spring, spilling steaming hot water into the marble basin. Avria was lowered in by the Drathar, who soaked his arms in doing so. He then shook his arms dry and pulled the veil from his pocket where he'd stuffed it after retrieving it from the floor of the library. He stood aside to cover his face.

Avria's anger was blunted. She sniffed and sat in the hot, soothing water while hands lifted her arms and washed away the last few days. She looked past the faces around her, she hardly heard their soft humming; she was somewhere else for a long moment. Her thoughts coalesced and she seemed to startle with realization.

"What did that sister mean I am not alone? Is he here?"

"No, he has not arrived yet. But he will soon. The core can feel his approach." Avria looked at the nearest face, and frowned.

"Then what did you mean?" She thought back to when the Drathar was worried about her refusal to eat—to what he had said to her. The lack of response provoked her.

"You should wait until the Mother Superior arrives and discuss it with her."

"I am with child, aren't I?" she asked. "I am with child and it's Eleran's child because it has great power." The sisters exchanged glances and two of them rose and vanished. The other one remained, rising to fetch a towel. She put it on the broad ledge of the marble tub.

"This is for when you are finished. You should soak for a while, it will do you good." In the wake of her exit, she left a whorl of inky mist. The Drathar was back in his chair, his face invisible behind his veil.

"You know, you answer me," Avria twisted in the tub, and clutched the ledge, her hair wet and clinging to her face. He stirred, the surface of his facial veil facing her.

"You are. It is a power I have never felt before."

"He told me so, you know. Long ago. He told me that a child of magic could only be born of two halves of the same soul," she whispered. "He told that when we shared our very first kiss." She twisted herself back onto her bum and leaned onto the side of the tub, propping up her knees.

"The Zsathri and their Hevra have always been infuriatingly prosaic in their interpretation of things; half souls, whole souls, those are all legends created by the Hevra—story-tellers all. The immortal beings are mad because they have lived unimaginably long lives. They were present before the first historical records. They are not mad because their souls are too great for their vessels. That is nonsense. It is well known by almost all magic bearers that power is passed through the blood. You were already imbued with power, Avria, from the moment you were born. Whether it manifests itself or not during your life, you have always possessed it. It was likely passed down from your mother. Her bloodline comes from a likely source. I'm afraid your father's line is ordinary."

"My father is not ordinary," Avria snapped defensively. "He is brilliant." The Drathar remained silent. She paused, and her irritation faded to curiosity. "So my mother could be a bearer?"

"Very likely. And she passed it onto you. Some people are born with power but it never quite surfaces or makes itself useable to them in a practical way. They would have more passive manifestations. But if your power is great, your child's power is great; and it is overt, for we can all feel it; those of us that possess the gift. So early in the formation of the child and the power of the tiny infant is already quite marked. If it were hidden power, like yours, like your mother's, we would not have sensed it." Avria's hand slid down to her tummy and she frowned. What would Offrin think of this child inside her; this product of Eleran's aggression? Would he love it? Hate it? Fear it? She swallowed and sank down into the water until it reached her lips. She remained there until the bath became tepid.

CHAPTER TWELVE – GRAVE MATTERS

Tinna did not take a coach. The coaches were consigned to the material goods and dogs, and were slowly making their way north, past the busy city of Loshan, around the great lake, following the ancient roads. Tinna was not patient for that sort of travel any more, not when she had Ledroran, for she could not turn down any chance to spend time with her old friend.

The massive dragon's crown shield could cover a small cottage and no longer had any large side openings, so it was like standing in a cave of sorts, with the view of the back and pumping wings. The cold snow blew like a funnel outside the shelter creating a dizzying tunnel effect she could scarce tear her eyes from. The dragon's body heat and the block of the wind made it comfortable enough for her to carry Istvan with her, swaddled in layers upon layers of warm coverings.

Taneth was still at Adremateen. Tinna worried that perhaps he was secretly angry about her decision to involve Phenmal in their marriage. She was careful however, to let him be the final deciding vote. She would not force it on him; she would be willing to let Phenmal remain as he was; a close family friend, if Taneth had decided against it. She guaranteed him she would not hold it against him, or make him feel bad for expecting a traditional marriage with his wife. She gave her husband the chance to tell her he did not like this idea. She knew it was selfish and she knew it was asking something difficult to a man she had been married to exclusively for twenty years.

There was no history of rifts; no cracks or fissures in their relationship to excuse her desire for Phenmal. They did not fight to speak of, except for silly things. Their relationship was harmonious most of the time. They spent a lot of time in different places these days; Taneth with his projects building and rebuilding; academies, archives, dragon rookeries. She was at Klatna, or embroiled in some political ridiculousness or other. Their marriage was not falling apart, it was... broadening.

Each one acknowledged these things during their long, forthright discussion of the matter. They were able to withstand the distances, the time apart as if it was not a matter to consider. They reunited into the natural rhythm of their lives and were happy when they were together—rare as it was. They still remained vastly passionate in their lovemaking. None of that would change, and as long as it didn't, Taneth did not seem to mind. Phenmal had been such a fixture in their lives, from the moment he first visited Thamatoc to find them after the burnings, and it was just natural to have him there, part of their most intimate discussions, mediating their disagreements sometimes.

Taneth had always been open minded and pragmatic. He saw this as adding a support system he regretted that he wasn't able to provide, and he did genuinely love Phenmal. There was one stipulation only; "Never the three of us", he told her. Tinna laughed and agreed wholeheartedly. Phenmal was definitely more dominant than Taneth. It was a refreshing change.

Of course, due to her close relationship with Ledroran, Tinna naturally discussed these things with him on this leisurely flight. She rarely had a chance to talk to him, except through a third-party summoner, which was like speaking through an interpreter; Summoners were naturally connected to the conduits through which Dragons spoke to one another, and could tap into them to relay messages.

Ledroran's size made him less bothered by the cold winter air. Because he loved Tinna, and enjoyed time with her, he took his time, his wings pumping slowly, often just gliding; his impossible size slipping through the crisp air with a languid grace.

Suffice it to say, AiTinna (he was the only one of Tinna's friends who used her traditional Thran appellation any more, and often, he dropped it these days), if I were fortunate as to be transformed into the tiny form of a man, so I could stand beside you on two gangly pink legs, I would hope you would make me a husband as well, he said, the words vibrating through his whole skull and shield, the bass reaching her bones.

"I'm not sure about the pink legs..." she shouted back. The dragon snorted.

I am no judge of beauty by human standards, I can sort of see it in some way; much in the same way an Araki can admire the beauty in one of his horses. Tinna laughed loudly and shook her head. I can see the beauty in a human or a similar creature—but to look at you is not what makes me love you. I believe I best qualify as your true love, for I love you entirely for who you are. I believe if I could somehow lift your soul out and put it in a comely lady dragon, I would surely be the happiest dragon alive.

"Oh, Ledroran, you're making me blush," she intoned loudly.

That, I very much doubt, he said with good humor. She laughed again. The dragon paused for a while, sighing deeply and pumping his wings to gain a bit of altitude so he could glide again. When he'd reached his desired spot in the sky, and let his wings ride the winds, the membranes of skin holding them aloft trembled on the hard gusts of air. His body remained perfectly still and level. He seemed to ponder things for a while, taking in all the things Tinna had told him in the last few hours.

Allow me to assuage your concerns, my dearest, sweetest Lady. You feel selfish for asking Taneth to share you with another man. Truth be told, my love, is that over the past twenty years, you have forced your husband to share you with countless things, Phenmal aside; like your rise to power for one; your relationship with me and with my kind; your part in the end of the burnings, your importance to the people of Thamatoc and the Araki. Of all the things that pull you from Taneth, there is at least one that he can grasp and see and in some essence, control. At least Phenmal is a known quantity; an actual, malleable, accountable thing. The others things are mostly unseen competitors and much bigger threats to your relationship than someone who's always been there—someone he already knows like a brother.

Taneth, of what I've learned of the squirrely fellow, is a man in search of rationality and fact. He finds that by insuring he knows as much as he can about his world, he can gain control over it to some degree. If he finds explanations for the inexplicable, he gives himself power over it. Phenmal, of all the elements that draw you away from him, is the easiest one to identify and decipher. He is no threat. I believe, If Taneth is angry at you about anything, if at all, it is how your life has separated so much from what it was when you were both younger, and you'd just met. He doesn't fear that Phenmal will take you away, Tinna. He probably fears that your life will diverge from his because you have become so important. How could he keep up?

"My goodness, dragon, who knew you were so insightful?" Tinna's eyes watched the swirling tunnel of snow beyond the arched opening. The wind did not pull hard. If he'd been moving faster, it might, but it was oddly comfortable inside his shield.

You did. You've always known. Tinna sighed and nodded, checking on her son, who slept comfortably in his bassinette, wedged against the warmth of Ledroran's head. She gazed down at him, and touched his warm, flushed cheeks.

Besides, what changes? A third person in your marriage; well, that's been going on for years. You share your bed with him? Seems a minor adjustment. As long as Taneth is not eventually excluded from those privileges and set aside, i can't imagine he has much to lose.

Tinna laughed a bit uncomfortably, unsure how to respond to the dragon talking about intimate subjects. She finally said in a loud voice:

"I am glad I have such a friend who would help me justify such a thing." The dragon laughed in the way dragons do, a snorting wheeze that the wind mostly carried away.

You are to be Queen are you not? You can do whatever you like, and the Araki people will follow suit, because you have proven to them you are their leader. The Adrei respect you, even your own people respect you. I'll wager, if you showed up at Miranne with a harem of men, nobody would even bat an eye.

All this proves to me is that you are more dragon than anything else, my lovely Tinna. Because we dragons all have multiple mates throughout our lives. We are liberal-thinkers, I suppose, like you.

Tinna's laughter rang out in delight at the image her friend Ledroran painted. She reached down and patted the base of his skull. How she adored this dragon.

"Oh, Ledroran, you make me laugh. You are such a good friend."

Likewise my precious Queen. He banked a bit and then leveled out. *I recommend you huddle in; we're about to hit a rough patch of air. It will be impossible to hear you until we are through it.* Tinna sat down and scooted back against his head, wrapping herself up in her blankets, and snugging herself against the baby's bassinette. The dragon's wings hit the first streams of turbulent air and pitched rather powerfully. The air gusted in from behind, and threw her hair about. A few times, the dragon fell by several feet, lifting Tinna off of his neck. She put her hand up and braced herself on the top of the shield, and held Istvan tightly to her. For a moment there was a lull in the turbulence.

634

Have you heard of the goings on in the northerly and westerly countries? I've heard of some skirmishes where towns and villages are casting out the gypsies and non-humans. A group of Adrei soldiers riding back from training west of Levra were pelted with rocks.

"No, I did not know this, Ledroran," Tinna said in shock.

I was just informed of this by my daughter as she made her way here from the coastal cliffs of our home. There seems to be some issues rising up with the remaining human communities. It looks like the High Throne has been busy undermining your rule already. It doesn't bode well, and I wonder how long before it erupts into something serious. Hayna tells me there are traveling troubadours sent out to tell the human cities tales of you in a negative light; to paint you as darkly as the Thran themselves, and to make it seem like you are no more than another, less evident attempt at an invasion.

"Gods..." The air grew rocky again and the dragon concentrated on that for a while, until he hit a smoother patch.

Your rule will prove itself to them. They have nothing to fear.

"I know that, you know that; but if the King has sent out hordes of tale tellers to rouse up the human communities, I'm not sure what I can do."

Speak to him I suppose, is the first course of action. Perhaps this can all be turned around before it is too late. Tinna could not believe what she was hearing. Was it really getting that bad out there? Everything looked so peaceful from high up. The sky became turbulent again and she felt the whole dragon lurch violently.

"How far do we have to go?"

Not far, Tinna. Another hour perhaps. She held on, hoping this bad air didn't accompany them the rest of the way.

The Keepers had sent a welcoming party to receive Tinna upon her arrival. She was shaken from the last hour of the flight, and in spite of her enjoyment of the special time with Ledroran, she was actually delighted to feel firm ground beneath her feet and she needed more information on what Ledroran had shared. She climbed down with the baby, and found two gentlemen awaiting her. Both of them bowed deeply at the sight of her and waited patiently as she moved towards Ledroran's eye so she could lay her hand on his cheek-plate and bid him farewell for now. Her residence at Miranne did offer her one advantage that she could not rebuke, and that was she would be able to see Ledroran more often. It was a better place for large dragons to land.

The gentlemen, as most humans were, seemed still a bit leery of the great beasts. Their memories were long, of the time when dragons had burned and destroyed the better part of their civilization, leaving humanity to languish against the growing power of the other races. There was much to resent; however Tinna had managed to help the dragons redeem themselves in some ways by involving them in the one day war to save Oromoii from invasion.

They stepped back warily when the massive creature lumbered over the thick curtain wall to find space to take flight again. Tinna called farewell to him and watched his form recede into the sky.

The representatives of the Keepers had been careful to remind these gentlemen, who introduced themselves to Tinna as ministers that they would be best served if they welcomed Tinna with open arms. And they did.

"Of course it's not quite... uh, considerate to the King to put you at residence in the palace proper, quite yet," one of the gentlemen declared, "however for now, we have secured you some lodgings at the Vedri House, which is more than suitable for someone of your stature; at least as a temporary residence." The one who spoke was a tall, lanky, boyish figure with thick sideburns that melded into a manicured beard. He wore fine garments, Taneth and Phenmal had pieces much like them for formal events, and over those, he wore a deep scarlet open robe, as did his companion. These were apparently the ministerial robes. The one on his friend had more intricate decoration in gold cording woven along the front panels and tall collar, giving Tinna the notion that the young fellow was junior to the other. "I am Minister Belval and this is Minister Dranai," the young man said. Tinna bowed her head to both, and heaved her son's bassinette onto her hip. She began to walk beside them as they led the way across the spacious bailey facing the palace.

"I confess, Ashru," the elder Minister Dranai intoned, "that I have heard much of your exploits already. Not simply by the talk in general that has been prolific since the war, but from a more direct source; a mutual acquaintance. The Duke of Zadrudas, in particular."

"Ah, Adracoor," Tinna smiled. She last saw him at Avria's wedding. The undercurrent of guilt in Tinna's head became heavier for a moment, as she thought of Avria, and she thought of Offrin. She frowned, and shook her head, trying to come back to the conversation. She'd become good at compartmentalizing things in the past years of her life; of taking all her worries about personal matters and putting them aside in a mental box to examine later, after she'd contended with pressing issues of great importance. With a slightly forced smile, she replied; "He is a good friend."

"His lady in particular, the Duchess Rhoa is as well."

"That she is," Tinna could not hide her smirk, the idea of Rhoa with such a title made her want to laugh out loud. No matter how many years had passed and no matter how much Rhoa had changed, Tinna always saw her as the gawky, silly, whining girl she first knew. The one who complained constantly, the one who fell in love with an invisible creature. It was difficult to envision her afterwards, a quiet, serious, grieving young mother whose perspective had lost its vibrancy and colour and whose soul seemed trapped and lost somewhere else part of the time. But a little part of the old Rhoa returned during the war, when she met her Duke; a grizzled, scarred, hideous man and Rhoa fell in love that day. She needed only a quick thought to decide to return to Zadrudas with him, and they were inseparable since. He called her his little red devil.

Adracoor was a rough character these days, but what she heard from him and from others that once upon a time, he was a part of the royal family, and quite the dandy. She knew what had changed him into the gruff warrior today and his face still bore the heavy scars of his suffering. Rhoa had never seen his days as a fop. She'd only known the hardened, rough-edged soul who could not believe any woman could ever love him with a face like his. His visage was riddled with terrible bad scarring and he was missing an eye. "I do hope to see them," Tinna smiled, her heart warming. She missed Rhoa.

"Oh, you most certainly will, most shortly. They await you at the Vedri house. The Duchess is most eager to see you again. They made the trip from the great isle the moment they got word you were confirmed to arrive her at Miranne."

"That's wonderful," Tinna exclaimed. They walked in silence for a while, still slowly making their way across the vast, empty cobbled bailey to one of the less prominent edifices surrounding this massive square. Istvan seemed to be getting heavier by the step. She wanted to rest. The ministers were kind enough to carry her other bags. She sighed and kept walking.

"I must say, my Lady, that I take it as a great recommendation that you have such respect from my old friend, Adracoor. He is an honorable and brave man."

"I know. I've seen his bravery first-hand."

"Yes, we all know the tale," the Minister laughed heartily, and paused, puffing out his chest and lifting his finger. "He tells it often;

of how he stood near the rise, watching the Thran army thunder towards his scant army. He'd already resigned himself to dying an honorable death in battle. He told of how your army all but materialized from behind him, and poured through his front line and flattened the Thran before his men could reach them. He recounted that at your command; dragons rained from the sky and burned the archery lines to a crisp."

"It didn't quite happen that way," Tinna chuckled. "His men fought among the Araki cavalry as bravely as any other. We certainly did not materialize. We nearly arrived too late. Thankfully the dragons were watching from above; veiled under cover of cloud, and urged us to move quickly. We flattened the camp as we rode through it, and came over the hill just in time to see the armies about to collide. Had we delayed only a few moments, there would have been many more losses on our side.

"And the dragons, well, they were there and they were many, but the ground dragons were as deadly as their flying brethren. The sky borne dragons were limited in what they could do. They could not bathe the melee in flames without harming their allies, so they focused on the lines of archers and also the berzerkers. Their columns of fire caused great chaos on the Thran side of the valley. Their infamous organized ranks and their time-tested strategies went up in flames."

"It is your intimate knowledge of those strategies that saved us, I am sure," he replied proudly. Tinna was highly animated as she spoke of the battle. It was a memory she cherished. No matter how reluctant she had been to lead the army that day, she was proud of how powerful a throttling they'd given to the Thran; an people whose entire culture revolved around war. It had humbled the arrogant women so tremendously; they'd offered Tinna their fealty in the end. She could see the appreciative smile on the Minister's face.

No matter how much she resisted what the Keepers were doing to her, she could not deny the satisfaction of knowing that she brought peace to this world twice, reunited the polarized races, and gave people like Adracoor and Dranai a second chance. She knew not all humans would look at her with the same reverence, but she would have to endure that. Humanity was still flailing for a foothold among the races again; and their best bet was not the leadership of their present King, who existed for self-indulgence alone. Because the Humans had become the minority of the races, it was logical that the dominant group's representative take the throne. Tinna was of both worlds. She was born human and gypsy, but now lived as an Araki.

She represented all. Their best choice was her. She knew this. It was the only reason why she didn't fight Phenmal more when he came to tell her to go to Miranne.

The group got underway again. "Tell me ministers, my companion and friend Ledroran mentioned some rather disturbing things to me today. He tells me the High King has sent out an army of people to misinform the human settlements about me and the people I represent. I understand human groups have been acting out, granted, in rather benign ways right now, against the Araki and the Adrei. Do the dragons have something to fear as well? Has the goodwill from the war somehow been undermined?" She paused and hiked the child up onto her hip. The ministers looked strained the moment she brought it up and they exchanged a worried look before the elder minister replied.

"Yes, there have been some rather disturbing actions made by the High King in his effort to hold onto power. His methods have been less than savory, and many in the ministry have been vocal about it. But since the war, the High King has been incensed by the improving attitude towards the dragons. He is not about to accept that humanity has become a minority. When he was crowned, what many do not know is that one of his first statements was one where he promised to put things back where they ought to be." he muttered. "We weren't sure what that meant, but when the first messages of the Keepers arrived declaring the appointment of a new High Ruler and demanding he step down, he redoubled his efforts to stop them by any means necessary."

"It doesn't mean everyone supports him by any means," the younger minister added almost frenetically, waving his hand. "Almost all viceroys support you; including the most difficult man, the Viceroy of Gheraine. Almost the entire ministry is in support of you; we all know what happened at Chrotrioth, we all know who you are. But the High King is a young and obstinate boy, who was handed the crown far sooner than he should have gotten it. His father was tired, and perhaps he already knew a new bloodline would be appointed soon anyway."

"I should be concerned then, that humanity might not be receptive of me now as their leader?"

"I don't know yet, Ashru, I speak to you in all honesty. I cannot speak for everyone anymore. Things have been changing so rapidly. But you can be assured that all of us that support your ascension to the High Throne will be working as hard as possible to smooth everything out and settle any misgivings the people we represent may have," Minister Belval assured her. Dranai nodded. Istvan woke up at last and started fussing. They made their way the rest of the distance to the house.

Tinna was never more relieved to see Rhoa appear at the door of this particular building; looking a contradiction in a gown so fine with her freckled nose and strawberry blonde hair. She looked divine, Tinna had to admit it. But far more importantly, she looked so happy. Finally. It took a moment for Tinna to realize she was not only glowing with happiness, but there was a rather telltale little lump forming underneath her flowing, columnar gown; it was still small, but it was there nonetheless. Rhoa was thoughtful enough to rush up and to take the crying toddler from her arms before even uttering her first word of greeting. Her eyes smiled and she kissed Tinna's cheek, and took her hand.

"Gods it's good to see you. You ground me. You remind me where I came from. Come, Adracoor is so excited to see you and we've had every fireplace stoked so it's warm and cozy. Little Ishty here can toddle about, I brought him some new toys and we can catch up," she rattled. "We also poured out some stiff apple brandy that the Keepers sent to you as a welcoming gift. They sent several cases!"

"Ah, they also bestowed some of the rare and delicious libation upon our ministry as well. Everyone took a bottle home last night!" Belval declared. Tinna smiled, she did like apple brandy. She wondered how the Keepers knew this, but then she realized that was a silly question. They seemed to know everything.

"When did this happen?" Tinna asked, pointing to Rhoa's little baby bump. Rhoa glanced down and blushed. She was only about two years Tinna's junior and like Tinna, she was having a second child later in life. Drashun would be shocked, Tinna thought. Avria was thrilled herself when she found out about the arrival of a new baby sibling.

"I realized I was with child shortly after the wedding. It was actually the formation of this lump that clued me in. I haven't had any of the other symptoms."

"Congratulations, Rhoa," Tinna smiled. Her joy was subdued and Rhoa noticed it.

"Is everything alright Tinna?" Rhoa asked, furrowing her brow and tilting her head. She hiked the child more snugly onto her hip and gazed at her dearest friend. Tinna, relieved of her burden, gestured for Rhoa to go inside and then followed with ease, nearly forgetting the two ministers who lugged her bags behind her.

They all entered the huge formal parlor and the ministers set the items down on the floor. The men politely took their leave with deep respectful bows to Tinna, and then wandered off to find the Duke, who was somewhere else in the house.

Tinna knew Rhoa's exuberance would be extinguished when Tinna would sit down, and in earnest, tell her what transpired since the wedding. She did not look forward to discussing it or bringing down Rhoa's happiness.

Rhoa's expression of shock and incredulity was one Tinna would have to work hard to forget. Rhoa's eyes glassed up and she pressed her hand to her stomach, which was swelling with the Duke's child. All she could do was croak out Avria's name before submitting to a flurry of sobs and hunching forward into them, her shoulders shaking. Her sobs were heard by her husband, who was in the adjacent room smoking from his pipe and talking to the ministers, and he appeared, the grizzled bear, his brow creased in concern. He knelt beside his wife, looking at Tinna in both confusion and accusation.

"What have you told her to upset her so?" he growled. Tinna hugged Istvan closer to her and opened her mouth to speak but Rhoa shook her head and accepted the handkerchief he offered her. She dabbed her eyes delicately, which still seemed so strange to Tinna, and then clasped her husband's hand.

"Avria's been violated," she blurted, "by her mage."

"What?" Tinna had to explain it all over again, and the pain of it was taking its toll. Rhoa rose and took the child again and rocked him as if he required comforting for this unsettling news. Tinna sat back and sighed shakily.

"And now you're here. As it always is—timely and convenient for everyone but you and yours," Rhoa said acidly. "Bloody Keepers," she finished with a snarl. She bounced the baby almost too hard in her frustrated state. Adracoor sat, his scarred face fallen and distant, trying to process what had happened to the girl Rhoa called her niece.

Tinna studied her old friend Rhoa. She had grown leaner in the last year. The gowns of the north suited her, but her freckled skin and reddish hair just seemed so un-duchess like. Her mannerisms were also still casual and easygoing as well. Tinna had managed to teach herself some refinement in the past two years, knowing it was necessary to deal with the politicians and advisors she often saw down at Klatna. Rhoa didn't have any political obligations to speak of; she was the wife of a Duke who no longer took interest in the entitlements of his rank. He ruled over his little Duchy isle country of Zadrudas in a much more connected manner than he had before the burnings. He knew his people, he cared for them, and they embraced his commoner wife with great aplomb, bringing him even closer to them. It wasn't unheard of nowadays to find him out in the field in the autumn, forking hay into the drays alongside the farmers. Tinna had heard lots of anecdotes that painted him as a man of the people. He was beloved.

Rhoa's husband had no designs on the throne or any more responsibility than he already had. His connection to the present King, a young nephew of his was tenuous at best. He was finished with the sedentary and indulgent ways of the old nobles and sovereigns. He'd seen too much, suffered too much to ignore his responsibility to his people. He was with Tinna now, only too glad to promise his loyalty to a Queen who stood to rule with fairness; and certainly for saving the rest of humanity from extinction by dragons.

In the past two years, Rhoa's family had become his. Thamatoc and its people, the greater people of Arak, who had come out in force to stop an invasion and to rescue the small human force that had been sent to stop it, they were his people as much as the Zadrudans were. He was incensed by the news of the beautiful Avria so egregiously violated. He turned and looked at Tinna. She looked exhausted and drawn. He thought perhaps few people had noticed her weariness, including his angered wife. He walked to her and looked down from his lofty height. Tinna found his one good eye so soulful and sweet, the expression of concern plain on his ruined face. He picked up the glass Rhoa had poured for her and gave it to her. It was a rich amber-colored brandy with the pungent aroma of apples emanating from the glass. Smelling it brought her to the lingering golden days of early autumn. Tinna drank it down in three swallows and then handed it back to Adracoor who raised his brows at her.

"You should rest," he recommended. Rhoa turned from her absent gaze out the window and nodded in agreement.

"I have to send a letter to Gavorre and Offrin, letting them know where we are and where things stand. I'm not even sure where they are, I'm hoping they'll be back at Thamat..."

"Tinna, you should rest," he said more forcefully. He offered his hand and pulled her to her feet.

"It's barely into the late afternoon..."

"Go sleep, you look exhausted. Red will take care of the little one." Tinna glanced at Rhoa and smirked feebly at her.

Rhoa laughed and shook her head.

"Go on, I'll have a servant show you where your apartments are," some shadow-like figures had already scooped up Tinna's bags and ferretted them away somewhere. She'd scarce seen a glimpse of them as they flitted about the place, but they were there; and evidence of it appeared in the form of a young man of about eighteen wearing some fine footmen's clothes who came when Adracoor pulled the cord.

He bowed deeply to Tinna, his eyes wide and curious about her. "Take the Ashru to her apartments. The child will remain here with us. See to it she gets something warm to eat before she retires," Adracoor instructed him. The boy nodded and backed out of the room, and gestured silently for Tinna to follow.

She climbed the stairs at his heels, feeling all of a sudden the weight of everything that had happened, and where things were. Her life was changing in so many ways. She was thankful for Adracoor, and Red, and for Ledroran, Phenmal and Taneth who were always at her side when she needed them. She missed Hanru and the dogs but most of all, she missed Avria's bright face. With a hard swallow she crested the first set of stairs and followed the boy down a long corridor. The dogs would be arriving with the rest of her things. She'd barely paid them any heed of late, and thought of Reega and her arthritic hips. For some reason that thought put her over the edge, and she started to cry. The boy remained tightlipped and uncomfortable as he led the sniffing Tinna down to her apartments. He pushed open the double doors to the palatial space within, and then bowed shortly.

"Evra will help you from here," he said. "I will see to it that some dinner is started for you." He ducked out and closed the door behind him. Hunched by the elegant fireplace was a slip of a girl who looked like Rhoa when she was seventeen; awkward and wide-eyed. She straightened and curtsied to Tinna

"My lady," she said. Tinna frowned. She did not want to be anyone's lady. With a sigh, she told the girl she wished to retire for the evening. The girl assisted Tinna into her night clothes and stayed to finish unpacking her belongings while the exhausted mistress drifted off to sleep in the center of the frigate of a bed, as if marooned on an isle alone.

CHAPTER THIRTEEN – ASSASSIN

It had been a long time since Tinna felt that shiver of wrongness. The tiny hairs on the back of her neck rose up and a frisson washed over her skin, bristling into goose bumps. Instinctively her hand slid soundlessly underneath her pillow. She was gratified to feel the familiar shape of the hilt of her poignard slipping comfortably and neatly into the palm of her hand, but her mind was instantly ablaze and she could barely think around it. The little knife never left her side; it traveled with her tucked into its little scabbard underneath her skirts in reach of her open pocket, and at night it rested underneath her pillow. This was a remnant of her assassin days and it wasn't going to go away.

She could hear the short, quick breaths of her baby son sleeping in his cradle at the foot of her bed, which she was able to make out as her instincts kicked in. She shut out the sound of her own heart and the rush of her own blood in her ears. She made an effort to relax away the tenseness this sense had created, to regulate her breathing and to appear at all costs, asleep. But her senses focused on the room around her. With her ears and her mind's eye, she listened.

She heard the breathing and she could tell where it was located in the room. She took a deep breath and rolled over, making a contrived sound of sleepiness as she turned. She turned her back to her intruder and then relaxed herself out, bringing her breathing back to the heavy, languid breaths of sleep while her hand tightened around the knife underneath her head. With nary a whisper the radiant heat of the figure closed in on her, her arsenal of senses focused on every little sound the person made. They approached warily, but also a tad recklessly. She wasn't impressed with their stealth by any means. This was not a good assassin. This person also smelled quite distinctive—there was nothing familiar in their subtle scent. This was a stranger.

She clearly heard the sound of metal being drawn ever-so-carefully from a hard leather sheath. As soon as her mind confirmed that this was the case, something else seemed to take over. She moved imperceptibly to pull her knife down in front of her without giving any clue her body even stirred in the slightest from the observer behind her. In the darkness of the room, she had many advantages over her would-be assassin. She closed her eyes and focused.

With a speed and precision almost impossible to believe, her arm jerked up and the knife was released. A grisly thunk was followed by the stomp and stagger of the person the knife just imbedded itself into; then a faint grunt before the noise of agonizing gagging. Tinna rose at her leisure. She pulled the covers aside and slid her legs off the side of the bed. Barefoot, in her long and elegant nightdress, she circled 'round towards the figure on the floor still writhing.

The darkness was momentarily obliterated by a blinding flare of a fire-twig being cracked in two, the flame flaring up before settling into a steadier yellow burn. She touched it to a lantern and then carried it to her attacker. Stricken and still struggling to breathe, a woman lay on the ground, her hair fanned out on the carpet in skeins of gold. She was wide-eyed and her feet were kicking as her hands wrapped around the hilt of Tinna's poignard, which was firmly embedded in the attacker's throat, the blade's tip protruding out the back of her neck, just left of her spinal cord.

"Hello there," Tinna said in a strange smiling whisper. Tinna's usually warm and sweet eyes were blank and hollow. Her black irises were bottomless and seemed to lack the presence of any light or soul. Her amusement was empty and therefore even more chilling and haunting. She knelt, holding the lantern out in front of her to get a better look at her assailant, sweeping her boundless gaze over the face of her attacker. The wide, frightened, light-colored eyes of the golden-haired assassin locked on Tinna and she kicked, struggling to breathe still. Tinna reached down and twisted the knife. The woman's breath gurgled as she aspirated her own blood. "I'm sorry I'm laughing but this is just ridiculous. They send you to kill a Kanindra?" she chuckled again, keeping quiet as not to wake the baby. "Did they tell you that? That I was once a Kanindra? A Thran assassin? I certainly possessed a greater proficiency at this work than you, dear clumsy, noisy girl," Tinna pulled the knife out and immediately put her hand on the wound, holding it shut. The woman gurgled and struggled, in shock; weakening by the second. She was drowning in her own blood.

"It's safe to assume you were sent by beloved King? In some roundabout way of course," Tinna asked. The woman nodded and blinked her pale eyes, coughing up blood that belched out onto her lips, flowed onto her cheek and then trickled onto the rug. "So this is the way it's going to be..." Tinna sighed. With a purse of her lips and a strange little shake of the head, she grasped her poignard and lifted it high above the girl's body. "I'll make it quick," she said with cool assurance, her empty, cold gaze on the girl. Her hand fell; knife and all burying the blade deep into the chest and cutting into the woman's heart. Her struggle ceased almost immediately, except for a few twitches and a final gurgling rattle of air escaping her lungs.

Adracoor stared at the body in disbelief. He'd seen Tinna in action, in a sword fight with a few opponents at once, but he didn't know this tiny woman had the strength and skill to plunge a knife into someone's chest, angled just perfectly so that it avoided the sternum and bury it between two ribs just enough to cut into the woman's heart. He was impressed and a little afraid. When she described how she'd lobbed the knife at the assassin from the position she was in, he had to sit down. All of this happened with such quiet that not even the child was awoken. He was utterly shaken and his skin tingled when he set his eyes on the woman standing barefoot in a night dress and dressing-gown, with blood caked on one of her hands. Rhoa simply raised her brow and nodded at him as if to say: See? I told you so. He still couldn't believe it.

The representatives of the Keepers sent a group of four guards to the site and they were busily managing the scene. Tinna was adamant that she wanted Araki soldiers at Miranne immediately and she commanded that Adracoor see to it the moment morning came. Rhoa was standing nearby, clutching her elbows and looking horrified at the dead woman on Tinna's floor. With perfect timing, they heard the familiar sound of dragon's wings passing overhead and Tinna suspired.

"Phenmal's here." She dropped her hands and then realized they were covered in blood. A strange, evocative expression crossed Tinna's face when she looked down at them. She went into the bathing chamber and poured water into the bowl from the decanter, scrubbing her hands clean.

Adracoor looked at his wife. "You were right; she certainly didn't need too much protection. I knew she was able, but I had no idea she was capable of this."

"She's capable of much more, mark my words," Rhoa said with a bit of a laugh. Tinna returned from the wash chamber. Her expression was peculiar.

"I want to meet this King first thing tomorrow morning," she whispered. "Do you think you can make it happen?" Adracoor shrugged,

"I can try. He isn't being receptive to any of the nobles and ministers who have been supportive of the Ashru," Adracoor replied. He shook his head once more at the body as the guards fumbled with it. He was bewildered that this tiny woman could make so much damage with so little fuss.

Phenmal entered a few moments later, already well-apprised on the goings-on. He'd known the moment he came into range of the house. His hand fell immediately onto Tinna's shoulder and she reached up and clasped his fingers.

"Seems you had a visitor?"

"A laughable one at that. Clumsy and unskilled," Tinna replied in a muted voice. Phenmal nodded. The guards finally were able to roll the assassin onto the sheet and they grasped corners and lifted her up. All that remained were the dark spots where her blood was absorbed into the carpet. "I wonder who she was."

They watched as the guards hefted her through the doorway. Tinna then turned and stood on her tip-toes to plant a kiss on Phenmal's lips. "I'm so glad you're here," she sighed. He kissed her again, more deeply this time. Rhoa gasped audibly and her eyes darted about in utter confusion. Phenmal smirked playfully and even a bit smugly and pulled off his frock coat, hung it on a chair and then reached up and untied his cravat. He tugged the long strip of fabric off his throat and tossed it over the chair, pausing to look into the cradle where Istvan slept peacefully. He then removed his waistcoat, loosened the cuffs of his shirt, undid the loop that closed the stiff collar under his chin and pulled the end of his long shirt out from under his fall-front trousers.

"Come now, you two going to stand about gawking all night or can I get into bed with my wife to be? I've been in the air for hours and I've been looking forward to this all the while," he asked, highly amused by the look of shock on Rhoa's face and the smirk on Adracoor's.

"Tinna, You and Taneth... You're not..."

"Everything's fine. I'll explain tomorrow," Tinna muttered, finding her expression amusing as well.

"Don't you want different a room, Tinna on account of the blood?" Adracoor managed to ask, guiding his wife to the door.

"It's just a little blood. Someone will be up soon enough to scrub it up as best they can. Off you go," she replied. They exited and the door latch closed behind them, Rhoa's shocked voice bombarding her husband with questions and speculation.

Tinna looked at Phenmal and her amusement melted away. "If this is the sort of thing I can look forward to in the next few weeks, I'm not sure I want to do this anymore. It's not that I can't handle the attacks, but I am already emotionally dead. My daughter is alone with a demon, her husband is goodness-knows-where getting into goodness-knows-what sort of trouble with the Adrei mage, Taneth is forgetting about me completely, the humans are starting to rebel against all of us, and you... well I don't have to be a Chaiva to know that you are just thinking about all the wrong things right now. Now the High King is trying to kill me. Wonderful," she threw her arms out.

"Get into bed," Phenmal ordered. She arched her brow dubiously and he marched over to her and put his hands on her waist, lifting her up and tossing her into the mattress. Tinna could not help but smirk to herself in delight as she watched his hungry eyes devour her and his legs kicking off his breeches. He was exactly what she needed, so she abandoned herself to him.

* * * *

Avria stared quietly into nowhere, her hands fallen still from her writing. The Drathar watched her intently with his white eyes. She sat in the general reading room copying books for her father. She'd taken up this task again with aplomb, her mind focused on the idea that she had a life inside her that needed her more than anyone. She'd come out of her shell and started paying attention to things again. She was comforted by the presence of the Drathar. He could feel her emotions towards him and her quiet admiration of him because he reminded her of Eleran on some level. He was happy with even a proxy admiration; for he admired her as well.

He knew her power was latent and passive, but he knew that like her mother, the magnetism was almost unnatural. Not that she was not worthy of great attention, she was a beautiful girl, all of her features seemed to be the epitome of what was desirable in a woman; the plump pink of her lips, the sweep of her brow, the smooth line of her neck, the press of her breasts against the fabric of her gown, the shape of her hips and the way her back curved out into a fine posterior that was impossible not to admire in its beautiful dance when she walked. Her mother was the same way; stamped from almost every man's idea of womanly perfection it seemed. But Avria and her mother also inspired less than rational attractions. Tinna somehow unconsciously kept her power under control, but it was there. Avria's was out of control and it had driven more than one man mad in their attempts to have her.

The Drathar was fairly certain he was genuine in his attraction to her and not under her spell, so to speak; but even if the latter were true, he could not object to it for now. She was filling his days with something he had never tasted before and he wasn't about to just ignore it. He did not feel obsessive about his regard for her. It was more natural than that. He watched her with a fervent affection behind his veil and guarded her with his soul. He was growing to love Avria just like every other man who took a moment to look at her.

"Endrin bloom," she said in a scratchy voice. She'd shaken herself out of her reverie and started writing again. She did this sometimes; she read things aloud to him as she went along. "...found mainly on the western shores of Oromoii and south to Gheraine, this coastal blooming beach-grass can be rendered into a powerful poultice that can draw out infection and pus from festered wounds or abscesses. That is disgusting," she wrinkled her nose. The Drathar was charmed. "Dry in conventional fashion, and then pluck the leaves from the base. In the mortar you should powder them and add a bit of water and the milk of the Hadram weed to bind the powder... Working it will create a malleable, clay-like paste. Make a little patty to cover the affected area and bind to the patient with a bandage. The poultice will absorb a good deal of the infection and pus and will swell with it, so it should be replaced at least within a day or if it has doubled in size," she mumbled, her hand moving.

"Does it even grow anywhere near where you live, Avria?" the Drathar asked. "Your father may have knowledge of it from what you copied, but it does him little good if this endrin bloom is not available to him locally."

"He can send away for some. He has friends everywhere now. And his schools, they educate people from all over. It could serve to..." she trailed off as the Drathar suddenly stood and turned to the

650

window. Her hand stopped moving, eyes wide, mouth partly open. The Drathar's shoulders squared and his chest seemed to widen.

"He's here, isn't he?"

"Something just tried to pierce the core. Either he isn't especially sharp or he is more conniving than I imagined,"

"He's a lot of things, Drathar, but Eleran is not stupid," Avria said. The Drathar's veiled face turned to her and he studied her for a moment.

"Get into your sitting room and close the doors to the archway," he said. A sister appeared out of nowhere, startling Avria. She looked at the Drathar and frowned darkly.

"He's attempting to cast a Kavarnoth spell. Arrogant thing. I'm taking her to the keep; he might get in," she said to the Drathar. The core has shrunk by at least a meter just with those two attacks."

"Where she goes, I go." The sister nodded and took his hand and then Avria's. With that, they were gone.

CHAPTER FOURTEEN – OFFRIN'S RETURN

Offrin and Master Gavorre arrived at Miranne with a small mounted military contingent of Adrei. It was late afternoon and the bevy of mounted soldiers rode into the quiet bailey of the palace towards one of the visiting dignitary barracks. They wore the red and white of the Ashru's army, Tinna's symbols emblazoned on the surcoats. Master Gavorre was not in saddle but riding in a rather small-sized caravan being pulled by two heavy ponies behind the twenty or so riders that entered the square. The contingent of Adrei was mounted mostly on showy black Hale ponies, which looked like small versions of the heavy-breed draught horses that were bred to carry ancient knights and their heavy amours. The large destriers that these ponies were bred to resemble were still used by the Kanreth Knights, a dying breed of mounted warrior that used two tremendously long swords to fight in saddle. These ponies, like the much larger horses they resembled were powerful creatures, raven black with rippling muscles, thick crested necks, feathered hoofs and dense, long manes and tails. Draped in the red and white colours of the army, they were a sight to behold.

Taneth, who'd arrived only the night before, smiled at the sight of them. Tinna's power had given the Adrei many resources to create a sizable military force and to equip themselves with this special breed of pony among other things. They were loyal to Tinna. The Adrei were a group of people made up of throngs of little people born to the Humans; sent as infants to live among their own 'kind' in communities called Auberges scattered about the same forestlands that the Araki occupied. Like the Araki, nobody paid too much heed to these hidden communities, so nobody really understood how large, spread out and powerful the Adrei had grown over the centuries. The secret came out about both peoples after the One Day War, when the Araki made it known just how much of a power they wielded when united.

The Adrei joined the Araki, small perhaps in size, but great in courage and numbers, they rode into battle against the Thran at the side of the Araki riders. Tinna had given them the official distinction of their own identity as a people after the war, and she had honored them and asked them to become a brotherhood of sorts with their Araki friends. The Adrei summarily agreed, and because Master Gavorre had already established a close relationship with the Ashru and her family, he was named as the representative for their people. The marriage of the Adrei man Offrin to the Ashru's daughter only further cemented the bond between these two groups of people.

Tinna had been called out to meet them when they arrived. A runner from the gatehouse had announced their approach. She, Phenmal and Taneth had walked out the main door and met the group as they clattered into the mostly empty square. It was a beautiful day, ice-cold but sunny, the sky a pristine blue with only a smattering of cirrus clouds. The wind was sharp. Tinna wore a large woolen cloak of deep navy blue with a fur-trimmed hood, over one of her more casual gowns from home, made of a soft burgundy wool trimmed in thin bands of gold silk. Offrin rode in front and they met almost smack in the middle of the square. A few ministers were scurrying across the cold space to meet somewhere and here and there a palace compound resident or servant ran quickly against the edge of the icy wind. Tinna held her hood on and waved to Offrin, who drew his mount to a stop.

Offrin looked quite furious for a moment, but his stiffness softened when he saw Tinna's drawn and exhausted face up close. She approached his mounting side, putting her hand on the mount's neck. On his pony, he was taller than Tinna. He was wrapped in a thick cloak of red as were most of the others, their hands bound in fur-lined black gloves. His feathered helm was tied in front of his right knee on his saddle. An emblem on the front of his helm indicated his rank of sergeant. He smiled wanly at her. "I came as you wished."

"I'm sorry for everything Offrin..." Tinna intoned. He lifted his hand to stop her.

"I know why you pushed me out of the way and I can't say I am pleased by the idea, but I understand. But you cannot deny me the right to protect her too. She is my wife, and I love her. But I know now the logic of it," he said, "My place is here." Tinna sighed in relief and stepped forward to embrace him. He leaned down and wrapped his powerful arms around her, hugging the tired woman tightly, his armor and mail ringing pleasantly together with his movements. His pony shifted on his feet. He withdrew, gathering his reins for second, taking a moment to drink in the features that reminded him of Avria so much.

"What's the situation?"

"I'm waiting on our Araki guards to arrive," she said.

"They left only shortly after we did. Lejreth Asnan told me he would be a half day or at most a day behind us. We did not stop for long; for us it was eight days of hard riding from Thamatoc. They should be arriving shortly depending on how long their rest stops were. In the meantime, Temret and I will stand in as watch until your men get here," he said. "Gavorre is sleeping. He picked up a right beast of flu several days ago and was suffering so much that I think he might have over-medicated himself. He's been knocked out most of the journey. This isn't the sort of weather for an elderly fellow to be out and about in."

"He was offered a quick ride on the dragon," Taneth interjected.

"He's like the old man over there," Offrin glanced at Phenmal, "he doesn't care for flying."

"Well, our hosts have provided him with comfortable lodging right next door to our residence. I'll wake him and get him inside," Taneth said. The scholar made his way to the back of the procession and started talking to the man who drove the coach. The assemblage then rumbled off towards the residential buildings.

"You on the other hand are to stay with us," Tinna said. Offrin nodded and dismounted, handing his reins to another of the mounted Adrei soldiers. He sent them off to the barracks with a nod and then followed the three back to the house. They were met by Rhoa and the child at the door. He greeted her with a nod and they all entered the vestibule. He shrugged off his cloak, which a servant immediately took. Rhoa led the group to the parlor, her face also stressed and anxious.

"Did Cennik make it alright?"

"Yes," Tinna told Offrin. He nodded, his face unreadable. "That red-haired woman was asking after him back at Thamatoc. I am tasked by her to relay him a message."

"He wasn't happy to come, but he's settled in nearby. He keeps in constant contact with the dragons these days. I'll direct you to his residence after you've settled in. I'm afraid that red-haired woman is going to be disappointed. He's already taken up with someone here. He's quite the roving wolf, that one. His reluctance to leave Thamatoc was quickly forgotten once he got here and spied some of the ladies that serve the palace." Offrin laughed through his nose, and then sighed wearily, scratching the back of his neck.

"I suppose it didn't take long for the King to act out against you," Offrin shook his head. "We departed the moment we got your message. In truth we were going to come north anyway the moment we heard you'd been sent to Miranne. The Master thought it advisable that he be present here as a representative of the Adrei and he imagined that a small showing of our militia wouldn't hurt," Offrin said. "He had an idea where the Chaiva might have sent Avria, but he realized it would be a waste of time for us to go. He convinced me of that as well after working hard to get through my furious determination." He pulled off his surcoat and his mail, and sat down by the fire, opening his hands to it for warmth. "I've heard some rumours that things are starting to grow uncomfortable between Arakis and humans in some areas. A large fight broke out at Ivridorp two weeks ago between some of the royal guard and a group of Araki horsemen who'd ridden up to provide training for some of the new Kanreth plebes."

"The King has been creating some tension among his subordinates. He certainly has been trying to influence his court and the ministry. He refuses to see me. I've been trying for more than a week. I'm not sure what the Keepers expect me to do; they said they'd take care of it, that's what they told Phenmal, so I'm just waiting. In the meantime, I remain here. I'm not sure how long he can continue to ignore me, but I thought if I brought some muscle into the palace grounds, he might take notice."

"Tinna, you must know that the Kanreth have declared their service to the Ashru. They have renounced their connection to the present Throne. In fact, we heard the rumour of the fight from them. We came upon them just leaving Loshan. They are on their way here as well. They heard why we were coming and decided to join us. They will arrive only after stopping at a training school in Vyanne to collect some of their friends. They will want to don your colours when they arrive." Tinna suppressed the urge to sigh in relief and smile. That meant something; an old and trusted institution; the trust and fealty of the Kanreth Knights would surely give those who doubted the Ashru peace of mind.

Tinna wished for the thousandth time that day that she was not the Ashru, and she was not stuck in this frozen city, in a noble house in its large, cool rooms, awaiting the condescension of a King who wanted her dead. Instead she thought of being at Thamatoc, spending a snowy day in her apartments with Phenmal in his chair by her fire smoking his pipe, speaking with Taneth in a low voice while she patted the dog's head. She wanted that back again more than anything. She certainly did not want laughable assassination attempts and an obstinate twenty-four-year-old king with tremendous skill for manipulation. *Has he not learned anything from his father's reign, when the dragons had nearly destroyed everything the Throne exacted power over? His guard is small and ineffectual against my own militia alone, let alone with the addition of the Adrei and the Kanreth. The total population of his people numbered less than an twentieth of the Araki alone. What did he hope to accomplish by riling up what was left of humanity? Having them all killed?* Tinna shook her head and sighed, utterly bewildered by the monarch's determination to remain in power when he had nothing left to rule.

Tinna's frustration was reaching a limit. The assassination in and of itself, she took care of quickly. It was a physical response more than anything. She reacted as she had been trained. Tinna had vowed to herself years ago that she would do whatever she could to avoid living a life even remotely like the one she lived before she came north. She did not want to see blood on her hands ever again. The reaction and defense against the attacker had been so ingrained and practiced; she'd done it before she really knew what she'd done. The knife had flown as if of its own volition. She'd killed the woman before she had a chance to think of other ways to deal with her. She hated that. She hated that she'd been trained so well she couldn't even control her own actions once things were set in motion.

The last time Tinna had killed, it was in a battle orchestrated by her own mother and she had taken the lives of most of her mother's personal guard. She almost allowed the beast within her to exact that same fate on her own mother, but Avria's voice had pierced through the specter of her inner monster and had stopped her before she'd lost her entire soul that day. She was so grateful that her daughter was a creature of such goodness and thoughtfulness, that she could recognize the danger of falling into the cycle of revenge. She was so grateful that this child of her heart could penetrate the shadow of death that had been programmed so well into Tinna.

She was furious at the boy King for unknowingly taking her back to a place she did not want to revisit for the rest of her life. And a part of her feared that she would have to be the instrument to rid the world of him for good. She had enough pressure in her life; she did not want to be an assassin for anyone any more. Enough was enough.

She looked at her son-in-law, who so carefully avoided asking the questions she knew he wanted to ask and she sat down across from him. Phenmal knew the moment she set her eyes on Offrin that she wanted to speak to him in private. He gestured subtly to Taneth with his chin to leave the room; "Join me for a smoke, Taneth," he said. He then grasped Rhoa's shoulders and ushered her out as well. Offrin and Tinna were not blind to the lack of subtlety of the exit and they both smirked at one another knowingly. Offrin's smile faded and he sighed.

"How is she?" he asked softly, still looking at his hands.

"I don't know," Tinna's voice cracked and she cleared her throat.

Offrin lowered his face and stared at his hands. He had no idea how to even talk to Tinna about what was going through his mind. All he could feel was the intolerable pain he had felt for all this time, from the moment she'd been hurt. He wanted so to go to her, and show her he loved her and would always love her, and that he in no way could blame her for anything. He wanted to show her that he could wait with her indefinitely until she healed, as long as he was with her. He wanted to hold her while she wept and to comfort and love her. He finally allowed himself to dwell on his emotions enough that he became overcome with them. His shoulders shook as he began to weep, thinking only of his wife's pain and her humiliation and of how alone she must feel.

"I always want to fix things; it's who I am. How will I ever fix this?" he said hopelessly. "She does not deserve even a shade of this unhappiness beset upon her; her sweet soul is not fit for this pain. How she must be suffering alone," he said through his tears. Tinna remained in her seat, gazing at him with her own tears barely under control.

"She will come through, Offrin. And her love for you has never wavered. Her greatest fear was that you would no longer love her." These words made him weep harder, and then he remembered himself and tried to collect his wits about him. He'd been holding onto this sadness for a while now, keeping it locked away as best he could. He had hope in his eyes when he finally met Tinna's. Her words had bolstered him.

"Then I shall show her that I love her no matter what happens. I only wish I could kill that... whatever he is, myself," Offrin growled, his ire barely contained.

"That whatever-he-is will meet the fate he deserves, mark my words. If not by the means Phenmal has offered, then at my hands. I have vowed never to let these hands see blood again, but for that, I would take his life without hesitation. I must have faith that the measures Phenmal has put into place will insure her safety. She has the guardianship of a Drathar, and that fact alone has given me leave to focus on all these other things."

"A Drathar? Really? I didn't think those were actual creatures. I thought they were myth."

"I'd never heard of them until I came north. A book Taneth brought me of Oromoii lore mentioned them. The creature seems quite unlike the book described; he seems almost human, but I could not see any part of him; he was covered from head to toe in black, and he had his face wrapped in black muslin. I could see in certain light, his eyes glistening behind the sheer fabric, his skin so pale; but his eyes looked white, with but a dot of a pupil. It reminded me of the wolves. I miss the wolves. I hope they arrive soon," she added distractedly. She stood and stepped over to the young man, putting her hand on his shoulder reassuringly.

"She is in the most excellent hands, Offrin. She will be fine and on her way here soon."

CHAPTER FIFTEEN - DRATHAR

"I don't understand. How could a mere Zsathri do this?" the mother superior asked. She folded over again in pain as did the six other women with her. The Drathar flinched and his presence seemed to darken. All of them surrounded Avria in what they called the Keep. It was a windowless, doorless chamber. Anyone who wanted to enter it had to have powers. The tall wooden paneled walls covered a stone one many feet thick, and around them the soil of the earth pressed in from all directions. The room was appointed rather comfortably, decorated like any common sitting room complete with a shelf of books. The lamps were lit, but no hearth offered warmth of a fire. She wondered how they even managed to get air in here.

Avria was sitting in a chair, her hands pressed together and resting on her lap. She was wearing a simple day-gown of the style she wore when in Loshan. It was white and the tiny bodice hugging her upper chest was ruched and thickly gathered. Below that, her skirts fell over her traditional pantalettes, shift, two layers of plain petticoats and snow-white thigh-length light woolen stockings. She wore a pair of plain black slippers. In the rush to get her to safety, one of the ribbons had come undone and lay twisted around her foot. She noticed it and bent down, lifting up her hem just enough to tie it around her ankle and secure it with a bow. Even at this moment of strain and physical discomfort as the Zshathri somehow managed to attack the core itself, the Drathar had to stop and admire the gracefulness of her movements and her astounding beauty of the sight of her dressed so delicately. That morning, he had enjoyed seeing her exit her chambers wearing the nice garments for a change. She'd been so shabby and tousled these past days. The thought of that creature harming her filled him with rage. The memory of her violation burned through his mind like molten rock. Another pang of pain passed through him and he felt something unusual in it. He paused.

"This is not the Zshathri alone..." he muttered. The Dreff sisters straightened and their six faces turned to him with expressions of confusion. Another pang of pain, and he lifted his face, talking through gritted teeth. "He has help. Do you not feel it? No Zshathri could do this—even one as tainted and unconstrained as he. No one has the power to undermine the core. It is the magic of a collective of four hundred at least. Who could? I can think of only a few creatures in this world that have the capacity or the power to even scratch the surface of the collective spell. Most of those most powerful creatures are... hobbled by the Keepers. But there is one being that can and has no controls in place; one being that can pull someone from the voids; one being that can wield so much power: the Hevra. They are helping him," he muttered in a dooming tone. The sisters peered at one another as they reflected on this and again they felt a wash of pain as another attack was cast upon their core.

"Yes. There is a taste of the ancient in these attacks. You are right brother. What do we do?"

"I am hobbled. But with help, we can prevent this. We must do a summoning to bring all the Drathar here. It might divert your power from the whole of the core and weaken it, but with all eleven of us here, even the Hevra would be challenged to get through to the girl. Even with our restraints, together we are powerful. But we must get them here now, and for that I need all the magic of all the Dreff," the Drathar said. The mother superior nodded and closed her eyes for a long moment. When she opened them, her eyes were marbled eerily in white, as Eleran's had done when he petitioned the voids for answers and power in meditation. The mother superior however was neither meditating nor in any way incapacitated by this connection. She turned her white eyes to the Drathar.

"It will be done. The sisters are prepared. Join the summoning. We must be quick. We will restore the core in a smaller area around us when we are finished. It will slow them down," she held out her hand and the Drathar reached for it. Avria watched as physical manifestations of their powers arced across the hidden space in misted flares of pale blue.

Then the room began to fill. One by one, new forms began to appear, the language of their bodies defensive and confused; ripped from wherever they were to this new place without explanation. One by one, Drathar appeared, all like Avria's guardian, swathed in black, some taller, some shorter all veiled and grave. The eleventh Drathar materialized and Avria's guardian let go of the mother-superior's hand; turning to his brothers he showed them in silence the answers

662

they needed. The sisters worked to communicate with the rest of the Dreff to refocus their magic on restoring the core, their eyes all turned white.

"The Hevra are strong. They now attack the sisters outside of the core to weaken it. I have ordered a retreat to those who still stand outside of its defenses. Their powers are ineffectual against the ancients," the Mother Superior said.

"We cannot kill them, what do we do?" one of the women asked in desperation. "They are killing my sisters!"

"We will remedy this. Concentrate everything you have on the girl. Keep her protected at all costs, and keep that core wrapped around her so nobody with power can see her or find her," the Drathar told her. She nodded. Avria watched them all vanish in their telltale puffs of black mist that dissipated so quickly. Her stomach iced over in fear. The sisters surrounded her in her chair and linked hands, throwing their heads back, their eyes all ghostly white. Twelve more sisters appeared in the room and made a circle 'round them. Avria lifted her feet up onto the chair and lowered her face into her knees, her arms clutching her legs and her hands tightly clamped together. She was terrified with the Drathar gone. All she could do was visualize the horror of Eleran harming her again. He was probably already well within the building, powerless, but searching; biding his time until his friends broke down the dampener that made him ordinary.

"Get out!" the Drathar shouted to his sisters. The nave where Avria had first entered the abbey filled by eleven people in a matter of seconds and the sisters that stood against the assaults were facing the doorway, hands aloft creating shields against which a collection of people pushed just inside the gaping doorway. The core had been pushed all the way back to the main edifice, and the attackers were now fully in view, no longer hidden by the forest.

Outside the shrinking core, the bodies of dreff sorceresses lay prone on the ground of the courtyard, their clothes and cloaks rippling in the wind. The first line of defense had fallen. The tear-streaked faces of their sisters protecting the inner core pivoted in shock at the appearance of the Drathar. Their hands dropped; they retreated, some by magic, others on foot, vanishing into the variety of corridors behind the rows of massive columns. The Hevra proceeded forward unhindered; Eleran leading the pack. He had remained with his protectors, biding his time while they undermined the core, hoping he could act quickly when they'd weakened it sufficiently. He would find Avria and take her out of here the moment the magical veil was torn down. The Drathar were fortunate. Eleran could have run ahead and gotten lost in the building, searching with naught but his eyes, but he was thinking this through, and he knew that separating himself from them gained him nothing, especially inside the labyrinthine building.

The Drathar had a clear image from Avria what the man looked like, but Eleran somehow grown a sinister air to him over the past weeks since he attacked the girl. His long black hair was loose and hanging heavily down the sides of his head, fanning out along his back and in front of his shoulders. His gaze was dour, his eyes upturned, sunken in deep sockets that were a reddish purple. His eyes were cold and menacing.

Behind him, the collection of beautiful, ethereal people followed; all with guileless expressions and wide, curious eyes; all had their hands up like claws, which they cut into the core with, piercing its invisible skin like the talons of a raptor. They halted when they saw the Drathar brothers before them, their hands dropping as curiosity filled their faces. They sensed their ancient roots, and immediately knew these were not simple creatures.

The air was thick with electricity, and the smell of ozone washed the space. Splashes of magical energy surged forth from their beings as they fought against the core from within, fighting to collapse it for the Zsathri. Eleran stopped too, looking bemused by the presence of the eleven black figures standing before them in a neat arc. Nobody really knew what a Drathar looked like anymore. Lore had made them into hideous demons. These eleven figures were a mystery to the intruders, but they did not miss the undercurrent of power emanating from these darkly clad figures as they drew closer together before them. They realized this power was present in spite of their being inside the core. It had no effect on them.

"Who are you?" Eleran asked. The figures remained deathly silent, waiting until every set of eyes was fast upon them. When the intruders all gazed in puzzlement at the ones inside the core, in an act of synergy, the Drathar tore off their veils and threw them aside. The veils drifted gracefully to the floor. Their cold gazes seemed to suck the colour from the world; drawing everything into them. The vortexes that drew the energies were merging into a violent maelstrom that spread out over the area before them and enveloped the sixteen people standing there, riveted to this spectacle and now trapped irrevocably by it.

There were horrified cries from the Hevra; two of them thought quickly enough to cover their eyes with their arms and turn away, but the rest were instantly rapt, gazing directly into the vortex and strands of misty light began to bleed out of their faces, from their eyes, ears and mouths, floating outwards, where the it stretched out into tendrils that merged into larger ones that undulated and extended like tentacles towards the Drathar. The Drathars' eyes absorbed them. The Drathar stood in wide stances, strong against the power of their magic, their shoulders hunched and their fingers clenched. The cries became piercing screams of horror as the essence of these ancient creatures was being sucked out of them in beautiful layered streams of luminous mist. They collapsed to their knees.

The devastation of the combined Drathar gazes spread, extracting the lingering souls and essences from the open eyes of even the dead and dying Dreff resting on the cobbles of the courtyard; shriveling up and making grey and lifeless the evergreens that hugged the edge of the square, bringing birds down from the sky to fall twitching onto the earth.

When the screams faded into silence, they relented, closing their eyes and stooping to pick up the veils they'd thrown down. They pushed back their hoods and quietly and methodically draped their faces. Only two of the Hevra were left with any sense or consciousness. Both were on their backs on the hard stone floor, weeping behind their forearms. Eleran himself knelt on the floor, staring blankly into nothingness. The essence of who Eleran was, of who he had ever been now resided inside the eleven souls of the Drathars; including the sum of his power. Tingling and surging now with the power of Hevra and Eleran and some of their Dreff sisters, the Drathar began to leave, one at a time until all that remained was the first. As they each vanished, the clouds of smoke they left behind were peppered with tiny figures and glyphs that spun and floated momentarily before vanishing along with the mist.

The remaining Drathar walked to Eleran. He reached out his gloved hand and tilted the Zshathri's chin up to see his face. He looked down into the empty eyes. Nothing remained.

"This is not how the story should end," one of the two remaining Hevra whispered through her tears, her flaxen hair tousled and her eyes red. "It was supposed to be happy. It was supposed to end happily," she insisted. The Drathar stood staring at her and her weeping dark-haired sister. They could harm nothing just the two. They no longer had reason to. Their story had ended.

Avria was huddled in her chair. Around her, the sisters dropped their hands to their sides and the mother superior nodded. The others vanished from the room, seemingly taking some of the limited air with them. Avria felt weak and wanted to breathe fresh air. The mother superior reached out her hand. Avria's knees dropped down and her feet touched the floor. She took the mother-superior's hand and stood.

"It's over," the mother said. Avria was suddenly blinded by powerful daylight. Unexpectedly, she was standing in front of the entranceway to the great abbey, the sunlight bright and white and pouring in from the open doorway. She shielded her eyes for a moment, squinting against it. And then her focus came back, and she saw Eleran kneeling in front of a scattering of unbelievably beautiful bodies, two of which wept and rocked on their knees, hands reaching out to touch the still forms of the others around them. Eleran was staring forward to the top of the nave where the three great windows cast their colored light onto the floor. He paid no heed to Avria. The Drathar stood nearby, his face pointed to the floor, his arms crossed.

Avria clutched the mother superior's hand at first, instantly filled with terror at the sight of the man she once loved. When she realized he was in a trance, she let go and padded forward on her little slippers. She came to stand in front of him, her head tilting sideways in puzzlement. She waved her hand in front of his blank gaze. "Eleran?" she asked weakly. He did not flinch. He stared steadily forward. When she tore her eyes from his beautiful, peaceful face, she noticed all of the people save two were in the same quiet trance, some lying on their sides, others flat on their backs, others sitting or kneeling like Eleran, all staring blankly at nothing. She turned her gaze back on Eleran.

"What's wrong with him?" she asked. The Drathar shook his head.

"It's what happens when a person's eyes meets our gaze. He is not in there anymore. Not the good Eleran, nor the bad one. There remains nothing but basic instincts like chewing and swallowing and breathing. He will no longer be of threat to you Avria. You may go home," the Drathar said, the regret at bidding her farewell well hidden in his words. Avria began to cry, her hands gripping each side of the Zshathri's finely hewn jaw.

She stood before him, peering searchingly into his empty gaze, which did not even lock onto her face but looked somewhere beyond. He was so beautiful. The evil in his eyes was gone, as was the love that had once filled them. He was a facsimile of what she remembered, a painted image. His face, the one she'd come to dream about and so secretly hoped to see again even when she accepted Offrin's offer of marriage was there, but he was not in it. Avria's grief overwhelmed her and she knelt in front of him, weeping and crying his name, "Eleran, Eleran," wrapping her arms around him and hugging him close; shaking his shoulders and calling his name again and again. Impassive and hollow, he allowed her to do this, sitting on his knees still, stiff and unyielding, vacant and hapless. "Say something," she whispered to him. "Say you are sorry. Say you are sorry for what you have done to us." But he remained silent. His gaze looked through her as if she didn't exist. She wanted to hit him, to claw at his face, to kiss him, but he wasn't there. This thing before her was innocent of crime, and incapable of love. She knelt weeping in front of him for a long time.

When her tears had run dry, she stood and wiped her eyes with the ball of her hand, hiccupping still from her sobbing. She couldn't even bid him farewell. Not to this thing. The Mother Superior came to her and put a cloak on her shoulders.

"Could we just walk back to my rooms?" Avria asked in a soft whisper through her hiccups. The mother nodded, and they made their way towards the corridor, the tall woman holding Avria's shoulders as they walked. The Drathar vanished without a goodbye, leaving only a cloud of mist and glyphs which too vanished as if he'd never been. The two remaining Hevra hovered over their brethren in confusion, trying also to draw them out of their stupors to no avail. The sisters then began to file out of the corridors into the nave to clean up the mess. There was a strange bristling sensation as the core began to wash outwards again like a great wave; unhindered now. Its size was only reduced marginally by the deaths of the eight sisters. The arrival of so many power-bearers into the nave sent the two remaining Hevra packing. Avria did not put a single thought into what would be done with the empty people now.

CHAPTER SIXTEEN – HOMECOMING

Phenmal was filled with a strange sense of apprehension when the Drathar arrived. Something oozed from his being, something barely controlled. He appeared without invitation in Phenmal's private chamber where the older gentleman was about to go to bed for the night. Their powers were unbelievably strong, but he felt even more powerful this time, like it was straining against the seams of his loose, draped clothing.

"What are you doing here?"

"The mother has cast you out of her bed for the first husband I see," the Drathar mumbled sardonically. He took the liberty of sitting down in one of the chairs and stretched out his legs. Phenmal did not answer him, and simply continued unbuttoning his waistcoat and loosening his cravat. "The girl is safe. The Zshathri has been neutralized." Phenmal's hands dropped and he smiled, nodding.

"Well done," he said.

"Your actions put her in greater danger. The Hevra took your intervention as incentive to assist the Soothsayer. The ancient idiots wanted to help him finish the story with a happy ending; to reunite their lost child with his beloved. Lives were lost," he said icily. Phenmal's smile faded and he bent his head down, his fingers rubbing along his forehead in frustration.

"It was a stupid idea. I thought they would stop him..."

"You were wrong. I cannot say you are to blame; you are not familiar with the ways of the ancient ones. They are mad and old and stupid from ten thousand years of idleness. They are mostly gone. There remains only a few now. Their power—the essence of the others resides in me and in my brothers; additional power that will probably cause the Keepers to attempt to impose even more controls upon us." The Chaiva nodded knowingly and sat down, his shoulders dropped in hopelessness.

"You killed the Hevra?"

"My brothers and I did not kill a single soul. We consumed them," he replied. "Our combined powers were able to overcome their resistance and to draw out their essence. No one of us could have done it alone. We broke one of our most stringent rules to save the girl; we gathered together in one place." Phenmal shook his head and sighed.

"You will likely see repercussions for uniting against the Hevra," Phenmal muttered, "for absorbing new power. I am sorry I put you all into that position with my recklessness," he said. "I merely wished to save the girl from more suffering." The Drathar visibly softened at the mention of Avria. Phenmal immediately knew she'd drawn his soul in and took ownership of it as aptly as the Drathar did to others with his gaze.

"In that, you were successful. She will no longer suffer at the hands of the Zsathri. He is nothing more than a drooling idiot now. As for my brothers and I, we will manage. She will leave the Abbey soon and she will need her family to make her whole again; her husband..."

"Yes, of course."

"I will go. I must go to the Citadel. Make an explanation. I have already been summoned."

"Drathar..."

"Yes, Chaiva..."

"Tell them your actions were inevitable and they were performed with the intent of saving the Ashru's daughter. They are protective of the Ashru. They see her as the salvation from a future they cannot see. Tinna will be happy now that Avria is safe. She can concentrate on the issues before her with peace of mind. Knowing this, they will surely understand your determination to keep Avria safe. I will send them a message of the like, with my gratitude for their allowing me to have your services." The two stared at one another for a long, pregnant moment, and then the Drathar nodded and disappeared. Phenmal's eyes widened at the sight of the lingering figures and letters left in the Drathar's wake. His skin rose into bumps as he realized what implications this seemingly benign little detail meant.

* * * *

The knock on the door roused Taneth and he was irritated to be pulled from being notched against his wife underneath a pile of warm blankets. He padded barefoot to the door, his long loose-legged pants waving against his legs and he tugged open the door to the bedroom. He found Phenmal in a state of partial undress in front of him. He rubbed the goo from the corner of his eye with his finger and squinted at Phenmal's candlelight.

"It's my night, go away."

"I have news of Avria," Phenmal retorted, shouldering his way into the room. Taneth shut the door, his fingers rasping through his beard, hiding his emotional response as best he could, but his breath was short and shallow. Tinna was just lifting her head up and blinking the sleep out of her eyes.

"What's going on?" she asked groggily.

"Avria is safe. The Soothsayer has been neutralized. The Drathar just came to me to inform me of this," he said. Tinna sat up, her face a shock. She then dropped back onto the bed and she released a sigh as if she'd been holding it in for weeks, her arms splayed out at her sides.

"Good, Phenmal. I thank you. For everything."

"She's as much family to me as she is to you."

"You kept her from being hurt again, and I love you for that," she said, her voice heavy with emotion. He could barely see her past the glare of his candle, but he knew her eyes were glassy with tears. He wished he could just crawl in there with her. Tinna sighed again, and rolled onto her side. "Phen, call on Cennik first thing. Get her here; and can you let Offrin know?"

"Of course my sweet beloved soon to be wife," he said, smirking at Taneth. The scholar rolled his eyes and crawled into bed, pulling the heavy blankets over his legs. Tinna laughed quietly and turned onto her side with her back to them both.

"Your message is delivered, now go away," Taneth replied with a grin. The older man nodded and waved his hand dismissively at them both, exiting the room. What an arrangement he'd gotten himself into. He shook his head at the thought. But at least there was honesty now; and freedom to speak one's thoughts.

He wandered down the corridor and crossed the central part of the house. Offrin was not consigned to stay in the guest barracks with the rest of his men. He was family, and he stayed with Tinna. The Araki guard had arrived the day before and four of them sat at a table in the large vestibule playing cards to pass the night. They glanced up as Phenmal crossed the mezzanine and the stairway into the wing where Offrin slept. Only one face was a familiar one from Thamatoc. The rest were people from other clans. The soldiers were serious now. Two years since the One Day War, and the Araki had started forming a true army, and training them alike. This was no longer the group of volunteer horsemen that had ridden into battle with little experience and a sword in their hands; these were true, experienced warriors.

Offrin was still awake, a book clutched in his hand when he answered the door. The news of Avria's safety filled his face with relief and he bowed his head for a moment to contain himself. He lifted his hand and laid it flat over the Chaiva's heart. He thought his gratitude loudly and clearly to the older man. Without another word he withdrew and closed his door. Phenmal felt good. In spite of his error in judgment with the Hevra, he had been for a rare moment the instrument of good news for a change. He was regretful he was not the one next to Tinna this night, but he had at last that satisfaction to take to his sheets at least. He made his way back to his rooms, in the morning he would order a dragon to fetch the girl he thought of as his own little daughter.

Avria watched Wye pass soundlessly beneath her; she knew it was Wye because it was the only town on that coast that was in view of the Isle of Gales. It was strange to see an Araki town that was not in the style of the clan villages. This town was of individual houses made in the human style, the angled rooftops all square and white with snow. Somewhere, her brother was down there with his wife Skye, and they were happy and ignorant of what had transpired for the rest of the family. Her heart hurt she wanted to see Hanru so badly, but instead she was told she would be going to the palace at Miranne. Before her, the forests of the Araki people spread vast and endless. The dragon banked to the right, and cast itself north. The cold had abated a bit, but not enough to melt the dry snow. It was a beautiful, clear day without a cloud for miles. It was not so frigid that Avria could not occasionally peer out and watch the landscape fly by. It astounded her that what would take days of foot or horse travel took only hours for the dragons.

Avria, in spite of the weight of her sorrow, could not deny she was pleased to see Eretrix swooping elegantly into the bailey. She could scarce hide her relief at departing the old abbey. Her bag was made heavier by a stack of papers she had managed to copy for her father—for that she was grateful; but the heavy ceilings and hunkering weight of the building and its shrouded core had made her feel uneasy. She regretted that the Drathar was not there to say goodbye, but she appreciatively bid the sisters farewell and did not look back. Instead she huddled against the back of Eretrix's warm head and tried hard to act out in her head her imagined reunion with Offrin and not a single of her performances ended without her succumbing to the tears of humiliation and culpability. Her guilt was profound.

She had admitted to herself that she had wanted Eleran back even when she had committed herself to Offrin. She felt shame for wanting to kiss his blank face, but she knew the man who had harmed her was not the man she longed for still. But her guilt for loving Eleran still was strong. Now she carried a child that was not Offrin's. A child conceived of an unwilling union; a child with unknowable power. She was without idea of what to say to him. Even though she felt lighter in leaving the Abbey, her stomach started to feel heavier and heavier the closer she got to Miranne. She hoped Offrin was not there so she could have some more time to prepare.

Avria's hopes were in vain. Eretrix found footing in the empty square at Miranne only to be greeted most gleefully by Igro who happened to be out stretching his wings when they arrived. It was late evening and everyone was preparing for bed; the royal city was quiet and settled. The light cast from the windows from the town circling the square glowed like a wreath of candles. Miranne's ancient moat still glimmered against the curtain wall, buffering the main square and bailey from the sleepy town that hugged up against it. The main palace dominated the center of the back wall of the square across from the main gate, wings stretching out like arms to meet the buildings on each side that were built up against the curtain wall. Pillars of fragrant wood-smoke rose up in amorphous columns through which Eretrix slalomed as she made her way to the destination.

A dark shape had slipped up beside them soundlessly in the air just before they landed, and then snorted. Eretrix barely acknowledged him, probably aware of Igro for a while now. Eretrix was markedly smaller than Igro, but both were formidable sights. The larger dragon sped up and landed before Eretrix, and he waited with barely contained exuberance until Avria stepped down before trouncing Eretrix playfully and rolling with her across the square. They made little mewling growls, their delight in this encounter most evident. Avria took a moment to observe this rare sight, using it as a perfectly acceptable excuse to avoid finding the people she loved. She was filled with dread. The playful dragons offered a brief respite, until someone shouted from their window at the dragons when their tousle took itself too close to their walls. The dragons ceased and greeted one another affectionately. Igro nipped at Eretrix demonstratively as he led her to the byre that had been set aside for visiting dragons. Avria smiled wanly and turned to find herself face to face with Phenmal.

She immediately dropped her bag and jumped up to wrap her arms around his neck, her sobs instantly soaking him. He hugged her to him and rocked her back and forth. "I've never been so happy to see you," she said through her tears.

"I don't know how I should take that..." he said with a touch of humor. She let go of her tight embrace and let him straighten again. She laughed and then wiped her tears.

"You felt my arrival?"

"Of course. And the dragons' as well. Igro likes the little red one very much. It was his abject joy I felt first when he sensed her approach. Then I felt you. You have nothing to dread my dear, come..."

"Please Phen don't read my mind," she sighed.

"It's too late. I know everything. I guarantee you there will be nothing more than pure happiness at the sight of you. What other burdens and secrets you may carry can wait until morning if you prefer. Offrin's heart is so open..."

"He's here?" she asked, her voice rising in pitch.

"He is. Master Gavorre is here as well, but he is incredibly ill. I think you need to set aside your personal reservations, Avria and keep an open heart too. He is your husband and he loves you inside and out. His forgiveness isn't needed for he holds nothing against you. He wants only for you to look at him with love, Avria." She began to cry again, hating that she's done little else but weep of late. Phenmal simply put his hand on her cheek and said:

"In your case, Avria, all the tears are utterly forgivable and justified. Come inside now. Nobody knows you're home yet, I thought it would be best if you had a moment to collect yourself first, rather than beset a horde of worried family upon you the moment of your landing."

"That is thoughtful of you, Phenmal," she smiled through her tears. He stepped aside and gestured her forth with his arm. With a shaky sigh, she walked ahead of him. He caught up and took her bag from her. She looked up at him gratefully and slid her hand into his.

Avria was almost suffocating between her two parents. Tinna covered her face in kisses and hugged her hard again, with Taneth clinging to her all the while. They were both teary-eyed and overjoyed to see her; trying hard to somehow absorb her shame and her sorrow into themselves so they could see happiness in her face again. She scarce got the bleary-eyed baby into her arms when Offrin burst into the room and then froze as if afraid. She felt little Istvan's hands tugging at her frizzed curls but all she could do was stagger a bit into a turn to see Offrin's face. Her soft smile melted away into something else. Istvan was carefully pried from her arm, and she let her hands fall to her sides. Offrin approached, gazing up at her searchingly. When he came before her she fell to her knees and wrapped her arms around his chest, her head pressed against his shoulder. He bent down and kissed the top of her head.

"Offrin..." she sobbed, "forgive me!" she cried.

"There's nothing to forgive, Avria," he replied, which only made her weep harder. All she could think of was her hope that Eleran could be saved, that he could be the Eleran she once knew, the Eleran she loved, and all she could feel was the wash of guilt for holding on to that hope even with Offrin's heart in her hands. Now she would have to tell him that she carried a child by Eleran, a child created when her most horrid memory of her life was created. She could not stop the tears as Offrin wrapped her in love that she was sure she was unworthy of.

Even after she'd been scooped up by her family and guided to her room, even after her mother tenderly helped her into some night clothes, promising a hot bath in the morning, even after Offrin had lay beside her, never once touching her in any way other than pure affection, and gazing at her until he finally succumbed to sleep, Avria could not shake her sense of guilt. She did not want to tell Offrin about the baby. She did not want to tell him that even though Eleran had done what he had done, that when she saw him kneeling there in the abbey, that all she wanted to do was to kiss him and find a way to bring the man she loved back. She felt like an awful person. In the light of the slow-burning fire, she studied Offrin. She loved him, she knew that. If she didn't, she would not be so worried about hurting him.

She realized that her guilt would be something she'd have to learn to live with; because she needed him as much as he needed her. She would not tell him what she thought and felt after Eleran hurt her. She would only tell him what she could not avoid telling him. In the morning, she would sit down with Offrin and reveal the existence

675

of the child. With a glance at Offrin's peaceful, handsome face, she turned over and finally fell asleep.

CHAPTER SEVENTEEN – PLAGUE

In the darkness of the room, the Drathar was invisible. His quiet form watched Avria in her fitful sleep. He ignored the person beside her who huddled close to himself, even in his slumber, careful not to trespass too closely to her body. The Drathar stooped by the bed so that his face was level with hers. His eyes studied her as she slept. Gently, he leaned forward and kissed her through his veil. Her eyes opened, and she neither withdrew nor objected. He felt her lips go soft, and press against his. She then slipped her hand out and lifted his veil so that their lips touched. The Drathar's soul melted as he kissed her. When her lips withdrew from his, he heard her whisper: "Thank you." He used his thumb to wipe away the tear shimmering at the corner of her eye, and he vanished leaving only his earthy scent behind.

* * * *

Avria awoke to the sound of shouting. It was muffled and the words were difficult to make out. Offrin was not present. Instead, a young girl entered and smiled shyly at Avria. She couldn't have been more than twelve years old. She was a willowy, reedy girl with long straight brown hair loose on her shoulders, and a small navy-colored gown with an apron bib pinned to the bodice, the wide front tied around her high waist.

She wordlessly gestured Avria through to the adjoining bathing chamber and discovered a hot bath awaiting her. She soaked for a while, still listening intently to the angered voices below her rooms. Offrin was there, as was Tinna and Taneth. Phenmal was probably there but he was not a shouting sort of person. He was probably hunched in a chair, looking on to the noise and chaos while occasionally calmly chiming in his opinion.

The girl, whose name was revealed to be Teya could barely find it within herself to speak, she was so shy. She wanted to simply help Avria and flee. Avria was put into her white dress again. Her mother had always frowned on having to wear the more formal northern garments. Northern women almost always wore long gowns, although the styles had changed significantly since Tinna's youth, and the gowns were infinitely more comfortable and free flowing and as far as Avria was concerned, much prettier. But her mother was a southern woman born from a matriarchal culture, and the woman there were infinitely more daring in their choice of clothing, including short little skirts and breeches like men wore. They believed in the power of the woman's body and flaunted it quite brazenly. Tinna however did not believe in flaunting; she believed in complete comfort. She did not want what she was wearing to come into her mind at all through the day, and so she wanted simple things. She was still resisting the new fashions she would invariably have to wear daily, remembering the common woolen gown she was wearing last night.

It didn't take Avria too long to get ready. She didn't bother much with her hair. It was still wet, so she combed it through, parted it down the center pulled it back tightly and rolled the rest up into a tight bun on the back of her head. No jewelry, no adornments, she got up and smiled at the girl and decided to investigate the sound of the discord below floors.

She slid quietly into the formal receiving room when she got downstairs and everyone fell silent when she came in, including a huge man of about thirty years who literally looked like a larger version of Offrin. He was shaved bald with a thin beard edging his jaws, his moustache trimmed close to his face. He had green eyes and an angry scowl which melted the moment he saw Avria, his mouth hanging partly open and his eyes locked on her pretty figure as she moved through the doorway and closed it behind her. Her spell was powerful and it brought the discussion to a halt. Offrin did not miss the man's reaction and he became visibly irritated by it, rising to greet to his wife.

"Avria, good morning," Tinna muttered in surprise.

"Hello mother. I wanted to know what the hullabaloo was about."

"This gentleman is sent by the King. He is the Sheerchai of the guard, and has been told to deliver us a message from his highness," she replied. "Come sit dear. Have you eaten anything?"

678

"No, not yet," she replied. She sat down next to her mother, and Offrin maneuvered himself into the space on her right. "It must be a long message, you've been shouting at one another for more than half an hour," Avria replied. The man snapped his mouth shut and looked a bit embarrassed for her observation.

"My pardons lady if our discussion has disturbed you," he said quickly, shaking his head.

"The gist of his message is that we are to ask the 'murdering scourge' dragons to leave the compound at once," Tinna said to Avria with an amused smirk.

"I don't understand; how is the King making such orders when you are to take his place?" Avria asked innocently.

"Our point exactly. It is the Keepers who choose the ruling family. They have appointed me to succeed this monarch. He is to step down and he is in no position to issue orders to me. I think it would solve many problems if the King would allow me to speak directly to him. Right now, I've been here almost three weeks and he hasn't said a word to me except through messengers. I will not accept his orders; nor will I accept his threat to send in dragon hunters if I do not comply. I have a contingent of men here from my army, from the Adrei army, and I have the Kanreth knights who are at my command. Also, I have mentioned this before, on the advice of the Keepers, I have the sum of the Araki mounted army standing by should I require their assistance, as well as a large fleet of the noble dragons and ground dragons. Do we truly want to end this in a scrap over something so arbitrary? Do we really want that? I ask this because if this is the case, the monarch will lose," Tinna said sharply, her laughter imbued with incredulity.

The messenger looked most frustrated, but he was now utterly distracted by the quiet presence of the girl. He sighed in frustration and shook his head. "I am here to deliver a message, I cannot provide you with any answers in the King's stead; I am neither his advisor nor his minister."

"Then as I said, your message to him in reply will be that I will only speak directly to him about these matters. The dragons are staying where they are, and I'm not going anywhere. I've said it before, and I say it now. I don't think I could be any clearer. Your lingering here and shouting at us is not going to change my answer. Unfortunately you will have to return to your monarch with an answer he will not be pleased with, but it is what it is, as they say. If your monarch has issue with our presence here, and those of our allies, he should take it up with the Keepers."

The man looked defeated. He was regretful he was the deliverer of this message, but he was still charged with service to the monarch. With a last lingering glance at Avria, who seemed distant and distracted, staring off into nowhere, he simply walked out without leave.

Tinna shot to her feet the moment the Captain left and made a sound of frustration. Avria was surprised to see her mother in a gown of the latest fashions. A gown of simple white gauzy muslin with mid-length straight sleeves, a ruffle on each cuff made of a fabric so sheer it was almost invisible, a V-neckline of heavily ruched panels coming together with an unpretentious wood-carved and gilded brooch underneath her bust-line. The skirts were gathered lightly up front as the ruched top ended and the gathers flared out, and in the back, a small train of heavily pleated fabric came up to a short, beautifully sewn bodice back. Her hair was up in a loose bun on the back of her head with a ribbon of gold wound around her head. It was a day gown with few embellishments. The white suited her, Avria thought. She sailed around the room to a sideboard and poured herself a stiff drink, downing it quite brusquely, a look of irritation plain on her face. It was from the several cases of fine apple brandy sent to her in congratulations for her arrival at Miranne; a gift from the Keepers. They had drunk most of one case already, it was delicious. It was the only thing the Keepers had sent at this point. Tinna had mentioned several times while imbibing this brandy that as good as it was, it was no substitute for the actual presence of someone from the Citadel.

"That damned fool of a King. What is his problem? Pride? I'll fix his pride..." she growled. "And where are those idiot Keepers? They pushed, pushed, pushed for me to come to Miranne, 'You must come at once! We need the Ashru there!' they said. Well I'm here! I came at the cost of everything dear to me! I'm here and I've been here and nothing has come of it! This is ridiculous!" she ranted, slamming down the glass goblet. "Phenmal I want answers! And I want to see that _____ King!" her expletive made all the brows in the room arch up in astonishment, even Phenmal's. He barked out in laughter and scooted forward to the edge of his tall wingback chair, where he propped his hands on his knees and looked at Tinna with amusement.

"Laugh all you want old fellow, I'm not staying here another day unless something is done. We make to leave in the morning. Pack up our things!"

"What?" Adracoor asked, finally chiming in. He also moved forward to the edge of his chair angled by Phenmal's side and put his mug of hot grog down on the table between them. "You can't just leave..."

"Why am I here? There's no reason at all for me to be here. The King refuses to step down; he refuses even to just speak to me; the Keepers promised he'd be taken care of, I haven't seen anything of these mysterious Keepers and yet I am to feel compelled to follow their orders. Meanwhile the longer they delay, the longer the King succeeds in spreading his lies and vitriol to the human settlements! I'm starting to lose my patience. I won't sit about anymore; I won't be threatened by a nineteen year old fool..."

"He's twenty four," Taneth corrected her.

"Whatever," Tinna waved her hand irritably at him.

There was a knock on the door and a face peered in, a worried face. It was Embri, an Adrei healer who'd come up at the behest of Tinna, who was worried about Gavorre. He seemed unable to pull himself out of his illness. The city Wiseman was too preoccupied with his work, and Taneth was about to leave again soon. So she called his local healer to assist. The healer had been there for several days, carried up on the back of Igro from Taruttee. He had been up to this point, isolated with Gavorre in his house where the old homeopath was still ailing quite terribly from his illness. She was surprised to see him.

"Your highness, I am sorry to interrupt." Tinna turned and her brows came together in puzzlement. "I'm quite concerned. I'd like to speak to you in private, if I may." Everyone including Avria vacated the room and filed out the door. Offrin tried to stay but the healer sent him packing as well, shutting the door behind him.

"I have a suspicion, your Highness, and it is a perhaps leaning more towards a certainty which I am not quite willing to accept myself," he said. He was a youngish fellow, perhaps within five years Offrin's age, about the same height as Offrin with long black hair tied back into a tail. He came to the height of Tinna's shoulder. She sat down to give them more of an equal footing. He seemed to appreciate it but did not move to sit down. He remained standing in the open area in front of the chairs, trying to formulate his words in an anxious way.

"Is Master Gavorre that ill, Embri?" The healer twisted his hands together and looked at her fearfully.

"He is showing some unusual symptoms, your highness," sweat began to bead on his brow. "I've never seen a case of it myself first-

681

hand, but I come from a long line of healers who have passed this down from generation to generation. Ashru—" he sighed, his brow wrinkling, "I have reason to believe Master Gavorre has been infected with the wormskin plague."

* * * *

Tinna's stomach turned ice-cold and her skin grew waxen in a matter of seconds. She almost wanted to vomit. "TANETH!" she screamed at the top of her lungs, rising shakily to her feet. The man burst into the room wild-eyed and looked upon her with trepidation.

"What is it?"

"Taneth," she could barely speak. "Get Phen, get everyone... anyone who isn't Araki. Get them... Oh gods, get them out of here now... Fetch Cennik at once!" she lifted her violently trembling hand to the window. She turned to the Healer, eyes wide.

"I don't underst... what's wrong?" Taneth muttered in confusion.

"How many of the mounted contingent came into contact with him?" Tinna asked the healer.

"He only started to show the symptoms of contagion this morning. The pustules have started to open and he has the telltale serpentine rash forming all over his skin. Seeing that cemented my suspicions, and I came over right away. He's been infected long enough that others who would have been infected would show the early flu-like symptoms if they were infected. Those who came into contact with him before, I do not see symptoms yet. His isolation in the coach might have a bearing on that. Once he's gotten to this stage, it's likely it will spread and spread quickly. It has already probably spread. The servants of his residence, for instance, all came into contact with him at some point, assisting me with his care during his fevered stage. I would propose not moving him at this point. It's too risky. I have washed myself down with hevla simply to bring you this message in person, but I would hope that nobody with human blood would touch me, I am surely infected but not contagious as of yet, but you never know. You never know with Wormskin," he said through a tremulous voice. Tinna's hand clapped over her mouth and she bit back her sob.

"Gods," Taneth muttered, finally understanding. He turned "Wormskin! Get everyone out. Avria, you must leave at once! Phenmal, call the dragons!" he shouted, his voice edged in panic. "Tinna, you must go as well. Immediately!"

"I am gypsy, Taneth. Chai-Opse. Even part-bloods are safe. Avria and the Istvan are safe," she said stonily. "You are not. Phenmal is not. Offrin is not. The Kanreth, the humans in all those houses outside this square are not," she said in a hoarse, broken voice. "Hanru is safe, the Araki are safe. The Adrei are not. Cennik! He is human! How will we summon the dragons without him?" Taneth shook his head, for once, speechless and stunned.

Phenmal appeared in the doorway, the stricken look on his face was even more horrified than anything Tinna could muster, for he had come to an alarming epiphany as he heard all of their thoughts.

"We are not in danger," he said. He walked to the sideboard and picked up the bottle of brandy. "None of us who drank this are in danger. The Keepers said they'd take care of the human king and they said they'd prevent a war between the races for the throne. I think now I understand how." He looked gravely at Tinna, whose eyes widened in horror.

"Why would they do that?" she asked as the reality of this situation washed over her. "Why would they set loose a disease that could make the human race disappear? Why would they do that?" she started to hyperventilate into sobs. Tinna could feel the numbness spread over her body, starting at the pit of her stomach and growing outward until she felt like she was floating. She did not feel the muscles go weak in her knees; she did not feel them give way. Her body fell and she landed hard on her kneecaps, her skirts billowing out around her; her hands falling flat and open on the woven rug, pale against the dark tones. A tortured, horrid cry escaped her lips and she slumped forward, tears flowing hot and fast. She hunched in on herself and wept... crying out "oh by the gods, why?" again and again, her shoulders wracking with sobs. Everyone closed in around her, hands reaching out to grasp her weakened arms. They lifted her into a chair where she was given water to drink. She sipped, her hands barely able to hold the glass. The idea of the devastation this disease would cause filled her with dread and a ghastly sense of responsibility. She gathered her wits as best she could.

"Get the Adrei and Kanreth out of here. Send them south to the forests. Evacuate the town around here as well; send them, oh gods, if they're carrying it they'll just bring it with them. Do we have any of that brandy left? Give it to the Adrei and the Kanreth. I don't know if we should move the humans out of the town, we risk carrying the disease outwards..." she rambled. "You must send out a directive to the Araki—use the last relay to Klatna to the delegate office. Close down all relays from human settlements into the forests.

You must direct all Adrei communities to shut down and be prepared to shoot an arrow into anyone who comes close to their communities from outside. Shut down the trade roads, shut down everything that moves people around. For at least four months." Tinna took another drink. Adracoor immediately rocketed out of the room with Rhoa at his heels. Rhoa had only made a late appearance to be confronted with this horror. Phenmal, Taneth, Avria remained while the Healer exited quietly and gingerly.

"The Thran! Warn the Thran! And the Gheraine... Oh Gods..." she fell into a whisper and sobbed again, grabbing Phenmal's hand.

"Can we not end it here by... I'd hate to say this... but if we disposed of the source..." Taneth spoke these words as if he couldn't believe they were coming out of his mouth.

"I highly doubt he's the only source, Taneth. How did Master Gavorre become infected? When?" Phenmal barked.

"He's been ill since he left Thamatoc, correct?"

"No, since we passed through Lemoram. He started getting sick in earnest the morning after we departed. He dined with a group of wisemen that night, and came home feeling quite unwell," Offrin said. "I wonder if all the wisemen are ill." Phenmal nodded knowingly and crossed his arms.

"Wisemen are largely from human settlements. They will carry it wherever they go. And Lemoram, with its host of visitors and students..." his voice trailed off.

"It's only a matter of time" Tinna replied, her voice breaking. She shook her head in disbelief.

"Four weeks for the disease to spread. That's what it took last time there was an outbreak," Taneth said matter-of-factly. "Four short weeks it cast itself across the continent and the isles and obliterated almost everyone that had human blood. The disease takes a while to fester, but in two months, this world could be nearly bereft of humankind."

"Indeed. It was the only solution," a new voice added.

An old man appeared at the door of the receiving room. Phenmal recognized him at once as Evankor, one of the younger of the Keepers. He was lowest ranked among them and therefore, subject to errands for the others. He stood in the doorway, his hands clasped, his clothing a bit dated against the newer fashions, his velvets looking garish, the gold-embroidered designs too fussy. He wore black slippers; dark green stockings, burgundy knee breeches that were loose around his legs, a gold waistcoat with elegant leafy whorls embroidered in ivory, and a burgundy frock coat of the old style. His white hair was carefully coifed into forward-sweeping whorls in a vain attempt to look stylish. He had dark brown eyes and a mouthful of perfect white teeth. His papery, wrinkled skin was marked with age spots. His eyes wandered about taking in everyone in the room, stopping abruptly again on Avria. They widened significantly and then they traveled down to her tummy where her hand unconsciously lay.

"Goodness gracious," he said absentmindedly. Avria's hand pressed onto her belly and she allowed herself to fade back behind the side of Phenmal's shoulder. The strange old man shook his head and tore his gaze from Avria, letting them fall on the horrified face of the new Queen.

"In three weeks we will all attend to your coronation, my dear. There was no avoiding this, we could not really foresee if the humans would revolt or not, but it seems there has been some success on the part of the young monarch in instilling a sense of righteous entitlement to power in his people. We were seeing rumblings of war and we did not want that for the Araki; to be humankind's death knell. It would be easier if we reduced their numbers one last time," he said openly.

Tinna thought about what she'd done to keep their secret all those years ago, and again she could feel her gorge rising. She sat back, glaring hatred at the old man.

"It will solve your problem with the King as well. It won't be long before they all start to show the symptoms. The servants that attended to the Adrei magician have done their job. No need to move anyone about, except of course to protect the Adrei," he added swiftly when peering at Offrin. "All known Adrei wells have been generously dosed with heeda, so your people will be safe. You can thank your loyalty to the Ashru for your people being spared, sir. We know how any of the Adrei being harmed would wound our beloved Queen." He turned his face back to Tinna. "Your knights can be easily protected with the remains of our gift of Heeda-laced Apple Brandy. Clever wasn't it?" He seemed genuinely proud of this exclamation, expecting nods and smiles in return. He looked disappointed when Tinna's eyes narrowed into two furious slits, and she gripped the arms of her chair, white-knuckled.

"What of the Thran? The Gheraine? They have no involvement with our throne!"

"They are human. They will be affected. It is inevitable. But like it has in prior outbreaks, they will be somewhat protected by the distance from Oromoii, with fewer losses, for certain. And those who are here, some will survive; the strong ones."

"And what dare I ask does the Trinity think of all this?" she asked acidly. They governed the Keepers—one representative from each of the three predominant races, "surely they could not sanction this mass murder yet again?"

"The Trinity no longer has a say on this matter, Ashru," the old man replied. "It became clear that there was an imbalance there many years ago," he said. "Our organization itself is a human effort with human leaders, and we understand this. We did not understand our priorities then; our responsibility to this world and the races of people that reside in it, but we do now.

"Thousands of years; humanity has not learnt its lesson. Not even recently, when they were dealt the most humiliating blow by the dragons, they still arrogantly believe themselves above other races. Perhaps the dragons never should have been stopped," he sighed lamentingly, "perhaps we would have been best served to let them finish the job," he said. Tinna's eyes widened in shock.

"Instead we saved what we could, and let the human leadership continue on. And in part we have had nothing but poverty and instability until the One Day War. We allowed our sacred lands to become vulnerable and weak—nearly invaded by the Thran. Now that the true peoples are given their chance to right the wrongs of humanity once and for all, the humans, even in their reduced numbers, are fighting it. Change must occur. It is inevitable. Our methods are drastic, but change will occur." He shook his head regretfully,

"Ashru, you must not be angry, this is not your doing. We are simply acting on what we must, to insure the survival of all races," he assured Tinna.

"You have made the people my responsibility, Keeper, now you tell me I should not feel responsible for what you are doing to them?" Tinna barked.

"Fear not, humankind will not be destroyed, Ashru. They will be humbled—which they should be. The plague has been a means of control for our troublesome race some time. It has worked in the past to make things right. The Chai-Opse have resurged and grown quietly and efficiently. Now it's their turn. It will give the world time to heal from the effects of humankind. You will understand in time. War would not be any solution, only a lot more work and pain and suffering to achieve what will ultimately be the same end. We are saving your armies the trouble." The entire complement of the room gazed at this old man with unadulterated hate and disbelief, faces aghast, unspoken rage hanging on their lips. He left them that way. He turned and exited.

"Wait just a moment!" Taneth shouted. He ran after him but when he reached the corridor, it was empty.

He returned to the room and looked at Tinna disbelievingly.

Tinna gazed at him and then at Phenmal, their eyes seemingly speaking a thousand words.

688

CHAPTER EIGHTEEN – THE FADING KING

Avria thought she was seeing things. It began shortly after the visit from the Keeper, and she was starting to think she was going a bit mad. But it was Phenmal who told her quietly that she was not suffering from delusions. The things she thought she saw did indeed exist. They were hovering. Shadows and watchers. At first she thought she was losing touch with reality. A slip of movement here, a flit of something there, always just out of the corner of her eye. She was stricken when she joined her family for a somber breakfast.

Nobody really knew what to do. They could not travel, lest they carry something out of Miranne, they could not think of anything else to do or anyplace else to go. So they stayed at Miranne until someone came up with a plan. It had been a week since the Keeper had come. Their household went oddly on as normal. They rose, they talked, they pondered, they slept, and they ate. It was a strange state of limbo as they waited for the next thing to happen; yet none of them knew what they were expecting.

But Avria, since the Keeper's visit, existed in a bizarre apprehensive state. Her instincts were prickling her, and these little nothings she saw were weighing her down. She stepped into the dining room, and Phenmal caught her darting gaze. Phenmal's searching eyes saw what she had seen, and he gave her a reassuring look and patted the seat beside him. Tinna, Taneth, Phenmal, Offrin, Avria, Rhoa, Adracoor and Istvan were seated around a large oval table, the baby on his mother's lap. Even Cennik was present—having partaken most generously of the brandy, he was in no danger. He was however, extremely morose, and he had come to join the others in this strange time. The center of the table was heaped with a variety of foods none of which anyone had touched yet. Everyone appeared to be slowed and made still by the idea of what was to come. They were horrified to be expected to go on with things like breakfast and dinner when the world around them was going to crumble at any given moment.

What was worse this particular day, was that Master Gavorre had succumbed to the disease only hours before. It was the news that woke the household. They rose all as a family and sat at the table staring at one another. Avria was beside herself. She loved the apothecary so much. She'd only just manage to stop crying, feeling hollow and drained, she sat, pale and wan, staring at nothing.

"I'm with child," Avria blurted. Even Phenmal looked startled by her sudden declaration, in spite of his knowledge of it. Offrin's face turned even paler but he did not say a word. Avria's eyes lowered to her empty plate and she sighed. "It isn't your child, Offrin." She looked at him and he was visibly having trouble containing his emotions. She was impassive. She was resigned to whatever the outcome. He could be angry at so many things, the injustice of having to raise a rapist's child, the fact that Avria chose to tell everyone at once rather than him in private; but he did not speak until he controlled all his anger. A part of him understood. Avria then reached for a bowl containing a clutch of shelled boiled eggs and spooned one onto her plate and watched it roll to the raised lip of the plate.

"It is not of your doing who fathered the child in your belly, Avria. It will have a loving home regardless," he choked out. Avria's waxen face gazed at her egg and her eyes misted up. Phenmal offered her a reassuring pat on the hand. Someone started eating; the sound of the silverware seemed to prompt the others. They ate in strained silence, the clatter of the forks and porcelain seemed almost deafening. Phenmal glanced at Avria and then and leaned in to her ear.

"You are not seeing things, Avria. I think they're watching you. Well, more accurately, watching your baby," he whispered. Her eyes met his and she furrowed her brow, but she did not speak.

"The Keepers have always been the controlling factor for almost every type of power-bearing creature in this world. Some do not fall under their dominion, the Zshathri Druidic Soothsayers, for instance; the Hevnelor, the Diviners and Thranic Sorceresses—but most do."

"What do you think they want by watching me?"

"There's no mistaking what's inside you, Avria. Anyone with even the smallest power can feel it. The most powerful creatures that I know of are the Drathar, and they require tremendous control to keep them in check. Without the harnessing spells, there's no telling what the Drathar are capable of; what anyone with powers is capable of. And that little baby already radiates something unequal to anything I've ever felt. The Keeper that came, he saw it at once. They will seek to harness your child, Avria. They will seek to control it and cover it with spells, as they do all of us." Avria remembered the Drathar for a moment, how he'd mentioned something about being hobbled. She hadn't understood what he meant until now.

"Each creature under the eye of the Keepers has figures etched into their skin. The more letters, the more power is required to contain them. I am certain that the Drathar must be covered—" he mused. He dwelled momentarily on the memory of the letters that had fallen away when the Drathar had left the room. Avria nodded. She knew the Drathar were indeed covered in letters.

"What would they do?" she asked, her hand falling protectively to her belly.

"They would take the child, Avria," he replied. "And hobble it with spells. They would raise it to serve them." Her dry, red eyes moistened instantly, and her lips tightened. Phenmal put his napkin on his lap and looked up.

"Tinna, I must say this to you. The Keepers; they are a danger to the child, to Avria," Phenmal blurted out. Tinna's eyes rose up and she looked at him in puzzlement. "The Keepers. They are a danger to this child. The child has powers; anyone with the ability can sense it. They will want to take it, as they do any child with powers, and use the child to their own ends, as they do me, and the others."

Tinna gazed at him blankly for a second and then put her teacup down. "Gods, I just want to go home to Thamatoc," she sighed, rubbing her temples for a moment.

She looked at Taneth, and then Phenmal, then her eyes swept over the rest, falling with an expression of tired, loving resignation on her daughter.

The woman then found her reserve of strength; she found it in her abject fury that was boiling just under her skin. She found it in her heart, and with it, she sat up straight and looked each and every person in the eye.

"I think we can all agree—the time of the Keepers must come to an end," she said with finality. She picked up her napkin from her lap and put it on her plate.

Tinna got up and walked out without uttering another word. It took only a moment for her to find her cloak and to don it, moving with quiet purpose to the door and exited the house.

There was less resistance to her arrival than she had imagined. The people of the palace were worried, some were already ill; some had simply abandoned Miranne at the first sign of the plague. Outside of the isolation of her household, Tinna was only marginally aware of the disease spreading around the palace grounds and beyond. She didn't want to know.

Tinna had walked into the great room to find nobody there. She turned into the next room, and the next, finding only one of the few remaining members of the court standing by a window in a great library, gazing out numbly. It was a great lady of one kind or other, a shawl tightly wrapped around her narrow shoulders, the folds of her gown tumbling out from its edge into a beautiful, rumpled silken train on the floor. She scarcely moved when Tinna approached.

"I am seeking the monarch," she said in her velvety voice. The woman's pale face turned to peer at Tinna, her drawn, wan features seemed sunken and hollow. She was sick, there was no doubt of it, her skin was waxen, her complexion pale and her eyes two dark hollows from which her golden brown eyes gazed out at Tinna. She was still dressed impeccably, as was expected of all of the royal court. Her hair, styled in a rather sizable heap on top of her head was all elegance with decorative ribbons and a several strings of glassy blue beads. She looked Tinna up and down and then sighed.

"He has fallen ill. As have many of us," she replied, "while your lot thrives in health and blush, how convenient," she said bitterly.

"This was not our doing," Tinna said uselessly. The woman turned back to the window where she watched some ravens pecking at a smattering of dried bread someone had thrown into the garden courtyard beyond.

"I don't care," she replied.

"I must speak to the King. Do you know where he keeps?" The woman turned to look at Tinna again, this time with accusation.

"They say you possess a cure to the plague. Is this so?"

"The Keepers gave us such a cure. We were unaware of it. But it can only prevent the wormskin, it cannot cure it. It is too late for everyone here who hasn't had this elixir." The woman's brow furrowed and her sunken eyes grew glossy with tears. She studied Tinna for a long silent moment.

"I never objected to the idea of your assumption of the throne. I welcomed it. I thought Oromoii could use some new blood, someone forward-thinking, someone strong and unselfish; someone who knew adversity and who knew pain as their subjects do," she hissed. "I looked forward to the day when the monarch would step down and you would come to live here. I looked forward to standing in your court," she muttered with anger, as if she regretted these feelings. "Come along, I'll take you to him." She turned and moved in a rustle of silk. Tinna followed, her lips tight, her brow furrowed.

The King was sitting in a chair, looking a lot more than his mere twenty-four years. He hadn't gotten quite ill enough to show the pustules or the rash, but he was well on his way. He sat in his chair by the window. Outside, it had started to snow again, and the sky was boulder-grey. His skin was almost the same value. The fire roared in the fireplace. The young man was wrapped up on two blankets, and his hand was clutching a thick clay goblet of something steaming. A spare girl was serving him, she did not appear ill. He turned to look at Tinna, and then his eyes seemed to smile at the realization of who she was. He ordered everyone out, and then pointed to a chair across from his. While she sat down, four people exited, the door clicking loudly as the latch fell into place.

He was a good-looking young man; younger than Hanru. His face was a bit long, but the jaw was strong and angled. His eyes had a liveliness to them. She knew he was charismatic and engaging to people. He was deathly ill. His face had a strange grayish tint to it, and his hands trembled. But his humor seemed intact, at least at the sight of the rival he'd worked so hard to discredit and avoid; even kill. "I suppose the people who were meant to keep you out are gone now?" he said with sardonic laughter. Tinna shrugged her brows and shucked the cloak off her shoulders. He looked at her elegant garments and scoffed at her.

"You have thrown off the common linens and cheap wools I see..."

"Nothing less can be expected from any self-respecting usurper," Tinna replied dryly. He smirked and sipped his hot drink, grimacing at its taste.

"As if this concoction is going to stop the wormskin plague," he declared, putting it down on the small table by the arm of his chair. "If I'm going to die, I want to die drinking what I want to drink." Tinna nodded and looked out where he was looking, at the movement of a dragon crossing the great bailey, and slinking into one of the large livery barns.

"I hate them," he said. "I was small, barely old enough to hold onto memories, but I remember them. I remember the fear and the horror as news of each new city destroyed by dragon-fire was delivered to my father. I watched a vital man fade and shrivel at the terror of it all. I lost so many relatives—hundreds of people, killed. For no good reason. Why did they do it? Why did they render my race into the shambles it is today?" He paused. "But you know. I've been told that you know why."

"They were only instruments," Tinna replied, "nothing more. I used to think the culprit behind all that death was one man, but I suspect now, it was no mistake that he came upon the information that he had; it was no mistake that he had found enough to raise the ire of the Trinity and the Keepers, no mistake that the dragons were set to do what they had done."

"Yes, I was told of your great feat by the damnable Driva that have done nothing but haunt my father and I since I was but a small child. The great AiTinna, the Thran Gypsy who stopped the destruction of humankind. Nobody told us exactly how, or why, but we were told that we should be grateful to you. Here she is in the flesh, the magnificent savior, come to laugh at me," he said bitterly. "And worse, you bring dragons with you, to add insult to injury." Tinna shook her head and leaned forward, resting her elbows on her knees.

"The Keepers set this plague upon you. The Keepers decided that Humanity needed further humbling, that you must go in this fashion."

"I never would have stepped down. They would have to kill me."

"They have," Tinna replied. He shifted in his chair, and for a moment, he looked as if he was going to fall asleep, his lids drooped and he wavered. With the plague, there were no coughs, no sniffles, there was only the fever that burned from within, that made you sweat, but took your warmth. He was shining in beads of perspiration, but he clutched his blankets tightly around him. He came-to again, and then looked at Tinna, a strange smile on his face.

"Now, you serve them?"

"I do not. And I mean to never serve them."

"I do not like you, Gypsy. The idea of such impure blood taking the throne after a legacy of a thousand years of my family's royal blood makes me ill. But I admit that if anyone belongs here after me, it's you; especially now, with this plague destroying so many lives. I don't like to think well of you at all, but I cannot believe you would just walk away. Not you."

"I don't mean to abandon Oromoii, boy, I mean to save it."

"It's too late for that," he laughed. "Unless you mean the Oromoii without the human race living in it."

"It might be too late his time. But it can be the last time. I mean to stop this sort of thing from ever happening again." The

King's pallid face turned to her; his eyes were bloodshot, watery and bleary. How pathetic he looked. He studied her.

"Why are you here?"

"I need something from you. Something I hope you are willing to give," she said; "Because if I do this, I will need your legacy to assure the remaining people that this was the right thing to do. The world has never known a time without them. The unknown may cause panic. The disease alone is something to fear, but if I am to step up after you, I will need their trust and your blessing. If they believe I've done something to harm them, they will not trust me."

"You mean to destroy the Keepers," he concluded with a bubbling, weak laugh. She stared at him in all seriousness. He then grinned and waved his hand;

"As if I could ever object! Look what they've done to me! To my promised one, to the children of my mistresses—they've killed us all!"

"I need you to order it. I need you to ask me to do it—to tell me that I must do it to avenge the people of this deed. I need you to declare that it was the Keepers that set this disease upon them; they must be exposed by the most credible means possible, and that is you! I need you give me freedom to act. I need you to will it as King." His brow furrowed and he struggled to sit up. Tinna stood and offered her hands. He looked up at her and nodded once. She slid her hands under his arms, and hoisted him up in his chair. He nodded subtly in thanks, and reached for the bell on his table. He rang it loudly.

"I'm dying. We all are. If I am to be replaced by anyone, it will have to be you," he said. "But you must vow to me you will do as you promised."

"If you know anything about me, young man, you would know that I do not break promises," Tinna hissed. His eyes burned into hers, testing her determination, trying to detect a wavering of her resolve. The lady who'd led Tinna to the King appeared.

"Fetch Rallnett if he can still move about," he said without breaking his gaze with Tinna, "Tell him I need him to scribe a royal order at once."

CHAPTER NINETEEN – TO END IT ALL

The family that surrounded Tinna sat in glum silence. Tinna stood in the center of the circle where they had all faced their chairs. The only sound for a few moments was that of the freshly applied wood popping loudly in the fireplace.

"I still don't understand why it has to be just you," Taneth mumbled, rubbing his temples. Phenmal shifted in his chair and frowned.

"I object to it as much as you, but not everyone can enter the citadel. We do not have time to fly an entire army there, nor can we send common assassins. Me, they know, and they will know my intentions at once. But Tinna, she is privileged. She is named and Keeper-appointed royalty now. She is not marked by the Keepers as I or the other magic bearers are. She will be able to pass through the gates with no resistance."

"What of the dragons? Can they not simply burn them where they sit?" Avria asked. Phenmal shook his head.

"As long as the old men are living inside the citadel, it cannot be destroyed."

"And nobody else can enter the gates besides Tinna?" Taneth reiterated.

"Maybe Avria. Or you Taneth. You are not King, but you are of the royal line now," Phenmal explained.

"I serve no purpose, I am no assassin," Taneth muttered.

"But I am," Tinna interrupted. "I am a Kanindra, after all. I cannot deny my heritage, my training. I am the best-qualified to do this task, in addition to being one of the only ones who can enter the citadel."

"How convenient," Offrin said sarcastically. Avria snorted through her nose, her brow furrowed in thought. Tinna shifted her weight onto her other foot, and clasped her elbows. The dogs seemed to sense her unease and they lifted their heads and made high-pitched whines from before the fire, both looking at her with their shining eyes. She looked back at them, her gaze softening, and a strange, whimsical look crossing her brow.

"When I get back, I want new puppies," Tinna declared. "Then I want to visit Hanru at Wye. And I want to spend the rest of the winter at Thamatoc, with occasional trips to Klatna. I will come here for the summer only. It is too high, too bleak, and too empty here. If I am to do this, to finally become what's been expected of me by the Keepers, I want these things.

"With the Keepers gone, nobody will argue with you."

"Why bother being Queen if you are getting rid of the Keepers?" Avria asked.

"Because the people look to me as Queen now, Avria. I am Ashru. I was chosen as Ashru by the Araki people. And what remains of humanity after the blight has passed will need someone to watch over them. I'm stuck with this role, with or without the Keepers. Only without them, I can rule by my own ethics, and not be guided by old men with none of their own." There was a long span of quiet.

"I suppose I should get Cennik then. He will need to call Ledroran," Phenmal blurted, standing. "I ask, as your husband to be, please don't get yourself killed. They are powerful men. I'm not even sure if they can be killed."

"There's one thing I'm good at, dearest Phenmal, and that is killing. I'll find a way. Sometimes the simplest means are the best ones. I will need a good, sharp sword."

"I can help you with that, Tinna," Offrin piped in. "The Kanreth are here and they are our friends. And they are equipped with some of the most deadly swords in the world." He said this grimly and stood. When he did, so did everyone else. Tinna watched them all leave and then followed. She donned her cloak and left the house, crossing to the great palace. She would sit with the King for a while, and keep him company.

Ledroran was quiet. Tinna, for a while, was worried for his silence. He mulled her words carefully. Cennik was not entirely cooperative when she called him, his messages to the dragons were tainted with his resentment for the loss of his people, and it was difficult to work around that—the dragons arrived reflecting his pain. They felt guilty, perhaps. Tinna feared she would lose one of the dearest friends of her life when the great dragon arrived. Bundled up in a woolen cloak, standing alone in the courtyard in front of the massive dragon, she waited. He seemed sullen and confused as he looked upon her.

The Trinity is dead, he finally said. Ejenat has been killed, our highest leader. The leadership of dragon kind now falls upon me. I am not sure if I want that responsibility, the dragon uttered.

"I can relate to that feeling, my friend," Tinna replied. "But the truth is, you have been their leader all these years already, Ledroran. The dragon sitting for the Trinity did little else but focus on the Trinity. The others have always looked to you." The dragon dropped his head, his one eye studying Tinna intently.

Now you want me to take you to the citadel, for reasons not given to me in your message, but I can easily deduce.

"They killed the Trinity," she replied matter-of-factly. "They have used you all extremely ill. They have all but erased the human race."

There are some who might think that was a heroic act.

"And there are some who believe that it should not be up to the Keepers to decide what should be the fate of an entire race." His great eye studied her some more, his hot breath steamed from his nostrils, and he tilted his head to look at her with his other eye. She loved the sight of him. She could not contain her adoration for this dragon, this creature that had carried her all these years. She reached out and put her hands on his muzzle.

"Ledroran, I have asked much of you. I have asked a great deal, I know. I understand this is against everything you are; the Keepers have always protected you. You have carried out their will without question because you, like everyone else, have always believed they had the welfare of all at heart. But with the murder of the Trinity's three leaders; this should show you that we have all been fooled—we've been deceived into believing that the Keepers were acting in our best interest. They have lost sight of everything. I need your help, Ledroran. After all this, we will need each other more than ever."

The dragon sighed wearily and groaned.

You did not have to convince me of anything Tinna. I know your honor better than anyone. I know what we must do. I am merely concerned. I am fearful of what is to come. A world without the Keepers is a dangerous world, Tinna. Everything will change. Our peoples will require a great deal from us in leadership, and your reluctance to reign, my dearest Tinna, worries me, because after this, you will have to stand in the stead of the King, and you will have to convince everyone that this was what you wanted. You must commit yourself, as I must commit myself, to what will come of all this.

She nodded. "I have resigned myself to what I am to do, Ledroran. I promised myself no more blood, but I am now left without a choice. If any of humanity is to survive, I am the only one left who will protect them from whatever is to come."

Then to the citadel we will go. Many of my brothers and sisters are to join us. The citadel, once you've done your work, must be destroyed. Its secrets are too dangerous to be permitted to fall into unworthy hands, especially when all of the bearers of this world will be amok.

Tinna didn't quite understand everything he spoke of, but she wasn't in disagreement. The Citadel would have to fall.

"Then we leave at first light," she declared. The dragon nodded and lumbered towards the byre. He was so large, he would touch the rafters and displace the other dragons in residence. She would have to order more space be provided for her dragon allies. She watched his huge form recede in the late afternoon light, and then turned back towards the residence.

Avria awaited her when she stepped through the door.

"Mother," the girl uttered quietly. "I am going to go with you."

"Absolutely not," Tinna snapped, gliding past her daughter. Avria grasped her mother's arm tightly and spun her to face her again. It surprised her to see her daughter do something so rash and forceful.

"They seek to harm my baby. I must go to ensure this threat is eliminated."

"I can handle it myself," her mother barked. Avria's grip tightened.

"NO!" she shouted. "I will go! I will go with you and stand beside you for once! I will go with you and I will share in the blood because everything should not only be your burden to bear! I will go!" she bristled, her voice raw and broken. She then calmed a bit, and her face softened. "Let me go, mother. My eyes are wide open now. I can be of help."

"I could not bear seeing you harmed, Avria. I could not bear that sort of grief."

"Then I will not be harmed," she replied. "Let me help," she said. "Let me take some of this onto me. Let me come so you are not alone in this." Tinna pursed her lips and nodded once before abandoning her daughter in the doorway. She did not want Avria to see her tears.

The sky was as blue as freshly bloomed forget-me-nots, and it was filled with dragons. Ledroran led the fleet of beasts westward, his passengers huddled behind his shield, mother and daughter. They held hands. Tinna's grasp was strong and steady, with no softness or warmth in it.

"It was important to have the approval of the monarch to do this," Tinna said out of nowhere. Avria looked at her questioningly, but did not have a reply. The girl, in breeches and the rust-colored sweater they both adored peeking out from her layers, gazed at her mother with a grim, straight line across the brow and a serious cast to her lips. On her belt she wore two basket-hilt daggers. These were the weapons she'd been trained to use for all these years. She'd never actually used them against someone else, but she knew she could manage well enough with them. She had no idea what her role was to be in all this, she didn't even think they'd survive, but she'd watched her mother take the brunt of everything these past years, and somehow, even with Taneth beside her, she was always alone with it. She wanted to take some of the burden from her mother's shoulders. She hoped she would not simply become yet one more burden for her to bear.

Tinna had a two-hand sword of mirror-smooth metal slung across her back. Her cloak and hood fluttered in the wind. She looked vibrant and young, but the look on her face was something Avria had only seen once before. Her expression was cool and distant. It was resolved and determined. It was cold. Avria had only experienced this once, at the conclusion of the war, when her own grandmother had challenged Tinna. She'd never seen her mother kill before that. She had no notion that her mother was capable of such darkness until then. Seeing it again chilled her.

Avria reached inside herself to see if she too could find that same stoic resignation, that single-minded purpose that would carry her through this. What she touched was the growing life inside her. It filled her with fire, thinking of the child being harmed. So tiny, so new, and it already had such great power. It was innocent. It was a part of Eleran that she could hold onto. It occurred to Avria why her mother was the way she was—so protective and determined. She knew her mother had always acted to shield Avria from the things that had hardened Tinna; the things that had taken some of her humanity away; to protect her from gaining the capacity to turn off her compassion and her kindness. She did not want Avria to become her. Avria finally understood. She wanted the same for her child. She wanted this child to live free of the pain she'd suffered, the loss, the

701

fear wrought by people who were supposed to love her. She knew now. She finally truly understood. She wanted this child, who would be so powerful, to understand innocence and goodness, and to never be forced to do the things she was about to do. She wanted to protect it from the darkness as Tinna had hoped to do with Avria. She squeezed her mother's hand, and looked at her squarely.

"I love you, mother." Tinna's coldness flickered, and for a fleeting moment, she was warm again. She smiled wanly in response and squeezed Avria's hand in return.

"My treasure," she said, barely audible over the wind. And then she looked forward and her eyes grew icy again, and her brow dropped. Tinna was preparing herself for the kill.

There was no resistance because nobody had expected them. It surprised Tinna that they were not sensed as Phenmal said they would be. There wasn't even anyone to welcome them. Ledroran dropped the women off at the gates of the lone citadel, which was quietly nestled on snowy hilltop, surrounded by osteal, ice-covered oaks. The dragons retreated for now, allowing Tinna to do her work. They would wait until Tinna and Avria left the citadel. Eretrix was there to watch for them. Tinna instructed Ledroran to wait until the sun was about to set, and if they had not appeared, that they should do their work whether or not Tinna or Avria had escaped the citadel. Ledroran grimly nodded, saying in a low, gravely dragon-whisper, that this reminded him of a time long ago, when they had done something much like this. Tinna smiled and snorted through her nose and turned towards the gate, Avria at her heels.

They crossed under the gatehouse and across an old-fashioned courtyard. There were no guards. Tinna had no idea where they were going; she merely took the paths that seemed most prominent, where the stone flags were most-worn and shining from use, and they led them both directly to the doors of the main hall, where only a polearm stood on its butt, leaning on the wall by the door. The door was cracked open, and the mother and daughter crept up to it, Avria's hand gently pressing the door open, which widened silently.

Inside there was the collection of little old men that Phenmal described. Every last one of them was present. They were all huddled around a fire in their chairs, their backs to the women. They were quietly sipping some tea, eyes focused on the flames. One of the old men froze, his shoulders tightening, and then the rest did the same in turn, each twisting around. Their eyes went straight to Avria's tummy—every last one of them. It was bizarre. Only after they all

702

had a good look at Avria's belly, then they looked up at the mother, and then finally, Tinna. There was a moment that they seemed to parse what they saw, when one of them finally said something:

"We did not sense you—how strange," someone muttered.

"You are an unexpected surprise ladies, unexpected indeed," one of the eldest of the old men said. "Where is Phenmal? He is not here."

"He has other responsibilities," Tinna replied. The old men began to stand in turn, some gazed upwards to the ceiling. Tinna's eyes followed, and to her astonishment, there she was, depicted in a somewhat stylized figure doing what appeared to be cutting through a tangle of vines with the sword she now had strapped over her back in its scabbard. Behind her effigy, images of her past two decades were displayed, the tail end of the events of the dragon-burnings among the earliest images; the figures moving the long band along the edge of the coffin-ceiling with languid grace. Tinna's eyes took in this wonder, studying her own face.

"What brings you here, honored Ashru? You and your beautiful, charmed daughter?" Tinna's gaze dropped, her look of bemusement quickly replaced by a blank expression. Her eyes darkened.

"I came because I have questions."

"Well, perhaps we have answers for you. Tea?"

"No thank you," Tinna replied, raising her hand. She stepped forward, approaching the old men, gazing into the eyes of each individual.

"Where are your guards?"

"We sent them away. We gave them Heeda, but in spite of our generosity towards them, they still acted with ingratitude towards us, angry perhaps that we had endangered their loved ones. We offered them a choice, to remain in service or to go. They chose to leave, so we sent them away."

"Can't say I blame them," Avria muttered bitterly.

"We are not entirely without assistance. Some of our servants have remained. You surely did not come all the way here to ask about the guards."

"We did not," Tinna retorted. She looked up at the moving mural again, unable to keep her eyes off of it. "Tell me, all of you were aware, all those years ago, who the perpetrator was that learned of the plagues that you beset upon this world. You knew where he was too, didn't you? You allowed him to continue." There was a pregnant pause, and then one of the old men walked to the tea urn, and poured himself a cup. Tinna wondered why the servants remained. Who would want to be around these murderous old bastards? He drank from the steaming cup and then said:

"Of course we knew where he was! Do you truly believe that we, who wield the most powerful creatures in this world, could be outfoxed by a mere mortal, an ordinary human? Of course not! We orchestrated it all. It was all destined to happen. All destined to take place," he pointed to the ceiling where the fresco with the depiction of Tinna hung heavily over their heads. Tinna's sword in the image hung heavily, blade down, the point moving slowly towards them.

"Do you not see what damage has been done?"

"We see only what benefits are reaped from the actions we take. We make the hard choices that must be made. This world is our ward, we must protect it; the races within it are our responsibility. It has always been so." Avria moved unhurriedly towards the side of the room where the windows looked out into the forests.

"What do you mean to accomplish, Ashru, coming here? You bring your daughter with you, endangering the life of the child within…"

"How would I be exposing her child to danger by coming here?" she asked, her brow rising in curiosity. "There is nothing here to fear, unless the danger of which you speak is you yourselves." There was a pall, a silence that lingered for a time and then one of the old men chimed in.

"It's odd that we did not sense your arrival Ashru. Odd indeed." Tinna dragged one of the chairs to face them, and sat in it, smiling with a touch cool smugness, her brow raised. Avria watched her from the side of the room, her fingers hovering over the cool hilts of her daggers.

"It's probably for the best. It's much better for us to arrive here without your being prepared to receive us."

"We would have been better hosts, for certain," the old man smirked—although she saw that each of them was beginning to show signs of alarm. They were finally realizing why Tinna had come. How deluded they must be, she thought, to imagine I would come for any other reason—to take tea. With a sword on my back no less.

She stood, and stretched. Her demeanor was changing right before their eyes; her cool reserve seemed to be barely holding back what seemed to be a boiling rage.

"My dear, I hope you do not intend on harming us," one of them finally uttered. "You do realize we possess great powers—and we have the protection of beings of great power as well."

704

"I don't see anyone else here, do you Avria?"

Avria shook her head, her face pale and drawn. Why she decided to come, she suddenly did not know. Why she thought she could do this alongside her mother, exact pain on old men—she felt irrational for even thinking so now. But then, as if sensing her doubt, a powerful surge of something radiated from her belly. She straightened and reached down to slide her daggers out of their sheaths. She watched her mother reach up to her shoulder and wrap her fingers around the hilt of her sword, drawing it out of the short scabbard and gracefully bringing it down in front of her.

"This will be the last time I will do something like this. I've been manipulated and toyed with enough. I am not your puppet. My family is not for you to control. I have accepted the future you have imposed upon me, to lead this land. But I will lead it without you. The time of the Keepers has come to an end." Her words were filled with ire, her eyes wide and empty.

The old men raised their hands up, and threw forth arcs of energy at both Avria and Tinna. Avria screamed and immediately covered her face with her arms, and hunched down into a defensive posture. Her body surged with power and she felt it radiate out from her core. She was surprised to feel no effect of their attack. All she felt was a power radiating outwards. At first she thought it was her baby, but she realized it was not. It was coming from the center of her chest. She warily dropped her arms, and stood straight only to find the arcs of white energy colliding against a wall of nothing all around her, just as it had when Eleran had cast a protection spell on her long ago; only this time, it came from inside her. She looked over to her mother through the arcs of light, and saw them passing through her as if they were but beams of sunlight. Mother and daughter exchanged glances, and in tandem, the lifted their weapons for the kill.

CHAPTER TWENTY – ROYALTY

Avria could not deny that she was gratified to set eyes on the Drathar again. With the sorrow and pain of these past weeks laden upon her, all she felt a desire for familiarity and comfort, and he reminded her of these things for some strange reason. Her eyes took his form in warmly. She caught his appearance out of the corner of her eye, turned her head and looked at him. She realized there were several creatures in the room with them now. When they appeared, she did not know, she was too caught up in the mess she and her mother were making. She saw the Drathar, and she knew it was the one that was her friend by the way that he stood.

She just idled there among the carnage she and her mother had wrought, one pale hand gripping the top one of the chairs facing the doorway. On the chair below her hand, the bleeding form of an old man hunched forward, still twitching. Her other hand rested lightly on the flat of her belly. Her daggers were on the floor at her feet, both awash in an enamel of blood. Above, the mural was roiling; the tangle of vines twisting and writhing, wrapping itself around the past; consuming it. Tinna was haggard. Her darkness had yet to dissipate and the appearance of the Drathar made her spin around to face him, holding up the bloodied sword, her fingers and fist dripping with red.

"You have finished your killing, Gypsy Queen," he told her. She glared at the dark-robed figure and then dropped her hands and blade. "You have done more than enough," his voice had a smile in it. Avria looked on in strange, ambivalent silence. The Drathar's ghostly hand reached up and he threw back his hood. Carefully he removed his tunic and threw it aside, showing the full of his pale chest and arms to the women. The letters on his skin were flowing across his skin as if being carried by a current. One by one they were disappearing, sinking away inside him like leaves dropping down into the depths of the water. "You have freed us all," he said. As the last of the old men gurgled his final breath, his skin became completely clear of the spells that bound him. They watched as each of the ancient magicians began to dissolve like a lump of sugar in hot water, their blood drying up and flaking into ash. "We had nearly freed ourselves, but not quite. Not entirely. The Hevra's power had almost been enough to loosen our shackles, but not break them."

"But now, thanks to you, the Driva, the Chaiva, the Summoners, bearers of all kinds, the lot of us—nothing holds us back any more. Nothing." His words were edged with a manic joy, but his features were unseen behind his veil which was still wrapped around his head to protect the women.

The old man in the chair by Avria suddenly melted into sand the colour of ash, filtering down into sheets of tiny, glistening grains that piled onto the floor and in heaps on the chair, some remaining on the armrests as his hands fell apart into myriad grains. The blood on Tinna's sword and her hands also fell away, and Avria's daggers, once glistening red, were polished silvery steel again, the sand now resting on the beautiful rug beneath their feet.

"They are so ancient, nothing about them is real anymore. Magic held them together, and now they are dead, they've fallen apart," the Drathar observed. He stooped and scooped up a handful of the sand. "Reduced to the basic elements that made them what they were." Avria dusted off the beloved sweater, the blood that stained it was now a powdering of sand. She smiled. She realized she must have believed she was going to die when she dressed that morning, for she wore the sweater with the idea that stains wouldn't matter in the end.

"What you have done here is what will allow you to rule the common folk unhindered; it is what will solidify peace with the rest of us. Be warned; my bearer brothers will not withhold their enthusiasm for their freedom—they are unchecked now. The magic-bearers are now without laws, without restraint. They will wreak havoc," he explained. "Our power is why these old men kept a tight leash on us all. Because they knew we would be the end of order and peace. So they found ways to control us all. But now there are no more Keepers. No more Trinity governs. There is only you and it is your act of mercy that will keep us from destroying everything. We are in your debt. Yours..." he paused and his ace turned to Avria. "And hers." She in turn gazed upon him in quiet concern.

"Act of mercy?" Tinna scoffed, "you call this massacre an act of mercy?" The Drathar laughed quietly, and moved around the room, stepping over the piles of sand that were once old men, his face angled down to take in the scene in all its grisly beauty.

"If you had any knowledge of the sheer number of people who were in their grip for centuries, you would know how many people you have freed today; the thousands of beings that were muzzled by their spells, stifled, chained by their tyranny. We are free now. They can no longer control us; no longer harm us. The Drathar, we are the most powerful. The others below us will respect us. I speak for all." He paused in front of Avria and boldly placed his hand on her belly. She did not withdraw; she merely looked down at his hand. "Even for this one."

"They were threatened by the power in your daughter's belly. They were terrified of it. They were going to kill her and the child. I came as soon as I felt it," he looked up at Avria's beautiful face, and he caressed her cheek with the tips of his fingers. "But you had it all under control," he said softly to her, "beautiful creatures." He then turned and strode to Tinna, casting his gaze upwards to the moving ceiling.

"They could not see beyond you in the prophesies of the Founding Keeper. It was he who was the first to propose and implement the hobbling and binding of the bearers; to understand our power and to use it to exercise their own ends. But the founding Keeper was not all-powerful. His seeing eye could not see beyond you. His spells could not see beyond you, Tinna because none of them knew that your sword would kill them. They could not see even there, where your figure holds a sword that points down to where they sit, that their time on this world was at an end. They could not know that your power, Tinna, was to be immune to theirs. You were born to defeat these old codgers. Avria possesses the same power. You were the only ones who could ever do this," he spread his hands to encompass the room, "You are the only creature able to end their tyranny. That was your fate."

"Everything is going to change," Avria muttered.

"As long as the Ashru and her line rule this land, there will be some measure of peace. We can all promise you this," he gestured to the figures standing around the edges of the room. They seemed so still the women had almost forgotten they were there. "It is the gift we offer you for freeing the bearers. I cannot control everything that my kind will do, but I can assure you of our best effort to protect the common folk and most especially, your line, Ashru," he told them. He then took Avria's hand, and lifted it up to his veil, where he kissed her fingers through the fabric. She gazed up at him, her eyes wide and warm at the sight of him. She could see a glint of light catch

709

his eyes beneath the veil. With a soft whisper that fluttered his veil he said.

"You and your child are especially dear Avria. I will be watching over the both of you." Once again, he vanished. Her hand was left poised in the air. One by one, the silent observers that had appeared only moments before stealthily followed Avria's Drathar and vanished in wisps of smoke. Tinna turned to her daughter, and shared a look of incredulity. They dusted themselves off, and walked through the silent citadel.

A young servant with dark wine-red hair and gold eyes appeared, drawn by the sound of their footfalls. Her face expressed severe alarm.

"I can't feel them..." she whispered in a strong Gheraine accent, her voice edged in panic. "Why can't I feel them?" The women stopped walking, and looked at her, their dark eyes taking her in. She was like a terrified mouse.

"They are dead. I recommend you run and find everyone else that still dwells here and urge them all to leave this place at once. In a little while, the citadel will be nothing but a burning ruin. Nobody will survive if they remain inside. The girl's frightened eyes flashed, and she scampered away, looking back at the women in fear.

Tinna and Avria made their way out of the citadel, happy to see Eretrix awaiting them at the edge of the trees, a shock of shining creamy red against the frozen, snowy landscape. Tinna and Avria climbed up onto the back of her neck and huddled up underneath her shallow shield. Up she went, into the sky, carrying them with her, her wings blowing clouds of snow-crystals with each pump until she finally got high enough to clear the tree tops. It wasn't long before the rest of the dragons had been summoned with their silent calls, and the women were delicately deposited on Ledroran's broad body. Dragons began to rise up from the forest like flocks of starlings. Dragons of all sizes, gained altitude and spiraled higher and higher above the citadel, circling and circling until the sky was black with them.

We enter a new age, Ledroran said. Behind them, a column of smoke rose up from where the citadel once stood, flocks of dragons still circling and blasting pillars of fire anywhere that was not already burning. It was a sight to see. Tinna and Avria sat against the back of Ledroran's skull. If they weren't it would be impossible to understand him in the wind. They watched the column of smoke recede, and the wildly careening dragons that continued to destroy everything that remained of the Keepers' home.

Tinna's hand slid over to her daughter's and they clasped onto each other. Her humanity had returned, and her eyes were glossed over with tears. She hadn't said a single word since they left the great temple that was now in ruins. Avria watched as Tinna's strength wavered and her grip tightened on her daughter's hand. It began with a tremor and then swallowed sobs. Tinna lost control. She lurched forward into the wind and began to weep. It was a sorrow that came from the depths of her soul. Her gut-wrenching sobs tugged at her daughter's heart. Avria was unsure what to do; she'd never seen her mother like this. She huddled onto her and gathered her close. Tinna crumpled onto her daughter's shoulder and then down onto Avria's lap where she cried and cried. Avria hunched over her mother, sitting her through her misery, fighting back the tears that threatened in her own eyes.

When her tears subsided she remained with her head on Avria's lap, hiccupping occasionally, staring out at nothing. Avria blankly rubbed her mother's back, touched and surprised that she was the one to give her mother comfort for once. She leaned forward and kissed her mother's cheek, and hugged her. She had no idea what awaited them when they returned to Miranne, but for the moment, they had some peace to simply be.

The coronation was a subdued occasion. The Magistrate, who was showing signs of illness, and several ministers who had been fortunate to have had the brandy were in attendance among a few others. The High King, looking old and frail, covered in lesions and rashes, had conceded his crown and handed it to Tinna from his deathbed. She was crowned in the company of only eighteen people; her husbands, her daughter, Offrin, the Duke and Duchess of Zadrudas and a smattering of other people. A message was dispatched across the countryside by Araki riders to inform the people of the coronation and to take an assessment of the damage caused by the virulent illness that ravaged the land.

The royal family moved into the main palace the day after the King died, but it was not long before the group headed south to Klatna, where Tinna insisted she would spend the rest of winter.

Taneth, being one of the few surviving human Wisemen, found himself falling into the role of leadership. The Keepers were no longer in control of the brotherhood, and the remnants of the organization turned to him for leadership. He accepted the mantle

711

with sadness, for all his work to rebuild had been hampered by the decimation caused by the plague. There were fewer resources now, fewer people to continue the hard work rebuilding the academies. He would have to rely more on Araki and Adrei now.

Only one in a hundred humans in Oromoii survived the plague in the end. The isolated communities of Gheraine and Thran and the southerly countries suffered fewer losses thanks to their isolation and scattered communities, but they were stricken harshly nonetheless. At this point, it was impossible to know what the damage truly was, but one could see it in earnest riding through the cities nearly emptied of their residents, surrounded by large swaths of newly planted forests of trees where the Araki people had buried the dead.

Within months, the Araki communities began to emerge from the forests, branches of certain clans spreading into the old, nearly empty human settlements. A number of towns and cities were simply abandoned by the survivors. The remaining humans did not take long to gather into small, insular, jealously guarded communities where they were unwelcoming and suspicious of non-human races. Others moved south and west to join the less-affected communities around Thran, Gheraine and the xenophobic and scattered peoples of Kytrine.

Ledroran had been accurate in his prediction; it was a new age for the great lands. But nothing could fully prepare any of them for what was to come. The effects of unchecked magic-bearers was far-reaching and a growing problem. It wouldn't be long before the fragile peace would come undone, and the magic bearers would begin to rain chaos on the world. With no limits to their actions, no accountability or restrictions as they once possessed, they became increasingly violent and dangerous. The citadel and its secrets were destroyed. Tinna's peace would come to an end, in spite of the Drathar's promises—it was only a matter of time. She only hoped that the child Avria carried was truly blessed with the promise the Keepers had feared—and he or she could somehow bring peace and balance to the world once more when the time would come.

For the time being, the new Queen of Oromoii did what she could to rule the land and its people with a fair, but firm hand. With the support of the Dragon King, Ledroran, and her family, she was not alone. Avria, who had always been such a guileless creature had grown grave and hard like tempered steel. Tinna knew she would make an excellent Queen in her stead when the time came. For now, they all waited for the child to be born, and for the balanced future that this child might bring.

END OF BOOK 3

Other available titles by Miranda:

Red Slipper Series:
The Wizard King
A Problem of Ghosts
The Beast with Silver Eyes
The Red Witch of Tirdonne
Coming soon – The Raven's Serenade

Blackroot

The Belletrist (Anthology)

www.mirandamayer.com

www.ingramcontent.com/pod-product-compliance
Lightning Source LLC
Chambersburg PA
CBHW050117030726
47505CB00007B/1915